Vampire Cherry

BOOKS 1-3

SOTIA LAZU

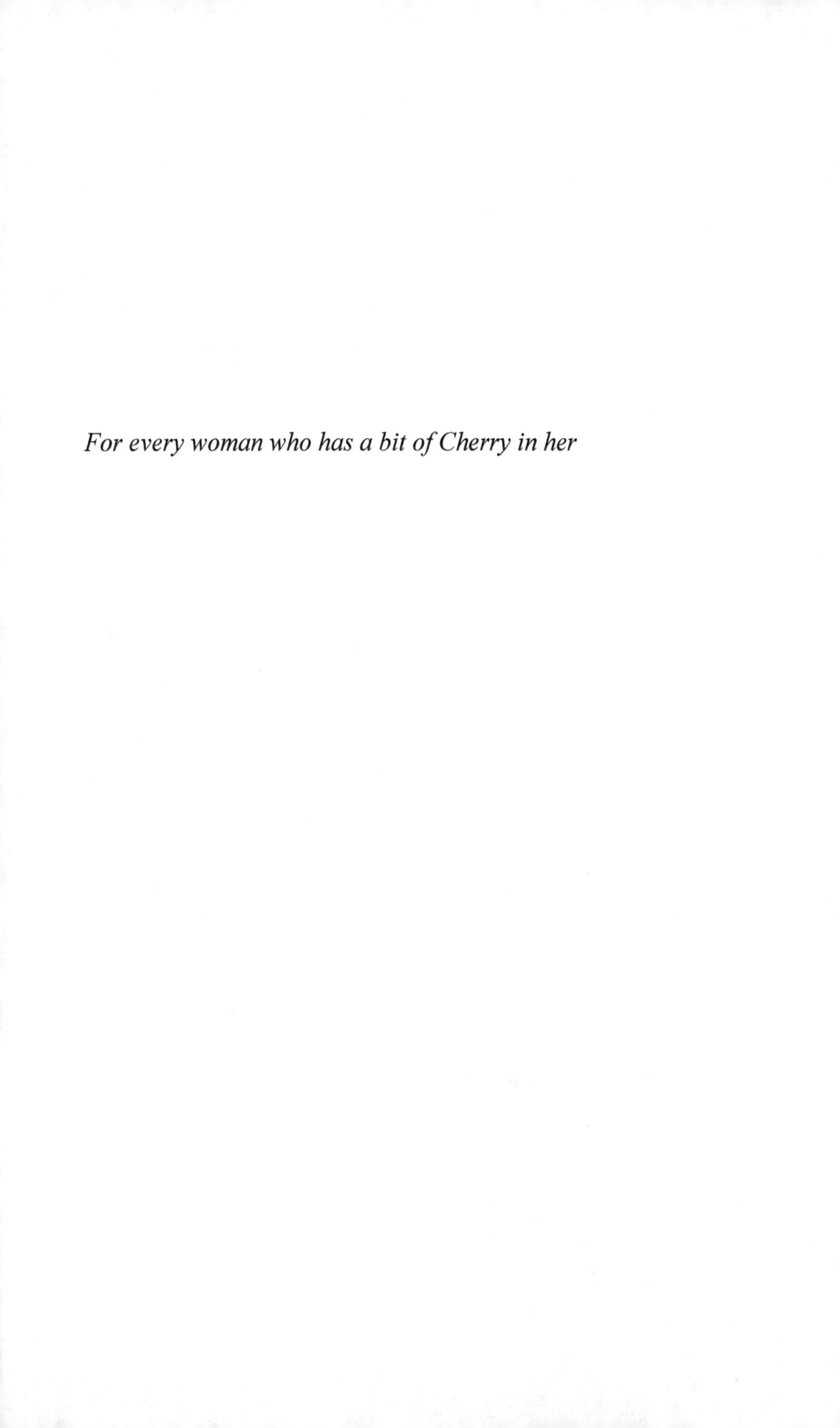

For every woman who has a bit of Cherry in her

Table of Contents

Book 1 11

Cherry Stem 11

Prologue 3

Chapter One 5

Chapter Two 22

Chapter Three 29

Chapter Four 44

Chapter Five 53

Chapter Six 72

Chapter Seven 80

Chapter Eight 99

Chapter Nine 107

Chapter Ten 120

Chapter Eleven 137

Chapter Twelve 143

Chapter Thirteen 146

Chapter Fourteen 152

Chapter Fifteen 161

Chapter Sixteen 176

Chapter Seventeen 198

Chapter Eighteen 204

Epilogue 208

Book 2 .... **213**

Cherry Blossom 213

Chapter One 215

Chapter Two 221

Chapter Three 229

Chapter Four 237

Chapter Five 247

Chapter Six 254

Chapter Seven 260

Chapter Eight 270

Chapter Nine 281

Chapter Ten 288

Chapter Eleven 297

Chapter Twelve 301

Chapter Thirteen...309
Chapter Fourteen..316
Chapter Fifteen..324
Chapter Sixteen..333
Chapter Seventeen...342
Chapter Eighteen..354
Chapter Nineteen..364
Chapter Twenty..376
Chapter Twenty-one..385
Epilogue 397
Book 3 ....**401**
Cherry Pie 401
Prologue 403
Chapter One 405
Chapter Two..414
Chapter Three..421
Chapter Four..427
Chapter Five 433
Chapter Six..440
Chapter Seven 448
Chapter Eight 453
Chapter Nine 458
Chapter Ten...468
Chapter Eleven 477
Chapter Twelve 484
Chapter Thirteen...492
Chapter Fourteen..498
Chapter Fifteen..507
Chapter Sixteen..514
Chapter Seventeen...521
Chapter Eighteen..528
Chapter Nineteen..535
Chapter Twenty 544
Chapter Twenty-one..551
Chapter Twenty-two...557
Chapter Twenty-three..564
Chapter Twenty-five 578
Epilogue 583

Book 1
Cherry Stem

Prologue

My mom always told me not to play with my food. I try to keep that in mind.

She never told me not to let my food play with me, however, so I would let tall, dark, and handsome—with gray eyes, a brilliant smile, and killer cheekbones—flirt with me to his heart's content. Then I'd let him take me to his place.

Then I'd feed.

By the time he woke up in the morning, he'd remember having great, anonymous sex and nothing else.

That was the plan, at least. That had *always* been the plan.

Until things changed.

Chapter One

I was about to leave my apartment, when there was a knock at my door. I opened it, and Dotty, one of the second-floor tenants, burst into the room.

We weren't friends per se, but she'd occasionally pop by for some girl chat. I'd told her I worked nights and that I needed my beauty sleep, so she wouldn't disturb me during the day, but she'd never before come by after nine in the evening.

"I need your help." She gasped for breath as she turned to face me, running a hand through her short, spiky black hair.

At nearly six feet tall, on the heavy side, and with a square jaw, Dotty never seemed to need anybody's help.

"What can I do?" I secretly hoped whatever it was could wait until my stomach was full. Her outfit somehow made me doubt my hopes would be justified; she looked ready to go out.

As did I, which I prayed she'd notice.

She bit her lip, then said, "The sitter was with Mark until now, but she had to go, and my date—ummm. I invited him upstairs for a drink, and he's waiting in the car." She blushed and sucked in a gulp of air, before blurting out the actual reason for her visit. "Can Mark stay here for an hour?" When she took in my short leather skirt and bustier that left little to the imagination, she pouted. "I guess not." With a sigh, she turned for the door.

Even though she turned slowly enough that I knew she *expected* me to stop her, I felt bad. "Okay, but only for one hour," I said to her back. I'd looked after him before, and he wasn't *horrible*.

The words had barely left my mouth when she opened the door again and let Mark, her pudgy six-year-old son, inside. "I owe you big-time," she told me over her shoulder, blew Mark a kiss, and rushed out before I could change my mind.

"Why aren't you wearing pajamas?" the boy asked, tilting his head to the side. "Did you just come back, like Mommy?"

I swear he would have had a brilliant career with the Spanish Inquisition, had he been born back then. Since I always believed in treating children like adults, I opted for the truth. "Nope. I'm going out as soon as your mommy picks you up."

"Why are you going out after dark?" His thin eyebrows were furrowed, the sharp expression looking out of place in the adorable roundness of his face.

"Why not?" I asked innocently. *Ha.* I beat him at his own game.

"My daddy says only bad people go out after dark." He crossed his arms in front of his easily breakable chest and looked at me smugly.

I understood why his mother never asked her ex-husband to babysit. "Your mommy was out until now," I said with a saccharine smile. "Is *she* bad?"

He apparently took offense, because he stomped his foot. "*No.*"

"Well, then, your daddy is wrong." There. I'd had the last word. How would he beat that argument?

"But it was *day* when my mom went out." Smug again.

I was tempted to try my brainwash gaze on him but thought better of it. Instead I said, "If you don't talk again until your mom comes to get you, I'll give you ten bucks."

He squinted at me. "Twenty."

I should have started lower, but it was too late for that now. "Fifteen, and you never tell her about our deal." Hey, I said I'd looked after him a couple times; I never said I was good at it. I'd have to find another way around his questions next time, though. He was getting expensive.

Dotty wasn't late to pick him up. She was disheveled and grinning like the Cheshire cat, but not late. I grabbed my keys, stuffed them in the front of my bustier, all but tossed Mark to her, and was out of there.

****

The Gridlock was one of my favorite bars, which meant I visited it only every couple of months. It wouldn't do to be seen leaving with a different man every night, especially if said man didn't remember me the following day.

Spacious and dimly lit, the Gridlock was decorated in black and shades of red. Drapes separated a few private stalls, and the upper floor housed the supersecret VIP area. Get your minds out of the gutter; the place wasn't a sex club. The VIP area was only secret because celebrities often chose it to unwind when they needed to stay away from the public eye for a while—no orgies took place there as far as I was aware.

What added most to the bar's appeal was its patrons—young professionals, not out to get wasted. Pretty people, who took care of themselves and looked and smelled good, relaxed on leather armchairs. A smorgasbord of dining possibilities, *and* the music was to my taste.

As was the bartender, but he was off limits.

Heads turned as I entered, but I maintained my cool. The outfit I'd chosen was at odds with the surroundings, but by the time I left home, I was in a hurry, and the club I initially had in mind was too far away. I might have gone through the trouble of finding another place that suited my attire, but a phone call earlier that evening had jarred me—always, *always* change your cell number after breaking up with someone, or they can bug you for years.

I looked cheap for the place, but it was too late to do something about it. Holding my head high and keeping from swishing my butt more than necessary, I made my way inside and pretended not to notice the glares a group of businesswomen in their thirties with impeccable hair, threw my way. I was there for a reason.

I moved toward the bar with deliberately slow steps. Gaze not lingering on a face for more than a split second, I tried not to broadcast that I was looking for someone to fulfill my needs for the night.

I spotted the perfect guy within twenty-five seconds of scanning the room. I'd never seen him around before. Believe me, I'd remember if I had. A head taller than everybody else, and with shoulders as wide as my bed, he leaned casually against the bar, holding a bottle of beer. Even at a distance, I could see his eyes were the same charcoal gray as his shirt, and fringed with long, dark eyelashes. And his gaze was locked on me.

The first phase of the plan was complete—the prey had seen me and was attracted.

Phase Two consisted of me feigning disinterest until he made a move. If I took the first step, he might deem me too easy, and as I'd discovered in the past, that wasn't always enough of an ego booster to make a man take me home. Although, if I played my cards right, it might be more than enough to make him follow me into the ladies' room.

With the rent deadline approaching, I needed money tonight almost as much as I needed blood, so a quick hit wasn't an option.

Oh, the blood thing reminded me there's something I should have said earlier.

My name is Cherry, and I'm a vampire.

Sadly, since L. A. wasn't brimming with job openings for an aspiring porn star turned vampire, I often found myself in need of cash. When that happened, I looked for someone to serve as more of a sponsor, rather than a blood donor. For the day, not indefinitely.

I'd been in a couple of adult movies; I wasn't a sex-worker. Most of the guys I fed on got nothing other than the *promise* of sex. If I was into them, I might do them as I fed, but I never did it because I thought I had to. Letting someone cover my expenses in the long run would change that dynamic.

As would falling in love with someone. A *breathing* someone, with a pulse and an expiration date.

It would screw things up majorly, which was why I never slept with the same human more than once since I became part of the living dead. *The living dead.* It sounds so very ominous, but some of us are nice.

And... I'm digressing.

One of the coolest vampire powers is mind control, which some swear is the best way to a healthy relationship. Personally, I prefer not having to wipe my lover's brain clean every so often. A steady, living boyfriend from whom I'd have to hide my true nature was therefore out of the question.

As for dating a vampire? No thanks. Too many relationship issues. The way I see it, knowing you'll be around for a *very* long time can make you extremely picky as to whom you want by your side.

Also, male vampires are patronizing, controlling assholes with superiority complexes.

And they cheat.

I admit to only knowing one of them that well, so call it an educated guess.

I approached the side of the bar farthest from the guy and ordered a Bloody Mary. Silly private jokes like that give me a weird sense of accomplishment. I know; I need therapy.

Drink in hand, I tapped my foot to the rhythm of the music and observed the crowd dancing—slowly swaying, to be more precise—while I mentally counted the seconds it would take for him to approach me. When he hadn't moved any closer after a whole minute, I turned and gave him the *squint.*

The squint is a leftover from my short days as a catalog model, before I decided on a major career change and made my first of two adult films. To achieve it, you narrow your eyes enough to make your gaze look focused and promising. Overdo it, and you look myopic. Combine it with a slight pout, and you have guys eating out of your hand.

Or flashing you a smile, as was the case now.

His smile was dazzling. Straight, white teeth—I'm a *vampire*; we pay attention to teeth—and a lower lip that begged me to nibble on it. And *oh* those cheekbones...

I clenched my jaw and made a show of turning away. *You want me, buddy? You have to come and get me.*

He didn't, but a fifty-something man with alcohol-laced breath and red-rimmed eyes appeared out of nowhere and cornered me against the bar. Just my luck. There was *one* person in the establishment who hadn't bathed for a couple of weeks, and of course he decided to make a pass at me.

"Can I buy you a drink, honey?" His words were slurred, and he stood too close for comfort.

I could have ripped his head off his shoulders within seconds, but I don't generally like violence. Placing a hand on his shoulder, to keep him at arm's length, I indicated my glass. "No, thanks. I'm set." I smiled, allowing a bit of fang to show. He couldn't possibly have enough credibility to expose us.

The drunk stumbled back, hands held up in the universal giving-up sign, at the same time the yummy male specimen made his way to us. Yummy's face fell. *Aha.* Hero complex.

"I was coming to save you," he said, "but I see you handled him yourself." His voice complemented the rest of him. Deep, masculine—the voice you'd want whispering dirty things in your ear.

The ball was in my court. "Maybe you should stick around, in case I can't handle the next one." I smiled. No fangs.

His grin gave me a better look at his pearly whites. Yup, still flawless. "I'm Alex. Alex Marsden."

"Cherry." No last name for me. There was no reason.

Up close, he looked even better. I figured he was in his late twenties, thirty tops, and worked out. His fingers, which I got a good look at when he raised his beer to his mouth, were long, and I couldn't help but imagine how his big hands would feel on me.

"So, what do you do?"

His question threw me. People didn't usually care what I did when I was dressed in leather and thigh-high boots. I wondered how he'd react if I said I was a lawyer.

I took a sip from my overpriced, alcohol-laced tomato juice. "Used to model. I'm between jobs now." Had been for a long time, since my maker hadn't bothered to ask about my future plans before turning me. At first I'd been really pissed off to wake up dead while at the peak of my career.

Meh. I may as well be truthful. I hadn't been at the peak, rather at the beginning. I'd filmed two *highly* erotic movies as an extra and had just been given the starring role in a third one. And the main reason I'd been pissed off for the better part of six years was that I'd been turned before getting the lipo and boob job I'd planned on pampering myself with for my twenty-fourth birthday. Now I was doomed to go through eternity without the flat belly and double D breasts Dr. King had promised me.

Alex nodded and looked me up and down. "You look familiar, and I don't follow fashion. Have we met before?" To his credit, his gaze didn't pause anywhere but on my face during his perusal.

Classic pickup line, although he might have seen me before. I couldn't really ask him if he liked porn, so I shook my head. "What do *you* do?"

"I'm a cop. Detective." He shrugged like he was saying *nothing special*.

A detective. This could be bad. These guys have good memories as a rule, and he might have seen my missing-person report. Still, I wouldn't panic. I'd gone from blonde to redhead for *Knotting Cherry Stem*—hell, I'd changed my name for it—and had bangs now and forever. No, he wouldn't recognize me.

And *no*, I'm not telling you my real name.

"Sounds exciting," I drawled, all wide-eyed. "You should tell me more." To stress how interested I was, I ran the tips of my fingers down his bicep. Nice and firm. Yum squared.

As if he didn't notice, he began saying something about my eyes. Most guys would be all over the chance to touch me back, but not him. I could see he was the type to really take his time with a woman, and it intrigued me. Would he take his time with *everything*?

I cut him off, pointing to the speaker booming overhead. "It's too loud in here. Maybe we should go someplace quiet?"

He arched his left eyebrow but put his palm on the small of my back. The touch gave me goose bumps, and that's a real feat when talking about a dead girl. "My place is quiet." Ah, he got the hint. Smart man.

As soon as I left my drink on the bar, he caught the bartender's eye and paid for us both. I didn't offer to cover my half, but I made a mental note to thank him properly once we were alone.

"Do you have a car?" he asked as I let him lead me to the exit. "You can follow me in it, or I can drive you back here…" His voice drifted off. What would he say? What could he say? *Later? After?* His sentence was better left unfinished.

"No car. I took a cab." Not all vampires can fly, but only because some can't fathom lifting off the earth and therefore won't focus their will enough to achieve it. *I* can. I'd flown to the bar, but I couldn't tell him that.

"Are you okay with taking my car? Riding with strangers, and all?" He was so thoughtful, and I had to try not to swoon until he added, "We could go to your place, if you'd feel more comfortable."

No no no no no. No. Bad enough that I was still going through with my plan though he was a policeman—but he was *so hot*, who could blame me? Bringing him to my apartment would take *risky* to a whole new level.

"I wanna see how a cop lives." A bat of my heavily made-up eyelashes, and the deal was closed.

****

The drive to Alex's place was long enough to get me wondering if he was some psycho killer, looking for a place to have his wicked way with me. If that was the case, he was so in for a surprise that I felt bad for him. Although the possibility of that being his agenda made me feel less bad for what *my* agenda was, which in itself was weird.

I've never felt shame or guilt for feeding off unsuspecting victims. *Never ever.* It's not like I do them any harm. Nothing like the harm that was done to me, anyway.

I'd met my maker at a party.

His name was Willoughby, and he'd been gorgeous and polite. Nothing like the grabby crowd my agent usually brought me into contact with. When he'd suggested driving me home, I'd been all up for it. Maybe the mention of a limo had added to the appeal.

We never reached my home. We started making out in the car—I remember giggling too much, because of the champagne—and things got heated fast. My sequined dress, extremely short to begin with, was bunched around my waist, and he had his hand between my legs, when I felt a sharp pain at my neck. I never liked hickeys, and I'd been supposed to begin shooting *Knotting Cherry Stem* the following day so I'd tried to push him away, but to no avail.

The shooting of *Knotting Cherry Stem* had been canceled, of course. I wasn't sued for breach of contract because nobody was able to locate me. Willoughby had dumped my lifeless body in an alley.

Alex didn't seem like the kind of man to dump someone in an alley. Maybe that was why I felt a pang at the thought of using him. A *pang*, mind you, not guilt. We, creatures of the night and all, don't feel such puny emotions. Just a pang when he opened the passenger's door for me; another when he didn't try to cop a feel while grasping the gearshift; another when he asked where I was from, how old I was…

Turning sideways in my seat, I took in Alex's profile. He reminded me of a Greek god—nose a bit too large, adding a masculine tone to a face that would otherwise be too pretty with the long-lashed eyes and pouty lips, and hair just long enough to curl over the collar of his shirt. The streetlights gave the black curls a shine that tempted me to run my fingers through them.

He pulled into a driveway, and I focused on the scenery outside for the first time since we got into his car. A nice street in Monterey Hills, with single and two-story houses. Not the kind of neighborhood I'd associate with a cop.

Then again, the house the driveway led to didn't look like what I'd expected a cop's house to be.

He seemed apologetic while telling me there had been a gas leak in his city apartment. "My mom's away for a few weeks and said I could crash here until it's fixed."

His mom? He'd brought me to his *mom's*? Okay, so she was away and his place wasn't habitable at the moment, but hadn't he heard of hotels? And how would I even enter the place? "She won't mind you having company over?" I asked, trying to decide whether to stick with him and see if I could go inside, compel him to take me somewhere else, or cut my losses and find another guy to get me through the night.

"Nah. I grew up here. It's as much my home as it is hers." From where I stood at the threshold, I saw a wistful smile grace his lips. "Plus it's always tidy and with a full fridge."

It was the smile that sold me. This place was special to him, and something deep inside made me want to see it. If he turned out to be a momma's boy after all, I wouldn't stick around for it to matter. That was one problem solved.

He gave a half shrug and held the door open for me. "Come in."

I lifted my foot over the threshold and met no invisible barrier. *Phew.*

Gesturing to his right, he indicated the living room. "Make yourself at home. I'll get us something to drink."

I couldn't get comfortable with all the frilliness and floral patterns surrounding me, but I tried. I sank into the huge sofa, crossed my legs demurely at the ankles, and waited for him.

An *uh-huh* came from the kitchen, followed by, "I knew she had liquor here." Alex poked his head out of the doorway that separated the kitchen from the living room. "What'll it be?"

My turn to shrug. "Do you have beer?" I didn't feel like making him prepare me a cocktail.

"Beer?" He mock scowled. "What kind of drink is that for a lady?"

I chose to believe he was kidding, and made a show of looking around. "Lady? Where?" If that wasn't an invitation, I don't know what would be, but Alex laughed. It was a nice laugh—deep, like his voice, rich, and hearty.

"All women are ladies until proven otherwise," he said with a wink before disappearing from sight.

I could explain why that was old fashioned and a tad sexist, or I could be proven otherwise. I seriously didn't want to be a lady tonight. Other than having the serious munchies, I was more attracted to him than I'd been to anyone since I broke up with my last boyfriend almost four years ago.

Alex brought me my drink and sat in the armchair to my right. That wouldn't do.

"Why so far away?" I asked. "And aren't you drinking?"

He shook his head. "I've had enough for one night."

He didn't explain his seating choice, and I was confused. He wouldn't have brought me here unless he was attracted to me, so why wasn't he doing anything about it? "So… are you seeing someone special?" I didn't know why, but I wanted to know the answer. And I wanted it to be *no*.

He took some time to reply. The look in his eyes made me antsy; it was too serious. Maybe he *was* seeing someone. Maybe he was married, despite the lack of a wedding band on his finger, or he lived with his girlfriend, and that was why he'd taken me to his mother's house. It would explain why he was reluctant to make a move.

It felt like forever until he spoke again. "No." He sighed. "I couldn't be more single. You?"

"I don't do relationships anymore." Not since I found Constantine in bed with his maker. Constantine, who promised to love me forever and then broke my heart.

Silence again. I hate silence sometimes. This was one of those times.

He opened his mouth, closed it again, and rubbed his temples. "I may be about to say the stupidest thing, but… I'd never pay for sex."

I looked at him, mouth agape. My first instinct was to go over our interactions and find what I'd done, to give him that impression, but I held back. It wasn't my fault he jumped to conclusions. He was an asshole, pure and simple, and the only thing that saved him from a full-on angry-vampire attack was that said angry vampire was too shocked to react.

"It's not about my job." He leaned forward, elbows on his knees. "I'm not going to arrest you or lecture you, though going after someone you know is a cop is stupid. I just thought we could talk." After a pause, he added, "I'm not paying for that, either."

I wanted to slap him, but that might end with his head flying into the wall and I'd hate to ruin the beige tapestry with bloodstains. "I don't charge," I said through gritted teeth.

"Come on, Cherry." He touched my knee in a brotherly fashion. "The clothes, the attitude…"

I hated the tears that sprang unbidden to my eyes as I jumped up and turned toward the door. "I'm leaving," I said. "You're an asshole." My taste in men seemed consistent, if nothing else.

He was fast for a human. And strong. He grabbed me by the arm and spun me to face him. "You're telling the truth." The incredulity in his voice gave my anger a fresh boost.

"A woman can't go out at night by herself to have a drink? She can't see a man she likes, and—and *want* him, without being a prostitute?" If I'd fed, I be beet red by then.

"Cherry, I'm sorry. I—all the leather and the way you came on to me… I thought—"

"What you *should* have thought was that you were about to get incredibly lucky." I shook off his hand. "Not anymore."

I kept glaring, even after he grabbed me again and lowered his lips to mine. Glared for all of a second before melting into the kiss. His lips were soft and moist and apparently magical, because while they were attached to mine, I forgot all about how he'd insulted me.

When I remembered, I pushed him back hard enough to send him flying into the chair he'd recently vacated. "Oh, now that you know it's for free, you want it?" I leaned over him and grabbed the arms of the chair, trapping him. "Well, you can't have it." I said the words slowly, my tone even. I can say with certainty that vampires can't kill with our eyes, since Alex survived the daggers thrown by mine.

"I wanted it from the start." He got in my face. "Just not the way I thought it was offered." His voice gradually lost oomph, until the last few words were whispered, his face a study in misery. "I *am* an asshole. You looked so pretty and so out of place, and I couldn't believe that you—" He ran his palm over his face. "I'm an asshole. And I'm so very sorry. Both for insulting you and for screwing this up. I'll drive you to your place, and you can forget we ever met."

There was no doubt in my mind he felt bad about what he'd thought and said, but he'd really insulted me. I should accept his apology and walk away. But maybe I shouldn't be hasty. I mean, he said he was sorry and called me *pretty*. Too pretty for him to believe I'd genuinely been into him. That had to count for something, right? Most importantly, though, I shouldn't care what he thought of me. I should feed, have fun, and get out of here.

This time *I* kissed *him*.

I wasn't in the mood for softness and hadn't been for a while. I pressed my lips against his violently and invaded his mouth with my tongue.

After his shock wore off, he took over, his languid pace lulling my sense of urgency. He cupped my face and withdrew enough that his breath merely caressed my lips.

I tried to kiss him again, and he chuckled. A mewling sound came from my throat. That snapped me out of my lustful haze long enough to push his hand away and crawl onto his lap. I wasn't the prey, I was the predator, and it was about time Alex knew that. Knees framing his thighs, I undid his belt and pulled hard enough that it came out, ripping a couple of loops in the process.

He unzipped his pants one-handed, bunching the fingers of his other hand around my thong and pulling it aside. Stretching awkwardly to reach his back pocket, he fished out a condom.

Since I couldn't explain why there was no need for it, I took it from him, ripped the packaging with my teeth, and slowly rolled it down his cock. I took my time touching and stroking his long, hard shaft, enjoying his gasps. He was hard *for me*, gasped *for me*, and that made me want him more. I had the sort of power over him that had nothing to do with physical strength or vampire thrall, and I relished it.

He grasped my wrist, stopping my movements. Time held still for a second, as our gazes locked. I could get lost in those eyes, and that was dangerous. I squeezed my eyelids shut, shifted my grip, and guided him inside me. I didn't want to look at his face; that might make this more than sex.

He closed his hands on my hips, lowering me onto him slowly. Inch by agonizing inch, he entered me, and I wanted nothing but to take all of him in. I couldn't be patient. The void inside me ached to be filled.

Alex wouldn't be rushed. "God you're beautiful. So beautiful." He caressed my hip bones with his thumbs, and I got goose bumps all over. "I want you so much. Feels so good being inside you."

His words wouldn't let me focus on the feeling of his cock. I kissed him, to shut him up. I didn't want to hear the pretty words, when he wouldn't remember saying them later. I just wanted to ride him until I saw stars.

He thrust upward, and I hissed. He was big, stretching me this side of pain.

I liked it, but it wasn't enough. "More."

He fisted his hand in my hair and pulled my head to the side, to graze my neck with his teeth. "I didn't prepare you," he whispered.

He hadn't needed to. I'd been wet since his fingers made contact with the skin of my lower back at the club. I tried to swivel my hips, to show him, but he held me still.

"There's no rush. Let me make it good for you." He pulled me backward and lowered his lips to my collarbone, his free hand fiddling with the laces of my top.

I couldn't imagine how he'd make it any better than this. Every nerve ending in my body felt exposed. His breath on me set my skin ablaze. "Fuck me." I slid a hand inside his shirt and dug my nails in his shoulder.

He bucked his hips and growled, but wouldn't move other than that. "Let me make it good for you," he said again, uncovering my breasts.

My keys fell with a happy jingling from where I'd stashed them in my cleavage; I'd left the house thinking there would be no undressing. Handbags, clutches, and the sort aren't easy to handle during an emergency takeoff.

Unaware of my self-ass-kicking, Alex fastened his lips around one nipple and rolled his hips. I could do nothing but moan as he pumped inside me slowly, his shallow thrusts synchronized with the pulls of his mouth. His tongue flicking my nipple sent a tingle down my spine, but it was his cock driving in and out of me that sent jolt after jolt of pleasure to my core.

His thrusts turned deeper, harder, stoking the fire he'd lit inside me. He turned his attention to my other breast, and his warm mouth made me shiver. I arched my back in abandon, offering more of me to his wandering mouth, his hold on my hip the only thing keeping me from falling backward.

I clawed the air, seeking purchase against his shirt and failing. The silky material evaded my fingers, until I stopped trying. I couldn't focus on anything but the pressure building between my legs.

Alex pulled me up by the shoulders and gathered me to him. The angle changed, and he rocked his hips faster, every stroke sending me higher on a seemingly endless spiral of pleasure.

His chest was sweaty against my breasts. My tender nipples throbbed as they rubbed against him. I nuzzled his neck, nibbling on the smooth skin over his pulse point. I wanted to penetrate him like he was penetrating me. I wanted to taste his blood. I wanted more of him inside me than I already had.

I ran my tongue down the column of his neck and loved the goose bumps that rose when I blew on it.

He bit me.

Blunt, human teeth dug into my shoulder at the same time he raised my hips and slammed me down on him again. His balls slapped against my ass, and I couldn't hold back under the sensations assaulting me. My body tightened, and the tension in my belly uncoiled in every direction, wiping out logic and turning me into a creature made of pure need. A scream of delight burst through my open lips, before I fastened my mouth on Alex's neck and pierced his skin with my fangs.

I tried to be gentle—if done right, a vampire bite can be painless—but his fierce thrashing under me and plunging inside me made me lose my mind. I drank and drank, drawing more of Alex inside me with every sip. Each pull on his blood made my pussy spasm and drew out my orgasm, his moans music to my ears.

For a few moments, it was like I was floating. My lips felt dry. I opened my eyes and had to blink a couple of times before my vision cleared. What had just happened was… *wow*. My fuzzy brain couldn't come up with a more appropriate word.

I licked closed the wound on Alex's neck. Then I cleaned my lips with my tongue and raised my gaze to his, getting ready for the moment that canceled the whole night— the moment to erase me from his mind.

He smiled and held me tighter, oblivious to what I'd done. His chest heaved with panted breaths. His heartbeat pounded in my ears.

I hated that I liked it.

I started to stand on leaden legs, letting his softening cock slip out of me, but his grip felt made of steel despite the blood I took from him.

"Stay," he said. Though worded as an order, it sounded like a plea.

"I can't." If I did, there might be no turning back.

He kissed me leisurely. Intimately. It was too much.

I gave in. "Only for a little while."

He shifted me sideways in his lap and gathered me to him, tucking my feet snugly between his thigh and the armchair. "I wish there was a blanket down here," he said. "Or do you want to go upstairs?"

Upstairs. Where the bedrooms had to be. Where he'd want me to stay longer. I should go. Right now.

I shook my head. "I like it here."

Laying his cheek on my head, he whispered, "I like it too."

I stayed here, cuddling with him, for longer than I should have. Unwilling to let go of his warmth, I listened to his heart rate slow to normal and his breath even out. Once he was asleep, I thought it'd be a shame to wake him and wipe his memory. Instead I watched him, until the angles of his face, the curve of his lips, and the smoothness of his brow were imprinted on my mind. I dropped my gaze to his neck. My bite mark was nothing more than a couple of dots, like pinpricks. I kissed my mark and inhaled Alex's scent, to complete my mental picture of him.

I never allowed myself to fall asleep anywhere but in my basement apartment and had to be there before dawn. The sun coming up doesn't make us narcoleptic, but it can make us nice and crispy, so I always made a point of checking the sunrise time online before going out.

Well…almost always.

I fell asleep.

Chapter Two

I awoke with a jolt. Sharp pain sliced through my right side. My arm hurt like it had been carved to the bone. I tried to lift it, see what the damage was, and had to bite back a scream. The pain became sharper, deeper, as if the flesh was peeling off.

The curtain, flimsy as it was, had blocked some of the sunlight, but not enough to keep it from burning the skin of my right shoulder and as much of that side of my back as wasn't covered by the armchair and Alex's arm. It stretched and felt about to tear open with every move I made.

I shrieked—an honest-to-God shriek I'd thought could only be accomplished by teenage drama queens—and jumped off Alex's lap to crouch between the armchair and sofa.

Alex snapped his eyes open. "What—"

"Room without a window?"

Why was he looking at me and not replying?

"*Alex.*"

His eyes cleared and became more focused after I barked out his name.

"Is there a room without a window in the house?" I hated to think of what would happen if there wasn't one. The sun was low enough now, but soon it'd be streaming in through the glass panes. Even if I managed to find a spot where it didn't directly hit me, I'd feel like I was in a furnace.

Cop instincts must have kicked in, because he stood, fully alert now, and pointed to the back of the house. "Second door to your left. Takes you to the basement."

I took off, leaving him to run after me.

"Cherry? What's wrong?" I doubted he realized he was yelling.

An unfiltered, stray beam of light found my foot when I paused to fumble with the door. My flesh sizzled, and I cried out.

Alex was by my side now, close enough to see my fangs.

Whenever vampires are threatened enough for instinct to overcome logic, our fangs pop out. It can prove immensely helpful when fighting another of our kind but is all kinds of inconvenient when dealing with the sun and a human bystander.

As I finally opened the door, I saw Alex's hand fly to his neck. Yup, this wasn't one of those times when auto-extending fangs would help. "You—you're... *What are you?*" he asked.

I slammed the heavy door in his face.

He called my name, then tried to push his way in. Yeah, good luck with that. The door locked from the inside, but even if I hadn't pressed in the lock button, all I had to do was sit on the steps behind it and lean my back against it, and it wouldn't budge an inch.

"What the fuck is happening, Cherry?" Kicking now.

I tried to check my shoulder burn but couldn't. Not because of the darkness—every story you've heard about vampires having night vision is true—but because of the position of the damage. It didn't matter; I knew it'd be healing. I'd fed well, and my constitution was good even without that. "Nothing. Don't worry," I yelled back. Well, that was convincing.

He grumbled something about his gun and a lock. Then silence.

Sadly it didn't last. His voice, calmer now, drifted to my ears. "Come on, Cherry. Open the door. I don't know what's wrong, but we'll figure it out." A pause. "Please." The word didn't sound like one he had much practice saying.

I haven't needed air in years, yet I still inhale all the time. Like at that moment, when I decided lying wouldn't help me. I took a deep breath. "I can't come out. The sun burns me."

"Are you photophobic?" It made sense for that to be his first thought.

It was my way out, and I should take it. I didn't. I respected him too much to lie—or maybe I'm the kind of woman who loses her mind when a gorgeous man offers her mind-blowing sex and then cuddles her until morning. "That too," I said. Before I chickened out, I added, "I'm a vampire."

The reaction I'd expect from someone after such a revelation would be to burst into laughter. Alex sighed. "A vampire?" He cleared his throat. "Seriously? Tell me more about it."

Wow. That was open-mindedness I didn't see coming. "Well, not much to tell." He didn't doubt me. He wanted to get to know me better. I tried to put my thoughts in order. "I need blood to sur—" Realization dawned. "*You don't believe me.*"

He tapped his fingers on the door, an impatient sound. "I'm sorry, it's… No. No, I don't."

What an ass. Instead of letting him think I was crazy, I decided to prove I was telling the truth. "Move away from the door," I said.

"Why?"

"Can you please just do that?"

I heard him take a step back, and I opened the door enough to show my face and slide my unscathed arm through the opening. I waved at him, then bit my lip and put my hand straight in the sunlight's path.

The burn was tolerable for a split second but soon made my eyes water. My flesh felt about to fall off.

Alex stared wide-eyed at my blistering knuckles, then my face. I clenched my jaw against the pain and lifted the corners of my mouth in a forced smile, letting my canines elongate.

He jumped away, knocked over a lamp that looked too expensive to be on such a tiny table, and fell on his ass.

I snatched my hand back and held it to my chest before closing the door again. "Let me stay in here until sundown," I yelled. "I promise I'll leave as soon as possible, and you'll never have to see me again." This time I was lying. He would see me one more time, so I could return his state of blissful ignorance by taking away his memory of the last few hours.

Nothing.

I listened. Surely I'd have caught the sound of feet running to the nearest exit. Unless he hit his head when he fell…

I was about to open the door again, when he said, "So it's Bram Stoker more than Stephenie Meyer?"

I couldn't contain a very eloquent, "Huh?"

"Your hand." As if that explained everything. "Stoker had the vampire thing down better than Meyer, right?" He sounded like he really wanted to know the answer.

Only a dead *and* buried person would have missed the buzz the latter's works had caused, and the former was a legend. "Stoker's definitely closer. I mean, sparkling? Seriously? Neither is completely right, though."

"What is he wrong about?"

I sighed. I shouldn't be telling him anything about my kind, but I'd buy some time by keeping him talking. He was a cop; his word had gravity. If he decided to tell people about me, someone might check his story out. I couldn't have that, so I had to keep him within reach until I could wipe him, and the best way I saw to do that was to convince him I wasn't a monster. I'd stall till sunset, leave the basement, and wipe his memories of me with the least amount of trouble.

Plus I hadn't really *talked* to someone in a long while.

"Um, where to start? We don't turn into wolves, bats, or mist—not to my knowledge—and we don't have a thing against God or anything religion related."

His gasp pissed me off. Here I was, trying to keep things between us civil, and he was upset one of the ways of hurting me was off the table. "Yeah, you can't use a cross on me." My tongue dripped venom—not literally; we don't do that either. "Pity, huh?"

"Don't be stupid," he said, adding to my ire. "Vampires seem to be repelled by crosses in most books and movies. I was surprised that, of all things, the religion part is a lie."

Were we really having a theoretical discussion about my vampireness? I shrugged it off and picked at the scab forming on my foot. "Also, we don't feel compelled to follow the orders of any head vamp." I thought that over again. "Well, there's a council that issues laws, but they don't micromanage."

"Hmmm." Typical can't-think-of-anything-to-say reaction.

"Yeah..." Typical reaction to can't-think-of-anything-to-say reaction.

Five, ten, *twenty* seconds went by, and then he said, "Do you kill people?"

"No."

"But don't you—"

"I've never taken a life."

I expected some expression of relief on his part, but he shot his next question. It wasn't an easy one. "Do you have mind-control powers?"

Unfortunately our superhuman speed does not include speed of thought. I could hear the wheels in my head turn as I tried to find the safest way to respond.

I must have taken too long, because his next words came out in a high-pitched voice I couldn't quite associate with his husky tones until then. "Did you... *hypnotize* me? Is that why I brought someone I thought was a prostitute to my mother's?"

He had no sense of danger; I could snap his neck, and if he kept accusing me of things, I probably would.

I don't use my mojo to get a guy to take me home. I've never needed to do more than swish my hips and smile lasciviously, or stretch and let my boobs do the flirting. His gall was incredible.

"No, *Einstein*. That was all you, wanting to *talk*. I didn't need thrall, to get in your pants."

"How do I know you're being honest with me?"

I couldn't believe we were having such a stupid dialogue. He couldn't know. And I had no reason to keep being honest. But being me got lonely from time to time, and since we were talking anyway, I wanted to be real. "Because if I'd used thrall, we wouldn't be talking about it at all."

"But you bit me." There went the upper hand. I'd lost it. Buh-bye, upper hand.

Begrudgingly I muttered, "Yes. Had to feed." Why was I hanging my head? I really did have to feed. "I tried not to hurt you." That was the closest thing to an apology any of my donors had ever gotten.

"You didn't." His voice lost some of its edge. "I thought it was a"—he cleared his throat—"an expression of passion."

I ghosted my fingers over the door in the wish-it-were-my-guy-instead-of-the-wooden-surface rom-com way. For a second, I allowed myself to believe he wanted it to be just that, and maybe I'd get a chance for a do-over.

"But I was a snack."

I got defensive, though his tone hadn't been angry. "I *chose* you, okay? I *slept* with you." I jabbed the air with my index finger, like he could see me. "I don't fucking do that." I barely resisted punching the wall to stress my point.

"Am I going to become like you now?"

"No." Maybe I should open the door and use my mind trick after all. Nothing else seemed likely to get him off that interrogation line.

"How do I know that?"

Again with the stupid questions. "It doesn't work like that. There's more to turning someone, and I'm not allowed to do it, anyway."

"Why?"

I didn't have to keep answering but decided to stick with it. "I was the last person to be turned before the new regime banned turning altogether." I was also the reason for the banning, since my asshole of a maker didn't realize I was sort of recognizable and had a family, unlike most people chosen for turning, so there was the possibility my resurrection wouldn't go unnoticed.

"You're the youngest vampire?" He huffed. "When were you made?"

"Turned," I said. "Six years ago."

"That makes you what? Thirty?"

"No." I added *dumbass* in my head. "It makes me twenty-four, forever."

I caught a buzzing sound, and soon he was on the phone. I didn't bother listening to both sides of the conversation—it's good that we can tune our senses up or down depending on our needs, or the abundance of stimuli would drive every last one of us crazy. My relief when I heard him say, "I'm coming over now," was indescribable.

He hung up and told me he had to go see a contact and then run by the police station. I found the fact that he explained both odd and endearing.

"I shouldn't trust you with the place," he said, "but I guess I don't have a choice."

My day just got better, except for one thing. "Will you tell people about me?" I hated how small and worried my voice sounded.

"Of course I will. Nothing says *captain material* more than a cop claiming he has a vampire locked in his basement."

"You know, you were a lot nicer before I put out." That shut him up as expected, so I continued refusing to acknowledge the fact that his attitude had changed after my revelation, and not after the sex.

Just before the front door slammed shut, I heard him mutter, "You better be here when I get back. This isn't over."

This couldn't have been *more* over, but I said nothing. When he got home, I'd wipe him and fly out of there, never to be seen by Alex Marsden again.

Chapter Three

"You've been missing for six years." That was the greeting Alex gave me when he returned to the house.

I could say *duh* or say nothing. I opted for the latter. It sure took him long enough to get back. At least I took a nap while he was gone. Nice of his mom to have a comfy sofa in the basement.

"I found your file, Cherry. Or should I call you—"

"No, you definitely shouldn't call me that." Bad enough that he'd found out my real name. I didn't want to hear it again. It belonged to someone who died, who had a family and a future. Still, I couldn't help but feel a little flattered that he'd searched for me, especially since it had to be hard without knowing my real name when he went looking.

"Okay, but I don't get why. It's a nice na—"

"Never. I'm not her anymore. And how'd you find that file?"

"Looked for models who went missing six years ago. You don't look like your picture." Conversational tone, calm voice—maybe we were done with the drama for the day.

"I better not, if it's the picture my mom put in the paper when she was looking for me. I've lost seventeen pounds since that was taken." I missed Mom every day that went by, and the thought of her brought tears to my eyes. I wiped at them furiously, mentally thanking God that sunset was near. I could feel it in my bones.

"I don't know. I think you looked adorable. Blonde, green-eyed, round cheek—the poster child for healthy upbringing."

Alex sounded—dare I say it—flirty, but I couldn't respond in kind. I *had* been brought up perfectly, by loving parents who wanted the best for me. I'd been a rebel, though, and left home for a life in the big city. And here I was, in the City of Angels, but with no life to talk about and no way of getting back to the people I loved without risking their lives.

The tears began flowing freely, and I couldn't contain a sob.

"Cherry? Are you all right?" Concern colored his voice, and I wondered what had happened to bring that about. He seemed to despise me when he left the house hours earlier.

I sniffled. I wasn't all right. Not even close. I was alone, and that wasn't likely to change. "I miss my mom, okay? The big bad vampire misses her mom. And my dad…" My dad, who'd supported me in everything—who acted as a peacekeeper when Mom and I had one of our stupid yelling matches over something menial—thought I was dead. I was only a couple of hours away from him, but I'd never again get one of his bear hugs. Unable to put my emotions into words, I thudded my head against the door.

"Can I… Is there some way I can help?" Alex asked.

"Don't worry. I'll get over it."

"Want to open the door? We can talk about it. I can hold you."

It sounded so tempting that I reached for the knob, but I stopped myself. I didn't want him to make me feel better. I didn't want to need him or anyone. I didn't want to be weak and sad.

"Why do you care, anyway? I bet you just want me to open the door so you can see what vampire flambé looks like." Under my breath but loud enough for him to hear, I added, "Jerk."

"I'm not that attached to the door. I could break it in and watch you burn if that was what I wanted."

Don't be reasonable, for fuck's sake; work with me. "Then what? You want a second round? I'm a good lay, huh?" The words tasted bitter. I was being unfair and unreasonable, but I needed some distraction from my reality.

"I'm sorry," he said, effectively silencing me. "I freaked out this morning. I was scared, I guess. I shouldn't have acted the way I did. I'm so—"

"*I'm* sorry." It was becoming a trend, him apologizing, and this time it felt wrong. He'd come back offering an olive branch, and I'd been nothing but bitchy. "I'm sorry I bit you, too. I just don't know of another way to stay alive; I need blood." The truth, pure and simple.

"Did you only wanna fuck so you could feed?"

"I wanted to *have sex* with you because I liked you. I didn't mean to spend the night, and I'm sorry I fell asleep." I really was. More sorry that spending the night in his arms had felt like the most *right* thing I ever did.

"You liked me?"

I snapped, thinking he was after some ego stroking. "Yeah, I liked you. You're hot. Satisfied?"

"You don't anymore?"

I felt like screaming. What did he want from me? That morning I'd been something he couldn't wait to get rid of, and now…

As if he read my thoughts, he said, "When I found your file, you became more real. You were once again the woman I spent the night with, not a vampire." Pause. "I liked you too. Still do."

Ah crap. "Well, that's a bummer." We were not supposed to like each other. We were supposed to fight and yell. And I wasn't supposed to want to kiss him again.

"Tell me about it. Hottest woman I've met in a while, and I don't know if I can trust her not to eat me." I could tell he wasn't exactly joking.

Though justified, his lack of trust stung. At least it solved my lust problem. I no longer thought about kissing him. He was attracted to me, but he feared me, and because of that, nothing could happen between us again.

I was trying to find something to say to lighten the mood when the sound of wood breaking reached my ears.

"What was—"

"What the—" Something cut off the rest of Alex's words and made him grunt in pain.

I burst out of the basement without a second thought. I had to save Alex from whatever harmed him.

As he told me later, the sun was already down when he returned. So much for vampire instincts—go, me. At the time, however, I wasn't thinking that I might be in danger—and just when my previous burns had healed.

A man in a black ski mask held Alex by the neck against the living room wall, his grasp not loosening despite Alex's struggles. I ran toward them, but a second masked intruder flew into me before I reached them.

He had no pulse.

The discovery shocked me enough that he managed to elbow me in the face and flip me on my back. I listened for the other burglar's heartbeat but got nothing other than the erratic thudding coming from Alex.

I tried to get up, but the guy straddled my thighs. I had to get him off me. I thrashed and kicked but only made him cackle. *Cackle*. Like a cartoon villain.

"Stop that, Cherry," he said, "or Mr. Marsden will get to watch me do naughty things to you." The lack of profanity and his matter-of-fact tone scared me, but not as much as his knowing my name did.

I forced myself to relax and tried to think. He knew who Alex and I were, so it wasn't a random burglary.

"There's a nice girl." The scary vamp on top of me caressed my cheek. I'd heard his faint British accent before.

Out of the corner of my eye, I saw the second vampire relax his hold on Alex, who panted for air. Before relief could sink in, the guy shook Alex like a rag doll.

Alex's head hit the wall with a sickening *thud*, and he slumped to the floor, his heartbeat weak but steady.

I went from scared to furious.

A small table lay on its side next to me.

I squirmed underneath the heavy man. I didn't try to throw him off. On the contrary, I rubbed my body against his. "If you know me, you know what I can do."

He closed his fingers around my neck and pulled me closer. "Haven't seen you in action, but I wouldn't mind a private showing." He slid his knee between my thighs. Gag.

I reached out and closed my fingers around one leg of the table. There was no way I could break it without him noticing, but wood doesn't need to be sharpened, to be lethal. Not if you use enough force.

I arched upward and rubbed my cheek against my attacker's neck. He roamed my body with his free hand, and I made an effort not to flinch away from his repulsive touch. "I have something in mind for you," I said.

"Oh, I'll get what I want. Don't worry." He raised his head to look at me, and I went for the throat.

I closed my jaws over his jugular, locking him in place. Before he could react, I brought the entire table up. Hoping I my aim was good, I plunged the leg through his back with all the strength I could muster. Flesh ripped and ribs cracked under the force of my blow. The next moment, my mouth filled with ashes. I'd heard staking led to instant death, but I couldn't imagine that a person could be there one moment and simply *not* there the next—nothing but a thin layer of white powder.

I didn't have time to pull back before the end of the leg hit my chest. Sputtering and blinking hard against the dust that was everywhere, I rolled to my side and looked around.

The second male vampire snarled and lunged at me. I was on my feet and swinging the table in no time. It caught him on the head and stopped him in his tracks.

"*You bitch.*" He took a couple of steps back. "I should have killed you after all."

That voice I knew. "Willoughby?" Impossible. He met the sun half-a-dozen years ago.

Before I could move, he was out the door, promising we'd meet again. "And the next time, I'll make things right."

Vampires can't faint, but I was as close to that as physically possible. I went to Alex on legs as sturdy as noodles, and let out a sigh of relief when he inhaled. I picked him up and carried him to the armchair we'd spent the night in. "Alex?"

To my relief, he opened those beautiful gray eyes of his. "Cherry?" His lips moved slowly. "Who were—? What—? *What*?" He let his head drop back and squeezed his eyes shut again. "Were they vampires?"

"Yes. I dusted one of them, but the other escaped." I took his hand between mine, and my heart clenched when he pulled away. I tried to keep my voice from wavering. "Are you all right?"

He looked at me with a rueful smile. "I'll survive." His voice was hoarse.

"You'd better." What was it with me and crying today? Tears filled my eyes again, making my vision blurry. Still, I made out the narrowing of his eyes as he studied my face.

"These are real tears?" When I nodded, he muttered, "I thought they'd be blood."

"I'm so sorry I dragged you into this. The guy who escaped was my maker. He was supposed to be dead. *Dead* dead. He must have been after me, and you were in their way." I shouldn't have spent the night. I shouldn't have—

"What's done is done." He touched the back of his head gingerly and winced. "Why did you help me instead of running?"

"Oh, I dunno. Because they attacked you?"

His eyebrow quirked, one corner of his mouth twitching before he elaborated. "They're your people. You should be on their side."

"That's not how it works. We're not a pack." He'd offered to hold me and keep the sadness at bay, before the attack. For that reason alone, I wouldn't lose my patience and bite him to shut him up.

"So what?"

"Do you help criminals out, 'cause they're human?"

He shook his head.

"I didn't think so. Besides, I like you more than I do them. Plus it's my fault they were here. They must have followed me to the club and waited until it was dark again, to make their move." My theory had enough holes to be used as a fishing net, but the gist of the matter was that I was to blame.

"I don't think they were after you," Alex said.

I reached for his hand again. He didn't avoid my touch this time, and I gave him a gentle squeeze. "What do you mean?"

"Can vampires enter someone's home uninvited?" He coughed like his lungs were on fire, and I wondered if he'd taken a punch or two before I came out of the basement.

I patted his back. "No. They have to be asked in by the owner. Unless the owner is dead, of course, in which case…" The horror of what I said made me numb.

Alex searched his pockets like crazy. "My phone."

I spotted the cordless lying on the floor and rushed to get it for him.

He snatched it from my outstretched hand, punched in the buttons, and brought it to his ear. His body relaxed after a couple of seconds. Not wanting to intrude on a family moment, I pretended to be preoccupied with my nails but watched him for signs of discomfort.

"Hey, Mom. The house is fine." He blushed and lowered his voice. "Yeah, I'm eating right. Mom, I'm thirty-two. I live by myself; I know how to… Yeah, okay." He nodded a couple of times. Rubbed his throat. "I promise. See you soon." A grin split his face. "Say *hi* from me too, and he better be taking care of you."

I didn't look at him until he caressed my knuckles with his thumb.

"She's fine," I said with a smile. His mother was unharmed, and he was being all chummy with the back of my hand. Things were looking up.

He cleared his throat and nodded. "Which proves my suspicion. They've been here before."

Another coughing bout took him over. I went to the kitchen, filled one of the glasses on the drying block with tap water, and rushed back. He took it with a shaky hand and a mumbled *thank you*, and downed the water greedily. Choking on the second gulp forced him to take it a bit slower, but he still finished the whole glass.

Reverting to cop mode happened instantly, in front of my very eyes. The line of his mouth hardened, his face becoming a stone mask. He was scary in a way that turned me on beyond words. "We've never met before last night, have we? You haven't…" He waved a hand by his head.

"No. Of course not."

"Then I was right. They were after me."

The idea seemed preposterous. "Why?" I didn't mean for it to sound like I didn't find him significant enough, but he scowled.

"I'm a *cop*, Cherry." The scowling lost its oomph by the way he rubbed his chest, as if in pain. He waved off my worry when I asked if he was all right, and said, "I go after bad guys. Most of the time, I piss them off."

I rolled my eyes and sat on the armrest, one foot tucked under my butt. "Supernatural bad guys? You couldn't piss off the normal mafia kind?"

His laughter caught me unawares. "It seems the supernatural is attracted to me these days." He was still chuckling when he cupped the back of my head and pulled me in for a kiss. Brief and casual, it felt like something I could get used to—if I weren't a vampire or he weren't a human.

He seemed to no longer resent my nature, and he was still attracted to me, but I couldn't allow myself to get comfortable with that idea. "Any clue why they'd be after you?" I tried to pull away, but he didn't let me.

"Been looking into a series of disappearances lately. Girls in their twenties. Beautiful, sociable, no direct family. They go to a club or a party, then nobody hears from them again."

I pushed against his chest and straightened up. "Willoughby—my maker—he turned me after a party. If he's part of it…"

"You think he's turning them?" His voice was flat, no emotion coloring it.

"I think you should look for them in Dumpsters."

"He's killing them?"

"That was his plan for me." Making my voice gruffer, I said, "*I should have killed you, bitch.* His words, not mine."

Alex narrowed his eyes and furrowed his brow. "We haven't found any bodies."

"Oh my God, I knew the other guy too. The one I offed? He lied the first time we met. He hasn't seen me."

Alex looked perplexed. Of course Alex looked perplexed. Alex didn't know, and I didn't make any sense.

"I was in a couple of films. Of the adult variety." Biting my lip, I turned away. "It was a long time ago."

It was the perfect time for him to say something, but he was quiet, even the wheezing gone from his breath.

"A long, *long* time ago." I needed to know he was fine with it. "Never mind. Forget about it. The point is the guy whose remains I'm now wearing was the one who found me after my turning. His name was Ted. Back then, he said he recognized me. That he was a fan." Alex was watching me, expressionless. I wanted to slap him. "Tonight he said he'd never seen me in action, which means he lied before. Also— hey—he was here with my maker. Isn't it too much of a coincidence?"

For the first time, I thought maybe my situation hadn't been an accident. *Maybe* I was supposed to have been found. "I remember waking up, hungry and disoriented. I'd just found my footing when Ted appeared. He made a big fuss about how he loved my work, and insisted he take me to the council. If he and Willoughby are a team now, they could have been one back then too."

My maker's insistence on leaving the party early also made sense with that scenario. Newly turned vampires don't rise until the next evening, if their turning is less than a few hours from dawn. My rising had to be the same night as my death, or Willoughby would have risked someone else finding me first, and my awakening taking place in the morgue.

"Are you sure it was him? Ted?" Nice. Alex would pretend he didn't hear the porn-related part.

"Yes. I knew his voice when he spoke, but I couldn't place it till now."

"Hmmm." He motioned for me to lean closer, and I did. He was hurt. Perhaps he needed me to help him up. He smirked. "Can I get my hands on either one of those films?"

I matched his expression. "If you beg, maybe." He licked his lips. He was about to kiss me again. Badness lay that way. Flirty territory was too shaky under the circumstances. I got back to the subject we should be concerned with. "We have to do something."

He grimaced. "I know. I finally have a lead, thanks to you, but I can't tell my lieutenant that *vampires* did it." He pulled me sideways onto his lap. "Any clue where we can find that guy?"

"I told you, I thought he was dead. Executed for turning someone recognizable." I loved how soothing his hands felt, caressing my back, yet I had to wonder how we got where we were.

His acceptance of my undeadness had to be due to my fighting on his side, but could we pick up where we'd left off the night before? A question for another time.

"A huge mess was stirred when I was found," I said. "The existing council at the time was overthrown. My turning was the reason for the ruling against any but the oldest of vampires turning people, and even they must have a special permit."

"Maybe you should start at the beginning." His chuckle sounded forced. "My head is spinning with all the random data."

I offered what I saw as a good alternative. "I can do better than that. I can make you forget that I—that *we*—exist."

He pushed me back. Not hard. Not a shove. He just grasped my shoulders and made me sit up, my upper body away from him. "No. You don't mess with my head. Don't even think about it."

I felt the need to explain, if not defend myself. "It won't be messing. I won't take away anything you need, just the—"

"*No.* You will take away nothing." He threw his arms in the air. "*God.*" Upset as he sounded, he didn't make me get off his lap.

"I'm only trying to help." Maybe, just *maybe*, I was sulking.

"Help?" He widened his eyes. "How? By making me forget important info about a case that may never be solved otherwise? By making me forget one of the best nights of—"

He clumped his mouth shut midsentence, but what I heard was enough to make me stop sulking. I got the point. And I liked it. Not that I could show my improved mood, with him scowling the way he was.

"I'll pretend you never offered to do that," he said, only slightly mellower. "Now tell me what I need to know about all this."

What *did* he need to know? "I guess I'll take it from the start." I bit the inside of my cheek. "I mean, I was sort of a celeb, I got bitten by a guy I met at a party, and until now I thought he left me for dead." Alex's gray-eyed gaze was locked on mine, making it exceedingly hard for me to remember what I meant to say next.

I can proudly say I managed, nevertheless. "Ted—vamp who went poof—found me, said he recognized me from my films, and took me to the council to record my turning."

"The council. You mentioned it before. What is it exactly? How does it work?"

I took an unnecessary breath, then let the air rush out noisily between my lips. "It more or less comes up with rules to be followed. And of course with the repercussions for not following those rules." Like for spilling my guts about our kind to a human. But it wasn't like he'd tell anyone while I was around, and I'd make him forget about us when I said *goodbye*, whether he wanted me to or not.

Alex looked at me, waiting for the interesting part, I guess. Too bad there wasn't such a part coming. "There are five council members. Used to be the oldest vampires that ran things, but after"—I pointed at myself—"well, most of the ones who overthrew them are younger."

"Why was the council overthrown over something an errant vamp did?"

That was a great question, actually. Why didn't I wonder about that before? Oh, right—I didn't bother with logic. What I cared about at the time was that I'd never have the perfect abs, that I was hungry, and that my career would never take off. "The story was that the old council should have come up with rules against random turning earlier, and that by not having done so they betrayed the ones they were appointed to protect."

"And the new council cares more?" he asked.

"I don't know. The services that took me in were established when vampires were first organized, but they're no longer necessary, since we don't have more fledglings, so they were… discontinued. That's the only change I know of."

"Services?" He tilted his head to the right and cocked an eyebrow. It was unsettling that I considered the movement a trademark of his, like I'd known him for a long time and not just twenty-four hours. "Like *social* services?"

I could see the idea of a vampire society with an infrastructure similar to that of humans amused him. "Yup." I popped the *p*. "*Vampire* Social Services. We called them VSS. They took in new vamps and taught us what we needed in order to survive." I paused. "There were also leaflets and a handbook to be memorized and destroyed before we left."

Alex gave me a full-blown grin, and I swatted his shoulder. "Don't mock, sir. It was helpful. I wouldn't have learned how to control the thirst or fend for myself without it. I'm not sure I'd have even wanted to." Constantine had helped me practice what I'd read, but it wasn't the time to mention him.

He caressed my back, his long fingers drawing soothing circles that drove the stress away. "In that case, I'm glad you had it." He leaned closer to me.

I wanted to kiss him, but there were things to be discussed. "I think I should talk to the council about tonight."

He sucked in his lower lip. I wished I were the one doing the sucking.

"Sounds good." His fingers crawled up my neck and began massaging my scalp. "And I should keep looking at what the missing girls had in common other than their age and looks. They didn't even all vanish from the same place."

The massage relaxed me, and soon I felt my eyelids drifting shut. "Can I take a look at their pictures? I know people. I could ask around, see if they heard anything about new fledglings."

"I can get you their files, but I don't want you to take any risks. He already saw you with me. If he finds out you're looking into this…" He stilled his movements and narrowed his eyes. "If he hurts you—"

That was another sentence he didn't get to finish, this time because I sealed his lips with mine. It was a spontaneous reaction. He was worried for me. Wanted to protect me.

"Where did that come from?" He didn't seem to mind.

I shrugged, unable to meet his gaze. "Felt like it."

With his index finger, he tucked my hair behind my ear. "I'm glad you did." His thumb brushed my chin, lingering at the corner of my lips.

There was too much tension, too much *something* I didn't want to identify between us. I wouldn't be able to handle it if he kept being so nice, so cute, so…

I looked around. The place wasn't wrecked, but we had stuff to do. Thank God for small favors. The smashed coffee table lay by a broken lamp, the overhead light reflecting off the scattered shards of glass and sprinkling tiny dots of light onto the upturned couch. Dust covered a doily I was sure had been handmade. The table I used as a weapon was remarkably unscathed—more than could be said for the curtains, one side of which had been ripped off the rail.

"Let's clean up." I hopped off Alex's lap.

He got up after me. "The front door lock is busted. I'll have to go buy a new one." He stood so close, I felt the heat of his body like we were still touching.

I nodded. Casually putting some distance between us, I picked up the doily and shook it, in an effort to get dusted vamp off it.

Alex turned the couch upright and replaced the cushions on it. "The bolt wasn't on, so I can use that to keep the door closed, but I can't lock from outside."

I studied the ruins of the coffee table, our glasses from the previous night miraculously intact on the floor. I tried hard not to stare at how his dress pants stretched over the curve of his ass when he bent down for the last throw pillow. I needed to get the vacuum and mop from the basement. Anything to keep from jumping him.

"Can you stick around until I'm back?" he asked.

I raised my gaze to him. Why did he have to look so adorable, looking at the floor, his hands deep in his pockets?

"Alex—" I wanted to say how bad an idea that would be.

"You know—so nobody robs the place? Of course, I won't be able to put in the new lock till morning. I'll need better light." He looked like the cat that swallowed the canary. The porch light was probably as bright as the sun. "You could spend the night. Stay here for backup if Willoughby returns. And we can talk about the case. See how to proceed with it."

Bad, *bad* idea, but I couldn't think of why. I wasn't wiping him yet, and he already knew we existed, so one more night wouldn't be a problem. "Sure." I tried to sound disinterested, though the thought of being with him a bit longer made me giddy. "I'll crash in the basement."

"Good. That couch turns into a double bed, so we can both sleep there."

I was torn between feeling stupid for not figuring that out, or giddy because he was suggesting we spend the rest of the night in bed together.

"You can—" He cleared his throat. "You can drink from me again if you need to."

As if his initial offer wasn't alluring enough. My mouth watered.

"I don't have to go in tomorrow, so we can stay here during the day too." He rubbed his chin. A day's stubble gave him a more rugged look.

Okay, okay—I was sold. "You'll have to get me something to wear. I'm not sleeping in leather again," I said, trying not to sound suggestive.

"I'm on it." Waggling his eyebrows, he moved toward the door. "I'll be right back. Feel free to start tidying up," he said over his shoulder as he crossed the threshold.

I called his name, but he ignored me. I hoped he'd be careful and stay safe. Willoughby wouldn't be going after him again so soon—not without backup, since he knew Alex had me to help him—but caution is always a good thing.

A door was shut between us once more, and I hadn't been the one doing the shutting. Still, I felt oddly optimistic as I skipped down the steps to the basement, to get the vacuum cleaner. I'd met an incredibly hot man with whom I'd had incredible sex, and he hadn't wanted me out of his life the moment he found out I was undead. For the first time since Constantine, I felt warm inside.

Vampires are not supposed to feel warm.

Chapter Four

Alex took a bit more than an hour to get back, which left me with plenty of time to kill, after the fifteen minutes it took me to clean up in vamp speed. Impressed? If the vacuum sucked harder, it'd take even less.

I was in the shower but clearly made out his footsteps on the stairs, even under the running water.

"Honey, I'm home," he called out.

I knew he was joking, yet the relentless romantic hidden deep inside me let out a *woot*. I opened the glass pane so he'd hear me. "I'm in here."

I didn't get to tell him I'd be right out, because he came right in. He wore the clothes he had on since last night, shirt untucked, and he was barefoot. He had beautiful feet, I noticed. Big, *male* feet with long, straight toes.

I had to get a grip.

Hiding my body seemed silly after we had sex, so I didn't. Not that he looked.

He dropped a duffel bag by the sink. "Thought you'd want clean clothes as soon as you were dry. Got a couple tees and sweatpants from my place. They'll be too big for you, but the pants have drawstrings. Should be good for the night."

Then he pulled his shirt over his head.

If I were human, the water filling my mouth and clogging my throat while I gaped at him would have drowned me. As things were, I was grateful I'd opened the shower stall door and could enjoy the view.

Most people look better when they're dressed than when they're out of their clothes. There are always flaws.

Something that needs covering up—a jutting stomach, love handles, scars, pimples. *Something.*

To me, Alex was perfect.

I ran my fingers down his chest and abs last night, but seeing the smooth, flawless skin stretch over rippling muscle made me ache to caress it. His shoulders were wide. I knew that already, but the way they rounded, leading to his flexing biceps, was a sight to behold. And that was what I did. I *beheld*, wishing he was closer, so I could press my breasts against his chest and see goose bumps rise.

I'd have kept staring at his six-pack for much longer if his fingers hadn't gotten in the way. Splayed across his abdomen and ghosting their way down to the front of his pants, they touched what I longed for. I wanted to lick my way along the trail of fine hair beneath his navel that disappeared inside his waistband. I sucked in a breath when he undid the button and another when he lowered the zipper to allow his slacks to fall to the teal tiled floor.

I followed them with my gaze, until he stepped out of the pooled fabric and toward the shower stall.

Toward me.

I bit my lip, barely registering the pain as I took in the muscled calves, the strong thighs, and finally his magnificent cock. He was inside me last night, but our hurry and my position above him didn't allow me to fully appreciate his... assets.

I did now. Springing from a nest of trimmed black curls, hard, darker than the rest of his body, long and thick and slightly curved to the right, Alex's cock beckoned with every step he took.

I was more than ready to respond to its beckoning when he joined me under the water jet.

Like staying here again became a good idea and telling Alex about vampires seemed preferable to making him forget he ever met one, having sex with him one more time now struck me as the only viable scenario.

I didn't care how he'd take me; he could press my face against the glass door, my back against the tiles, or have me on all fours. I just wanted him inside me. I tried to wrap my arms around his neck, but he got hold of my wrists, stopping me.

My face must have shown my confusion, because he smiled. "The water is cold," he said.

"Don't like it much hotter than this." Ignore what you read in most books. Vampire body temperature makes us sensitive to heat, not cold. For him, I turned the faucet a bit to the left.

He turned the water off altogether. "That's better."

I watched, mesmerized, while he took his time uncapping the shower gel, pouring some of it in his palm, and capping the bottle again.

He put it back in its place and rubbed his hands together until they were covered in foam. "Turn around. I'll do you first."

Oh, the innuendo in that last sentence.

Uncaring that I'd lathered and rinsed, I turned my back to him.

"Pull your hair up," he said.

I twirled my red tresses into one thick curl and tucked it at the side of my neck.

It wasn't enough. "Hold it up with both hands and don't let go." His voice brooked no argument, and I was more than excited with his take-control attitude.

I did what he asked, trembling only slightly when he closed big, strong hands over my shoulders and massaged the lather onto my skin. He pressed his thumbs against the back of my neck, digging his fingers rhythmically into the muscle and releasing knots I didn't know were there.

Moaning my approval, I let my head fall forward. His hands went to my shoulder blades, spreading the foam there before moving to my back. He followed the line of my spine, his palms and knuckles taking turns in working my flesh. I barely kept my footing as he slowly stroked his way down to my ass before kneeling behind me.

He ran a finger between my ass cheeks and chuckled when I reflexively clenched. He pressed a finger lightly against my asshole. "Don't worry. I'm not going here—today."

I wanted to come up with some smart retort, but he began massaging my inner thighs. His thumbs almost touched my pussy. I jerked back toward him, trying to rub against them. I craved his touch a bit higher. Just a bit…

Argh. He moved on to the backs of my knees, which nearly buckled, and then to my calves. I was wet, and not just from the shower. His touch set my skin on fire, and I squeezed my thighs together, needing friction to ease my need. It wasn't enough. It felt like nothing but Alex would be enough ever again.

When I couldn't take more teasing, he stood and ordered me to face him. His voice sounded husky and strained. Thinking I would finally get what I wanted, I complied eagerly.

Alex had something else in mind.

He prepared more lather and rubbed my throat. The pressure from his hand combined with the silkiness of the foam to make me light-headed. He was so close, his breath warmed my skin. I tried to lower my arms and grab him—wanted to smash my lips against his, climb him and impale myself on him—but a shake of his head told me not to.

"Trust me," he said.

"Why should I?" Despite my flippant answer, I knew that frighteningly, inexplicably, I did. I would angst over that later, once I was satisfied and had the luxury to worry about my budding feelings for a mere mortal.

"Because I know how to make your body sing." Cocky, but a proven fact. "Now no more talking."

Nodding sapped my strength. My entire being felt tense, not from the strain he chased away with his magic touch, but with anticipation of what would happen next. Where would his hands go after my collarbone? I couldn't believe I stood there while he made my body react any way he pleased. It had been a long time since I granted anyone control over me, and I found it hard to do so now. Then again, it was so long since anyone evoked such lust in me, since I enjoyed anyone's attentions like I did Alex's, that I couldn't find it in me to be anything except passive.

That would change if he took much longer.

He feathered the heels of his palms over my nipples, making them rise in hardened peaks.

I arched my back, pressing my breasts against his palms, and reveled when I realized his hands trembled. His heart thundered, and his jaw was clenched. It took as much effort on his side as it did on mine, to maintain the slow pace he'd imposed.

Good.

Gaze on mine, he cupped my breasts and kneaded them. He rolled the nipples between his fingers. His breathing sounded labored, but his movements weren't rushed. He lowered his hands to my stomach and got on his knees once more, this time in front of me, to soap my belly and thighs.

I pushed my hips forward, craving his touch on my pussy. He didn't disappoint. He snaked his hand between my legs and glided it back and forth. His touch didn't linger, but it didn't have to. Each stroke raised my temperature and made me rub against him. My legs trembled. I felt empty. I needed him to fill me and soothe the ache in me.

He massaged my clit with his thumb and slid it inside me, but not deep enough. I let go of my hair and placed both hands on his head, trying to stay upright, as well as hoping he'd use more than his fingers on me. Instead he withdrew and finished lathering the front of my legs. Then he rose and reached behind me for the shampoo.

"You shouldn't have let go of your hair," he said. "Now it needs washing too."

He kept his lower body away from mine till now, not letting me feel him. When his hard cock brushed my stomach, I hissed. He seemed unaffected, fully focused on making lather of the jasmine-scented liquid.

He proceeded to work the shampoo into my hair, and I couldn't help but look down at him. Our bodies touched, his length rubbing against me at the same time his arms moved so he could massage my scalp. I wanted to drop down onto my knees and take him in my mouth.

Too suddenly, he stopped and took a step back. "My turn."

I thought he meant I should treat him to the same pampering he treated me to. Wrong again. When he held me at arm's length and poured shower gel down his body, frustration made me see red.

He washed himself fast, with not even half the care with which he'd washed me, yet his hands caressing all of him was the most erotic thing I'd ever seen. Tan skin gleamed against white foam and made me lick my lips.

He closed his fist around his shaft. In a circular motion, he coiled it from the tip to the base of his cock once, twice, before returning to his abdomen. A groan escaped me.

I think it was what finally made him break. Or maybe it was his plan from the start to do things the way he did next. He turned the water on, folded one arm around my waist, and cupped my neck with his other hand, to bring me to him. I stumbled and clung to his biceps, to keep my balance. They were made of steel. Once I was flush against him under the jet, he lowered his face to mine for a kiss.

His posture held such urgency, I expected him to devour my mouth, yet his kiss was gentle. Almost timid. He brushed his lips against mine with tenderness, before tracing their seam with his tongue. I opened for him, meaning to deepen the kiss, but he wouldn't be hurried. Suds and water cascaded down my face, getting in my eyes and mouth, but I couldn't have cared less. Alex gasped for breath, but he wouldn't stop kissing me. He leisurely explored my mouth until I felt like my feet didn't touch the ground.

And then they no longer did.

Alex lifted me in his arms and turned the water off with a nudge of his elbow. I don't know what he was about to do next, but I didn't wait to find out. As he maneuvered me in his arms, I lifted my legs, wrapped them around his hips, and let myself sink on his dick.

"Cherry—" He lost his footing but regained his balance and turned so I was pressed between him and the glass wall. "You really shouldn't have done that." His eyes glinted with mischief.

"Um, if it's about the condom thing, can't get pregnant and not carrying any nasty germs." I moved against him.

He chuckled and grabbed my ass with both hands, stilling me. "I thought we could use a bed this time."

I tightened my inner muscles' grip on his shaft. "Beds are overrated."

His body tensed, his grip on my ass becoming punishing. I must have made some sound, because he relaxed his hands and whispered an apology before claiming my lips. This time his kiss was hungry, demanding. He bit my lips like he was trying to devour me, and began driving his cock in and out of me.

Water didn't make for the best lubricant, but I liked the friction. I loved being sandwiched between a hot man and a cool glass pane and being thoroughly fucked.

Only it didn't feel like mere fucking.

Alex was rambling. I wasn't sure he knew what came out of his mouth, but I heard it all. I was beautiful, perfect to him. He never wanted to hurt me. The openness and honesty of his face, the awe in his eyes as he sank and withdrew from my body was overwhelming. For the second time in as many days, he offered me much more than just sex. He offered me companionship. Comfort. He promised me a tomorrow.

I wasn't sure I deserved it. I knew I couldn't handle it.

I leaned my head back and cried.

There were no sobs, only tears falling down my cheeks, pooling at my neck. Tears that seemed to cleanse me of all the bad that had accumulated inside through the years.

He noticed, despite my already wet skin, and ceased his movements. He caressed my cheek and asked if something was wrong. I wanted to ease the worry in his voice but could do nothing other than shake my head and rock my pelvis, urging him on. I couldn't tell him he'd touched me deeper than anyone else. I didn't know why I was crying. I only knew I was happy and terrified at the same time.

He took my hint and started fucking—no, *making love* to—me again. He lifted one of my legs higher and plunged inside me faster. His mouth found mine, and he swallowed the choked mewls that escaped my lips.

He was deeper than before, but that wasn't enough. "More."

My wet back made funny sounds against the glass, but the only sound I cared about was Alex's heartbeat.

He panted into my mouth, slamming his hips against mine. He hit all the right places with every move of his pelvis. That was all that mattered.

"Come for me, baby," he whispered. His breath quickened.

I was close. All I needed was…

Not losing a beat, he slid his hand down the length of my body, all the way to where we were joined. "Come for me," he said again, pressing down on my clit with his thumb. "*Now*, Cherry."

The earth-shattering pleasure seemed to short-circuit my brain, white fire bursting through my veins. I locked him in place with arms and legs while I rode out my orgasm. My legs shook and my hands trembled, while my body convulsed against him. Stars blossomed behind my closed eyelids, as rapture washed over me.

His thrusts, rhythmic until then, became erratic, jerky, when he gave in and let go. He came inside me, the heat of his cum making me shudder one last time, but he didn't stop moving until his cock was half erect and his heartbeat had slowed to normal.

I have no clue where he found the strength to remain standing, but he toed the stall's door open and carried me out of the bathroom and into the next room, where a large double bed took up most of the space. The rest held a desk and a bookshelf in one corner, the latter decorated with pictures of a young boy. *Alex.* "Your old room."

He nodded and laid me gently on the bed before collapsing next to me. "Gimme twenty minutes, and we'll show this room things it never saw before."

My lips were too numb to form a coherent reply. I giggled.

Swallowing a gulp of air, he looked at me, head tilted to one side. "Something funny?"

I shrugged, still laughing.

His eyes glinted. He shook his head. "As soon as I regain feeling in my legs, I'll show you it's not nice to laugh at people."

I silenced him with kisses. Tried to, at least.

Before dawn, he carried me to the basement, where we spent more time exploring each other's bodies. I fed, but only after he reminded me I hadn't in more than twenty-four hours. He insisted he'd had something to eat while he'd been out.

When I drifted off this time, I knew I was safe in Alex's arms, the rise and fall of his chest soothing against my back.

I also knew another thing—I was falling hard.

For a human.

I wished I wouldn't come to regret it.

Chapter Five

I was just done relooping the laces through my bustier's tiny eyelets, when the bedside light was switched on.

"What's with the leather again?" Alex lay on his side, propped up on one elbow, his cheek cradled in his palm. "I brought you clothes. You can wear those around the house."

I pursed my lips, thinking of the contents of the bag he'd brought. Not the most flattering fit. A dazzling smile blossomed on his lips, and I had to smile back.

"Or you could wear nothing." He waggled his eyebrows.

I looked away. If I spent a couple more seconds looking at the curve of his hip, his white teeth nibbling at his lower lip, or the way he invitingly caressed the sheet in front of him, I'd forget what I had to do, and jump back under the covers with him. "I have to go." My traitorous gaze returned to him.

He turned on his back and pulled the sheet up all the way to his chest in a gesture so prudish it'd be funny if I didn't want to rip the covers off him. "To the council?"

I shook my head. "No. Someone else first. I want to see if he can arrange a meeting." I'd showered again but hadn't paid enough attention to towel drying, and it was a bitch putting my boots on, which worked out fine since fighting to pull them up meant I didn't have to look at him.

"*He?*" Out of the corner of my eye, I saw him run a hand through his hair. "Should I be jealous?"

My worry that maybe he should be, that my meeting Constantine was a horrible idea, was what made me snap at him. "You have no right to be jealous." I shouldn't feel bad for saying that; he wasn't my boyfriend.

Ha. The boots were finally in place. I trained my gaze on him.

Alex nodded.

Right. So I felt bad. And I'd pop by my place to change into something less sexy before visiting my ex. "Will you be okay?" I expected him to say I had no right to ask that.

He surprised me. "It depends. Will you be back?" He wasn't facing me, but I made out the muscle ticking in his jaw. I liked knowing it took effort for him to be so calm and civil—and God, did that make me a horrible person.

I should keep my distance. Especially after the way I felt last night. I should go see Constantine, have a quickie for old times' sake, and only contact Alex when I knew something about the case. "Don't you plan on going home at some point? Oversee the repairmen?"

Why did he have to have that boyish grin? "Nope. No need to. Gas company guys know what they're doing." He shrugged. "And I have everything I need here." The look he threw me indicated he was referring to much more than groceries. "So will you be back?"

"Yeah. It won't take long." Not if my brain still worked after seeing Constantine for the first time since I broke up with him.

Alex held out a hand to me. I closed the distance to the bed, took it, and leaned over so I could kiss him goodbye.

****

Constantine's human butler, Wesley, opened the heavy mahogany door. There was no sign of recognition on his ancient face even after I gave him my name. It stung that he didn't remember me—not like he'd seen me almost daily for two years.

He let me in and told me Constantine was waiting for me in his *boudoir*. His smile when I groaned at the thought of meeting my ex in his bedroom took twenty years off his wrinkled face. "I suggested the parlor, but when Master Constantine is set on something, there is no talking him out of it," he said.

Tell me about it. I'd been yelling at the stubborn ass to leave me alone for four years now. Constantine didn't relent one bit in his pursuit and still called me at least twice a week, to see how I was doing and ask if I'd reconsidered.

I followed the human inside with a nod, trying not to scoff at *parlor*. Why would a vampire need one unless he was a pretentious bastard? Never mind, I got my answer right there. I scratched out the thought that I'd considered his flashiness part of his charm when we were together. I'd been too smitten to be objective.

Not staring at the blatant expressions of wealth along the corridor that led to the stairway took a lot of effort. The tapestry was embroidered with what I knew was real gold. I couldn't help but compare my ex's lifestyle with Alex's. It both relieved and scared me that in my mind, Alex won, hands down.

The thick carpet enveloped our feet, drowning out the sounds of our footsteps as we took the stairs down.

Constantine heard us, nevertheless. "Come in, darling," he called from behind the closed door of his bedroom. "We won't be needing you, Wesley."

The old man reached for the doorknob, but I placed my hand on it and shook my head. "I got it."

I expected him to insist, but he gave me a small bow, his joints creaking, and disappeared up the stairs faster than I considered possible.

I so didn't want to open that door.

The knob felt cold under my palm, uninviting. I turned it and pushed anyway, to reveal a sight that would have taken my breath away, if I had any.

I'd called before dropping by, in hopes Constantine would be decent by the time I went to his mansion. I ought to have known better. The light of at least ten dozen candles showered a room twice as big as my apartment, in the center of which stood a bed double the width and length of a king-size.

The deep-purple silken duvet matched the color of the walls and made stark contrast with Constantine's naked upper body.

He was waiting for me *in bed*.

Fortunately he was covered from the waist down. His long legs were bent at the knees, and he had one arm folded behind his head, the other lying loosely at his side. His hair, long and golden, framed his head, making him look like an angel. I knew no angel would be as wicked as he was or have as perfect a body.

His height—I confess, I like my men tall—and absurd sexiness were the only similarities between him and Alex. Alex's well-built body and short, wavy hair, that perfectly black that even the best colorist wouldn't be able to duplicate, brought to mind a Greek god. Constantine's lean and sinewy frame, his long blond hair, and blue eyes made me think of a Norse deity. One that pillaged and made love for hours.

That was definitely not how I should be thinking of him.

I couldn't move. Couldn't enter the room or back out of it and run like I wanted to.

He reached out, much like Alex had when I left him earlier that evening, and beckoned me to him with his index finger.

For a moment, seeing his bare skin gleam in the candlelight, I forgot everything. I forgot how he crushed my heart underfoot after I gave it to him. I forgot that he was a cheater and that he filled me with insecurities even before I knew he was sleeping with someone else. I shut the door and stepped closer.

His beautiful, sexy, promising smile was what snapped me out of it. It was too self-satisfied for my taste. That lift of his sensual lips said, *I knew you'd come to me*. Once upon a time, that would have been enough for me to strip and jump him. Now I was glad I'd taken the time to go by my apartment and change into a pair of blue jeans, a hoodie, and sneakers. It was a small victory that I hadn't dressed up for him.

I stopped at the foot of the bed and said, "We have to talk."

He pouted, and I felt like a loser for wanting to pull his jutting lower lip between my own. "Do we have to?" he asked.

Why would he still have an accent? He'd been in the States for a couple of centuries, long enough to speak like he was born here. Was he keeping it only to make me want him?

"Yes. We do." Go me, for sounding so sure.

"Can't we kiss hello, first? That's what my people do."

"You're not Italian, Constantine." That wasn't even his real name, not that I could talk. He'd changed his name when he moved here, going for something more sophisticated. "Your people probably decapitated one another as a greeting." Okay, I was being stupid, but all that hotness put me on my defensive mode.

He laughed, and the sound felt like a caress. He used to laugh like that when he reduced me to a pile of goo after hours and hours of amazing sex. *Gah.* Could I stop thinking about that, please? I hadn't been the only one he liked goo-ifying.

"How about a kiss because you want to, then?"

I scowled. I didn't want to kiss him, did I?

"I guess that's a *no.*" He raised his arms in defeat. "Fine. We'll talk, then." I was about to sigh in relief, when he folded the quilt back from his legs and slid out of bed.

He was naked.

And hard.

And walking toward me.

Telling him to put something on took all the self-control I possessed, and I was drained by the time he draped a dark-blue robe over his shoulders. It didn't hide anything, but if I opened my mouth to tell him that, I'd drool.

There was nothing in the room we could sit on except the bed, so I reluctantly parked my butt at its edge. I had to hop a bit to manage that, but I did so as gracefully as possible and locked gazes with him. Big mistake. He was the only vampire I knew whose eyes changed color according to his mood. Their current violet meant he was hungry. And not for blood.

That was the way his eyes had looked every time his lips sought mine. Every time I took him inside me.

That was the way his eyes had looked the day I found him balls-deep inside the woman who'd created him.

I didn't need the visual that came to mind uninvited. The she-devil had been on her knees, facing the door, and he was slamming inside her, making her breasts bounce. She'd seen me first, smirked, and urged him on, which he had no objection to until he noticed me. Even then, when he'd frozen, she kept fucking herself onto his cock.

I had to focus on what was important, not the way he'd had his face buried in her golden mane. "I need you to arrange a meeting with the council."

"I need you too." He covered my hand with his and brought it to his chest, over his heart. "This almost beat when I was with you." He sounded sincere, which was unsettling.

What was more unsettling was that I cared. I tried to speak, but nothing came out of my mouth. Unless you count that mewling sound I wished I could take back.

"This is serious, Constantine." This time I formed words, but my voice lacked conviction.

"This is serious too." He moved between my legs and guided my hand down his front, to his cock.

I pulled away like I'd been burned. "No. *That*"—I pointed to his groin—"is *stupid*. You don't want me. You just hate having lost me."

"I hate having lost you *because* I want you."

"To complete your collection?" Why was I letting him pull me into that talk? We'd had it over the phone, more times than I could count.

"Because I can't live without you."

"You're already dead. It doesn't matter."

"I made a mistake, Cherry. I've apologized a million times, and I will apologize a million more. It meant nothing."

Yeah, sure. It meant nothing. According to him, that was why it had happened often—because it meant nothing. "*Vampires are overly sexual beings*," he kept telling me, back when we were together. "*We are driven by our passions and our lust*." When I said that made us animals, he countered that it made us superhuman; the way we let our wants dictate our actions held us above society's rules and conventions.

I'd said that was bullshit, and he'd said I was too young to know better. I'd wanted him to be monogamous, something rare in our kind. He'd made an effort for me, which was why he'd only been fucking Ádísa. *Because it meant nothing.*

Well, it meant a lot to me, and I said so now, as I had then.

He grabbed my wrist, and when I moved to slap him with my free hand, managed to trap that too. "I love that you're so stubborn."

Then the asshole kissed me.

It was nothing like the kisses Alex and I exchanged the last two days, although it did have the same bone-jellifying effect. It was dominant and possessive, and I didn't want it.

For four years, I'd avoided meeting him, despite calls and letters that begged me to do so, because I'd been afraid I'd give in to the passion he always ignited in me. And before Alex, I probably would have. After Alex, however, hot and irresistible as Constantine might be, it was only my body that wanted him. The body has its own memory. It remembers how a touch made it shiver once—remembers how it felt to be taken by an experienced lover.

Sadly for my ex, those memories weren't enough to overcome the memory of his betrayal, or the memory of another lover, a considerate one, waiting for me.

I freed my hands and shoved him back so hard, he'd have flown across the room if he were human. As it was, he barely saved himself the embarrassment of falling on his ass.

"You don't get to kiss me." I stabbed the air with my index finger. "You don't get to touch me and make me want you. We've been over this."

"I love—"

"You don't get to do *that*, either. You'd convinced me I was nothing without you, and you hate that I know better now."

His face hardened, and I had the niggling suspicion I wasn't entirely right on that account. Not that I cared. I didn't. *Wouldn't.* Even if part of me wanted to hug him and hold him close.

"You're not getting me back, Constantine. Ever." I hated that he squeezed his eyes shut with something akin to pain at my words. I hated that I cared.

He tightened his robe around him. "I'll let you know when I've spoken to the council."

I nodded. "Thank you."

"They may ask what it's about." He turned his back to me and walked to the door. I reassessed my earlier reflection on similarities between him and Alex and added one. They both swaggered with a feline grace that made me feel like a klutz.

I followed, happy my legs were steady. "I think there is a rogue out there."

His step faltered for a split second.

He opened the door and held it for me. "If you change your mind—*ever*—I will be waiting."

"I won't." I couldn't do more than whisper, but I was reasonably confident that I meant what I said.

He bobbed his head once. "I will be here, regardless."

I cupped his chin, allowing myself to take in the lines of his face, his cheekbones, his high brow, his square jaw. "Thank you."

I was halfway up the stairs when he said, "Please be careful."

****

I was too stressed to fly after leaving Constantine's place, so I took a stroll, let the night air calm my nerves.

The way things had been going the past couple of days, it made sense that my little walk would end up frazzling me even further.

The conversation with my ex went well, all in all. I felt bad for causing him pain, but at the same time, I felt vindicated. Besides, I'd hurt him less than he hurt me. At the end of the day, we'd been mostly civilized, had long-overdue closure, and he would talk to the council for me. I hoped they'd agree to see me, and that they weren't the grudge-holding type.

When the new council was first formed, they asked me to voice my approval of them when interacting with other vampires. I didn't refuse, but I didn't socialize with any vampires other than Constantine, so it's not like I really helped them. I hoped the former lack of active support on my part wouldn't make them think twice about helping me now.

I flared my nostrils as a car drove slowly by. The driver, fortunately alone, was drunk but extremely polite when he stopped and asked if I needed a lift. I locked gazes with him, declined, and ordered him to go straight home and never again drive inebriated.

The alcohol on his breath and the smells of the night—trees, flowers, a cat or two, the earth itself—made me think of another smell. Blood. The emotional roller coaster seeing Constantine put me through had me on edge, and I needed to feed.

A couple turned the corner, coming my way. They were holding hands, and the boy, who couldn't be older than seventeen, with saggy hair and baggy clothes, leaned to whisper something in the girl's ear. She laughed, her earrings jingling, and turned to him for a kiss, her auburn hair catching the streetlight and showing red streaks.

Red.

Blood.

I could have a quick snack on the spot and be on my way without either of them remembering what had happened. Their throbbing pulse called for me to do just that. I didn't even have to go for the neck. A nibble on the bend of the arm would be more than fine.

No. Even if they didn't remember the violation of a happy, carefree moment, I would. I didn't want to burst their bubble. They had a few more years ahead, before they absolutely had to face the cruelty of the world. My stomach protested my altruism, but I ignored it.

They smiled when they passed me by, and I returned the smile, fully meaning it. I

I'm a really scary vampire, aren't I? But they were so cute and so obviously in love.

Love. Love is something beautiful, something that should be treasured, and something not all people find in a lifetime. Many take it for granted, failing to recognize its magnificence. I am not one of them. I know love needs nurturing to thrive, and at that moment, I felt too scattered to focus on that nurturing. If I let myself go, what I felt for Alex would become deep enough, but I doubted I'd be able to handle it. Perhaps once I had my shit together, if he was interested in something more than sex and could wait that long…

Time was something I had in spades, barring an impromptu staking, decapitation, or burning, but Alex was mortal. Even if he fell head over heels for me, he would one day want more—a family, someone to grow old with. I would never grow old with anyone.

Thinking of Alex made my head hurt. It wasn't just my future that turned complicated when I tried to factor him in, but my present too. Would I drink from him again? Another rumble from my belly reminded me I should drink from someone, and soon. The thing was, I couldn't wrap my mind around going to a bar or club and hitting on anyone other than Alex. Sinking my fangs into someone else's throat and sucking wasn't appetizing at all, for some reason.

Some reason? Ah, how I love my denial. Still, I couldn't feed on Alex for a third time in a row. Could I? Especially when I wanted to keep whatever was between us casual?

Most importantly, would anyone see me if I started smacking my forehead repeatedly?

I decided to go with the third, least appealing option where dinner was concerned, and say *no* to my hand's urge to meet my temple. I glanced backward, to make sure the couple was out of sight, and took off.

****

Once the VSS had deemed that I was able to take care of myself, I'd been given a nest egg and the boot. The nest egg hadn't been enough for me to re-rent my old apartment, but that wasn't why I'd had to move. The guidelines say returning to our previous life is frowned upon, and *frowned upon* usually leads to staking in our crowd.

The money had, however, been enough to pay the first four months of rent for this underground studio with no kitchen. I'd bought a microwave oven for reheating the occasional cup of packaged blood, placed it on my bedside table, and I'd covered my culinary needs.

I got a bag of blood from my emergency stash in the teeny-tiny freezer that came with the teeny-tiny apartment, and warmed it. By the way, reheating frozen blood doesn't make the stuff tasty, just bearable.

I could have asked Constantine for a sip or two. Feeding from another vampire keeps us going for at least two or three days. It makes no sense, considering dead man's blood is poison to us, but it's true. And Constantine had been my donor many times in the past, so technically it would have been wrong to ask him. If I had no conscience.

Then again, I doubted he would have been very giving, without demanding something in return. I lifted my mug to my lips and took a mouthful. *Bleah.* I'd forgotten how bad frozen food tasted. Pinching my nose, I gulped the rest of the liquid down and went to the closet-sized bathroom to rinse my cup.

Deciding what to do next was hard. I could stay home and watch reruns, or I could keep my word and go to Alex, as I promised. Alex, who was waiting for me. Alex, who seemed unfazed by the weirdness that was my reality, and who treated me like I was special. Alex, with whom I'd spent the whole day in bed, going through pictures from his childhood, laughing, and making love. Alex, on whom I was developing a crush, though I tried hard not to.

Alex, with whom I couldn't be for more than a few measly decade—far too short a time for someone destined to live forever like I was—before his body betrayed him and he inevitably passed away, as all mortals do.

I couldn't do that to myself. Crush or not, I had to get out as soon as possible. As soon as we figured out his case.

But I promised.

I checked my cell phone. No missed calls. Nobody sought me out in the two days it lay under my bed, where I'd thrown it. It didn't surprise me. I shoved it in my back pocket. Constantine would call to let me know what he'd arranged. I grabbed my backpack, stuffed some clothes in, pulled my hair into a ponytail, took a deep, unnecessary breath, and opened the door.

I couldn't spend the rest of Alex's life with him, but there was no danger in enjoying his company for a few more days.

Plus there's safety in numbers, and two is a bigger number than one.

And I promised.

****

It was odd, seeing Alex in the kitchen. I hadn't associated him with that room. I'd thought he'd be more at ease in a luxurious bedroom, with dark colors and lavish fabrics. No, I didn't have a specific one in mind.

Nevertheless, he seemed comfortable among the spotless white countertops, flipping an omelet in the air when I walked in. So comfortable, in fact, that he was doing so wearing only an apron. What was it with naked men today?

"Does your mother know you wear her clothes?" I lifted one corner of my lips in appreciation of the view.

He threw me a smoldering look over his shoulder and wiggled his ass. "I like how airy this thing is."

We managed to keep a straight face for only a second or two, before cracking up.

I placed a kiss on his shoulder, hung my pack on the back of a chair, and hopped on the kitchen counter. "Saw you fixed the front door. You might consider locking it too. Anyone could walk in."

"I'll lock up tonight, so we can sleep without worrying about burglars." He added grated cheese to the omelet, and I watched it melt.

"So I'm staying tonight too?" I asked. Don't judge; I was there already.

"Unquestionably." He slid the omelet out of the pan and onto a plate he'd set to the side. Switching the cooker off, he turned fully to me and captured my lips with his.

"Good." I returned his kiss, internally thanking whoever was listening that Alex didn't have a vampire's sense of smell. Constantine's scent lingered on me, and we hadn't even had that much contact.

Alex looked at the plate, which gave out a divine aroma, and then back at me. "I forgot to ask if you can eat. Food. Solid food?" His perfect teeth trapped his lower lip.

I tore off a bit of fried egg with my fingers, dropped it in my mouth, and made a show of chewing and swallowing it. "It does nothing to sustain me, but I can have it." I ran my tongue over my front teeth. "It needs a bit more pepper." I like spicy food.

"It does not." He mock glared. "I make a mean omelet, and you'd better get your butt in a chair if you wanna have any more of it." He pointed at the table, which was set for two, a candle in the middle. "I'll make a salad and be right with you."

The whole thing was bizarrely cozy and sweet. I did as he said, making myself comfortable at the table and crossing my legs at the ankles, all prim and proper. Was that how being with him would be? Would he always remain so very wonderful? And why was I torturing myself? Vampires don't get to share *always* with humans.

"I like you," I blurted.

He furrowed his brow. "I thought we'd established that."

I nodded. "Felt like saying it." Oh God, I was sixteen again.

Looking at me meant he wasn't watching the knife, which missed the tomato and found the pad of his thumb instead. "*Ouch.*"

I was beside him before he got to the *ch.*

"It's nothing," he said, raising his hand toward his mouth.

I was faster. I took hold of his palm and lead his thumb between my lips. I licked the wound, sealing it, but he didn't pull his hand away. When I looked up at him, I was stricken by the way he watched me; it was intense and warm and full of something more than lust—which was utterly, indisputably *wrong*.

He averted his gaze, and I let his thumb go with a *pop*. "The omelet is getting cold. We should eat." If I sounded any cheerier, I'd barf.

"Yeah. Better forget the salad and dig in." He took the omelet to the table and pulled out a chair for me.

"Naw, I'll finish it. You sit." I was done with the tomato and chopped the lettuce by the time he began protesting. He gave in and took the seat across from mine.

Finding a bowl for the salad took a rather long time, because Alex stared at me with a hint of a smile instead of telling me which cupboard to look into. I scraped the salad from the chopping block into the bowl, snatched the pepper mill, and batted my eyelashes at him.

He chuckled as he served his creation to our plates. "Have at it."

I sank back in my seat and twisted the mill over my plate until one more speckle of pepper would make me sneeze. Then I tried the eggs. I may be exaggerating a bit, but that omelet was the best I'd ever tasted. We shared it while playing footsie under the table. Yup, I was sixteen, all right. And loving it.

Until things turned sour, as they almost invariably do.

Washing a sizeable bite down with cola, Alex asked, "How come you only stopped the blood?"

I had no idea what he was getting at, and it must have shown on my face.

"Aren't you hungry? You haven't eaten since late last night."

I worried he'd want me to drink from him again if I mentioned the frozen blood. I didn't want to get used to his taste, when I wouldn't have it for long. "I can take it a bit longer. And you need to build up your strength." Hoping I sounded blasé enough, I stuffed a forkful of salad in my mouth. "This is filling, as well as yummy." All that was missing from my performance was a satisfied tummy rub.

His fork clanked against the plate, where he let it drop. "You're lying. I see it in your eyes." His lips were quirked in a smile, but his tone was serious.

I turned the double-crossing things to the table. "Am not."

"The question is *why*."

Sighing in resignation, I took his hand in mine. "When I went to pack, I had a bite. Frozen stuff."

"You can have more of mine later if you want." He caressed my knuckles with his thumb, seeming relieved. "How did the meeting go?"

I shrugged one shoulder, focused on chasing a piece of lettuce around my plate. "It was fine. He'll call me when he hears from them."

"So do I get to know who he is?"

My hesitation indicated guilt, and I wasn't guilty, damn it. "My ex. His name is Constantine." Eh, I felt guilty.

"I see." Alex didn't speak again, switching his attention to his food. When his plate was squeaky clean, he pushed his chair back, stood, and left the room.

It took a couple of seconds for me to make up my mind on whether to follow him or not. If I didn't, he might think I didn't care. If I did, he might feel suffocated. Rock, meet hard place.

While evaluating my options, I factored in a very significant parameter—I was stronger and faster than he was. If he tried to pick a fight or leave the house, I could easily hold him still until he shut up and listened to me. Though why I had to explain myself, I really couldn't say. It wasn't like we were an item.

My chair screeched against the floor, the sound a million times more annoying to my ears than to a human's. Then I was on my feet, walking slowly to the living room. I'm talking real slow, not slow for a vampire. I dragged my feet because, although I'd done nothing wrong that night, I didn't want to talk about Constantine. Nothing good could come out of it. What was more, I didn't want to lie.

Alex sat in *our* armchair—funny that I felt we had shared custody of the thing—rubbing his face with his palm.

"Do you wanna—"

"My last girlfriend broke up with me eight months ago," he said to the wall behind me. "My life was too *adventurous* for her. We'd been together for a year and a half, and I was gonna ask her to marry me. Letting go of her was the hardest thing I've ever done." Amazing how a man his size seemed small at that moment.

The sadness in his voice made my throat constrict. I moved farther inside the room and leaned my thigh against the side of the couch, crossing my arms in front of my chest. I wanted to tell him I was sorry to hear that, yet I said nothing. *Sorry* wouldn't cover the extreme dislike I felt for the woman who'd wounded him, though I'd never met her. Still, it wasn't up to me to help him heal; I was nothing but a passerby in his life.

He shrugged, but his face had clouded. His nonchalance was an act. "She said she'd never be able to keep up. That she was leaving me for my own good. She said she was sorry and that it hurt her too. I didn't believe her. I couldn't get how the fuck she could leave me if it hurt her to do it."

I didn't want him to finish that story saying that he finally understood what she'd been talking about, that now he knew what being with someone too fast for him felt like. The conclusion was unavoidable though. He was only telling me about her as a preface to calling things off with me. What other reason could he have? In all my deep contemplation of the future, I'd failed to take one thing into consideration—delayed freakout. Alex had been fine so far because the goings-on hadn't sunk in. Until now.

I let my head fall back. At least I wouldn't have to worry about leaving him; he was making my choice for me. I should be feeling relief instead of that numbness spreading from my fingertips toward my chest.

"She broke my heart to the point I thought it'd never mend again. I didn't even go on a date until I met you," Alex said.

I felt the need to interject, delay the inevitable. "It's not like we're dating." Good job, Cherry. *Great* job.

He might as well not have heard me. "The thing is"—

I dug in my biceps. Despite *knowing* we could be nothing to each other, I didn't want to hear what *the thing* was. Couldn't we forget *the thing* for the time being?

—"I want us to."

Okay. Rewind. Let's talk about *the thing*. "Huh?"

"I want us to date, Cherry. I want to take you out and come back home with you, but"—

Ah, the *but*. I should have known it was coming. *But* he couldn't handle it. *But* we weren't good for each other. *But* it wouldn't go anywhere, so we ought to save us both the trouble.

— "I'm not going to let another woman in, just so she can eventually hurt me. I want to know where you stand. How available you are, emotionally." He rolled his eyes and let his hand land heavily on the arm of the chair. "Fuck. I sound like a chick." At last he turned to me. "No offense."

"None taken," I said without thinking about it. I hadn't had time to take offense anyway. My mind was too busy trying to become pliable enough to bend around the unfathomable idea that Alex wanted to see more of me.

"What I'm saying is that there's something here." He wagged his index finger between us. "But I don't want to make more of it than it really is. I mean, if there's someone else…"

"I see." He wasn't saying we couldn't be together. I wanted to bounce. I refrained because really, we couldn't. But he wanted us to give it a try—and wasn't this a wonderful *but*?

"And?" He drew out the question, staring at me. Why was he staring? Had I done something wrong?

"And?" I batted my eyelashes, trying to buy some time. It was up to me to define what we had. Oh God. I *suck* at definitions. Doubly so when the definition I feel like giving is completely inappropriate.

"And would you like to say something?" His eyebrows shot for his hairline, his face such a contrast to the apron, I'd giggle if he hadn't just opened his heart up to me.

There was no one else, but that wouldn't be enough of an answer. I started at the beginning. "I met Constantine shortly after I was turned. He was my sponsor." The blank look from Alex made me elaborate. "He was the one in charge of me. He taught me how to choose my prey; how to deal with missing my family; how to not let the thirst take me over." And I fell so in love with him, he became my whole world—which Alex didn't need to know.

"Constantine made me stop hating what I'd become. He was there for anything I needed. He showed me fighting moves and made me read. Reading was what distinguished us from savages, he said. We became lovers." We had been more than that. He'd made me happy, and in return I'd let him suck me into his whirlwind of an existence.

Alex's mouth twitched almost imperceptibly, his eyes darkening a shade.

I shouldn't linger on that subject. "We were together for a couple of years, until I walked in on him with another woman. We hadn't seen each other since, until tonight." That didn't feel entirely honest. "We spoke on the phone lots, though."

Alex still stared at me. I hadn't answered his question. "It was weird seeing him," I heard myself say. *Weird* was an understatement. "But I'm okay. And nothing happened." That was as much as I could say about my emotional availability. I wanted Alex, and yes, I was over Constantine. Mostly.

No, I wasn't in the best place for a relationship. Yes, I wanted to give it a try anyway. No, I couldn't do what I wanted. There were repercussions for me to consider.

"Can you see yourself with him in the future?" There was cop face again, only this time his worry seeped through the mask's cracks.

"I… No. I don't think so." I hated the doubt in my voice. "I'm not in love with him anymore, but he's important to me. I'd like for this to be something, Alex. *Us*. I just don't think I can be what you need." There. Full honesty. My cards were spread on the table.

The room was so silent once I stopped talking, I tapped my foot to make sure I hadn't gone deaf. I wasn't what Alex needed. He had the chance to make a family with a human who'd grow old with him. Nevertheless, I wanted him not to let that stop him. Hey, I'm dead, but I'm still a woman.

He leaned forward, hands on his knees. "I'll go by the office in the morning. Get you the pictures." That was a change of subject if I ever heard one—or so I thought, until he spoke again. "We'll talk about this more once we've solved the case. Fucking will tide us over till then." He winked.

If any other man spoke to me like that a couple days after we met, no matter how carnal his knowledge of me might be, I'd snap at him. Instead I laughed. Alex tone showed he didn't mean it as a slight, and it was nice laughing with him—easy, pleasant. He made it possible for me to be carefree, when my head was filled with problems to be solved.

"Was that a *no*?" He gave me a lopsided smile.

I licked my lower lip and walked to him, swishing my hips with every step. "It was a most definite *yes*."

The future was so very far away that moment.

Chapter Six

My knight in shining armor, Alex brought the portable television downstairs before leaving for work, but daytime TV wasn't enough to keep my mind busy. My thoughts returned to my current situation despite my efforts. As a last resort, I started counting the bricks in the room.

I was halfway through the third wall, when I heard a car pull up and soon steps rushed along the driveway. Friend or foe?

I knew it was Alex when I heard the key in the lock. Willoughby would have no qualms busting through another door.

If it weren't for the evil sun, I'd have flown up the stairs to meet Alex and thank him for saving me from my boredom. As it was, I jumped out of bed when he switched on the light, planning on smooching the breath out of him as soon as he set foot on the landing.

His grim expression stopped me in my tracks. "We had another disappearance last night." He kissed my forehead and passed me by to drop an armful of folders on the bed.

I looked at my feet with their ever-perfect red toenails, ashamed that my worst crisis last night had been which hot male to sleep with.

"She doesn't fit the pattern. A bit older and rather… Well, she isn't a match, physically." He hastened to add, "Not that she's ugly."

"Maybe her disappearance is not related?" I tucked a strand of hair behind my ear and blew my bangs up off my eyes—really inconvenient hairstyle to carry indefinitely.

Shaking his head, he sat on the bed and patted the mattress next to him. I sank down by his side, rubbing his neck with one hand while he opened the first folder.

"She disappeared from a nightclub." He didn't find what he was searching for, so he checked the second one and let out a huff before tossing that aside too.

His shoulders were full of knots, so I slid behind him, legs outside his, and used both hands to massage him. "Maybe she wanted a change of scenery and will show up eventually?"

"She has a kid. She wouldn't have left him willingly," he said in a low voice, shuffling through more papers. I was about to point out that there are some horrible mothers in this world when he cursed under his breath. "Finally."

An uneasy feeling in the pit of my stomach made me stop what I was doing and glance over his shoulder at what he held up. It was a passport picture, and not a recent one.

"Theodora Williams," Alex said. He didn't have to.

I knew the big, earnest eyes looking out at me from the face with the prominent angles. Her hair was longer than she'd worn it since I first met her, her cheekbones sharper, her neck slimmer. Still, there was no doubt in my mind. Even in a photograph taken something like ten years earlier, I recognized the girl.

Dotty.

Alex was still talking, but I wasn't listening. His voice was background noise, lost as I was inside my thoughts. Was Dotty randomly targeted, or did my maker know where I lived? Who my friends were? Doubt and self-recrimination were circling in my mind like sharks in a tank, and in these circumstances, I wasn't a good swimmer.

"I know her," I said after several long moments. "She lives in my building. We're friends. Sorta." It couldn't be a coincidence.

He turned, trying to meet my gaze. When he couldn't, he rose and sat again, this time facing me. "I'm sorry, Cherry. We'll do everything we can." He reached for my hand, and I let him take it but couldn't accept the solace he was offered.

"Mark. Where is Mark?" I couldn't believe I hadn't asked that sooner.

"With his dad. Dad went to drop the kid off, and there was no sign of Dotty. They waited, but she didn't show. The boy said she was out with a guy she'd been seeing, but we have no name or description."

"Can't you find him from her phone records?"

"We're waiting for the judge to sign the subpoena."

Waiting. I wasn't good at waiting. I pulled away from his touch. "We have to do something. I think it's because of me. 'Cause we're looking into this case."

His other hand found my shoulder and squeezed reassuringly. "Don't do that. She was unlucky. We'll—"

"No." The word came out so harsh, it reverberated off the walls and came back to me like the snap of a whip. "This has nothing to do with luck, bad or otherwise. She doesn't fit the profile. You said so yourself. She isn't young enough and has family. If she was indeed taken by Willoughby, it can't be for the same reason. It's to get to me, like breaking in here was to get to you."

"But we don't know why the others were taken." There he went with the sense-making again. "We still don't know why *you* were turned."

"You think my turning is connected?" I was already half-convinced it wasn't random, but six years had passed since. What he was suggesting was…

"I do." He drew circles on the back of my hand with his thumb. "And I'm going to find out how."

I stood so quickly that I'd have felt dizzy if I were alive. "We can do that later. We will. First we have to find Dotty." I itched to sink my teeth in the throats of those responsible for it all.

"*We* will do nothing until it's dark outside." Alex headed toward the stairs.

"Where are you going?"

"Gotta make some phone calls."

I wondered what good it would do but said nothing. I paced while waiting for him to come back down. I couldn't shake the feeling that I was the reason Dotty was in danger, and I was restless with the need to act. Wouldn't stupid dusk ever come?

"...one of you can come in." Alex got in my way, snapping me out of my internal musings.

"What?" I had no clue what he was talking about or when he'd returned to the basement. Vampiric senses, my ass.

"I said, at least we know only one of you can come in."

"Where?"

"In the house," he said. "*This* house. Only one vampire can come in—other than you. My mother said two guys came by a few days before she left. They were selling cable service. She's had no other visitors that she didn't know."

I was perplexed. As was becoming a habit, he read my facial expression all too well. "I told her there was a burglary in the neighborhood," he said. "Asked if she'd seen any strangers around."

I nodded. "Is she sure?"

"A hundred percent. She's a hell of a gossip. The cable guys refused to say anything about themselves, and it struck her as odd. They were also very insistent about coming inside the house but didn't stay for more than five minutes once she invited them in." He ghosted his knuckles down my cheek. "Are you okay?"

"No. I want to go by Dotty's, see if I can find anything out."

"We've already spoken to her son and her ex-husband."

Of course they had, but I could find out more than Alex's colleagues had. "Mark said she was out with the same guy she'd been seeing for a couple of weeks." I should have asked her about that guy last time she wanted me to babysit. "Sure none of our neighbors has seen him?"

To his credit, Alex didn't look upset that I more or less questioned how he did his job. He shook his cell phone in the air. "Called Lieutenant Roebuck again. Nothing yet. We'll keep asking around, but there's not much to go on. Guy might as well be a ghost."

"I have to go, Alex."

"No, you don't. What's more, you can't. Her place is filled with cops. They're talking to her neighbors. If you show up, they'll ask questions, and if they need to talk to you for hours, they won't be understanding of your sun allergy." His voice rose gradually. "Let us handle it, all right?"

"No. It's not all right. I *need* to do something about it, and you can't stop me."

"Cherry." His tone was pleading now. "Please try to understand. It's our job."

"Well, you're not very good at it, are you? Those girls can attest to that." I regretted the words the moment they were out of my mouth.

His face fell and closed up at the same time. He was still looking at me but with narrowed eyes.

"I'm sorry," I whispered. "That was cruel."

"You think?"

"I'm sorry." I leaned my forehead against his broad chest. "I hate being unable to help her."

He wrapped his arms around me. "I know the feeling. I promise my guys are doing their best. They're gonna turn the place upside down, to find clues about her guy."

The calmness that washed over me when he embraced me was unsettling. I couldn't let myself lean on him like that, when he wouldn't be around for long. "I still believe I can do more," I said, trying to pull away. "I know her. Your guys don't. And poor Mark must be scared to death."

"He's with his dad." He wouldn't let go.

"His dad is a first-class jerk, Alex. Please let me go."

He sighed so deeply, my head rose and fell against his chest. "Can you get in and out of her apartment unnoticed? The kid may tell you more than he did the officers, but he's not alone."

"I can make others not notice me." I hung my head and looked up at him through lowered eyelashes. He'd made his thoughts on mind control clear.

He surprised me by kissing the crown of my head. "You're not going to hurt anyone." It wasn't a question or a demand, more a statement of fact, yet I felt the need to reassure him.

I met his gaze and gave him a weak smile. "I'll…
compel them to look elsewhere. No harm, no foul."

He chuckled. "Fine. You can *compel* away. Just don't
get into trouble."

"I won't. Honest."

****

The uniform in front of my building was in his mid to
late thirties and impeccably groomed. He leaned against the
glass door, obviously bored. I could relate. I'd twiddled my
thumbs most of the day too, waiting for it to be dark outside.

He snapped his head my way when I started up the
steps. Huh. He wasn't as out of it as I initially thought.

I caught his gaze. "I'm not here," I said. "You never
saw me."

His eyes went blank. "I never saw you."

I nudged him aside and crossed the threshold.

The two cops outside Dotty's apartment were equally
easy to get off my case, as was Mark's dad, a short, tubby man
with beady eyes and thin lips—I don't know what Dotty ever
saw in him.

Finally certain my presence wouldn't be remembered, I
walked to the boy's bedroom.

Mark rushed me and wrapped his arms around my
waist the moment I opened the door. Gone was the snotty brat
whose ass I wanted to kick every time I babysat him. He was
just a lost little kid now, and I was the only adult he felt close
to. He buried his face in my belly and let out a choked sob that
broke my heart.

"It's okay, big guy. We'll get your mom back." I
caressed his hair. "We will. And she'll be fine. You'll see."

"Will the scary man let her go?"

I wouldn't have made out his question without my
enhanced hearing. What did he know? "What man, Mark?" I
wanted to see his face, but he might find it easier to talk
without facing me.

"He came to my window earlier. Said—" Another sob,
and then he wouldn't talk despite my urging him.

77

Only a vampire could have appeared at his second-story window, and I bet my bottom dollar I knew who it had been. "Did the man have big, pointy teeth?"

Mark sniffled.

I decided to resort to extreme measures. "Look into my eyes, sweetie."

He did, his face open and full of trust. The hope mirrored there made me feel guilty, but not enough to stop me from using my abilities on him. "Tell me exactly what the man said."

His eyes glazed over. "You're a good boy, Mark, and that's why I won't kill your mom. But you have to do something for me too. Tell Cherry to get her boyfriend off my case. If you tell anyone else you saw me, I'll come back for you." The voice that came out of his mouth was his, but deeper, like he was imitating an adult.

I knew beyond the shadow of a doubt whose disdainful tone I heard.

Willoughby.

Mark trembled like a leaf, and I clutched him to me harder. I would find the stupid vampire who thought he could mess with me and mine, and I'd turn him to dust, like I did with his buddy.

"You *are* a good boy, and I'll get your mom back to you." I slid down to kneel before Mark, never tearing my gaze from his. "You must believe me and not be sad."

He smiled—not the cocky grin that resembled his dad's, but a sweet tilt of the lips that was a hundred percent Dotty. "I believe you."

I kissed his cheek and told him not to tell anyone he saw me. I trusted him not to, though I'd stopped the gaze lock by that point.

He grabbed my shirt before I could go. "Dad wants me to stay with Gran for a while. What if Mom comes home and doesn't find me?"

Dotty had mentioned her mother-in-law lived in Bakersfield, far enough for Mark to be relatively safe. "I'll tell your mom where to find you. Don't worry."

He wiped his nose on the back of his hand and nodded.

****

I rang Alex's doorbell and waited. My phone vibrated in my back pocket. I pressed the little green button and brought it to my ear.

"Constantine." I said his name flatly, instead of a greeting. *Hey* or *whazzup* wouldn't cut it.

"Cherry." It sounded more like *Chérie*. It pissed me off without real reason.

"Did they say yes?" There was no need for niceties; we both knew why he called.

Alex opened the door, and I motioned for him to be quiet as I walked inside and let him close it behind me.

"Indeed." Constantine sighed. "Where are you?"

I ignored his question. "When?"

"Now." I detected impatience in his voice. "Where are you?"

"Not your business. Where?" The council's private meeting chambers have always been hush-hush. They hold hearings in safe houses, but never without an appointment and never at the same place twice. Last I'd seen them, they'd been in an old warehouse.

Only a handful of people knew how to contact them, something I found at odds with their purpose. Rulers are supposed to know their subjects. Also, I hate being considered anyone's subject. That said, I assumed their agreeing to meet me meant I was in the inner circle. Sort of.

"Come by the mansion. I'll take you to them," Constantine said. So no inner circle for me.

Alex frowned, and I turned my back to him to whisper into the phone. "I don't want you there, Constantine. Thank you for arranging it, but I don't need you to cover my ass."

He tutted. "First off, I prefer your ass naked. Secondly, *they* requested I be there."

Bullshit. It wasn't a *they* that wanted him at the meeting; it was a *she*. A bitch, who happened to be one of the council members. *Ádísa.*

"I'll be right there."

Chapter Seven

As it turned out, I wasn't the only one to grumble.

Alex insisted on coming with me, but I couldn't very well present him to the council and say, *Hey, peeps. This human knows all about us, but it's cool.* Not if I liked my head where it was—and it just so happened my shoulders were kind of partial to it.

"Are you sure it's safe?" He stood at the open door, blocking my way out of his mom's ground-floor bathroom. Arms stretched over his head, he held the door frame and rolled his shoulders and neck. His heartbeat betrayed that he wasn't half as relaxed as he appeared.

"Yes"—an endearment was about to roll off my tongue, but we weren't there yet—"Alex. It's safe. They're the council. The good guys."

He snorted, the sound carrying more snark than any nonverbal response should. "What about the warning?"

The thought had bugged me since I left Mark behind. "The warning was about *you* backing off, which you said you would. Plus, I don't see how he'd find out I'm meeting the council."

"You do realize I'm not officially withdrawing from the case, right? Just lying low?" He sounded concerned. "That doesn't mean the department is going to drop it. There are people looking into this as we speak."

"I know," I said. "And it's not like you and I are gonna sit on our hands in the meantime. We're just going to be more subtle."

"Still, maybe going with him—"

"Isn't a good idea," I finished his sentence. I had no time for jealousy and territory marking now, although I might enjoy Alex and Constantine comparing their machismo at a less panicky time. "The council asked for him, and they will know what to do." I wholeheartedly hoped they would. If they couldn't help, Dotty wouldn't be Willoughby's last victim.

"Fine. If you want to go, go." There went the cool act, right out the window. He didn't raise his voice, but there was an edge to it. "If you're not back by dawn, I'm coming after you."

"I'm going, and I'll be back way before dawn." Not that he'd know where to begin looking. I rummaged through my bag, for a bobby pin. My nowhere-near-natural, bright-red hair color was damaging enough for my credibility in front of the vampire ruling body. I had to at least pull the bangs back.

Ah, there it was.

"Fine," Alex barked once more

I had the pin in my mouth and was trying to hold the front of my hair up, to secure it. "Fine," I spat back around the hairpin. I finally got my bangs where I wanted them and tried to pin them in place. No luck. My hair isn't great at staying in place unless copious amounts of hairspray are involved.

Alex plucked the thing out of my grasp and shoved it in my hair so hard that, at a steeper angle, it would have gone through my scalp.

"Ow." I ducked away and turned to glare at him.

"Sorry." No, he wasn't. The corners of his mouth lifted. A smiling Alex was a good thing, so I wouldn't hold this against him.

I pinched his ass and begrudgingly returned the hug and peck he gave me. They felt too much like *goodbye* and made me want to burrow into his embrace and forget about the meeting.

I couldn't. "I'll be back soon."

"I'll be here. Told Roebuck I'm following a lead, so I won't have to go by the department until we know something about the case. And I've got research to do." He pointed to the folders strewn all over the coffee table. "So I'm clear, though, I don't like this."

As I walked out the door, I couldn't help but wonder how much harder letting him go for good would be, if leaving him for a short time felt so bad.

****

Constantine waited for me at the door, dressed this time. Can't say I wasn't a bit disappointed over the lack of bare flesh, but most of me was relieved to see him in his black dress pants, designer black shirt, and purple tie. A vampire dressed in black and purple. *Stereotypes-R-Us.*

He looked scrumptious, dressed up—don't get me wrong—and with clothes covering his body, I had less trouble focusing on his face.

I tugged at the end of his ponytail. "My, my, aren't we all spiffy for the meeting." I wasn't jealous that he'd spent time becoming even more gorgeous than usual because he'd see Ádísa. Wasn't jealous at all.

He narrowed his eyes and looked at me top to bottom and up again. He didn't seem pleased, and I instinctively ran my hands down my blouse. It was a nicer top than the one he last saw me in, but the jeans and sneakers were the same. When he clucked his tongue, I wished I'd bothered to wear something fancier.

"Does your human keep you too busy to clean up properly?"

I be offended, if his tone didn't hold a hint of covetousness. *Touché.* Er…I mean, I won. He was jealous, *and I wasn't.* "What human?" I asked with an innocent smile.

"The one I can smell all over you." He flared his nostrils, and *damn*, that was too sexy to be legal.

Mega-oops—I didn't shower after this morning's sexcapades with Alex. The council would smell him too. Not that they'd care, but I hated the idea of them knowing what I did earlier today.

I batted my eyelashes at Constantine. "Are we driving? If we're flying, you'll have to tell me where we're going." I'm so smooth when I want to be. *Not.*

He didn't fall for my attempt at changing the subject. "Last time… He pursed his lips, then closed his eyes. "I didn't realize he was more than food." When he opened them again, he looked at me like he saw right through me.

His irises had turned nearly black, a color I hadn't seen them before. They were mesmerizing. His expression changed—no distinct movement, just the barest tensing of muscle. I can't explain it, but it was the most vulnerable I'd seen him. A knot formed in my stomach. I did whatever this was to him.

"Constantine…" What was there to say?

He pinched the bridge of his nose, and when he withdrew his hand, there was a smirk that didn't reach his eyes. "We're flying."

I had no time to react when he pulled me to him and cupped the back of my head. For a moment, I was sure he was about to kiss me—and not sure at all that I'd stop him.

Instead he pressed my face to his chest. "You're not allowed to see where we're going."

Why all the secrecy? Not like the council would be visiting the place again. Snuggled in his arms, with the night air swishing around us, I didn't voice my thoughts. I leaned against his body and trusted him to lead me to our destination.

In retrospect, that might not have been my best idea ever. I hadn't felt dizzy after a flight since my first takeoff as a vampire, but I was light-headed by the time we landed. It might be the flight, or I could blame it on Constantine drawing circles on the small of my back with his thumb and moving his lips against my hair, like he'd been whispering a secret.

The flight it was, if I wanted to get any sleep that day.

My knees buckled when Constantine let go—the way knees do because of uncontrolled landings, and nothing else— and he grabbed my shoulders hard enough to leave bruises. Good thing bruises fade fast on us.

I found my footing and pulled away, but his grip lingered. "I'm not letting go," he whispered.

He wasn't talking about my shoulders. "It'll be hard for us to walk this way." Keeping my voice steady and my tone light took a lot of concentration.

"But it will be fun." He ghosted one hand up my neck and traced my jawline with his thumb, stopping a hairbreadth from my lower lip.

I turned my cheek to him, doing my best to gather my wits and figure out where we were. We stood on what seemed to be the runway of a deserted airport.

"We'll be late," I said to the tarmac, refusing to meet Constantine's gaze.

****

The good news was I was too rattled by the moment I shared with my former lover to let the idea of facing the five vampires whose word was law frighten me. Plus they were supposed to be on my side.

Mostly.

That last word flashed bright neon in my head, as soon as the first of the council members walked inside the cold room, in the middle of which a tiny scrap of a human man had seated Constantine and me.

Ádísa glanced at me, a smirk on her full, red lips. She would have headed the council if the job description depended on age. Legend had it she was a Valkyrie, a *chooser of the slain*, who'd escaped Odin and renounced Valhalla, the Old Norse version of warrior heaven. I was convinced she'd created that legend herself because she loved being the center of attention.

With her long blonde hair braided at the sides of her neck, and her barely-there leather getup, she looked the part as she regarded Constantine with a small smile. Her breasts were too firm to spill over her bra-like top, even if they looked like they were about to do just that. Whether because of awesome genes or Odin's favor, she'd never curse herself for not getting a boob job in time.

In her wake came Gheorghios. Second oldest of the council members, he'd for a while followed the arch-bitch's example and tried to convince people he was *the* Saint George, who'd slain the dragon. Even one-day-old newbies knew he'd

84

pulled that out of his ass, yet nobody would dare say so in his presence. Unlike his story about his past, his viciousness and quick temper were never disputed.

His hawkish gaze landed on me like an actual physical weight, and I strove not to show my discomfort. I couldn't smile; he might take it as insolence. So I met his gaze with the best combination of respect and earnestness I could muster. I guess I did well enough, because he nodded at me and my escort and took a step back, to stand on Ádísa's right. The way they lined up made me think of a beauty pageant. *And now, our next contestant, in dark 'n' gloomy wear.* I shushed the thought. This wasn't the time to giggle.

The urge to squirm was overwhelming. I wasn't there to get judged, but I felt every part the naughty schoolgirl, appearing before the school board—an extremely strict school board, with a propensity for bloodshed.

I calmed down a little when the third of the five we were to meet strutted our way and graced me with a full grin and a wink. He shook hands with Constantine and took his place at Gheorghios's side. John—Johnny Boy to his friends—had been turned in his late teens and dressed as if he was still in them. His jeans were faded and ripped, his boots heavy and with metal fronts, his T-shirt snug. Barely a century undead, he'd accumulated a great following and had gained the respect of friends and enemies, despite being known as a pacifist—something not guaranteed to gain you status among our kind.

I'd spoken to him once before. He was the one who approached me for that spokesperson deal in the past, and he was as mellow as vampires come, in spite of the bad-boy exterior.

Hui Zhong, following close behind, was the exact opposite. Her china-doll appearance, complete with a silk robe—which I'd called just that and had been glared at, 'cause "*it's a* hanfu"—belied her bloodthirsty nature. She'd been turned in China in the late 1800s, and her kills during her fledgling days rivaled the number of deaths from the plague epidemic, which had conveniently covered said kills.

She didn't smile, frown, or even look at us. A demure bow, aimed at nobody in particular, was all the acknowledgment we received. I found the act too much, like the outfit, but I resisted the eye roll I felt coming. I'd heard she carried a sword under that robe—hey, it's my head, and I say it's a *robe*—and I didn't care to find out for sure.

The last vampire to walk in before the door was bolted on the outside was Benjamin. He was a paradox, in that he'd been turned in his sixties and had been one of us for only seventeen years. There was a theory that he'd been recruited for the council to appeal to a different demographic. Hui Zhong was supposedly there for the same reason—diversity. The new council advocated it, and that was the basis of its power. One look into Benjamin's flat eyes, however, and one could see the cold calculation and single-minded determination that gained him his position.

He'd been the instigator of the coup that ended the old council, and the first to dust one of them. One moment he'd been one of those present at the hearing about my irresponsible turning, the next he'd been yelling that the council was inadequate and driving a wooden stake through the oldest vampire's heart in the ensuing melee.

He scared me shitless.

With Benjamin in place, a semicircle was formed around me and Constantine. A black semicircle, with the exception of Hui Zhong's colorful attire. A shiver ran down my spine. Constantine found and squeezed my fingers. I squeezed back. There was no reason for worry. They were scary-ass, all right, and I had to tell them something they wouldn't like, but they wouldn't turn their wrath for the rogue against us.

Right?

"State your name, please." The man who'd told us to sit was now between us and the council. He looked at me expectantly and waved a pen over a pad. He didn't seem nervous enough for being in the presence of so many of us. I certainly felt more apprehensive than he looked.

"Your name?" he asked again when I took a whole entire second to reply.

"Cherry Stem."

Someone snorted; I'm not sure whether it was at my screen name or because of what I'd done on said screen. Either way my money was on Ádísa having made the rude sound, but I didn't glance her way. The secretary, or whatever Little Man was, squinted at me before jotting down my name.

"Is your reason for requesting an audience political, ethical, or personal?"

I'd rocked multiple-choice quizzes in high school and was about to say that, when Constantine nudged me with the heel of his shoe. "I am not sure," I said. "It affects all of us, but it's not political."

The guy narrowed his eyes again. "Ethical, then?"

I shrugged. "Sure."

The pen scratched the pad once more. "And who vouches for Ms. Stem?"

Umm, what was that?

Before I could say I had no clue someone was supposed to vouch for me, or what said vouching was about, Constantine spoke up. "I do."

"Are you sure?" I muttered the question under my breath without looking at him, but the council members no doubt heard it.

He wasn't perturbed, of course. "Yes. They needed someone to vouch that you had a valid reason for asking to see them. I did. They know and trust me."

I tried not to dwell on the fact that, last time I checked, only *one* of the members knew him well enough.

I smiled at the human, who cleared his throat to get our attention. "Yup, he's the voucher, all right." By his frown I assumed a bit more formality wouldn't hurt. I beamed a smile at him, grateful I didn't have a pulse. If I did, it would be racing now.

Constantine's name was noted down—he didn't give his real name, either—and we were done with the formalities. The human moved to the side and sat behind a little desk.

I turned to the standing vampires, studying each face briefly. They all looked at me in expectation. *Don't waste their time*, I told myself, yet my brain froze. How was I to start?

I wet my lips and went for it. "I have reason to believe a rogue vampire is turning young women." There. Like pulling off a bandage.

I expected some reaction to my statement—a widening of the eyes at minimum, maybe a gasp—but all I got were blank looks.

I hate blank looks. "A woman in my apartment building went missing, and I overheard the police talk about how that fits a series of other disappearances."

They still not said nothing. They didn't even blink. John gave me an almost imperceptible nod, so I went on. "The thing is, the day before the disappearance, I was attacked by one of us. He was masked, but I recognized him as Willoughby. My maker. I thought he was dead."

Benjamin spoke. "Willoughby? That's highly improbable." His frown made him look even scarier than before.

"It was him. He said he should have killed me."

"But your attacker was masked." Hui Zhong's voice was light, like a chirp, and neutral.

"And I'm sure more than one of us has thought about killing you." Ádísa was friendly as always.

I huffed. I had to tell them the whole story, or a version of it that would keep me out of trouble. The lie I'd decided on wouldn't cut it. "I was with a man. A human." Constantine tensed beside me, but I couldn't do this *and* spare his feelings. Besides, he and I weren't together. "I was at his place for… dinner, when Willoughby broke in. He attacked us both."

I should have told them about Ted too, but I didn't want to admit to dusting him. "I didn't realize who he was at first," I said, "but then I recognized his voice. The man I was with turned out to be the detective investigating the disappearances. See? It all makes sense. Willoughby must have planned the attack. He must have gotten a member of the family to invite him in the house earlier on, or he wouldn't be able to enter."

The synchronized bobbing of heads with matching skeptical expressions was a funny sight, but I didn't feel like laughing. "I wiped the human. After." I sounded convincing enough. "I don't understand how Willoughby is still around, how he escaped when we all thought he was executed, but I think he's out there killing or turning women, and—"

"Thank you for bringing this to our notice, Cherry. We'll look into it." John smiled at me, eyes twinkling, and the knot in my stomach loosened. I had at least one ally in a high place.

"*If* there's something to look into," Gheorghios added, and Hui Zhong raised an eyebrow—the first expression I'd seen on her face so far. Benjamin was frowning. The lines of his face deepened, and the result was disconcerting.

I hesitated. Should I tell them about Dotty's son getting a visit from the kidnapper? My instincts told me not to. As far as I knew, said kidnapper wasn't aware his message was delivered, and that might keep Mark safe for a bit longer. "Could you let me know if you find my neighbor? Her son needs her." I was asking for a lot, but I liked Dotty.

"We're done here. You may go now." Ádísa, ever helpful, waved one hand toward the exit.

I was about to object—beg, if I had to—when John said, "We'll keep you posted."

It was more than I could have hoped for, although I was still planning on looking deeper into Dotty's disappearance.

Ádísa stressed her dismissal by folding an arm behind her head, arching her back, and yawning.

I never had illusions concerning my appearance, nor did I have any complexes. I'm not a stunner, but I'm pretty and can turn heads with little effort. And makeup. All in all, I have confidence in my looks, despite my handful or two of extra pounds. When Ádísa stretched, that confidence wavered.

Seeing her exhibit how much I was boring her should be insulting. She probably meant it that way. The only thought that crossed my mind, however, was that *I* would probably cheat on me with her. Toned abs, high cheekbones, bee-stung lips, golden mane—and we've covered the boobs, right? Her curves looked preordered, and knowing they weren't pissed me off to no end. I pinched the inside of Constantine's bicep, just because he'd let her seduce him.

Since I was pinching, I kept my hold on him as I rose to leave. Constantine stood next to me and gave the council a little bow, before placing his hand at the small of my back and guiding us toward the exit.

"Not you, darling." She even *sounded* gorgeous, damn it, her voice throaty and melodic.

Constantine turned to her. "Pardon?"

I took a couple of steps forward, fully aware ignoring her was impolite, yet not caring.

Then she said, "I thought maybe you'd like to see me home," and my feet ceased moving.

To his credit, Constantine didn't jump at the suggestion. "It isn't gentlemanly to let the lady I'm escorting return home alone."

"We're not in the eighteen hundreds anymore." She laughed. "I'm sure your little friend can find her way home."

Little friend? Grrr!

"She can't, Ádísa. She doesn't know where we are, nor should she find out." Nice. He'd pretend to be protecting the council? He lacked the balls to tell her he didn't want to go anywhere with her?

Unless he did.

Constantine must have sensed my irritation, because he reached over the distance between us and put a hand on my shoulder. It had a calming effect. I realized he was protecting me by trying not to piss her off. I was happy my back was still to them. I doubted she'd appreciate my face-splitting grin. And it was face splitting. It made my jaw hurt.

"Rowland can drive her, then." There was such finality in her tone, Constantine argued no more.

The human all but ran to my side. A peek over my shoulder showed me the others had left. The sneaky bastards hadn't made a sound. Ádísa held out her arms for Constantine. She met my gaze and blew me a kiss.

Bitch.

****

Constantine was safe and would probably enjoy himself, if he wasn't already. I'd be safe too, despite having been blindfolded as soon as I stepped out of the building.

Still, refraining from bitching took all the energy I had. The council hadn't shown interest in what I told them. I was tired, hungry, and my hot ex, with whom I had unresolved issues, was practically vamp-napped by your stereotypical femme fatale.

The latter wasn't my worry; it just annoyed me.

The ride was quiet and uneventful. Rowland wasn't the world's best conversationalist, but he was nice enough to offer me a reheated bottle of blood when I mentioned I hadn't eaten in more than twenty-four hours. I needed to feed so badly, the packaged meal didn't taste half bad.

When I entered the house, Alex was sprawled on the couch, his bare feet propped on the armrest. The lower half of his face was hidden by the folder he'd been working on when sleep overtook him, and he was snoring lightly. Seeing him made me forget all about Constantine as a wave of affection washed over me. Coming back to Alex was like coming home.

My heart expanded at the thought of doing that on a daily basis, and I shook my head to get rid of that mental image. Neither the time nor the subject matter was right for daydreaming. I plucked the folder from his fingers and left it on the floor so I could lean over him, to touch my lips to his.

He smiled without opening his eyes. Just a quirk of the lips. He was still asleep; I could tell by his breathing.

"Want to come to bed?" I whispered in his ear. My tongue trailing along it was just an accident, honestly.

The response I got was an adorable furrowing of his brow and an even more adorable scrunching of his nose.

"Alex?" I caressed his stomach, first over his shirt and then under it, loving the feel of his heat and smoothness. "Come to bed with me?"

He fluttered his lids and stirred a bit. Snaking an arm around my waist, he pulled me to him. "No," he mumbled, burying his face at the crook of my neck.

Being held bent over wasn't the most comfortable thing in the world, even for an immortal, so I draped a leg across his hips and crawled on top of him. "I'll carry you if you don't get up."

Idle threat—I could pick him up and carry him but had no intention to—yet it worked. Alex blinked at me drowsily. "You'd better be joking." He found my waistband, bunched his fingers around the loop at the back, and gave it a playful yank.

I giggled. "Only one way to find out." I started to get off him, but his hold on me didn't budge.

He caressed my cheek tenderly with his free hand. "You okay?" His eyes were serious and completely awake when I looked up at him.

I nodded, nuzzling his palm.

"Will they help?" He pulled the hair band from my ponytail and ran his fingers through my hair again and again.

"Uh-huh." Too tired to elaborate on the meeting's result, I let my head drop on his chest and melted into his touch. I'd fill in the blanks in the morning, since he didn't have to go in. Whoever kept tabs on us should take that to mean Alex was off the case, and Dotty would be safe until we got her back.

"Good." He trailed his thumb under my chin, so he could lift my face to him. When his finger feathered over my mouth, I wrapped my lips around it and sucked it in, like I had the previous night.

This time there was no omelet going cold, and I'd let no doubts hold me back. One more night wasn't forever, but it was one more night. For all I knew, it was all we had.

My jeans weren't accommodating for impromptu romps on the couch, especially with Alex obviously unwilling to move and me unwilling to lose touch with him long enough to stand and get rid of them. I had to work around them.

I squirmed in his lap, feeling him hard and thick between my legs. He drove his slim hips against mine, making me wish it was his cock I was sucking instead of his thumb. His gaze was fixed on my lips, his tongue all but lolling out of his mouth. The desperate moan he let out, a sound I'd heard men make before but which didn't touch me so deeply in the past, made up my mind for me. Without a word, Alex had conveyed such urgency that I decided to let his need come before mine.

I let go of his thumb and placed a kiss on the inside of his palm. Then I took hold of his other wrist and raised both his hands over his head. "Hold on and don't let go," I said with a wink, closing his fingers around the armrest. "It will be a bumpy ride."

He bucked beneath me. "This bumpy?"

"You don't know the half of it." I caressed his cheek. His stubble pricked at my fingertips. I used both hands to trace the sides of his face and continue down his neck to his smooth chest. I wanted to bury my face in the crook of his neck and inhale his deep, masculine scent until I got light-headed. Instead I bunched his T-shirt in both hands. "How attached are you to this?"

He barely had time to say, "Not very," before I pulled. The fabric shredded with a ripping sound and exposed his toned abs. He sucked in a breath, the muscles of his stomach clenching and becoming even more lickable. He strained not to move, his biceps bulging inside the short sleeves, and looked at me under hooded eyelids—all male, and all mine.

Maybe I could take my jeans off really, really fast?

Nah. I leaned forward and trailed my tongue down his throat. His skin was salty. A clean taste that made me want to savor more of him. He shivered and craned his neck to the side, spurring me to close my teeth over his jugular and nip lightly.

Alex groaned and rocked his hips. Finding and pinching his nipple, I pressed down on him, the seam of my jeans at just the right spot to make the friction pleasurable. We both hissed—okay, maybe I was louder than he was—and I moved back a little so I could lick his stomach without spraining my neck.

I blew air over the wet trail my mouth had left. The change in his breathing and heart rate would have made *snapping* my neck worth it. His chest rose and fell rapidly, and I realized I instinctively matched his intakes of air. By the time I undid his buttons and kissed below his navel, he was trembling. I looked up at him. His eyes were narrowed with concentration, and veins popped in his arms.

I'd had men want me before. As a human, I'd been in those circles where getting ahead meant giving head, and as a vampire, I'd had my share of conquests. Men had tried to charm, con, blackmail, or buy their way into my panties, but none of them had wanted me as badly as I could feel Alex did at that very moment. Not even Constantine, who'd been an experienced and considerate lover, and who I knew had loved me.

I shooed my former lover's memory out of my head. It was easy to do, with Alex's long and hard cock so close to my mouth. I wanted to wrap my lips around him and feel his silkiness on my tongue, feel his pulse throbbing in my mouth. I wanted to taste him when he lost control.

But I wanted him to beg first.

Alex had been the one doing the exploring during the few days we'd been together, and I thoroughly loved seeing how he responded to my touches now that it was my turn to play. I crawled between his legs and pulled his jeans as far down as they could go. It wasn't enough to expose all of him. I nibbled at the soft, smooth spot above his hip bone, and he mumbled something that sounded like *fuck*. I liked that, so I treated his other hip bone the same way, taking the opportunity to inhale his distinctive *Alex* scent under that of his shower gel.

He swayed his hips, and his cock nudged my cheek. Ignoring him, I placed an openmouthed kiss right next to his shaft, where it lay partially constricted on his lower abdomen. I trailed my fingernails over his length, and he tried to push against my palm, but I was faster, withdrawing it.

"Cherry, come on." He panted, his voice raspy. He raised his legs, bending them at the knees, and pressed his feet to the cushion.

"What?" I flicked his erection once with the tip of my tongue.

"You know what." His lower body jerked up from the couch when I did it again, and he said, "*Evil.*"

Stroking his inner thigh over the denim, I nodded. "I *so* am."

His muscles were tense, stretching the fabric and making me want to rip his pants off too. He amazed me by not releasing his grip on the couch when I licked along his cock. Though he did threaten me with revenge, unless I sucked him off immediately.

"I didn't hear the magic word." I sat back on my haunches, a silly giddiness overtaking me. "Without the magic word, you don't get a thing." I smirked, pleased with myself, and tickled his stomach with my nails. "Say the magic word."

"*Now?*" He growled, trying to move his legs.

I held on to them. "That's not the magic word." Since I was being childish anyway, I tickled his side when he stopped thrashing.

His eyes were the darkest gray I'd seen them so far, but he seemed as amused as I was. "Then what is?"

"*Please,*" I said smugly. That was my mistake.

"Well, since you're asking for it nicely." His hand flew to my hair and fisted in it. He used his grip to press my face to his cock.

I laughed. I'd never laughed during sex before I met Alex. I was usually too busy being the sultry seductress or the eager student. The latter was with Constantine, who'd always been teaching me, both in and out of bed. With Alex, it was different. He felt lighter, for lack of a better word.

He laughed too, stopping only when I closed my lips around the head of his dick and licked a single, salty drop of precum from its tip.

Not needing to breathe is a major asset when it comes to going down on a man. Nevertheless I couldn't do much with his jeans in the way. I made a valiant effort to take all of his cock in my mouth, but the angle was wrong.

As I was getting frustrated, Alex whispered, "Not attached to the jeans, either." I tugged on them sharply, and they were out of the way, framing his thighs with their front torn.

I took his cock down my throat and sucked. His balls were heavy. I cupped and rolled them in my palm. Both his hands were in my hair now, fingers tangled and tugging. I loved the illusion that I couldn't break free from his grasp.

He used his feet to propel his thrusts in and out of my mouth. He didn't hold back, but then, he didn't need to. I welcomed his frenzy. The sounds he made while his dick, slick with my saliva, slid forcefully between my lips filled me with a sense of power that had nothing to do with physical strength. This strong, assertive man was reduced to meaningless cries of ecstasy because of what I was doing to him. Holding him still, I sucked harder, withdrawing enough to circle his cockhead with my tongue.

His grasp on my hair intensified, and I thought he meant to push back in, but he didn't. Instead he pulled me up and gave me a fierce kiss. "Turn around," he said.

I was so lost in enjoying his pleasure that I didn't understand what he was talking about.

"On your knees. Face the other way."

Ah. I turned and braced myself on the opposite arm of the couch with one hand, undoing my fly with the other.

He yanked my waistband halfway down my thighs, and in a single thrust buried his cock inside me. He didn't pause when I cried out at the suddenness of his intrusion—not that I wanted him to. He fucked me with almost punishing force, my position making the friction between us more intense, despite how wet my pussy was. He gripped the back of my neck and pressed my face down against the cushion.

The change in angle of penetration added to the pressure building in my lower belly. The couch's fabric scratched against my skin, but only heightened my pleasure, as did Alex's roughness. I reached down to stroke my clit. Each move of his hips, each touch of his fingertips, each thrust of his cock made a claim over my body. I was his to take, his to fuck, his to please, and I wouldn't have it any other way.

I loved this dominating side of Alex as much as I loved his easygoing one. And I wouldn't linger on the *love* part.

"Who's fucking you, Cherry? Who are you going to come for?"

"You, only y—*oh God.*" A crushing wave of pleasure bowed my back and made my head light. The tension inside me finally broke. It felt like a vial of adrenaline was poured in my veins. Without warning, my senses became more acute, my hold on them gone. Alex's scent filled my nostrils, and the drumming of his heart thundered in my ears. I could make out the slightest change in pressure, where he dug his fingers into the back of my neck. The hairs on his legs tickled the oversensitized skin of my thighs. My pussy pulsated. My stomach tightened.

The force of my orgasm made my body shake. I tried to look at Alex over my shoulder, but all strength had been sapped out of me. My vision blurred. I squeezed my eyes shut and bit the cushion, trying to stay grounded. It didn't work. I expanded and expanded until I was nothing but light and color. I flew and I fell, my limbs light as feathers and made of lead.

Alex slammed his hips against me once, twice, three times, and then spilled himself in me, hot cum dripping down my inner thighs.

We slumped down and stayed there, until I could feel my legs again. He wrapped an arm around my waist, gathered me to him, and lay back, peppering kisses on my shoulder. I wanted to roll over and face him, but his hold wouldn't budge even after his cock slipped out of me. He hadn't been at his chattiest after sex so far, but there was now a tension in him I didn't like.

He spoke before I could ask if something was wrong. "That last part… I don't know where it came from." He interlaced my fingers with his, brought them to his mouth, and brushed his lips over the knuckles.

"It's okay. I liked it." I let the *l* roll on my tongue for emphasis.

"I'm lying." He sighed, stroking my stomach.

I sucked it in—not my sexiest body part. "What about?" Post-coital Cherry brain doesn't work at full capacity.

"I do know where that came from." The words, though whispered, were crystal clear. "You and your ex. You saw him, then came here all frisky. I guess I was jealous." Before I could respond, he went on. "And don't tell me I have no right to be. I want you, damn it, and I can be patient, but I won't be left here again while you're out there with him."

I should have been offended by how little faith in me that statement indicated. I knew how it felt to have been betrayed, however. It made people more guarded. It took something from them.

Dropping the pretense that I couldn't break free, I used my vampire agility to flip on my stomach. What I said right then and there could make or break what we had. "Alex"—I waited until he looked at me—"I was frisky for you. I'm not going to screw around." It wasn't possible for us to be in a relationship, but whatever we had was for two players only. He opened his mouth, and I silenced him with my index finger on his lips. "I know what we have is… Well, it's a wait-and-see thing, but I'm only waiting to see things out with you."

His smile shone on his face for a moment, and then he was kissing me again.

We barely made it to the basement before sunrise.

Chapter Eight

I needed to sleep. My brain was fuzzy, and my body felt too exhausted to keep my head up while Alex talked. I found the perfect solution in confiscating his pillow and placing it on top of mine to hold my head propped up as I lay on my side. My mind didn't benefit from the more upright position. It still wanted to shut down.

Alex nudged my shin with his foot. "*Hey.* I didn't sleep while you were telling me about your meeting."

"Mmm."

He'd been a good little trouper and paid attention while I'd described how my night had gone, and he'd had all the right reactions, including a disgusted face when I'd mentioned Ádísa's behavior after explaining who she was. It was by all means my turn to listen. And I tried to. Honestly.

"Tell me." I turned my face to the pillow to hide my yawn.

"Like I said, I got a call. Your friend's case has another thing different than the rest."

I blinked drowsily. "What's that?" He'd better tell me soon.

"She left her cell phone behind. Not on purpose, most probably. It was found under the couch at the club where she was last seen. They're working on locating her boyfriend and checked her calls. No outgoing calls after noon, but her last incoming one was from a private number. They're working on tracing that. Meantime she had a missed call that night. Apparently from a modeling agency."

That woke me up. He was sitting up, and I had to crane my neck to look at him. "A modeling agency? I didn't know Dotty modeled." I was ashamed that I didn't think she could model. Like Alex had said, she wasn't ugly, not by a long shot, but she wasn't extraordinary looks-wise, either. My shame deepened when I realized my train of thought assumed I'd been something special during my modeling days.

"Weird that she didn't mention it. You said she's your friend. Anyway, I'll be checking that out first thing in the morning." He touched his lips to my cheek and slid under the covers, facing me.

"This *is* the morning," I mumbled.

Chuckling, he glanced at his watch. "Yeah, but I doubt Sheena's Models is open at six thirty."

"Sheena's Models?" It came out squeaky.

Alex arched both eyebrows. "That's the agency. Why?"

"Sheena was my agent."

I've never believed in coincidences.

****

Alex promised not to go see Sheena by himself before sunset, and I slept like the—wouldn't you know it?—dead.

What interrupted my slumber was a curse coming from the floor above. I sprang upright and instinctively reached for Alex. After the first few seconds of disorientation, I realized he wasn't in bed. As a matter of fact, he was the one who'd done the cursing. I could hear nobody else upstairs. Maybe he'd jabbed a toe or something, while making me breakfast. The thought of him cooking for me made me smile.

"It's the only way," Alex said.

So he *was* talking to someone. I tried not to listen in, but his next words piqued my curiosity.

"If you don't suspend me, I'm leaving the force."

Resisting my natural instincts was futile. I settled my head back on the downy pillow and eavesdropped.

"You know you owe me," Alex said. "I was in a bad place, and it worked out well for you. This is *my* case. Let me work it the way I know how."

I couldn't make out the other side of the conversation.

"Just do it, okay? I'll deal." Pause. "Thanks." The last word was whispered.

The next sound was of footsteps approaching.

I kept my eyes closed when Alex sneaked back into bed. I didn't know how extensive his detective training had been, but even if he was trained to recognize when a human faked being asleep, I had no breathing he could listen to, in order to call my bluff.

He snuggled behind me and buried his face in my hair. I couldn't tell if the sigh he let out was of contentment or frustration.

I pushed my body against his with a *mmm* sound, and he pulled me closer. I mmmed again when he kissed my shoulder. He cupped my breast, and I shifted so he could catch a glimpse of my face. Scrunching my nose, I asked, "What time is it?" My voice came out thee right amount of groggy.

"Eleven thirty. You can sleep some more." His hand roaming my body indicated he wouldn't mind if I didn't.

"Are you going to work?" *Come on, buddy. Fess up. Don't lie to me.* The latter became a chant in my head for the brief moments until he replied.

"No. I'll nod off too." As if to prove he had every intention of doing so, he stopped caressing me.

I was aware of the irony of wanting him to come clean, when I was deceiving him, but it was about self-preservation. My first priority was making sure I didn't trust someone else who'd lie to me. I'd have time later to feel bad about it. "Right. You're not going in. Following a lead..." There was his opening, and I hoped he took it.

He didn't. "Yeah." The single whispered word sounded regretful.

With any guy before Alex, I'd have let them go on, dig a bigger hole for when I dumped their asses into it. Since Constantine made me trust him and then duped me, I regard men lying as the norm. I expect to be lied to; it fits into my world theory. For Alex, however, I did something out of character. I gave up my efforts toward an Oscar-winning performance. "I heard you. On the phone."

I expected him to make an excuse or be upset I eavesdropped. I couldn't blame him if he was, but I was relieved when instead he said, "I didn't want you to have to worry about me too, with everything else happening. Wanted you to believe I had things under control."

I turned within his embrace. "I only heard what you said. Wanna talk about it?"

"Roebuck wouldn't let me investigate what I found out unless I let him in on it. I said I had a source I couldn't reveal—that it's big and lives are at stake if the department is involved—but he's stubborn. He offered to come by and talk about it. I can't drag more people into this." He cupped my cheek and tucked my hair behind my ear with his fingertips. "Thought about asking for a leave, but I can't take days off in the middle of a case. Finally asked him to suspend me, so I could do what I wanted."

"But he wouldn't." I walked my index and middle finger up his torso, then along his collarbone. It wasn't a sexual touch, more an *I'm here* one. If my touch afforded him half the comfort his afforded me, it would help him open up.

He shook his head and closed his hand around mine, stopping me. "He refused to. Said they needed me. So I had to play dirty. First I threatened to quit, and then I reminded him he owed me. It was a low blow." He rubbed his face with his free hand. "I can't believe I did that. I'm such a prick."

"You're not." I kissed his cheek.

He turned away. "I shouldn't have said what I did. It's not even true."

I didn't ask. Going against my nature, I remained silent until he began talking again.

"Roebuck was my partner. I was going through my dark phase when promotions were up. It was too soon after my breakup with Marion." I assumed that was the ex. "Anyway." He sighed and wet his lips.

My gaze was drawn to his mouth before I returned it to his eyes, feeling guilty for thinking naughty thoughts at a time like that.

"We scored close enough on the test, but my performance had taken a plunge. Roebuck got the promotion to lieutenant and deserved it, but he's felt bad about it since. And now, like the asshole I am, I rubbed it in."

I couldn't watch his self-kicking any longer. "You did it for him. If he got involved—if *anyone* got involved—there'd be more people missing. Dying."

"I'm still an asshole."

I batted his shoulder. "That's irrelevant."

His lips twitched, and then he did what I was hoping for. He smiled. "You always know the right thing to say, huh?" Before I could come up with a self-satisfied reply, he tickled me and kept tickling until I squealed.

****

Alex brought Mexican food, which was spicy as hell, and I took immense pleasure in his terrified response when I offered to blow him after stuffing my mouth with what seemed like my body weight in jalapenos.

Those moments of intimacy that had more to do with enjoying each other's company and wit than with sex were when I knew beyond the shadow of a doubt that I was half in love with him already. I loved the tiny little wrinkles that showed around his eyes when he smiled. I loved the long lashes that shaded his prominent cheekbones. I loved how he lowered his eyelids coyly before saying something raunchy that would make me blush if I had blood circulation. I loved the way he spoke with his entire upper body, his shoulders, arms, and long fingers stressing his points as eloquently as his deep voice.

Those moments made me want to cry. The way I felt about him was why I should leave him. I couldn't stand watching him grow closer to death every day, and the idea of turning him was preposterous. Alex's humanity was part of him. To take that away, together his chance of fathering children that would turn out as wonderful as he was, was something only a monster would do.

So I focused on the *now* and the time we had together until the case was solved, but as the hours passed, I felt him become antsy. Strangely enough, I also loved that his mind never veered far from the case. His sense of honor wouldn't allow him to have fun at the expense of people in danger. Spending time with me while waiting for a clue was one thing. Wasting time with me once a clue had landed in our laps was another. After a point, he began taking trips upstairs to check if the sun had gone down, as if he couldn't trust the Internet any more than he could my inner clock.

I, on the other hand, was in no hurry for dusk to come.

I was in no hurry to hear Sheena admit she had something to do with my turning. I'd trusted her. She was the first person to be genuinely nice to me when I moved to the city. She'd found me the apartment I lived in before I died, and booked my jobs both as a model and in the… other industry I tried to make a name for myself in. For a long time, I felt bad about not telling her I was still around, and now I found out she might have been involved in what had happened to me. I didn't want to face her, but I couldn't let Alex deal with her alone. It might be dangerous.

"It's dark outside," Alex yelled from the top of the stairs.

I barely groused on my way up.

To his credit, he was holding the door for me when I got there.

****

"I can fly us over, you know." As much as I dreaded meeting my old agent and friend, a forty-five-minute drive would only fray my nerves more.

Alex, who was locking the front door, froze mid key-turn. "You can fly?"

"I didn't mention that, did I?"

He finished locking and looked at me. "No, you didn't. How?"

"I don't know the mechanics. No sprouting bat wings or anything. I just want to take off, and I do. An open mind is essential, the handbook said."

"I see. While that sinks in, let's drive there." He pressed the button on his car key, and the car's lights flashed twice. "I don't like flying," he said, getting the car door for me. That he admitted it, instead of coming up with a lame excuse, gained him extra brownie points but still wasn't enough for me to admit I was afraid of what we might find out. I folded all of my five-feet-four into the passenger seat, and he shut the door.

We hit traffic almost immediately. Insert frustrated groan.

Stillness isn't something that comes naturally for me. I know, I know—vampires are supposed to have perfected stillness. I think it's something paranormal romance writers came up with, to add mysterious allure to their heroes and heroines. Or maybe the notion came from someone who's met Constantine. Either way I don't do still; I'm a fidgeter. I play with my hair, the hem of my top, the belt loop of my jeans, my jewelry, and occasionally tap my foot and/or fingers on the nearest available surface, which, at present, was the casing of the car window.

My nails aren't long, but they're always manicured—yay to having been turned right after full-body pampering—and they're noisy.

Disturbing was the word Alex used.

"Sorry. Didn't mean to get on your nerves." I stopped tapping my fingers, but soon began twitching my foot, and from time to time, connecting with the middle column.

"Okay, what's wrong?" Alex peeked at me before returning his attention to the road. "It's the first time I've seen you so jittery."

"Yeah, well, you haven't seen all that much of me, have you?" *Nice, Cherry.* I gave him a sheepish look. "I'm sorry. I'm being a bitch."

"That's irrelevant."

"Smooth, Marsden." Still, I felt more relaxed with his attempt at humor.

At the traffic light, he put his hand on my thigh, his warmth doing nothing for the cold I felt inside. "Seriously, what's the matter?" he asked.

Closing my eyes, I let my head roll to the side until my forehead leaned against the cool glass.

I was done with my shift at the bakery and was helping myself to a doughnut with extra glaze on it, when a woman behind me said, "I'd enjoy the fuck out of that if I were you, honey. If you're to work for me—which you are, and are going to love—that's the last of those babies you're gonna have in a long while."

I turned to bitch slap whoever dared come between me and my dessert, but the smile on her lips stopped me in my tracks.

"I bet you want to be a model, don't you?" she asked. "Or an actress? Isn't that why you came to the city?"

Mara, the bitchy waif who had the evening shift, snorted. That made my decision for me. I took a big bite of my doughnut. "What can you offer me?" I asked.

The woman's smile widened. "The world, darling. And I'll start with a ride away from this place."

I opened my eyes again and focused on the *here* and *now*. "Sheena. If she handed me to them… It hurts." I blew out my breath noisily, fogging the window. "I know it's silly. It's been so long, but—" At least she'd let me keep having doughnuts for a while.

"I get it." He squeezed my leg, and I knew he wasn't just saying that. He got me.

A look at him, and I was back in swooning mode, the knot in my stomach temporarily forgotten. Even if Sheena betrayed me, Alex wouldn't. He *got* me.

But for how long?

Chapter Nine

For all my anticipation and dread, reaching the modeling agency proved anticlimactic.

I'd imagined Alex ringing the doorbell and moving to the side, allowing me to step forward. Sheena would open the door, dressed in a possibly purple pantsuit, professional smile in place. When she saw me, that smile would waver until it was replaced by a look of shock and fear. She might try to slam the door in my face, but I'd be faster. Sticking my foot into the opening of the door, I'd say, "Hello, darling," my voice cool as a cucumber.

I should have let Alex in on my fantasy confrontation. Since I didn't, he got it wrong from the start, ringing the bell but not budging an inch, so I had to stand on tiptoe, for the top of my head to be visible over his shoulder. The door was thrown open by a blonde I'd never seen before, a distinct expression of disinterest on her face. "Can I help you?"

Yup. Anticlimactic.

I mean, don't get me wrong—the sight of Alex flashing his badge at the girl and telling her we had some questions was a thrill in and of itself. He ought to have turned the badge and his weapon in, but he was being naughty about it, and I didn't mind that naughtiness at all. I wished we were alone. Seeing him like that, jaw clenched, shoulders squared, body posture imposing, I wanted him to take me right there, on Sheena's Models' doorstep. Or I could jump him.

Nah. I couldn't. I was introduced as a consultant, and sexually assaulting a detective wouldn't be very consultanty.

The blonde said her name was Barbara Greg, and she was Sheena's assistant. She invited us in and asked if we'd like a beverage. We followed her to the waiting area but politely refused her offer of coffee or tea.

"We would like to speak to Ms. Herring," Alex said.

"I'm sorry. She isn't in."

Alex brought a notepad and pen out of his jacket's inner pocket. "Do you know when she will be coming in or where we might find her?"

She shrugged. "Well, she left two days ago and said she'd be gone indefinitely, so no."

I felt like a balloon someone punched a hole in. All the mental and emotional prep work I'd given myself on the ride was sucked out of me, leaving behind a sizeable gap and a sense of floating—not as in being joyful and weightless, but rather like having no anchor or purpose. It was a sickening feeling, and I wanted to punch the wall. Irrelevant to my personal history with her, Sheena was our best lead so far, our greatest chance to find Dotty and the other girls. I couldn't believe she wasn't here.

"Are you aware of her current whereabouts? Where did she go?" Alex tapped his pen on his notepad, while I stood against the wall, playing not-here cop. A slight twitch of his eye was the only indication that Sheena's absence bothered him too.

"She said she'd visit family, out of town. I don't know where," Barbara said nasally, pouring herself some coffee. The smell of hazelnut wafted to my nostrils. I'd have loved some but saw enough cop shows to know accepting something to eat or drink from someone you were questioning seemed unprofessional. "I haven't been working for her long enough to ask for details." She shrugged again, her breasts threatening to pop out over her constricting top.

"How long is *not long enough*?" Alex smiled, and I leaned carefully to one side, to see what he was looking at. Her eyes, not her cleavage. I caught myself nodding in approval. Good man. The ludicrousness of concerning myself with petty jealousy when so much was at risk didn't escape me.

"Almost three months now." The blonde turned to me, and I straightened as fast as I could. "What is this about?" Worry was drawn on her pretty yet overly made-up face.

Alex ignored her query. "Ms. Herring went on a vacation, leaving behind an employee with less than three months of experience?" His voice was gentle, coaxing, rather than prodding. *Amaze me with how good and deserving an employee you are*, it said.

She frowned. "I'm excellent at my job, Detective Marsden. I don't need to defend my employer's choices."

"I don't doubt your abilities, Ms. Greg." Alex smiled reassuringly. I tried not to harrumph.

"It's *Miss* Greg." She smiled back. "Better yet, call me Barbie, Detective."

Barbie, for fuck's sake.

"Miss Greg, then." Alex produced a pack of pictures from the same pocket as the notebook. "Have you seen any of these girls before? Maybe one of them has worked with your agency in the past."

Barbie barely glanced at Dotty's picture before she put it down and looked at the second missing girl's photograph. My heart sank when she showed no signs of recognition. My ears didn't pick up the slightest change in her heart rate. She wasn't acting. Second girl got a *no* too, but we sort of had a winner with the third one.

"Her." Barbie's lacquered, one-inch nail—how could she type with those things?—tapped the picture of a stunning girl with short raven locks and prominent eyebrows that brought out the green specks in her hazel eyes. "Liza Mills. She was here… a month ago? Let me check my appointment book."

She opened her top drawer and brought out a humongous folder, holding a pack of letter-size sheets. Each page had a mug shot stapled on it.

Barbie noticed me looking at the photos. "Sheena insists on candid shots of everyone we interview."

I knew that. I was just wondering if my picture was still here somewhere.

I begrudgingly admitted Barbie might be better at her work than I pegged her for. She found the girl immediately. The only info under her shot was a cell-phone number.

"Here she is."

"This contact number is all you have?" Alex reached out, and Barbie placed the open folder in his hands with a nod.

He flipped through pages, and I tried to be inconspicuous while stretching my neck to see the photos attached to them. "The other forms are filled in completely, as far as I can see," he said. He hadn't looked through everything, though. Maybe there were other girls with just their numbers jotted down, girls who hadn't disappeared yet and could be saved.

She wrinkled her nose. "I book the appointments and fill these in when the girls come. I was on my day off when Sheena met with her, though, and when she gave me the form to file it, she said not to bother with anything else."

"Do you mind if we hold on to this for a couple of days?" He graced her with that smile that made me want to be his slave. "I could get a warrant, but I see no reason to."

"I have it all in electronic form. Even scanned the pictures. I'll print you a copy." Barbie preened. "I keep telling Sheena we're in the age of technology."

Well, that was easy.

While the printer worked its little mechanical heart out, making a sound that bore an eerie similarity to grunting, Barbie looked at the other missing girls' photos and ruled out everyone else.

I started moving toward the front door, when Alex asked, "What's your work schedule, Miss Greg? Do you work Saturdays, for example?"

Why did he want to know that?

Her grin was big enough to show her gums. "I'm here every Saturday and most Sundays, but I have the afternoon off one week from today." Her face fell, which gave me an odd sense of joy. "But I can't leave the office—not with Sheena gone."

"Is it a fixed weekend every month or did you need that time off for a specific reason?"

"No reason. Sheena gives me an afternoon off each week. This week it was day before yesterday, when I last saw her."

When anyone last saw Dotty.

"And you haven't heard from her since." It was a mixture of a statement and a question. Pen poised over pad once more, Alex waited.

"She called me about half an hour before you showed. Asked if anyone had been by looking for her." And she hadn't thought to mention that so far. Finally she asked the million-dollar question. "Is she in trouble?"

She would be, when I found her. Before I did something stupid like say that out loud, Alex asked, "Does your phone show caller ID?"

****

The area code of the last incoming call was proof positive that Sheena had lied about going out of town. She had to know her assistant wasn't the sharpest tool in the box too, since she hadn't bothered calling from a private number. Still, it would have taken us a while to trace the call if I hadn't seen that number on my cell phone's screen enough times to know it by heart.

Sheena had called from her *house*. She had a private office there, with its own line, which was in her ex-husband's name. She only used that for nefarious purposes, such as organizing the shooting of adult films without her name showing anywhere. I ought to know; I'd been involved in said nefarious purposes.

Once again we were in Alex's car, but this time there was no traffic delaying us. The scenery was no longer urban, buildings having given their place to trees that appeared to run by my window at full speed. The colors changed too, from gray to green, to yellow, orange, and red. I knew Alex couldn't see the hues as well as I could in the darkness, and for a moment I grew wistful. There was an entire world he couldn't be a part of, just as I couldn't completely belong in his. The thoughts I'd tried to drive away for the finite time we had together resurfaced in my mind. We weren't meant to be. He thrived in the sun, while I could only live under the moon. The sooner his case was over, the better. We could both get back to reality.

His hand brushed my thigh when he closed his fingers around the gearshift. He flashed a brief smile my way, and I wouldn't trade that smile for the world, not even to save myself sorrow in the future.

I would if it was to save *him* sorrow in the future, though. Just as I'd go against his wishes and take away his memories of me if he refused to let go when the time came.

****

My agitation rose with every step Alex and I took on the cobbled walkway that led to Sheena's front door. I could have sworn that walkway was a lot shorter the last time I visited. Now it felt like years passed before we stood on the red, bow-shaped welcome mat.

I remembered that mat. Sheena had told me my hair matched it, once I'd changed its color for the never-shot movie I was to star in. In the darkness, I saw the vibrant hue clearly, and it made me want to rip it to shreds. In some irrational way, it was another reminder of how she'd betrayed me.

Oblivious to my train of thought, Alex wiped his feet meticulously.

I snorted. "You couldn't have stepped in some mud? Dog poo, even better."

"Sorry?"

I wasn't sure if he wanted me to explain my demand-like question or if he was apologizing. I shrugged. "It's okay."

He put his hand on the small of my back, and like the first time we met, electricity flowed between us. This time, it had a different result than to raise my lust for him. His touch now was soothing, comforting. I melted against his side.

112

"Is it?" He gave me a questioning look, wrapping his arm around me, to press me to him. "Are *you*? I don't need you for this. You can wait in the car. You should, officially."

I rubbed my face against his shoulder, then nodded. "Yeah, well, you shouldn't be here, officially. Let's get this over with."

He let go, gave me a peck on the lips, and rang the doorbell.

I allowed my hearing to expand to its vampiric limit and easily made out the ring reverberating throughout the house. Then I heard scuffling.

"Someone's moving inside," I whispered. My phone vibrated in my back pocket, startling me. Whoever it was could wait.

"Ms. Herring? Open the door, please. Police." Alex sounded very police-y, indeed.

There was the scuffling again, like feet dragging. Like someone being sneaky on the wooden floor. The sound wasn't coming toward us. "Back door," I blurted and took off. Not literally. I didn't have to fly, to round the house faster than a human could cross it. I was waiting outside the glass door of the kitchen when the door pulled open.

Sheena burst out and straight into my waiting arms. I grabbed her waist. She dropped the backpack and laptop case she was holding and fought me blindly. I didn't let go of my grip on her waist.

With her eyes squeezed shut, she screeched like a banshee. I lifted her off the ground to subdue her, and she did her best to lodge her pointed shoes inside my shins. Why on earth would a woman try to escape while wearing high heels? *Vanity before safety.*

Then she kneed me on the hip.

I adjusted my grip and moved behind her. That way she couldn't get me with her hands and knees. Still, she wouldn't stop trying to claw at me over her shoulder or get me with her heels.

Alex approached, gun in hand. I shook my head, and he halted but kept his weapon pointed at her.

Sheena shrieked and bucked. Her long nails found my face, and one of them gouged my cheek. It stung enough to make my eyes tear up, but I held on even as her fuchsia jacket ripped.

"Ms. Herring, I have a gun pointed at you. We just want to ask you some questions." Alex's voice of reason wasn't working. Sheena didn't cease her thrashing.

"Sheena, cut that out. You're not going anywhere until you talk to us." My fangs had come out, and my *s*'s were kind of whistly, but I sounded menacing, nonetheless. The scent of my own blood made me moodier than before.

"*Let me go.*" She stomped on my foot with her heel.

The jolt of pain was sharp but not debilitating. I held her at arm's length. "Why did you hand me to Willoughby?" I shook her before spinning her to face me. "Why?" I was certain I was yelling, but the last reached my ears as a whine. "I thought you were my friend."

She stopped fighting, and her body sagged. Easing one eye open, she said, "Cherry?"

"Yeah." I could have said something wittier, but for the second time that day, my expectations had little to do with reality.

Like I said, I expected shock and fear when Sheena laid eyes on me. Now I saw shock there, all right, but no fear.

She reached for me again, yet not to hurt me. She touched my face. My shoulders. My hair. I didn't know how to react. She wasn't trying to wound me or defend herself.

Finally she squeezed me to her. "Oh thank God, you're okay."

****

Her living room hadn't changed since I'd last been there. Every piece of furniture, as well as the walls and carpeting, still made a statement—the owner had a loud personality.

Then again, the owner herself was a testament to that.

Sheena had on a pair of fuchsia pants and a matching jacket which now lacked two buttons, with a fuchsia and lime-green silk top. The set might have looked appropriate for Halloween on me, but it complemented her mocha-colored skin perfectly. Her matching makeup was messed up, mascara-tinged tears making tracks on her blush.

She'd asked if we wanted coffee or something stronger but we'd both refused anything, so she was the only person in the room with a drink in hand. Scotch. Straight up.

"I'm so glad you're okay," she said for the millionth time, reaching across the couch to pat my knee.

I traced the scratch already healing on my cheek but didn't respond. I was still so gobsmacked, I could only stare. If Alex hadn't pulled me inside the house by the hand, I'd have probably still been out in the garden, trying to figure out why Sheena acted happy to see me.

Alex, my knight in shining armor, took it upon himself to point out the mistake in her statement. "She's far from okay, Ms. Herring. She's dead." His glare was anything but professional.

Sheena sniffed. "She's walking and talking. It's more than I thought she was. Ergo, she's okay."

Ergo. Leave it to her to find the oddest time to use a pretentious word. I shook my head. Alex was right. I wasn't okay. I'd spent years alone. Even when I was with Constantine, I had no friends, nobody to be silly with, no shoulder to cry on. I couldn't see my family. Couldn't let them know I was still around, still the same person they'd brought up, except for the undead thing. I never wanted kids before I was turned, but knowing the choice had been taken away from me made me long for the possibility of one at times.

I could have been worse off, I guess. Could have been gone forever. But so much had happened to me because of her.

I looked at Alex and felt a smile tug at the corners of my lips. Some of those happenings hadn't been bad.

I no longer felt like killing Sheena. "Why did you do it?" It was the thing I needed to find out first.

"I didn't know I was doing something." The words came out soft as a breath. "That guy asked to meet you.

Nothing bad was supposed to happen to you." That she didn't knowingly lead me to my death loosened the knot in my stomach the tiniest bit.

"Something did happen, though." I thought Alex meant to urge her to say more, but a glance at his face showed me he was still beyond pissed off. "Of course, you thought you were just whoring her out." He spared her none of the formal courtesy he'd offered her assistant. This wasn't an investigation any longer; it was as personal to him as it was to me.

Sheena hung her head. "Willoughby was good looking, well mannered, *rich*. I thought he'd be good for her."

How could she have thought a guy named *Willoughby* could be good for anyone?

Alex sat on the armrest next to me, gun lying on his thigh. He hadn't even let go of it to hand Sheena her bag and laptop before we'd come inside. I squeezed his free hand.

"Why didn't you do something when you heard I disappeared?" I asked Sheena. I wanted to believe she'd initially acted with my best interest at heart, but there was no excuse for the rest. "Why did you give him more girls?"

"I didn't *hear* you disappeared." Her voice was louder, exasperated, and she was still not looking at me. "He came here and he said what happened to you would happen to me if I didn't help them or I went to the cops. He—he *bit* me." Her free hand twitched on her lap.

I didn't want to feel sorry for her, but until recently I'd thought of her as a friend. I couldn't just delete that. Instead of trying to figure out my feelings, I focused on how her words answered one of my upcoming questions. She knew about vampires. "And you let him do it to others?"

"He promised me they'd be kept happy. That he'd offer them things." I could tell she was trying to convince herself more than us. "There were some who didn't have much of a future on the runway, or at all." I remembered the entry with just a picture and number that her assistant gave us. "Others that he'd specifically suggested I approach. He'd call and tell me what he had in mind. I arranged the meetings."

"Knowing they'd die?" It was possible I could still find it in me to snap her neck. Deep down I wanted not to have found out about her involvement, even if that shot down our chances of recovering the young women.

"Knowing they'd live forever," she yelled, raising her gaze to me. "They'd stay pretty forever. They wouldn't get a single wrinkle, and they'd be rich. Nobody would miss them. I was helping them."

"What about Dorothea Williams?" Alex's question fell heavily in the quiet that had followed Sheena's outburst. "She has a son." I was grateful the wrath etched on his face wasn't aimed at me. He was mortal, and therefore physically weaker than me, but seeing him like that, I knew he'd be lethal if he chose to.

Sheena's complexion turned ashen, and her lower lip trembled. "I didn't want to give him Dotty. I wouldn't have signed her if he hadn't made me. He told me where I could bump into her. I had to make it seem like my idea. He couldn't approach her on his own, because she was cautious of going out with strangers, being a mom and all. After I met her—she was so nice. He said she'd be the last one. That it had to be her. I introduced them about a month ago, and they went out a few times. When nothing happened on their first date, I hoped he wouldn't... You know."

I motioned for her to continue, but my mind reeled. If Willoughby was the guy Dotty had been seeing for a month, then he'd selected her before finding out about me and Alex. Before there *was* a me and Alex. Willoughby had been keeping tabs on me. But why? The question was drowned out by a flood of guilt. Whatever the reason, it was *my* fault Dotty was gone.

"When he called and demanded a new girl for next week, I told him I wouldn't do it anymore. That he'd promised I wouldn't have to. I asked him about Dotty. He wouldn't talk about her, but I knew if he wanted a new girl, it meant Dotty—" Her voice, high-pitched by that point, broke, and her next words were muttered under her breath. "She was so nice."

Hearing Sheena say *was* twice drove a sharp spear of cold fear through my heart. "She's dead?"

"I tried to call her, to get her to break things off with him, but she didn't answer. I thought I was too late. Isn't that why you're here?"

I didn't realize I was almost crushing Alex's hand until he cleared his throat and tried to pry it away. I let go. "We just know she's missing. Do you know anything about where he might be taking the girls?"

"No. I swear. I was too afraid to ask for details, and he never told me anything." She downed the rest of her drink, and her hand trembled when she leaned forward to leave the glass on the coffee table.

"Have you seen anybody else with him?"

"No. Never." She chewed on her lip, and flakes of the supposed color-stay lipstick peeled off on her teeth.

"Do you have his number? Any way to contact him?" Alex produced his notepad, but Sheena shook her head.

"He always called me, and from a private number. Set the time and place, and asked for what he had in mind. He'd meet them at clubs or parties. The names the girls were to ask for were different every time."

Made-up names. I wondered if they were worse than *Willoughby*, though that had to be his real name. Or at least what he went by in the vampire circles. It was what they'd called him during my trial.

Alex asked for her phone. "Maybe he'll call again," he said. She gave it to him immediately.

He didn't ask her to specify the names Willoughby had given her on occasion. It made sense; we had no use for them. We were back to square one.

I rose, and Alex followed my lead. Nothing more to do here.

Sheena pushed herself off the couch with both hands, wavered, and finally managed to stand. "What about me? What are you going to do with me?"

Alex looked at me, and in that moment, I knew beyond the shadow of a doubt that he'd be fine with shooting her and burying her in the backyard if I asked him to.

A small part of me would be fine with it too. Sheena had pulled the world out from under my feet, and I couldn't forgive her for that. Before that, however, she'd made my world a better place for a while. "Get out of town," I said. "For real this time. If I see you again, I'll kill you." I wouldn't. I'm not a killer. But I'd do my best to make her miserable.

She nodded. "For what little it's worth, I'm really sorry. I didn't want any of this."

I believed her, but I didn't care.

****

My phone buzzed again on the drive back, and once more I let it go to voicemail. I curled up in my seat and let the rocking motion of the car lull me to sleep.

I awoke briefly when Alex was getting me out of the car. He said something about taking care of me. He was human and fragile despite his size, and I was a vampire and basically immortal. Still, his words made me feel safe. Alex's strength came from within, and it could move mountains.

Nothing bad would happen to me again as long as he held me.

Chapter Ten

Lying naked in bed, pressed against a hard male body, provided the best distraction from depressing thoughts. The body being Alex's, chiseled to perfection and warm to the touch, added an extra reason for me not to want to get out from under the covers to retrieve my buzzing phone.

It was still in my jeans pocket, where Alex left it when he'd undressed me to put me in bed, and the jeans were folded on a chair, a few feet from where we were. The distance seemed vast when crossing it entailed disentangling myself from Alex.

"You're not gonna get that?" His breath caressed the back of my neck, making me itch to leave the blasted call alone.

I let out a puff of air and brought his palm to my lips, so I could place a kiss on it. "You heard it?"

"You don't need enhanced hearing for that. I think I put your keys in the same pocket. They're jingling." He caressed my cheek with his thumb.

"I don't want to get up." The words were drawn out and nasal.

Alex ignored my whining. "I heard it earlier too. May be an emergency."

I doubted that. The caller hadn't been persistent enough; they'd let hours go by between tries. I should have checked my missed calls, but I'd honestly forgotten about them till then. "The only people who have that number are Sheena, Constantine, Dotty, and the council." Ignoring Alex's grumbling that he ought to have it too, I went on. "It's too early for any of the vampires to be calling me, and Sheena wouldn't dare to."

I was out of bed as soon as the last word left my mouth.

Dotty. Dotty or her kidnapper—I refused to think of him as her killer—could be trying to contact me. I grabbed my jeans. My fingers might as well have been sausages, the way they refused to be agile and pluck the stupid phone out of the stupid denim. The buzzing stopped.

I finally found the phone, when it started vibrating again. I let out a surprised squeal and looked at the name blipping on the screen.

My mood plummeted. *Constantine.*

There went the possibility of crawling back next to Alex and having me some early-day sex. Unless I ignored the phone. If it was urgent, he'd text me when he saw he couldn't reach me. I pressed the little red button and sent him a ready-made excuse message. *Can't talk. Text in case of emergency.* Then I turned and smiled at Alex, who was sitting up and looking at me intently. "Nobody important." A glance at the unanswered-calls list showed it had been him earlier too, but I had no voicemail alert.

Alex's features hardened, his deduction as to the caller's identity so obvious, I might as well have heard it click into place.

I put my phone back and did my best seductive prowl up the bed, but he seemed preoccupied. When I straddled him and lowered my face to his, he said, "I've been thinking..."

Shit. Nothing good ever followed that line. Sitting back on his thighs, I looked at him with a pout. "If this is about Constantine, I told you—"

"Nothing to do with him." Yeah, right. That was why he spat out *him* like the word was drenched in lemon juice. "We've been going about this all wrong."

"Huh? Like how?" I scowled hard enough to almost put my eyebrows in my line of sight. How could we have been doing the sex wrong?

"We've been looking for clues, when we don't have a theory." So it really had nothing to do with Constantine. "We have to take this from the start."

Did I mention I was straddling him naked? And he wanted to talk shop?

I slid off his body and covered myself with the sheet. "So let's." Suppressing my sulking took some effort, but being upset that he could disregard my blatant pass at him was stupid when he wanted to discuss something about the case.

"First off, you were turned—we assume by accident—and left for dead. A vampire who *happened* to be your fan *happened* to come by and spot you. Right so far?"

"Right." Where was he going with it? We knew Willoughby and Ted had been working together.

"Okay, so the question is *why*? Turning you, dumping you, and supposedly discovering you was too big a mess. Why would they do that? What did they hope to accomplish?" He might have been directing the questions to himself, his voice was so low.

"A law against turning people was established?"

Alex arched an eyebrow, his look saying what his mouth wouldn't dare to—I was an idiot to believe that. "I doubt that was what they were after, since they're still turning people."

I crossed my arms, trapping the sheet against my breasts. I wished the cloth could protect more than my nonexistent modesty and warm more than my skin. The ice-cold fingers gripping my still heart showed no intention of melting, however. That I was warm and safe mere moments ago compounded my sense of dread. Things were so fucking volatile. "We don't know that," I said in a small voice.

Whether he sensed my need for reassurance or because he too needed the contact, he placed his palm between my shoulder blades. I leaned into his touch. "You're right. We don't know that. Yet that's not all they managed, is it?"

I curled in on myself and hugged my legs. Laying my cheek on my knee, I focused on enjoying his caress. "No, it's not. The old council was overthrown, and a new one replaced it." They were the ones to benefit the most from my turning. Nobody controlled or even questioned them.

"If your turning was indeed prearranged, they had to be involved. They were supposed to get Willoughby executed and didn't. The same people you went to for help." His tone held no accusation, yet guilt was added to the cluster of negative feelings that made a home in my belly. Alex had warned me not to trust them, but I'd insisted they were the good guys. Now they knew we were on to something.

They probably knew about Alex too, which put him in even greater danger. It was one thing for a single rogue vampire to be after us, and another altogether for the enemy to be the council itself.

"The council wouldn't need to outlaw turnings if they planned on continuing them. They could have found another way to go about overturning their predecessors. This must all be a coincidence." Unless they had another agenda.

He tugged at a strand of my hair. "You said yourself we don't know they're turning the girls. If they are, maybe not all council members are in on it. *Probably* not all of them are in on it, or they'd have killed you when you went to meet them. Still, even one of them is enough of a threat."

They knew where to find us. The lack of a new attack might have been meant to lull us into a false sense of safety.

"There's something else your theory doesn't explain," I said. "Assuming they're taking the girls, why are they doing it?" And what could we do?

"We'll look into that. First we have to find a safe place. Maybe my apartment."

I scrunched my nose. "Which floor is it on?"

"What does that matter?"

"If it's not an underground one, you obviously wanna see me go up in flames."

A vibration made me jump. This time there was no procrastination. I elbowed Alex in the ribs trying to answer it. The call would act as a distraction from the scariness, regardless of who was on the other end of the line.

Only, when the music kicked in, I realized it wasn't my phone. My ringtone wasn't "Paparazzi."

With a fleeting thought at how our provider rocked for allowing for reception in the basement, I looked at the tiny slip of a cell phone inching its way toward the edge of the coffee table we used as a nightstand. The screen flashed an innocent white light.

Alex stared at it too, but he stopped me when I climbed over him to get it. "What if it's him?" He wasn't worried. He was asking if I had a plan.

I knew what course of action would appeal the most to me. "I tell him to give me Dotty, unharmed, or I dust him?" I asked with fake cheer.

Alex reached out and picked it up. After one glance at the display, he shook his head. "Out-of-area." We were both whispering.

"Let it go to voicemail."

We remained silent until the cell stopped ringing. We could have waited for an alerting text, but Alex was no more patient than I was. He narrowed his eyes and pressed 1. The phone looked fragile in his massive palm. When his index pushed down on it, I was sure he'd break it. He didn't, and he managed to turn the speaker on too. I silently prayed Sheena didn't have a PIN for accessing her messages.

Alex pressed 1 once more, drew me so I lay on his chest, and held the phone between our ears.

"*I want a blonde tomorrow night. The swimsuit model, if she really is no older than twenty-three. Tell her to meet me in the VIP section of the Dark Sun at eleven. Ask for Mr. Erebus's booth. If she doesn't show, I'll come for you.*" The voice was flat. Emotionless. Willoughby's.

I shivered, and Alex tightened his grip on me. He waited for a heartbeat, then tossed the phone back on the table, and cradled me. "We'll get him." He kissed my forehead. "We'll get him, and he'll pay."

"How?" The human justice system wasn't capable of containing or handling a vampire, and more innocent blood would be shed when he escaped.

"Same way his friend did."

I was happy I couldn't see his eyes. Judging by his tone, the darkness in his expression would scare me more than the notion of one or more council members being after us.

"So we're going to the Dark Sun tomorrow?" I brushed my lips along his collarbone.

He nodded.

"And until then?"

"We're staying here."

I looked up at him, shocked. "What about finding a safe place?"

"Even if the leak's fixed, my apartment is on the seventh floor and facing east. Windows with gauzelike curtains all around. Yours?"

"We don't need an invitation to enter another vamp's place. Dead people have no threshold to keep the supernatural away." I averted my face when he tried to capture my lips. "We don't have to hide together. You could stay at your place, and I'll stay at mine." Not my idea of fun, but I didn't want to risk Alex's life more than I already had. He was strong and trained to fight, but he was still human.

He cupped my chin and turned me to him, our faces so close I went cross-eyed trying to look at him.

"We hide together, we fight together, and—if we have to—we run together," he said. "Only Willoughby can get in here without an invitation. If he does, we can take him."

He sounded so certain, I allowed myself to relax and get lost inside the cocoon his words and presence built around us.

The semblance of safety and comfort only lasted until he said, "I think we should look through the folder Barbara gave us."

With a groan, I let him get up and bring the blasted thing over so we could flip through the pages. There were ten more entries that only held pictures and numbers. Ten more young women who'd been selected for vampire snacks—or worse. And those were only the ones Sheena's Models had lined up for Willoughby. Nothing assured us my former agent was his only supplier.

"This blonde has the proportions of a swimsuit model." I pointed at a young woman's picture. Her measurements were jotted hastily next to the photo.

"I didn't know models came in different categories."

So he thought I was in the same league as Gisele? Could he be more awesome? I felt bad for having to correct him. "They do. Runway models as a rule are really tall but less curvy. Swimsuit models are curvier and often more athletic." And catalog models, like once-upon-a-time me, can be shorter than runway and more girl-next-doorish.

None of the girls in the pics were among the missing ones, and Sheena had said there weren't supposed to be more, so who were they? *Alternatives*? Had she been presenting Willoughby with a buffet? I couldn't think of what to do about it. We couldn't start calling them and warning them off a potential supernatural kidnapper or killer.

"Maybe you should take this to your guys?" I said. "They can do more to protect them than we can."

"My guys are the ones who told us about Sheena's Models. Roebuck has probably gone by the agency by now and has a copy of this in his hands. I was hoping there'd only be a couple more possible victims so you and I could follow them." That last sentence was uttered under his breath, like he was talking to himself. He closed the folder and dropped it to the floor by the bed.

"So Roebuck knows we've been by asking questions too."

"Yup." The single word sounded like a whip cracking.

"Uh-oh?"

"Uh-oh."

How long would it take Barbie to tell *them* Sheena had called in? How soon would they trace that call to Sheena's house? I hoped Sheena had the good sense to follow my advice and leave town. If not, she'd have some explaining to do. The kind that results in people being locked up in loony bins.

It was the least appropriate time for sex. Someone I cared about was missing, people I trusted had betrayed me, and Alex and I were in grave danger.

But I needed something to keep my body and mind occupied, and I needed that to be Alex. Whatever came next, even if we were both going to die soon, I needed to feel him inside me again. I needed to cling to what we had, before someone took it away or I had to give it up.

Nuzzling his wide sternum, I slyly tugged at the sheet between us with my toes. Even if we did nothing, I wanted to be touching all of him.

He untangled my hair with his fingers, brushing it to one side in the process. "Cherry, that's not a good idea right now," he said, caressing my back.

"Dunno what you're talking about," I muttered against his skin and flicked my tongue over his nipple. Lifting my hips, I pulled at the covers.

When I lowered again and started rubbing against him, he grasped my shoulders. "Stop it. This isn't what you want."

I stopped, but not because he said so. Well, actually, I *did* stop because of what he said, but not because I agreed with him. "Says who?"

"I do." He folded his arms around me and rested his chin on top of my head. "You're not doing this because you want to. You're doing it because you're scared and worried."

"Now you're telling me how I'm feeling?" I rolled off him, taking the sheet with me.

"Don't be like that." He turned on his side and reached for me, but I shook his hand off.

"I'm not *being* like anything. This is how I *am*, which you wouldn't know since you've known me for all of five seconds." I was being unreasonable, but I *was* scared and worried, and I'd been alone for too long to feel comfortable admitting it to another person. Sharing my fears didn't come naturally. I needed action. I wanted sex to keep my mind off all the badness.

"Okay then." He grabbed my forearm and drew me to him, rolling onto his back at the same time. "Hop on." There was no hint of lust in his words.

"Wha—huh?"

He patted his thigh. "Changed my mind. We're doing it after all." Taking advantage of my surprise, he coiled an arm around me and lifted me onto his lap.

"Ah, now you're doing me a favor?" I batted at his arm. "*Lemme go.*" I could have been free in a blink of an eye and across the room in one more, but that would have defeated the purpose of my winning the argument.

He raised his eyebrows, giving me the distinct notion he was mocking me. "Isn't that what you want?"

"Not like this." I'd been upset when he'd declined sex, but my mood now galloped toward *livid*. What was wrong with him?

He didn't let go, stroking my breast with his free hand. "How, then? Do you wanna maybe give me instructions? Write them down, so I don't forget? Since I've known you for all of five seconds."

Narrowing my eyes, I wagged my index finger in front of his face. "Maybe I should. Maybe then you'd get it *right* for a change." It was a stupid, petty, *mean* thing to say, and a lie to boot. When it came to sex, Alex was nothing but toe-curlingly praiseworthy.

I expected him to start yelling right about then. Maybe call me names.

He didn't.

He snatched my finger, which had been left to hover in front of his nose, and bit it.

It didn't hurt, but it shocked me into stillness. I don't know how stupid the astonishment on my face looked, but it had to be very, because Alex laughed.

"God. You'd say anything to pick a fight, wouldn't you?"

Hiding my relief that he didn't take my words seriously, I retrieved my finger and tucked my hand under my armpit. "I wasn't trying to pick anything. You just pissed me off." I halfheartedly tried to slide off him, but gave up when he stroked my hip with his thumb.

"Yes, you were. You're freaking out and wanted to get me to either fuck you or fight with you." He saw right through me. He was all kinds of wonderful, and I was an idiot for being such a bitch.

In lieu of an apology, I muttered, "I'm a little stressed. I didn't mean what I said."

"I know." He gave a smug smile. "I knew from the start."

Men. "Well, then, why didn't you play along and let me have my fight?"

"I promise to do so in the future, once in a while. Sometimes I may even put out."

"*Hey.*" I slapped his chest, but there was no feeling in it. With what he'd said, I no longer needed sex or an argument to forget my fears. He'd mentioned a future and had done so in such a natural way that while I was in his arms, I could imagine us having one together. My bubble was firmly back in place. "Could you put out now because I want you to, because you're very, very hot?" I asked.

He shook his head. "Are you still hoping to take advantage of me? Wouldn't you rather just talk?"

I grabbed my pillow and smacked him in the face. My victory was short lived. He dug his fingers into my ribs and tickled me mercilessly. Attempting to flee his attack without using the unfair advantage my vampiric powers afforded me, I didn't notice him pull his pillow from behind his head until it hit me sideways.

"Oh, now you've done it." I twisted my body so I faced away from him and began tickling him on the soles of his feet and behind his knees, keeping him in place with my thighs. That got me a slap on the butt.

I turned to glare at him, when I made out another sound among his chuckles. "Was that your stomach rumbling?"

He shrugged. "It's long past breakfast time."

"Long past lunchtime too." I pushed at his outstretched form. "Go get something to eat. I don't want you going all scrawny on me." Not that I could fathom the possibility.

He sat up and gave me a quick kiss before getting out of bed. "What about you?"

"It's still sunny outside. I'll be here, waiting for you. In the *nude.*" Like I'd give up on early afternoon frolicking so easy.

"Aren't you hungry?"

I was but didn't want to drink from Alex all the time. I'd stick with packaged meals as my regular diet and only feed from him on occasion. "We'll go by my place before the Dark Sun, so I can change. I'll have a microwave dinner then."

"You can drink from me. Always. I mean, unless you don't want to. Don't know if it's a same-meal-different-day thing for you." He said it in a low, unsure voice, and it once again dawned on me that I wasn't the only one with insecurities.

"Blood isn't just sustenance," I said. "It's an experience. Some see it differently, but for most it's sexual to a degree." I tried to find the perfect simile, failed, and settled for a close second. "I remember thinking chocolate soufflé was heaven when I was human. For me taking someone's blood is like eating chocolate soufflé off his naked body, only better. It fills my stomach, but it also turns me on and rejuvenates me. I could never get bored with licking chocolate soufflé off *your* naked body."

I paused to make sure he was with me. "I want to take only from you, but it may hurt you. *I* may hurt you. If this is a regular thing, it may weaken you, or you may become addicted to the endorphins released in your body when I bite you." I was talking as if we could go on the way we were, but I didn't feel like I was deceiving him. Was it possible I was deceiving myself, by thinking I'd walk away after we found Dotty? Not what I ought to be thinking. "Do you get what I'm saying?"

Alex nodded again, yet I saw the *but* forming in his eyes before it reached his lips. "But you don't take more than a pint at a time. That much is replenished within twenty-four hours. And if I was to get hooked on your bite, wouldn't it have happened already? Wouldn't we have seen it?"

The handbook had a section about addiction. It said addicted humans could go through depression or even experience physical pain if they weren't bitten regularly. It also said the craving would show after the first bite. "I guess."

His expression was serious. "There won't be any microwaving tonight."

****

With the door closed behind Alex, I picked up my cell. It wasn't like I was hiding something. I'd just rather escape the awkwardness of talking to my ex in front of my current lover.

Two clicks later, I was dialing Constantine.

It rang for a long time, before he finally answered. "Now, *I* don't want to talk to *you*." His words were drawn out, like he was half-asleep. His drowsy voice had the same effect on me as Alex's drowsy voice. Maybe I had some condition that caused overhorniness?

"Very mature, Constantine. I couldn't talk earlier. Was it something important? Did the council—"

"You may find this hard to believe, but I really don't want to talk to you right now. I'm in the middle of more pleasurable things." A throaty laugh from the background— correction, a laugh that sounded like the woman laughing had something *in her throat*—accompanied his words.

I didn't have time to be indignant before he hung up.

Ádísa. He was in bed with Ádísa again. Or was it still? Had the two of them jumped into bed straight after our meeting and stayed there until I called? I wouldn't, couldn't, shouldn't care. He was safe and obviously pleasured, if not happy. Good for him. I glared at my phone like it to blame that a certain horny bastard hadn't changed. *So much for him not letting go,* something whispered in my head. I gritted my teeth against acknowledging the thought and the stinging it brought to my eyes.

I was still nude, but my naughty mood was replaced by a murderous one. I wished that she-devil was the council member involved in the whole mess, and that I got to dust her. It'd be a challenge, with her age and warrior past in the way, but I'd figure it out.

"A little help here?" Alex's voice snapped me out of a particularly satisfying daydream that involved Ádísa begging me for mercy.

I ran up the stairs and opened the door for him, careful to stay behind it and away from the sunlight.

He inched in and didn't miss a step on his way down, despite juggling a heavily laden tray. The tray held a bowl of what appeared to be a mountain of cheese and exuded a mouthwatering scent, together with two plates, cutlery, and a pepper mill. A very slim vase with a paper rose in it was wedged snugly between the plates, to be kept from toppling over.

"Pasta and a flower for my lady." He grinned and set the tray in the middle of the bed with a flourish. "I would have gone for a real one, but I wasn't dressed for outside."

Denying the urge to bite his bare ass, I sat on one side of the bed. He took a seat opposite me, cautious not to shake the mattress more than necessary.

"Prepare to be amazed." He filled the plate closer to me and then placed the bowl on top of the empty one. Throwing a wink my way, he stuffed a huge bite in his mouth.

A gorgeous, naked, kindhearted man treated me like a queen, and I was about to give him up because we'd be incompatible at some point down the road. Was that rational?

"Eat. It'll get cold." He spoke with a full mouth, using his fork to jab the air above my plate.

I did as he ordered, but not before I overindulged myself with the pepper mill. I brought a forkful to my mouth under his watchful eye and couldn't hold back a moan of approval.

If his omelet the other day had been good, his pasta was excellent. He'd chopped carrot, zucchini, and onion finely, and as he explained while I chewed, mixed that and an egg with the pasta while the latter had been steaming hot, which effectively cooked the egg and left the veggies crispy enough to make the end result yummy. The whole thing was then buried under an insane amount of cheese and sprinkled with a bit of parsley.

I was halfway through my serving when I realized he hadn't even touched his food after the first bite. "What?" I tried not to display the contents of my mouth.

"I know we said we'd talk about us after things settled, but I called my mother when I was upstairs, to ask where she had the onions—"

He'd talked to his mother? It had to have been while I was talking to Constantine, for me not to have heard him. *Was trying* to talk to Constantine, that is.

"Cherry, baby, you're great, but you need to stop zoning out." He was looking at me with good-humored exasperation.

The rest of my bite went down unchewed. "I'm sorry. I'm sorry. You were saying?" His calling me *baby* hadn't gone unnoticed. There was a peculiar warmth in my stomach.

"Eh, the moment's gone now." He gave me a dismissive wave and focused on his plate.

I was such an ass for not paying attention to the wonderful, beautiful, sexy, intellig—God, I needed to work on my focusing. "No, tell me. *Please.*" Whatever it was he wanted to say would be huge. It would play a major role in something. All my instincts screamed I needed to know.

"It's nothing." He picked a piece of pasta with two fingers and popped it in his mouth. "My mother asked why I was home in the middle of the day, and I told her I took this week off, to spend it with my girlfriend. It was supposed to be a white lie, get her off my case, but I liked the sound of it."

His girlfriend. He thought of me as his girlfriend. I hadn't been something so innocent to anyone in a long while. It was surreal that I could feel happy amid all the danger, and that in turn horrified me. There was so much more than my unlife at stake.

I knew Alex had told me so he'd see my reaction, but I couldn't give him what he wanted just yet. When we'd finally be done with the case, I'd have to decide whether we could be together or I should go ahead with my original plan. He didn't know about that, though, and I wanted to keep it that way.

I began to smile, stopped, and ran my tongue over my teeth to make sure no sneaky piece of parsley was stuck on any of them. *Nope.* I beamed at him. "Did you tell your mother you're not putting out?"

****

I'm a natural blonde. Well, used to be a natural blonde. Now I'm a very *un*natural redhead, a shade so striking, it stays in the mind of the casual observer—also known as any guy I choose not to leave a place with, when I go out for a snack. That's why, on occasion, I do my nightly prowl in a wig.

In that apartment, my wig collection was in the right-hand side of my closet, and it was extensive and fabulous.

I was in a skintight silver minidress and had set aside the killer Jimmy Choos, for which I'd used my vamp gaze on a bank manager just the previous month. The dress made it a bit hard for me to kneel, as did the nice and pointy piece of wood I'd taped to my inner thigh. I managed nonetheless, and was now carefully going over the blonde wigs, trying to choose the perfect one without getting the rest of them tangled up.

"What about this one?" I held out a honey-blonde one with as natural a curl as it comes when wigs are concerned, and looked over my shoulder at Alex.

"What was that?" He lay on my bed propped up on his elbows, wearing the shirt he'd had on the night we met. His hair was tousled to perfection, and his gaze was trained several inches lower than what I was showing him.

I realized the dress was not covering even a little bit of my rear, so I pulled on its hem with my free hand. My efforts at modesty were in vain, but at least Alex looked up. "The hair. Do you think it'll work?" I said. It would, in principle. The club would be crowded and the music too loud for Willoughby to realize the blonde waiting for him wouldn't have a heartbeat.

"It's a bit too conservative for what we're going for." He crossed his legs and returned his gaze to where it had been before I demanded his attention.

I scrunched my nose. "You're right." Looking for something more bleached provided three alternatives. Highlighted, short, and feathery was rejected. Longer hair would hide more of me. The second was shoulder length and light yellow, but one look at Alex shaking his head made me discard it. The last one constituted a *eureka* moment. A near-white hue, it was silky smooth, completely straight, and came down to my waist.

I tried it on and studied my reflection. Yes, I have one. We all do, and thank God for that, or applying makeup would be mission impossible. The whole thing with vampires casting no reflection only held true when mirrors had a real silver coating at the back. I don't know why we can't see ourselves in silver; it's not like we're silver intolerant, like werewolves are. What I do know is that it's a good thing I was turned after that era, because my vanity didn't fade with death, and I don't think checking myself out on other surfaces would have comforted me—not like I could walk around with a window pane or a lake in my purse.

I grunted at what the mirror currently showed me. "I'm like a ghost in this." I looked at Alex, who shrugged.

He was looking at my butt again. I found it endearingly annoying. What was more annoying was that my self-made broomstick-turned-stake dug into my flesh, the way I squatted.

The lighter the shade of blonde, the fewer people it looks good on. Some complexions, mine included, are too pale to pull it off without the end result looking like someone threw them in the washing machine, and others are too dark for the hair to look anything but alien contrasted to them. It was extremely thoughtless of the powers that be to give me the combination of hair and skin they did. Couldn't they have read a copy of *Cosmo,* prior to blending features together?

Still, there was a way for cosmetics to fix what nature had messed up.

I applied foundation, thinking of how that golden-white blonde worked on Ádísa. Not that I'd ever seen her without makeup on. For all I knew, she looked like Scarface in a wig. *Nah.* The woman was naturally gorgeous, and it was a good thing her personality was that of a cockroach. If she were nice, I'd have to despise her more than I already did, and I wasn't up to such a Herculean feat.

Speaking of gorgeous blonds, Constantine would have called back by now if he needed to talk to me. I pulled my phone out of my cleavage and checked for missed calls—not that I wouldn't have felt them buzz. Nothing.

I added blush and proceeded with a generous amount of charcoal eye shadow, ignoring the questioning looks Alex threw my way.

I was done applying a double layer of mascara and about to finish it all up with cherry-flavored lip gloss when Alex said, "Don't. It'll smudge when you feed."

Why didn't I think of that? The upcoming confrontation with Willoughby had killed my appetite, but I still had to eat before we left. "You're a wise man, Detective Marsden." I stood on tiptoes to give him a peck on the lips on my way to the freezer. Out came a pack of frozen blood.

Down on my hand came Alex's huge palm. "You're not eating that."

I withdrew my hand and popped the package in the microwave. "You need all your strength tonight. Make that offer to me again when we get back. I promise I'll say *yes*."

He didn't press the matter more, but I knew he'd hold me to my promise.

Chapter Eleven

We were at the Dark Sun at a little after ten, to scope the place out.

The mountain of a bouncer outside the VIP section raised a meaty palm when we approached. "Reservation only, this way." Sweat glistened on his forehead and marked him as human.

"I'm Mr. Erebus's guest. Is he here yet?" I said.

The guy checked the list in his other hand and shook his head. "Says here party of two." He looked at Alex. "He's not going in."

I looked at him, smiled, and said, "Yes, he is. And you're going to make sure we get no trouble for it." I used my slow, mesmerizing voice. Alex could have flashed his badge, but we were trying to stay under the radar.

"Of course he is," the guy said with a goofy grin. He barked orders into his headset, and a busty brunette with barely more than a bikini on came to lead us to our booth, where a bottle of champagne awaited.

Willoughby's seduction style hadn't changed since we met. I parked my ass on the edge of the semicircular leather couch. Since my maker wasn't there yet and Alex was busy locating the fire exits, I took the opportunity to assess my surroundings.

For a place with such a name, I'd expected the Dark Sun to be a bit less perky. Then again, for an exclusive club, I'd expected its patrons to smell a bit less of perspiration. The stench of it was everywhere, and it was too early in the evening for the sweaty bodies undulating around us. The women wore

clingy, sexy outfits, but the majority of men looked bored. I
didn't get it. Why weren't they interested? Had to be a case of
overabundance of supply, bringing value down.

One pop song followed the other, but my mind wasn't
on the ambience. We still had time until the rendezvous, yet
Willoughby might have also arrived ahead of schedule. It'd be
in my best interest to spot him before he saw me.

"Dance with me." Alex's breath caressed my ear, his
whispered words more of an order than a request.

"No." My refusal had nothing to do with the reason we
were there. In all honesty, despite the weight loss that preceded
my turning, when it comes to dancing I feel like the chubby
teenager who didn't get a date for prom. Whenever I think of
myself doing anything more than nursing a drink and gently
swaying on the dance floor, I get a vivid mental image of the
hippo in the tutu from Disney's *Fantasia*. "Cherry doesn't do
dancing," I said, trying for a joke.

Alex wrapped his arm around my waist and lifted me
so my toes barely touched the ground. "Come on. You're too
tense. You're supposed to be a wannabe starlet, out for a good
time, not the best-dressed wallflower in the establishment."

He ground his hips against mine, urging me to follow
their motion. It should be sensual. It *would* be sensual if I
weren't as graceful and pliable as a brick wall. His words gave
me an out, though.

"I'm also supposed to be here for him," I said. "Alone.
Not dry humping you on the dance floor."

He let me find my footing and withdrew his arm but
didn't move away. "Well then, you have to play the room."

I knew what he meant, but that didn't mean I liked it. It
had been a long time since I last flirted for the sake of flirting,
and I felt rusty and old. I reclaimed my seat. "And *you* have to
keep some distance." I wanted him out of the line of fire, so to
speak.

His hesitation was evident in his eyes, and it wasn't
like I didn't share his worry. Honestly, though, if Willoughby
recognized me before he was close enough for me to press the
sharp piece of wood against his chest, there was no way Alex

would stop him from fleeing. If, on the other hand, Willoughby got close enough and chose to attack me despite the danger to himself, Alex could do nothing to help me.

Speak of the devil, and he appears. As soon as Alex took a couple of steps back, I saw someone swaggering my way.

I lowered my head so my hair hid as much of my face as possible, and looked up through my eyelashes. Yup, it was Willoughby all right. He was taller than average, but not as tall as Alex, with perfectly parted, chestnut hair and chocolate-brown eyes. He was dressed to the nines, as if he were going to the opera and not a nightclub, and had on that self-satisfied smile that once upon a time seemed classy to me but now paled in comparison to Alex's grin—and even Constantine's smirk. And why did *he* keep popping up in my head?

Willoughby took his time approaching and appraising me at the same time. I sucked in my stomach and made a show of crossing my legs, careful not to reveal my weapon, yet positioning my left thigh so I could grasp the stake easily. I didn't realize my mistake until it was too late. There was no way for him to sit right beside me unless I moved deeper into the booth, and that would give him time to recognize me. It left me with only one option.

The moment he stood in front of me, I looked up and smiled. "Hey, you."

From the corner of my eye, I saw Alex close in behind him. Stupid man. He shouldn't stand between a vampire and his escape route. Without thinking, I grabbed the stake and threw myself at Willoughby. I wrapped an arm around his neck and held the stake between us, pointing it at his heart. I hoped the crowd would see it as an overexcited hug.

"I have a pointy stick between your ribs, and I'm not afraid to use it," I whispered in his ear, certain he'd hear me despite the music. "Now, pretend you're happy to see me and walk me out of here. We have some things to talk about."

"Cherry. Always a displeasure to see you," he said. "Didn't you get my message? I have your friend. If you hurt me, she is as good as dead."

He sounded unperturbed by my threat, so I pressed the stake in a fraction of an inch, hoping it stressed my point. "I think she's dead either way. And who said anything about killing you? We just want you to answer a couple of questions." Uh-oh. *Major* uh-oh. Why did I have to go and say *we*?

He caught my slip of the tongue at the same time I did. He grabbed my waist, spun to his left, and spotted Alex, who with his alert stance stuck out like a sore thumb. "You're actually working with the *human*?" Willoughby asked.

I was grasping for a witty comeback, when Willoughby threw me on Alex, as the latter was pulling out his badge.

I bounced back, and with a fleeting look at Alex, started after my maker, who was getting away.

Willoughby could have fought me and probably won. He was older and stronger, and I gave a damn about the humans around us while he didn't. So why was he running?

Behind me, Alex yelled, "Police. Make way." I didn't turn to see how that worked out for him.

Willoughby disappeared among the humans. I couldn't fly after him, with so many eyewitnesses here. If I failed to brainwash even one of them afterward, our kind might be at risk. So I ducked and I rolled and I sidestepped, and the distance between me and Willoughby grew.

He disappeared through the fire exit, while I still waded my way through the crowd.

I was helping up a girl I'd tripped in my efforts to get to Willoughby, when Alex caught up with me.

His eyes were restless, scanning the crowd. "Are you okay?"

I wasn't sure if he was asking me or her, but I nodded.

"What the fuck is wrong with you?" The girl looked too young to be out and drinking. She tugged her top away from her chest. It was soaked. "My mom will throw a fit if she sees this. Does vodka come off silk?" Yeah, she was okay too.

Alex flashed her his badge. "I think you should go home and start washing it now."

"*Hey.* I'm over twenty-one." She rummaged in her purse, but he stopped her with a hand on her wrist.

"You're not. Don't make it worse by showing me a fake ID." When the girl turned away with a huff, Alex grabbed my arm. "Let's go. We have one more chance of finding him."

I frowned, unsure what he had in mind.

"He thinks Sheena sent us. He's probably going after her now. We can catch him at her place. If she's smart, she took your advice and skipped town, but we have to hurry in case she didn't."

I was slightly upset he thought of it before I did. I let him lead the way out the door but didn't keep my mouth shut. "You know, it was pretty stupid of you to try to block his way out."

"Seriously? You think what *I* did was stupid? You jumped on him."

"Yeah, well, I tried to surprise him."

"And how did that work out for you?"

"He was definitely surprised. And he couldn't dust me in the middle of the dance floor. He could have snapped your neck, though. You didn't have to play the hero."

"I'm pretty sure I've told you this—and numerous times—but I'm a cop. I'm supposed to go after threats to society, and that's what I did."

"Well, you didn't have to. I'd have it under control if he hadn't seen you."

"But he did. And I had to act before he hurt you or anyone else."

I couldn't blame him for that. He'd done his job and followed his protective nature. "I guess we both did what we thought best," I said. "Just please be careful next time."

"You too. No more leaping into trouble. Though you were kinda brilliant." He pulled me to him and kissed me hard, until I found my hips bucking against his.

Seconds later, when I told him we wouldn't be waiting for his car, he retracted his last statement.

Once we were airborne, a thought made it through the adrenaline fuzzing my brain—why was Willoughby shocked to see Alex with me? He'd referred to Alex as my boyfriend when he sent me that threat via Mark.

Altitude doesn't do much for carrying sound, but I thought I'd try to share that thought with Alex. Looking up at his face, however, made me decide to leave it for later. He was paler than me, and his eyes were squeezed shut. He more than *didn't like* to fly.

I was contemplating that, when the wind stole my pretty wig, which had until then been a real trouper and stuck to my head as if with superglue.

Thank goodness Sheena's house was soon within sight. I lowered us as gently as possible and pretended her red doormat held me too entranced to pay attention while Alex emptied the contents of his stomach a few feet behind me.

Chapter Twelve

I had every intention of letting Alex save face after his projectile vomiting by allowing him to kick open Sheena's front door, but he said stealth might be a better option.

I tried the doorknob. Surprisingly it turned and the door swung open. *Nice way of staying safe, Sheena.*

I was prepared for Willoughby to jump out at me, but not for was something solid landing hard at the back of my head as soon as I set foot over the threshold. *"Ow."*

I twirled to see Sheena squinting at me in the darkness, a frying pan in hand. "I thought you were him." Her tone didn't hint at a profuse apology.

"What the hell are you still doing here?" I slammed my hand on the light switch, and the hallway brightened. I heard movement behind me, and out of the corner of my eye saw Alex blocking the entrance with his body, his back to us. I resumed glaring at Sheena. "I told you I'd kill you if I saw you again."

She didn't seem half as disheveled or as drunk as she'd been the previous night. "Well, one of you's gonna do that, anyway. Better you than that creepy asshole."

I grabbed the pan from her hand and smacked her thigh with it. It was not a playful smack. If I'd gone for her head, she might have gotten her wish to die at my hand. "You shouldn't be here. He's coming for you."

"I thought you didn't care." That sounded mocking.

"She obviously does." Alex sounded pissed off. "Fuck if I know why. So why don't you tell her why you're still here, so we can figure out what to do next?"

Sheena let out an indignant sniff. "Well, I couldn't book a flight out without using my credit card, and my limo can be easily traced." Crossing her arms over her chest, she returned my glare. I noticed for the first time that she was in silk pajamas and high-heeled slippers. The woman had no intention of leaving town.

"You could have taken a bus," I said.

She looked more horrified at that prospect than at having her throat torn out by either me or Willoughby. "A bus? I wouldn't be caught dead in one of those. Nope, I'm staying put."

Uh-huh.

Alex closed his hand around my bicep as I felt the handle of the pan bend inside my fist. I let it drop. It clanged, and I winced.

"Sheena, you're in danger. Don't you get that, you idiot?" I was no longer in control of my voice. A human could hear me from the next house over—a vampire from anywhere within a five-block radius.

She planted her hands on her hips and lifted her chin. "Why do you care? I thought you wanted me dead. I don't want to run, and he won't scare me into doing what he wants any longer. I'm not going anywhere. Let him come."

I had no answer to that. I think I growled. She took a half step back, and Alex turned to face me. The extra space she'd given me wasn't a bad thing; I had some thinking to do. I'd considered killing her myself hours earlier, but the version of her that stood in front of me at that moment was the version I'd known and loved. She was the woman who didn't give up, who fought for what was hers, and I'd considered her a friend. I wanted to keep that woman safe, despite what she'd done.

Once we dealt with Willoughby and I knew the fate of the girls she'd handed to him, I'd see what I'd do with her. In the meantime, we had to forget our plan about cornering my maker at her place. I couldn't go up against him if I had to protect two humans at the same time. My priority became taking Sheena to safety.

Where might that safety be, though?

The answer made me grin so wide, I knew my fangs showed. "Alex, grab her."

Before Sheena could protest or even blink, Alex had her in a hold she couldn't escape. And before *he* realized what was happening, I had my arms around them both and was rushing us out the door.

"Cherry, what the hell are you doing?" Alex asked through gritted teeth.

I gave him a quick smile and kicked at the ground. "I'm taking us up, up, and away."

Chapter Thirteen

According to some vampire lore, turning into a vampire means losing one's soul. That's not the case in reality. We keep our souls and remain the same people we were prior to our turning. What changes is our perception of limits.

You see, humans know their time is finite, and no matter their belief system, the majority go through life keeping in the back of their minds the thought that they'll one day be judged. Vampires consider ourselves immortal. To us, judgment day is so remote it loses its significance.

What's more, remorse goes away with time. If we're not careful, our consciences loosen after the first few centuries, allowing for ever-increasing transgressions. Eventually we act like the soulless monsters we're believed to be, not because we are inherently evil, but because we reach a point where we have no fear of consequences.

Or that's what Constantine told me in one of our first meetings.

I definitely felt pretty evil *and* soulless as I rang his doorbell.

Knowing Constantine's eclectic tastes and need for quiet, I was confident Sheena would get on his nerves in no time, with her flashiness and her incessant chattering when she got excited—and she'd be excited all right. She'd be spending a few days with a drop-dead gorgeous vampire who meant her no harm.

I could cackle.

Alex had taken his second flight a bit better than the first one. No physical reaction this time, but his eyes were glazed over as he stood on Sheena's other side and waited for the door to open.

I reached around her and squeezed his hand. "How are you doing?"

"I'm fine. I may barf on your ex, but that'll make up for the rest of my night." His thin smile took away from his joke.

As soon as we'd landed, I'd explained to him and Sheena that nobody would think to look for her at Constantine's, since he was sleeping with one of the council members. Sadly neither of them was convinced of my ex's loyalty to me. I knew he hadn't been, wasn't, nor would ever be loyal as a boyfriend, but I was also one hundred percent certain he wouldn't betray me when it came to something so important. He'd been there for me from the beginning. Taught me. Supported me. Even after we broke up, he wouldn't stop checking in, making sure I was doing okay—when he wasn't trying to get me to give him another chance.

Most of all, though, he'd been the one who'd held me day after day while I wept over losing everything and everyone I'd loved. He'd helped me keep my humanity and not give in to the temptation of the easy way. For that alone, I trusted him.

The door was finally answered, and Wesley appeared, his attire crisply ironed, in direct contrast to his wrinkled face. He gave us a little bow. "Ladies. Sir. May I help you?"

"*Hi.*" I expected him to wince at the informality of my greeting, since he hadn't at what Sheena and I wore, but he only quirked his lips upward, so I went on. "Is Constantine around?"

"I'm afraid not, Ms. Stem." At least this time he remembered me. "If you wish, I can relay a message, however."

There went my evil plan down the drain. I couldn't tell him what I wanted. Constantine would be warned and have enough time to find an excuse not to take Sheena in by the time I finally got in touch with him.

Alex jumped in. "This is Ms. Herring, who's wanted by some *very* bad people." He pushed Sheena a forward. She batted her eyelashes, and I had to try hard not to giggle.

"Yes. Very bad," I said. "We were hoping Constantine could take her in for a few days, until we take care of them?" It was my turn to bat my eyelashes.

Wesley chuckled. "You can tone down the charm, both of you." I could tell my companions were as shocked as I was by his temporary slip in decorum. If he winked, I might faint. His face straightened again. "I will make sure Ms. Herring is made comfortable with us while you go about your business." He took Sheena's hand and ushered her inside. "Come in, dear. Aren't you freezing in those clothes?"

It hadn't occurred to me to feel bad for making her fly in nothing but her pj's. Hey, I owed her for the frying-pan-to-the-head bit.

"We'll find you something warmer to wear," Wesley said to her before turning to me. "I will tell Master Constantine to contact you when he returns. And if those very bad men you mentioned are of your"—he glanced from me to Alex and back again—"*special circumstances*, rest assured they cannot enter this property without my permission. The deeds to the house are in my name."

I muttered my thanks, and the door slid shut.

Alex wouldn't hear of flying again, so we used my cell to call a cab that drove us back to the Dark Sun. By the time we picked up his car, Alex's color was back, as was his usual good mood, so we stopped at a twenty-four hour place and he really did buy the eggs to make me the promised dessert.

When we parked in front of his mother's house, I had on a face-splitting grin, which only got wider when my phone buzzed and I saw the caller was Constantine.

"I know she's annoying, but you have to keep her safe for a while. Just for a few days," I said in lieu of a greeting.

"Hello to you too, Cherry. How was your night?"

If he cared, he could have asked me that when I called him earlier, but he didn't, did he? He'd been too busy with What's-her-Name. "Went from fine to crappy to fine again, thank you. Did you hear back from the council?"

He let out a tortured sigh. "Not exactly. Can we meet?"

"What? Now you have time for me?" Oh shut up. I resent the implication that I'm petty.

"I always have time for you, Cherry. Some things are simply beyond my control."

Right. Like whom he fucked and how he talked to me when he was with her.

"I'm deeply sorry if I offended you." His words were belied by his irate tone. He hated apologizing, but I wouldn't listen to anything else he had to say unless he did so. "Please believe that I had my reasons. I called you as soon as I became available."

"I bet you did. What's up?" My legs were crossed in a very unladylike manner, with my right ankle resting atop my left knee, and I was tapping my foot against the dashboard. Alex clasped a hand over its top and held it immobile.

"Now see who's impatient," Constantine said. "I called you first, if you recall. You didn't pick up. I haven't been home in forty-eight hours because of you, and when I finally get here, I find an insufferable woman waiting for me. She's been my guest for a little over an hour, and she's already emptied half my liquor cabinet, Cherry. You owe me, and you'll repay me by waiting. Tonight I'll come to where your human lives. After sunset all right with you?"

I glanced at Alex, who wasn't looking at me but made no move to get out of the car, either. "You're not showing up here."

Constantine was unperturbed. "Will you tell me where he lives, or will I have to find out by myself?"

Even if I ended up going with the leaving-Alex-for-his-own-good scenario, I didn't want Constantine to know more about him than he absolutely needed to. "Will you shut up and listen to me? I'll meet you if I have to, but somewhere else. I can come by your place." I doubted Alex would appreciate the alternative I offered my ex, but the first option was worse.

"I guess that means I'll have to follow my nose," Constantine said. "This will probably make me testy when I meet him, so you two lovebirds better keep displays of affection to a minimum."

He hung up before I could protest.

I doubted he could really find us; his sense of smell was enhanced, but he couldn't go roaming the city, nose in the air. He could always ask Rowland where he dropped me off after the council meeting, however, and I didn't want to have to test that *testy* thing, no pun intended. If Constantine and Alex had to meet, I wanted things to go down as smoothly as possible.

Beside me, Alex said, "I'm guessing he didn't shut up and listen, huh?"

Texting Constantine with the address and making it explicit I thought he was a giant ass, I said, "He didn't. He'll be by at sunset." Phone stuffed in cleavage once more, I opened the passenger door.

I was out of the car when I noticed Alex hadn't moved from his seat. I walked to the driver's side and threw his door open. "Come on, there's plenty of time until then. Let's make it count." None of the badness could touch us for a little while longer, and I needed to be lost in him once again. Needed to feel his touch, to connect with him one more time before whatever tomorrow might bring.

"He'll be by? Here? How does he know where *here* is?"

There was no use in lying. "I let him know where we're staying." Before the red flush creeping up Alex's face had time to translate into yelling, I added, "Not that it was necessary. He smelled you on me last time we met. If he's half as possessive as he used to be, he's followed your scent here."

"Possessive? Are you his?" His face betrayed nothing. If it weren't for his heartbeat rising, I'd think he was making idle chitchat.

I should have been honest and owned up to how I felt about Alex. I should have told him there was no reason for him to be jealous of my past. I didn't. It was bad enough that I knew. Saying it aloud would make my choice even harder. Instead I threw back my head and laughed.

It wasn't nice of me.

I can totally admit that I loved every minute of his jealousy, just as I loved every minute of Constantine's advances. I was convinced Constantine's interest in me had nothing to do with feelings. He cared about me but wasn't in love with me. He only wanted me because he wasn't used to losing. That didn't make the passion of his pursuit any less flattering, however. It was simple mathematics—one Cherry plus two gorgeous men equaled one giggly Cherry with a heavily petted ego.

Alex didn't see the situation in the same positive light. He grabbed what little fabric was covering my breasts, pulled me down, and crushed his lips to mine for a kiss much more possessive than Constantine's attitude could have ever been.

I didn't stop laughing until his hand found its way between my legs and got rid first of the stake and then of my panties.

By the time our lips parted, I'd made my choice. Not about whom I wanted to be with; there had been no doubt there. I'd decided what I was willing to sacrifice for Alex. Now it was all up to fate.

Chapter Fourteen

The front seat was cramped, but I am nothing if not flexible, so I did my best to pass one of my legs over Alex's thighs until I could make myself comfortable in his lap. Ignoring the steering wheel digging into my back was difficult but not impossible.

My efforts had just panned out and I was more than enjoying myself, when Alex whispered, "Call him back and tell him not to come."

"Come? Who?" There was only one person I cared about coming—*me*.

I sat there and watch my chances of coming fly out the window as Alex withdrew his hand from my pussy and used it to push at my shoulder so he could look into my eyes. "Call Constantine"—he pinched one nipple over my dress—"and tell him not to come here. We don't need more vampires with invitations to this place."

His voice was as close to enthralling as any human's could be, but I didn't appreciate that he used our sexual *connection* like a mind-altering tool.

I got off him as awkwardly as I'd straddled him, which was embarrassing for a vampire, and was out of the car straightening my dress in a heartbeat. "Constantine is *not* a threat," I said. "But I get it if you don't want him inside your mother's place, so I will meet him out here. Is that okay?" Not waiting for his response, I turned toward the house.

"I don't want you meeting him at all. It could be a trap." He came out after me.

"It's not." I let out an exasperated sigh and sat on the hood of his car, elbows on my knees and feet perched on his bumper. "It's Constantine. I've known him for years, and he's not going to double-cross me."

Alex stood in front of me. Every muscle of his body was tense, his wide and generous lips drawn into a thin line. Though nothing could make him unattractive, I didn't like the look of distrust on him. "You said yourself you hadn't seen him in years." The distrust in his voice was no less annoying. "His maker is in the council. For fuck's sake, Cherry, *think*."

He made some valid points. It made sense that Constantine would be in on all the badness. He had the ins with the council and had sort of kept in touch with me via the phone after our breakup, so he knew where I lived. If we went further back, it had been really convenient that I'd gotten such a stud of a mentor, with whom I'd developed a romantic relationship. Assuming he'd been involved with Ádísa the entire time and that she and Willoughby were on the same team, it could all have been a plan to keep me under his thumb or to keep tabs on me.

Except I knew in my heart that it wasn't.

Constantine had his share of flaws—hell, he had several people's shares of flaws—but he was nobody's pawn. I could see him going above and beyond if the whole scheme had been his idea, but not because someone else put him up to it. And I could definitely *not* see the whole *let's turn someone people would recognize so we can overthrow the council and install a new one* being his idea, since it didn't make him part of the new council.

Unless he was the brains of the operation, and Ádísa was his pawn ... Hmmm. That might be worth looking into.

No. I knew Constantine. He'd helped me fix a bird's broken wing so I'd stop crying. I refused to be pulled into conspiracy theories other than the one we were currently tackling. There were bad guys among the ones ruling our kind, and they were out to get me and Alex—who was still rambling, by the way—but my former lover wasn't one of them. Despite everything, for the time we were together, Constantine had loved me in his own way.

Alex's grip on my arm brought me back to the *here* and *now*. "He could be how they're keeping track of you. How Willoughby knew where you lived and where to find Dotty."

Okay, I hadn't reacted when he implied I wasn't thinking, but bringing Dotty into this was a low blow, especially when he'd insisted her kidnapping wasn't my fault.

I poked his chest with my forefinger, only not hard 'cause that would have either sent him flying toward the house or broken his rib cage. "I trust Constantine." I emphasized each syllable with one more poke. "He's lousy when it comes to fidelity, but I trust him not to hand us to Willoughby or the council. If that was what he had in mind, he could have done so when I told him I suspected there was a rogue among us. He could have killed me before I ever left his place. I'm meeting him whether you like it or not." Kicking Alex's car would be childish, so I refrained. Barely.

Alex grabbed my wrist and loomed over me. "I don't like it, but if you're meeting him anyway, he's coming inside. He may wanna grab you and fly you to the council, for all I know." *Brilliant.* Typical male. He took a predetermined thing, twisted it around in his brain a couple hundred times, returned it to its initial shape, and served it up like it had been his idea to begin with.

I filled my lungs with air I didn't need and let it whoosh out. "Sure. If you insist." No sense pointing out to him *that* had been the plan in the first place.

"I want to keep an eye on him," he said, as though I still needed convincing.

I shrugged. Whatever. If Constantine was up for a fight, Alex would be useless, but *whatever*. I was too tired to get into another argument. Mentioning Constantine's vampiric powers would make Alex think I was putting down his humanity. Male ego, when faced with any perceived threat, can lash out in all directions, and the first collateral damage is usually rational thinking.

I started to stand, but Alex planted one fist on either side of my thighs. "I wanna keep an eye on you with him."

"I told you, there's nothing going on between him and me."

"You did. But there's also nothing going on between me and you, is there?" Really? After being patient for this long, he wanted us to have the talk now? Out in the open?

I feathered my fingers over his cheek. "We said we'd figure this out later."

Instead of replying, he snaked one hand between my thighs and ran his fingers along my flimsy thong. "Do you want me?" he asked. I barely had time to raise an eyebrow in question before he pushed two fingers inside me. "Do you want me, Cherry?"

I swallowed. "You know I do, but—" We were outside his mom's house, on top of his car. Even I knew that wasn't right.

"Because I want you. All the time." He withdrew his fingers and made a show of licking them clean.

Hell, it wasn't *my* neighborhood. "Show me," I whispered, pushing my hips upward. I wanted more of him. I reached for him, but he held me down.

"Sit back."

I did and waited for his next move.

It didn't disappoint.

He grabbed my thighs and pulled me to the edge of the hood. The hem of my dress slid up and bunched around my hips, exposing more of me. I leaned back, propped on my elbows.

"I want you wanting only me," he said. "Thinking only of me." He traced his fingers along my collarbone and slipped down one strap of my dress. "I want you always trembling under my touch." The second strap caressed my shoulder on its way down, raising goose bumps. He cupped one of my breasts, his palm warm against my skin. I pressed against him, and he pinched my nipple until it was hard and aching. "Like you are now."

Alex leaned over me and took my other nipple in his mouth, in turn flicking his tongue over it and grazing it with his teeth. Alternating between warm, wet softness and sharpness kept me on the edge. I pushed against his mouth and whimpered when he stopped caressing my other breast to trail his hand lower, over my stomach, down my belly, and between my thighs, setting each spot he touched on fire.

He raised his head to look into my eyes. "And I want to be the only one touching you here." He stroked my pussy over the tiny triangle of fabric.

My arms quivered, and I tensed in anticipation of more.

"Watching you squirm." He pushed the thong aside and used two fingers to circle my clit again and again.

The pressure was right, but his fingers moved too slowly. An ache in my core screamed for more. I was wet and lightheaded, and I had to have his fingers or his cock inside my pussy before I combusted with need.

He pinched my clit, spicing my pleasure with enough pain to make me moan. I lay back, my arms no longer able to hold my weight.

"I want to be the only one tasting you." He knelt in front of me and pushed my legs up and farther apart before spreading me open with his thumbs. His tongue entered me, and I bucked my hips. He used his warm mouth to map every inch of my pussy, sucking on my clitoris, fucking me with his tongue, grazing his teeth over my inner thigh and labia. My senses were in overdrive. I could smell the night air, see the stars even when I let my eyelids drift shut, feel the tiny speckles of dust beneath my fingertips. Above everything else, though, I feel the heat in my pussy, each touch of Alex's tongue and teeth adding to the pressure inside me.

I brought my legs up and draped them over his shoulders. When he pressed the tip of a finger coated in my juices against my second entrance, I'm pretty sure I dug a stiletto heel into his upper back. I was kind of protective of my ass, but with Alex eating me out the way he was, I didn't resist the intrusion. A second finger found its way past the outer circle of muscle, adding to the burning sensation consuming my lower body. Just when I thought it was too much, he replaced his tongue with his free hand.

I gathered every ounce of strength I could and lifted my head to look down the length of my body. Alex was fucking me with both hands and watching my splayed body with reverence, the likes of which I'd never seen before.

"I want you." My lips and throat felt dry. "Only you. Make love to me." I no longer cared we could be giving the neighbors an after-hour show.

He crawled up my body and undid his belt and jeans. I tried to help, needing him inside me as soon as possible, but my hands felt lax. He entered me slowly, ignoring me when I clutched his buttocks urging him on.

I didn't want it slow, but not because I couldn't deal with the feelings I associated with it. I was just so close, I'd burst if he didn't make me come. "Please."

He wouldn't be rushed in taking his pleasure or giving me mine. His cock slid in and out of my pussy languidly. My body tingled. I mewled and panted and begged, and he still didn't change his rhythm.

The tension inside me reached a plateau. I needed *something* to let it all out. I rocked my hips faster and tried to wedge one hand between our bodies, to rub my clit. Alex stopped me, pinning my wrist to the hood of the car.

I groaned.

"I want you to bite me." He draped one of my legs over his arm so he could spread me even wider.

His cock sank deeper than before, rubbing the bundle of nerves inside me with every down stroke, and I no longer cared about right and wrong. I tangled my fingers in his hair and buried my fangs in his throat, coming the instant his blood touched my tongue. The flavors erupting on my taste buds combined with Alex's thrusts to flood my pleasure centers with pure bliss. I was rolling on a cloud of endless euphoric sensations. My body pulsed with life. I wanted Alex to keep fucking me forever while I drank him in.

I forced myself to let go after a few sips, afraid I'd rip his flesh, the way I bucked and quivered. He thrust faster and harder, until he suddenly pulled out, and I felt warm, thick liquid coat my lower belly and inner thighs.

"I want you to smell like me." He kissed me, effectively silencing any protests.

What he did was petty and childish after what we'd shared, but I didn't mind. Because I loved him, and that meant loving his pettiness and childishness too.

Yes, I loved him. Silly, given how little I knew him, but love can flash like lightning, striking you down in a split second. Tonight managed to wipe out my noble intentions of sacrificing my happiness for Alex's normalcy. If all we had left together was one day, it was still worth an eternity of memories. Up to now, I tried to convince myself leaving him was the safest bet, but my heart would be broken without him one way or another. Perhaps I should take what he gave me and be with him for as long as we could make it work, or as long as he lived.

And perhaps now was time for him to know how I felt.

I took a deep breath, filling my lungs with useless air that felt invigorating nonetheless. "I—"

"It's getting chilly out here. Want to move this inside?"

His question drowned the words I meant to say. They were too huge to be said as an afterthought and too small to be allowed to get in the way of our investigation.

Sometimes there's only one specific moment. One opening. If you lose it, you may lose everything. I knew it, still I chose not to tell Alex I loved him.

"Yeah. I'm sleepy." I yawned. "Dawn is approaching."

He rose and held one hand out to me. I took it and smiled to myself when he wrapped his long fingers around mine. My palm looked small and pale, fragile inside his darker, larger one, and for the first time, I sensed it wasn't just an illusion. Alex's power wasn't physical, but it was there, and he held a ton of it over me.

****

My eyelids had just drifted shut, when an earsplitting ringing assailed my eardrums. It tore me from the blissfully hazy space between wakefulness and slumber. My relaxed state had loosened my control over my senses—Alex's cell ringing an entire floor above us, sounded like it was inside my head and trying to get out.

I tuned it out and half rolled off his prone form, to shake his shoulder gently. "Your phone."

I was sick and tired of getting woken up by phones, by the way. Next time we turned in, I'd personally make sure all telephones in the house had the ringers switched off.

Alex's reply was a mumbled grumble.

"I can't bring it to you. It's upstairs. Sunshine-filled upstairs. Get up." My nudging, not very gentle this second time, had the desired effect of at least getting him to open his eyes. The caller was persistent; the ringing continued while Alex took his time getting to his feet and climbing the stairs.

I could pretend to have learned my lesson and say I chose the high road, but I the reason I didn't listen in on his conversation wasn't about ethics. I was simply too sleepy to pay attention. I made myself as comfortable as possible and dozed off again.

When Alex returned to the basement, I awoke long enough to hold up my arms to him, thinking I'd have to get up too. Instead he joined me in bed once more. "Roebuck warned me to stay away from his investigation," he said. "Either that or cover my tracks better. If he hears about me looking into it again, he'll sic Internal Affairs on me."

Sleep weighed heavily on me, making it hard to remain alert. The possibility of Alex being investigated by Internal Affairs, however, was too important for me to give in to my drowsiness. "Can he do that? What will he say?"

He gave me what looked like the facial-expression equivalent of a shrug. "That I'm acting outside the law. Pursuing my own interests. He doesn't need to make it stick, just have them up my ass."

I felt my brow furrow and consciously relaxed it. Vampires don't get wrinkles, but we do get tension headaches. "Doesn't he owe you?"

"Says it's for my own good. That I'm in over my head, working this alone." He turned me so my back was to him and enfolded me in his arms. The hairs on his forearm tickled my chin.

I found that oddly comforting. "Maybe you should lie low for a while, to get him off your back," I said. "I can take it from here." Not that I knew what there was for me to take. We were more or less running in circles and chasing our tails so far. Sure, we'd made some progress, but until we found out more about which council members were involved, there was nothing we could do.

"We've covered that," he said. "The answer is *no*. Now sleep. I want to catch some shuteye." He kissed the back of my head and tightened the sheets around us.

I pushed one of my feet between his shins. "Yes, sir."

I'd screwed up his sleeping pattern—turned his night into day, and vice versa. It'd be bad when the case was over and we didn't absolutely *have* to spend day and night together.

That last thought was depressing enough to keep me up the rest of the day.

Chapter Fifteen

I doubt Alex would take as long to prepare for a date as he did to receive Constantine.

He didn't shower, and his scowl when I mentioned I'd like to freshen up deterred me from doing so either, but he took his time applying gel to his hair, only to muss it up to what he considered perfection. His hair looked adorable—and exactly the same as before he painstakingly separated and positioned the curls to show he just got out of bed—but I was too busy biting back my comments about what a girl he was being to say anything about it.

The best part was when time came for him to put a shirt on, and he realized he'd have to do his hair all over again, because the neckline of the tight white T-shirt he chosen—with comfort, not muscle definition in mind, I'm sure—dared touch the top of his head.

That was when I decided the sight was too much for me. I put on a pair of skintight jeans and a sleeveless top that wasn't revealing enough for Alex to think I put extra effort into looking enticing for my ex's sake. I did put on some lipstick, though, and I used one of the makeup-removing pads I never left home without, to erase the smudges of eyeliner and eye shadow from the previous night that had formed around my eyes. *Not trying too hard* didn't mean I had to look like a clown.

Alex's deodorant suffused my nostrils. If he didn't shower so Constantine could smell me on him, the deo dulled that effect significantly, since vampires don't have intense body scent to begin with. Still, Constantine would smell Alex on me. I hoped that wasn't a bad thing.

The doorbell rang right on time. My former lover was a gentleman—when he wasn't banging a two-bit ancient whore.

I looked at Alex. I could be at the door before the spray can in his hand touched the shelf above the sink, but the Alpha dog in him would no doubt find that insulting.

He placed his palm at the small of my back. "Let's not keep our guest waiting." His smirk was scary.

I spun to face him. "Promise you won't do anything stupid."

His gray eyes looked almost black. He stared at me for a split second, before the hardness melted from the corners of his mouth and his lips parted in a boyish grin. "I promise not to do anything stupid *first*."

It would have to do.

I stepped aside for him to lead the way, and my gaze fell to the back pocket of his jeans.

There was something there I thought I'd left in the car.

The stake I made for Willoughby.

****

I missed Alex's reaction when he opened the door, because I was too busy doing a double take at the vampire on the doorstep.

It was Constantine all right, but the version of him smiling at us was one I hadn't encountered so far. His hair, loose, cascaded over his shoulders, which were bare except for the straps of his tank top, and his arms hung relaxed at his sides, thumbs in the belt loops of his faded jeans. Tan cowboy boots completed the ensemble. I didn't even know he owned a pair of those, or any kind of shoe that wasn't patent leather and polished until you could see your image in it.

He stood underneath the porch light, the halo forming around him carving his shape out of the night behind him in stark relief. I bet he was fully aware of how the luminescence added to his natural gorgeousness.

"What's with the disguise?" I asked. Focusing on how out of character he appeared was better than focusing on how hot that out-of-character-ness looked. And it looked *sizzling*.

He studied me as if I were naked, and for a moment I felt just that—naked and exposed to his shameless charm, with no defense but the human beside me.

Alex, more polite on his worst day than I was on my best behavior, held out his right hand. I knew he'd rather clench it in a fist, but he kept his tension out of both his posture and his voice. "Alex Marsden." He could afford to be polite; his saliva wasn't threatening to spill down his chin.

Constantine widened his eyes in surprise for an instant, before he shook the proffered hand. "Constantine," he said. He didn't offer his last name, and Alex didn't ask.

When neither of them broke the handshake or said something as dishonest as *nice to meet you* after a couple of very long seconds, I realized the greeting was, in fact, a macho territorial thing. Good thing neither of them was literally Alpha *Dog*, or I'd have a pissing contest to deal with. I hoped Alex wasn't trying to establish dominance by squeezing Constantine's palm, because if Constantine squeezed back, Alex's hand would soon look like raw burger. I listened. Nope. No sound of crunching bone.

I shifted my gaze from their clasped hands to Constantine's face and saw he was sizing Alex up. They were the same height, give or take a quarter of an inch, but Constantine cocked his head back and to the side, so he was looking down at Alex. One glance at Alex revealed he was appraising the competition as well. *Fun, fun, fun.*

I was about to pipe up and ask what the urgency of the meeting was all about, or just tickle their sides—anything to break the stalemate—when Constantine raised one corner of his upper lip enough to show a long white fang. "Aren't you going to invite me inside, Mr. Marsden?" He used his mesmerizing voice.

Fuck. Why didn't I see that coming? Why didn't I warn Alex not to hold his gaze?

Because to me, Constantine wasn't the enemy. What was more, since Alex wasn't my prey, I overlooked the fact that he *was* prey to Constantine.

Before I could snap Alex out of the mind hold my ex imposed on him, Alex said, "Come in, Constantine."

Which the bastard did, sneering when Alex got out of his way and motioned for me to do the same. "You will remember I made you invite me inside but believe this is the last I will mess with your free will," Constantine said. "No matter what Cherry tells you."

Way to cover his bases. Would it be my fault if I grabbed the stake from Alex's pants and went for a certain overconfident vampire's heart? I settled for glaring instead, but with the same lethal intention.

Alex nodded. When he spoke next, his voice was clear. "I believe you, but so you know, I have a stake in my pocket." My man and I were in sync.

Constantine, made himself comfortable in the armchair and stared at the front of Alex's pants.

It was the perfect opening to get back at him for being a jerk. "Stake's in the back pocket. That's all him." I felt both men's stunned stares on my back as I made my way to the kitchen. "Can't do this without a beer. Too weird. Anyone else want something?" I said over my shoulder.

Alex asked for a beer too, and Constantine said he'd like a scotch if I didn't have any blood. Scotch it would be, and I'd be naughty enough to water it, just 'cause I could.

"I'll be right back. Meantime, play nice." Not that I trusted them to do so, which was why I tried to hear everything they said while I was gone.

Unfortunately, keeping the beer from fizzing out of the glass took up enough of my concentration that I missed whatever made Constantine laugh. That he laughed was enough to worry me. Did he decapitate Alex? Was he now showering in his blood, like I bet used to be his customary dance of triumph once upon a time?

Balancing all three glasses on a tray, I pushed the kitchen door open with my foot and returned to the living room as fast as I could without becoming a blur to the human eye or spilling the drinks.

The danger of spillage was more imminent when I stopped than it while I'd been in motion; the sight that greeted me made me think the world was spinning backward. I mean, I asked the men to play nice but didn't honestly expect the level of *nice* I came upon.

Constantine was sprawled in the armchair, looking at the ceiling and shaking his head in disbelief, while Alex half-sat on the armrest of the couch and nodded vigorously. "That's what I thought she was, man. It was an honest mistake. You'd have thought the same."

Hearing me approach, my former lover raised his head in a motion that reminded me of a serpent ready to attack its prey. Did that make me a helpless little mouse? Nah—a bird. Better be a bird.

"Maybe our lessons in sophistication didn't do as much good as I'd thought." He narrowed his eyes, but not before I saw the glint of mirth in their irises.

"Your lessons in landing my mark worked like a charm, though," I said, not skipping a beat. For once I was extremely grateful I had no circulation and was spared the embarrassment of blushing from either the memory of the misunderstanding between Alex and me during our first encounter, or that of Constantine's… lessons. I placed the tray on the coffee table, handed Constantine his liquor, and passed Alex his beer. Then I took my own and sat on the couch next to my current boyfriend, my arm draped over his thigh.

"What were you wearing, that our dear Alex thought you were a working girl?" Constantine was so not dropping the subject. *Argh.*

I'd make him drop it. "How's Sheena doing? Are you two getting along?" If my grin was any wider, my face would split in half and each part would roll off my skull.

Constantine took a sip of his drink and grimaced. "To be perfectly honest, Ms. Herring is a pain. She asks questions about everything, flirts with me shamelessly, demands constant attention, and is *loud.* Other than that, she is fine and sends her regards. She is not why I'm here, however."

"She's not?"

He shook his head. "Ádísa is."

I didn't like the sound of that. Did she send him?

Alex tensed and leaned forward. Out of the corner of my eye, I saw the top of the stake jut out of his pocket. I moved my hand from Alex's leg to his shoulder, then ran it down his back, all the way to his waistband. I didn't think we had much of a chance if Alex was proven right as to Constantine's loyalties, but if it came to that, we'd go down fighting.

"What about her?" Okay, so I couldn't have possibly said *her* any more disdainfully.

"She and another of the current council members are the ones who organized your turning." I couldn't believe his calm.

I curled my fingers around the stake but not so I could free it from its denim sheath. Holding on to it was like holding on to reality itself. Hearing my suspicions confirmed shocked me more than meeting Santa or a village of Smurfs could.

"How long have you known?" I asked. *Please…*

"I found out after you and I broke up, but she'd been the one who insisted I become your mentor." He cradled his glass with both hands, staring at the amber liquid as though it held the answer to some invaluable mystery.

If he didn't look at me soon, I'd get up and slap him. "Did she insist you fuck me too? Say you *love* me?" I all but forgot about the man beside me. His warm presence became nothing more than a part of the surroundings. All I saw, felt, tasted was betrayal. First Sheena, now Constantine. How much of my life before and after my turning was a lie? The question swirled in my head, drowning out another one trying to form there.

Constantine looked to my right, and I followed his gaze to Alex's face. Alex looked grim but showed no intention of leaving my side or changing the route of the conversation. I was grateful for his understanding, and at the same time, wanted to yell at him for having no insecurities when I was teeming with them. I readjusted my grip on the stake, but Alex reached behind him and covered my hand with his.

The stake wasn't my connection to reality.

He was.

"She wanted me to make you fall for me. She hadn't planned on the opposite happening," Constantine finally said.

There was no doubt in my mind he didn't miss any of the interaction between me and Alex. Both Constantine and I knew who the better man in the room was.

"That's why she did her best to seduce me back to her." Constantine downed the rest of his scotch in one big gulp. "Once you and I were over, she promised me power to keep me with her, but when she told me what she'd done… I really did and do love you, Cherry. I'd do anything for you, including sit back and let you be happy with a human."

I waited for a comment from Alex, but none came. Too numb to hold on to my beer, I left it on the table. I didn't know how to react. My eyes burned with the sting of tears, and there was an itch in my throat that would lead to hysterical laughter if I let it out. My ex gave me his blessing and confessed his love for me in front of my current love interest. Who, by the way, took it all in stride and let us talk things out. Civilized, huh?

I couldn't let Constantine's declaration of love get to me. "When she told you what she'd done—what?" His eyes were a stormy blue, earnest and tormented, when he raised his gaze to mine, but I pressed on, keeping my tone cool. Detached. "You were with her again after the meeting with the council. And last night." My jealousy wasn't the issue; I wanted him to know I wasn't buying what he was selling.

I saw him grasping for words before he said, "I was with her because I had to be."

"Am I supposed to feel sorry for you? Poor thing. It must have been horrible, fucking her again and again." I was disgusted. How could he sit here and expect me to listen to this?

"That's not how it was."

The waver in his voice did nothing to melt the ice in mine. "Who else from the council is in on it?"

"I don't know. I only know someone is, because Ádísa told me so." He held up a hand to shush my protest. "Let me tell you things as they happened, all right? Please hear me out?" At my nod, he went on. "When she bragged to me about how she attained her position in the council by having you turned, I didn't hold back. I made my displeasure with her rather obvious, and went as far as threatening I would tell the council about her actions.

"She laughed and told me to go ahead. That it would be my word against that of two council members." He addressed Alex now, maybe seeking male camaraderie. "That would help neither me nor Cherry, so I tried honey where vinegar failed, to find out more so I could have a case against her. I approached her again, made a public apology, and finally got back into her good graces, managing to pass off our fight as a lovers' spat. I told her what had enraged me the most was her lack of confidence in me." He locked gazes with me once more. "I'm not proud for sleeping with her when you and I were together, but I swear to you, the only reason I ever touched her since was so I could bring her down."

"She bought the love-struck puppy act," I said. His charm was indisputable, and Ádísa's ego wouldn't let her doubt his adoration of her.

He nodded. "She still doesn't tell me about what she does, but she's not meticulous about hiding it, either. She believes I'm oblivious. What I've managed to find out is that Willoughby is her childe too. You're right about him turning young women, although I still don't know why. I followed him once, after he visited her, and saw him take a woman to a house on the other side of town from Ádísa's. I didn't see the woman leave while I was there, and I stayed till just before sunrise. I went back the following day, but the place was deserted. I've only seen him twice since, but he keeps disappearing on me."

Willoughby's threat to Mark came back to me. *Tell Cherry to get her boyfriend off my case.* Could he have meant Constantine? But we broke up years ago. I wanted to slap my forehead. *Years* ago? Willoughby was probably *old* old, both *olds* measured in centuries. Four years to him were like a week to me.

I squeezed Alex's hand. "Willoughby didn't mean you. He knew Constantine was after him all along. That's why he was surprised to see you at Dark Sun." The implications of what I was saying hit me full force, and I turned to Constantine. "He knows you're after him."

"It doesn't matter anymore," Constantine said. "Last night I overheard there are some fledglings and a human in Ádísa's basement."

Alex and I jumped up as one. The human had to be Dotty, and the sooner we got to the fledglings, the less the influence Ádísa and her bastard would have on them. Without the right sponsor, the girls could become remorseless killers. "Why didn't you start with this little bit of info?" I asked with a snarl, as Alex demanded instructions to the bitch's abode.

Constantine's eyes blazed at me, brilliantly blue. "If you answered your telephone, I'd have told you much sooner. And my timing doesn't matter. We cannot go there for at least one more hour. Ádísa wanted to be alone, and she's given her staff the night off. She's going out to feed at nine. I say nine thirty is our best bet for getting in and out of there with as little trouble as possible."

I didn't want *little* trouble. I wanted *big* trouble, and I wanted to be the one causing it. The rational part of me knew he was right. I was dying to know what Ádísa needed her privacy for, but the fewer vampires we had to fight, the better our chances of survival. We couldn't exactly spy on an ancient vampire and expect not to be noticed.

"We leave here at nine," I said. "I need to go by my place first." Once the girls and Dotty were free, we could go back and settle things with Ádísa once and for all. With any luck, the three of us might beat her, but I needed sturdier shoes if I was even going to *try* to kick her ass.

"We're going in tonight because he said so?" Alex indicated Constantine with the hand holding his beer. "If he gives me the address, I can go get Dotty during the day, when it's safe. Assuming she's really there." He looked at

Constantine. "No offense, man, but I trust you about as far as I can throw you."

Constantine grinned. "If I said the same, it would be a great compliment."

I scoffed. "Shut up, Constantine. We get it—you're strong. Alex, Ádísa is not defenseless during the day. Even without humans protecting her, she wouldn't have gotten this old if she were stupid." Constantine agreed, and I continued. "She'll be as lethal as always below ground level, which is where the girls are. Plus you can't drag the new vamps out in the middle of the day, and we have to save them from her clutches too."

Alex seemed unconcerned with them, which, to be honest, bummed me out. I didn't want him to consider vampires expendable. These girls were significant to him before their turning. They ought to matter now too.

He did that nibble-worthy clenched-jaw thing. "Fine. Then let's get backup. Aren't there any other vampires you can trust?" His question put him back on my nice-boys list.

Those of the council not working with Ádísa should be the obvious answer, but who was beyond suspicion? "We could try Johnny Boy." I looked to Constantine for confirmation.

He shook his head. "We don't know which of them is on her side."

"One of the council members?" Alex asked, eyes wide. "Haven't we agreed they're not the good guys you thought they were? Think outside the box, Cherry. You've been around for six years. Haven't you made any vampire friends?"

It sounded too much like an accusation for my liking. "Six years aren't an eternity, and we're not the friendly kind. Also, I don't know if you've noticed, but my taste in companions has been sort of poor."

Alex shrugged in what looked like agreement, and Constantine scratched his chin with his middle finger. If I didn't know he'd never stoop as low as that, I'd think he was flipping me the bird.

"You've been around forever," I said to my ex. "What about your friends?"

He stretched and graced me with a bored gaze. "I don't do friendships. I do politics." I ignored the sharp pain through my side. He probably didn't do relationships either. Or feelings, despite his statements earlier. Not that I cared. Whatever we had was in the past.

Alex raised both arms. "Going in with *his* friends wouldn't make me feel safer. We need people we know are on our side."

"There aren't any." There was the police, but— "None we can risk, anyway. We are all we've got. Deal with it." It came out harsher than he deserved, but there was no way for me to take it back. I needed air. It was stupid—I didn't need to breathe—but I needed air. And why were the men being so civilized? Shouldn't they be a lot growlier with each other?

"I still say we're walking into a trap." Alex didn't raise his voice, but there was a finality to his tone. He lifted his beer to his lips and gulped half of it down before setting it aside. It seemed he'd put an end to the subject.

I needed to be out of there, away from the two of them, from the responsibility knowledge brought in its wake, and from the doubt eating at my insides. Alex could be right, and if he was, I was endangering much more than myself by stubbornly choosing to believe Constantine.

But if Constantine was telling the truth…

I worried my lower lip with my teeth, aware Alex wasn't going to like what I'd say next. "I have to go. I *am* going. Can't risk Ádísa moving them." My body gravitated toward Constantine's, which I only realized when I felt him caress my inner wrist.

I pulled my hand away and rubbed the skin, as if he'd burned me. The touch had felt too familiar, too comfortable for my liking. Everything about his demeanor was far too comfortable for my liking. He'd waltzed in here like he owned the place and divulged information that turned my world upside down.

Slowly, with measured steps, I positioned myself so the three of us formed a triangle of equal sides. I needed the distance from both of them if I was to take the best course of action without letting personal feelings influence me.

Alex tried to reason with me once more. "Okay. Try to see things from where I'm standing, please. My vamp girlfriend's"—there was that word again; I smiled despite myself—"undead ex appears at my place to tell her he loves her, has always loved her, but he was planted in her life from the start by the woman who ordered her turning, in order for that woman to gain power."

I was forgetting something. What was it?

Alex was unfazed. "He's still that evil woman's lover—though she's responsible for the turning of more innocents—but he's somehow not involved in the whole mess and wants nothing but to bring the bad woman and her accomplices down. At his own risk. Only it has to happen tonight. How believable is that shit?"

Constantine didn't stop nodding during Alex's recap and jumped in before I could answer. "Not at all, and I more than understand your skepticism. I have no assurances to offer you, Alex. You may believe me, or you may choose not to. The fact is I've told you the truth." Folding his hands on his lap, he perused each of us in turn.

"And if he hasn't and I don't come back, you're going to torch his place first thing in the morning," I told Alex, without a trace of humor.

Constantine let out an indignant protest and was ignored by both of us.

Alex looked at me, one eyebrow arched.

I couldn't meet his gaze. "You're not coming with. If something happens, one of us has to be here, to do something about it all." My arguments made sense, but I knew Alex would think I was keeping him from doing his job.

To my surprise, Constantine did nothing to make the awkward moment worse. Instead he put our discarded glasses back on the tray and headed toward the kitchen without a word. He'd undoubtedly hear us from there too, but his attempt at discretion was unexpectedly gallant.

Alex remained silent until we heard the kitchen door closing. Then he said, "I'm not letting you go alone."

I opened my mouth to point out it wasn't up to him to *let* me do anything.

"It's not a case of *me man, you woman*, and it's not about jealousy. Not after last night. This is about you and me being in this together, and I'm coming whether you like it or not." He frowned and ran one hand through his hair. "Hell, I'm coming even though *I* don't like it!"

"You don't understand. Any self-respecting vampire can sniff out a human. A council member will have you drained in a second if you so much as set foot on their front porch." I might be exaggerating, but they'd at least have his memory wiped, if they felt charitable. Plus Alex wouldn't be of much use if the proverbial crap hit the metaphorical fan; I was much stronger than him. There was no way of saying so without wounding his ego, and I didn't want us to part on such terms, when I couldn't be sure I'd see him again. "We need someone to—"

"Tell the world our story?" He let out a bitter chuckle. "Cherry, if they take you down, I'm next. Not like I can ask for reinforcements. Nobody would believe me if I started blaming vampires for the disappearances. And I'd hate myself if something happened to you and I wasn't there. I know you're stronger, and so is the guy pretending not to listen in on our conversation, but I'm fast and a sharp shooter. Even if bullets don't kill vampires, they can hurt them."

"Alex—"

"You don't even know we'll only be up against vamps, anyway. Maybe she lied about sending her staff off, or Constantine did. I can help. You can take me with you or let me drive around all night, searching for a house spooky enough to belong to an ancient vampire, but I'm not sitting on my ass and letting you do the fighting without me."

He cupped my cheeks with both palms, and I let him raise my face to his. His features looked blurry through the tears fringing my eyelashes. Blinking the tears away didn't help clear my vision as he came closer until our noses touched. "Nod if we're clear on that," he said.

I nodded and smiled against his lips as they closed over mine. What did I do to deserve such a guy in my unlife?

Constantine reappeared a few minutes later, more serious than ever. "All three of us are going, then?"

"Yup," I said.

"Maybe Alex should drive there? We don't know what shape the fledglings and human will be in."

Alex nodded and jotted down the address Constantine gave him. "I'll park a couple blocks away and meet you there."

My ex turned to me. "I suggest you and I fly by your place first, since you want to change, and meet Alex outside Ádísa's."

If Alex had any objections about the detour, he wasn't vocal about them. I suspect his fear of flying had something to do with that. The three of us didn't speak again until the grandfather clock standing on the far wall of the dining room chimed nine.

****

Constantine was uncharacteristically hands-off during our short flight to my apartment.

He held on to me, but not like when we flew to meet the council. Despite our proximity, there was a sense of detachment that wasn't there before. It gave me the chance to clear my head, and I was grateful for it. Instead of breathing him in, I let the scents and sounds of the night fill my senses until there was no room for doom and gloom. By the time we landed, I was ready to take on anything.

He kept a respectful distance while I unlocked my door and entered, unnecessarily waiting for me to ask him inside before joining me in the space that served as both my bedroom and living room. I saw the covert peeks he took at my quarters. He didn't have to be so discreet with his disapproval; I knew my whole studio apartment could easily fit in his bathroom.

He was playing nice, which wasn't easy for his snarky personality, so I let him entertain himself while I looked for my tall buckskin boots. With their thick leather exterior, they were as sturdy as they were cool. I wanted them covered with Ádísa's ashes before the night was over.

I was pulling the left boot up my calf, when Constantine cleared his throat. I expected him to finally stop holding back and say something about how brilliant it was that they now made pocket-sized rooms or something, so I didn't pay much attention.

"Do you love him?" he asked. "Alex?"

I hopped around on one booted foot, to stare at him.

His eyes were the color of the winter sky before heavy snow. He didn't wait for an answer. "If you do, don't miss out on even one moment with him. We think there's always time, but there isn't. And he's human. If he won't turn… Just don't waste time, Cherry."

I crossed the room and hugged him. He certainly wasn't my favorite person at the time—didn't make it into my top ten of favorite people, and I was friendless—but it felt like the only thing to do.

Chapter Sixteen

Waiting for Alex outside the wrought-iron gates gave me all the time in the world to ponder the unfairness of her living in a manor and Constantine having a mansion, when I was stuck with a frigging underground studio. Maybe I'd get to upgrade too, in a couple of centuries. If I survived the night.

And where was that man, anyway?

I sighed with relief when Alex rounded the corner. Nothing could have gone wrong this early in the plan, yet the knot in my stomach had become tighter the longer he'd been out of sight. He reached us and gave me a smacking kiss on the lips, which left me with a silly smile and Constantine with a disapproving frown. I pretended not to notice. Nobody cared about *his* approval.

The gates were to keep humans out, I guessed. I was about to propose Alex hold on to me so I could float us over the fence, when Constantine leaned on the gates, and they opened.

"The latch hadn't caught," was his answer to my questioning look. "You really should be more observant, *Chérie*. Having night vision is a gift. Not using it is remiss of you."

"Good thing you're with us, then," Alex said. "It's so handy that you notice the little things." I'd bet my favorite pair of Louboutins that by *handy* he meant *prearranged*. Judging by Constantine's frown, the implication wasn't lost on him.

No reason to allow things to escalate between them. I weaved my fingers through Alex's and pulled him after me, inside Ádísa's garden.

The beauty that greeted us was like nothing I faced before. Flowers formed islands of color through which meandered cobbled pathways. Grape hyacinths and lavender mixed with blood irises and lilacs, making purple in all its shades the prevalent color. Batches of pink peonies and yellow freesia, hot orange gerberas and velvet red roses broke the uniformity with their vividly contrasting hues. And those were just the ones I could name.

I can't describe how vibrant colors look to us at night. They're not as they appear to humans in broad daylight. It's like the colors are three-dimensional, deeper, exposed through a special filter. The colors of the flora around us, framed in the white pebbles shaping up the pathways, composed what I imagined the Garden of Eden would look like.

And like that garden, this one hid a snake in its heart.

Already distracted by the exquisite panorama, I didn't want to add fragrances into the mix, but my nostrils flared, seeking the scents against my better judgment. The mixture of dizzying aromas affected me the way I expected it to, only about a million times more strongly.

Next thing I knew, Alex and Constantine were shaking me. I forced my eyes to focus and waved off their hands.

"What happened?" Alex was in my face, whispering urgently.

"Sensory overload," Constantine said just as quietly. "Ádísa built this garden as a defense mechanism. I'm sorry. I should have thought to mention it, but I've been here so many times, I'm used to it by now. It masks her scent when she's hunted, and vampires who haven't been here before and don't know to block the stimuli are overwhelmed."

Alex looked around. "By what? Vegetation?"

How could he call the miracle of nature around us *vegetation*? A voice in the back of my mind whispered, *He is human.* I wanted to weep for him. His short lifespan in itself meant he would miss out on so much. Now I realized how much more his mortality deprived him of. There was no reason for me to explain what he could never experience for himself, so I nodded. "Vegetation. She's charmed it."

Constantine kept quiet and helped steady me so we could move on. He squeezed my shoulder after a couple of steps, but I didn't turn his way. Whatever solace he offered was not welcome.

Alex clasped my hand and halted us once more. "But why would vampires cross the garden on foot? I get why *you* have to—human with sensitive stomach here." Wrinkles formed on his forehead, as he frowned in a self-deprecatory manner. "But you could fly if I weren't with you."

"We'd walk anyway." I hoped my smile looked reassuring. "Flying over another vampire's property is considered hostile action."

He gurgled back a chuckle. "And breaking into their home isn't?"

Constantine beamed an unexpected grin. "Vampire law. What matters to us is that, if someone inside sees us fly over, they'll be prepared for a fight and allowed to attack first. The way we're approaching now, our purpose might as well be a social visit."

Alex shook his head. "Vampire law is stupid," he murmured, "and if someone's in there, we'll be getting a fight anyway, the second we pick their lock." Still, he began moving again, squinting against the darkness.

Knowing the power of the garden helped me focus on the task at hand. Extending my hearing and keeping the rest of my senses on a tight leash, I placed one foot steadily in front of the other. No matter how careful we were, I cringed every time our shoes made contact with the ground. The pebbles rubbing against one another sounded to me like a burglar alarm, and any vampire left in the manor would be alerted to our approach.

A few feet before the main entrance, I held Alex to me and flew us over the rest of the distance and the stairs to the front door. Constantine followed our example. We managed a near-perfect landing, but Alex's feet hit the marble deck before mine did, since he was taller.

The thud his shoes made wasn't deafening, but in the stillness of the night it might as well have been a gunshot.

Afraid we'd been heard, I pushed him behind me and scanned the periphery, expecting someone to jump at us from the bushes around us. Just as I began to relax, I noticed Constantine stood stock-still, staring at something over my shoulder.

Dread filling me to the point it felt like my heart might start beating again, I turned toward Alex.

The door behind him was ajar, and Johnny Boy's face peeked through the opening, his index finger slicing his smile in half.

I took a step backward and collided with Constantine, who was trying to get to Alex. *Get to Alex.* Alex was in danger. Johnny was too close to him.

I looked at Alex. In the split second it took Constantine and me to find our footing, he'd ducked and pulled his gun on Johnny Boy.

"Alex, get away from him."

But Johnny Boy hadn't moved. The look he was giving us was amused rather than threatening. "When you two are done with the slapstick, get the human and come in. And for God's sake, keep it quiet. I heard you when you were still at the gate."

I gaped at him, while Constantine placed his body between Alex and the door. "What are you doing here?" he asked.

"Same thing you are, I suspect. Looking for condemning evidence." Johnny Boy winked at him and turned to me. "Well, are you coming in or not?"

I took Alex's hand and followed Constantine inside. Johnny closed the door after all of us.

"The rest of the council didn't seem moved by your warning about a rogue," he told me, walking ahead and motioning for us to go with him. "Me—I'm not used to ignoring beautiful women."

Alex groaned. "Oh great. Another one."

Constantine patted his back, which had me doing a double take. Those two were *comrades* now?

Johnny kept talking, as he led us deeper inside the house. "Willoughby was easy to trace, once I got hold of his turning file. I found out Ádísa was his maker and thought maybe she'd helped him evade his punishment. I tried to talk to her several times, but she avoided me, and the council wouldn't condone a formal investigation. So here I am." He turned and grinned over his shoulder. "And here *you* are."

Here we were, indeed. I looked around. The place was the baby of extravagant wealth and abysmal taste. The amazing garden outside couldn't be Ádísa's creation if this room reflected her decorative preferences. The lushness of the setting bordered on vulgarity, with her obvious efforts at a burlesque style drifting toward the grotesque.

Plush fabrics of clashing colors covered the walls, Venetian and Grecian masks pinning them in several places so they formed folds before draping to the floor. Animal heads stared at us with glassy eyes from around the oversize fireplace, and heavy chandeliers, interspersed as much with polygonal crystals as with horns, dangled over our heads, more reminiscent of guillotines than ornaments. And don't get me started on the furniture. Really. *Don't.* A woman who chose to decorate her living room this way wouldn't surprise me if she slept in a bed made of human skulls.

She'd shared that bed with Constantine. On more than one occasion.

Since I couldn't share my distaste with my ex, I aimed my grimace of disgust at Alex.

He mouthed something and tilted his head toward Johnny Boy.

Huh? I mouthed back.

He widened his eyes and mouthed the same four words again. *I don't trust him.*

Well, neither did I—not completely—but there wasn't much we could do. I shrugged, hoping to convey that exact message.

Johnny stopped in front of an open door. "I've checked everywhere else and found nothing," he said. "This leads downstairs. I was on my way there when I heard you. Once we reach the landing, we should split up. Cherry, you and I go left.

Constantine and the human can check the other side. We'll meet back here when we're done."

His plan wasn't the best, and not only because it involved my ex and current flames, alone, in a dark basement. I was about to suggest an alternate division of forces, when Constantine said, "I'm not going with the human. He's Cherry's problem."

Not knowing whether to be thankful or upset, I went with indifferent and snatched Alex's waistband. "We'll take right."

Constantine winked as I passed in front of him to climb down the stairway. "Good luck," I told him in a cheery voice.

"You too," replied Johnny Boy. It sounded flat, despite reverberating on the walls of the narrow corridor.

****

That level of the manor was almost barren in contrast to the upper one. The stone walls were naked except for lit torches every ten feet or so, and the floor was gritty underfoot. Despite the years she lived and the fortune she amassed, let alone the furniture she picked for her living room, Ádísa was still a warrior at heart and had chosen a frugal style for her chambers and private space.

I glanced at the lit torches once more. Something felt off, but I went ahead and rounded the bend in the corridor.

I ran into a cold male body, the collision hard enough to make me bounce backward. If I were to judge the living status of the man in front of me by his eyes, I'd pronounce him as dead as his temperature indicated he was.

I knew better.

I tried to scream, but he covered my mouth with one hand and grabbed Alex's neck with the other. The council member who scared me the most had a firm grip on both Alex and me. "Make a sound, and I snap him like a twig," Benjamin said. "Is that clear?"

Alex gasped for breath. He kicked at our captor to no avail. I could possibly get away with nothing but a bruised jaw, but I couldn't do much to help Alex; Benjamin stood with his arms spread, so we couldn't reach one another.

"Is that *clear*?" Benjamin asked again.

It was possible that Constantine and Johnny had heard Benjamin and were rushing to our rescue, but I couldn't afford to wait for knights with sharp canines, who might or might not show up. I nodded. Benjamin's palm was disgusting against my lips. It felt dead-dead. Touching my lips to it was like touching them to wax. Cold wax, not the kind I used to get rid of unwanted hairs when I was alive. It was odd, since he and I had to be the same temperature.

"Will you keep quiet if I let you go?" He dug his thumb into the soft tissue underneath Alex's jaw, making him tilt his head back and wince.

I nodded again, more vigorously, my gaze glued to Benjamin's dirty thumbnail.

"Good." He squeezed my face once and pulled away.

"You're the one working with Ádísa," I said as soon as he loosened his grip on Alex. My tone was as accusatory as I could manage without raising my voice.

He gave me a bewildered look. "I'm here to take her down. The bitch will get what's coming to her. She'll pay for what she did to my daughter."

"Your daughter?" My turn to be taken aback. I never imagined he'd have a family.

Though his eyes weren't as wide now that he could breathe again, Alex looked as shocked. He didn't need to know who the man in front of us was; at first glance, Benjamin seemed incapable of human contact.

"She was killed a few days before you were turned. I knew a vampire had done it, but I could do nothing about it." Benjamin's face now showed more emotion than I thought possible, becoming almost human instead of the carved-stone mask it usually resembled. "The death of a human meant nothing to the council. I wasn't supposed to keep in touch with my family after my turning, anyway. Ádísa approached me the night before Willoughby's hearing and promised me the one responsible would meet the sun if I helped her."

Things were falling into place. "That's why you were the first to attack the old council." I remembered Benjamin jumping up and hurling accusations at them, urging spectators to join him in bringing them down. "The one who killed your daughter," I whispered. "Was it…?"

He nodded. "Willoughby. He was supposed to dust for what he did to my little girl. She was twelve. I only had a year with her before I became a vampire—too little time. I couldn't give her up, so I watched over her and my wife as much as I could. Then he—" His voice cracked, and I was shocked to see a tear run down his cheek. "When you came to tell us he was still around, I confronted Ádísa. She called me an idiot for believing you. I looked into it anyway, and once I discovered Willoughby was her childe, I knew for certain you were right. A maker would never have their offspring killed."

Yeah, tell Willoughby that.

Benjamin shook his head. "She lied to me from the start. For all I know, she was the one who ordered my little girl killed, so she'd get to me. I could be the reason my Virginia died." His face crumbled, and it was as if he shrank, the wind knocked out of him.

I didn't know what to say. I was frozen in place, watching pain destroy a man I'd considered emotionless.

"We're going to bring him down. Her too. For everything." Alex sounded hoarse. Of course he did. He was suspended by the throat for the second time since we met. Hanging out with me didn't do much for his wellbeing.

Benjamin nodded again and let Alex go. "Come with me and keep your voices down. She'll hear you."

"She's here?" That was bad—so *very* bad.

Benjamin walked by me, toward the direction Alex and I came from. "Yes," he said over his shoulder. "I didn't see her leave. I meant to hide until she was gone, then break in and wait for her to come back, but I didn't have the patience. Thought she'd be underground, but all I found were some newly turned vampires. They may be the girls you're looking for."

What about Dotty? "Did you see the human woman too? Thirties, tall, with short hair?"

He shrugged. "Saw someone. She was restrained. I don't know if she's who you want. She was asleep, I believe." With that he was out of my field of vision, around the corner.

Alex and I hurried after him. I wanted to ask where she was and rush to her, but our chances of helping her and the rest of the girls would be much greater once Ádísa was out of the picture. Then another thought occurred to me, and I wanted to smack myself for not having it sooner. "We need to warn Constantine and Johnny Boy." I stopped Benjamin with my hand on his arm.

He frowned. "Johnny is here too? But he didn't believe you. Or me."

He didn't? Then why was he there?

Oh shit.

I was so stupid, letting myself be fooled by Johnny Boy's friendly act.

He'd conveniently appeared at Ádísa's the same night as us, with a story that would work if he weren't a council member. Why would he be looking for proof of her guilt by himself, when he could order someone else to do it for him?

And why didn't I think of this sooner?

He said he'd looked everywhere upstairs for the girls. If he had, he'd know Ádísa was still inside the manor. But of course, he knew that from the get-go. He'd wanted me to go with him and leave Constantine with Alex, because he wanted to take me to her. He was leading Constantine into a trap.

Unless my ex was in on it.

No. Constantine was the one to insist I stick with Alex. Whether he suspected something or not, he definitely wasn't in cahoots with Johnny. And I had to warn him before it was too late.

"Let's go." I started running toward the stairs, where we said we'd meet the other two, barely holding back for Alex to keep up.

Constantine and Johnny weren't at the bottom of the staircase, and we wouldn't find them in any of the basement rooms. Without thinking, I climbed the stairs and burst into Ádísa's living room of horrors.

****

"I suggest you don't come any closer." Johnny smiled amiably, as always. He sat on the armrest of the chair I noticed on our way in. The thing was uglier than ugly, from its winged back to its clawed feet. Ádísa stood behind it, leaning against its back and tapping her sharp nails on the upholstery. Willoughby flanked her other side, his arm folded around Constantine's chest, the stake in his hand pressing over Constantine's heart.

They made for a very evil—if totally clichéd—tableau. I sort of felt bad for Ádísa. For all she had going, she seemed desperate to prove her superiority.

Still, her guys were armed, so I froze in my tracks, as did Alex. Benjamin, however, unconcerned with my former lover's unlife, shoved me aside and lunged for Ádísa with a roar.

Johnny raised his arm. I heard the *thwack* of the cord releasing but didn't have time to warn Benjamin. An arrow shot out of the mini crossbow in Johnny's hand, sliced the air, and found Benjamin's heart.

Benjamin turned to dust mid-leap. One moment he was lifting off the ground, about to close the distance to the woman who promised him retribution for his daughter's murder but used him as a pawn, and the next he was a thin cloud of dust descending toward the inappropriately colorful carpet.

Alex's gasp reached my ears. It was the first time he saw someone dust, since he'd been knocked out when I offed the vampire at his mother's place. I wanted to make sure he was okay, but I didn't dare avert my gaze from Willoughby's hand.

"Why?" I muttered, unsure of what that *why* was about. Why did they kill Benjamin? That was kind of easy to figure out. Why were they turning the girls? Why was Johnny teaming with Ádísa? *Why...?*

Ádísa replied to the obvious question. "He was dangerous. He had to be put down." She looked between me and Alex. "You are dangerous too."

185

"We've done nothing to you," I spat out between gritted teeth. She was a council member, and we were nobodies. No reason for her to fear either of us. "You were the one who ordered me turned and had him"—I pointed to Benjamin's remains—"help you overturn the council. And you had Constantine keep an eye on me. Why?"

"I am not going to explain myself to you or to a human." She straightened up and went to Constantine.

"Why take the girls?" I asked, unfazed by her turning her back to me. "Or me? You could have turned anyone. Why set up this scheme?"

Willoughby mustn't have noticed how bad guys in movies die after presenting their elaborate plans to the white hats. "These girls are precisely the type rich, powerful men go for," he said with a grin. "Place them in the right spot at the right moment, and they can bring those men to us."

Huh? "So this was about money?" That was absurd. Ádísa had to be richer than Midas.

"No." Ádísa's tone was scornful. Apparently she wasn't above explaining herself if that meant pointing out my idiocy. "It is about power. Turn a few men at key positions, kill a few more after they sign over their companies to their latest significant others, and we rule the world."

I gaped at her. "You're planning to take over the world with an army of what? Five gorgeous, undead escorts? Ten?"

She scoffed. "You're assuming we limited ourselves to Los Angeles."

"Why didn't you turn those men to begin with? Why involve the girls?"

"The ones we're after are hard to get close to. They have people monitoring their every move. Turning doesn't happen within seconds. It's one thing for Bill Gates to disappear for a whole night after an appointment at his office, and another for him to *ask* not to be disturbed because he's spending the night with a conquest. And the girls are trained to be conquests. Men in power have to hunt their prey."

"Bill Gates is married," was what came out of my mouth. My mind couldn't process what I'd heard.

"Why did you break into my mother's house?" Alex asked from behind me.

Willoughby smirked. "We needed to know what progress you'd made with the case. I followed you there before, and she told us you'd be there alone. We were planning on wiping you, but she"—he pointed at me—"got in the way."

"Well, you shouldn't have messed with me. Why turn me?" They'd turned me and let me loose. I didn't even fit the type they were after.

Willoughby opened his mouth, but shut it again at Ádísa's glare.

"What? No more playing the James Bond villains?" I asked.

Blank looks all around. These people lacked basic pop-culture knowledge.

"You know—answering our questions so we aren't left wondering after we escape and kill you?" I acted braver than I felt, but I wasn't exactly trembling in my boots. Their displays of power made them less scary than the ideas of them I'd had in my head.

"Not as if we're risking anything. You're as good as dead." Ádísa arched two perfectly shaped eyebrows. With an order from her, Willoughby dropped his arm, and I let out a sigh of relief. Imminent danger to Constantine was averted.

Probably.

Ádísa locked her gaze to my ex's and said, "I knew I could count on you to bring her here."

The ground opened under my feet, and my stomach plummeted. Constantine betrayed me? I stared at him, certain Ádísa was playing me. She had to be lying.

Constantine was silent. Why wasn't he denying her words? He smiled at her, and I almost took a step toward him before the memory of Benjamin's perma-death stopped me. I'd have to kill the double-crossing bastard later. Because I *would* kill him, for making me trust him and letting me down.

Again.

Ádísa went on. "I knew you had a soft spot for her. I saw you watching, listening... waiting for the right moment to turn on me. I arranged for that moment to be tonight." She whispered the last part, but all nonhumans in the room must have heard her loud and clear.

A sense of peace washed over me, at odds with the situation. Constantine didn't betray me. She used his feelings for me against me, but it wasn't his fault.

I didn't get to relish my relief.

Ádísa made a show of pulling a sharpened stake out of a hip holster and dragging it along Constantine's cheek. "What is it with the women in your family, Cherry?" she asked.

It took a couple of seconds for me to grasp that she was talking to me. The women in my family? I didn't have the faintest idea what she meant.

"No matter. Your allure worked against you this time. It got you where I wanted you. It's such a pity Constantine will share your fate, but maybe I'll get to keep your new friend." She meant Alex.

I growled. "You'll leave all of us alone."

"Or else?" Her smile was too sweet and innocent to be sincere.

Constantine spoke up. "How could you think I would betray you? After all we've been through? Don't you know I love only you?"

I opened my mouth to say I was sorry, I should have known better, when it dawned on me he was talking to Ádísa. And then he did more than talk. He cupped her face, pulled her to him, and shoved his tongue down her throat.

Ádísa lowered the stake and plastered her body against his, all but dry humping him.

This was like the set of a supernatural soap opera, with the leading characters changing allegiances and lovers before every commercial break. "Now *that's* been cleared up, will you tell me why it had to be me? I mean, I know you needed someone recognizable for the whole council-overturning scheme to work, but I was a minor celebrity at best. Why not go with a big name?" I said.

Oh, for the love of God, could she just answer me and stop sucking face with my ex?

Nobody paid me any attention except for Johnny Boy, who leveled his crossbow in my general vicinity. From the corner of my eye, I noticed Alex moved so he stood half behind me. He wasn't a coward, to be using me as a shield, so I hoped he had a plan in mind.

"*Hey.* I'm talking to you, you harpy. And what do you know about my family?" I yelled the question, both in hopes the other vampires would turn their attention to me, and on the off chance I got a reply.

It worked. Ádísa pulled back from the lip-lock, clearly about to say something. Only she didn't get to.

Constantine, still cupping her face, twisted.

I heard a *crack.* Her spinal cord snapped as easily as a twig. Constantine kept twisting and pulled upward, until he tore her head from her neck with a squelching, ripping sound.

He *twisted* her head *off.*

Despite knowing better, I expected blood to spurt. There was none. In the blink of an eye, Ádísa's body formed a pile, her stake landing beside it with a dull *thud.* Constantine was left holding thin air, his palms covered in her dust. His face contorted, lines marring his beautiful features. His eyes filled with tears. His pain seemed physical.

I wondered if it really was—if there was some sort of metaphysical bond between maker and childe that hurt when severed. Would I feel what Constantine did now if Willoughby was really executed? I didn't know; they don't cover *maker extermination* in the handbook. I'd find out firsthand, though, if Willoughby did us all a favor and died tonight.

I could ask Constantine later, but I didn't want to. He appeared devastated. Lost.

Then he met my gaze.

Producing a maniacal grin, he spun and caught Willoughby's wrist. He took advantage of the other man's shock, to move the stake away from his own chest.

"You killed her." Willoughby's face was a mask of fury, but his eyes held the same devastation Constantine's held for that split second after he killed Ádísa.

Constantine didn't speak, but used both hands to bend Willoughby's wrist backward. He pushed, and the stake was shoved into Willoughby's chest. Willoughby took a couple of steps back but didn't dust. The stake must have missed his heart. I looked at Johnny as he was about to shoot me. I saw it in the tensing of his eyes, the tightening of his finger on the crossbow's trigger. I ducked to the side at the same moment Constantine kicked the armchair into Johnny and rattled his aim.

An arrow buzzed by, not close enough for either Alex or me to be at risk. If Constantine didn't jar Johnny off balance, I'd be history. Before relief could settle in, Alex pulled me behind him and brought up his gun. This was why he'd hidden part of his body from view—so the others wouldn't see him reach for his weapon. Well, there was no reason for him to hide anymore. The fight was on.

I tuned down my hearing just in time. Alex's gun went off, and the sound had to be deafening to the other vampires in the room. Johnny looked pained even before Alex planted bullet after bullet in his chest. Johnny Boy's inability to take aim again allowed me to approach Willoughby and Constantine, who were wrestling on the floor.

I grabbed Ádísa's stake from where it lay beside them and crawled toward Johnny. The armchair acted as a shield against stray bullets. Alex was still shooting Johnny when I stood behind the vampire and plunged the stake under his ribs and through his heart.

Something whizzed past my head. My cheek burned. Alex almost shot me. "*Hey.* Watch it."

"Are you all right?" Alex crossed the room toward me, holding his gun up.

"Not thanks to you." I rubbed my cheek and checked my hand. No blood, not that it'd leave a scar even if there were an open wound. Dust clung to my lips and eyelashes.

He stopped a couple of feet away from me and took me in. "You seem fine from where I'm standing."

"I'm lucky you ran out of bullets." I tilted my head toward the other two vampires and motioned for Alex to stay where he was. He nodded, and I rushed to help Constantine. I was looking for an opening, when Willoughby brought up his knee and crashed it squarely into my ex's crotch. Constantine folded over with a groan, and Willoughby rolled him off and took flight.

Constantine was on his feet before I could decide whether to chase Willoughby or look for the missing women. "Go find the fledglings," he said. "I'm going after him."

Dilemma solved, I kicked at Ádísa's ashes, watching as my boot scattered them. I'd wanted her to tell me why she hadn't picked someone better known and what her comment about women of my family meant, damn it. And I'd wanted to be the one to rip her head off—or something less brutal but equally final.

Resigned to knowing I couldn't have everything, I stole a kiss from Alex. "Let's get the girls and get out of here."

****

I stared down the iron door barring our way to the first room in the basement. Anything could be behind it, but I was ready for *anything*, so that worked out fine. "I'm going in first. We can't be sure what shape the newly turned vampires will be in. For all we know, Ádísa, Willoughby, and Johnny have been starving them into obedience. If they're in the room, half-crazed with hunger, you'll be the perfect snack for them."

Wisely, Alex didn't put up an argument.

I put my ear against the door for the third time. I couldn't hear evidence of life on the other side, but that didn't mean Dotty wasn't in there. Even if the door weren't thick enough to conceal a heartbeat, Alex's heart pounding would definitely cover it.

I tried the doorknob, but it wouldn't budge. Not surprising. I didn't expect the thing to be unlocked anyway. "Hello?" I said, and jumped when two distinct voices returned my greeting.

"Hold on, we're here to get you out." My mind reeled at the possibilities of what would greet me when I entered the room. Would the women be chained up? Tortured? The mental picture of naked, bleeding bodies lying on the cold floor made me flinch. *Oh God.* With a curse, I grabbed the knob again and rattled it. Nothing. Alex was out of bullets, so I'd have to break the door down.

"Hold on," I yelled again, swearing to myself I'd make sure they were properly taken care of from that day onward. I'd make it the point of my unlife to help them forget whatever pain was inflicted on them for the first weeks of their existence as vampires.

I took a step back, steeled myself, and shoved at the door with my shoulder, putting all my weight into it. I accomplished jack shit on my first effort, but the second time was the charm. The moment my body made contact with the iron surface, the door gave way, emptying me into the room. I didn't bust in; it was opened. From the inside.

I landed face first on a sheepskin rug, in front of a pair of feet with perfectly painted orange toenails. The legs attached to those feet went up for miles, and from my position I saw more of their owner than I wanted to. I raised my gaze to her face. It looked familiar.

"Oh look. They brought us a chick," the tall girl standing above me in a forest-green silk robe said.

I'd seen those hazel eyes before, in one of the pictures Alex showed Sheena's assistant. Intense eyebrows, short black hair… *Liza. Liza Mills.*

She looked a lot more interested when she took in Alex helping me up. "And who are you?"

"He is off limits." I bounced back to my feet, confusion forgotten at the thought of him being in danger. "Nobody bites him."

"I'd say," Alex murmured.

"I wasn't going to," Liza said. "Like I'd feed on a human."

Huh? Humans are our food source.

I glanced around and saw two more girls watching us. They were dressed the same way Liza was, only in different colors, and looked the exact opposite of the prisoners I expected to find. The room wasn't what I'd pictured, either. It wasn't big, but it was every girlie girl's fantasy, with cosmetics and hair products lining all surfaces except for the two sets of bunk beds. I was prepared for a medieval torture chamber but found myself in a sorority house.

"We're here to save you," I said. Now, how to convince them they needed saving?

"Are you a missionary?" the blonde sitting cross-legged on one of the beds asked. "I've dealt with your kind before. I have to tell you Willoughby says our souls are in no danger from our turning." She was clutching at the lapels of her robe, keeping them closed over her breasts and paying no mind to how much of the rest of her was on display.

The third girl sat at a vanity, braiding her dark chocolate brown hair in a manner similar to how Ádísa often wore hers. "Where is Willoughby? He was supposed to feed us today." Done with her hair, she tossed her braid back and turned toward me.

"Yeah. Did he send you instead?" asked the blonde.

I had no clue why she'd think I was there to feed her, but I was thankful she only asked me, and not Alex. That, and what Liza had said about not feeding from a human, indicated Willoughby kept the girls on vampire blood. It sort of made sense, since vampire blood is more nutritional, but I didn't get why he didn't even tell them humans equaled food.

Willoughby was obviously trying to gain their loyalty. Cultivate an actual maker-childe bond. I wouldn't be resentful just because he obviously took far better care of them. I wouldn't.

Then again, any care was better than dumping someone in an alley after their turning.

All three fledglings looked at me like baby birds looking at their momma. A momma about to tap a vein for them. This so wasn't happening.

I had to tell them the truth, and I doubted they'd like it. "Willoughby took off. And Ádísa is dead."

"Oh my God. What happened to her?" Liza seemed about to cry. "Where did Willoughby go? Is Johnny okay?"

I wanted to bang my head on a wall. Instead I shook it. "Dead too," I whispered.

"We'll tell you all about it," Alex said before I could say more—like how I was the one responsible for Johnny's new status. "First we have to get you somewhere safe."

"Are we in danger?" Liza was the most vocal one. The other two girls approached us, and I didn't like how they seemed to be measuring Alex. Whether they meant to bite him or not, they most definitely seemed hungry for him.

Constantine appeared at the doorway as I took Alex's hand in mine. "He got away," he said, his gaze roaming the fledglings. "Are they all you found?"

"Just told these girls their maker disappeared and the other two people… taking care of them are dead." I spared him a glance that I hoped warned him not to disagree. He nodded, and I said, "Can you fly them to your place? We'll look for the rest and Dotty, and then come find you."

"To my place?" He scrunched his nose in dismay. "Cherry—"

The young vampires hissed in unison. The blonde took a step back. "You're Cherry?" Her fangs were out, but she sounded funny more than menacing. "We've heard about you."

Well, this was odd.

"You want to stake us, don't you?" The brunette stood in front of the blonde. "Don't worry, Sally. I won't let her get to you."

I turned to Liza, whom I deemed the brainiest of the three. "Listen—I don't know what Willoughby and the others told you, but I have nothing against you. They were the ones who took your lives from you. They did the same to me. I'm on your side. I'm here to rescue you."

"From what? Luxury?" The blonde one, Sally, wrapped her fingers around the brunette's bicep, stopping her from nearing me. "Don't, Carrie. She's dangerous."

I was about to throw a fit. "I'm *not* dangerous. I'm not the one who turned you so you could fuck and kill men for their estates."

Blank looks all around. *Awesome.*

Constantine held his hands up. "I will explain everything when we get to my mansion. You ladies seem to need to feed. I will take care of that too. If you'll get dressed and follow me." With a small bow, he stepped outside.

I was waiting for protests, but none came. Not taking their eyes off me, the girls hurried to the closet. Alex turned away, and I was left to watch bouncy boobs getting squeezed into revealing tops and perfectly shaped tummies being sucked in for skintight jeans to be zipped up.

I remembered the plastic surgery I never had, and stood there sulking as the girls exited the room, mindful not to come too close to me.

"Come find us when you're through looking around," Constantine called out over his shoulder, wrapping an arm around Carrie's waist and the other around Liza's shoulders. Sally seemed at a loss for a second, but then she grabbed his waistband and the four of them were soon out of sight.

Alex grinned. "Do you think he'll take care of all three of them?"

I scowled. "We have to find the rest of them and Dotty." Constantine *could* take care of all three young ladies. Also, I could *gag*. Sheena would probably be her annoying self enough to keep any sexing from happening till we met up with them.

And I didn't care.

I led Alex to the next room.

That door wasn't locked from the inside, and it took three kicks and a shoulder wedge for me to open it.

My previous fears came to life when I saw Dotty chained to the far wall, her jeans and frilly blouse torn in several places. She was thinner than when I last saw her. Her nose had bled at some point. Rust-colored stains covered her front, and a crust of blood blocked what I saw of her right nostril.

Her nose wasn't the only part of her she'd lost blood from, though. Even from across the room, I made out the raw and angry bite marks on the insides of her elbows and her wrists. I bet there were more on her neck, but I couldn't see them, the way her head was tilted.

At least her jeans were still on. Whatever happened to her, she at least wasn't violated *that* way. Nobody would have bothered dressing her afterward.

Fury fought with nausea inside me. They didn't need to have her chained up, hanging from the wall like a side of beef; they could have thralled her into submission. They could have licked her wounds closed, for fuck's sake. I wanted to weep for her—for what happened to her because she was unlucky enough to know me.

I wished Constantine hadn't lost Willoughby. I wished he'd caught the sadistic creep and brought him to me, so I could mete out some justice.

"Dotty?" I whispered. "Can you hear me, honey?" Her heart was beating, thank God, and her chest rose and fell, albeit slowly. She was alive, and that was all that mattered.

The shackles looked sturdy. I could probably break them, but I might injure Dotty more. Luck smiled at us when I noticed a small key on the bench to my right. "Help me," I said.

Alex ran to her side and propped her up, while I undid her bindings. She slumped against him, and he maneuvered her so cradled her body in his arms. "I'll wait here while you search the other rooms."

With a grateful, shaky smile, I left him and his precious cargo and went to tear down the rest of the doors in the basement.

I found nobody else. A second preppy room, like the one we found the newbs in, was empty. As, predictably, was Ádísa's bedroom.

I returned to Alex and carefully took Dotty from him.

"You'd better fly her to Constantine's," he said. "She needs to be looked after as soon as possible."

I wasn't sure I could take Alex with. Dotty was still out for the count, and I'd have to hold her with both arms.

He shook his head, as if reading my mind. "I'll bring the car."

I thanked him, and we made our way outside. He kissed me when we got to the front gate. It was awkward with Dotty between us, but he managed a lingering kiss, full of promises.

I reciprocated with equal fervor. With the bad guys out of the way, we had a future, and I was keen on starting on that as soon as I had Dotty restored to her healthy, vibrant self, and back with her son.

I gazed at Alex one last time before I took off. He looked at me with a secret smile that made his eyes twinkle. My chest swelled with love that warmed me up inside. I wouldn't let another opportunity pass me by. When I saw Alex later tonight, I'd tell him I loved him.

I tucked Dotty's head under my chin, smiled back at him, and launched into the night sky.

Chapter Seventeen

I waited at Constantine's for three hours.

I shouldn't have waited that long. I should have known something was wrong when Alex didn't show within the first thirty minutes. I should have felt it.

I didn't.

I was too preoccupied with worrying over Dotty, who didn't wake up even after Constantine and I closed her wounds. Sheena helped me clean and change Dotty into warm pajamas and didn't freak out once during the whole thing. That she wasn't drunk or even tipsy spoke volumes about the truth of her resolution to be strong and finally deal with things she avoided for a while.

I was busy helping Constantine feed the three girls, then explaining to them why we killed two of the vampires treating them as royalty. His patience with them was surprising, as was the firm yet kind way he dealt with all the excitement our revelation caused. They were still wary of me but at least seemed open to the possibility they were lied to by their maker and his friends. It was more than I could have hoped for.

By the time I realized Alex was taking far too long, it was almost two in the morning. I tried his cell phone, but it kept ringing and ringing until my call was forwarded to his voicemail. *"I can't pick up right now,"* his recorded voice informed me, *"but if you leave your name and number, I'll get back to you as soon as possible."*

The pit of my stomach gave way, and the world tilted. I wanted him to get back to me *now*. Where was he? Did he have an accident while speeding to get to me?

"Don't be silly." Sheena stopped my pacing with a hand on my shoulder. "Have some of this." She offered me a cup of the tea Wesley made for us all. The poor man felt useless among the drama until Constantine set him on tea duty.

I didn't take it. The stupid stuff wasn't going to fix anything.

"He probably went by his place to shower and left his phone in his car. Maybe he's set it on silent." Her efforts to reassure me were valiant but ineffective.

"He would have called me." He wasn't taking a shower. No shower took that long. "He wouldn't make me wait like this." I should call his place or his mother's, but I didn't have either number.

I shoved my phone in my pocket and made sure Dotty was tucked in where she lay on the couch. "I'll go find him."

Ignoring Constantine's protests that I couldn't leave him with three pissed-off women and a crazy one, I ran out the door and was in the air in seconds.

****

I could have gone to his mother's first. Hell, I *should* have gone to his mother's first, but I didn't want to waste time doing things in what might be the wrong order. Determined to start at the beginning, I flew back to Ádísa's, landed in front of her manor's gate, and flared my nostrils until I caught his scent.

Nose in the air, I followed Alex's trail around the corner he appeared from earlier tonight and into a well-lit street lined with two-story houses, their gardens trimmed to perfection. There, under a streetlight, I saw a familiar car.

My feet almost kicked up sparks, as I covered the distance to the car at full speed, hoping against hope that Alex was just taking a nap behind the wheel, the exhaustion and excitement of the night having finally caught up with him.

He wasn't behind the wheel or in the backseat. I punched through the lock of the trunk, to pop the lid open. Not there either.

The unmistakable scent of his blood wafted to my nostrils. It didn't come from the car but the gravel. A closer look revealed a couple of dark droplets. Alex had been here, and he'd been bleeding.

Something happened to him as he was about to get in his car. I tried telling myself it could be something as small as a nosebleed, but I knew better than to let the lack of more blood appease me.

I couldn't have been too far when he was hurt. I should have heard him call for help. *No.* I should have been there with him. I should have saved him from whatever harmed him.

Willoughby.

The thought made me panic. Every hint of rational thought I might be capable of got choked out. I tried to think of other possibilities. Alex could have been hit by a car—*no*, there would be more blood. He could have been mugged, although the sight of his gun should be enough of a deterrent for any aspiring mugger, who wouldn't know it was empty. He was a cop; he'd manage to at least pull his gun on his attacker.

If his attacker was human.

I could no longer hide from the truth. Willoughby got to him. My maker came back after he escaped Constantine, and he got Alex alone. In my mind's eye, I saw him pinning Alex to the car and closing his jaws over my Alex's jugular.

Did he kill him? I shook my head. Alex had to be alive. He had to be alive for many, many years. We had to make each other happy.

My vision blurred with tears. Wiping my eyes and cheeks furiously, I let my sense of smell overtake my other senses, not hoping for much. If Willoughby flew Alex out of here, it would take me forever to find him.

The scent hit me again, and I frowned. Willoughby carried him away on foot? What for?

The streetlamps were too bright. A cat howled from atop a nearby trash can.

He did it for me to follow them. It was a trap for *me*.

****

I stood at the entrance of Alex's mother's house, working up the courage to make my way inside. I didn't know what I'd find, and for the millionth time considered calling Constantine. He would be more than useful an ally in a confrontation like the one I was about to have with my maker.

Calling him would be the wise thing to do, but not knowing in what condition I'd find Alex meant I couldn't wait. I squared my shoulders and tried the door. It wasn't latched, which added to my unease as I stepped into the living room.

Empty.

The entire house smelled like Alex, so I no longer trusted my nose to lead me to him. The ground floor was empty. I threw caution to the wind and rushed to the basement, only to find it in the same state I remembered it—bed unmade and Alex-less.

That left the upper floor. Had to be where Willoughby was holding him.

I flew up the stairs, and the stench of blood slammed into me like a sledgehammer. It was no longer a hint or a trail. It smelled like a bucketful or two, and it came from Alex's old bedroom.

But I couldn't make out a heartbeat.

A piece of paper was pinned to the wooden frame of the door. I snatched it.

> *You took something of mine. Now I took something of yours. I hope he's still alive when you find him, so you can watch him die.*
>
> *W.*

It was written in ink, not blood, the handwriting sophisticated and elegant.

My fangs dropped.

I didn't bother hiding them again.

"I swear, I'll kill you." My words echoed back to me in the narrow corridor. A low *thump* snapped me out of my shock

201

and led me to the entrance of the room. Another *thump* followed. It *was* a heartbeat, slow and unsteady.

Reluctantly, I opened the door.

I saw him.

My brain at first refused to make sense of the sight. It couldn't accept that the crimson sheets weren't really red, but soaked with my lover's blood. I couldn't believe the naked torso, covered with wounds, belonged to the man I loved. I couldn't grasp that I was seeing his life essence seep away from too many cuts to count. Willoughby didn't feed from him, or there wouldn't be so much blood. No. The sick bastard took his time slicing and biting Alex, for the sole purpose of torturing and killing him.

I hoped Alex had been under a thrall or unconscious during his ordeal. He had to be, or someone would have heard and called 911. On second thought, I wished someone did. Alex's chances of survival would be higher. His pulse was too weak. Even if I called now, they'd be too late.

I climbed on the bed next to him and raised his head in my lap, willing him to wake up. "Come on, baby. Open your eyes. Please, open your eyes and look at me."

I was crying again—still—begging him to stay with me, warning him not to dare slip away from my grasp, when we were so good together. "I want to be with you, Alex. Please, look at me. *Look at me.*" I was rambling. I took off my top and tried to wipe him clean.

I didn't want to lick his wounds closed. I didn't want his blood in my mouth, even if it was to save him. So I spat on my hands and rubbed them on every inch of him, pressing everywhere, to stem the flow. His blood slid between my fingers, too precious and too elusive.

"You can't leave me, not when I just found you," I whispered.

Not a twitch.

"Open your eyes, Alex. Open those beautiful eyes. Wake up. We'll make you good as new. Just look at me. *Please.*" I was lying, to him and to myself. There was no way to make him good as new. Though he wasn't losing any more blood, I could see and hear that there was too little left in him. He had but minutes to live, and I could do nothing but watch him go.

Wrong.

There was something I could do.

Unsure of whether it was the right thing, or if it would work anyway, I used my fangs to pierce my inner wrist. Forcing his lips open with my other hand, I held my wrist to them and squeezed a few drops of my blood into his mouth. If the handbook had it right, that ought to be enough.

It didn't appear to be.

Alex's eyes never opened.

Not when I kissed him and told him I'd rather have another moment with him than an eternity alone. Not when I shook him and watched his curls, usually carefree, cling to his skull, matted with his blood. Not when I finally said I loved him.

I moved him off my lap and lay next to him, turning his face so his mouth was a hairbreadth from mine.

I was still begging him to open those long eyelashes of his, when his last breath caressed my face.

I kept begging long after his heart stopped beating.

Chapter Eighteen

Constantine showed up near dawn. He said he called me several times, but I couldn't remember hearing my phone ring. Not that I'd care, if I did.

"He won't wake up," I told him, trying to clear my throat. It was sore, and I guessed my mourning hadn't been as quiet as I thought. "I tried. I gave him my blood. But he won't—" A sob cut me off, and I shook Alex's still form hard. "Why won't he—"

Constantine wrapped his arms around me, pulling me from Alex. "Hush, baby." He hadn't called me that in years. Once upon a time, I melted when the word escaped his lips. Now I wished it was Alex whispering it in my ear.

Constantine tried to calm me down, but I wouldn't listen. His words couldn't penetrate my sorrow. Couldn't diffuse my guilt. Alex was dead because he'd met me.

"—light outside."

I turned to Constantine in a fury and shoved him halfway across the room. How could he talk about anything other than the loss I suffered? He grabbed my forearms when I went for him again, and held me to him while I flailed.

He didn't let go until I stopped fighting his grip. "We have to go before it's too late." He was right.

I couldn't care less.

He obviously caught on, because he hauled me over his shoulder with an exaggerated sigh and moved to the window. Finding fresh strength, I thrashed and kicked. Not that it did me any good; his grasp was made of steel.

"I'll be back for him." He pinned my legs to him with both hands. "I promise."

I didn't believe him, but it didn't matter. He could take me wherever he wanted. Protect me from the sun. Hide me at his estate so the remaining council wouldn't come after me when they found out I killed Johnny Boy. He could keep my body from dusting, but I'd still be dead inside.

Alex was gone, because of me.

Everything I let myself hope for—love, a future—was wiped out because I was stupid. Alex never heard me say I loved him, because I was too selfish to admit it aloud.

Back at the mansion, I sank into an armchair and curled into myself. Sheena tried to comfort me, but I would have none of it. I didn't deserve to be comforted. I'd brought Alex into a world filled with death and left him there to be swallowed whole.

I was wallowing in misery when Dotty opened her eyes and started shrieking. Constantine was at a loss. Her wails became louder every time he tried to approach her, and she wouldn't stay still long enough for him to catch her gaze. Seeing me calmed her down but didn't help us decide what to do next. I mean, were we supposed to tell her the truth or try the all-powerful mind wipe?

In the end, it was my call to let her choose for herself.

We filled her in on the entire story and let her decide if she wanted us to make her forget.

She did.

She didn't want to remember a single thing she'd been through, but most of all, she didn't want to know there was such a thing as vampires, or that I was one of them. I took her memories of the last few days away and, when she came to, fed her a story about Constantine and me being secret agents who were in charge of solving her kidnapping. Other than being a part of that secret organization, VSS—feel free to laugh—Constantine was also a doctor. He assured her she didn't have to worry about her loss of short-term memory, as it was trauma induced.

She swore not to mention us or our organization to anyone, including the cops. Since Willoughby had an invitation to her home and we couldn't be sure if he'd go after her again, we promised to drive her to her mother's, where her son was still staying, as soon as the sun went down.

She wouldn't wait that long, and I couldn't blame her. I wished I could be there when she was reunited with her son, but my wishes weren't what counted now. I hugged her goodbye, promised to check in on them soon, and called her a taxi, which Constantine gladly paid for.

Dotty and Mark would be fine, and I'd be around to make sure of that. I would accept no more losses.

That last thought landed me back in my reality and snuffed out my glee over seeing Dotty back to her normal self. At least she still had a life and the option to lock the boogeyman out of it.

I *was* the boogeyman. I was the thing hiding under the bed, skulking in the darkness and luring good, brave people to their death. Their horrible, painful, lonely death.

I hid my face in my palms and sat there, praying I could take the last few hours back—or maybe even the last few days. I would have never met Alex, but at least his smile would still be brightening the world.

****

"Cherry, it's time."

I lifted my head and looked at Constantine through blurry eyes. Time for what? I blinked to bring him into focus. Exhaustion must have overtaken me, because I was now lying on the couch. I hadn't realized I drifted off.

Constantine wiped my hair off my face with gentle fingers. "Do you want to come with me?"

I didn't know what he was talking about. I shook my head. I didn't want to move; I wanted to waste away and leave behind the pain tearing me up inside.

"He's going to bring Alex," Sheena said with a tender smile. "Are you sure you don't want to go?" Her palm on my shoulder was more than a show of support. She was gently pushing me up.

"Alex is dead." There were no more tears in my eyes, but they were choking my voice. "I don't want to see him like that. Not again."

Constantine frowned. "Cherry..."

In my sleepy state, it was harder for me to block his voice out.

"Cherry, didn't you hear me earlier?"

Instead of replying, I closed my eyes.

He grabbed my upper arms and shook me gently. "Listen to me. You know newly turned vampires don't rise if their turning was close to dawn, so they don't burst into flames when they greet the morning sun."

I knew that. Three hours from sunrise was the theoretical limit. The meaning of his words finally sank in. "If Alex's turning was successful, he'll only just be waking up now." Oh God, I should have remembered that.

Constantine smiled gently. "Do you want to come with me?"

I nodded gingerly and sat up, but doubt stopped me from standing. "I can't. What if he's not...?" Not alive. Not turned. Not happy with the choice I made for him. Scratch that—I didn't care if he was so mad at me he never wanted to see me again. All that mattered was for him to still be part of my world.

"I'll bring him to you." The softness of Constantine's tone surprised me, as did his certainty.

"Thank you," I said.

"I would do anything for you. You know that." I did, but I couldn't focus on what it meant. I could have Alex back. I could have another chance. I could even have forever.

Soon I'd know if Alex was gone or not.

Epilogue

Less than forty-eight hours ago, under Sheena's worried, watchful eye, Constantine turned my emotional switch from *devastated* to *hopeful*, and then proceeded to make good on his promise.

Alex wasn't gone.

In Constantine's words, "he was looking around stupidly" and nearly ripped Constantine's arm off when the latter tried to feed him. Still, Alex was composed and clean by the time the two came back to Constantine's.

I heard the door open and stopped myself from wearing a moat into the floor with my pacing. Alex stopped in the doorway and met my gaze. It took great effort to hold back from tackling him. I studied him carefully, trying to spot any difference between his new self and the man I knew and loved. I searched his eyes for a hint of resentment. There was none. Only love shown in the smile he gave me.

Unable to put my relief into words, I flew into his arms, which closed around me. "I love you," I said, the words long overdue. I clung to him and kissed him the way he deserved to be kissed, declaring my love every time our lips separated.

Constantine cleared his throat. "I've made arrangements for the young ladies to spend the night in my quarters, so I can ensure they are comfortable," he said. Such an altruist. Snort. "You may settle in the guest wing. Don't make me regret my hospitality." *Or else* was implied.

We didn't.

Not last night, anyway.

From what I've seen so far, Alex has taken to his change well enough. He's tamed the hunger already. I guess his first feeding from one of us and his preexisting ethical code helped with that, but I still dread what will happen if he needs to feed from a human.

The council doesn't know about his turning, and we're planning on keeping it a secret for as long as possible. That way, if he decides to keep in touch with friends and family, he'll just have to come up with an explanation for his newfound intolerance to sunlight. We haven't yet talked about how he wants to deal with work and his mother. We haven't talked much in general. We had other priorities.

Alex refused to give flying a chance, said he's too grounded for that, but I convinced him to let me fly him to his car last night—and I listened to him grumble about his trunk being busted.

We drove to his mom's place. I hated cleaning up the mess in his childhood bedroom. The sheets reeked, and the mattress was soaked all the way through. There was no way the blood would be washed away from them, or from my memory. We stuffed the beddings in garbage bags, which we drove to the nearest dumpster, praying nobody noticed us.

The powers that be were listening, as I suspect they have been since Alex and I first met.

The room stank only slightly less like a slaughterhouse after the second thorough cleaning with bleach, and we decided to leave the windows open for the night, hoping fresh air would help.

I insisted we fly back, but Alex wouldn't hear of it. The lid of his trunk is now kept closed with several layers of duct tape.

Back at the mansion, we ran into Liza, who demanded to know when Constantine would be back.

Who knows?

He's meeting the remaining council tonight in hopes of convincing the dusting of two of their members was necessary. I offered to go with him, but he wouldn't let me.

I hope he succeeds. If he doesn't, we have to go underground for a long time, and by *underground* I don't mean his humongous and luxurious basement.

"The girls are asking for him." Liza pouted prettily.

Right. *The girls.*

All three of them have become far more attached to my ex than is advisable. I wonder what will happen when we find the rest of Ádísa and Willoughby's would-be undead army. Will Constantine start a harem? He said yesterday that he plans to keep them with him until he figures out a solution with the council. I think he just loves having three gorgeous women falling over themselves for him.

Let him. I have Alex.

We promised Liza we'd let her know if we heard from Constantine, and pushed our way past her, holding hands.

Sheena was nowhere in sight, as expected; her internal clock is the opposite of ours. Night equals sleep time to her body, and I see no reason for that to change.

She isn't in a hurry to go home. On the contrary, yesterday afternoon she mentioned she'd arranged for some of her clothes to be brought in. "If you run, I run," she said. "I'm safer with you." I think Wesley gave her the idea. He's taken her under his wing and would probably hate to lose her company.

She doesn't have much to fear. There's been no sign of Willoughby, who probably thinks he's exacted his revenge. It's actually unfortunate, because I want to find him and make him answer the two questions plaguing me. I asked Constantine, but he has no idea why I was chosen as vampire zero, so to speak, or what Ádísa's comment about my family meant.

Sheena isn't concerned with all this, of course. She insists Willoughby may come after her at any second. I think her reason for sticking around is, in fact, also Constantine. The man is going to have his hands full for a while.

I don't feel sorry for him. I'm too busy enjoying my time with Alex.

****

210

I haven't fed and yet can't be bothered. I'm sprawled on my back in Constantine's bed, trying not to think about where I am and what I'm doing.

I look at the man between my legs and tangle my fingers in his black hair. "We shouldn't." I drift off, pleasure turning my next words into a moan.

Gray eyes meet mine. "Will you relax? He'll never know."

Of course he'll know, and he'll probably kill us both, or hand us over to the council to do that for him.

We were only supposed to go to his room for Alex to borrow clean clothes. But Constantine's bed is just so huge. We were unable to resist.

Constantine was sickeningly nice to me since he hauled me away from Alex's dead body, but I doubt he'll keep being nice once he smells my little carnal reunion with Alex in his bed.

I try extremely hard to care about that, while Alex pumps three fingers inside me, his tongue flicking my clit.

I fail. Spectacularly.

Later, exhausted and sated, I trace Alex's jugular with my tongue. Graze my teeth over it. He grabs my hair and presses my mouth against his flesh, but I just nuzzle it.

"Didn't your mother ever tell you not to play with your food?" he asks.

She did indeed. All the time. I let out a deep, throaty chuckle and sink my fangs into the smooth column, letting his rich blood fill my throat. I have all I need, and I'm where I want to be. I'm happy.

I hope I'll feel the same way when Constantine returns with news from the council.

If he returns.

He still hasn't called, and I can't say I'm not a little worried. For all I know, despite his charm *and the fact that he's right*, the council executed him on the spot and the remaining members are coming for us.

They can't come inside this house, thanks to Wesley.

Even if they do, Alex and I will handle it.

Book 2
Cherry Blossom

Chapter One

I like big beds.

I like wide, comfy mattresses that allow me to stretch to my heart's desire and roll over as many times as I please. What's more, I like bedmates that don't take up the space I lovingly maintain around me.

Alex wasn't that kind of a bedmate.

Alex was a cuddler, which I more than appreciated after naughty-times, but suffocated me in my sleep, when the weight of an arm pressed my chest down or a hard body kept me from turning around.

He also snored from time to time, which made no sense, since he no longer needed to breathe. I guess old habits die hard.

I wouldn't have made a big deal out of any of these things this morning, if I didn't wake up to Alex spooning me from behind, both of his arms wrapped around me like steel bars, and his voice whispering in my ear, "I want you to meet my mother."

And I certainly wouldn't have kicked him off the bed, if he didn't add, "And I want to meet your family."

****

"What did you do that for?" Alex rubbed his head where it had impacted with the wall. He was still on the floor where he landed, staring at me.

I sat up and bunched the covers around me, still not fully believing I did what I did—or that he actually said what I heard.

"Cherry? What's up? And *ow*, by the way." He didn't seem as pissed off as I'd be in his place. "Did you have another nightmare? Think I was Willoughby again?"

His concern made me feel bad. To be honest, I never had nightmares of Willoughby. At times when Alex was too clingy in my sleep, however, I may have elbowed him in the ribs or kicked him in the shin and afterward implied I thought he was my maker, haunting my dreams. He was having nightmares of his turning too, so he believed me.

I shook my head. "Not him," I said. "Different nightmare. About you wanting us to meet each other's folks."

That got him fuming in no time, which worked out quite well, because I wasn't feeling all lovey-dovey.

"Why's that so bad? My mother's been hearing about you for two months now. She wants to meet you." And *this* was a glaring example of why we should let our family think we died after our turning. If the vampire council caught a whiff of Alex's staying in touch with his mother, they might resort to extreme measures.

Then again, they'd have to know he was a vampire, for them to even care, so it was a moot point. After the havoc that resulted to his turning, the vampire council reinstated the Vampire Social Services, to help tighten the bonds within our community. They also decreed a census, to record all vampires currently in the United States. We'd kept Alex's change in status a secret, to avoid dealing with the repercussions of breaking the law against turning new fledglings.

"What if she doesn't like me?" 'Cause loveable as I am, this was always a possibility. I didn't voice my worries that I might not like her. "And you can't meet my family. *I* can't meet my family again. They think I'm dead."

"They think you're missing. Finding out you're still"— he scrunched his face—"*around* would be the greatest thing to ever happen to them." He was using his rational voice on me, something that probably worked when he interrogated suspects, but which I hated when I was feeling unreasonable. He got on his feet and dusted plaster off his hair. "And my mom will love you. Just like I do."

Yeah, okay. Play the *I-love-you* card, why don't you? "We'll talk about it," I said. "I'll ask Constantine what he thinks. He knows the council better than I do, and they like him." If they didn't, they'd have publicly executed him for admitting to killing two of their own. Instead, they had him join them. "If he thinks it's safe for me to go home, we'll visit my family."

There was no way my ex would condone something like this. It was reckless and might endanger us all—plus he might be acting cool and superior, but I could tell he wasn't happy with my relationship with Alex.

Alex must have realized Constantine would say *no*, because he kicked dejectedly at the floor and came back to bed with a scowl on his face. "I'll talk to him too. Maybe I can convince him," he said, standing in front of me in his birthday suit.

He could certainly try. Meanwhile, I'd do my best to make him forget about the whole thing.

I smiled, slid to the edge of the bed, and let the covers drop, to reveal a state of undress that matched his. I traced the lines of his body—hard muscle under soft skin that shivered ever so slightly under my touch.

His gaze was locked on mine, as I replaced my fingers with my mouth down his stomach. I loved the texture, the smoothness of his skin. I feathered my lips along his hipbone and felt his legs tremble. I loved his body's involuntary responses. Smiling to myself, I brought one hand around him and dug my nails into his buttock, pushing him against my face.

He rudely interrupted my efforts at driving him crazy with anticipation, by stepping back, grabbing my knees, and laying me flat on the bed in one smooth move. Before I could voice my protest, he was kissing me.

I arched upward and wrapped my legs around his hips, but he resisted, his body hovering above me. "No." The single word was heavy with promise.

He kissed me again, teasing my mouth open with his tongue and finding mine. The kiss deepened, as did my need for him. When he sucked on my lower lip, I ran one hand down the length of my body and between my legs, where I wanted him the most.

He closed his fingers around my wrist and forced my hand to the mattress. "Be a good girland don't move." His cool breath tickled my ear.

It's not like me to submit without a fight, but the lust burning in his gaze stifled my rebellious side. I tangled both hands in the sheets, to keep from touching him.

His mouth moved down the side of my neck, kissing and licking the area over my jugular. I wanted him to bite me. I wanted to push against him. I held back. He barely let a fang graze my skin and chuckled at the whiny sound that escaped my throat.

The bastard.

He made his way down my body with his lips and fingers, pulling sighs and moans out of me with every kiss, every caress, every nip. My nipples hardened at his touch. My stomach tightened. Every nerve in my body screamed for more, but he refused to give it. By the time his face was at the apex of my thighs, I craved him beyond reason. I couldn't be held accountable for my actions if he didn't sink inside me immediately.

Only Alex wasn't done teasing me.

He closed his teeth over the sensitive flesh at the inside of my thigh without breaking the skin, and sucked while pushing a finger inside me.

My hips flew off the mattress, and my eyes watered at the pressure building up in my belly. I needed just a bit more. More pressure. More friction. I needed him to add another finger and pump them both. I needed him to eat me out. I needed him to—*Oh God...*

He didn't do what I wanted but he didn't withdraw, either. Instead, he splayed the fingers of his free hand on my stomach to hold me down and pierced my skin with his fangs at the same time he pressed his thumb on my clit.

I thought I was going to scream, but only a hoarse whisper reached my ears when I managed to form a word. "Please."

He either didn't hear me or ignored me. He drew lazy circles with his thumb around my clitoris and slid his finger in and out so slowly, I couldn't get the *more* I needed. He kept pulling at my blood, and the sensation was enough to drive me to the precipice but not to throw me over.

Pleading obviously didn't work, so this time I went with an order. "*Now.*"

Alex was not in a compliant mood. He stopped touching me entirely and raised his gaze to mine, making sure I watched as he licked his lips. Once he had my undivided attention, he lowered his head again and slowly ran his tongue along my cleft.

That was when I stopped being nice.

I grabbed his hair to anchor him to me and began grinding against his face, urging him to go faster. Harder. If he wanted to play *Hold off Cherry's Release,* I'd take matters in my own hands.

I was so close—so *fucking* close—when he forcefully removed my hands from his head and rolled me over.

Now we're talking.

The bed was too tall for my knees to reach the ground, and my legs dangled awkwardly. I tried to find purchase on the floor with my toes, but Alex nudged my thighs apart with one knee, throwing me completely off balance, and pushed inside me.

Can't say I complained about the manhandling. Perhaps I would have, if I weren't enjoying it so much. I've always loved seeing Alex's mild manners put aside and this dominant side of his come out in the bedroom—bathroom, kitchen, public place, wherever.

He dug his fingers into my hips and lifted me to meet his thrusts. I didn't have time to push my body up with my arms. My face was rubbing against the mattress, but all I felt was the fire he stoked inside me with every plunge. Every time he withdrew, I clenched around him, trying to lock him and the pleasure in place. My fangs popped out, and I bit at the sheets, uncaring that I'd leave holes in them. I was nearly there nearly there nearly—

Alex's movements turned jerkier, shorter. He draped his body over mine, letting go of my hips so he could wrap his arms around my torso. I let him draw me to him and tilted my head to the side, to get my hair out of the way.

The moment his fangs pierced my throat, everything I wanted, everything my body craved for suddenly flooded my senses, short-circuiting my brain. I couldn't tell which of us was trembling. All I knew was that, pinned to him, torn sheets hanging from my mouth, I felt my body shudder with waves of pleasure until I could no longer keep my eyes open.

Alex obviously had problems controlling himself, too, because his knees buckled, and we toppled forward, his teeth and cock still inside me.

In my fuzziness, I barely registered his tongue gently licking the wounds he'd inflicted, before he rolled to the side and gathered me close. It's possible I purred with delight. This was one of the times I not only didn't mind the cuddling but welcomed it.

I don't know if I drifted off or just zoned out, but I'd been too engrossed in my efforts to distract him, to realize someone else was in the room.

Until Constantine cleared his throat.

Chapter Two

Asking my ex if he'd watched my current lover and me having earth-shattering sex would lead to all kinds of awkwardness, so I opted for yelling at Constantine to get out of the room and go wait for us in the kitchen.

He left with the huff and flourish that accompanied him since he became a member of the vampire council.

"Come on, before he pitches a fit." Alex tossed my jeans and a top on the bed.

I ignored the clothes and watched him slide into his own jeans. The sight made up for the cramped sleeping arrangements. "He can wait." I stretched on my back and reached with my toes for one of his belt loops. "I think you should come back to bed."

"And I think you should stop avoiding him." He was right. I was avoiding Constantine. I bet Alex didn't know why, though.

I wasn't sure why I did it. I only knew I felt odd being couple-y with Alex in front of my ex. It was like I rubbed his face into my happiness with a man who wasn't him. The lingering looks Constantine gave me from time to time didn't help much, either. They weren't looks of longing. He studied me, as if dissecting me. Trying to read my mind. He never said a word against Alex—or *for* him, to be honest—but his general disposition had turned snarkier. Gloomier. Not that he'd been a ray of sunshine to begin with, but sensing I was the reason for his change made me feel bad.

"I can't deal with his smartassness first thing in the morning," I said. Pulling the covers over my head acted like an end to the conversation. Or so I thought.

Alex drew the covers away and leaned over me, now fully dressed. "Get up. Stop being a five-year-old. He may have something important to tell us."

He had a point. Constantine or his people—council members always have *people*—might have finally spotted Willoughby. With a groan meant to show my displeasure, I got up and put on my clothes. "Let's go," I said and led the way.

****

Constantine sat at the table, entirely out of place in the spacious, well-lit kitchen. It wasn't his age that put him at odds with the modern tiles, shiny lacquered-wood and glass surfaces, and metal elements. He looked mid-thirties and hot, his long blond hair framing an angular face devoid of wrinkles. Only his blue eyes betrayed he'd seen much more than his smooth skin and casual attire indicated.

His jeans and white T-shirt weren't too stylish for him to be in a place where food was prepared and served, so that couldn't be it either.

Eyes narrowed, I studied him until realization sunk in. It was his posture that made him clash with the surroundings. He held his back straight, shoulders square, and chin up, as though he were royalty sitting on his throne, waiting for peasants to bring forth their offers.

I *so* wouldn't be one of them.

"Nice of you to finally join us," he said.

"Like we had a choice." I'd *known* he'd be sarcastic. I should have come up with a reply that had more bite.

Liza, who was never too far from Constantine, threw me a scolding look from her perch on the kitchen counter, her black eyebrows furrowed. She was absolutely gorgeous and had been an aspiring model when my old talent agent delivered her to my maker, who wanted to add her to his undead army of models.

222

Alex, Constantine, and I rescued Liza and two other fledglings from Ádísa and her cohorts. Constantine took the girls in, and they more or less worshipped the ground he stood on.

Now I itched to tell Liza I'd been in Constantine's life much longer than she had, and could therefore speak to the man she viewed as a god any way I pleased, but it seemed petty. Instead, I returned her look and took a seat across from my ex. Alex pulled out a chair between us, turned it around, and straddled it.

"Talk," I said to Constantine.

"Would you like something to drink first?"

I looked around. "Where's Wesley? I could go for some coffee. And maybe eggs." Constantine's human butler and his incredible cooking skills were among the perks of living at the mansion. Normal food doesn't sate our hunger, but we enjoy the hell out of it.

"Wesley is busy. Liza has brewed tea."

"Then no, thanks."

Next to me Alex shook his head. "I'm good. What's up?"

"There has been a possible sighting of Willoughby." Constantine motioned at Liza, and she hurried to refill his teacup.

Gag.

"I can't say more at this time, but you should be getting ready for a trip at short notice," he said.

Alex nodded, unperturbed as always by Constantine's exaggerated air of mystery.

I wasn't that big a person. "You got us out of bed to tell us someone's seen the bad guy, but not who or where? What's next?" I deepened my voice to a basso. "It will rain one day in the near or distant future." In my normal pitch, I asked, "Was that doomsday-worthy enough for you?"

"Cherry, this is all I can tell you right now. You have to trust me. What matters is we may have a clue as to his surroundings, if not his intentions."

"A clue you won't share with the class."

"I'm sure he'll tell us more when he knows more." Alex placed one hand over mine, which I'd apparently fisted without realizing it. His effort at soothing me had the opposite result.

"He knows more now." I locked my gaze on Constantine's. "Don't you?"

Constantine shook his head and smiled ruefully. "When did you become so cynical?"

I scrunched my face in mock concentration, then widened my eyes. "*I know*. Must have been about the same time I found out you lied to me and our relationship was a sham. Yup, that was the exact moment."

His eyes were a stormy midnight blue that usually meant anger or extreme pain. Yes, the man came with preinstalled mood-rings on his face.

I wasn't being fair. His maker had appointed him my sponsor. She wanted me to fall for him, and it hadn't taken long for that to happen. But at the time, Constantine didn't know Ádísa had ordered my turning. And contrary to her wishes, he'd really loved me in return. Weeks ago, he insisted he still did.

Liza walked up behind Constantine and laid both hands on his shoulders. Until that moment, I'd only thought of her as Head Concubine. I'd assumed all they shared was sex and blood. Apparently, I'd been at least partially wrong there.

How well she knew him astounded me. Though Constantine's posture didn't change, Liza noticed the subtle increase of tension in his body, like I did. Thing was, I couldn't tell if Constantine's discomfort was out of guilt over the lies he'd told me in the past—for which he'd atoned by killing his own maker—or because he really knew more about Willoughby than he let on.

I didn't want it to be the latter. Not when he'd been regaining my trust. My stomach clenched at the possibility. Instead of asking him, I said, "Fine, be mysterious. But while we're here, can you remind Alex we're not supposed to keep in touch with our families?" Might as well get one problem out of the way.

The tiny lines of tension around Constantine's eyes smoothed out, and he relaxed his jaw. Was it me, or did my ex seem relieved by my change of subject?

Before Constantine could speak, Alex piped in. "I want Cherry and me to meet each other's folks. I know it's not something vampires do, but I'm still alive as far as my mother knows, and I don't see how Cherry's family would be anything but ecstatic to see her again. She was never declared dead, just missing, so she can tell them she was off finding herself or something."

I didn't expect the matter-of-fact way he'd presented his case to do him any good. What he was asking went against council policy. No way would Constantine condone it.

Constantine smiled, his irises now faded to their normal light blue. "We have been doing things our own way for a while now." He shrugged, apparently oblivious to how my mouth gaped at his response. "I don't see why you shouldn't do as you please, as long as you're careful. I will, however, be joining you when you visit Cherry's parents. As a precautionary measure, in case things go awry. I'll have to make some arrangements first, but we should be able to leave by the end of the week."

It was obvious from Alex's eager expression that he'd go along with anything to get the go-ahead for his silly fantasy. I didn't exactly view things the same way. It was weird how readily Constantine had agreed.

"Precautionary measure?" I asked. "You plan to mind-wipe them, if our little reunion is threatening to the vampire community?" Meaning if my parents somehow realized I was undead, freaked out, and threatened to tell the world about our existence.

The look he gave me was full of scorn. "No." The word sounded like it was mentally accompanied by several non-flattering adjectives. "What I had in mind was that you'll have a member of the council with you, in case another vampire realizes what you're up to. My presence will make your visit legitimate." I could swear I heard him finish his sentence in my head with, "You idiot."

"Oh." Because, what else could I say? He only had our best interest at heart, and I really should stop being so suspicious of him. If he said it was all right, it probably was. "Okay then, I guess."

Constantine grinned. "Besides—the three of us on a road trip? Think how much fun it will be."

Yeah, he was hiding something, all right. All this cheer wasn't normal. "What's in it for you?" I asked.

"Just the pleasure of your company." His mocking tone and arched eyebrow didn't exactly vouch for his sincerity.

"And what else? Why come with? If you plan on hurting my parents—"

He slammed one hand on the table, making all of us jump. Outbursts were no more like him than cheeriness was. "I'm not planning on hurting anyone, you stubborn woman. I'm coming with, because you'll need me there."

I had no response for that.

Liza's face fell. "Can't I come with you?" Her big green eyes shone with unshed tears. She was really going to cry, because Constantine would be away for a few days? Or because he'd be with me?

But I had a boyfriend…who was glaring daggers Constantine's way. Oh-kay.

Constantine tugged at Liza, until she rounded the chair and faced him. "You know Carrie and Sally need you," he said, his tone grave. "*I* need you to stay behind and take care of our girls."

She preened at his show of trust, and I felt bad for her. I'd been there, ready to do anything for his approval. I hoped it ended better for her.

****

For all his outstanding qualities in and out of bed, Alex wasn't above snarking.

"So I ask nicely, but all it takes for you to agree is Constantine's permission. Good to know," he said with fake cheer, as soon as our bedroom door was closed behind us.

226

"Thought you got what you wanted." I turned my back to him, kicked off my slippers, and went to the closet in search of my sneakers. I'd promised Sheena I'd catch a late movie with her, and I'd rather focus on that than what Alex was saying.

"No. Constantine got me what I wanted. And you said nothing when he said you'd want him there."

"He said I'd *need* him there, and he's right. He knows our laws better than me, and he can protect us from the rest of the council. You were the one who thought talking to him about it was a good idea."

He shoved his hands in the pockets of his jeans and rolled his head from side to side. "Yeah… I'm being an ass. I'll call my mother and tell her we'll go by tomorrow evening. She can't wait to meet the girl I'm constantly talking about."

Oh, *goodie*. With or without Constantine's approval, the idea still held no appeal. "Isn't it too late for you to call her? Maybe you should do it in the morning and give her a couple days' notice."

"Notice for what? She'll just be making dinner."

My right sneaker was in front of me, but I couldn't see the left one. I crouched down and started rummaging through the shoes that littered the floor of my closet. "I don't know. *Notice.* Where is the stupid thing? Sheena will kill me if I'm late."

Sheena wouldn't say anything, even if I stood her up. She still felt guilty for being the one to introduce me to Willoughby, though she didn't know what he was at the time.

Alex walked up behind me, bent down, and closed his hand around the second of my shoes, as if by magic. "My mother's always ready for guests," he said, holding it out to me.

I grabbed it and squeezed my foot inside without bothering to undo and redo the laces. "Call her in the morning." By then, I might have found an excuse to avoid that get-together. With a quick peck to his lips, I rushed to the door. "We'll talk when I'm back. We're meeting the guy from the blood bank after the movie, so I'll bring some blood home. Maybe you can try it?" He still refused to drink human blood, saying vampire blood kept him sated for a longer period of time.

I believed he saw drinking human blood as the last step to no longer being human.

Fast as lightning, Alex pinned me to the door, his body hard against my back, his arms framing my shoulders. "I only want *your* blood," he whispered harshly, his face in my hair. His erection digging in my back was the least of my concerns.

"Okay, the mood swings? Not doing it for me. You go from mellow to seeing red in no time. Is something bothering you? If you want to talk about it, I can call Sheena and cancel." I prayed he said yes and finally talked to me about how he really felt about being a vampire. He'd told me how powerless he'd felt when Willoughby drained him—how he hated the fear and the nightmares that followed—but not a word about what he'd become.

He pumped his hips against me. "It's bothering me that you're not naked."

Trying to fuck issues away was my thing. Alex usually insisted it solved nothing. Seeing him resort to the same cheap trick raised a wave of anger inside me.

Let go," I said. "I have a show to catch."

He stepped back, and when I turned, his arms were up. Whether in surrender or resignation I couldn't say. Something clenched in my gut. His lack of a heartbeat wasn't the only thing different after his turning. I wanted to believe the rest of the changes I saw in him would smoothen out, as he got used to his new reality.

I pulled him down by his shirt and whispered, "Be good." Then I touched my lips to his once more and went to find my friend and ex-manager.

Chapter Three

The movie was nothing noteworthy, but mind-numbing and jolly was exactly what I needed for my head to clear. By the time the ending titles rolled, I'd decided to let things unfold as they would. I'd meet Alex's mother and bring him to my childhood home. My lifespan would be too long for me to worry about every little thing.

My stomach clenched at the thought of facing my parents, but I put on a huge smile. "You up for ice cream? I'm buying." Actually, Constantine was. Since he'd achieved council member status for something we'd both done, he was giving me half of the stipend that came with the position.

Sheena arched an eyebrow, her dark eyes glinting. "How very generous of you."

Pretending not to notice the sarcasm in her voice, I smacked her ass. "You want lobster, you got to gimme some sugar."

She kept a straight face, but I could see a grin tilting the corner of her lips. "Tempting though it may be, I'll have to refuse. Ice cream will do."

By now, we'd reached the ice cream stand. "One of those." Sheena pointed at the largest cups available. "I'd like two scoops of caramel and one each mocha and vanilla."

"I want a cone, straight up chocolate, please," I said.

The teen behind the counter asked if we wanted any toppings. I refused, but Sheena hid her ice cream under thick layers of whipped cream and added a cherry on top. How the woman remained slim was beyond me.

"You're a cheap date." I indicated her cup with a tilt of my head.

She shook her head, glossy black curls bouncing. "And you're using cheesy lines that send the feminist movement decades back. How you got not one, but two gorgeous vampires to fall for you is beyond me."

"They're old fashioned. I just smiled and nodded a lot."

"I see. Now it all makes sense. *Hey.*" She batted my hand away when I tried to pinch the maraschino that crowned her humongous dessert. "So, you and Alex are meeting the in-laws, huh?"

"Don't wanna talk about it." To stress how *much* I didn't want to, I stuffed my face with more ice cream.

"Wanna talk about how your new and old beau are disconcertingly civil with each other?" So she'd noticed too. If I were still human, those two would give me heartburn.

"Would such a discussion entail hypotheses of a future threesome with said beaus?"

She took her time cleaning drops of vanilla from her hand with her tongue. "I doubt it."

"Then no."

"Okay, you choose the subject."

I gave it a moment of consideration. It had been a long while since Sheena and I last had a girls' night out. Hell, longer since we'd been friends.

She'd shown up at the bakery I worked for when I first moved to L. A. and offered me a job. She helped me lose weight, managed my career, and soon became my only friend.

She'd also been the one to hand me and the three vampettes now living with us to Willoughby and his associates. She'd been afraid for her life, and her remorse was genuine. Since she'd moved into Constantine's mansion, she'd been doing her best to help the fledglings. I'd finally accepted her apologies, and we were rebuilding our friendship from scratch. That night in the city was supposed to help us bond over silliness—and possibly alcohol.

I didn't want to be a party pooper and ruin the fun mood, but I had nobody else to talk to. "I'm worried about

Alex," I finally said. "He insists everything is fine, but won't touch human blood."

"Isn't that a dietary choice?"

I shook my head. "It's more than that. It's like he resents having to feed off humans—which is totally rational, only he has to get over it at some point. I'm not saying he should go killer-sucker. I just wish he'd seem more at peace with his new nature. Being with him is like riding a roller coaster."

"Are we talking about the crazy vampire sex?" She stuffed a spoonful of caramel in her mouth, but not before I saw her smirk.

I glared. "I'm serious. Lately he seems ready to snap at the smallest thing, and I believe it's because he can't accept himself."

Her gaze softened. Lost its teasing edge. "And you feel guilty."

"And I feel guilty." I forced that new nature on him. He never had a chance to refuse it. Not having consented to my own turning, I hated that I hadn't given him a choice.

"My poor idiot." Sheena held her ice cream away from her body with one hand and pulled me into an awkward hug with her free arm. "You saved his life." I started to protest, and she shushed me. "So he's brooding a bit. Beats being dead. If he can't deal with his current existence, there are always exit strategies."

I pulled away. "I'm not killing him."

"I'm not saying you should. I'm saying he's a grown man who knows his options. If he doesn't feel like being the evil dead, he can take a nap on a park bench right before sunrise. That he hasn't so far means he's dealing. It'll take a while until he's fully there. Now let's go see Blood Guy and get home. I need to pee."

"You have such a way with words."

"It's a burden, but I carry it with elegance."

"Obviously. But maybe you should sit somewhere and wait for me? Somewhere with a ladies' room, so you don't have a little accident? The meeting place is more than a couple of blocks from here."

She shook her head. "Better idea—you fly me home, I make Margaritas and wait for you?"

"Only if you're sure you won't pee on me."

"Oh, shut up. I'm a lady."

Laughing, we walked into an alleyway, and I did my vamp-lift-off thing. It's really nothing more than willing your body to rise above the ground, but it only works if you believe you can win a fight against gravity, and not all of us are open-minded enough to manage it.

Sheena made a run for the bathroom as soon as we landed at home, and I took off again for my meeting.

****

Blood Guy, known to his friends as Frank, was a blood bank employee and my first success story in compelling. He was the first person I'd ever managed to use my vampire gaze on without turning him into a complete puppet or making him think I was crazy. In his mind, I worked for a hazardous materials disposal unit. I called, and we met behind the bank, where he handed over bags of blood that needed to be destroyed for whatever reason.

I'd only been using him sporadically in the years since Constantine had taught me how to feed from live donors without endangering them. With four fledglings to keep fed and happy, however, I'd recently added Frank's number to speed dial.

"You're late." He checked his watch, as if to make sure he had it right.

"I know. I'm sorry. You know how it is."

He nodded, though he had no clue how it was, or what *it* meant. He always nodded, because we always had the same dialog. I hadn't compelled him to greet me that way every time he saw me; I guess creating a pattern in our transactions reassured the rational part of his brain.

"You park close by?" he asked. "Bag is heavy." That too was part of our usual rapport.

"Round the corner." I took hold of the dark blue duffel he carried. "Thanks."

"Sure you don't need me to help with that?"

"Nope. Got it. Thanks again."

"See you next month."

I gave him a little wave and waited until he was back inside the building. As soon as I was certain I was completely out of his field of vision, I kicked at the ground and was airborne.

I entered the mansion from the basement and stowed the blood in the freezer Constantine had installed in the ensuite I shared with Alex. That floor housed our room, the gym, and the huge-ass bedroom and white-marble bathroom Constantine shared with the three fledglings, while the upper floors of the mansion boasted two living rooms, four and a half bathrooms, a kitchen, and a *parlor*—let alone Wesley's apartment. When I asked Constantine how come he didn't want a more livable basement apartment for the daytime, he said we weren't supposed to live during the day. Bleak, huh?

I pulled my red hair back in a ponytail, secured my annoying fringe to the side with a bobby pin, and rushed upstairs. The whirring of the Margarita maker acted as a homing beacon, leading me to the kitchen.

"I'm home," I said as I entered the room. "Bring on the booze."

"Thought you wouldn't be back till later." Alex leaned against the stove, arms crossed over his chest.

"Oh, hi. Yeah, didn't Sheena tell you? We decided to do the alcohol-binge part of the night here." I approached and rose on my tiptoes to plant a kiss on his lips. He didn't return the greeting. "Is something wrong?" I looked around. "Where's Sheena?"

"Needed to get something. Asked Wesley to drive her. She'll be back soon."

I took a step back. He looked tense, and there was some sort of menacing wave coming off him. His eyes seemed cloudy, like he wasn't really seeing me. I wanted to touch him but refrained. I'd never before felt unsettled in his presence.

Now it was as if he'd raised some sort of force field around him.

"Alex? Everything okay? Are you hungry?"

He shook his head and smiled, but the sense of wrongness was still there.

I wasn't afraid of him. He was my Alex. He was dealing with things his way.

I was relieved to hear footsteps behind me. "I heard the car," Constantine said. "Sheena is back, so let's leave the ladies to it, Alex. We can spar, if you feel up to it." He was training Alex to control and utilize his superhuman strength, but the two never let me watch.

"Yup, you should go," I said with false cheer. "I won't be too late. Wanna catch up on some girly stuff." And maybe shake off the weird feeling suffocating me.

Constantine placed his hand on the small of my back, and I let out a sigh. Whatever his reason for doing it, to me it meant he realized I was uncomfortable, and reminded me he was there for me. Little things like this made up for his snark and his occasionally sour disposition.

Alex grabbed the front of my shirt and pulled me to him. Before I could react, he closed his lips over mine and pushed his tongue into my mouth in a kiss that felt more like raw hunger than love. "See you in bed." His eyes were clear now, and the roughness of his voice sent goose bumps of the nice kind down my spine.

Lust and unease fought inside me, making my gut clench. "Yes, Mr. Caveman." Once I regained my balance, I turned and followed the two men out with my gaze, enjoying the view. Even the compounded yumminess of their broad shoulders and narrow hips didn't calm my nerves, though. Something had really been off there for a while, but as long as Alex was crazy about me, nothing was beyond fixing.

Sheena ducked inside. "Is it safe to enter now?"

"When wasn't it?"

"When male bravado had replaced the oxygen in the room." I arched both eyebrows, and she went on. "Remember how your beaus were insufferably polite to each other?"

"Yeah..."

"Well, you can forget it. Don't know exactly what they were talking about, when you dropped me off, but they seemed a heartbeat away from pulling their cocks out and measuring them—not that it'd be an objectionable sight, but you catch my drift."

"They were fighting?"

"More like posturing and staring each other down. I asked if we had fresh strawberries, and they all but growled at me. I found what I was looking for and started making our drinks, but then Alex pushed Constantine away, and Constantine grabbed him by the throat, and I had to sneak out and beg Wesley to drive me around for a while. Even the vampettes stayed away, and you know how they go gaga over topless Constantine."

"Constantine was topless?"

"Because that's what you need to focus on?" She flicked my ear with one long, lime-green fingernail. "Those boys are playing nice when you're around, but they need to realize they're both parts of your life now. Either that, or one of them has to stop being part of it."

I didn't want to think about the latter, but starting a conversation out of the blue about how they both meant a lot to me—*in different ways*—seemed stupid. "Maybe the field trip will do us all some good?"

"Field trip?"

"Ah huh."

"The three of you?"

"Yuppers."

Sheena cracked a smile. "You really are trying for that threesome, aren't you?"

Though it wouldn't be the worst possible outcome I could fathom, as far as the three of us were concerned, my hopes for the trip were simply that the two men in my life would do some bonding, and I'd get some peace of mind.

Sheena didn't seem very convinced when I said so.

The first Margarita mix had turned into watered down slosh, so we made a fresh one and proceeded to consume it with the fervor of college kids on their spring break.

****

Alex was already in bed, when I turned in for the day. The smell of his shower gel wasn't strong enough to disguise the smell of blood. His blood. I guessed his sparring with Constantine hadn't exactly been tame. Maybe that was good. If they resolved their issues on the training mats, everyday unlife would run more smoothly.

He turned and pulled me to him as soon as I was under the covers, and I let my body melt in his embrace. The alcohol I'd imbibed was sufficient to give my vampire constitution a pleasant buzz and dull my worries. "Are you okay?" I whispered. "Sheena said—"

"Shh. Sleep." He touched his lips to the side of my neck and tightened his grip around my waist.

I hugged him back, resting my head on his unmoving chest. "I can't. I'm worried. I know Constantine isn't your favorite person, and you certainly aren't his, but this is his place, and we need him." Alex tensed, and I ran my fingers along his brow. "For now at least. He's really not that bad, once you get used to him. What happened between the two of you today, anyway?"

"Don't worry about it." He caressed the side of my face. "It'll be fine. Now can we please get some sleep? I'm beat."

He hadn't exactly answered my question, but I felt hopeful. I kissed his collar bone. "'Kay. Goodnight. I love you."

"Love you too."

That was all that should matter.

Chapter Four

I woke up with Alex inside me.

He'd often used his mouth or fingers to tease me awake in the past, but never his cock.

Now I found myself lying on my stomach, Alex sliding in and out of my pussy in slow, deep strokes. I smiled. *The perfect wakeup call.* I tried to turn and look at him over my shoulder, but he twisted one hand in my hair and pushed my face to the pillow.

So we were playing rough. *Nice.*

I tilted my hips upward. The angle changed, and with it the friction. Alex's cock felt longer inside me. Thicker. Hitting all the right spots. I pushed back, urging him to go faster.

He slapped my ass. "Stop moving."

"Make me."

His grip on my hair turned punishing, and he began thrusting inside me hard. Too hard. I planted my hands on the mattress and bucked against him. "You're hurting me."

He pulled out, and I expected him to say something, but he didn't. Instead, I felt strings of cool cum shooting on my lower back.

I dug my nails in his wrist until he let go of me. "What the fuck, Alex?"

"I'm sorry. I must have lost control. Are you all right?" He touched my shoulder gently.

I slapped his hand away and rolled onto my back, not caring if I stained the sheets. "No, I'm not fucking all right. What do you mean you lost control?" It was then I noticed his gaze was unfocused. He seemed stoned. "What happened?" I asked, worry threatening to dilute my anger.

"I don't know. I'm sorry. I thought I was dreaming. Didn't know I was really…"

"You were dreaming of using me as a sex toy?"

He cast his gaze down.

"Was it even me?" Or had he been fucking someone else? An insane stab of jealousy sliced through me.

"I don't know, all right?" His voice was high pitched, infused with a note of panic. "Did I hurt you badly?"

"I'll survive. Just don't let it happen again." It felt too little. I had to say more. He'd fucked me like I meant nothing to him. Like he didn't care if it was me or any other hole there for him to take his pleasure. He'd made me feel small. Insignificant.

I wasn't sure I wanted to tell him he had such power over me.

He nodded, black locks falling in front of his grey eyes and making him look like a lost puppy.

"I need to hit the shower." And think. I needed to think. Something was wrong with Alex, and I had to figure out what before it was too late. I wasn't afraid of him; he'd stopped the moment I'd said he was hurting me.

Or my pain had gotten him excited enough to come.

No. This wasn't—

"This isn't me," he said, echoing my thought.

I hoped it was the truth and this wasn't a side of him he'd kept hidden until now. But if it wasn't him, who was it? Did it have something to do with my turning him?

I got out of bed and took the sheets with me to the bathroom. Wesley did the laundry, but I could at least shove it into the hamper.

I turned the water on and adjusted it to room temperature before getting under the shower jet. Even with the roar of the water in my ears, I heard the door open. The next moment, Alex pulled the curtain out of the way and stepped in behind me.

"I'm sorry," he whispered in my ear. "I'm so sorry. I never wanted to hurt you, Cherry."

"I know."

His hands slid around to cup my breasts, then down my stomach, doing nothing more than caressing. "I'll spend the rest of eternity trying to make it up to you, I promise."

Logic dictated I shouldn't be feeling safe in the arms of a man who minutes ago was out of control, but this was Alex. I was safe with him. He was going through a rough patch. I'd been there too, freshly turned against my will and having to adjust to an entirely different existence.

I sighed and turned in his embrace. Shit happened. If that was the worst of it, we'd be okay. "You won't need to try for that long. The next ten to fifteen minutes should do."

"Yes, Ma'am." He kissed his way down my body and spent the rest of the shower on his knees.

By the time we came out, I was squeaky clean, thoroughly pleasured, and much less worried.

Until Alex told me to get dressed, because we were off to meet his mom in a little over an hour.

****

I wouldn't suggest meeting your boyfriend's mother for the first time *after* you've died. It's practically a given that she'll find you too pale, and your hand will be too cool to the touch.

Well aware of it, while getting ready to meet Alex's mom, I'd made sure to feed so I'd at least raise my temperature for a while—which isn't to say I didn't worry on the drive to her place. And all the way from her driveway to her front door.

"I should have worn something more dressy." Alex had insisted my black skinny jeans and emerald-green silken blouse were perfect for a casual family dinner. At the time, I agreed. "Maybe we should reschedule?" I turned to look at Alex, who stood behind me as if to keep me from fleeing.

"Baby, I already rang the doorbell. Do you want us to make a run for it?" He tangled his fingers with mine and kissed the tip of my nose.

I opened my mouth to say *yes*, and then realized he wasn't being serious. "You're a meanie."

"Ah come on. You know you lo—Hey, Mom."

I swiveled around. The door was open, and a woman stood there studying us, a cheeky smile on her face. I liked her instantly. I'd seen pictures of her from fifteen or twenty years ago, but when Alex told me she was in her mid-sixties, I expected to see an old woman.

Mrs. Marsden appeared a decade or so younger than her real age. She was about my height, slim, and beautiful. She had Alex's midnight-black hair and steel-grey eyes, but I could see no other similarities between her and her son.

She wrapped her arms around Alex's neck, so she could plant a firm kiss on each of his cheeks. "About time you came to visit. I was arranging to take you off my will."

I winced. I was the one who'd delayed this visit.

Alex grinned. "You wouldn't do that. I'm the apple of your eye."

Mrs. Marsden turned to me. "See how he takes advantage of his poor old mother's love?"

Now was the time to say something smart. This was my only-chance-at-a-first-impression moment. "Old?" I asked. "But I thought *you* were his mom." *Nailed it.*

"Oh, I knew I'd like you." She beamed at me. "I'm Sylvia. Come on in."

I smiled, a weight lifting off my shoulders. Yes, it was still scary meeting my boyfriend's mother, but she wasn't trying to make it harder for me. "I'm Cherry. And these are for you." I offered her the flowers we'd gotten for her.

She took the bouquet and pulled me in for a hug, which I wasn't prepared for. The flowers were squished between us. I caught my balance and returned her embrace awkwardly, hoping my breath didn't smell of blood.

"Come on in. I've made meatloaf." She looked at me. "You're not one of those vegetarian people, are you?"

"Far from it." Alex squeezed my hand. I squeezed back, and we shared a smile. If only she knew.

"I love meatloaf," I said, and we followed Sylvia inside.

I hadn't been to the Marsden residence since the day after Alex's turning, when he and I had cleaned up the evidence of his death. I expected to feel repulsion being back there—expected the stench of his life's blood to assault my nostrils.

I was in luck. The only memories that came back to me as we crossed his mother's living room were of our first nights together. Having incredible sex in the armchair and falling asleep, still linked. Alex's first realizing I was a vampire. Spending the day following Willoughby's attack in each other's arms.

I inhaled deeply, wanting to breathe in all the scents that made this house part of the man I loved.

Meatloaf was a nice addition to them.

"I hope you don't mind eating in the back yard," Sylvia said, leading the way through the kitchen. "It's such a lovely evening. You can see all the stars."

"That's a great idea." I clutched Alex's arm. The back yard was where we'd burned the sheets he'd bled out on, but it was okay, because he was still here. With me.

Sylvia had set the table with a checkered red tablecloth that reminded me of my own mom. What was it with me and memory lane tonight?

I focused on the meat, and saliva pooled in my mouth. "Sylvia, this smells divine."

She smiled. "Good. Sit, sit. Alex, I forgot the wine. Could you get it? It's by the sink."

I took a seat and watched as Sylvia piled two thick slices of meatloaf on my plate, topped them with gravy, and added mashed potatoes and salad on the side.

"Dig in," she said. "You could use a little extra weight."

Yeah, I loved her.

Alex served red wine and sat opposite me, leaving the seat at the head of the table for Sylvia, who slid in it gracefully.

I tried to be lady like and not overload my fork, but I wanted my first bite to have a bit of everything. And it did. It was perfect—juicy meat, creamy mashed potatoes, and crisp lettuce with the perfect balance of seasoning, olive oil, and balsamic. A little orgasm in my mouth.

Sylvia chose that exact moment to ask, "So, Cherry, Alex tells me you used to model. What do you do now?"

I'm not going to tell you the food lost its flavor, but it certainly turned dry enough to stick in my throat. I coughed and hit my chest with my fist.

"She's doing some private investigating, Ma. And she's good at it." Alex handed me my wine, and I downed it in one gulp. I'd done private investigating *once*, but his version of things sounded better than, 'She's an unemployed vampire.'

"Right. I forgot that's how you two met," Sylvia said.

From what Alex had said, I seriously doubted she was the sort of woman who'd forget anything. She was being a mom and trying to find out as much as she could about her son's girlfriend.

"Are you all right, Cherry?" Her voice was laced with concern.

"I'm fine. Couldn't resist stuffing my mouth, and it went down the wrong way. But yeah, P.I. is me. It doesn't pay that well, but I meet interesting people."

Alex preened, and Sylvia laughed. "Any exciting cases lately? My son used to keep me entertained with police stories. I sure hope his leave from work doesn't last much longer."

It probably would. I could see no way for Alex to return to the force and manage to keep his undead status a secret.

"I'm sorry to disappoint, but I'm on vacation too," I told Sylvia. And I planned to stay that way for as long as possible.

"Yeah, we decided to take the same time off. Get to know each other better," Alex added. He wasn't as happy about it as he pretended to be, but work-talk was something he'd been avoiding. I was glad to see it didn't bring him down now.

As a matter of fact, he seemed more at ease than I'd seen him in weeks. It warmed me up inside and confirmed my suspicions. In familiar settings, he was still himself. The newness of his situation was what caused his change in behavior. All we needed was time.

"Well, that sounds promising. Do I sense commitment in the near future? Maybe a grandchild, before I'm too old to help raise it?"

"*Mom.*" Alex gaped. I could see my blood rising on his cheeks.

"Oh, shush. Cherry can tell I'm not going to be pushy about it. Can't you, dear?" She didn't give me time to answer. "It's just that Alex has been badly hurt in the past, and—"

"I'm not planning on hurting him, Sylvia. *That* I can promise you." But only that. I couldn't promise her a grandchild. Ever. I'd taken that possibility away from Alex. Adoption was an option, in theory. But even if we decided to go that way and managed to compel a court into believing we were fit parents, how could we bring a child into our lives?

Sylvia patted my hand. My gaze found hers, and in it I saw all the worries of a single mother who wanted the best for her son. I wanted the best for him too, but I wasn't sure I knew what that was.

Alex broke the awkward silence. "You wanted to meet Cherry, so I brought her—knowing full well you'd embarrass me. When am I meeting Mr. O'Connor?"

Sylvia blushed.

"Mr. O'Connor?" I asked, arching an eyebrow. Alex had told me about him, but I felt like joining in his teasing of his mom.

"He is…" Sylvia didn't seem to know to know how to finish that sentence.

"He's Mom's boyfriend."

"That's so juvenile, Alex. Don't call him that." Sylvia made a moue of distaste.

"Okay. He's your gentleman caller. Your love interest?"

She gave him a light slap on the shoulder. "Cut that out. I get it. You want me out of your business, or you'll butt into mine. Mr. O'Connor and I are seeing each other. Taking things slowly."

"Not too slowly, I hope. You're not getting any younger."

"*Alex.*" Sylvia and I said in one voice.

"What? No brothers or sisters, before I'm too old to help raise them?"

Sylvia threw her hands up. "You're incorrigible. Eat while it's still warm, and I'll try to keep the discussion to harmless subjects. Like the weather. How do you like the weather, Cherry?"

"It's lovely," I said, "and so is the food."

Once we were done with the main course, Sylvia brought out a platter of pineapple upside-down cake, which Alex and I gleefully obliterated. By the time she walked us to the door, Alex carried a tinfoil packet with leftovers for the next day, and I was utterly taken with her.

She was so much like my mom, I couldn't help but give her a hug on my way out, careful not to put any strength to it. "Thank you so much, Sylvia. It was a pleasure meeting you." Out of the corner of my eye, I saw Alex sigh in relief.

"The pleasure was all mine, hon. Now try to keep him good, you hear? And if he gives you any trouble, call me."

I gave her another gentle squeeze, and then stepped back while she and Alex said goodnight.

"That wasn't all bad, was it?" Alex asked, as he backed the car out of his mom's driveway.

"Nope. Your mom kicks ass. I'm glad you insisted we come see her." Also, it was fun having some time away from the mansion and its drama.

"Told you she'd love you. And I'm sure your folks and I are going to hit it off."

Why did he have to go and remind me of that? Trepidation trailed cold fingers up my back. "You sure I can't change your mind about that trip?"

"Positive."

"I think I may try anyway."

The look he gave me was nowhere near playful. "Knock yourself out. I doubt it'll make a difference. We're off, as soon as Constantine says we can go."

"We'll see." I opened the window a bit and gulped down an unnecessary breath of fresh air, steeling myself for what I wanted to ask him. "Alex, is there anything you want to—you know, talk about?"

"Like what?"

"Like, about how you'll never be able to give your mom the grandchildren she wants?"

"Can't say I ever gave that a thought before, either."

"Yes, but then you could, if you wanted to. Now you're a vampire. A freak of nature. No beach outings for you. No tanning. No Sunday afternoon barbeques. And no babies in your future. You're not gonna get to be a daddy." I was sad to ruin the lovely evening we had, but I needed to hear he was okay with the decision I'd made for him.

"Cherry, let it go. Sun exposure is bad for humans too. And I don't know if I wanted to be a father anyway."

"But I took the choice away from y—"

He hit the steering wheel with both fists, hard enough to make one side of it bend visibly. "Will you stop saying that? I *had* no choice. I was dying. *Dead.* Now I'm here, because you saved me. I won't get into this with you again, so get over it. I'm *fine.*"

I sat back and closed my eyes. If he was so *fine,* then what was with the outbursts? And why was he still refusing to drink human blood or have a serious discussion about permanently leaving the force? He wasn't fine. Not by a long shot. What I hated most was that I couldn't help him until he decided to open up. I could just be there for him and love him.

And introduce him to my parents.

Who'd spent the past six years thinking I was dead.

Fuck.

I tried to keep the thought at bay, but it still killed my good mood. When Alex asked if I felt like going for a drink, I told him I'd had an emotional day and would rather go straight home.

"Are you sure you're all right?" he asked when we reached the mansion. He pulled up to the entrance and tapped in the key code. The heavy steel gate slid open with a surprisingly faint sound, and we drove in.

"Yeah. I feel like spending the night in bed. Maybe I'll catch up on my reading."

Alex snorted.

"*Hey.* I do so read."

"Sure you do. So you won't mind if I leave you alone? I owe Constantine a rematch."

"You never told me why things were so tense last night," I said casually.

"I'm a sore loser. You know that." His chuckle sounded forced.

"I know. I just don't want there to be any bad blood between you and him."

"We're fine."

That was obviously all I'd get out of him on the subject. Maybe Alex wasn't the one to ask what had transpired. Good thing he wasn't the only one who knew the truth.

We walked to our room holding hands. It felt nice. I watched him put on his sweats and kissed him for good luck before he left to find Constantine.

Then I kicked off my high-heeled booties and flopped on the bed. I switched on the forty-two inch TV that hung on the wall across from me and let my mind be lulled by what passes for entertainment these days.

Chapter Five

Vampire hearing is about a hundred times more acute than human is. As with our sight, we're lucky we can regulate it, or we'd run the risk of bleeding eardrums.

Like, for instance, when a piercing screech and the banging of a door reverberated through the entire floor.

I jumped up and rushed out of the room, letting the ongoing cries lead me. Was it Sheena? Had something happened to her?

Had one of the vampettes snapped and attacked her for blood? Constantine was supposed to keep them in check. I rounded the corner to his room and saw Liza banging on the closed door.

"Sally, come out, and we'll talk about it," she said.

Nothing but wailing from the other side.

"What happened?" I asked.

Liza slammed her open palm on the door. "*Sally.* Don't make me break down the door. I doubt Constantine will appreciate the mess."

I wasn't surprised when she ignored me. Before we saved the girls from Willoughby and his cohorts, he'd convinced them I wanted to destroy them. Though they'd come to realize he was a creepy liar and a killer, and they no longer screeched in fear every time they saw me, they still didn't hold me in the highest regard.

Carrie leaned against the wall behind Liza, shaking her head. Her dark chocolate-brown hair was swept into a loose bun. I much preferred this hairdo to the Ádísa-inspired braid she used to sport. Carrie might still be a little wary of me, but at least she no longer idolized the woman responsible for her and her friends' deaths.

"What's wrong?" I asked her.

"Sally is being a brat." She rolled her eyes, but her full mouth was drawn in a thin line. She was worried. She and Liza were always protective of Sally, who was the most innocent and doe eyed of the three.

Liza turned to me now. "We were watching one of those makeover shows, and she flipped out. She doesn't want to be a vampire any longer."

"I don't," came Sally's voice from the other side of the door. "I'd rather die."

"Well, you can't do that in there, honey. There's no way to."

"I'll starve myself," Sally yelled.

"Get Constantine," I mouthed to Carrie, who nodded and took off toward the gym. To Sally, I said, "That will take a long time, and you know we'll get you out before then."

Liza glared. "Are you telling her to find a faster way to off herself?"

Was that what I'd done? I don't always do well under pressure. "Okay, don't open the door," I said to Sally. "Just listen to me for a few, yes? None of us wanted this. I don't know about Constantine, but nobody asked me if I wanted to die and become an undead chick, who can never drop a pound. Alex was brutally attacked and left for dead in his parents' house. I loved him too much to let him go, but I'm still not sure I did well to force this existence on him."

My voice broke, but I went on. "What happened to you was wrong and unfair, and I swear Willoughby will pay for it. He'll pay for what he did to all of us. But there are perks too, and you need to focus on them. Can you do that? Sally?" I listened, but only muffled sobs reached my ears. "Maybe we should break the door," I said and rattled the knob.

"Maybe you shouldn't." Constantine's voice came from right behind me. I turned and bumped into his very naked chest. Why did he and Alex have to spar topless?

Great. Now I had mental images of the two of them wrestling, glistening torsos rubbing together.

Of course, there was no sweat trickling down Constantine's pale abs. Vampires don't perspire. We drool, though, and I had to check myself, to make sure I wasn't doing just that. "Where is Alex?" My voice was cool. As cool as his skin, *that I was still touching.*

I looked up and met his gaze. His expression was flat, but there was a twinkle of mirth in his eyes. "He's doing his stretches, hoping he'll fall to the floor more elegantly next time I throw him across the room," he said.

My thoughts shifted to the way more appropriate image of Alex stretching, muscles rippling along the tan skin of his chest and back. Yum. Constantine and his state of undress no longer frazzled me. I'd just been caught off guard.

"Can you talk her out of there?" I pointed at the door.

Constantine nodded. "Sally? Can you please come out? I want to help you, but I can't, unless you let me know what's wrong." His voice was honey sweet and thick and intimate.

He spoke to me in that lover's voice a long time ago, but I never before heard him use it on any of the girls. I didn't know what happened between them behind the closed doors of his bedroom, but in my presence, he treated them more like beloved nieces. Though there was no mistaking the lusty looks the three gave him, all he seemed genuinely interested in was their well being.

Hearing him urge to Sally to talk to him, I realized he enjoyed more than their company. Did they all share his bed at the same time, or did they take turns?

So *not* something I wanted to dwell on.

"Sally, please open the door. You know I only want what's best for you, baby," Constantine said.

It felt weird hearing him call someone else baby, but there was no stab of jealousy. Good. My subconscious was catching up to reality.

Sally threw open the door and literally flew into his waiting arms. "We'll fix everything," he whispered into her hair.

We all heard.

"Maybe the rest of you ladies should give us some privacy?" Constantine said.

I reluctantly followed Carrie and Liza down the corridor.

"You coming upstairs?" Liza asked. "We got Wesley to order us chicken nuggets. You don't wanna miss his face when we dig in. The man prefers watching us drink blood than eat junk food."

Ruffling Wesley's feathers was always fun. The old human was always the epitome of decorum, though he had his naughty side. More than I liked the idea of witnessing his horror at our culinary faux pas, I was happy Liza wanted to include me. Maybe I was slowly becoming part of their group. It'd be good not to have to deal with their resentment while we shared a roof, and to be honest, I kind of liked them.

I smiled. "Sounds good, but maybe later. We just got back from a kickass meatloaf dinner."

She nodded. "Later."

Carrie threw me a finger wave over her shoulder, and they took the stairs up, while I headed for my room.

****

I'd changed into shorts and a T-shirt, when there was a knock on the door.

"It's open," I said, wondering why Alex would bother knocking.

Constantine poked his head in. "May I come in?"

"Sure." I had on more than I usually wore to bed, but I didn't want Alex to find me naked when he turned in for the day. Sally had seemed perfectly all right until her breakdown, and wondering if Alex was going down the same path put me off the mood for sexy times.

"Damn. You're dressed." Constantine pushed the door open all the way and sauntered inside, stopping by the foot of the bed. Lean and wiry, graceful and light-footed, he reminded me of a jungle cat zeroing in on its prey.

He only had his sweatpants on, and the way they hung low on his hips revealed there was nothing underneath but smooth, pale skin.

It was annoying how good he looked. I mean, I shared a bed with a gorgeous, chiseled man, who usually didn't bother with clothes around me, yet Constantine's body was nothing short of a work of art. Each curve, each angle, each line seemed perfectly thought of in advance, as though by a sculptor set out to carve the flawless male specimen.

And his every step showed he knew that.

Eh, at least he no longer frazzled me.

"How's Sally?" I asked.

"Better. I reminded her of some of the pros of being a vampire."

"Like stamina in bed?" My grin was genuine.

"No, you wicked creature. Like how she will never have to worry about wrinkles." He scratched his chest in a manner that was too sexy not to have been rehearsed. "This isn't why I called on you, though. I wanted to let you know we're leaving as soon as you're packed tomorrow evening. Alex is driving us, and I've arranged for supplies. Pack light, will you?"

I nodded. "Is this really a smart idea?"

"Packing light?"

"Stop acting obtuse—we both know you're not. If I do need to spell it out for you, though, do you believe visiting my parents is the right thing to do?"

He stepped closer and sat on the edge of the mattress, by my side. "I know this must be scary for you, but it's clearly important to Alex. If you don't think you can handle it, you only have to say the word. I'll tell him I changed my mind and won't allow it. But if you want to see your family again, and all that's holding you back is fear, I have your back."

"I know." A tightness grew in my chest, where my heart no longer beat.

"Perchance 'thank you' would be a more appropriate response? 'I don't know what I'd do without you' might also work."

"Yeah, yeah, you rock." I tugged at the end of his ponytail, the tightness giving way only slightly.

Constantine was the only vampire I knew whose irises changed color according to his mood. When they were the dark blue of the winter sea, I felt like he could see right through me. Now he narrowed his eyes and gave me that look from which I knew I couldn't hide. "We're going, then?"

"We're going."

"And you're happy with Alex?"

The question startled me. "Well, that was out of left field. Why wouldn't I be?"

"Just checking."

"Has he said anything to you? Is that what the thing last night was about? Sheena said the two of you were ready to go for each other's throat."

"That was nothing. Boys being boys."

"When the boys have the strength of bulldozers, it's not exactly nothing."

"He was setting his boundaries. It's inevitable in situations where two dominant males share the same space."

"So you don't think he's unhappy and lashing out?"

"He's not the one I care about." His irises swam with different shades of blue. I'd never seen them do that before.

"Constantine, don't…" What? Don't care about me? I'd already asked him not to, especially after the way things ended between us. It didn't seem to work.

He shook his head. "It's not something he said. He seems on edge. Constantly alert—ready for war, even."

"It's the cop in him."

"No, it's more than that. It's as if he knows something's coming, but doesn't know when to expect it."

"What's coming? What do you mean?"

He sighed. "I make no sense, even to myself. Ignore me."

Yeah, *that* would be easy. "I can't keep on ignoring things, Constantine. I've tried to wait out Alex's issues, because his world just turned upside down, but you don't have that excuse. Tell me what's coming."

He closed his eyes. When he opened them again, the swirl of emotion was gone. "I don't know. I swear. Alex seems to, however, and he's preparing for it."

There was the frozen fist clenching around my heart again. "I don't know what to do, how to help him. He says he's fine, everything is fucking *fine*, but I can see that's a lie. He won't feed except from me; he won't officially leave the force. It's as if he's trying to convince himself nothing's changed. Like he believes being a vampire is a phase, and he'll eventually outgrow it. I can't explain it any better."

"It must be his defense mechanism—how he's dealing with this transition. You know it's too big a change for someone to accept all once." His voice was soft, and I wished I could tell him how much his reassurances meant to me without leading him on.

"You're probably right."

"As is usually the case."

I smiled. "Wisdom comes with great age, after all."

"Yes, yes, I'm ancient. Ha-ha." He sobered. "Will you be all right?"

"Yup."

"And lightly packed by dusk tomorrow?"

"I'll try."

"Good." He kissed me on the forehead and stood. "Alex will be here as soon as he's done licking his wounds. I'm ashamed to say I wiped the floor with him."

"You're so not ashamed to say so."

"You're absolutely right." He gave me that bone-jellifying smirk of his, but something was lacking. Despite his smart-mouthed responses, his whole demeanor seemed more subdued than usual.

He was at the door, when I asked, "What are you keeping from me?"

"Nothing to do with Alex, I assure you."

Chapter Six

Alex was all smiles when he came back. Given Constantine had kicked his ass, his cheerfulness was surprising, until I realized Alex had to already know we were leaving in less than twenty-four hours. Part of me begrudged him for insisting on meeting my parents after I'd told him how awkward it would be for me. Another part was grateful I'd get to at least give them some closure. Those two parts fighting brought me as close to a migraine, as vampiricaly possible.

I watched Alex throw clothes into a duffel bag and tried to focus on how the muscles in his arms and back bunched and relaxed every time he bent over, and how his sweatpants stretched over his ass.

Even then, my mood wouldn't improve. "Can you at least stop whistling?" I asked.

"I'm sorry; I didn't realize I was." He seemed sincere enough, so I bit down on a bitter comment about his being off key.

"It's okay. I'm just antsy about tomorrow. I don't see any possible scenario, in which my parents don't freak out and call an exorcist, if we tell them the truth."

"We don't have to tell them everything, Cherry. All they need to know is that you're still around, seeing a great guy"—he made a sweeping gesture, encompassing himself head to toe—"and that you're happy. Any parent would be ecstatic to know their child is well and happy."

"Never mind that said child dropped off the face of the Earth for six years," I muttered.

"There are ways of explaining that. A drug problem, a cult, a spy career—"

"You're hilarious." Despite my sarcastic reply, I could feel a smile tugging at the corners of my mouth.

"Then wait till you hear my best idea yet." He mimicked the sound of a drum rolling. "You ready?"

"Doubt it."

"Alien abduction. How's that?"

"Brilliant. It might land me in the loony bin faster than the truth would."

He laughed and pulled me close for a kiss. His lips, soft against mine, were as effective in melting away some of my worry as his words were. "We'll figure it out. We'll figure it *all* out. Don't worry."

"Constantine said the same thing."

Alex stiffened, but only for a moment. "See? With us two, you have nothing to fear."

Yeah. Nothing. Except for the moment they turned on each other. "As long as you both play nice, I couldn't ask for better allies." I buried my face between his neck and shoulder, and let my fangs graze his skin. It was my way of showing him I wanted him, even in the midst of all the crazy.

"As long as you're in my bed, I've no reason to be anything *but* nice." I could tell he didn't mean it as a threat, but something in his tone rang a warning bell.

"And if I'm no longer in your bed?"

In lieu of an answer, Alex picked me up, shoved me against the wall, and wedged his hips between my thighs. When I opened my mouth to protest, he closed his lips over mine. It was nothing like his previous effort to reassure me. No soft pressing of lips—rather, sharp teeth and probing tongue. The hunger he poured into the kiss was frightening in its intensity. If I had a breath, he would have stolen it away.

He ground his erection against my mound and kneaded my buttocks with his palms. "Never gonna happen. You're mine forever," he said when he finally pulled back.

Lightheaded, I found my footing and straightened my shorts. I...didn't really have an answer to that. It sounded romantic, something a lover was supposed to say, but felt more primal than I was comfortable with. I forced myself to smile. "Let's finish packing. Before we start planning forever, we have to make it through the next few days."

"We will. You'll see. Your parents will be thrilled, and they're going to love me. And once we have their blessings, maybe we could move things forward. Make sure our relationship is going somewhere. There's no reason for us not to have a life, just because we're dead."

He was obviously in Lala-land.

When Constantine had been my sponsor—a sort of mentor the now defunct Vampire Social Services assigned to fledglings—he'd kept telling me eternity would make me see things differently. For the first time, I clearly got what that meant. Vampires aren't *people*-people. Our dietary needs aren't the only thing telling us apart from humans. Alex still didn't understand that. He thought we could play house indefinitely.

And I was burdened with the responsibility to show the man I loved that his life had changed a great deal more than he realized.

Sadness filled my heart. Had I lost too much of my humanity, or was Alex trying too hard to hold onto his? Instead of lingering on that and slamming reality in his face, I allowed him to pull me into his fantasy, where we moved into our own little place and got a dog and made friends with the neighbors. It was a beautiful daydream. Alex's eyes sparkled with more life than I'd seen in them since the night of his turning, and when he laughed at our imaginary dog's imaginary antics, I found myself joining him.

By dawn, my worries were at the back of my mind. We got into bed, and Alex cuddled me from behind. There was nothing sexual about his embrace. He held me, and I drifted off feeling safe and happy.

Until a deep growl snapped me fully awake.

I rolled to face Alex, but he was faster, pulling my body beneath his and pinning me to the bed.

I thought he was going for some kink, until I met his gaze. His eyes looked vacant. He dug one of his hands into the soft flesh of my stomach and squeezed my windpipe with the other. *Oh, God.* There was a monster holding me down, wearing my lover's face.

I clawed at his hand, raising bloody welts on the skin, but he wouldn't let go. Panic rose inside me. I was in no danger from lack of oxygen, but the way he balanced his weight on me was beyond painful.

I tried to call his name, wake him up—he *had* to be asleep; it *had* to be a nightmare; this wasn't my Alex—but could manage nothing more than a whisper.

I couldn't talk to him.

I couldn't scream for help.

Now that he too was a vampire, he outmatched me in physical strength like a two hundred and ten pound human man outmatched a hundred and thirty pound human woman. I could possibly toss him to the ground in a karate match, but couldn't fight him off when he already held me down. I kept trying to buck him off me anyway. Tears welled in my eyes, and sensory memory convinced me my legs had gone numb, though I rationally knew it wasn't possible for a vampire.

"Alex," I mouthed, "please."

I don't know if it was my silent plea or something else, but his weight was suddenly off me. He disappeared so fast, I couldn't follow him with my gaze. I heard the bathroom door slam shut. His voice came muffled from the other side. "Nightmare. What the fuck...? This isn't me. This isn't me. *This isn't me.*"

The desperation in his voice scared me more than his attack had.

I didn't know what to do. I wanted to put as much distance between us as possible, but the daylight held me captive in the basement, and I wasn't going to seek refuge in Constantine's room.

I didn't need to run or hide. Alex wouldn't attack me when he was fully conscious. He had a nightmare and fought back, not knowing it was me.

But my throat still hurt from his grip.

The water stopped running in the shower and another hour passed, before I realized Alex wasn't coming back anytime soon. I kept telling myself I was in no danger if he returned, but I couldn't relax. The thought of him getting back into bed while I was asleep sent a jolt of fear to my very core and kept me awake.

I couldn't be afraid of my lover. He never wanted to hurt me. It wasn't him.

Whatever his nightmares were about, they were messing with his head and they were messing with me. I thought of going to him and forcing him to come clean, but I was too much of a coward to confront him. Besides, I was sure I knew what he was dreaming of. It was his violent turning. Lying in his childhood bed. Bleeding to death.

All because he'd met me.

I didn't want him to talk about it, because I didn't want to hear him blame me.

I busied myself, unpacking and repacking our bags for the trip. Most of Alex's t-shirts were in dire need of better folding anyway. Being surrounded by his clothes, by his scent, gradually mellowed me out.

When he finally left the bathroom, the sun was down. He smelled of shower gel and deo, his hair was tousled to perfection, and his smile was wide. It was like nothing had happened.

He shouldered both our bags and held out a hand. The same hand that had hurt me. "Shall we?" His gaze was pleading.

I remembered him leading me out of *The Gridlock* the first time we met, his palm on the small of my back. His touch always made me feel safe, even when he was a human and physically weaker than me, and his long fingers gave me pleasure countless times.

I was beyond pissed that he'd pretend nothing had happened. I wanted him to come clean about his nightmares— or night-terrors, or whatever the hell he saw in his sleep that turned him into a savage animal. I wanted to smack some sense into him.

But I refused to fear his hand.

Promising myself I'd confront him as soon as we returned from our trip, I nodded and placed my palm in his. "We shall."

Chapter Seven

"But what if something comes up I can't handle? Sally may have another breakdown." Liza's voice was reasonable, but her gaze betrayed her worry.

I winced, the memory of Sally's sobs still fresh in my memory. Liza wasn't sure she'd remain focused on the perks of her newly acquired vampirism. To be honest, neither was I.

"Sally will be all right, and you'll have Sheena and Wesley here to help you. I'm sure you won't require any assistance, though. You're as capable of maintaining balance in the manor as I am." Constantine trailed his index finger down the perfect slope of her cheekbone and leaned down to place a lingering kiss on her lips. I'm pretty sure she sniffled when he broke away.

I averted my gaze, not wanting to intrude. It was odd, waiting outside the front door with Alex, while Constantine locked lips with all three young vampires. Wesley wrapped his arms around Carrie and Sally, and Sheena touched Liza lightly on the shoulder.

"It's okay. They'll be back soon," Sheena said.

Liza nodded and looked at me. "Call when you get there."

"Will do." I smiled. Our forced cohabitation was evolving into a tentative friendship, and I liked it.

Don't know how I'd feel if it were my house we'd all camped in, but Constantine didn't seem to mind the company. That wasn't the case from the beginning. When I'd sneaked Sheena to his place, to save her from Willoughby, Constantine had found her insufferable. He wasn't exactly thrilled when I'd volunteered him to take in the three fledglings either. Still, he'd offered Alex and me a place too, when we needed to lie low.

Of course, now he had a steady supply of lovers who didn't demand exclusivity, a verbal sparring partner in Sheena, an actual sparring partner in Alex, and... me. I wasn't sure where I fit in, but I was in no hurry to find out.

If anyone was to be bothered by the new living arrangements, it should be Wesley, who took care of everything and everyone, but he'd repeatedly commented on how brilliant it was having new blood—of sorts—enter the mansion.

Goodbyes exchanged, the three of us hopped in Alex's Chrysler. I rode shotgun, while Constantine made himself comfortable, sprawled in the back seat.

"Anybody feel like a snack?" he asked, tapping the portable fridge next to him.

"Cherry's brought her own," Alex said. "I'm pretty sure she emptied the kitchen cabinets on the way out."

"Someone's in a good mood," I muttered. It was going to be a delightful four-hour ride to San Luis Obispo.

Not.

Halfway there—about fifty miles from Santa Barbara—I was hungry for blood, on edge, and sick of Alex's running commentary on the scenic coastal route. He wasn't our damned tour guide. He and I weren't at a chit-chatty place. I didn't know what place we were at, but it felt cold and lonely. I was about to reach out and smack him in the mouth, when I caught Constantine's gaze in the rearview mirror. His face looked drawn, but the understanding in his tired eyes shocked me.

He gave me a tight smile and leaned his head against the window. "Alex, can you please shut up about the plunging mountain line and put some decent music on? We'll have enough talking to do when we get there."

Instead of snapping at him, Alex grinned and put on a CD. "Forgot you were probably around when the coastline formed, grandpa."

Constantine gave him a one-finger salute through the mirror, and rock music filled the car. I knew the song, but didn't lip-sync to it, like I usually did to protect the innocent from my vocal grandeur. Instead, I let it act as white noise, allowing me time with my thoughts. And my worries.

I had gone along with the men's plan because I loved Alex and wanted to do this for him. And I really loved the thought of seeing my parents again, after so long. On the ride, we came up with an amnesia story for why I'd fallen off the face of the earth for half a dozen years, but I wasn't entirely satisfied with it. It didn't explain why I didn't go to the police, who'd have matched me to my missing-person file, or why I wouldn't be able to visit during the day.

Right now, the best case scenario in my head had my parents ignoring my excuses, thinking I'd been kidnapped and brainwashed, and calling the police on Constantine and Alex.

Why had I waited this long to go back to them? Why had I followed the council's stupid rules? They were my parents. They loved me. Even if I told them the truth, they'd accept me.

Would they?

"It's all going to be fine," Alex said and let go of the gear shift to take my hand. "They'll be ecstatic to see you. Stick with the amnesia angle, and we'll be fine."

"If I hear the word fine one more time, I may scream." I shook off his grip.

"It'll be great. Wonderful. Amazing."

I snorted. Sure it would. I'd say, "Mom, Dad, I'm alive. I was in an accident that nobody heard anything about, then had amnesia, and now I'm here in the middle of the night, to introduce you to my boyfriend and my ex—who really has no valid reason for being here." Mom and Dad would hug me, and we'd all rejoice.

I sighed and let my head fall back.

Constantine closed his large palm on my shoulder. "We'll figure it all out. You deserve that."

Where was the snark? Where was the jackass, who cheated on me and tried to pass it off as natural for our kind? Or the pain in my butt, who had a comment about everything I said or did under his roof?

Why couldn't Alex and Constantine settle in their respective roles as doting boyfriend and calculating former lover, and stop messing with my head?

Because life would be way too easy, if they did.

"Either of you feel like a snack?" Alex asked.

"Not hungry," I said. I was famished, but we might as well get it over with.

"What about you, Cee? Care to sample the locals?"

Now they were on a nickname basis, and Alex was joking about feeding on humans? I wasn't sure I'd be able to wait till we were back to confront him.

"Nah. I'll bag it," Constantine said.

I turned to look at him over my shoulder, brow furrowed. "What did you say?"

He shrugged and pulled a blood bag out of the mini-fridge. "My new protégés come with an entirely new vocabulary. I grow old ever learning many things."

Protégés.

Not sex kittens.

Right.

Alex said something that sounded like 'soul on.'

"Huh?"

Whatever explanation he gave went unheard. I was too busy wondering why it bugged me that while Constantine and I had been together, I'd been the only one doing any learning.

****

It was well after midnight, by the time reached my home town.

"Can you give me directions to our hotel, or should I look it up?" Alex held up his phone.

"I know how to get us there," I said. "I… Maybe we should go straight to my parents' place?" Now we were close, I was getting antsy. I needed to see them. See they were okay. See their reaction when they realized I was back.

Feel their love.

For the four years since Constantine and I broke up, and until fate threw Alex my way, I'd been alone. My only concern had been to make it another day. Find another guy to feed on. Compel someone to cover my rent. It was a routine I'd gotten used to, and found hard to leave behind, when Alex barged in my life demanding truth and feelings and commitment.

Now I accepted there could be more to my unlife than eternally smooth skin. I had a man who loved me, friends, and a kickass place to call home.

I needed to know if I could also have my family.

"I can't say this is the best time for a visit," Constantine said. "We could unpack, maybe feed, and wait until sundown tomorrow?"

I shook my head. "If we don't go now, I'm not sure I can go at all." Anticipation and fear rolled inside my stomach in a jumble.

"Cold feet?" Alex squeezed my thigh.

I chuckled, no longer caring he'd been an ass. His touch reassured me. "That's putting it mildly."

"Lead the way, then."

I did. I gave him instructions all the way to the house I'd grown up in.

For the latter part of our trip, all I'd heard had been the growling of my stomach, but I forgot all about my hunger when I saw the freshly paved driveway. I'd walked, skipped, and sneaked along this driveway so many times.

We parked and got out of the car. The moment Alex slammed his door shut, a small light appeared on the first floor of the house, where my parents' bedroom window faced the street. My night vision kicked in when a dark shape formed behind the curtain. My mother stood there, and I could tell she looked our way.

I ran my fingers along the collar of my shirt. Maybe I should have worn something less casual than a shirt and jeans. Would Mom approve of my new hair? She always liked its natural blond, and this red was too fake.

Stupid thought to have. She wouldn't notice the hair. Her only daughter was home.

More lights came on. I rushed to the front door forcing myself to only use human speed. Alex fell back a couple steps, allowing me some space, but Constantine caught up with me and grabbed my forearm as I reached for the doorbell. I'd psyched myself enough to go through with it, and he cut me off.

I let my annoyance show on my face. "Seriously?"

"There's something you should know," he said, apparently unfazed by my glare. "I made a promise a long time ago. I tried to figure a way around it, but I couldn't break it."

"Just spit it out, please. Better yet, save it for later."

It was as though he didn't hear me. "Anyway, I haven't known for long, either. Only found out a week ago. After I joined the council, I did some digging. It wasn't easy. There was essentially no digital footprint."

Alex cleared his throat. We both turned to look at him. "You're rambling," he told Constantine. Constantine never rambled.

"I know. The thing is, it wasn't my choice to—" Before Constantine could finish his sentence, the door was thrown open to reveal my mom. Her hair was pulled back in the high, untidy bun she always favored. There were thin lines around her light brown eyes, and her roots showed her hair was really mostly grey under the chestnut dye, but other than that, she looked like I remembered.

My mouth went dry. What could I say? Hi? Greetings, human? Or maybe, I missed you?

I'm sorry?

I wouldn't be able to set foot in my family home without being invited in; my name wasn't in the deeds.

I stood there staring at my mother, my lips moving but not forming words.

She smiled, and her face lit up. "What took you so long?" she asked. I barely had time to register her lack of surprise, before she threw her arms around me and pulled me into a tight hug. Too soon, she withdrew and held me at arm's length. "You've lost weight. Looks good."

What the fuck? She hadn't seen me or heard from me in years, and that was the first thing she said?

I opened my mouth to voice my thoughts, but Mom let go of me and gave Constantine a kiss on the cheek. "I didn't dare contact you, after everything. Should have known you'd find her and bring her home."

Huh? I exchanged a perplexed look with Alex. At least someone looked more confused than I felt.

Constantine ducked his head like a shy school boy. "I'm so sorry, Kathleen," he said. "I didn't know she was your daughter until last week. I should have seen the resemblance, but the eyes threw me." The words were whispered, but I heard them loud and clear.

Was that the night of a million surprises?

"Yeah, she's got Greg's coloring," my mom supplied as coolly as if she were talking about the weather.

"Um, excuse me?" I lifted my hand in the air. "How do you two know each other?" What was happening? My ex and my mom seemed perfectly at ease around each other, like old friends. They better not have been anything more, or…

Yuck. I shook off the thought and focused on something else. If my mom had known Constantine for a while, she had to have noticed he didn't age.

"Is it—" Dad showed up behind Mom, pulling his robe on over his pajamas. His eyes lit up when his gaze landed on me. "It is you. Finally. Welcome home, Princess. Let me look at you. You're so beautiful. God, I've missed you." He tied his robe's sash, wrapped his arms around my waist, and twirled me in the air, like he used to when I was a little girl. "Ruby said you'd come back. Your mother was sure, but I missed you."

I was too shocked to ask what my mom's younger sister, Ruby, had to do with it all. I gave my dad a gentle squeeze, trying not to think of how I could twirl him far easier than he could me. "I missed you too. Lots."

"She's here now, hon." Mom patted his shoulder. "Come in, everyone."

She moved toward the kitchen, and I rushed after her. "What about you? Did you miss me?"

Someone—probably Alex—rested a calming hand on my back. I stepped out of reach. I didn't want to be calm.

My mom swiveled around, eyebrows arched. "Of course I missed you, sweetie. Why would you think otherwise?"

"Oh, I don't know. You haven't seen me in six years, and all I get is, 'Hi. Took you long enough. Yay, weight loss?' Don't you fucking care I'm back?" I felt like crying. For years I'd hated being unable to let them know I was still around. I worried they'd be devastated by my disappearance, and now she acted like I'd been on a planned vacation.

She gathered me close and kissed me on the forehead. "I care more than you'll ever know. I waited up for you every single night since your disappearance." I tensed before giving in. She still smelled like apples, cookies, and fabric softener, only a million times more intensely than she used to.

She smelled like home.

Unshed tears shone in her eyes, and I finally saw what my disappearance had cost her. "There's so much we need to talk about," she said. "We missed you like crazy, but we always knew you were all right. Let me get you all something to drink, and we'll explain everything." She gave me one of her trademark glares. "And mind your manners. No more using the f-word while you're under our roof; I didn't raise a punk."

I nodded and turned to the table, needing some space to compose myself. My gaze fell on Alex. He leaned against the kitchen wall, stiller than I'd never seen him before, and as obscure as his large frame allowed. I linked my arm through his and pulled him forward to stand by my side, happy when the dejected look slid off his face.

At the same time, my dad held out his hand. "We all seem to have forgotten our manners tonight. I'm Greg. My wife's Kathleen. Any friend of Gerri's or Constantine's is a friend of ours."

Constantine let out a low chuckle at the sound of my human nickname. I narrowed my eyes at him, and he gave me a wicked smirk.

Alex took Dad's proffered hand. "Alex. Nice to meet you." Not like he was surprised to hear what I was really called; he'd found my missing person report file, including all my personal info, the day after we'd first met.

Constantine made himself comfortable at the table. "Alex is Cherry's boyfriend. I have wanted to tell her everything since I found out, but couldn't until I contacted you. And of course your number isn't registered. When Alex insisted we visit you, I seized the opportunity to have you explain."

"Cherry?" My dad arched both eyebrows.

"It's what Gertrude goes by these days," Constantine said, before I could speak.

I wasn't little Gertrude Mosby any longer—hadn't been in a long while—and my new name was only one in a list of changes I'd have to fill my parents in on.

"I'll explain," I said, "but later. First, Mom, how did you... How do you know Con—"

Mom turned from the fridge, and the words died in my mouth, as I saw what was in her hand.

Three bags of blood.

I felt my jaw drop. "What's that?"

"Judging by the time, I guess...brunch." She looked at Alex. "You are like them, right?"

"I don't really..." Alex seemed at a total loss, which funnily was exactly how I felt.

"Alex is new. He isn't yet comfortable with our ways," Constantine said. "Your mother knows," he told me. "She and your father both."

No shit.

"I can't believe you didn't tell me you knew them," I hissed at him. "I thought you were done hiding things."

"I didn't hide it. I couldn't tell you."

"Don't blame Constantine. He promised to not tell a soul we know about your kind, and he's a man of his word," Dad said.

So yelling at my ex would have to wait. First I had to figure out if he'd compelled my parents into thinking him trustworthy.

Mom popped the bags in the microwave oven and set it for half a minute, before placing three mugs on the counter. "How about some tea, then?" she asked Alex.

"That would be great. Lots of sugar, please."

I let go of him and ran both hands over my face. "Okay, this is too weird for me. How did you know about me? About us, in general?"

Dad pulled out chairs for us all, and Mom handed us the filled mugs. "I'll tell you everything. Sit. Drink." She fleetingly caressed my cheek, her touch tender as ever, grounding me.

I took a seat and cupped my drink with both hands. I didn't know what I'd hear, but my world would never be the same again. Hell, it had already changed. I'd just found out I'd wasted years I could have spent with my family, for no reason. They knew what I was. I wanted to blame Constantine for it, but I believed he hadn't known sooner.

Alex sat next to me and placed a hand on my shoulder. I rubbed my cheek against his knuckles and steeled myself for whatever truth was coming my way.

Chapter Eight

"I—I don't know where to start." Mom gave us a watery smile.

"Try the beginning." Dad winked at her, and they shared a look that made me happy deep inside. Whatever else had changed, my parents were still as perfect a couple as I remembered them being.

She nodded. "When I was five, back in Ireland—"

I frowned. "In Ireland?"

"Yes, I grew up there."

"How come I never heard of that?"

"Really not what you should be focusing on, honey." Mom shook her head. "A month after my fifth birthday, to be exact, my mother and I were attacked on our way home from visiting a friend. My mother shoved me behind her and begged our attacker not to harm me. The woman completely ignored me, but went straight for my mother's neck. It was after sundown. I remember her opening her mouth, and her canines gleaming in the moonlight, long as my pinky. And I remember my mom collapsing and blood spurting on my good dress."

"A vampire?" I whispered.

"Not just any vampire," said Constantine. "It was Ádísa."

"You know her?" Mom asked me. She looked horrified.

"I did, Mom. She was… She had me turned." Mom gasped, and I clasped her hand. "She can't hurt any of us anymore. Constantine took care of her for good."

Tears shone in her eyes, and she mouthed a silent thank you to him.

Constantine shook his head, as if killing his maker was nothing worth mentioning. "She was set on having your grandfather as her consort," he said to me. "When he wouldn't cheat on his wife with her, Ádísa decided to simply eliminate the competition. My maker always was a sore loser."

That was unbelievable. "Ádísa was after grandpa Geoffrey?" And grandma Ross had won? I cheered inwardly for the woman I'd never met.

"She had already tried to seduce him, but he wouldn't leave us," Mom said. "I never found out whether he briefly gave into her advances or not. My mother never said. Maybe she didn't know. Anyway, Constantine witnessed the attack and heard your grandma cry that she didn't want to leave her baby girl—me—an orphan. He…"

"I turned her," Constantine said flatly. "I was no innocent. I'd done my share of indiscriminate killing, both as a human and as a vampire, but she… I couldn't let her die on the side of the road, covered in dirt, with her toddler watching."

"You turned Cherry's grandmother?" Alex sounded both incredulous and furious. I covered his palm with mine, and he sat back, but he was obviously still on edge.

"My grandma was a vampire? And you were her maker? Why didn't I know this sooner?"

"I told you"—Constantine sounded impatient—"I had no idea you were her granddaughter. I didn't recognize your family name."

"But you knew my dad. You must have known his last name."

"Listen to the whole story, and you'll understand," Mom said. "The important thing is he saved her."

I stared at Constantine. He returned my gaze, unfazed by my scrutiny. Every time I thought I had the man figured out, he showed me another side of himself. As he'd done a couple months back, when I thought he'd betrayed me for Ádísa, only to watch him behead her—his own *maker*—to save Alex and me.

Or maybe he wasn't all that chivalrous, and my grandma had been even better looking than Mom told me. Aunt Ruby was supposed to look a lot like her.

"Hold on." I looked at my mother. "What about aunt Ruby? How was she born? She's almost six years younger than you. Was grandma pregnant when Constantine turned her? But then she couldn't have— How…?"

Mom and Constantine exchanged a look. To me, she said, "Stop interrupting. We'll get to that."

Hard as it was, I managed to keep my mouth shut. I'd keep my questions for when they were done talking. I had no doubt there would be more things to ask by then.

"After I turned your grandmother, I took her and your mother to your grandfather and told him the truth about what I was. What his wife had become. I gave Geoffrey a choice. He either helped me keep her turning a secret, or I told the council about her, and she disappeared from her family forever. To his credit, Geoffrey wouldn't give up on the woman he loved.

"He helped me keep her in the basement and feed her, until she tamed her hunger and could fend for herself. Then I helped her, your grandfather, and your mother relocate to London. We stayed in touch as they kept moving to a different city every five years or so, to avoid people asking questions. Your mother met Greg, who was visiting family in Cardiff, and soon she was pregnant with you."

"Greg and I got married first," Mom interjected.

"Yes, yes. Everything was done properly, of course. Anyway, once Geoffrey passed away, things changed."

"Oh God, please tell me you didn't sleep with my grandma."

He smirked. "I always loved my women feisty."

My horror must have shown on my expression, because Constantine laughed. "I never saw her that way, and I'm sure she never thought of me as anything other than a friend. What I was going to say was that, with Geoffrey gone, nothing kept your grandmother on that side of the Atlantic. When Kathleen decided to follow your father back to the States, your grandmother came too, and we decided to sever all ties between us."

"We trusted Constantine, but phone calls and letters leave a trail, and we didn't want to take any chances," my mom said. "Three months after you were born, we moved here and changed our family name."

"I didn't see either of them since and had no clue you were Kathleen's daughter when I met you. I'd still have no clue, if Ádísa hadn't made that comment about the women in your family," Constantine said. "It was then I started looking into things. Your grandma managed to steer clear of our vampire registry, since she wasn't turned in the States, and your parents stayed off the grid. It took a lot of digging before I found out you were Ross's granddaughter. Or, I should say, Ruby's granddaughter."

Ruby's granddaughter? "Aunt Ruby isn't your sister?" I asked Mom. My eyes felt about to pop out of my skull.

She shook her head.

Alex draped an arm around my shoulders and squeezed my arm. I more than appreciated his silent support.

"She's your mother?" I asked. "Ruby is Grandma Ross?"

Mom nodded. "She changed her name to Ruby after my father died. Said she wasn't the same person any longer."

"Well, fuck."

Dad laughed at mom's glare. "The girl got a shitload of family secrets shoved down her throat. Let her deal with it her own way."

I didn't see how he could make light of it. "Nobody thought to tell me all this before? I mean, *you knew vampires exist.* People in horror movies die all the time because they don't know the paranormal is out there, and you knew and didn't warn me?"

Dad's face fell. "We thought we were protecting you by keeping you away from that world."

Yeah, that hadn't backfired at all. I bit back the sarcastic retort when I saw the pain in his eyes. He and Mom did what they did out of love, and Constantine kept his mouth shut out of loyalty to them.

Their noble intentions didn't make me any less upset, but they did make me less verbal about my feelings. My head was spinning. This was all too much. Ádísa had attacked my grandma before having me turned. My former boyfriend was my grandmother's maker, as well as a family friend. I took a sip of the blood and made a face. It was cold and tasted of anticoagulant, yet I found it easier to swallow than what I'd just heard. I decided to take things one at a time.

"Aunt—*Grandma* Ruby visited in the middle of the day. How come she walked in the sun?"

Constantine's head snapped toward my mom. "She did what?"

Mom nodded again. "She has a secret brew that makes her tolerate sunlight. I keep a few bottles of it around, just in case. I've added it to your blood and Alex's tea, but it needs about three days of steady consumption to start working for more than a couple hours at a time."

Alex switched into detective mode before our very eyes. A determined look descended over his previously perplexed expression, and he let go of me so he could lean forward. "She has a secret brew? She came up with it herself? Is she a chemist or something?"

Mom shook her head. "Herbs. I've seen her mix them, but didn't recognize any, and she wouldn't share the recipe with anyone. Not even me."

That muscle on his jaw ticked. "And have you tested the limits of the brew? How long do the effects last at a time, once it kicks in?"

It was obvious he had more questions, but Mom held up a hand. "I don't know how she came about it, but she did. It was long after we moved to California. She returned from one of her trips in the middle of the day. Any testing that was to be done, she did herself.

"Anyway, she needed to stay below the radar, since your vampire council didn't know about her turning and she didn't know what they'd do to her if they found out. Trying to be prepared, she began keeping tabs on the council members. She keeps her vampire life away from the family, so she never let me in on how she does things, but she eventually managed to hack into the VSS archives and began recording new turnings."

This was incredible. "My grandma has solved the sun-allergy issue *and* is a hacker?" Ha. Coolest granny ever.

Constantine chuckled.

My mother cupped my chin, and the tenderness in that small gesture filled some hollow part in my chest. "She saw your birth name come up. Your father and I were devastated, but she convinced us it only meant we'd get you back eventually. When she tried to get more information on your whereabouts, she found the system had crashed."

"Yeah, the VSS was shut down soon after my turning," I said. It had been one of the consequences of my turning, actually. The old council, who'd established it, was overthrown by those protesting my semi-public turning. The new council members—including the two serial killers with world-domination aspirations, whom Constantine and I had dealt with—had decided to ban all new turnings. Without new fledglings, there was no use for the Vampire Social Services, the sole purpose of which had been to help newbies get used to their new life. "That's where I met Constantine. He was my sponsor."

"We had no idea. Your grandma never found out where you were. I've been waiting to hear from you since."

"Oh, Mom." I turned and buried my face in the crook of her neck, drinking in her familiar scent that I'd always associated with safety. When I raised my head again, I had to blink back tears. "I wish you hadn't killed Ádísa," I told Constantine, "so I could rip her head off myself."

He rubbed his temples, and I felt a pang of shame. Whatever else his maker had been, she'd been his near-constant companion for centuries, and he'd killed her for me. I owed him not to discount that sacrifice.

"So first grandma gets turned, and then I do. What are the odds?"

My mom let out a forced little laugh. "It's not just you two. I'm the only lucky one, I guess."

"Why do you say that?" Constantine asked before I could.

"My own grandma disappeared before I was born, but there were rumors she'd been slaughtered by a beast," my mother said.

Huh. The women in my family seemed prone to brutal attacks. When Constantine had proven his loyalty to me, not her, Ádísa had asked what it was about women in my family. My gaze locked with Constantine's. There had to be something there. But what?

Mom yawned, and I realized it was way too late for the humans among us. I sighed. Delving further into my family's past would have to wait one more day. My life was shaken enough as it was. Maybe I could spend the downtime raging at Constantine for keeping all this from me. His promise had been necessary to keep my parents safe, but I was no threat to them. He should have told me. And I really needed to yell at someone.

"Look at the time," I said. "We better get going. The hotel Constantine booked is close by, so we can be back here right after sunset. We'll pick things up then."

"Nonsense." Dad stood and pushed his chair back. "You're staying here."

"Dad, there's no room for us."

"Actually, there's a bedroom and extra pullout sofa in the basement," Mom said. "And we've installed a small bathroom. It's a little cramped, but you should manage for a few days."

The choice seemed as out of my hands as my unlife apparently was. I gulped down the rest of my blood, trying not to taste it, stood, and left my mug in the sink. "Well then, I guess we're staying. We just have to get some stuff from the car."

"Alex and I can fetch that," Constantine said.

"I'll help the boys. You ladies go make the beds." Dad kissed me on the forehead. "Goodnight, Princess. I'm so happy to have you back." He was so adorable, I didn't tell him *the boys* would probably need no help carrying the entire car.

"'Night, Dad. It's good to be back."

Mom wrapped one arm around my shoulders and led me down the hall. "You know," she said, tugging on a strand of my hair, "red really is your color."

It really was good to be back.

I'd been shocked and disconcerted—and was still more than a little pissed off at everything the people in my life had been keeping from me, but I was ultimately happy to be home.

Mom kept the subject light while we made the double bed. She told me Dad made her a small vegetable garden in the back yard, and how she'd love to have a cherry tree, but the climate wasn't right. I let the sound of her voice caress my ears. It had been forever since we last chatted about little, everyday things. It was so comfortable and soothing.

"Are you taking the sofa, or are you and Alex sharing the bed?" she asked, when we moved to the pullout.

There went the easy chitchat. "We live together," I blurted, smoothing an invisible crease on the bottom sheet. "All of us. Well, not *that* way. I mean, Alex and I live together *that* way, and there's also Constantine and three young vampires. And my friend Sheena."

"Is that all?" Mom was completely expressionless as she tucked in the corners.

"And Wesley. That's all."

She sat on the bed and pulled one corner of the light summer blanket on her lap. "Is it… Is it an actual relationship? Constantine has explained about vampires and polyamory."

"What? Oh, God, no. *No.* It's Constantine's place, and Wesley is his butler." I went on to explain the circumstances that lead to us all sharing a roof, and soon I was telling her about Alex's insistence we meet each other's parents.

"Oh, he introduced you to his mother? Things are serious, huh?"

I resisted the urge to say 'deadly.' "Pretty much, yeah. I don't know if he and I have the same ideas about the future, but we're as in love as can be."

Mom smiled and let out a rushed breath in what could only be relief. "So you're happy."

I sidled up next to her, so I could feel her warmth. "I am, Mom. And I'm so happy to see you and Dad again."

She placed a butterfly kiss on my temple, and I felt her smile.

Chuckles from the upper floor reached my ears. "The boys are back. You should go to bed."

She nodded and squeezed me, before getting up. "See you tomorrow, Gerri."

I didn't correct her. She needed to know some things hadn't changed, and if calling me by my old name helped, I'd play along.

****

"I swear to you, the only reason I didn't tell you was my promise," Constantine said when the humans of the house went to bed. "You have to believe me, but I understand if you don't. I've betrayed your trust before." His kicked-puppy look was as effective as Alex's.

My anger deflated. There was no use yelling at someone who didn't fight back, so I chose my next words carefully. "I get why you did it, but I still don't like it. I'm asking you one last time—is there something else you're keeping from me?"

"Yes." He didn't hesitate.

"Are you fucking serious?" Alex took a step toward Constantine, but I stopped him with a hand on his stomach.

"I want to know what it is," I said.

Constantine nodded. "Give me twenty-four hours to check the validity of my information, and I'll tell you."

"Twenty-four hours," I said. "And you never keep things from me again." I wanted to add 'or else,' but had nothing to threaten him with. I had to trust he didn't want to disappoint me again.

I had to trust a lot of things those days.

Constantine bid us goodnight and said he'd call home and let everyone know we were all right.

Alex got frisky as soon as the bedroom door was closed behind him. I didn't share his enthusiasm. Not with everything we'd found out.

Not with Constantine *not* sleeping right outside.

"My parents," I whispered. "They'll hear."

"I'll be quiet as a mouse." There was that smirk again—the one I didn't like. I'd never seen it on human Alex's lips. Constantine assured me we didn't lose our soul when we turned. I certainly felt the same person—if a little more street smart—but that nasty curving of Alex's lips made me wonder if that rule was universal.

Well, hello, paranoia. Constantine and my parents had hidden things from me, and now I was suspicious of everyone.

"I still feel weird," I told Alex. "I haven't set foot in this house in years, and I get laid the first time I visit?"

"That's not what bothers you." He undid my buttons so fast, I didn't realize my shirt was open until he peeled it off me. "You don't want *him* to hear."

I was too emotionally drained to get into a fight about his stupid jealousy. I framed his face with both palms and slanted my lips over his. "I don't want *anyone* to hear. I don't want an audience when we make love."

He undid my jeans and shoved them down with his knee. "You didn't mind an audience when you were in porn."

"And we're done here." I pushed him back hard enough to make him stumble and pulled my jeans back up. I told him about my past from the beginning, and he accepted it. I gave nobody the right to judge me for my choices, much less someone who claimed to love me. "You and Constantine can share the bed. I'm taking the sofa." I was so furious, I'd have sent him packing right there and then, if I didn't believe he was dealing with some sort of identity crisis.

Still, that excuse was wearing thin.

He got in my way, puppy eyes at full force. "I'm sorry, baby. I didn't mean it. It was supposed to be nasty-sex-talk. I guess I went overboard."

"You did."

"Forgive me? You know I love you."

"I know." But I wondered what his definition of love was these days.

He pulled me against his chest and kissed me gently on the lips. "We both know I've got the foot-in-mouth syndrome. Apparently dying doesn't cure that." He laughed, but I wasn't amused.

"Listen, Alex, I'm tired. I need to rest, and I need to figure out how to deal with everything. I'm really not in the mood."

He ran a hand down my spine and cupped my ass, oblivious to how genuinely angry I was. "I could try to get you in the mood."

"No."

"Sure?"

"Positive."

"Damn."

"Yup."

"Can we at least cuddle? And maybe I could have some blood?"

I couldn't say *no* to that. I burrowed in his arms and let him feed from my neck, until exhaustion got the better of me. "I need to be horizontal ASAP," I mumbled.

Alex tenderly licked his mark, then lifted me and carried me to bed. He dug in our overnight bag for my t-shirt and pair of shorts that acted as pajamas, and helped me into them. "Sleep tight," he said, spooning me from behind. "I'm here. Won't let anyone hurt you."

It sounded like an odd thing to say, since we were no longer on the run, but I was too tired to give it much thought.

Chapter Nine

Not used to keeping a human time schedule, I lay in bed for hours, staring at the wall and wondering if anything in my unlife was what I believed it to be.

I'd suspected before that Ádísa had issues with my family, but my grandma and me sharing the same fate had to be significant.

I already knew my turning hadn't been at random. A couple months ago, Constantine had confessed Ádísa had instrumented my turning and arranged for him to become my mentor. She ordered him to make me fall in love with him, and he was very successful in his mission.

Although he also fell for me and claimed he still loved me, she managed to seduce him while he and I were still together. I broke things off, and Constantine tried to get me back for years, before Ádísa's promises of power made him return to her side. That was when he found out about her role in my turning.

In the end, he chose me.

I remembered Ádísa threatening him with a sharpened stake for helping me.

"What is it with the women in your family, Cherry? No matter. Your allure worked against you this time. It got you where I wanted you. It's such a pity Constantine will share your fate, but maybe I'll get to keep your new friend."

She'd meant Alex, and I had no doubt she'd have gone for him too, if Constantine hadn't rid the world of her vile presence.

Alex tossed and turned beside me. Nightmares again. I couldn't blame him. Just weeks ago he was viciously attacked and left for dead. I thought I lost him, despite giving him my own blood.

Until Constantine brought him back to me.

"I really did and do love you, Cherry. I'd do anything for you, including sit back and let you be happy with a human." At the time, Constantine was playing the long game; Alex's life was finite, while my ex and I were immortal.

But Alex wasn't human any more, and Constantine was still letting me be happy with him.

Thinking of it was more taxing than thinking of Ádísa, so I steered my thoughts back to her. Assuming the rumors about her having been a Valkyrie—or as old as one—held merit, Ádísa was already ancient by the time my great grandmother was attacked. Too old to obsess about a woman she met a hundred-odd years ago.

Maybe I should look into our family tree. Go back further.

My vampire inner clock screamed that the sun was up, but I couldn't wait until the evening. Waiting is the thing I do worse. I even iron better than I wait. I sneaked out of bed, wrapped a blanket over my shoulders, and flew upstairs. Dad was gone for the day, but Mom was up and about, and she hurried to shut the drapes as soon as she saw me.

"Gerri, you shouldn't be up. The potion hasn't started working yet."

"I couldn't sleep. And please call me Cherry, Mom. I'm not the girl I used to be." My voice broke, and her hand trembled as she adjusted the blanket so it covered my head too.

"Big bad vampire or not, you'll always be my baby girl."

I could spare a few moments to be just that, so I burrowed into her embrace and stood there, listening to her heart beat. I hadn't realized how much I'd missed this. It had to be one of the reasons the council forbade fledglings contact with family members. Seeing my mom, having her hold me, reminded me of all I'd lost. Because of Ádísa.

She was no longer around, so I was going to find Willoughby and turn him to dust for the life he'd taken away from me.

I don't know how long Mom and I held each other, but when we let go, I felt an inner peace I hadn't experienced in a while. "I need your help," I said. "I need to figure out how far back Ádísa's thing for our family goes. What caused it."

"Hell hath no fury like a woman scorned," my mother said.

"All this, because Grandpa didn't choose her? If she was the one who attacked your grandmother, there had to be something before that. Do we have any old family photos? Notepads? Anything you can dig up? Maybe we could ask au—Ruby?" I couldn't really call her Grandma.

"She's in Europe for the next few months. She calls me every few days, but I can't reach her in the meantime. There are some boxes in the attic I've never gone over, though. I think I remember her lugging them around every place we've been."

"The attic it is, then."

She shook her head. "No curtains up there. You better stay here, while I go get the boxes."

I raised the edges of the blanket, forming batwings. "Nah, I'll brave it."

Mom smirked. "I haven't dusted in a while. There could be cobwebs."

Scary-ass vampire or not, I won't approach a spider, if I can avoid it. "I'll wait right here. You take your time."

She laughed and pinched my cheek. "I see immortality hasn't changed *some* things."

"Nope, spiders are still on the top of my phobias list."

"Good thing you have a good man to squash them for you now." Mom winked.

"Yeah, I'm lucky." I smiled, but my eyes stung.

"Uh-oh. What's wrong, honey? You seemed fine last night."

Mom could always see right through me. Even over the phone, she could tell when something bothered me, which was why I'd only been calling her sparingly once I'd decided to get into adult movies. I hadn't known what to say if she asked me about my career, just like I now didn't know what to tell her about Alex and me. Only this time, I wasn't afraid she'd disapprove of my choices. My fears and worries were too vague to be put into words.

"Nothing," I said. "This whole Ádísa mystery is stressing me out. Can you please get the boxes now?"

"Of course. I'll be right back." She kept stealing worried glances at me on her way up.

****

The boxes weren't a couple. They were eight, and one of them was as tall as me.

Mom got hold of an old hooded robe, and we replaced my blanket with it for ease of movement, before I followed her back to the attic. The robe was thick, but made no difference to me temperature wise, since vampires emanate no body heat. I pulled the hood up, kept my head down, and followed my mother's feet around the cluttered space, praying there'd be no spiders. With the two of us working together, it still took several trips up and down the stairs.

We began going through the boxes one by one, but their contents were in no order we could discern. In the end, I emptied them around us in messy piles. I could see the annoyance in my mom's gaze. She said nothing, but I knew her inner neat freak was having a stroke.

"I promise to put everything back myself," I said. "And I'll vacuum."

"Good." She heaved a sigh. "Now let's see what we have here."

For three long hours, we waded through old, faded pictures and frayed documents. Of the ones with dates scrolled on them, the oldest seemed to have been written sometime in the 1440's. The month and last digit in the year were nothing more than smudges on the fragile parchment, but I had no idea what was written on the legible parts of the note either. "I think it's in Italian."

"We can have Constantine translate it." Mom plucked it gently from my fingers. "Seems to be a letter to a Francesca."

"Was she our ancestor?"

She shrugged. "I don't know. Doubt Ruby would either, this far back, but I'll ask when she calls."

It made no difference either way. I found more notes and letters in the same writing and stacked them neatly one on top of the other, without bothering to look at them twice. As I lifted the tenth one in a row from the mess around us, a separate piece of paper fell from inside it. As large as my open palm, it landed face down by my foot.

Milano, 1447, it read on the back. I flicked it over and saw a drawing of a woman. It was a portrait, and not a very detailed one. The hair was pulled back, and she showed too little cleavage for what I'd known of Ádísa, but it could totally be her. I searched the drawing for a signature or name. Nothing but the place and date.

"I'll get Constantine. He might know where she was around that time," I said, shedding the robe. The sun was low enough by then that I no longer needed the extra cover, and the basement had no windows anyway. On the way down, I thought of waking Alex too, but maybe some rest would make him less confrontational.

At the entrance to the basement, I froze. Constantine was sprawled on the pullout, an arm over his eyes. The sheets only covered the bottom half of his body, and the part that was visible was naked. And smooth. And pale. And perfect.

Admiring beauty wasn't cheating, I told myself, but I still didn't let myself gorge on the sculpted abs and pecs, or the broad shoulders. What I focused on was his face. I hadn't seen him so serene in years.

Then again, I hadn't watched him sleep in years, though it hadn't been all that long since I'd last seen him naked.

"Constantine," I whispered, "we found something you need to see." No response. "Constantine?" I leaned in and lightly touched his arm.

Eyes still closed, he flipped onto his stomach, driving the covers lower and exposing the top half of an exquisite—and very naked—ass. I trained my gaze to the ceiling. I hated his habit of sleeping naked. Couldn't he have worn underwear for once? I considered going back up and having my mom fetch him, but that'd be an entirely new level of awkward.

"Is there some specific reason you're here at this ungodly hour, or are you just admiring the view?" His voice was muffled by the pillow.

I didn't take the bait. "You really need to get up. Have to show you something we found."

"Go away."

"No, seriously. You have to come with me."

"If I get out of bed with you here, I'll get accused of indecent exposure. What's more, I'm quite certain your boyfriend won't appreciate my reminding you what you've been missing."

I could say Alex's cock was just as big as his, or I could be a grown up. And damn it, it was a hard decision. "We found a drawing that might be of Ádísa. Do you know where she spent the 1440s? And wasn't there a war in Milan around that time? I think I remember something from The Borgias, but I was never good with dates." Naked asses make me ramble. Deal with it.

"What are you on about?"

He began to roll over, but I turned around before I saw more than a girl in a monogamous relationship should see of her ex. It didn't help much. I still recalled every detail of his naked body from his last attempt to seduce me, right after Alex and I got together. It didn't work then, and it wouldn't work now.

"Mom and I have been going over old family stuff. We found a drawing of a blonde woman, along with some letters. They're in Italian, but I looked for her name. She wasn't mentioned anywhere."

"That's because she was going by Adalgisa back then. I think I remember her being in Italy for part of the 15th century, but not exactly where. It's not as if we could Skype back then."

A rustling came from behind me, then springs creaking, and finally the sound of a zipper.

"You decent?" I asked.

Constantine heaved a sigh. "Constantly. Whether I want to or not."

That was true. He'd been way more decent than I'd had the right to expect him to be. He'd opened his mansion to Alex and me, never made a pass at me, and now joined us in this family-reunion-turned-quest-for-answers-to-an-age-old-mystery.

"You know, you're a good guy, deep down," I said and led the way up.

"It's a burden I carry with style."

Chapter Ten

I watched Constantine's face for a reaction, when my mother showed him the picture we'd dug up. All I saw was curiosity, while he perused every line. In the end, he agreed the woman on the picture could be Ádísa and spent the next hour and a half poring over the letters we'd decided were from that time.

"Nothing." He set yet another letter aside and readjusted his long, blond ponytail. "These are all from a gentleman named Mario to his young wife, Francesca, telling her how hard being apart from her is and how he longs to hold his daughter in his arms for the first time. I expect his wife is an ancestor of yours?"

"Your guess is as good as mine," Mom said.

I pursed my lips. "Probably, for the letters to have ended up here. You didn't find anything weird in them, Constantine? Anything about a seductress trying to have her wicked way with him?"

"Nothing of the sort. I'm sorry." He looked sorry. Sorry and sleepy. "Wait. This is in different handwriting." He tilted his head to the right, narrowed his eyes, and leaned in to snatch the corner of a letter, barely visible beneath a pile of similar pieces of paper.

I should have noticed. Mom and I watched, as Constantine's expression grew cloudier with every line he read.

"It is from Francesca's mother, telling Mario her daughter was found dead. Savaged by what they believed to be a large animal."

"Ádísa. Has to be her. This goes too far back. Do we have a family name? Something that could help us figure out if Francesca belonged to a branch of our family?"

Constantine shook his head. "She only signs as, *Your Bereaved Mother in Law.*"

So we knew Ádísa might or might not have been responsible for the death of a woman who might or might not have been our ancestor, six hundred or so years ago.

Which amounted to zilch.

"I got you out of bed for nothing, huh?" I asked Constantine.

"It appears so." He scowled. "But I may actually be able to help after all. Kathleen, is there a computer I can use? One with an internet connection?" I raised an eyebrow, and he chuckled. "Being a council member comes with certain…perks."

My mom led us to Dad's study room and logged on the computer. The perk Constantine had in mind turned out to be the council's database, complete with detailed profiles on all USA-registered vampires. Finding Ádísa's file wasn't hard, but the first entry on it was in the 1700s, when the first vampire governing body was put together and began issuing laws.

"Shit," I said, perching on the edge of the desk. "Is *nothing* easy with this woman?"

"Some things used to be." Constantine smirked.

I made a gagging sound.

"There's only more thing we could try, although I'm not sure what you're after," he said. "Assuming it was her, what good will knowing for sure do?"

"Try it. I want to find out how far back her grudge goes," I said.

"Went," he said.

"Huh?"

"How far it *went*. She's gone now, Cherry. Maybe you should forget about her and focus on spending time with your family. Soon you'll be able to go out during the day. Think of that and stop wasting energy on someone who's no more than dust."

"You're right, but I can't. I won't relax until I know why she hated us so much. Besides, Willoughby is still out there. How do you know they don't have the same agenda?"

"Willoughby?" Mom asked.

"My maker," I said. "He's Ádísa's childe and helped her with—with everything."

"About that…" Constantine's face darkened. "I told you there was a sighting. Go get Alex. He should hear this too."

"He should hear what?" Alex's voice came from behind me, and I snapped my head up. I hadn't realized how close to Constantine I'd drifted, until I saw Alex's gaze go from one of us to the other.

"I was waiting for confirmation, so as not to unnecessarily upset you, but it's official. Willoughby has been spotted in the area. Just two blocks from here, in fact," Constantine said flatly.

"What the fu—" I cut my question short at Mom's glare. "What the hell, Constantine? He might have come after my folks. Why didn't you say something sooner?" He and Alex were set on testing my limits. Couldn't a day pass without one of them driving me nuts? "You didn't think I might need to know that?"

"You had enough on your mind. I did not want to add to it."

I pretended not to notice Alex's smile. It wasn't as important as the realization I'd been making the same mistake over and over, allowing the two of them to think I needed someone to protect me. I couldn't blame Constantine for not knowing better. When we got together, I was a fledgling who depended on him for everything.

It was up to me to make sure he understood things had changed.

"New rule," I said, locking my gaze to his. "Now on, nobody makes my choices for me. You don't decide if I need to know something. If it concerns me even remotely, you tell me and let me deal with it. Is that clear?"

"I'm not reckless." Constantine scoffed. "I had people watching, ready to interfere and let me know if he reappeared."

I kept staring at him.

"Cherry—" He sighed. "We're clear."

Alex was still smirking, when I turned to him. "That goes for you too."

He nodded.

"Constantine, you said you had people. Who? We have vampire spies near my parents' house?"

"And humans," he said.

"Can they be trusted?" Alex came up next to me and draped an arm casually around my shoulders.

"Yes."

"Why are humans aware of our existence? Why do we have the whole stupid rule saying our families shouldn't know vampires exist, if there are other humans who do?" I asked.

"They're bite junkies." Constantine saw my questioning look and elaborated. "A sort of adrenaline junky, only with a more specific hit. They love the danger of having a vampire at their neck, as much as the euphoria brought about by controlled blood loss. They're usually among society's castoffs, willing to do anything for a fix."

"And you trust them?" I couldn't believe my ears. "Addicts aren't the most reliable sources."

"That's why the council doesn't take action against their existence. Because they lack credibility, they do not really pose a threat to us."

"And where do they say Willoughby is now?" Mom asked.

Constantine shrugged. "I have all my contacts in the area looking for him. He won't stay hidden for long."

"But the fact that he's here could mean Ádísa's issues with my family aren't in the past. Not really," I said.

Constantine huffed. "Let me pursue that alternate avenue I mentioned earlier."

So pretentious. I rolled my eyes, but didn't comment. Whatever his methods, he usually yielded results.

And he was hot—which didn't matter, because Alex was hot too, and I loved Alex. Solely.

Constantine left the room, thumbing the screen of his phone. I was tempted to eavesdrop, but held back. Now he knew I didn't need a protective bubble around me, I trusted him to come clean about whatever his call entailed.

Eerie silence, thick and heavy, filled the living room. Alex watched me quietly, which made me fidget. I fidget when I'm nervous, and his gaze unnerved me although I'd done nothing wrong.

"Sleep well?" I finally asked.

"Not enough." He looked around. "Must be the new surroundings."

Mom looked from one of us to the other. "Tea?" she finally asked Alex. "Or are you going back to bed?"

He beamed his most adorable smile her way. "I'd love a cup, thank you. Don't think I can sleep again. I'll come help you, and you can tell me embarrassing stories about Cherry's childhood."

Sneaky was the word that came to mind. I didn't like thinking that about Alex. He was simply being nice to my mom and seizing the opportunity to get to know her and me better. I'd have done the same in his shoes. It didn't mean he wanted to pick her brain without me hearing.

Constantine reappeared, a deep vertical line furrowing his brow. He seemed more contemplative than upset, as he tapped his phone against his palm, then slipped it in his back pocket. "That was Hui Zhong," he said. Hui Zhong was one of the two scariest council members. She'd been turned near the end of the 1800's and had gone on a spectacular killing spree before getting a grip on her hunger. You wouldn't know it to look at her China-doll appearance, but she was rumored to have been deadlier than the plague, back in the day.

"She said she knew nothing more about Adísa than we do, but she'll ask Gheorghios and call me back."

I resisted the urge to make a face. As scary as Hui Zhong was, Gheorghios was worse. Vicious and quick to anger, he always seemed to me like the kind of man to slaughter first, ask questions later. Then again, appearances can be deceiving. The council member I'd trusted most, Johnny boy, had been Ádísa's cohort, while Benjamin, who'd always made me uncomfortable, had turned out to be nothing more than a grief-stricken father looking for his daughter's killer.

They were both dust now, with Benjamin's position in the council taken over by someone I'd never met, and Johnny-Boy's by Constantine. Ádísa's spot was still open, and I prayed it'd get occupied by a peace-loving, knitting old lady who preferred watching cat videos on Facebook to plotting world domination.

"What exactly are you looking for?" Alex asked.

"More on Ádísa's past," Constantine said. "Anything to indicate what brought about her resentment for this family and whether Willoughby is planning to continue pursuing whatever nefarious plans she had."

"Sounds solid." Alex nodded. "Kathleen and I are making tea. Want anything?"

"I wouldn't mind some blood, if it's not too much trouble."

"None at all."

And there we were in Lala-land again, with the boys playing nice and creeping me out.

"I'm going to take the boxes back upstairs," I said. I used full vampire speed to stuff the contents back inside, then took my time carrying them to the attic.

Dad got home, and we all did our best to have a normal dinner, with Mom being extra chirpy and bubbly as she filled him in on the night's events. She'd cooked her signature pot roast with baby potatoes and accompanied those with a salad I didn't even glance at.

"Lucky we don't have to breathe between bites." Alex chuckled, and I realized I was wolfing my food like I'd starved for weeks.

"I've taught her not to play with her food." Mom batted his shoulder playfully. He answered with a boyish grin, and I liked that their short time together had brought them closer. It was important that my mom really like him.

I washed my bite down with some blood and daylight-serum combo. "I'm sorry, but this is so good. Better than I remember." It was the truth, but might be due to the enhancement of my senses more than to my mom's cooking skills—which were generally indisputable.

"It is delicious indeed. Kathleen, do I detect a hint of rosemary?" My ex, the foodie, ladies and gentlemen. I didn't listen to my mom's reply, too busy helping myself to a couple more slices of meat.

"Leave room for dessert," Dad said. I picked up chocolate chip cheesecake cupcakes on the way."

My favorite. I smiled. He smiled back. We all wore similar expressions of joy, as the conversation slid to a halt.

My expression was forced. I couldn't enjoy my lovely dinner, when there was so much we didn't know. So much we might have to deal with. I was convinced the lynchpin to the mystery was Ádísa's connection to my family. Once we figured that out, everything else would fall into place.

I sighed and decided to bite the bullet and ruin the faux-pleasant mood. "We should—"

Alex cut me off. "I don't want to be the party pooper, but I was thinking. About all of this." The shift in conversation seemed sudden, but the way he squeezed my knee said he understood I needed it.

To my mother, he said, "I know we're going by the theory that Ádísa was the monster who killed that lady in Italy as well as your grandmother, but why would she have spared you? If she had something against the women in your family, why not kill you too, when she attacked your mother? The connection is too flimsy. I'm afraid you could be seeing too much into things."

Constantine nodded. He swallowed his mouthful and wiped his lips with a napkin before he spoke. "That's a good point, Kathleen. Have you caught sight of her since she attacked your mother?"

"Ádísa would be hard to miss," I said, the roast going rubbery in my mouth. "With her height, long blond hair, usually mostly-exposed bouncy breasts, and her legs for miles—"

"You sure *you* didn't lust after her?" Constantine asked.

"I just got to take a good look at her," I whispered. "You know, when she was naked underneath you?" That shut him up.

"Thank you for the graphic description of her attributes"—Mom either didn't hear the last part of my comment or chose to ignore it—"but it wasn't necessary. I could never forget her. Haven't seen her since she turned Ruby, though."

That was weird. Not counting Francesca, who had lived and died centuries ago, Ádísa had apparently gone after my great grandma, my grandma, and then me. Did her attacks have some intricate pattern? Why would she have skipped one generation?

Alex held up his index finger. "I may be feeding into the paranoia here, but what about the men?"

"What about them?" I couldn't tell where his detective brain was going with that.

"Ádísa had issues with the women in your family, but what about the men? She was after your grandpa, right? Then she tried to get your ex. And succeeded." I didn't appreciate the reminder of Constantine's infidelity any more than I appreciated Alex's self-satisfied smirk. "Maybe she's after your men."

Our men—not only mine. "Dad, have *you* seen her?"

"I'd think I'd remember a tall, blonde warrior princess." Dad kept his gaze to his plate.

"Unless you weren't meant to," Constantine said.

I turned a questioning gaze to him.

He wiped the corners of his mouth with his napkin. "Humans can be mind-wiped."

Only not always perfectly so. Another vampire could bring the hidden memories back.

"Can you make him remember?" I asked.

Constantine nodded. "It's relatively simple. We can do it now."

Dad sat upright, fork still in hand. "Not sure I like the idea of you poking around in my head, trying to dig up memories that probably aren't even there."

Constantine's gaze softened. "Greg, you said you'd think you'd remember a tall, blonde warrior princess."

"Yeah, so?"

"Nobody said she was a warrior." Constantine arched a blond eyebrow.

My dad sucked in a breath, tension practically oozing from him. After a heartbeat, his shoulders sagged. "Do it. I'm ready. Whatever you need."

Before Constantine could work his mojo, Mom grasped my father's arm. "Tomorrow," she said. "I know we need to do this, but not now. We're having a nice family dinner, and Ádísa is dead. This can wait." I didn't blame her for stalling.

"No," Dad said. "We do this now. If this woman did something to me, I want to know."

Mom nodded in defeat, but Alex spoke up. "If you met Ádísa, whatever she made you forget wasn't pretty. Keep your blissful ignorance one last night. Enjoy the evening."

I squeezed his hand. "Alex is right. Eat up, I heard something about cupcakes. Then you go to bed, and we'll clean up in here. Maybe go for a walk after. It's a beautiful night."

Mom agreed with a sigh of relief, and she and my father soon left for bed. My parents still didn't have a dishwasher, but doing the dishes using vampire speed was a piece of cake for the three of us. Sadly, it lacked the sense of calm I used to get from menial labor in my human days.

"Let's go get that air," Alex said, as soon as the last glass was wiped dry and replaced in the cupboard. He tugged at my hand. "You coming, Cee?"

"I think I'd like to be alone for a while," Constantine said.

"See you later then. Call if you need anything; we'll be right outside." Alex went for the door, pulling me after him. I'd come to dinner barefoot, and didn't bother putting on my shoes as I followed him out the door.

Chapter Eleven

Outside, Alex asked, "You want to fly, don't you?"

I did. "How'd you know?"

"You're fidgeting. I know what you look like when you want space." He gave me a half-smile. "And you tend to take off, when normal people would take a stroll."

I ran a finger down his chest. "What about you? You hate flying."

He shrugged. "I don't have to come with, if you need to be by yourself. I can drive around, or do some after-dark hiking. Maybe visit the National Forest."

I loved him even more for being so understanding. "You sure you don't mind?"

His mouth found mine, and he nibbled on my bottom lip. "You need your alone time. I get it. Just be back by four, or I'll come after you." He narrowed his eyes in a mock-villainous scowl.

"Thank you." I kissed him again. "I love you."

"I know." He smacked my ass playfully. "Now go. Worry that pretty little head of yours till you're satisfied, then come back to me."

"Always." I let him walk to the entrance of the driveway, before I took off. I had no destination in mind. Just needed to feel the cool night air against my skin. And avoid dealing with my feelings.

At least I was practically a pro at the latter.

I ended up perched atop Agape Church. Agape means love in Greek, my father told me when I was a kid. For a long while, I'd thought I'd never have love in my life again. Now I did. I had Alex. I had my family back.

I had Constantine.

I should be feeling a lot happier than I was. Yes, horrible, unimaginable things could come up tomorrow, but my parents wouldn't allow the past to ruin their relationship. I shouldn't either. Only, I couldn't stop wondering why Ádísa had gone after my grandpa, possibly my father, and then Constantine.

I couldn't stop wondering how much of Constantine's betrayal—the betrayal that had broken us up more than four years ago—had really been his fault. And if it had been some kind of maker juju Ádísa had put on him, had he really been in love with me since we first got together? And was he still?

The past sucked. Most importantly though, it was over and done with.

I let myself slide down the shingled roof and fell to the ground, loving the rush of adrenaline despite the certainty I'd land on my feet.

The earth squelched under my bare toes, moist with the anticipation of rain. I decided to make a run for it.

I reached my parents' house well before four, but Alex was waiting for me outside. I jumped in his arms and bit the side of his neck. I grazed the skin, and the taste of his blood awoke a new hunger in me. I didn't want to feed; I needed to reestablish our link.

"I want you," I said.

"What about your parents?"

"We don't have to go inside. There's a shed in the back."

"And Constantine?"

Any answer I gave would be wrong. I closed my lips over his, to shut him up. I couldn't think about Constantine when I was about to make love to Alex. I dragged him to the shed and undid my jeans with one hand while pulling at his fly with the other.

"I need to be rough," he said.

"I want you to."

He bent me over a pile of logs and shoved my jeans down to my knees. A harsh tug, and my panties were gone. The night air caressed my pussy, and then Alex drove inside me all the way to the hilt. I dug my fingers in the wood. Splinters bit at my skin, and two of my nails broke, but I didn't loosen my grip. They'd grow back in the morning, and I needed the pain. I relished it. Physical pain took my mind off my emotional turmoil.

Alex withdrew and plunged inside me again with enough force to make me lose my balance and scrape my legs against the logs. I could smell blood from the tiny cuts. It turned me on more. "Faster," I growled.

He found a punishing rhythm that soon had me crazy with lust. The first drops of rain pattered on the roof, the sound not loud enough to cover that of Alex's flesh slapping against the back of my thighs.

My pussy throbbed, my head felt light, and I was ready to fall off the edge, when Alex bit down on my shoulder, over my t-shirt. The bite was savage, tearing fabric and skin alike, but it was what I needed. With the first couple of pulls of my blood, he sent me spiraling toward my climax.

I was still floating, still fluttering around him, when he used his hands to rip the shirt open wider so he could lick the wound closed. "You're mine, Cherry. Say you're fucking mine."

The rain started in earnest, and the ground smelled of new life. One of my favorite smells. "I'm yours."

"*Not his.* You're mine." He swiveled his hips and began thrusting faster. Deeper.

I tried to adjust my position, uncomfortable now that the afterglow of my orgasm was fading. Alex grabbed my hair and pulled my head back, straining the muscles in my neck. "Not fucking his." He spat each word out.

I didn't need to ask who *he* was. "Yours."

He buried his fangs in my throat and sucked until my legs felt weak. Then he pulled out of me, and I felt his cum drench the tattered remains of my top and my exposed back.

My body was sated, but my mind was reeling. For all the niceties and buddy-routine, Alex felt threatened by

Constantine, and his jealousy was affecting his behavior. That was what all the mood swings were about. Sheena had been right. He and Constantine were only civil to each other because they had to be. My parents' obviously liking my ex didn't help matters any.

Worse, I didn't know how to change that.

All I could do was keep showing Alex he was the only man in my life.

It'd be easier if that were the case.

Feeling dirty and guilt ridden, I let Alex help me to my feet and drape his own shirt over my shoulders. Arms around each other's waist, we walked back to the house and to the ground-floor bathroom, where we had a quick shower together. We tiptoed to the basement like naughty teenagers on a school night, making sure to remain completely quiet as we passed by where Constantine slept.

Safe within the confines of our bedroom, I trailed my fingers along the wound on my throat. It was already healing, but still throbbed. It felt out of place.

I didn't bother with pajamas, and neither did Alex. We lay back to back, but our feet touched. At some point, I heard Constantine say goodnight. I hadn't realized he'd been awake when we'd sneaked past him.

Alex didn't seem to hear, and I didn't answer. For all Constantine knew, I'd already gone to sleep.

Chapter Twelve

A knock on the door me woke me up, and I realized I was ravenous. I did a mental check of my state of dress and made sure Alex was covered.

"Come in," I said.

Constantine pushed in the room, holding a tray with baked goods and three steaming mugs. "It's ten past sunset," he said. "Kathleen brought us breakfast."

I nudged Alex, until he opened his eyes. "Food," I said and sat up, gesturing for Constantine to come closer.

He approached on Alex's side of the bed and handed him the tray, then lifted one of the mugs to his lips. "Whatever the secret ingredient is, it makes blood taste even crappier than the anti-coagulant does," he said. "How is it in tea?"

"It tastes a bit like sage. Or old oregano." Alex shrugged. "Not that great either way."

My mouth was already crammed with chocolate-filled pastry.

Constantine snatched a croissant. "Finish up and come find us in the living room. Your father is back. We're ready."

That almost made the chocolate goodness lose its yumminess. I had to take another bite to get it back.

"We'll be right up," Alex said.

We finished eating, emptied our cups, and got dressed.

Alex came up behind me and caressed my back. "It'll be all right," he said. "Whatever your dad remembers is in the past. She can't hurt any of us now."

I knew he was right, but I still dragged my bare feet to the comfy couch I'd spend a big part of my teenage years on.

"Good morning," I said to my parents, though it was evening. I'd done that before too, after a late night out with my friends. I sat in the corner of the couch and pulled my feet under me. The comfy pillows hugged my body as if I'd never left, and for a moment it was as though the past six years of my life had never happened.

Only they had.

My father was in his favorite armchair. He looked a little pale, but smiled. "Let's see what I've forgotten," he said.

Mom stood next to him, holding his hand. "It'll be fine. Whatever it is, it'll be fine."

Constantine set one of the dining room chairs opposite my dad and took a seat. "Look into my eyes, Greg," he said. His voice had that deep, unearthly quality it got when he was enthralling someone.

Dad raised his gaze, and his face went slack.

"Greg, no matter what comes out of this, remember you are not to blame."

My mom bobbed her head in agreement. Having seen what Ádísa was capable of, I hoped she really believed it.

"You're not responsible for the things she made you do," Constantine said. "Will you remember that?"

"I'll remember," my dad replied in a flat, lifeless tone.

"Now focus on my voice. You and I are the only ones in the room. Nothing you say will hurt the people you love. Be completely honest. Have you met the woman we talked about yesterday? The tall blonde?"

"Ádísa."

"Yes. Do you remember meeting her?"

"I"—Dad's face distorted in agony—"don't know."

"She's told you to forget her. Forget everything that has to do with her, hasn't she?"

My father groaned.

"You're hurting him." My mother sounded scared. I jumped to my feet, but Alex stood and took her free hand before I could. I sat on the floor between them and Constantine, and smiled reassuringly at my dad. I wasn't sure he saw me, but I wanted to believe my proximity offered him and Mom some comfort.

"It's okay for you to remember," Constantine said. "You're allowed to. You're safe now. Tell me about meeting her."

"She said it's okay?" It was eerie hearing my dad sound so lost.

"She did. She said you can tell me everything."

Dad nodded. "Okay. I'll tell you everything. I met her when Gerri was eight. I had to stay late at work. On the way back, I saw a car stopped on the side of the road. A woman asked for help. It was her. Ádísa. I helped her change her tire."

"I remember that night," Mom said. "He came back covered in mud and said he'd slipped and fallen in the rain."

I remembered too. Mom had yelled at him for practically ruining his suit. The noise had jarred me from my sleep, and I'd padded to their room. My dad's face had broken into a huge smile when he'd seen me, and my mom had softened. They'd let me sleep between them that night.

"She was pretty," my dad said. "Beautiful. And she invited me to her hotel room. I said I was married. Had to get home to my wife. Ádísa got angry. Then she…" A tear sprung from his left eye, and I watched mesmerized as it coursed down his cheek to his chin.

"What did she do, Greg?" Constantine whispered.

"Maybe we should stop." I didn't want to hear more. Constantine should stop asking questions. He had to leave my dad alone.

"She looked into my eyes and told me she'd make me feel good. Better than my wife did. She bit me. It hurt, but she said I shouldn't fight, so I let her. She kissed me and pulled me down to the ground. She undid—"

"No need for details." Constantine sounded upset. I didn't know if he was jealous of Ádísa, or worried for my mom's sake. "Did you… Did you go all the way?"

"All the way."

Even though I'd been able to tell what his answer would be, my stomach lurched. Ádísa had mind-zapped my father into fucking her. Into cheating on my mother. I felt sick. This couldn't have happened.

Dad was all out crying now, the flow of tears at odds with his composed expression. "And then she told me to meet her again the next evening."

"I thought he was at work." Mom pulled free from Alex and covered her face with her palm. A surge of relief washed over me when I saw she hadn't let go of my dad's hand.

"Did you see her a lot after that?"

"Every evening for a month. After a while, she didn't have to tell me what to do. I'd hate myself and still do everything I knew she wanted. Then she'd tell me to forget until next time, and I'd go home. I'd leave the monster and go home to lie next to my wife."

"He had nightmares." Mom let out a sob. "He'd cry in his sleep. I should have known."

"You couldn't have," Alex said. It came out choked, but his tone was reassuring. "*He* didn't know. He probably felt something was wrong, or that something was missing. Maybe he acted strangely, but his conscious mind had no idea of what was happening."

Constantine glanced at Alex, brow furrowed. I guess he didn't expect him to be so insightful. I knew better and was glad Alex was there for my mom when I was too crippled by shock and revulsion to be of any use. My heart ached for her, but more so for my dad. Recalling the memories was tearing him up inside.

"How did it end?" Constantine asked.

Dad smiled. "She asked if I loved her. If I would leave Kathleen for her. I was lucid enough to say hell no. What she'd made me do… I couldn't love a monster. Not when I had Kathleen."

"I'm amazed she let you live," Constantine said.

"She was furious. Said she'd drain me right there and then. I begged her to let me go. For my wife and daughter. Then suddenly she smiled. She said I could go and not come back. Said to forget her. That she could wait."

My head spun. My stomach roiled in disgust at what that woman had done to my family, and that didn't allow for the loathsomeness of her having slept with both my father and my ex.

I tried to refrain from lingering on that last part, as Dad went on. "I left. I forgot all about her. The nightmares stopped."

My mother shook her head. "Not completely."

"You'll have no nightmares of her again," Constantine said. "Ádísa raped you. You did nothing wrong. You'll remember it all, but it will no longer affect you. Now she's gone and can never hurt you or yours again. *Ever.* You're free from her. And now you're free from me."

My dad blinked rapidly and looked around, until his gaze focused on my mom. He pulled her in his lap, and they cried in each other's arms.

Constantine turned to me, and I saw the toll the whole thing took on him. His eyes were red rimmed, his lips tight. He stood, and before I could think about it, I leaped up and hugged him. "I'm sorry," he murmured against my hair. "I'm sorry I let her get to your family. To you."

"Not your fault," I whispered. My body was numb.

He withdrew, and Alex pulled me in a tight embrace. "Shhh," he said. "It's all behind you now."

I disentangled myself from him. "It's not only what she did to my dad. It's what she said when he turned her down. She said she could wait. Even when I was eight years old, she was planning on ruining my life. On having me turned. Why? Just out of spite?"

"I don't know." Constantine shrugged.

"Well, I'm planning on finding out," I said.

"We need to locate Willoughby." Alex traced circles on my shoulder with his thumb. "He's the only one who might know."

"We can get on it tonight. Now." Constantine seemed in a hurry to leave, but he didn't move.

I dropped to my knees in front of my parents. "Will you be okay?" I asked them.

My mother twirled a lock of my hair around one finger and gave me a warm smile. "We'll be great. Constantine told us how he rid the world of that woman. She's gained nothing." Her eyes still shone with tears, and the neckline of her shirt was soaked, but she seemed to mean in.

"I love you." I smiled. My eyes burned, but I held the smile in place. We'd deal. All of us.

"We love you too, Princess." My father smiled too. "And we *will* be great. I feel lighter already. Thank you, Constantine."

"Think nothing of it." Unlike my dad, my ex seemed burdened with the weight of the world.

I wanted to hold him again, but it wouldn't go down well with Alex. "Thank you," I mouthed. I should say more, but the words weren't there.

I thought I heard him say he was sorry again, but his lips didn't move.

****

I watched Mom and Dad head upstairs. As soon as they were out of sight, I said, "We're going after Willoughby. Tonight. Constantine, any leads? Where do we start?"

"I suggest we start by scanning the neighborhood. If he is watching, we show him we are not sitting ducks. Odds are he will come to us. I do not believe he was sighted without his knowledge. Not when he managed to completely disappear for months. He wanted to lure us here." He could have shared that insight sooner. Along with other things.

Alex nodded. "I thought of that too."

"Either of you could have said something." My answer lacked bite. I was too mentally exhausted.

"It's just a theory," Alex said.

Constantine got the door. "Shall we?"

Within less than forty-eight hours, we'd found out that the ancient vampire who orchestrated my turning had been after our family for years, and she'd raped my father's body and mind. I felt drawn to Constantine on a level I couldn't explain; Alex had Mr. Hyde moments; and my aunt wasn't really my aunt, but my grandmother. Who was also a vampire.

Oh, and we were probably about to walk into a trap.

I needed a moment to process all that and analyze my dad's trip down locked-down-memory lane until it made sense to me. And I wanted a sounding board who had no horse in this race.

"You two go. I need to make a phone call," I said. "I'll catch up."

"Walking the streets alone two nights in a row is inviting trouble, especially if Willoughby's really still around. We'll wait for you outside." Or Constantine didn't want me to be alone after what we'd learned. I'd have expected Alex to be the one to object.

I nodded and waited for them to leave the house. Then I took a couple of unnecessary breaths and called Constantine's private landline.

Sheena picked up. "Have they killed each other yet?"

"No, but I'm tempted to off them both, for different reasons." I filled her in on what we'd found out and how much of it Constantine had known for a while.

Sheena snorted. "God. Men who pull that for-your-own-good crap drive me crazy. He's lucky he looks so good."

I laughed.

"And how's Alex? Going berserk, every time you and Constantine are within two feet from each other?"

"The paranoia factor keeps rising," I said, "but we're still holding strong."

"Promise you'll be careful," Sheena said.

"Don't worry about me. My guys have my back."

"Not the part of you they're interested in. You still promise."

"I promise."

"Good."

I hung up and returned to the living room. The sound of soft laughter drifted down from above, and I let myself hope things really would be fine. If my parents could share a laugh after the evening's revelations, anything was possible.

I pulled on my sneakers and stormed out. "Ready. Let's go." I slipped my hand in Alex's and silently prayed it wouldn't be long before this cloud pressing down on us dissipated. And what better way to speed that process than by finding and killing my maker? The grin on my lips felt slightly demented, but not forced.

Chapter Thirteen

Constantine, Alex, and I spent the next few hours patrolling the neighborhood, while pretending to enjoy a leisurely stroll. We meandered around my hometown in not-so-companionable silence, which I occasionally broke by pointing out a landmark or something I'd associated with my childhood.

"It's a beautiful place," Alex murmured, when we reached Santa Agape. "The whole town, I mean. A place to raise a family."

From the corner of my eye, I saw Constantine pick up his pace, allowing us some semblance of privacy.

"Alex," I said, "I'm sorry."

He gave me a questioning look. "For what?"

"You will never have the family you dreamed off." I had to be blunt. Our vague discussions about the future didn't seem to sink in, and after seeing my father cry for what was done to him, I was in no mood for subtlety.

"You don't know that." He shrugged. "There are other ways."

"No." I stepped up in front of him and held his gaze. "You can *never* have a family. You're no longer human. Children deserve to be kept away from our darkness."

"But with your grandmother's brew—"

"We'll still be vampires, even if we walk in the sun. The darkness is inside us. What will you tell your son or daughter, the first time they see your fangs pop out? They'll scrape a knee, have a nosebleed, and you'll vamp out instead of being there for them."

"Cherry—"

"*Never.*" I hated being that harsh and seeing the hurt and disappointment on his face, but there was no gentler way to break reality to him. I needed him to realize there was no maybe, no grey area, about this. "You're a vampire now. Not a human with a taste for blood. You don't get to live like them."

Constantine had tried to tell me that, repeatedly, and I'd shut him off, refusing to acknowledge the truth in his words. I'd been so wrong. On many things.

Alex nodded and kissed my temple. "You're right. I need more time to adjust to this change. Need to relearn how to think. How to be. You know?"

"I know." I found his lips with mine and kissed him gently.

"Maybe some tender loving can help speed up the process?" He nibbled on my lower lip.

"Not out here. When we go home. But you'll have to be quiet."

"Quiet as a vampire."

I laughed half-heartedly and swatted his ass. "Let's go. We have another ten blocks to cover."

I spotted Constantine by the creek. He was squatting next to a huddled figure. The wind blew the other way, and Constantine's face was averted, so I couldn't make out what he said, but the figure nodded. Constantine turned to us, and the moon shone on his face, revealing blood-smeared lips.

Alex tensed, flaring his nostrils. The human—had to be—stood and walked away.

Constantine used a handkerchief he pulled out of his pocket to wipe his mouth, and met us on the side of the road. "I promised him a bite for information," he said.

One of the bite junkies Constantine told us about.

"And? What did he say?" Alex sounded impatient, but I was sure the sight of blood had unsettled him. Feeding only from me was bound to become a problem sooner or later.

"He heard a girl was found nearby this morning. She was alive and lacking any physical signs of an assault, but appeared disoriented, and her blood-cell count was remarkably low.”

“And he found all that out, how?” I narrowed my eyes. I didn’t see the guy being into investigative journalism.

“His cousin is an EMT. He was first at the scene and followed the case.”

“So we’re sure her attacker was a vampire?” I asked.

“I’m certain it was Willoughby,” Constantine replied.

“How?” Alex asked.

Constantine kept his gaze on me. “The girl was a redhead with bangs.”

I took a moment to gather my thoughts. “That’s not exactly proof.” Even if it felt like a punch to the stomach.

“Forgive me, if I don’t require more evidence. We obviously have to stay vigilant—maybe sleep in shifts once Ruby’s potion takes hold, in case he has humans helping him.”

Alex nodded. “Cee’s right. We can’t risk it.”

I shrugged. There was no use disagreeing with the both of them, especially when I was still reeling at the thought of Willoughby attacking someone just because she had the same hair color as me.

“At least she’s alive.” Alex’s voice was laced with relief.

“Maybe we should go by the hospital? See if she remembers anything?” I asked.

Alex shook his head. “I don’t think it’s a good idea. For all he knows, she’s dead. If he’s following us, and we lead her to him, he may decide to finish the job.”

“She was really quite lucky. Willoughby isn’t known to leave his victims breathing,” Constantine said to him. His eyes were narrowed in speculation.

“Maybe she has a message for me?” I asked.

“As Alex said, we cannot risk leading Willoughby to her, if that’s not the case. Let us wait until the potion takes effect. Then we can visit her during the day.”

That made sense. We went on with our search, but found no sign of my maker in the surrounding area. I suggested we go looking downtown; San Luis Obispo has a rather lively nightlife, and nothing makes for better hunting grounds than nightclubs full of college students.

"He let the girl live. That has to be significant." Constantine tapped his chin with one finger. "He's not killing. He wants our attention, and he will have to stick close by to ensure his success."

I had to agree with that.

My thoughts veered back to the young redhead I'd never met. Whoever she was, she'd been incredibly lucky. Willoughby hadn't been all that gentle with me or with Alex; neither of us had survived his attack. His latest victim had been found in the daylight and had apparently been responsive, if disoriented, so she was still human. Still alive. If she was turned within three hours of sunrise, she'd remain dead until the next sunset, and if it happened earlier in the night, she'd be up and around by morning, but the sun would fry her.

Yup. Very lucky, indeed.

We were almost home, when Constantine's phone rang. Without breaking stride, he swept his forefinger across the screen and brought it to his ear. "Gheorghios, I did not expect you to call me back so soon."

I closed my hand into a fist with the thumb and pinkie extended, and shook it by my ear, waggling my eyebrows. The weird gesture was meant to ask for permission to listen in on the conversation. Constantine wouldn't be able to tell if I did, but I'd been brought up with manners.

He nodded, and I expanded my hearing.

Gheorghios was saying, "—if there's any truth in it."

"Tell me what you heard, and we'll look into it." Constantine came to a halt.

Alex and I stopped walking too, and I widened my eyes at Constantine. I wasn't sure letting Gheorghios know we were together was a good idea.

"We?" Gheorghios asked.

Constantine snorted. "You have been a council member longer than I, Gheorghios. You know we each have our people." Good save.

"Of course."

"So, if you please…?"

"Yes, yes. As I told you, all I know is a legend that some of the oldest among us believe to be about her. I cannot vouch for its validity."

He paused, but Constantine remained silent.

"According to legend, Ádísa was a Valkyrie who fell for a mortal," Gheorghios said. "She was supposed to collect his soul, but the man promised her his love, and she let him live. Odin, the father of the Norse gods, made her human as punishment. She would only be allowed back in Valhalla, if she brought with her the man's soul, but he had to give it to her willingly. Ádísa said she did not care about immortality; she would live out her human years with her lover. When she went to him, however, the man told her he was in love with another woman. He'd lied to Ádísa on the battlefield.

"Ádísa was enraged, but she no longer had the power to harvest his soul and take it to Odin. She begged Odin to take her back and reinstate her powers, and he said he would do so only if she managed to gain the man's love. Despite her pleas and promises, the man showed her nothing but scorn. He gloated over having fooled a Valkyrie.

"The thought of growing old and dying alone terrified Ádísa. Crazy with loss and sorrow, she found a vampire to turn her immortal again, and then killed the man who betrayed her. When she offered his still beating heart to Odin, the father of gods finally took pity on her. He said there was a way for her to return to his side. She had to win the heart and soul of a man pledged to a descendant of the woman the human chose over her."

I caught Constantine's gaze. He frowned. "So am I to believe in Old Norse mythology?" he asked Gheorghios. "I lived those times. I don't remember any Valkyries around for my death."

"Believe what you will. I only told you what I have heard. I know of no one who asked the lady herself and survived to share her answer."

"I see. Thank you, Gheorghios."

"Just remember your promise."

What promise?

"I do."

"When time comes, I shall call on you," Gheorghios said, and Constantine terminated the call.

"What promise?" Alex asked before I could.

"Nothing significant. Vampire politics." Constantine waved him off.

"You were a Viking," I said. That he was actually ancient never ceased to amaze me. "Ever hear of that legend before?"

"Not that I recall. What do you two make of it?"

I didn't know what to think. I wasn't sure what I'd heard. Was all this possible? "If we believe what Gheorghios said—and that's a big 'if'—I guess my great-great-great-several-times-back-grandma could have been the other woman. It would explain Ádísa's mania to destroy my family, and especially her hatred for me. I was turned before I had any kids, and she didn't know Ruby isn't dead, so I was her last chance. The last of our bloodline. She needed to seduce a man who loved me, to get her place back. But seriously, do we even believe this story? I mean… gods and Valkyries?"

Constantine's face fell. "Improbable though it seems, it would explain a lot."

I put two and two together. "Was this why Ádísa had me turned? Why she told you to make me fall in love with you?" It wasn't the most appropriate conversation to be had in front of Alex, but propriety wasn't my main concern right now.

"Possibly."

"She had to know you'd fall for Cherry too," Alex said. "It wouldn't have worked otherwise. She had to steal you from her."

She had stolen him, hadn't she? I'd found Constantine fucking her on the bed he shared with me. Her face shone with triumph, as she'd looked up at me. "She thought she'd won," I whispered.

But she hadn't. Because Constantine's heart had remained mine.

It still was, if I were to believe him, despite the three young vampires spicing up his nights lately.

I don't know if Alex caught the longing in Constantine's gaze. It only flickered there for a second, but that was enough for a knot to form in my stomach. Constantine and I had been Ádísa's puppets for years, our relationship constructed and shattered by her hand. I saw him clench both palms into fists and then relax them.

"Once again, glad you killed her, man." Alex patted Constantine's back. I couldn't tell if he was oblivious to my ex's discomfort, or was trying to alleviate the tension.

Constantine's reply was too low even for my vampire hearing to pick up. He didn't speak again till we were home. Neither did Alex and I. My parents were asleep, but there was a platter of sandwiches and three cupcakes waiting for us in the kitchen. We grabbed a bite and drunk our fill of Ruby's magic potion—Constantine and I with blood, Alex with more tea.

Alex tried to boost our spirits by suggesting daytime trips once the ability to walk in the sun kicked in. Where he found the strength to remain upbeat was beyond me, but it was equal parts endearing and annoying. I can't speak for Constantine, but my mood wasn't improved.

Chapter Fourteen

Sex was the furthest thing from my mind, when I finally stretched my body on the mattress. My lack of sleep caught up with me, and all I wanted was to close my eyes and wake up in a week.

I couldn't blame Alex for not sharing my vision. He was better rested than me. Better fed too, since I had packaged blood as sustenance, while he drank straight from the source—also known as me.

"Are you too tired?" he asked, raising the hem of my t-shirt and rubbing circles on my back.

"Mm-hmm, but what you're doing feels nice."

He kissed me behind the ear. "I can let you sleep, if you want."

My mind said yes, I'd truly appreciate that, but my body already responded to his touch. "I'm up for some gentle lovin'," I said and smiled into my pillow when Alex blew cool air down my spine.

"What my lady wants, my lady gets." Slowly, almost lazily, he ghosted his fingertips down the length of my body, lighting my skin on fire with feather-light caresses. "I love touching you," he whispered in my ear, his breath warm with my blood.

I rolled on my side, facing away from him, and pushed my body into the curve of his. The planes of his chest and abs felt like living marble against my back, as he ran his open palm from my throat to my breasts, and then down my stomach. His fingers were rough, callused with years on the force, but his touch was as soft and tender as the kiss he laid on my shoulder.

I spread my thighs in invitation and draped a leg backward over his thigh, opening myself to his exploration. He briefly cupped my mound over my panties before he returned his attention to my breasts, slowly kneading each in turn.

"I want you," I said. "Gently, but now."

He chuckled in my hair. "You're the personification of patience."

I growled. "In me. Now."

He pulled my underwear to the side and slid inside me slowly, filling me up until his pelvis was flush with my ass. Then he began the exquisite torture of gliding in and out of me one inch at a time, stoking the fire inside. I rocked against him languidly, both turned on and lulled by the swaying rhythm of his strokes.

There was no moaning, no panting, just a steady, quiet climb to pleasure.

He slipped two fingers between my folds and circled my clit in tandem with his thrusts. I could stay like that forever—my body tingling with sensation, and Alex pumping slowly inside me.

My orgasm had a different idea. It sneaked up on me, and the waves rocking me suddenly sent me crashing over the edge, the assault on my pleasure sensors so immense, my vision blurred. My limbs went rigid with the effort to contain the feeling of utter bliss.

It couldn't be contained.

Among the craziness and chaos that was my life, this connection with Alex—this perfect synchronicity of our bodies—kept me in check. Because of him, I could be happy.

"I love you," I said.

He spilled inside me as, tears sprung from my eyes. This man was perfect for me, and I was so lucky to have found him at a time when everything around me was collapsing. So lucky his turning hadn't taken away everything that made me love him.

"I love you too," he said. "So very much."

I drifted off still linked to him. Still happy.

My dreams wouldn't let my happiness last. In them, Alex finished his declaration of love with another woman's name.

Ádísa.

I snapped awake, feeling an eerie cold. It was a weird sensation, to say the least; due to our low body temperature, vampires are way more sensitive to heat than cold. "Alex?" I whispered.

Nothing.

I turned to look at him, but his side of the bed was empty.

"Alex?" I said again, as if calling his name could conjure him out of thin air. He was probably taking a shower. But I heard no sound of running water. Inexplicable dread dug talons in me.

I got out of bed and pulled on my jeans, not bothering to change my top or wear a bra. My cell phone lay on the floor by the bed. I picked it up and checked the time. Almost seven in the evening. The sun was low, but not down yet.

Careful not to make a sound and wake up Constantine, I left the room and climbed up the stairs. At the ground floor landing, I sucked in a useless breath. Now we'd see if Ruby's potion really worked.

Scrunching my nose in anticipation of scorching pain, I held my hand out to a patch of light.

Nothing.

A beam of bright afternoon sun sliced my palm in two. Painlessly. I turned my hand, fingers up, and waved it through the light. Gentle warmth caressed me. I didn't need more proof. Ruby had done the impossible; she'd given us back the day. Now I was going to make sure Alex didn't do anything that would stop him from sharing it with me.

I was out the door in no time, despite Mom's warnings that the potion's results were short term at first.

At the end of the driveway, I sniffed the air. Bad choice. I hadn't been out in daylight in a long while, and even the scent of freshly cut grass was different than it was at night. It was disorienting, until I decided to tone down my sense of smell and try another way. A quick glance around revealed no onlookers, but I'm not sure the existence of witnesses would have stopped me from taking off.

Maintaining a high enough altitude that I would look like a large bird to anyone happening to look upward, I scanned the surrounding area. There he was, entering the woods. I made as inconspicuous a landing as I could and hurried after him. It wasn't hard keeping track of him; he was walking at zombie pace and seemed more asleep than awake. I thought of calling out to him, but something held me back. I wanted to see how it all played out.

I waded through the trees after him, scrunching my nose every time I stepped on a dry twig or my movements sent a bird or little animal scurrying. I needn't have worried. Alex was oblivious to my following him. Gradually, my steps became bolder, until I was only a couple feet behind him by the time the trees began giving their place to tall shrubs.

We'd reached the edge of a small clearing, strewn with grass that seemed to have been stepped on once too often, the green blades no longer making an effort to stand. The place seemed as good a picnic spot as any, complete with a handful of logs that came up to my knee and could be used at seats. We were lucky there were no families around, in case the sleepwalking vampire in front of me woke up feeling grouchy. Alex sat on one of the logs, his moves deliberate. I rounded the clearing until I was almost facing him, trusting the foliage to conceal me.

Had he come here before? When? When I'd gone flying by myself? I'd have seen him. Before I could figure that out, he spoke. "Are you there?"

I thought he was talking to me and took a step forward, before I realized his eyes were closed. I'd been right. He was sleepwalking.

Someone apparently responded in his dream, because Alex smiled and turned his face upwards. "Don't worry," he said. "Nobody knows. It's our secret." He nodded.

He seemed so absorbed by whatever reply he got, for a moment I was convinced someone was speaking to him. I looked more intently, trying to make out a shape. Nothing. The forest had gone quiet around us too. I rubbed my arms. Despite the mild weather, I was chilled to the bone. And getting more creeped out by the minute.

Alex opened his eyes, and I thought he finally woke up, but his gaze was unfocused. "Cherry loves me." He said something else, but it was little more than a breath, and I didn't catch it.

I heard a hiss and looked around, but the sound had come from Alex. He was smoldering. Like, literally. The potion was apparently wearing off, and plumes of smoke wafted off him. No longer mindful to stay hidden, I ran to him, calling out his name. He sat there, smiling, so I threw him over my shoulder and flew us home as fast as I could, trying to keep his face shaded and praying nobody saw us.

When I returned Alex to safety, Constantine was up, prowling the limited space of the basement like a caged animal. "Is it true? Did you really walk in the sun?" He sounded like a little boy asking if Santa was coming. "I wanted to see for myself, but the older we are, the more brutal the sun."

I couldn't help a fleeting smile. "Yes. But it wore off fast, and Alex is burned."

Constantine was all-business in no time. "What do you need of me? Blood?" He reached for Alex's prone form.

I shook my head. "I've got this. I'll need to run something by you after I feed him, though, so maybe don't go too far."

"Or I could stay here and help you."

I wasn't very comfortable with him watching as Alex drank my blood, but I needed to pick his brain about the one-sided conversation I'd witnessed. I sat on the pullout Constantine used as a bed, and my ex helped me lay Alex down so I cradled his head on my lap. I popped a vein in my forearm with my fangs and held the wound against Alex's lips. He remained motionless, but I could see his throat working, so he was swallowing at least some of it.

"It will not be enough," Constantine said. "Our bodies do not work the same way human bodies do, and our circulation is much slower. He needs to suck to keep the blood flowing, or you'll heal before he feeds."

"He will. Give him a minute."

A couple of seconds passed, before Alex's mouth turned firm against my skin, and soon his fangs extended. In as much pain as he had to be, with patches of skin on his face and arms burned almost to a crisp, he was surprisingly gentle reopening the wounds I'd made, and sucking my blood.

"You are too calm for someone whose lover was minutes from turning into charcoal," Constantine said. His tone was glib, but his gaze searched my face.

"Once I got him inside the house, I knew he'd heal." I was right. Blackened ashy flakes peeled away, and tissue rejuvenated in front of my eyes.

"He was lucky you were there, although I cannot fathom why the two of you decided on a midday stroll all of a sudden." Constantine arched a mocking eyebrow, but dark violet swirled in his blue eyes. The way they changed color, betraying his emotions always mesmerized me. From past experience, I knew violet came with a primitive lust, completely inappropriate for our current situation.

Another thing for me to lock away deep inside and pretend not to have noticed.

I turned back to Alex's face and gently removed my wrist from his mouth. His face looked tired, but the flesh was now intact. Perfectly smooth.

"We didn't go for a walk," I told Constantine, gazing at him again. "Alex was sleepwalking, and I followed him."

"Sleepwalking?" Constantine's eyes were their normal clear blue now, his focus on the information I provided.

"Yes. It was weird. He was walking like he was a puppet on a string, but purposefully at the same time. More robot than zombie, if you know what I mean." Constantine nodded, and I went on. "He stopped in the middle of the forest, sat on a log, and began talking to someone I couldn't see." I shivered—which I rarely ever do since I died.

"That *is* weird, as you so eloquently put it. *Freaky*, even, as Sally would say. Did you make anything out? What did he say?"

"He said nobody knew… something. I don't know what he was talking about, but I think it was a secret. Could be about his turning?" And he'd said I loved him, but there was no reason to bring it up.

"Has he done this before? Does he have nightmares in general?"

"Yes to the nightmares, no to the sleepwalking. At least, I think it's a no. We'd have noticed if he'd walked out of the mansion in the middle of the day, right?"

"Maybe we should ask him?" Constantine indicated Alex with a tilt of his head, and I saw Alex's eyes were open.

"You're awake." I ran my fingers through his hair. "You scared me. I'll start locking the doors when we sleep."

"What? Why?"

"You up and left, with the sun still high in the sky." Constantine tutted.

"I did?"

"It was in your sleep. Do you remember what you were dreaming of?" I whispered.

He sat up abruptly. "No. You, I think. And Willoughby. It's all a blur."

"Do you remember the secret?" Constantine asked.

Alex's expression went from alert to slack and back again in the blink of an eye. "Secret? What are you talking about?"

I glared at Constantine. Alex was in shock; we shouldn't be grilling him until he got his bearings. "You mentioned a secret when you were mumbling," I told Alex. "It was probably nothing. Dreams don't always make sense." I leaned over and touched my lips to his.

"Yes. I remember now. It was… It was the vampire council, and they were asking who knew I was a vampire. I told them it was a secret and nobody knew. I was terrified."

No. He'd been smiling at the time. Conspiratorially. Had he lied to my face, or did he actually remember wrong? Something in my chest tightened, liquefying my insides. My gut was telling me not to trust him.

He took both my hands in his, and drew circles with his thumbs on my knuckles. His touch sent an unpleasant tingle spreading up my arms. "I'm sorry I worried you. I guess my subconscious made me want to distance myself from you, to protect you."

I don't need to breathe, but I felt suffocated by his proximity. I forced a smile. "All's well that ends well. And now we know Ruby's potion has started working, so that's something."

Also, I was now certain he was lying. Asking him about it wouldn't help, when the lie had spilled out so easily, so I had to watch him and pray he had good reason to keep the truth from me.

Alex grinned, our previous discussion already forgotten. "Does that mean we can have a picnic?"

"It still wears off too fast, but in a couple of days…"

"Good." He pulled me to him for a kiss that lasted a couple seconds more than was appropriate in front of company. By the time we parted, Constantine was no longer in the basement.

Chapter Fifteen

We were in the kitchen, having a civilized meal with my parents, and all I could think about was how Alex had lied. I couldn't fathom the reason. What could have been so bad about his dream that he was afraid to share it with me?

I tried to make sense of what I'd seen in the clearing, but something kept nudging at the back of my mind.

He'd been walking, not wandering. He'd meant to go to that specific spot. Sure, it was possible he remembered it from our search for Willoughby the night before. He was a cop, trained to be perceptive and remember details. But had one short jaunt through the woods been sufficient for him to memorize the path? Even the stupid log he'd sat on? He hadn't stumbled once.

I needed to look up how sleepwalking worked. Maybe he actually saw the scenery around him, and I was driving myself crazy for no reason.

"Want some more pasta salad?"

"Huh? Yeah, thanks." I lifted my plate for Alex to serve me two more heaps of the yummy combination of pasta, smocked tuna, corn, carrot, dill, and capers—with enough mayo to clog the arteries of the humans at the table.

He studied my face. "Are you all right? You haven't said a word since we sat down."

Dad piped up, always to the rescue even after all the years I wasn't around to be his little girl. "She's probably still excited about walking in the sun. It's been a while."

It really had, and I didn't even have time to enjoy its warm caress on my face. Not with Alex being a weird robot from planet Weirdo.

The thought I couldn't quite form glided just past the edge of my conscious mind. I tried to snatch it, but it swam away, fast as lightning. Stupid thought.

"Yeah, everything's been so overwhelming." I smiled at Alex and gave his hand a light squeeze, before turning my full attention to the food. "This is really good."

Mom beamed. "I knew you'd like it. And I have ice cream for after."

It was a lucky thing we couldn't gain weight after our death. Not so lucky that we couldn't lose any, but oh well.

"Are you going to look for that man again tonight?" Mom always had a way of making things sound normal. The homicidal vampire who'd turned me and left Alex for dead was now *that man.* Just like Ádísa was *that horrible woman,* and I was still alive.

Alex's fork hovered in front of his mouth for a second too long. He didn't like the idea. Maybe a confrontation with Willoughby scared him. Maybe that was what the dream and his irregular behavior had been about.

Sadly, I was sure he'd been enjoying himself at that clearing.

Worse, I was afraid whatever he kept from me was sinister. Something he wanted to keep to himself, not to protect me from.

My phone rang in my pocket. I was entirely too willing to let it go to voicemail, but it might be something important. I pulled it out. Constantine's home number.

"Everything okay?" It would be Sheena. I couldn't imagine Wesley or any of the vampettes calling me instead of Constantine.

"Here yes. There… not so sure." I could picture one perfectly shaped black eyebrow arched in reproach.

"We're managing." I pushed my chair back. "I'll be right back," I said to my table companions and went to the living room. The more distance between me and the other vampires, the better the chances they wouldn't listen in on my conversation. They both supposedly had better manners than that, but I wanted to keep my ass covered in any case.

"Alex is being weird," I whispered in the receiver, once I was reasonably sure of my privacy.

"Maybe he's sniffed out Willoughby," Sheena said. "Wesley told me to call you. He tried tall-blond-and gorgeous, but the call wouldn't go through. We got word your maker is there and planning something nasty." She pronounced the word as nay-stee, pouring gallons of distaste into it.

I knew she used theatrics to cover her fear of him. He'd threatened to kill her more than once, after all.

"Do we know specifics?" I asked. "Like maybe where he's staying?"

"Do you want his bank account number too? No, we don't know specifics. There have been sightings of a tall, dark, and handsome vampire terrorizing that area. Resident vampires have taken it upon themselves to clean after him, but nobody wants to go up against him."

One sentence had spawned a myriad questions. I decided to start with what I deemed as most important. "Terrorizing? There have been more attacks than the one we know of? Are the victims dead?"

"Don't know who you know of."

"A young redheaded woman."

Sheena blew out her breath noisily. "Hon, he's attacked three young women, and they're all redheads. Good news is they're alive, and the vampires of the area have made sure they don't remember their attacker."

So much for the red hair being a coincidence. It's impossible for us to get migraines, but I swore a spot behind my left eye throbbed. I pressed the heel of my hand against my temple, willing away the phantom pain. "Why?"

"Because there would be chaos, if the whole town knew undead monsters walked among them? Why do you think?"

I wanted to return her snappishness, but reminded myself it wasn't Sheena I wanted to kill. Slowly, as if talking to a child, I said, "No, I mean why does he leave them alive and not bother to alter their memories? That's not his usual MO."

"Maybe he wants to cause chaos? How should I know how a psycho vampire thinks? Just, please stay safe."

"I will." I was about to hang up the phone, when another question popped up. "Sheena, how do they know it's him?"

She snorted. "He's the only vampire unaccounted for in the census, and the description matches his."

"Is *tall, dark, and handsome* all they've got? What about his clothes? The color of his eyes, maybe?"

"I have to check up on that, but I think Wesley said he looks casual and inconspicuous. Nothing that sticks out too much. I'll get back to you on the clothes—and I doubt anyone got close enough to see his *eyes*, Cherry."

My fingers went numb, and I almost dropped the phone. Casual was not a word that would ever describe my maker. It did, however, fit another tall, dark, and handsome *unregistered* vampire. "No need." I tried to sound calm, but my voice shook. "Won't make a difference anyway. We know whom to look for."

But did we?

"Call me if there's any development," Sheena said. "And tell Constantine to check in more often. Mini-yous are having withdrawals, and it's like PMSing to the power of bitch."

I laughed, but my heart wasn't into it. "I'll tell him. Talk soon, babe."

"And call me if you manage that threesome."

This time my laugh was a little more real. I hung up and turned around.

Constantine leaned against the wall. Vampires can be stealthy, but it still amazed me how a man his size could move around so quietly. He was close enough to touch, and I bet he'd heard Sheena's naughty parting words.

Fuck.

Or not, if I didn't want Alex to kill us both.

The thought sobered me. Alex and killing was nothing to joke about. Not if my train of thought wasn't widely derailed.

"I need to talk to you," I said to Constantine in a hushed tone. "But not here."

"Are you going to try and lure me into the threesome your friend mentioned?" His voice was as quiet as mine. "You know I won't need much convincing, but I'm rather certain your boyfriend will be less open-minded."

So he wasn't going to let that drop. Eh, I was still free to bypass it. "Something is seriously wrong. Maybe we can find some way to sneak away for a few, later? I don't want Alex to hear."

He shrugged. "Then speak freely. His mother called, and he stepped outside to take it."

I inhaled deeply—I may not need air to survive, but I need it to speak, and I had to get the words out fast. Before love and loyalty stifled them and risked everything and everyone around me. "I think it's Alex. I think he's the one attacking women."

Constantine arched an eyebrow. "Your gallant knight? What makes you say that?"

"I don't have specific proof. Just a gut feeling. He's been acting weird. Hiding things, bringing up obstacles to finding Willoughby... Remember he was the first to say we shouldn't go see Willoughby's victim at the hospital? Maybe he was afraid she'd recognize him. And according to Sheena, Wesley spoke to someone who said Willoughby has attacked two more redheads in the area. Only he doesn't wipe their memories. The locals do."

And who were the local vampires in San Luis Obispo? How come I hadn't noticed any nocturnal neighbors when I still lived here?

Then again, I hadn't noticed my *grandmother* was a vampire—or that she was even my grandmother.

"Willoughby must have a reason for doing that. To create panic, possibly, or draw out the local undead population for whatever purpose. What does that have to do with Alex?"

"Your spies only think the vampire doing it is Willoughby because of his physical description and 'cause he's the only one whose whereabouts aren't recorded in the census."

"So...?"

"They said he's—as Sheena put it—*casual and inconspicuous*."

"That would be out of character for Willoughby. He is a pretentious prick, after all." The words were ironic, coming from someone who lived in a mansion, but at least Constantine deigned to wear jeans and a T most days.

"Also, kind of important, Alex isn't even *in* the census," I said, pulling my thoughts away from Constantine's stylistic choices.

Constantine pursed his lips. "What you're suggesting is highly improbable. We—You've been with the man near constantly."

"Except for when he sleepwalked. What if he's done it before?"

"He didn't back home. He'd have burned to a crisp. Even if he'd found a way around that before the potion, there are alarm systems in place at the mansion. He couldn't have wandered off."

"Plus we'd have heard about more attacks," I muttered. "It doesn't make sense. Why here? What triggered his sleepwalking?"

"It could still be a stand-alone event, Cherry." Constantine gave me a smile that would have been reassuring if I didn't know him enough to make out the doubt in his eyes. "He could have dreamed of something that made him walk to the woods."

I huffed and blew my bangs out of my face. "It's more than that. I know it. Something has gotten to him." Could be the same something that had toned down Constantine's sarcasm since we got to my hometown. My family? The sense of belonging... or not?

"If that's the case, what has changed in his circumstances? Think, Cherry."

"If it's not late-onset fear of commitment, it could be Ruby's potion. He could be allergic, or something." Fuck, I really didn't want the potion to be at fault. I wanted us to keep taking it.

"I somehow doubt it's either." Constantine inched closer and traced his thumb along the wall, right by my shoulder. I sensed his need to touch me, but couldn't allow myself the comfort of his touch.

I took a step back. "Whatever it is, we have to watch him. Constantly. I think whatever he's dreaming of is making him dangerous. Maybe it's that he won't drink blood. Maybe his subconscious craves it, and he goes after humans in his sleep."

He dropped his hand and nodded.

"Honey?" Mom's voice came from the kitchen. "Will you get the boys and come back to the table? It's dessert time."

"Sure, Mom," I called back. To Constantine I said, "At least there have been no fatalities, right?"

"Right." There was sorrow in Constantine's gaze. The kind I'd expect to accompany really bad news. I was grateful when he said nothing else.

I exited the house from the back door and rounded the side toward the front porch. Alex wasn't there. I backtracked and checked the other side. Nothing. He wasn't in the shed either.

I could feel panic rising inside me with every minute that passed. "Alex? Where are you?" I called out. Constantine came up behind me. "Can you try his cell phone?" I asked.

"Already on it." He brought the phone to his ear, but a moment later shook his head. "Straight to voicemail."

"Shit. What if he heard us? He must be devastated, thinking he might be the one who hurt those women." I started to take off, but Constantine was next to me in a flash.

He grabbed my forearm and held me in place. "Cherry, there's one possibility we haven't considered."

"What?" I was barely listening, needing to go after Alex immediately, before he did something stupid, or Willoughby found him and decided to finish what he'd started.

Constantine shook me lightly, until I met his gaze. "His actions may not have been subconscious," he said.

"What are you talking about?" I didn't know my voice could be pitched so high. Why was he stalling me? I'd lost Alex before, when my maker had bled him to the brink of death and left him for me to find. I couldn't let it happen again.

"Cherry, there's a chance Alex didn't run because he found out what he's been doing, but because we did."

At first, I couldn't wrap my mind around the meaning of Constantine's words. Then it slowly sank in. "You think he's been hunting and keeping it from us on purpose? No. You didn't see him in the woods. I did." And I'd seen him smile when he'd said I loved him. I hadn't liked that smile.

"This does not mean there isn't more you don't know. Have you wondered why Willoughby bothered following us here, instead of making a move while we were all tucked away in the mansion?"

"I… No."

"I have. And why did Alex insist to meet your folks, when he hasn't spent one minute since we arrived trying to get to know them?"

"He talked to my mom. We've all been busy. What are you getting at?" I tapped my foot impatiently.

"Maybe he's aware of his actions. I'm not suggesting he's gone rogue. Perhaps Willoughby has gotten to him somehow. I don't know… I just want you to be caref—"

"*No.*" I shook off his hold and narrowed my eyes. Fear sliced through me, at the thought he might be right. Alex might be hurting people consciously. Wanting to hurt me.

I don't like being afraid. I hate the helpless feeling that comes with it. The unease in my stomach. The uncertainty. The despair. So I did what I do best with emotions that make me uncomfortable, and funneled it into anger. "I knew you weren't as cool with Alex as you pretended to be, but this is really low. Pretending to worry about me? Saying maybe he's working with Willoughby?"

"Not because he wants to. There have been stories in the past of vampires messing with other vampires' minds. And you should be careful around him. It can't be a coincidence that he targets women who look like you." He reached for me again, but I pushed him back.

"Maybe he thinks he's feeding on me when he attacks them, *because he always feeds on me*." I refused to believe Alex would do these things consciously, or that he'd be a danger to me.

But he'd lied about the dream.

And he'd been weird.

"Or maybe there's another reason," Constantine said, and I was furious at him again, for making me doubt Alex's sincerity. Alex's love for me.

"Right," I said. "He subconsciously wants to drain me, while you only want what's best for me. Is that it?"

"Cherry, I'm only trying to protect you."

"Weird, 'cause I remember feeling pretty fucking devastated, when I caught you screwing someone else. The same someone who had me killed. Maybe you could have tried to protect me then."

Shock and hurt contorted his beautiful face, and a numbing cold spread inside my chest, but I didn't stick around to hear what he said next.

Chapter Sixteen

Alex wasn't in the woods. I know, because I spent five hours looking for him there. I flew over it and I hurtled through it, and I almost got shot when I scared one of San Luis's finest, patrolling the area in the middle of the night. I didn't have the time to play Scared Tourist Lost, so I compelled him enough to make him look the other way, while I fled toward the town center.

I revisited every place we'd checked for Willoughby, and even went by the hospital, where I was told my sort-of-lookalike had been released.

Asking about a patient whose name you don't know has to be hard when you're not a vampire. All I did was use my vampire gaze to get one of the nurses on shift to tell me about the redhead they'd found near the creek, before I deleted all signs of me from her memory.

A bit after six in the morning, I returned to the house, to see if Constantine had had any luck.

I ran into my mom at the door. Shit. Last she'd heard from me, I was joining her and dad for dessert.

"*Mom.* I'm so sorry about last night. We—"

"Don't worry, hon. Constantine explained someone called about… that man"—she spat the words out—"and you went to investigate."

She waved one hand dismissively, and I finally realized she really had no idea about the sort of monster Willoughby was. She might have seen her mother nearly killed by a vampire, but she expected Alex, Constantine, and me to defeat Willoughby. For her it was a matter of time.

I also realized Constantine didn't want to worry her with Alex's disappearance. I'd follow his example.

"Did you find anything?" Mom asked.

I shook my head. "I was hoping Constantine may have heard something more, since… since Alex and I went looking."

"He left shortly after you did. Said he would check out the local nightclubs." She gave me a cheeky grin. "I'm not sure if he's looking for Willoughby or a good time."

So Constantine had stuck with his insane theory. While I'd been looking for a guilt-ridden Alex, my ex had been searching for a hunting one.

I forced my lips to mirror Mom's expression, while inside I seethed with anger. If I were human, my temples would be throbbing. I wanted to bust Constantine's stubborn head as much as I wanted to bust Alex's inconsiderate one. Maybe I should smash them together. Then they'd both stop messing with my peace of mind.

"You may be right," I said. "I'll rest a little before going back out. What are you up to, so early in the morning?"

She reached for a woven bag she'd left at the doorstep, and held out a pair of pruning scissors. "I promised Ms. Wilkins to help her with her gardening. She was so kind, when we thought you weren't coming back, and I like helping her. If you need company, I can call her—"

"No." I shook my head. "Go. I'll probably sleep for an hour and then meet up with the guys."

"If you're sure." She kissed my forehead.

"I am." It'd be easier for me to scurry around, if I didn't have to hide my panic. I watched her head out, wondering what she'd tell Ms. Wilkins about my return.

I'd find out soon enough. Now I needed to feed, and possibly sleep for an hour or so. No longer than that. I couldn't let more time pass by than absolutely necessary.

Constantine returned alone too. He avoided my gaze. I didn't speak to him. It was two hours after dawn, and I was wild with fear.

Alex could be anywhere.

With every minute that ticked by, I forgot I'd ever been upset with him. Worry gnawed at my unbeating heart. Last time I waited for him for hours, it was because he was dying.

No. This time was different. He was somewhere moping, but reason would overcome his horror of what he might have done, and he'd be back soon. When there was no sign of him by half past ten, I went looking again. I couldn't fly this time, because my vision was blurry with tears. I wouldn't be able to handle it, if something else happened to Alex only because he had the misfortune of knowing me.

I stayed out until the heat became near-unbearable. Only it wasn't in an *oh-God-I'm-burning* way. More like I needed a cold drink and a thick layer of sunscreen. Even so, it was too much after I'd spent years in the night.

I went home for a shower and another hit of blood with Ruby's brew, and was about to brave the bright outdoors again, when Alex sauntered into the living room.

"Isn't the sun amazing?" he asked. "Hadn't realized how much I'd missed it." He wore his best boyish grin, but his eyes held a near-wolfish glint.

I threw myself in his arms. "You're okay. *God.* You don't know how worried I was."

He pulled back. "Why?" He seemed genuinely confused.

I smacked his shoulder, possibly a tad harder than would be playful. "You left without a word and stayed out all night. And then, this morning, you could have burned to ash."

He circled my waist with one arm and nipped at my throat. "I was careful. And I'm perfectly fine, as you can see."

He raised his head and smiled as I looked up. He was more than fine. He was glowing with health and looked better than ever. I sniffed the air around him and had to cover a shocked gasp with my hand, when the familiar sweet and coppery scent hit my nostrils.

"You fed." I tried to keep my voice emotionless. Really, I did.

He pinned me with his sharp gaze, his grey eyes holding none of their usual softness. "Is that a problem? I thought you wanted me to."

I did, but in a controlled environment. Preferably controlled by me. "I did. I do. But you were completely against it. What changed your mind?"

He gave me a one-shouldered shrug and grazed the top of my breasts with the fingertips of his free hand. "Not sure. I felt like trying something different. Maybe you're right. Maybe I should embrace my new lease on life and not try to hang on to the human I used to be."

I shivered. That didn't sound half as cool as it had when I'd suggested it.

"Maybe I should become more like Cee," Alex said, between kissing my neck and nuzzling my hair. "He seems to have a good grasp on things."

"What did you do?" I tried to step back and look him in the eye, but he tightened his hold and swayed us from side to side. "He seems to still have a good grasp on you, too." His words made a mockery of the lovers' dance he was leading our feet on.

I pushed at his chest hard enough to get free. "What did you do?" I repeated.

"Went for a walk and had a bite. What's gotten you all riled up?"

I searched his eyes, hoping to find them blurry. It'd all be better if he was in some kind of trance. They were clear, but shone feverishly.

"Who did you feed on?" I asked. "Were they on drugs?"

He smacked his lips. "I sincerely doubt it. She looked clean cut. A good girl, all in all."

She. My gut clenched. "Where is she now?"

"Left her where I found her." He arched a dark eyebrow. "Breathing, before you ask."

"Did you wipe her memory?"

"No, but she never saw my face, and I doubt anyone will believe her, if she starts talking about vampires."

I winced, both at his callous indifference and at the thought of what I should ask next. "Alex, was she a redhead?"

"Don't remember. What if she was?" His expression, already distant, turned stony.

"Alex, look at me."

He did, crossing his arms. "What am I supposed to see?"

I chewed on the inside of my cheek. "Did you overhear my conversation with Constantine last night?"

"Why? Do you two have secrets?" He narrowed his eyes, his full lips a thin white line.

"No. Nothing like that. I was telling him you haven't been yourself lately. After you walked in the woods… You may be doing things in your sleep that you don't remember afterward." I paused, extremely uncomfortable at what we needed to discuss. How do you tell the man you love you believe he's turning into a monster in his sleep? "Perhaps you're feeling some resentment toward me. Your subconscious could be blaming me for your death, and this is how your id is acting on it. Or whatever."

His expression softened. "Cherry, I love you. I'm not blaming you for anything. Willoughby killed me; you just showed me another way to live." He cupped my neck, and I raised my face to him. "As long as I know you love me, I'm happy," he whispered against my lips, before claiming them for a kiss.

He used one hand to bring me flush against his body, and then drove it downward, until he was kneading my ass. "Want to go downstairs?" he asked between kisses.

I nodded and nuzzled his cheek. I was anything but horny, but needed the connection sex established between us. "I'll let Constantine know you're back."

"You're telling him a lot lately. Have you also told him about my nightmares? About the time I got confused? In bed?"

He meant when he'd attacked me in his sleep. When he'd hurt me. When he'd attacked me in his sleep. Unease sent ice gliding down my spine at the memory of being unable to fight back. The need to connect turned into the imperative to distance myself.

I gulped, but schooled my features to remain placid. "That's between you and me, and it's in the past. He's out looking for you, and I don't want him accidentally walking in on us when he comes back."

Moving behind me, Alex slid his palm to my throat, and then down to my breast. He tweaked my nipple, where it stretched the cotton of my top. "We could stay right here and try to be fast," he whispered in my ear, pressing his erection in my back. His voice was sweet, but dark and sticky, and with a bitter undertone, like burnt caramel.

"You're crazy. Mom or Constantine may show up any second now."

"Then we better get to it." He slid his hand inside my jeans and pressed at my clit over my panties, grinding his hips against me. "You're already wet."

I usually was, around him. My body reacted to his touch instinctively. I rocked against him for a moment, before gathering my wits and stilling his wrist. "Alex, no. Let me make this phone call, and we can go where we'll have some privacy."

He managed to move my underwear aside and slip a finger inside me. "You mean where your precious Constantine won't see and get jealous."

His words stunned me long enough for him to add a second finger.

"Maybe he should watch." He pumped the fingers inside me and palmed my breast. "Maybe he likes to watch. Maybe he'll finally realize you're mine."

A moan reached my ears. My moan. I shouldn't be doing this here. I shouldn't be doing this at all. There was something wrong with Alex, and I wasn't letting his sexiness distract me from it. I pulled his hand out and squeezed my thighs together. "This is ridiculous. He and I have been over for years. He knows I'm with you. I haven't exactly been subtle about it. You go downstairs, and I'll be with you in a sec." I tried to sound seductive, despite the unease making my stomach roil.

He shrugged and licked his fingers clean. "If you're not down in two, I'm coming to get you." His nonchalance would have pissed me off, if I weren't already busy being worried sick.

I watched him swagger toward the basement entrance, and then typed a text to Constantine. I wasn't going to risk Alex's overhearing what I wanted to say.

Alex is back. You may be right. If you say I told you so, UR dead. Come home now. And plz interrupt.

"You coming?" Alex yelled.

"Be right there." I infused my words with a throaty sultriness I didn't feel.

The front door flew open, and Constantine entered. He gave off a vibe I wasn't used to, but I couldn't spot what was different about him.

Not knowing with the fuck was wrong with my guys was becoming a trend lately.

"You're back," I said for Alex to hear.

"I am. Is Alex well?" Constantine's blue eyes asked if I was all right.

I shook my head. "He's fine, thank God. He even fed." I widened my eyes, hoping he understood the last bit of info didn't make me as happy as I pretended to be.

Constantine frowned. "That's good to hear. And everything went smoothly? How did he decide to take that step?"

"You can ask the man yourself," Alex said from behind me.

I turned and watched him approach in long, slow strides. He only had his jeans on, their top button popped, letting them hang low on his hips.

"It was about time I lost my training wheels. And yes, everything went smoothly," he said, stopping next to me. He wrapped an arm around my waist and gathered me to his side a little more forcefully than necessary. "And now we know we're all well, you'll excuse us, Cee." He pulled me backward, and I threw Constantine a glance I hoped conveyed how much I didn't want to be alone with Alex right then.

If I had to, I was prepared to fight Alex off, but I preferred to avoid violence and get to the root of the problem.

Constantine didn't miss a beat. "I'm afraid your little reunion will have to wait." He might be a lot of things—conceited self-serving bastard topping that list more often than not—but he wasn't stupid. "As a council member, I'm afraid I am required by law to debrief you after your first feeding. I need to know who she was." He tilted his head and studied Alex's face. "I assume she was a she?"

Alex nodded, and Constantine went on. "Where you found her; how you approached her; how many pints you imbibed; what condition you left her in; what precautions you took to protect your identity and our kind. We must address all those issues and make sure you didn't cross any lines with the locals."

"Everything is fine. I found her in a coffee shop near the university, and she was alive and still standing last I saw her. This can wait." Alex caressed the length of my arm down to my wrist and tangled his fingers with mine. "Let's go, Cherry."

"You're going nowhere until I get answers." I don't believe I'd ever seen Constantine so serious or so commanding before. It was like he'd unfolded to a height even taller than his six-feet-three. His square shoulders appeared carved in stone, and his voice boomed. "I am the one who allows your continued existence, against vampire law. I am risking everything by keeping you hidden from the council. In my home, nonetheless. You *will* tell me how you spent the hours we wasted looking for you, and you will hope none of it displeases me."

Alex matched Constantine's posture, his own chest puffed. For what felt like an eternity, they stood there, staring each other down. Despite their similar height and Alex's being at least ten pounds heavier, it was soon apparent he wasn't going to win this match. Constantine's gaze was pure steel, forged through the centuries, while Alex's was iron. Hard but brittle.

And he broke.

I could tell the moment he decided to concede, from the way his body relaxed, his back slumping the smallest fraction of an inch, his eyes mellowing. He hooked his thumbs through his belt loops, not so inadvertently pulling the jeans even lower, until I could almost see where the happy trail that began under his navel ended.

"Okay," he said. "I guess Cherry will have to wait a little longer. Let me give her something to tide her over."

Before either I or Constantine could react, Alex dipped me backward and gave me the mother of all Hollywood kisses.

If I were in the mood, the kiss would have *really* gotten me in the mood. Now it felt awkward and stilted, and too much like a show for my ex's sake.

If it was actually meant to upset Constantine, it didn't work. He didn't even bat an eyelash. "And now that's settled, let her get some sleep. She must be exhausted after looking for you for this long." He motioned for Alex to enter the kitchen ahead of him.

I saw Constantine type something on his phone as he followed. A second later, my own cell buzzed in my pocket. A text from him.

Are you all right?

I replied, my thumb flying on the virtual keypad.

Scared. And still hoping you're wrong.

He threw me a smile over his shoulder and typed something else before leaving my line of sight.

I'll take that as an apology.

He closed the door behind them, leaving me to my mostly unpleasant thoughts.

<h1 style="text-align:center">Chapter Seventeen</h1>

It took only the minimum amount of effort for me to convince myself listening in on Alex and Constantine was a good idea.

I stretched out on the living-room couch, eyes shut. If anyone walked in, or barged out of the kitchen in a huff, I would appear to be asleep. In truth, I adjusted my hearing until I made out the soft sound of sneakers dragging along the kitchen floor.

Alex pacing, probably. He'd seemed more agitated than Constantine.

"Where did you go when you first left the house?" Constantine asked.

"For a walk. It was a starry night. I thought I'd let the romantic in me roam free." Sarcasm laced Alex's reply.

"What made you leave in the first place? Kathleen said your mother was on the phone. Did something happen?"

"Do you really care about all that, or are you trying to keep me away from Cherry? Like with the sparring?"

"We've already had this conversation. Repeatedly. I thought the last time I broke your nose you finally believed I wasn't after her."

My eyes flew open. So that was what their antagonism had been about back at the mansion. Alex had openly accused Constantine of trying to get between us. And a broken nose, more than once? Sure, it was nothing for a vampire, and I got why Alex wouldn't want to tell me about his stupid jealousy, but why hadn't Constantine said something? That was one twisted sense of male solidarity.

"I have no reason to keep you and Cherry apart. I wouldn't have offered you my hospitality if your relationship bothered me." Constantine's tone was impatient more than reassuring. "Why is it you think the worst of me? Nothing would have been easier than getting rid of you, back when you were human. Or during your turning. I did not have to bring you back to the mansion, when I found you freshly turned. I didn't have to come for you at all.

"Cherry wouldn't have known if I… took care of things. She was so distraught when she found you half drained by Willoughby, she thought feeding you her blood hadn't worked. I could have told her you didn't make it through the change. I took you in when I didn't have to. I am training you, to ensure you can survive in a fight against others of our kind. I even disregarded the council and allowed you and Cherry to meet each other's parents. You should know you can trust me by now."

"For her. You did all of that for Cherry, not 'cause you're my friend," Alex whispered.

Constantine lowered his voice, until I had trouble making out the words. "Of course I did. I would do anything for her, and that includes becoming a true friend to you. Now stop being a child, and tell me why you left last night."

Unbidden thoughts invaded my mind during the pause that followed. Constantine would do anything for me. I knew that already, though, didn't I? Everything he'd told Alex was true. Constantine didn't have to save Alex from walking in the sun when he first awoke as a dazed, disoriented fledgling. Didn't have to feed him his own blood to help regain his strength. Didn't have to put us both up and watch us be happy together.

Assuming Alex and I could still be happy. Or together.

What seemed like a lifetime ago, when Alex was human and Constantine was the man who betrayed me, my ex played the long game—allowing me to be with Alex for however long that lasted. Now he had nothing to gain, but still he helped me.

"I left because I felt suffocated." Alex's voice fished me out of that downward spiral. "My mother was asking about

Cherry's family and when I'd pop the question, and all I thought about was Cherry's words in the woods. How we can never have a family. I don't want a family, but I have to explain it to the woman expecting grandkids from me. And then she asked when I'm going back to work, and I don't fucking know that either. I needed some space, so I left."

"So you left. Without a word. When you knew Willoughby was out there." Constantine's skepticism didn't surprise me. Alex's excuse would have worked if I'd used it, since I tended to flee when faced with things I didn't like. But he was usually the one who attacked problems headfirst.

"I wasn't thinking," Alex said.

"I find that hard to believe. You've been trained to think. You think for a living."

"Yeah, well, I snapped, okay?" As he did now, his answer loud enough to carry, even if I weren't using my vampire hearing.

"Where did you find the girl?" Constantine asked.

It took me a second to follow that change in subject, but Alex was faster. "A coffee place. Didn't notice the name. She stood alone by the restrooms, watching a group of students laugh and talk. I pretended to go to the little boys' room, then doubled back and grabbed her from behind. I whispered in her ear that I'd kill her if she made a sound, and she let me pull her into one of the stalls. She never saw my face. I drank until she was weak. Her heart was still beating. Told her to keep staring at the wall until ten minutes passed, and I left. I didn't risk us. Satisfied?"

A shiver ran down my spine at his dispassionate account of how he'd threatened, scared, and fed on a young woman who'd done nothing to him. He'd sworn to serve and protect people like her, and until recently couldn't have entertained the idea of sinking his fangs into anyone but me.

What happened to him?

"Was she a redhead?" Constantine asked.

Alex snorted. "I don't know. Wasn't paying attention to her hair."

"Really? Was it short? Pulled back? Didn't you have to get it out of the way to reach her throat? You'd think its color would have registered."

"It didn't."

"All right." Constantine sighed.

"Are we done?"

"Not quite."

"What else do you need to know? If I enjoyed it? How warm her blood felt on my tongue, compared to Cherry's?

I was done. I didn't want to hear how he'd felt, drinking from someone else—if he'd gotten hard, like he always did when he fed on me.

The rational part of me reminded me how much more potent vampire blood was. Humans were warm and soft and yielding, but their essence didn't pack the zing ours did. It didn't provide the rush Alex felt every time he drank from me. Human blood wasn't as thick, or as infused with power.

But it tasted different every time.

Before Alex had been killed by my maker, I'd tried to explain to him what it felt like feeding from him. I said it was like licking my favorite treat—chocolate fudge—from his naked body. I could never get bored of it.

It didn't mean he saw things the same way.

This thought process was driving me crazy, and there was no room for more craziness in my existence. Willoughby had to be dealt with, and we needed to get to the bottom of whatever was eating at Alex. My relationship issues could wait. If I'd learned anything the past few months, was how to prioritize.

Sometimes I even practiced what I'd learned, and for now, my priority should be to clear my head and relax. Perhaps catch up on sleep.

Every fiber in my stupid body said I needed to confront Alex, though. I had to tell him my—*Constantine's* theory and force him to come clean. Whatever he'd done, we'd deal with together. There were no fatalities. No permanent damage. He hadn't exposed us.

We could come back from this.

Assuming Alex wanted to.

The iciness in his voice earlier, the lack of emotion in his gaze when he'd told me he'd fed, the way he'd responded to Constantine's questions—all indicated whatever had gotten hold of him had sunk its claws in deep. A confrontation wouldn't help, until I knew what we were dealing with.

If it was an external factor, and not some previously hidden side of Alex now rearing its ugly head.

How well did I really know him? We'd only met a little over two months ago, even if it felt like years with everything that transpired in the meantime. He could very well have always harbored a mean streak. A shadowy self that enjoyed hurting others and getting away with it.

Maybe a side that enjoyed hurting me.

Could his darkness be mere jealousy? How far back did he begin changing? How did I not notice?

For the first time since I began suspecting something wasn't right with my lover, I thought of how he'd looked at me when I woke up to him having sex with me. The way he'd taken me in the shed. The way his eyes had clouded when he'd thought he had good reason to be upset with me or Constantine. What Sheena had told me about him and Constantine duking it out back at the mansion. It could all be connected.

It *was* all connected.

My stomach plummeted, and my head felt light. How hadn't I realized it?

And when did it start?

When Alex and I first hooked up, he said he'd had a bad relationship in the past, with someone who couldn't take his way of life. He told me he didn't want to fall for someone who had baggage, and I promised him Constantine wouldn't be an issue.

Did I lie?

Since my breakup with Constantine, I didn't allow myself to consider getting back together with him. And now I was with Alex, I would never think of returning to my ex. Despite knowing the end of our relationship had been choreographed by his maker.

That didn't change anything.

Neither did the realization Constantine truly loved me and always had, even when he cheated on me. He believed what I thought was a cheap excuse—that eternity is too long to spend it monogamously, and sex has nothing to do with feelings.

It wasn't an entirely crazy theory. Who knew how I'd feel if I'd been around as long as he had?

Nope. I wasn't going there.

I was in love with Alex.

But my assurances obviously didn't suffice. He became more possessive by the day, gradually losing the gentleness and stability I'd come to love. Jealousy shouldn't have been enough for him to start attacking women out of the blue, though. Not enough for him to be so rough with me—and the more I thought about it, the more his roughness seemed a display of power, and not a manifestation of his uncontrollable lust for me.

If I was to keep my sanity, I had to believe there was more there. I had to believe Willoughby was somehow involved. That Alex's Mr. Hyde wasn't coming to play. I needed someone to tell me whether vampires could control each other's mind. I couldn't be sure Constantine would have let on, if he knew anything more than the rumor he mentioned, but he'd have taken advantage of it a lot sooner. Possibly to convince me to forgive his betrayal. Pity my grandma was in Europe. Judging by the filter she'd concocted, she knew things your garden-variety vampire didn't.

A door slamming shut brought me back to reality. Moments later, my mom was there, arms laden with groceries.

"Hey." I stood to greet her, wondering what store was open in town in the middle of the night. Oh, wait. I was up in the middle of the *day*. In a sunlit room.

I stole a moment to bask in the glow, and promised myself I'd be going on that picnic with Alex as soon as we'd figured things out.

"Are the boys home?" Mom asked. "Any news on Willoughby?"

There was no reason to worry her. There were enough of us losing sleep over the whole situation. "They're both back, but we got nothing on Willoughby. Alex was out till now. He decided to test the potion." I spread my arms in the sunlight. "As you can see, it works." I forced a smile as I took most of the bags, and then waited for her to open the door to the kitchen. I wasn't crazy about the idea of facing the men in there, but I wouldn't be a refugee in my childhood home.

Mom arched both eyebrows. "He was out till now? It's past noon. Next time he decides to check if something works, maybe he should do so in less lethal conditions." She spoke loudly on purpose, to make sure Alex picked up the admonition.

"You're absolutely right, Kathleen. I was too excited and didn't think." Alex sounded contrite, but I didn't buy it.

"All's well that ends well." She rinsed her hands in the kitchen sink, wiped them on a dishtowel, and set the electric pot on, before ducking out again.

Fixing my faux smile in place, I ignored the conversation behind me, made a beeline for the fridge, and began unloading cans and bottles.

Mom's process was one of the things that had mercifully remained unchanged by time. She put on the kettle for tea, and left to change into house clothes and shoes, before starting on lunch. This was my chance to talk to her alone.

"Whatcha making?" I asked in my cutest voice, as soon as she was back, in her yoga pants and extra large T-shirt. Alex and Constantine had been eerily silent, and I wanted them out of the kitchen and to a place where they could safely stop repressing their grievances, before they exploded.

"I was thinking of pasta with fresh tomato and basil sauce. Did you have something else in mind?"

I shook my head, studying Alex's stony expression and Constantine's stiff posture out the corner of my eye. "I can help. For old times' sake. Maybe start with peeling the tomatoes?"

Mom grinned, and the years slid off her, until she was the thirty year old who tucked me in when I was a little girl.

"I've missed that," she said and tilted her head toward the tomatoes neatly piled in the top shelf of the kitchen trolley. "You better get started, if you want actual lunch today."

"And maybe the guys could spend that time sparring?" Somewhere far, far away from mortals, if possible.

For the first time since I entered the kitchen, I turned to them. Alex still appeared impassive, while Constantine gave me a speculative look.

"If Willoughby is planning an attack, we all need to be at our best," I said. "He's older than all of us. I know I can't win in a fair fight with him, but you both could improve your chances with some training. You could use the back yard."

Constantine nodded. "I wouldn't mind some playtime in the sun. Alex, are you up for it?"

Alex stood, all but kicking his chair back. "Going to wipe the floor with you, old man." The words were playful, but his tone wasn't.

"Have some more of the potion first?" Mom glanced at me as she spoke to them. I gave a tiny shrug. Surprisingly, she said nothing until we were alone.

Until the very moment we were alone.

The door was still ajar when she mouthed, "What was that?"

I held up a palm and waited until I heard heavy footsteps tread down the porch steps, before telling her of the suspicions Constantine and I shared.

She sank in a chair, waved me to the one next to her, and listened in rapt fascination, while I detailed the instances on which Alex allowed me glimpses of a man I barely recognized.

"So you're saying something may be driving him literally mad with jealousy?" she asked when I was done.

"But in a weird, exaggerated way. If you could see his eyes... I can literally see him transform into someone else."

"You think it's something paranormal." It wasn't a question.

"It's either that, or he's always been this way and didn't have time to show it before. I don't want to believe it, Mom. You don't know how kind he is."

"He's been nothing but a perfect gentleman to me and your father. To you too, as far as I know. If he's laid a hand on you, I'll be really disappointed in him." Her gaze was so hard, she might as well have said she'd shower him with acid. For a moment I could believe she'd kick his ass if she believed he'd hurt me. She certainly looked as ferocious as a momma bear whose cub was facing a threat.

"He hasn't. He wouldn't. I'll tell you if he does." I winked, hoping it reassured her.

"Good. Now what are you going to do about it? How can you find out for sure what's causing this? And are you still waiting for Willoughby to come to you, or are you going after him?"

I shrugged. "We still don't have a plan, and we can't come up with one until we know we can count on Alex not to flip sides. I guess Constantine and I could try going after Willoughby without Alex, but I'd rather keep a close eye on him at all times."

"And you won't know what he'll do until you figure out what's happening to him."

"Exactly. Which is why I wanted to ask you if Ruby ever said something about vampires practicing mind control?"

Mom looked at me questioningly. "I thought you already knew. Don't they teach newbies anything these days?"

I felt a tingle of hope before I realized she'd misunderstood. "I mean controlling other vampires, not humans."

She furrowed her brow. Beside her, the pile of unpeeled tomatoes mocked us. If we didn't get started soon, we wouldn't be on time.

Which seemed to apply to everything as of late.

"Nothing?" I asked her. "Does she have some sort of diary? Notes? Something on the PC maybe." Light-bulb moment. "Where did she write the recipe for the daylight potion?"

Mom shook her head. "She doesn't trust anyone with the recipe. Once she perfected it, she destroyed all her notes on it. She has no files on this computer—only her laptop, and that's with her."

No luck there, then. "Damn it. I was hoping for precedence of vampires being controlled in their sleep. Guess it was a long shot."

"Oh, wait." Mom jumped up, and my unbeating heart leapt in my chest. "I remember Ruby saying she had the weirdest dream, soon after we moved to the States. Constantine came to her, to check if we were okay. She told him he couldn't really be there, and he said he'd tasted her blood, so all he had to do was go to sleep focusing on her. It was all very surreal for her. I didn't think of it sooner, because she had no doubt her imagination had made the whole thing up. But maybe…"

My eyes felt about to bug out of my head. If that was the case, could Constantine visit the dreams of anyone whose blood he'd tasted? Would they know if he did?

Would *I* know?

That was a question for another day. "Could there be more you don't remember? Maybe if I hypnotized you?"

"No, I'm not forgetting anything. Now that I recalled the conversation, it's as clear as if we had it yesterday. You should ask Constantine for details. If he was really there, he'll know."

I didn't want to ask him. I'd have to ask why he didn't say anything sooner, and that would only lead to badness.

"I think I'll try it myself," I told Mom. "See how that goes. Can you please not mention anything for now?"

She nodded. "But honey, if you need help, you can ask him. I trust him completely."

So did I, which was scary, because he wasn't a paragon of honesty. If he didn't lie, he withheld the truth. The end result was the same.

The men returned for lunch, and then disappeared again. Not that I minded. It gave me more time to figure out how to emulate what my mother said Constantine could do.

From what Mom said, Constantine had simply focused on Ruby at the right moment. I fell asleep thinking of Alex more than once, but I never landed in his dream, so I guessed it worked the same way flying did. We had to believe we could do it, and will ourselves to follow through.

Tonight I didn't feel like sleeping next to Alex. My skin prickled at the thought of him touching me, making love to me, when he felt like a complete stranger. I lay staring at the ceiling, as he came out of the shower, and I kept my gaze from diverting to what the towel around his hips left uncovered. Namely, most of his amazing body. Not looking straight at him didn't help. Even if his wide shoulders didn't butt into my peripheral vision, I knew by heart every inch of his hard pecs and cut stomach, sprinkled with a dusting of dark hair.

I was generally happy my hormones hadn't died when I did, but that moment, they mainly pissed me off.

Luckily, Alex passed out the moment he hit the mattress. Constantine had worn him out thoroughly. Or maybe it was the excitement of the day, and he'd wake up rested and back to himself in the morning. If wishes were horses…

I needed my beauty sleep, but my body wasn't yet used to my return to a human time schedule, despite my exhaustion.

Also, trying to find a way to spy on my lover, in case my maker had him under a spell, wasn't really conducive to relaxing enough to fall asleep.

Fun.

Not.

If I didn't fall asleep I couldn't enter Alex's dreamland—assuming I'd even manage to if I did sleep.

I got comfy on my back and threw one arm over my eyes, trying to focus on all that was good and kind about Alex. All that I loved about him. I needed to remember these things anyway, whether my plan worked or not. For my sake.

Our first night together. He initially thought I was a prostitute, and invited me home for a lecture, instead of the naughty times I had in mind. The naughty times were had after all, and what enraged me at the time was now our private joke.

He was always so open. So willing to talk about his feelings. So ready to trust me. To love me. To make me his priority. My chest expanded with the love I felt for him.

He'd stuck with me after he'd seen me sprout fangs. After he'd found out my true nature. He loved me despite losing his life as punishment for being my lover.

He introduced me to his mother.

He—

He sat on the same log, in the same clearing. In front of me.

I was asleep.

And inside Alex's dream.

Chapter Eighteen

The sensation of peace is all encompassing. No. All pervasive.

It's an unnatural peace. Forced.

Alex sits in the sun, only a handful of feet away. I could reach him in a human heartbeat, but my feet are cemented in place. My inability to move doesn't scare me. It somehow matches the tranquility of the forest.

Utter tranquility. Disturbing.

No wind rustling the leaves. No birds chirping. No wildlife whatsoever. It's like nature is in a coma. Makes sense Alex doesn't spend time recreating forest sounds in his sleep, but everything else seems a perfect copy of reality.

He raises his gaze, and I suck in a breath when he looks straight at me.

"You came." The smile on his lips is the exact same I saw when I followed him to this very clearing in real life.

What? He expected me?

Before I can ask, a female voice comes from right behind me. "How could I not? You know how I feel about you."

I know this voice. Where do I know this voice from?

I try to turn, to see who spoke, but I'm rooted in place. Worse, I have absolutely no control over my body.

A burst of cold spreads through me, from my chest outward, tying my stomach into a knot, making my throat clench, and numbing my fingers. It's gone as suddenly as it appeared, and I'm left looking at the back of a blonde head. The figure in front of me gradually comes into better focus and assumes shape as it nears Alex, adding to the distance between us.

A thick blonde braid draped over one shoulder. An almost bare back, pale and smooth. Voluptuous hips, swathed in barely-there strips of see-through gauze.

Ádísa. This figure can't belong to anyone else.

Why is Alex dreaming of her? He only saw her that one night, when she tried to kill all three of us. Constantine ripped her head off and turned her to dust, but she apparently had plenty of time to make an impression on Alex by then.

We certainly talked about her a lot lately. Alex's subconscious is probably messing with him.

I realize she must have passed through me. Was that the cold I felt all the way to my core?

If this is Alex's dream, how can the image of Ádísa bring forth a physical reaction in me?

She reaches him and sinks down to her knees by his side. "I'll always come to you. Always put you first." She trails a hand up his... calf? I can't really see from where I stand.

"Can you say the same for Cherry?" she asks.

Sick to my stomach, I wait to hear his response.

"Cherry loves me."

Is this some weird déjà vu? A replay of whatever he was dreaming when he sleepwalked? This is the time to check if I'm doing this right. Ruby was able to see Constantine when he shared her dream.

"Yes, Alex"—I smile—"I do love you. I'm here. Can you hear me?"

He doesn't bat an eyelash or look at me. His face is turned to hers, but from what I can make out, he's still smiling.

The clarity of the dream strikes me. I've never dreamed in such detail. My gaze is drawn to the blue sapphire gleaming on the cleft of my arch enemy's throat.

Details. Not as important as what Ádísa is busying herself with. And she's undoing Alex's pants. She makes herself comfortable between his thighs and pushes her hand inside the opening of his jeans.

I gag. "Alex, I'm here. Stop her. Send her away."

Still no sign he hears me. His eyes drift shut, and his head rolls back.

The bitch meets my gaze, and the look she gives me is the same as when I caught Constantine and her in bed together.

Triumphant.

She feels triumphant. In Alex's dream.

Something is even more wrong than I suspected.

I sense another presence, and again try to look behind me but can't move. This one isn't threatening—I don't think. It's just there.

Always looking at me, Ádísa licks her lips. "Does she appreciate you like I do, Alex?" She raises his shirt and kisses his navel. Alex moans. "Would she put you above everyone else?" Her sharp nails leave red lines on his side. "Even Constantine?"

"Cherry loves me." Alex stills her moves, and I silently squeal in delight. Then I realize he hasn't removed her hands from his body.

It's a dream. Just a dream. I can't be jealous of a dream. Even if it's of the woman who destroyed my life and was the reason Alex lost his.

"But does she love you enough?" Ádísa asks. "I would love you enough. You could fix it, if you did what I told you. Then you could have it all."

What? What did she tell him to do? It feels important.

So many things are important, but I can't tell why—like that Ádísa is less real than Alex. Less substantial. She's still more solid than I am.

Alex moans. It sounds like he's enjoying himself, and I'm glad Ádísa's hair now hides whatever she's doing to him.

Shit. Is she…?

I can't watch, while she has imaginary oral sex with my boyfriend, and I can't leave him here.

Focusing on my love for him, I shout, "Alex, wake up."

Yeah, that doesn't work. No sound makes it out of my lips.

"Alex." Nothing again.

I close my eyes and scream in my head. "Wake up. Wake up. Wake up."

Nope.

I have to wake up. Now. Eyes open, damn it.

Alex lay on top of me, legs tangled with mine. He was hard against my core.

Hard for her.

I grabbed his shoulders and shook him harshly until he opened his eyes. It wouldn't be fair of me to knee him in the balls over something that ultimately wasn't his fault.

"Bad dream?" I asked.

He rolled to his side and took me with him. "Yes. I'm sorry if I scared you. Wanted to feel you." He caressed my stomach and brought one of my legs over his hip.

"This doesn't seem scared." I pumped my hips against his erection once, and then tilted them so my lower body didn't touch his.

"It was fucked up. I think everything we found out about Ádísa got to me. I dreamed she was trying to convince me you didn't love me, and she was pretty damned persuasive. She tried to seduce me, and I sat there, powerless. Even enjoying it. But it wasn't me. I didn't control it, Cherry. I'm sorry. You know you're the only one I want."

Relief washed over me that he didn't lie. I held his chin and looked into his eyes. They were open and lucid. He knew it was me in bed with him. As things should be. I arched my neck and rubbed my heel up the back of his thigh. Despite all my fears about what was happening, I needed to feel the closeness that bound us when we made love, and the man in front of me was the lover I trusted, not the madman trying to replace him. Ádísa's memory might have turned him on, but I'd reap the benefits and enjoy the hell out of them.

And I would ignore how petty it was that part of me wanted to make love to Alex so I could one-up her.

"Love you," he mumbled in my hair.

"I love you too." Not like he could control his dreams, right?

I pulled him to me and lay back, so he was covering me once more. He propped himself up on one arm and caressed my face with his free hand. "You're so beautiful," he said. "Perfect."

His voice and gaze held such awe, I almost teared up. He was back. The man who'd made me overlook my decision to never fall from a human was in bed with me, planting butterfly kisses on my lips and eyes. He nuzzled my hair and licked a trail down my neck. I'd gone to bed in a tank top and a pair of boy shorts, and it didn't take long for Alex to find his way inside both. Before I knew it, my top was bunched around my waist, and my shorts were hanging from one ankle.

"Touch me." Alex gently led my hand to his cock.

His long, hard shaft throbbed against my palm. I closed my fingers around it, unable to circle it all, and slid my palm up and down its length—squeezing on the upstroke, the way I knew he liked.

He groaned. Grinded against me. "Just like that."

I kissed his jaw line and pulled his earlobe between my teeth. Nibbled on it. "Tell me what you want," I whispered.

"I want to taste you."

I withdrew my hand and spread my legs wider.

"Not there," he said. "I want your blood."

I wrapped my arms around his neck and folded my legs over his hips, so the head of his cock nudged my entrance. "I thought you fed tonight."

"Nothing tastes like you." He pushed forward slowly, until only the tip was inside me. "Nothing measures up."

His words meant more than I cared to admit. He didn't prefer human blood to mine. He didn't miss the warmth.

I hadn't lost him.

I arched my body, trying to take in more of him.

"I need to taste you," he said again.

I tossed my head back, clearing the hair from my neck and baring my throat to him.

He needed no further invitation to sink inside me to the hilt, just as his fangs sliced into my neck. The euphoria of the double penetration was unsurpassable as always, and I gave into him, allowing him to mold my body to his, prolong my pleasure as he took his. I let him take me and take from me, while I fell off the edge again and again, until I could no longer control my limbs.

"Wow," I murmured when he finally stopped moving inside me. I was so lightheaded, the words fell out in a jumble.

Lightheaded. From blood loss.

He was still pulling on my blood.

"Alex. Stop." I couldn't manage more than a whisper, but I knew he heard. He had to have heard.

Why wasn't he stopping?

"Alex? Baby? You're draining me." This came out on a breath and had no more impact than my previous words had.

I didn't have the strength to even panic properly, let alone push him off me. How much had he drunk? I lay there, feeling my second life slip away like my first had. Only this time, it was at the hands of someone who loved me.

I felt sorrow for Alex. By the time he realized he'd taken far too much, I'd be nothing but ash. That was what happened when we no longer had blood in our veins. The end result was the same as if we'd been staked or decapitated.

He'd be so shocked.

No.

Screw Alex's shock. I loved him, but I wasn't going to spend my last moments of existence lamenting his hurt at causing my ultimate demise. I tried to raise a hand and slap some sense into him, since he wasn't listening, but my fingers barely rose from the sheets, before my arm flopped down numbly.

Fuck.

This was it. This was really it.

Alex's weight lifted off me all at once, as though he flew upward. Which, I realized, he did. He flew in a short arc, before landing across the room with a hollow thud.

"Are you all right?" Constantine's face took up my visual field. He looked worried. Why was he worried?

Right. I was half dead.

And completely naked.

Eh, I couldn't let that bother me.

Constantine was more chivalrous than I gave him credit for. He pulled the covers on top of me even before popping open a vein in his wrist. "Here," he said. "Drink."

The classic cologne he preferred caressed my senses. Tobacco, wood, and leather, with dark, spicy undertones that kick-started my sensory memory. I scrunched my nose. "No. Can't." Drinking from another vampire was too intimate, and he and I weren't at that place anymore, however familiar his scent. Hadn't been in a long while. "We broke up." My voice was no louder than before, but he apparently had no issues making out my words clearly.

And why was my brain glitching? Who cared if we weren't together? The man was trying to save my life. "Never mind," I more mouthed than said, before opening up for what he offered.

God, I'd forgotten how good his blood tasted. I don't know if blood ages like wine, but his was richer, thicker, and more fragrant than Alex's. Not that I spent much time thinking about it after the first few drops touched my tongue. I latched on to his self-inflicted bite and sucked greedily. My eyes slid shut, as I felt strength return to my body with every gulp.

"Of course it's Constantine. It's *always* Constantine," I heard Alex say. A growl vibrated in his chest.

I wanted to tell him he should be thanking my ex instead of being all grumpy about his intervention.

No, I wanted to kick his ass for making that intervention necessary. I was done feeling sorry for Alex and worrying he wasn't all right. Done tiptoeing around his feelings. Whatever was happening to him, he had to be a man about it and come clean, not risk my damned life because he felt too embarrassed to own up to it.

I was, of course, too busy feeding to answer him as he deserved, so I kept scolding him in my head while I focused on the task at hand.

A door slammed shut, and I assumed Alex was having a hissy fit. Whatever. Once I was done here, I was totally giving him a piece of my mind. The guilt trip I'd been on since assisting his turning was now over, thank you very much, and our last stop was Reality Check.

The mattress dipped by my side, and I opened my eyes to Constantine half-lying next to me, propped up on the arm not acting as my feeding tube. He looked even paler than usual.

Shit. Now I was overindulging myself. I took one last, ladylike sip, and licked the wound closed. "Thank you."

"Anytime." Constantine smiled wanly. I could see this had gotten a lot out of him.

"I took too much, didn't I?" I tested my limbs. They all seemed to be in working order again. At least I could bring up my knees and turn to my side, to better look at him.

"That's not it." He used one finger to tuck my hair behind my ear. My bangs fell back in place, as always. What had I been thinking, cutting bangs to shoot a porn flick—sorry, adult movie? At least by dying the day after my visit to the salon, I'd have mostly well-styled hair for as long as I roam this earth.

And I was digressing again. Constantine narrowed his eyes at me. "You're having an internal monologue, aren't you? One of those weird ones."

I shook my head. "I haven't done that in years."

Liar.

Shut up.

"Are you okay to get up?" I asked him, to get out of my own head. I didn't want to kick him out. I just wanted to get to Alex, before he continued on his idiotic path of secretive self destruction.

"Right as rain." Constantine started to get up, but I reached for his hand.

"If it's not that I took too much, then what?"

"Nothing. It has been a while."

I wanted to ask if he meant since he'd fed me or since we'd been in bed together. I kept my mouth shut.

He nodded curtly, as if agreeing with something only he'd heard. "I will be right outside. You get dressed, and we shall speak to Alex together."

If *shall* came to play, things were dire indeed. "I'll be right out. And hey, now I can enter your dreams—or I guess I already could, since I had your blood before." I don't know what possessed me to say that. Did I want to let him know I knew? Was it a half-assed attempt to alleviate some tension?

Whatever it was, it worked to reinstate Constantine's usual posture. He rolled his shoulders and stood in one slow, liquid motion. Watching me, he licked his lips and rolled down the sleeve he'd lifted for my sake. "Who says you ever left them?" he asked in the deep baritone he'd once used to whisper in my ear what he was about to do to me.

I still felt Alex inside me, but my whole body gravitated toward Constantine. It was the result of drinking his blood. No other explanation.

"On second thought"—he cleared his throat—"I will go find Alex and wait for you upstairs. Don't take forever."

I barely had time to say okay, before he was out the door. I was still half naked, when he opened it again.

I had my back to it and was pulling up my jeans. "What did you forget?" I asked, turning around in time to see him dump Alex's prone form on the bed. "Constantine, what did you do?" Not that I could blame him for punching Alex's lights out.

"*Nothing.*" He sounded incredulous. "This is how I found him, on the pullout. If I wanted to finish him off, I wouldn't have brought him to you afterward. What am I? A bloody cat?" Constantine rarely lost his cool enough to curse, and his use of the British curse word would have cracked me up, if it weren't for Alex. Lying on the bed. Apparently unconscious.

I could see nothing wrong with him. No wound. No blood, other than the smear of mine around his lips. "Did you try to wake him?"

"No, my first instinct was to shoulder his weight and parade him around the house."

His sarcasm felt familiar, safe, and allowed me to think of other, more important things. "Will he be all right?"

"You know how it is with us. If we're not dust, it's fixable."

I nodded. "I have to go back in," I said.

"Excuse me?"

"His dream. Before he..."

"Yes?" The single word brimmed with impatience.

"Before you stopped Alex, I followed him into his dream. Ádísa was there, and"—I huffed—"I think she was about to blow him."

One corner of Constantine's mouth tagged upward, and I saw his effort to rein in the smile threatening to blossom on his lips. "Not to speak ill of the dead, but she tended to do that to people a lot," he finally said.

Yeah, it was so nice having his usual, cocky self around, instead of the kind, understanding one. Only not. "She was *trying* to get him to say he'd leave me for her. I think that's what she wanted. There was something he had to do, and then he'd have it all, as she put it."

Constantine's eyes lost their playfulness, and his mouth hardened. "What did he say?"

"He kept repeating that I love him, but she was feeding into his jealousy of you." I rolled my eyes. "Yeah, okay, it's no secret he's jealous of you. With no reason whatsoever, I might add."

His smile was no longer suppressed. "Of course. Please, do go on."

"Not much to say. I woke him up before things escalated between them, and he said he must've been affected by all the talking about Ádísa."

"It is a possibility."

Memories of the dream kept coming back to me. "But it was somehow more than that. It seemed like she could see me, when he couldn't. I need to go back in, see if I can talk some sense to him there."

"You said he couldn't see you."

"Yes, but this time you'll tell me how it's done. The right way."

Chapter Nineteen

Constantine paced the length of the room. Repeatedly. It was becoming annoying and didn't let me relax enough to sleep. Let alone how disconcerting it was seeing him stressed. The man was usually cool as a cucumber, both figuratively and literally.

"Remember to stay focused on Alex," he said, coming to a stop at the foot of the bed.

I looked to where my fingers were interlaced with Alex's, and then closed my eyes again. For all Alex and I had been through together, the touch felt unnatural. "I don't get why this is necessary. You were miles away when you dream-bombed Ruby."

"I was already ancient by then. I *knew* stuff."

"*Stuff.* Eloquent. I see the company you've been keeping lately has rubbed off on you." And possibly all over him.

"Will you focus? Remember—only *you* can control yourself. It may be his dream, but you can be active in it. It's a matter of will."

I closed my eyes. "You told me." As I'd suspected, I was supposed to use the same trick I did for flying. Visualize what I wanted to achieve, and believe it was possible. The reason most vampires can't fly is because they can't believe they're able to defy gravity by sheer force of will. I'm generally very selective with what I consider impossible. A certain threesome, for example.

"Cherry? Are you okay?"

"No, I'm not. I'm trying to sleep, and you won't shut up."

He grunted, and I briefly cracked open an eyelid to see him glaring down at me.

"Maybe you shouldn't be here?" I said.

"Not an option. He might attack you again."

"Yeah, 'cause he looks so scary, all unconscious like this."

Constantine frowned. "Perhaps I should try to put you under."

I almost sat up at that. "Like, with vampire mojo? You can actually mind-control vampires? Why didn't you tell me? It would fall into the things-that-concern me category."

"Hush. It has nothing to do with vampirism. I worked with a travelling magician once. He taught me the ways he used to reduce tension and hypnotize select members of his audience."

Pop went my eyelids again. I had to see if he said all that with a straight face.

"Oh, will you sleep, already?" he asked.

"Show me."

"I'd rather drain you again." He ran his tongue over the tip of his elongated fang.

"Whatever."

Neither or us talked after that. I tried hard to focus on Alex, but remembering all the good stuff wasn't so easy this time. The badness was too pronounced and too recent for me to push aside.

I'm ashamed to admit it took a while before it dawned on me that the center of my focus didn't necessarily have to be something positive. I had to zone in on Alex. The specific aspect of him that drew my thoughts was immaterial.

I remembered the way he crowded Constantine in the kitchen. The way he'd grabbed me earlier. How he didn't seem willing to pay heed to my objections, but kept pushing. Touching me.

How he'd been drinking from humans who looked like me.

How he'd almost drained me, after doing nothing to stop Ádísa from blowing him in his dream.

I felt my feet slide. Dead leaves beneath my bare soles.

The smell of rain—

I'm in again.

I'm not standing; I lie sprawled on a heap of leaves. They're slimy with dew, but I can't spare the time to be disgusted.

Two feet away stands Willoughby, arms crossed over his chest, his impeccably white shirt glinting in the moonlight.

"Finally," he says. "I was almost certain you'd manage to fuck this up too." His words are loud as a gunshot in the absolute quiet surrounding me.

I can move. This time I can move. I need to remind myself, before I manage to scramble backward. I look around. It's the same clearing, but in the night it seems dreary. Even malicious. There's still no sound reaching my ears. Not even the squelching of the leaves and dirt under my toes, as I propel my body farther from my maker.

My head hits something hard. A tree. I blink, and Willoughby is closer. Close enough for me to—

I kick out my right leg with all my force.

It doesn't move.

I call on every dredge of inner strength I have. I know this is possible. I did it mere seconds ago. I can move. I can control my actions. I can kick Willoughby on the shin.

No, I can't.

"What did you do?" I try to ask, but the words remain trapped inside me.

Relax. I need to relax. This is just a dream. If I can't control it, I'll wake up.

Willoughby throws back his head and releases an uproarious laugh. "She actually thinks she will somehow survive this."

I don't know who he's talking to.

Wait. I know who he's talking to.

The queen bitch floats toward us, her stride more elegant than her muscled legs ever managed in life or unlife. "Let her hope. It will make her defeat all the more delicious."

Alex materializes next to her, as though out of thin air. His body is first a shimmer. A splotch of light in the dark. The splotch grows and solidifies. She's holding his hand.

I try to look at my hand, the one holding his in the real world, but my fingers aren't in my line of sight, and I can't move my head. I'm trapped here, unable to even close my eyes when Ádísa cups Alex's cheek with her free hand and guides his mouth to hers.

"This time you'll do it," she whispers against his lips.

A fist clenches around my unbeating heart when Alex melts into the kiss.

"This is just a dream," I chant in my head.

Willoughby gives me a scornful look. "How wrong you are."

If it's Alex's dream, how can my maker know my thoughts?

"You won last time," Willoughby says, "but it was sheer luck. Your precious Constantine won't be able to save you this time."

What's everyone's obsession with Constantine? He wasn't saving me when he ripped Ádísa's head off. He was saving himself. She planned on offing both of us. All of us— Alex included. I scowl at Willoughby, hoping my gaze shows exactly what I think of him.

"Oh, you may speak. This will be the last time we hear your annoying voice anyway," he says.

I test my vocal cords by clearing my throat. Sound comes out. Instead of wasting it on my maker, I call for Alex.

Alex, who is still kissing her, his palms curved around the weight of her full breasts.

He doesn't stop kissing her. Doesn't stop squeezing the perfect creaminess I'm seeing way too much of.

"Alex, please," I whisper. The sight of him responding so eagerly to her advances is breaking me in a way his almost draining me earlier couldn't have done.

Wake up. I have to wake up, if he won't.

"He can't hear you. Ádísa has him now." Willoughby says her name as if she's more than his maker. A goddess, perhaps. "He belongs to her. You can scream his name till you lose your voice again, but this time she's won. Pity you won't be around to see her become her true self again."

For a change, my mind latches onto the important detail. "Where will I be?" I ask.

Willoughby raises both arms, palms up. "Everywhere. You'll be scattered by the first gust of wind, once Alex finishes the job."

"The job?"

"Choosing her, and in doing so, killing you."

Fuck, I need to wake up. Now. Wake up and tell Constantine what Willoughby is planning. Alex's subconscious is trying to warn me through his memory of Willoughby, and if his subconscious still cares, I can appeal to the rest of him.

"Alex," I call out again. "Please stop. Please remember who you are. What you know about her. This isn't you."

Only, whoever it is, he's obviously enjoying himself, even as Ádísa rips open his T-shirt and scratches a line from his collar bone to his navel. It's a shallow cut, barely bleeding. Alex hisses in an unnecessary breath and tangles his fingers in her hair, to bring her mouth to his chest. "Lick it," he says, voice gruff with what I recognize as lust.

I've lost him this time.

"She's obviously won. He's with her now. Choice is made. Why does he have to kill me, too?" I try to stall for time, unsure what I'm hoping for. Divine intervention can't reach me here.

Why can't I wake the fuck up?

"You will never wake up again, Cherry. God, you've always been so dense." Ádísa nuzzles Alex's stomach, but looks straight at me, the sapphire around her neck lighting her face with an eerie blue glow. "We're not figments of Alex's imagination. His subconscious isn't doing this." She glides a palm down the front of his jeans, and he bucks his hips against it. "I am really me, and it's really Willoughby holding you

down, like the powerless little cunt you are." Turning her face up to meet Alex's gaze, she says, "Let me touch you. Please."

If she's telling the truth, there's no getting out of this. My only advantage over her in the real world is that she's dead, which isn't the case here. There's two of them, ancient and half-past crazy, and only one of me. I can't count on Alex to take my side, even if I don't believe he'll really help them.

I need a weapon.

The only thing I can think of is Ádísa's ego.

"Makes sense," I say, "that even when you control someone's dreams, you need to beg for their affections."

She doesn't take the bait. Her lips are fixed in a smug smile, when Alex pops his fly and pulls his jeans down his hips.

I can't close my eyes, so I settle for rolling them. "Your hold on him only works when you're touching him. I remember you using sex to win Constantine over too, and he ended up dusting you for me."

This time her smile falters, but it doesn't fall from her face. "Constantine fell for your innocent act. The women in your family seem to have the damsel-in-distress bit down to a pat. Alex is smarter than that, though." She closes her hand around Alex's cock, slides it to the base and squeezes, until the head turns an angry purple. "Aren't you, lover?"

Alex moans and begins fucking her fist, one hand pulling on her hair, pushing her head downward. I almost wish she'd take him in her mouth, so I don't have such a clear view of her pleasuring him. What she's doing to him is essentially rape. Even if he's a willing participant, his consent is not informed. He thinks he's dreaming, while according to her, this is actually happening.

"Alex." I make one last effort to concentrate on everything that's passed between us from the moment we hooked up until he started changing. I need to believe he can feel the love I try to broadcast his way, and break her spell.

For a split second, I think I may have succeeded. He inclines his head toward me, and his eyes hold immeasurable sorrow. "Cherry loves me." His voice holds no conviction. He grabs Ádísa's wrist, stops her, but his hips are still thrusting forward. "I can't. I love Cherry," he says, louder this time.

Ádísa frees her hand and stands.

Is she giving up?

No. She pushes at his shoulders, until Alex takes a step back and lets her lower him to the ground. He opens his mouth to talk, but she hushes his protest with a finger across his lips.

"I love Cherry," he says once more.

She smiles. "Not enough, though."

I expect her to straddle him and compound my misery, horror, and disgust, but she passes her palm over his face. "Sleep."

"Didn't you get the memo?" I snark, therefore I am. "He's already asleep. We're in his dream. And if you're done perving all over him, it's time for us to wake up and for you to go back to being nothing but a memory." Is that a quaver in my voice?

I've almost forgotten Willoughby, until he speaks. "You still believe you'll wake from this? That there is an after *for you?"*

I snort. "There's obviously an after *for her, and Constantine twisted her overly made-up head off." Until now, I've more or less been flying by the seat of my pants, going for the what-if scenarios. 'What if Alex's subconscious kind of hates me?' turned into, 'What if psycho bitch and her boy toy are really real?' and to, 'What if I can keep her talking?'*

Now I realize that, to see where the latter may lead, I have to focus on the hows.

"How is she here, anyway?" I ask.

Ádísa approaches us. I can see Alex's prone form behind her, his face placid and body limp. "She is *eternal." The bitch says.*

I laugh. "Not the tune you played when Constantine got rid of you."

"But I'm still here." Her calm grin is disconcerting.

"So you say. Prove it."

"I need prove nothing to you, girl." Her voice turns deeper, older. It bounces off the trees surrounding us, as though they were walls, and reaches my ears in a rumble. "I

*am who I am. You can only see my aftereffects, and you will—
as have those who came before you."*

*There we go with the riddles again. "Are you being
cryptic on purpose," I ask, "or simply unable to carry a
normal conversation?"*

*I don't see her move, but I feel the sting of her slap on
my cheek. Tears of anger burn my eyes. I've never felt so
vulnerable. Not even last time she tried to kill me. I won't give
her the satisfaction of showing it, though. "So it's door number
two, then." If I could, I'd toss my hair back.*

*Ádísa kneels in front of me. Initially I'm irrationally
afraid she'll kiss me too. She seems about to, with how close
she brings her lips to mine. "Maybe I should fuck one of you.
See what all the fuss is about." She scrutinizes my face. "Nah.
I think I can live with not knowing." She stands again, and
now I'm looking at a pale thigh. Creepy crawlies make their
way up my spine, when she says, "I'd rather get rid of you."
Alex's subconscious can't possibly be making up the hatred in
her tone.*

*"But why?" My bravado deflates as the certainty she is
who she says, and not a faded memory, takes root.*

*She walks backward, until I can look into her face.
"Because I'm done, Cherry. I'm tired of seeking your line up
and down the world, vying for the attention of mortals whom I
wouldn't spare a second glance. I'm fed up with rejection upon
rejection, for the sake of the same women who ultimately
spawned you. That's why I had Willoughby turn you."*

*To my left, Willoughby preens as if she's given him a
compliment. 'Cause bleeding an unsuspecting woman dry in
the back of a limo, while making out with her, is apparently an
accomplishment.*

*I don't voice my thoughts, because Ádísa is still talking.
"As a vampire, you'd be the last of your line, and I could focus
my efforts on you. I mean, look at us. How hard could it be to
convince someone to leave you for me?"*

Too hard, as it turned out.

*"I guess I could have waited for you to have a loving
boyfriend, and then killed you. That way, I could take
advantage of his grief, but I tried killing the women before. It*

never works. The men won't get over them. Constantine didn't, even after you made it clear you didn't want to see him again. It's been what? Six months?"

"Four years plus change—but who's counting?"

"Whatever. You were together for less than it takes me to braid my hair. You should have been nothing to him, yet he killed me for you."

Ah huh. "So you are dead."

"Not as dead as you'd want me to be. Tell me, Cherry Stem, what is it about women in your family that makes their men so loyal?"

This is the complete question. Now I finally know what she meant last time we'd met. "Maybe we simply don't fall for men who would go for deranged murderous bitches," I say.

She gives me a strange look, devoid of the anger I expected. "I will never understand the attraction, and I've made my peace with it. I just want it all to end, and I want to return to my rightful place. It is why I planned for Constantine to become your lover. Stealing him back would seal the deal and release me from this limited shell." She looks at her immaculate body with as much disdain as I usually save for my belly rolls.

If she dislikes this form, how stunning did she originally look? Never mind. I don't want to know. I have enough complexes already.

"So you wanted to get your Valkyrie cred back, but Constantine threw a wrench in your plans when he wanted to win me back." I can't entirely suppress my smugness.

"Valkyrie? You believe that?" She laughs, the sound too beautiful to be coming from a creature as evil as she is. "Valkyries don't exist. I was so much more. So much stronger. I brought men to their knees, and they begged me to kill them with my love. I was a succubus, favored by Satan himself."

My turn to laugh. "I see death has amplified your delusions of grandeur."

She acts as though she hasn't heard me. "Constantine was one of my greatest disappointments. No matter what I did, his soul was never far from yours. And this is why I'm going to take Alex from you." There's the devious smirk that makes my stomach lurch. I don't believe for a moment she was what she claims to have been, but she's still lethal.

If I'm to save Alex, I have to save myself first. "You have him. Now leave me alone."

She shakes her head. "What I have is a man convinced the woman he loves is in love with another. He may do many interesting, deliciously depraved things with me, but he hasn't chosen me. Not until he kills you."

"But that's—"

"A loophole." Her smile is like a shark's. "The way the condition was worded, he has to kill you for me, because I say so, not because he loves me."

Fuck. Can we get back to trying to wake up?

"It won't make a difference what you do." Willoughby's face appears impossibly close to mine, his pupils taking up most of his irises. "This dream is my playground. What I say goes, and I say Alex will drain you for her. For my maker. She will return and bathe in your blood."

"I thought I'd be drained by then. Best she'll be able to do is snort my powdery remains." My boldness is completely fake. Right now, I don't believe there's a way to survive this dream. Not unless Constantine figures out something's wrong and magically jumps in here with me.

"You can jest all you want, but the result will be the same." Willoughby snaps his fingers, and my limbs shift. Lift. Straighten. My ass glides up the tree trunk I butted my head on, until the entire length of my body presses ramrod straight against that same trunk.

"Alex will drink you to death, proving Ádísa's victory." Willoughby brushes invisible specks of dust off his shoulders. He takes his time unbuttoning his sleeves and rolling them up to his elbows. "Then I will carve out his heart with my fingers and offer it to her. She will be restored, and after I'm done with your friends and family, there won't be anyone left to remember you ever existed."

I try to swallow past the knot in my throat, but find it impossible. Killing me won't be enough for the twisted dynamic duo. They have to obliterate all traces of my passing *from this world. "How are you doing this? You're not even Alex's maker, I am. I should have more power over his dreams than you do. Constantine said you can visit the dreams of someone whose blood you've tasted. But to control them?" It's imperative I understand before I die.*

"I am more than a thousand years old, Cherry. I know more than you ever dreamt of."

"Constantine is older than you," I say.

"But he hasn't spent that time learning. Researching our nature. That's why I knew how to bring her back." His eyes are burning with fanaticism. He'd lay his life on the line for Ádísa. There's no talking sense into him. "The only thing I didn't know was that Ruby walks in the sun," he says, "but now our dear Alex has informed me, I am certain your mother will eventually tell me all I need to know, to duplicate Ruby's elixir of life."

"She doesn't know how," I whisper.

"She doesn't know she knows. I can dig into her memories. It'll be painful, of course."

My dead heart constricts in my chest, but I can't let myself believe he can get to my mother. I have to trust Constantine to protect her, as he's done before.

"With you out of the way and the curse broken, Ádísa and I can finally realize our plan," Willoughby says.

Right. The world-domination thing. I'll give you one guess how that went down last time.

If your answer was, 'Like a lead balloon,' congrats, you have more common sense than your run-of-the-mill megalomaniacal vampire.

"Let's take over the world today, Pinky," I mutter under my breath. I look at Ádísa. She's standing over Alex, looking down at him with pure hunger. I'm not sure she'll spare a moment's thought to Willoughby, once she's back to her true nature—whatever that may be—but he won't believe me if I try to warn him.

Constantine will stop them. He will. He has to.

"No, he won't."

I should have realized sooner. The fucker can read my mind.

"It's not that hard. You basically broadcast your thoughts. More to the point, I already told you this dream is mine to play with."

"Then why don't you get on with it? Have Alex kill me, if you think you can." I have no doubt he can, but at this point, death may be easier than listening to these two planning my demise, and I'm not going to beg them for my life.

"Oh, we first had to make sure you'd convince your lover to do what we need," Ádísa says.

Huh?

"He'd never kill you because I asked him to." She fiddles with the end of her braid, the gesture almost innocent. "But if I told him the only way to ensure you stopped wanting Constantine was to drink all your blood, he might."

I narrow my eyes. I can do that much now, even if I can't flex my pinkie.

"Oh, wait," she says. "I've already told him that's the way to your heart. I've made sure to keep him company in his dreams for a while. I've warned him about Constantine's efforts to steal you back. Fed into his jealousy. But he needed to hear it from you. And now you've spent your precious last moments thinking how Constantine could help you. Only Constantine. He'll be the one to save your parents. He'll stop Willoughby and me. Such faith in a man who's betrayed you."

She tuts. "Pity Alex heard those thoughts as clearly as we did. He's heartbroken, the poor dear. He'll do anything in his power not to lose you. Even if it means killing you."

No. I have to wake up.

I have to open my eyes before Alex does. Open my eyes open my eyes open my eyes open my eyes

I opened my eyes to complete darkness.

I was awake. I had to let people know what was happening. I tried to get off the mattress—why was it wet, anyway?

I wasn't in bed.

Chapter Twenty

I smelled moist earth and dead leaves, and the electricity in the air that usually meant a storm was near. Before I could focus my night sight, I heard a rustling.

"Constantine?" I croaked.

"Guess again." My vision adjusted in time to make out Alex's disdain. The storm was in his eyes, as his fangs popped out, the right one nipping his lower lip enough that a drop of blood welled up to the surface.

"You'll be mine," he said and planted one hand on my mouth, silencing my scream. "Shhh. It's okay. Things will soon be as they should."

I shook my head from side to side as violently as I could, but it didn't stop Alex from grabbing a fistful of my hair, yanking it to one side until my neck hurt, and slicing his fangs into my throat. The memory of him doing the same thing earlier—how being incapacitated and waiting for death had felt—made my panic flare.

This time there was no doubt in my mind he'd finish me off. The long pulls he drew of my blood proved he was determined to.

His body squashed me to the wet ground. We were in the forest. The fucking clearing. How had he brought me here?

I let my own fangs descend and buried them into the flesh of his palm. Surprised, he yanked it away. He only stopped drinking to say, "Scream if you want. Call for Constantine. He's not coming this time. Nobody is." He was set on finishing what he'd started.

I screamed until my voice was hoarse and my throat raw.

I screamed until I no longer had the strength to pull in my lungs the air necessary for another call for help.

Alex kept drinking.

What undid me—what made my gut hurt and revolt at the same time, was the way he stroked my face while he did so. Tenderly. Lovingly. He really believed this was the way to truly be with me.

We were both doomed.

"Alex," I whispered, "I never cheated on you. I never would. Ádísa made you believe I still wanted Constantine, because she needs this. She needs you to kill me."

He pulled back, wiped his mouth on the back of his hand, and looked at me incredulously. "Kill you? I'd never hurt you. I love you." He seemed wounded at the thought. "I'm consuming you. Making you mine."

My fault for not filling him in on the basics of vampirism. I spared a thought to lamenting the loss of VSS. Under the old council, the first thing VSS taught every fledgling was ways we could die, and being drained of blood stood prominent among those.

"You *are* killing me. Once you've drunk the last of my blood, I'll turn to dust." Was it possible to reason with him? Was there still hope? "Ádísa wants you to believe this will make our bond stronger, but she's lying. Why would she come on to you, if she wanted us to be together? She's using you to regain her Valkyrie status." Easier to believe in Valkyries than Succubusses. Succubi. Whatever. "Don't you see?"

Doubt clouded his eyes. "She said you'd try to persuade me not to do it. That Constantine's hold on you is too strong, and you don't want to break it."

I coughed, the strain to keep talking quickly sapping the last dregs of my energy. "She's a liar, Alex. A fucking liar. She wants you to kill me. It's her endgame." Had my eyelashes always been so heavy?

"Hush, baby. You're confused. You just relax, and I'll make it all okay." He touched his lips gently to mine.

"No, you won't," I said in a breath. "She made you attack women who looked like me. She made you doubt my love. And now she's making you kill me. We're all her puppets." With every word, I felt my second life slip away.

He snapped his head back, his expression bouncing from stricken to horrified. "I'm killing you?"

I tried to nod. Speak. Nothing. I hoped he read my blink correctly.

He shook his head, like a horse shaking off a horsefly. "That's— No. I'm not. I'm giving us another chance."

"Says who?" Only his vampire hearing could catch that; my voice was barely audible.

"Ádísa. She said you still love Constantine."

"She lied. Now she wins." My lips were numb. Frozen. Near impossible to move. "I love you," I mouthed, before I could no longer keep my eyes open.

"Cherry? *Wake up.*" He lifted me from the shoulders and pulled me to him. I forced my eyelids open a sliver. His gaze was clear. Ádísa and my asshole of a maker didn't control him in that moment. "This isn't working like she said it would," he yelled.

No shit, Sherlock. I felt like laughing, but it was too much effort.

"I love you too, baby. Fuck. I'm such an idiot. Fuck." Alex scrambled upright, holding me to him. "Blood. You need blood. Then we'll—"

I didn't hear the end of that sentence, because I was harshly thrown back down. I felt rocks digging into my back. Leaves scrunching under my weight. Grass scratching my bare arms.

Dazed, but with adrenaline giving me a second wind, I looked around. Willoughby had tackled Alex to the ground. He sat on Alex's stomach and pummeled Alex's face with his fists. Alex kept trying to block or return the hits, but Willoughby moved fast as lightning, his eons of experience putting Alex's police training to shame.

Hey, stop that, I thought I said. I made no sound. I made no move. I lay there and watched my maker rain hits on my lover, berating him for being unable to follow through.

"You had one job," Willoughby said. Alex blocked a punch to his temple only to gain himself another in the nose. The crunching sound raised my hackles. "I incapacitated Constantine for you, and even dragged her all the way to the middle of nowhere." My maker closed his fists together and brought them down full-force into Alex's sternum.

He'd kill him, and then he'd have to kill me himself, to keep me from going to the council. There was a twisted sense of vindication in the thought Ádísa wouldn't be getting her loophole salvation after all.

Alex and I would still be dead, but you win some, you lose some.

"You have to stop getting into these damsel-in-distress scenarios." I knew the voice, and I knew the cologne scenting the pale skin of the wrist filling my vision.

Constantine.

"Bite, woman. Take enough to stay awake, while I clean up your mess."

Of all the arrogant, sexist things to say… When I bit into his vein, I made it hurt a little. I took barely half a pint, the whole time watching the pitifully uneven fight unfolding in front of me. Willoughby was too busy turning Alex's head to pulp, to notice the three of us were no longer alone in the clearing.

I didn't bother to lick the wound closed. "Go," I said. "I'll be okay, as long as you keep him away from me."

Constantine didn't have to be told twice. He literally flew into Willoughby's body, lifting him in the air and slamming him down on a log. It was the one Alex had sat on, when he'd sleepwalked to this clearing. I hoped Constantine broke the asshole's spine.

Willoughby scissored his legs in the air, kicked, and twisted his body, torque setting him upright, as Constantine reached for his head. Spine intact, then. Bummer. Judging from the murder in Constantine's eyes, that wouldn't remain the case for long.

Alex tried to sit up, but before he could lift his body off the ground, Willoughby avoided a high kick by Constantine, produced a stake from his jacket pocket, and slammed it into Alex's upper chest.

"Alex. *No.*" This time my voice was loud. My throat still hurt, but not as much as my heart did. It took an eternity for me to realize Alex hadn't dusted. Willoughby hadn't found his heart. He'd merely—*merely*—staked him to the ground.

Constantine tried to repeat his attack through the air, but this time Willoughby was prepared. He rolled to his back and kicked both legs into Constantine's stomach. It was like watching a superhero movie, with bodies and fists taking off and descending like rockets, kicks connecting with the force of minivans, and nobody making enough headway to be deemed the winner.

I absentmindedly noticed the real forest came with real forest sounds. A squirrel scurried up the tree to my right and scared a bird into flight.

"Ádísa wanted to take care of you herself, but she'll have to settle for my avenging her death." Willoughby managed to smash a knee into Constantine's lower back, making him jackknife backward.

"She will not have a say in the matter, because she is not coming back. Ever." Doing a close resemblance of a backflip, Constantine grabbed Willoughby's lapels—seriously, who wore a button-down to a fight in the woods?—and sent them both hurtling into the thick foliage surrounding us.

"Oh, she is." Willoughby knocked him backward, his entire bodyweight behind the blow. "Even if I have to slice your whore's throat and let the blood drip into Alex's mouth." He feinted to the left, and when Constantine mirrored him, dove toward me.

"*No.*" Constantine's roar was deafening. Willoughby was almost upon me, when Constantine wrapped both arms around his waist and pulled him away.

My maker used the momentum to roll around and pin Constantine to the ground beneath him. They were inches from me, and I was powerless to stop Willoughby from locking Constantine's head in a vice-like grip.

"You'll dust for what you did to Ádísa," Willoughby said. His eyes held the same murderous glint they had in the dream, as he began twisting Constantine's head around.

"*Cherry.*"

I glanced up to see Alex grasp the stake buried in his chest. It's funny what the mind focuses on in times of grave danger. I saw his knuckles turn white with the effort it took to drag the piece of wood out of his flesh. As soon as it cleared the wound, he tossed it to me in a high arch, and his head fell back, his last reserves of energy depleted.

I raised my hand and prayed his aim would be true. There would be no second chance to do this.

The moment the rough, unpolished piece of wood touched my palm, I closed my fingers around it. With strength and precision I didn't know I still possessed, I swung and slammed it into Willoughby's back.

I felt flesh give way under the pointy tip, muscle shred, and bone shift.

And I felt his black, shriveled heart tear.

I felt it. Inside my own chest. I'd died and come back before, but had never experienced the violent ripping sensation I did now. Or the sad, *sad* hollowness that unfolded in my chest. Was that how it felt when someone's maker died? If I hurt like someone stomped on my stomach and squeezed my throat at the same time, when I'd barely known and completely hated my maker, how had Constantine felt when he'd ripped his own maker's head off? She'd been his companion. His lover. His love.

A puff of dust exploded all over Constantine and me, getting into our eyes and mouths, and dispersing the blackness inside me, until it was little more than a dull ache. I spat out the foul, bitter taste, but could feel a ferocious grin threatening to split my face in half.

We'd done it. We'd fucking done it. The bastard who'd ended both my and Alex's lives was no longer.

Exhilaration faded away, giving its place to exhaustion. I wished I could pass out, so one of the men would carry me home, but A) I'm a vampire, and we don't pass out when we're tired, and B) no way was I giving Constantine fodder for more damsel-in-distress jokes.

Alex crawled to me, and Constantine sat back and let him gather me in his arms. My ex's gaze was watchful, and when Alex tried to offer me blood, Constantine stopped him with a gentle shake of his head. "You look as if you spent the night in a meat grinder, and you've been staked. Let me."

I looked up at Alex's face. It was beginning to heal, but it was still bloody and raw, his nose at an odd angle. He glanced at me, then Constantine, and I was relieved to see no hint of speculation or distrust in his eyes. "I've taken a lot of her blood," he said. "I have enough to spare. You've already fed her."

"Twice," Constantine said, "but I don't need as much as you do to sustain me."

"Yeah, yeah, you're ancient." My joke fell flat. I let them maneuver me into Constantine's lap.

"Do you want me to fix your nose for you?" he asked Alex.

"Nah, I got it." Alex closed his fist over the bridge of his nose and gave it one hard yank, twisting his wrist. "Fuck."

I was pondering whether to ask how much pain he was in, or tell him it served him right, when I felt Constantine's tongue on my neck. I shivered at the cool, wet stroke. "What..?" My voice came out way too breathy, for someone who'd been through Hell and back.

"Just taking care of your wounds." His voice was emotionless, but his grip on my arm quivered. The intimate gesture had rattled him.

It had rattled me too. "How did you find me?" I asked. "Us."

"I'll always find you," Constantine replied.

His words soothed and unsettled me at the same time, but before I could ask more, I felt a whisper close behind. It was the same sensation I'd had in Alex's dream—the familiar-yet-not presence. I snapped my head around, almost head-butting Constantine. Nobody was there. "Did you feel that?"

Constantine gave me a smile too wide to be honest. "I'm sure I don't know what you mean."

Before I could explain or demand a straightforward answer, Alex kneeled by my side and took my hand. "I'm so sorry, Cherry. I'm willing to spend eternity making this up to you."

Constantine cleared his throat. "Let us start by getting her back to her feet. Then you two can patch things up, while I take the time to sunbathe, like it is going out of fashion."

I half chuckled, half choked at his choice of phrasing.

"You want my wrist again?" he asked.

The way I sat, my face so close to his, drinking from his throat would have been infinitely easier. Natural.

Dangerous.

"Yeah," I said.

I opened his vein, careful not to spill a drop or cause any unnecessary pain. I drank and sealed the wound. I tried to keep the process clinical and remain detached from the feelings and memories drinking from him a third time in a row brought to the surface. It wasn't easy, with our bodies pressed together.

"Ready," I said and used Constantine's shoulder as a prop to get myself upright.

Alex tried to drape one of my arms over his shoulders, but I shied away from his touch. It wasn't a voluntary reaction. I've said before that the body has a memory of its own, and sometimes it overcomes reason. I knew Alex hurt for hurting me, but my body couldn't take his proximity.

His face was healing, but I was thankful his still swollen eyes hid his feelings when he gave me a brisk nod and walked ahead to lead the way out of the woods.

Constantine helped me along the path. "You'll be okay," he said. "Both of you."

"I know." I told myself it was exhaustion that made me cling to him, not the need for reassurance. "Thank you," I whispered.

He looked away, but not before I saw the thin line of his usually luscious mouth. "I would have come sooner, but I was detained."

"Detained?" I tripped over a fallen branch.

He held me up, his arm wrapping tighter around my waist. "Willoughby came by your parents' house. He must have compelled one of them to let him in."

I halted and turned him to face me. "My parents? Are they—?"

"They're fine. They were sleeping when I left. Both breathing; I made sure. Willoughby probably didn't want to kill them until he got everything he needed."

I wouldn't think of the lengths he might go to make my mom tell him the recipe for the potion. I would focus on my relief he hadn't harmed them.

"I didn't realize he was there until he burst in the basement bedroom and ordered Alex to take you to the forest. We fought, and he staked me to the wall." Constantine clacked his tongue. "Apparently Ádísa would love that."

"She totally would." A short laugh burst out of my lips.

He chuckled and looked somewhere behind me. "You realize she is to blame for everything. Alex was her puppet."

My eyes stung. I rubbed my face with both hands and wasn't surprised to see blood and dirt on my palms when I was done. "I know." I wasn't happy she could make him her puppet, though.

"Good." He tucked me to his side, and we caught up with Alex, who'd almost reached the end of the tree line.

Chapter Twenty-one

We made it home with the gray light of dawn and went straight to the basement. It wouldn't do to freak out my parents with our blooded and bruised appearance.

"You hit the shower first," I told Alex.

He complied without a word, and a fist gripped my insides, threatening to rip me apart. I should say something soothing to him, but I didn't want to.

Constantine watched Alex shuffle his feet to the small bathroom. I stepped aside to give Alex wide berth, and Constantine pinned me with his gaze.

"Resentment is a nasty thing. Sneaky," he said, when the door was safely closed between us and Alex. "It burrows inside you and makes a nest. It festers there and rots your soul."

"Same goes for jealousy," I said. "At least there's a good enough reason for my feelings."

He crossed the room to me. His six-foot-something towered over my five-foot-four, but I didn't feel threatened, even when he leaned close and trapped me between his body and the wall.

He brought his lips to my ear. "And you're saying Alex had no reason to be jealous?"

I heard water running behind me. Alex showered a few feet from us.

Constantine feathered his lips over the shell of my ear. He smelled of his cologne and blood and moist earth. I closed my eyes and let my head drop back. I owed it to him to be honest, but I didn't know how.

In the end, I said, "I never gave him reason to." It would have to suffice.

Constantine inhaled deeply in my hair, and then touched his forehead to mine. "That I don't think you should condemn him for things beyond his control doesn't mean I have given up on you," he whispered.

His lips were a hair's breadth from mine. He'd kiss me. Did I want him to?

He stepped back, and relief and disappointment warred for room inside me.

He trained his gaze to the floor. "We cannot control what we feel. What we want. Fortunately, in most cases we can control what we do about it. In the end, Alex chose you."

I nodded, quietly.

"You should shower after he's done," Constantine said. "I'll use the upstairs bathroom." He left me no time to reply.

I waited for Alex to come out, holding a pair of sweatpants and a Tee for each of us away from my body, so I didn't stain them. He came out, wrapped in a towel. We avoided each other's gaze, as I handed him his clothes.

I took the fastest shower in history. I didn't want to smell Alex's blood and body gel any longer than I had to. It jumbled up my brain, sending warm and fuzzy feelings to my belly and jolts of terror through my core.

I pulled on my pants and shirt, and fled the bathroom.

Alex gathered our torn and blooded clothes into a pile, and we shoved them into the big garbage bag Constantine brought downstairs with his own tattered clothing. I braided my wet hair hurriedly, and tried to apply some makeup on my neck but gave up. There was no reason to put effort into hiding the bruises. They'd fade and disappear all together after a good feeding.

I took in Alex and Constantine's faces. Alex's cheeks had deep gashes, and the bones seemed broken. His nose was swollen, and angry purple blotches circled his eyes.

Constantine only had a few cuts on his forehead, but the knuckles of his left hand looked like raw hamburger.

By comparison, the two bite marks on my neck, were nothing.

A hole in the wall of the bedroom marked the spot where Willoughby had skewered Constantine to the wall. Despite all his scheming, that was all the lasting damage he'd managed to do today, and it would be fixed with some plaster and paint.

I felt hysterical laughter bubble up my throat and clenched my teeth together. That wasn't all of it. Alex, Constantine, and I were still here, my parents were still alive, Ádísa was still dust, but something else had been irreparably dented.

My relationship with Alex.

****

We found Mom in the kitchen, preparing breakfast.

"My God, what happened to you?" Her gaze zoomed in on Alex, then took in Constantine and me.

"We got Willoughby," I said.

Mom wiped her hands on her apron, and rushed to hug me so fiercely I thought my bones creaked. "Are you okay?" she asked.

"We're fine. Well, not fine, but nothing a little blood won't fix."

"You should see the other guy." Alex's chuckle turned into a groan. "I can't even laugh."

He'd tried to kill me. Twice. Still, he was as much a victim as I was. I patted his shoulder, and he rubbed his cheek on my knuckles. Maybe my body could forgive, if it couldn't forget.

"Sit. I'll get you blood and some tea," Mom said.

"Don't bother with tea for me. I'm good with blood too," Alex replied.

Mom gave him a questioning look, but got two bags of blood from the freezer and popped them into the microwave. She returned her attention to the skillet in time to salvage five strips of crispy bacon.

"I decided to expand my diet," Alex said. He waited for me to sit first, and then took the seat across from me, leaving Constantine to sit next to me.

"Willoughby is no longer a threat," Constantine said.

"Not thanks to me," Alex muttered.

I'm not sure Mom heard, but she kept nodding as she poured the first large spoonful of pancake batter in the griddle, without cleaning the bacon grease. My mouth watered.

Dad joined us for breakfast, and between us, Alex, Constantine, and I told them what had happened during the night. Alex had the most trouble with it, but his description of the systematic brainwashing Ádísa had done in his dreams was honest.

I cut in before he told them of the first time he almost drained me. "Willoughby and Ádísa made him take me to the woods, but he shook off their control and helped keep Willoughby busy until Constantine came." The more time passed since our fight with Willoughby, the more I thought Alex and I might work things out. If my parents knew the disturbing details, there would be another hurdle for us to overcome, and we already had enough of those.

I reached across the table for Alex's hand, but he fisted it before I could clasp it. He frowned and opened his mouth, but closed it again without speaking.

"And where is she now? Willoughby is dust. Does she have other progeny that could come after you?" Dad asked.

I froze for the second it took Constantine to shake his head. "No. If there was another *childe* of hers out there, we'd know by now. Even if she's not entirely gone, she is no longer a threat. She's suspended somewhere, inert without Willoughby to bring her in touch with the living and undead. There is no way left for her to return to life."

Phew.

"So what now?" Mom studied my face. "Do you have to go?"

I looked at Constantine. "Do we?"

"You can stay for as long as you want. You slew Willoughby, and once I return to L. A. and inform the council, you'll be one of the cool kids." His grin was full of mischief.

"I've always been one of the cool kids. Your stupid council just didn't know it." I held out my plate, and my mother served me a neat stack of pancakes.

"*Our* stupid council now."

So I was going to become a member of the ruling body. Cool. There were some things that needed changing. Especially the stupid rule forcing fledglings to disappear from their families.

Alex was silent until then. Now he asked, "What about me? Am I still the secret bastard of the vampire clan?"

His words lacked bite, and Constantine didn't react to the snark. "I think between Cherry and me, we can convince the others of your value, as well as of the need to allow your continued employment. One of our own in the Los Angeles police force should be handy."

I expected Alex to be happy at that, but he seemed pensive, eyebrows drawn low and nostrils flared.

"So you're staying?" Dad asked.

"I guess so." I smiled. Some tender loving care from my parents would go a long way toward healing us all.

At least, I believed so.

For the next two days, we all stayed with my parents, who coddled us and plied us with packaged blood and Ruby's potion.

After the first couple of feedings, our bodies were fully recovered. Even the holes in Alex's shoulder and Constantine stomach, where Willoughby had run them through with stakes, were completely healed. And Alex now fed solely on bagged blood, which other than a great step toward his full acceptance of his vampire existence was a relief to me. Although at times I missed his more gentle bites, I wasn't sure I could bring myself to feed him.

I did enough soul searching at night, when he slept on the floor by the bed we used to share, to know I still loved him and wanted to make our relationship work. I wasn't sure, though, how long it would be before I could enjoy his touch again. Or even endure it.

I wasn't the only one feeling uneasy. Alex walked on egg-shells around me, treating me as if I were made of porcelain, and Constantine made himself scarce while I was awake.

Their behavior drove me up the walls and kept me from fully enjoying what should be a relaxed time. I tried to mend our relationship, but seemed to be doing something wrong.

The nicer I was to Alex, the more distant he became. We didn't have a single exchange during which he looked me in the eye. His gaze was usually drawn to the floor or ceiling, and he avoided talking about what happ— *No.* What Willoughby did to us. I was fed up with his behavior before too long. Yes, we weren't at a good place, but if he wanted to ever make things right, we needed to talk about what happened, not dance around it.

I was still not used to sleeping at night. After fighting to doze off for what seemed like hours, I sat up with a huff. "Alex, about Ádísa…"

He sat on the floor by the bed, not even pretending to try to sleep. "No." He shook his head. "It's too soon. You need to recover first, and—"

"*We* will never recover, if we don't deal with what happened. Alex, I want to be with you. Look at me."

He swung his arm to the side, slammed his fist on the wall, and grimaced when I winced. "I'd say I'd never hurt you, but we'd both know it's a lie," he said.

I got up and approached him slowly, as I would a wounded animal. "I don't believe you'll hurt me again. I know what happened wasn't your fault."

"Wasn't it? She came to me, yes, and I'll even accept she had some psychic influence on me, but she'd have achieved nothing if I wasn't jealous of Constantine."

"Cons—"

"I know you say you and he are in the past, and I believe you believe it, but he loves you, Cherry, and he's a better man than me. Not that it's hard these days."

"It's not a contest. I chose *you.*"

"But would you choose me again?" He didn't give me time to answer. "Should you? Ádísa persuaded me with lies and compulsion, and Willoughby urged me on, but I knew I was hurting you. Even if I didn't believe I'd *kill* you, I was still trying to force you to choose me. *Force* you, Cherry."

"I want to be with you." I kept saying that, but after what had transpired between us, I mostly wanted to be by myself for a few days. "My mom said I could stay another week or so. More like, she said she'd hunt me down if I didn't. You and Constantine go home, clear the air between you, and when I get back, we'll start over. I know we're both hurting, but I don't blame you." Not consciously, at least.

"Why didn't she haunt Constantine's dreams?"

"What?" I needed a moment to catch up to what he meant.

"Ádísa could have haunted Constantine's dreams. Why didn't she?"

I thought about it. "Willoughby hadn't drunk his blood."

"But she had, and Willoughby had hers. Cee—Constantine told me that would have worked too. But she didn't go to Constantine, because she knew he would never turn against you."

"He's older, Alex. He'd know she was lying."

"Maybe he's stronger. Maybe he loves you more. Either way, he wouldn't have failed you like I did."

I didn't know what to say, to counteract his argument. Especially without hurting his already wounded ego more. Constantine was stronger, but that was only because of his age.

As for the other thing— "The reason doesn't matter," I said. "Maybe she didn't want to risk it, since he killed her. You know what? You should stay too. Constantine can go, so the vampettes don't take their withdrawal out on Sheena and Wesley, and you'll stay. We'll start over. Maybe date a little. Do things the right way this time." We'd slept together and fallen in love before getting to fully know each other. A new beginning might fix everything.

Alex shook his head. "Dating won't fix this, Cherry. I'm sorry. I can't. I have to go."

"Back to the mansion?" I knew that wasn't what he'd said, but I needed to hope things would get back to how they were.

"Cherry."

His hushed utterance of my name did it. It broke the dam. So far, I had found an excuse for him, every step of the way. He'd been thrown into my world unprepared. His turning had been without his consent. He was forced to leave his apartment and cohabitate with my ex, among several other people living at the mansion. He was used by an ancient valkyrie—or whatever the fuck she used to be—and her lackey.

But now *he* wanted to leave me, and he didn't even have the decency to yell and have a proper fight about it.

I'd fix that.

"What? Am I making this hard for you? What happened to your promise to make it up to me? You hurt me. Repeatedly. And you think the way to atone for it is to run away? Excuse me for not liking that solution one fucking bit." I'd raised my voice and wasn't surprised to hear a knock on the door.

"Not now," I said.

"Yes, now." Constantine made his way in, as if he owned the room. He had a knack for that.

"We're trying to have a conversation here," I said.

Alex hung his head. "I've already spoken to Constantine about it. He agrees it's for the best."

Just when I thought he couldn't piss me off more. He went to Constantine before he talked to me? And Constantine had—what? Given permission to Alex to dump me? "Does he, now?" I glared at Constantine. "I bet he's only thinking of what's best for our relationship. Or maybe you're being played by yet another ancient vampire."

"I resent that implication." Constantine's lips didn't even move. They were frozen in the most uncomfortable smile I've ever seen him sport. "I am actually trying to salvage your relationship."

"By driving us apart. Makes sense." It had nothing to do with helping us and everything to do with his feelings for me. There was no reason bringing said feelings up in front of Alex, though, when I was trying to convince him there was nothing between Constantine and me.

"I'd already made up my mind when I went to him," Alex said. He stood and took an uncertain step toward me. He dusted the seat of his jeans. He was always fully dressed around me now. "The night Constantine killed Ádísa, she said Los Angeles wasn't the only city they'd been hunting in. With the council's sanction, I'm going to look for other fledglings she and Willoughby were hiding from us."

"The council knows about you?" After all we'd done to hide his change from them? I was dumbfounded.

"You and I do. We're both members now," Constantine said with a shrug. "You and I witnessed Willoughby turn Alex three days ago, before he tried to come after you again, and you took him out."

He'd said this would happen, but I didn't know how to react. What did it mean? What would be my responsibilities? I opted for my usual way of dealing with overwhelming situations—humor. "Do I get a crown?" I asked. "'Cause I really want a crown."

Constantine gave me a look fraught with disapproval, but his eyes were smiling.

"Well, I don't sanction Alex's leaving. He has to stay. We have to work things out."

"I need to go, Cherry. These fledglings need to be brought in and shown they can be good, despite Ádísa's doctrine. If I help them, I help me. I'll learn control as I teach them. I won't trust myself with you unless I know nothing can get to me. That I'm more than my new nature. We can't work anything out until I've found myself again. You and I keep saying I wasn't myself lately, but who was I? Who am I really, now that everything I've known is different?"

Sadness funneled into hurt, and then into anger. "And you're just now figuring out you've changed? You've been a vampire for months."

"Yes, and I pretended everything was the same, but it's not. To be good enough for you—to be the best I can be—I must first figure out a way to be me. This new me. Undead guy on a liquid diet."

"You can be you with me," I said quietly. I'd lost my oomph. Alex was determined, and I wouldn't stoop to begging.

Constantine reached for the door handle. "I will let the two of you hash it out."

"Don't bother," I said. "We're done." I turned to Alex. "Go, but I'm not going to wait for you."

"I wouldn't expect you to, but I *will* return, and I *will* try to win you back." To Constantine, he said, "You hear that? Take care of her, make whatever move you're going to while I'm gone, but I'll fight for her when I'm myself again."

Constantine shrugged. "When Cherry comes back to me, it will not be because I won by default—because I was the one to stay behind. She will come because she burns for me."

I expected a punch to fly his way. Alex gave him a tired smile instead. "You're a weird fuck, Cee, but I can see what she likes about you."

I shook my head in disbelief. I was *there*, while they talked about me like I was a prize to be won. "You're both weird fucks, and I don't like either of you very much right now." Though the discussion turned me on.

"You, pack your bags," I told Alex. "Go, do your thing, and we'll talk when you're back." Something dawned on me. "As a council member, I order you to check in with me when you get to each new city. I want to know where you are at least once a week. Got it?"

"Will do."

"And you"—I poked Constantine in the chest—"better get back home. Your little girlfriends are driving Sheena crazy." I left the room, unwilling to watch Alex get ready to leave. Leave me. "I'm staying with my folks for a couple weeks. I need the time off," I called over my shoulder, already halfway up the stairs.

I didn't see Alex off. Mom said Constantine would drive him to the mansion, to get a bigger suitcase and more clothes, and then take him to the airport. Constantine didn't come see me before he left either. He asked my folks to let me know my room at the mansion would be waiting for me.

<h1 style="text-align:center">Epilogue</h1>

I'll go, sooner or later, but it's been ten days, and I still hate the idea of leaving. Having breakfast with my parents in the morning, in a house devoid of vampires, drama, and politics, feels good. Normal.

I've missed normal.

Mom makes tea, and after Dad goes to work, we prepare lunch and fill each other in on the last six years.

I do most of the talking.

I've told her everything—about my short-lived career in porn, about my turning, about what Constantine meant to me and what he still means to me. About Alex. This time I even told her about the change in his behavior toward me and why he left.

I think she's team Constantine, but first and foremost, she's team Cherry, and that's what matters. She even calls me that now, having accepted everything that's changed about me.

My dad knows less, but enough to realize I'm no longer the little girl who left home to make it as a model in the city. I'm still *his* little girl, though. He makes sure to bring me a cupcake every evening, and I'm finally glad for my vampire metabolism, after years of whining about being unable to change my body.

Last night, Alex called. He's been in San Francisco since he left. Nothing definitive has come up, but he believes he's on the trail of at least one member of Ádísa and Willoughby's army of undead hotties.

It was the second time he called—the first was to say he landed safely. We didn't speak about us this time either. I've come to realize there really can't be an 'us' right now. I hate to say it, but he made the right choice in leaving. Distance has to soothe the hurt that's there. Soften its edges. When we can look at each other without seeing the past, maybe we can start building again, if there's enough foundation left. He seems to be on the right track to finding himself.

I turned in soon after we hung up. The downside to living with my parents is that I'm worn out well before midnight, and tonight was no exception. The moment my head hit the pillow, I was out like a light.

I lie on a beach chair, a strawberry daiquiri in one hand, a romance novel in the other. The warmth of the sun caresses my skin, and a light breeze ruffles my hair from time to time. The only sound disrupting my sunbathing is the gentle, languid sloshing of the sea against the shore.

I've had this dream before. I know the book is blank, but the frozen daiquiri tastes like heaven, the sweetness and tartness of fresh strawberry elevated by the kick of alcohol.

I sense a presence that wasn't here last time, though. I look around, and here's Constantine, strolling along the beach toward me.

He stands over me, in a pair of scruffy jeans he'd never wear if I were awake. No shirt. No shoes. The sand gleams golden between his toes, but it's the pale perfection of his broad chest that draws my gaze. "I miss you," he says. "When are you coming home?"

He feels so real, I know I'm not dreaming of him. He's sharing my dream—or is he usurping it?

I put my drink aside, lower the book to my lap, and push my sunglasses atop my head. "I thought this was supposed to be me-time," I say squinting up.

"You can have you-time at the mansion." He shades his eyes with his palm, and a cloud covers the bright sun, shedding a grey tint over my surroundings.

"Are you controlling my dream? That's not playing fair." I'm not upset, just curious. "You said you didn't know how."

"I'm only doing what I have always done," he says. "Watching out for you."

"Pretty stalkery of you." Part of me wonders at my calm acceptance. Then again, not everything has to make sense in dreams. "Now if you don't mind, I have several months of tanning to make up for."

"This is a dream."

"Exactly. Only place I can tan. So unless you're here to put lotion on my back, or have something else to fess up to..." I give him a little finger wave.

I expect him to make some remark about the lotion, but his expression closes, becomes more guarded. He crosses his arms and rests his chin on his chest. "I promised to never again keep something significant from you, and something came up that I believe falls into that category."

"Next time use the phone." I reach for my book again, but he drops to his knees and traps my hand between both of his.

"Ruby visited my dream," he says. "She heard about Willoughby."

That stings. "She could have called me. I know you two go back a long time, but I'm her granddaughter. You'd think that'd count for someth—"

"Cherry, she says you could become human again."

"What?" My whining is forgotten in an instant. Hope blossoms in my heart, but I stomp on it before it takes root. There's no turning back from being undead. If there was, I'd have at least heard rumors about it. "That's not possible." Is it?

He snaps his head to one side, then the other. "Shit. I must wake up. Tell nobody of this and don't call me. We can't talk about it over the phone. Just come home."

I nod, and he's gone.

I need to wake up.

Now.

Book 3
Cherry Pie

Prologue

"Cherry, can't you see he's lying through his teeth? I can, and I'm on a different continent."

Alex had his reasons for being suspicious, but Constantine wasn't lying. Things would have been much easier if he were.

I wouldn't have to die again.

But I'm starting the story in the middle.

Let me fix that.

Chapter One

I open myself to the scenery around me, until the stitches holding it together glow a pure white. The sunglasses holding my hair back from my face are useless against this light, but I don't want to dim it, anyway. I need to take it in.

The sight is beautiful in its eeriness.

I focus on a single point along the seam between golden sand and blue morning sky. About where the overhead light switch should be. It doesn't give, but it will. I've been practicing since I was trapped in Alex's dream.

I use my finger to draw a bright-red thread over it, and snap it with my finger. I tug, and my strawberry daiquiri fades to transparency before it's gone completely. The book on my lap follows it to oblivion. The wind has dropped, and the waves no longer lap at the shore. They're frozen in place until I pull again, and then they melt into the sky that in turn gives its place to the white of my bedroom walls.

I close my eyes and smile when the beach chair beneath me yields into something softer. Fluffier. I open my eyes again and—

I blinked away my much-needed sleep. Did Constantine have to drop into my dream tonight of all nights? His timing sucked.

Speaking of timing, I should start keeping track of how long it took to enter and exit a dream. I practiced every chance I got and was improving—another reason I was so tired; I needed to let my mind switch off once in a while—but I wanted tangible results.

Maybe I'd ignore my ex's new bout of drama and sink back into my dream.

Sure.

I'd forget he said I could be human again, so I could catch some shut eye. 'Cause I was cool like that.

Not.

I kicked the sheets off and stood. My inner clock told me the sun was still down for the count, which meant so were my parents. I didn't want to sneak out of their home without saying *goodbye*, but if what Constantine said was true, I couldn't wait to get more details out of him.

I pulled on my jeans and sneakers, and wore my hoodie over Alex's T-shirt I'd been using as a pajama top. His scent was barely there after ten days. I didn't know where we stood, other than that we weren't a *we*, but I liked feeling close to him at night. And it was a comfy shirt.

I scribbled a quick note for my parents on a Post-It and pressed it to the fridge door with the heel of my hand.

Constantine needs me at the mansion. I'll be back tomorrow, for my stuff and a proper farewell. And I'll need pancakes. Lots of them.
Love you both,
Cherry

It was a three-and-a-half-hour drive back to L.A. without traffic, but traffic didn't apply to me and neither did driving. I was flying there. I pulled my hair into a tight bun and raised the hood, to minimize damage, and took off.

The crisp night air felt refreshing on my skin and called up memories of the warmth of the dream. The heat had been at its strongest when Constantine was there.

And when wasn't that the case?

As trees and hills gave way to wide open road beneath me, my mind flew forward, to the mansion and the man waiting there.

Constantine didn't reach out before tonight, respecting my time with my family. I appreciated that, but until I dreamed of him topless beside me, I hadn't realized I'd missed him. It was weird. We broke up years ago, but the last few months he'd been a constant in my life, and I liked having him around.

Another thing to sort out if I wanted a future with Alex. Which I did.

With the exception of his… dark period, Alex was the yang to Constantine's yin. He was open with his feelings, unafraid of commitment, and with a moral compass so strong, you could count on him to always draw a clear line between right and wrong.

Constantine was all about gray areas and fuzzy limits.

And I was confused.

Not about which of them to choose. Constantine was history—though who knows what would have happened between us if Ádísa hadn't planned and executed our breakup?

Not what I should be considering.

The hazy scenery beneath me gained shape. I cut into the smog, thankful I didn't have to breathe. I began my descent, careful to keep away from the lights. Not easy in downtown L.A. but doable around Constantine's mansion.

My feet met solid ground at the same time, and I brought my body to a perfect halt. Can I get a *yay* for bending the laws of physics?

I lowered my hood and let my hair loose. It felt stiff, and I bet it looked it, but this wasn't a social call.

Constantine said I could become human again.

How?

And why wasn't I ringing his doorbell and asking him?

I pressed the button by the wrought-iron gate and smiled at the closed circuit camera, waiting for Wesley, Constantine's aging human butler, to buzz me in. Flying all the way to someone's front door unannounced is considered an aggressive move among our kind, but I wasn't afraid Constantine would see it as such. I was simply being polite. He was waiting for me, but I wasn't staying here yet. Or again. Or at all, depending on how our chat went.

"Come to the parlor. We'll watch the sunrise." Constantine's voice came from behind me, instead of from my left, where the intercom was.

I spun on my heel. Nothing. The acoustics out here were wonky.

The latch clicked, and the gate slid open. "I didn't come for the sunrise," I muttered under my breath, though I couldn't wait to see it. Couldn't get enough sun since my grandmother's potion made it possible for me to walk in daylight. If only I could tan…

I followed the path to the front door and let myself in. Wesley poked his head out of the kitchen, and a smile brightened his lined face. He looked tired. I couldn't blame him; he'd been taking care of too many people for a while now.

"You've been missed," he said. "Coffee?"

"I missed you too." I returned the smile. "And yes, please." No need to tell him how I took it; he'd made me coffee more times than I could count, both when I dated Constantine and in the months Alex and I stayed here.

I padded softly on the plush carpet, as I trailed through the ground floor, praying I met nobody else before I talked to Constantine. I'd love to catch up with Sheena, and the little masochist in me missed the three fledglings Constantine sort of adopted on the day he decapitated his maker, but I could do without diversions until I had answers.

From past experience, odds were Constantine would be less than fully dressed, so I wasn't surprised to see him in nothing but a pair of silk pajama bottoms. I crossed the threshold to the spacious parlor at the exact same moment the rising sun appeared through the glass panes taking up three sides of the room. The rays that a couple weeks ago would have reduced Constantine to ashes now set his pale skin ablaze with red, orange, and purple hues. The muscles in his wide sternum stood out in stark relief, and his blue eyes sparkled.

He was magnificent.

I didn't try to hide my ogling. He expected it. It wouldn't surprise me if he'd timed my entrance specifically for this.

I blinked, and whatever thrall he held over me evaporated. He was still stunning, but now I could focus on things beyond that. "You said I could become human again?" I asked.

"I did."

I was looking right at him, but I didn't see him move his lips.

"Finally, she catches on. I've been dropping hints for a while." His lips never parted.

"How are you doing this? Are you messing with my mind?"

He held my gaze. "I've broken my promise," he said, and this time I watched him form the words. His serious tone was a far cry from the seductive purr he usually opted for when shirtless. "I've kept something important from you."

Ah, now I got it. "How long have you known I could be turned back?" I glared. Would he never learn? Omissions and lies always came back to bite him in the ass. And I wouldn't think of that thing's perfect curve.

"No. Not that. I informed you of the possibility as soon as Ruby told me about it. There's something else." His mouth stopped moving, but the words kept coming. "*When two vampires who've killed their own makers exchange blood, they get a sort of telepathy.*"

Shock and surprise short-circuited my brain.

"*I killed Ádísa, and you killed Willoughby,*" he said. In my head. "*And then—*"

"You cleaned my wounds and fed me your blood. Three times."

"*Yes. And you don't have to speak aloud. I can hear your thoughts.*"

This was too fucking much. He'd crossed lines and pushed my limits time and again, but to be able to straight-up pull thoughts out of my head? No. "You do that, and I promise to hurt you so bad, you'll taste it for eternity. My thoughts are mine. No trespassing. Got it?" I refused to use my inside voice.

"Cherry, I would never disrespect you this way. You have to believe me."

"Do I?" I was tired of believing him. Of trusting him. More tired of reminding myself not to. "Don't tell me you only found out about this now, too." Oh, he knew for a while. He'd insisted on giving me *his* blood when Alex tried to feed me.

"No." He said this aloud. "I've known for years, and after Alex… After you were hurt the first time, I couldn't overlook the opportunity."

"To bind me to you?" I asked. The arrogance was strong with this one.

He frowned. "Of course not. To never let you get hurt again. Wherever you are, whatever happens, you'll be able to reach me at the speed of thought. Think about this, Cherry." His eyes pleaded with me to forgive him, and I found myself wanting to.

"You should've let me choose for myself." I was tired of people thinking they knew what was best for me.

"You were drained. There was no time to discuss it."

"You could have come to me later."

"I didn't think that far ahead." He stood and scratched his chest, his bicep bulging. He used his body as a distraction, but I knew all his tricks, and they wouldn't work this time.

"You're lying," I said. "You jumped at the chance to have an in with me, and you knew it when you told Alex you wouldn't be my default choice. Games. It's all about games with you."

His blue eyes darkened to near black, as he narrowed them at me. "There was nothing game-like about seeing you drained in your parents' basement, with your crazed lover still inside you, and knowing I could have prevented it. You'd be dead now if I didn't act."

I arched an eyebrow. "Alex might have stopped."

"You don't believe that any more than I do, but I'm not talking about then. How do you think I found you in that clearing?" Where Willoughby made Alex bleed me out.

I remembered wondering about that at the time, before more pressing matters had demanded my attention. Like surviving. "But you hadn't had my blood then. You only licked my wounds clean after," I said.

"When I gave you my blood the first time, I held you. Your blood was all over me, driving me insane. I knew the effects wouldn't last if I only tasted it, so I went for it." He raked his fingers through his long blond hair.

"And at the clearing?"

He held my gaze. "You'd almost died twice, Cherry. I wouldn't leave it to chance. I took enough to know this bond would last. That I wouldn't lose you again."

I should be livid. He'd made the decision for me. Twice. *To protect me.* As if I were a helpless little girl, and not a vampire who could stand on her own two feet—and kick ass, when need arose.

But his last words… His eyes, swirling with color that I knew corresponded to pain and hunger and even love…

He didn't want to lose me, and more than once he'd gone above and beyond, to keep me safe and happy.

I closed the distance between us and touched my lips to his cheek. *"I forgive you."* I tried to think it at him, unsure how this worked.

He slid his hands up my arms, his touch lighting my skin on fire. When he reached my shoulders, he dug in his fingers, holding me to him. *"I'll make you happy, if it kills me."*

The emotion in his words slammed into my chest and made me lightheaded. It took all my willpower not to think of a response. I couldn't trust myself not to project it to him, and I didn't know what it would be, when my gut reaction was to lose myself in him.

But that way lay badness.

He nuzzled my cheek. "I made so many mistakes as your mentor. I fancied myself a sort of Pygmalion and tried to sculpt the perfect woman out of you, when I should have spent our time together letting you know you already were perfect. *Are* perfect."

He'd approached me as my VSS-assigned mentor and had done his best to teach me all he could, but I never shook the feeling he found me lacking. That I couldn't compare to the Valkyrie who made him. My insecurities intensified when he cheated on me with her, and they didn't go away even when he killed her for me.

He'd said he loved me—before and since—but this validation filled my stomach with butterflies.

"You really think I'm perfect?" I whispered against his ear.

He shifted to touch his forehead to mine. "You're beautiful, and you're smart. Funny and brave. A hellcat, in and out of bed. And your heart… This world has broken you down and stomped all over you, people have hurt you and betrayed you, and you *still* see the good in them. You see the good in me. Fuck yes, you're perfect." And then, with the slightest tilt of his head, he found my lips and claimed them.

Soft, full lips glided against mine, before his talented tongue slid between them and caressed my own. I melted against him, my heart absorbing his words. I skated my palms up his sides, enjoying the hardness of muscle beneath his smooth skin.

It was incredible.

I was kissing Constantine again, after so long. After I was sure he and I were done.

When I'd been thinking of another man.

I said I wouldn't wait for Alex, but part of me wanted us to fix things. To regain the normal, easy relationship we had before Willoughby and Ádísa threw us the mother of all curveballs.

With great reluctance and even greater regret, I broke the kiss. "Too soon," I said.

He ghosted his thumb over my cheek. "Will it ever not be?"

I had no reply for that. "Is it okay if I stay here?" I asked after a second.

"Of course." His smile lit up the room.

"And you'll tell me about the whole vampire-to-human reversion thing?"

The smile wilted. When it reappeared, it didn't reach his eyes. "Anything to make you happy."

Chapter Two

I took a sip of the coffee Wesley brought me, and bit back a moan of appreciation. His brew could wake the dead—I vouched for it.

"I'm ready," I said. "Tell me everything."

Constantine nodded. "My last year as a human, I was one of a select army of Viking warriors, sent to guard the Byzantine emperor Vasilios the Second. It was the late tenth century, and we were known as the Varangian Guard." He'd reverted to his most cultured tone, the one unaffected by me and the three vampettes who taught him things like *OMG* and *WTF*.

He cleared his throat. "During the battle of Abydos— you might know it as Hellespont—"

I wouldn't know it as anything; I had no clue whether it was a place or an artifact. Plus, I was still doing the math, to calculate his exact age. He'd been turned in his early thirties, so… I'd always thought of him as ancient, but I guess he was only eleven hundred years old or so. *Only.*

"—we were fighting the rebel Bardas Phokas, when a sword sliced through my side. I dispatched of my attacker and was forced to seek shelter in the catacombs of a monastery. There, among the robes of a deceased priest, I found a scroll. At the time, I didn't know what its significance was, but I held on to it nonetheless."

I arched my eyebrows. "You were wounded and in a place filled with dead people, and you decided to keep a piece of paper that meant nothing to you?"

"*Parchment*, Cherry. It was old, and it called to me." He gave a rueful smile. "And it was in my hand when I died."

I leaned forward. "That's when Ádísa turned you?" I ached to reach for him and was grateful for the coffee table acting as a barrier between us. Touching him again wouldn't lead to good things. Correction—it'd probably lead to great things, which would be bad.

"Indeed. I remember the cold stone beneath me and the smell of mold in the air. When she leaned over me, I was sure she was a Valkyrie, come to take me to Valhalla."

She'd cultivated that myth for a while. Before I dusted her childe and co-conspirator, Willoughby, I found out she was really a succubus, who lost the Devil's favor when she fell for a mortal and failed to get his soul.

"What was Ádísa doing there?" I asked.

"She thrived on war. She joined the guard looking for blood and mayhem."

"But—" *She was a woman*, was what I meant to say. I must have thought it too loudly.

"Viking women never shied from battle."

"Makes sense." I could picture her slaying people, running them through with a sword, or tearing into them with her bare hands.

Constantine's gaze was vacant, as if he'd been transported to that time so long ago. "She was beautiful and fierce, and when she offered me immortality, I didn't refuse her. She sealed my wound, her lips cold against my fevered skin. She closed her mouth over my throat, and I wouldn't mind dying in her arms. I hadn't felt a woman's touch since I left my wife behind."

The shocks wouldn't stop coming. "You were married?"

He sighed. "I never saw her or my two daughters again. Never went back. I was dead and reborn that night. I buried my name together with my past." His eyes were dark and stormy with pain.

"Do you want to talk about it?"

He shook his head. "I loved them. I left. I died. I expect so did they."

I wouldn't press for more. This was his story to share.

"When I woke up, I was disoriented and ravenous. She fed me her blood and we spent the night together. I was enthralled by her beauty and ruthlessness. We joined the fight side by side and fed on our enemies and our warriors alike. By the time the battle was done and Phokas was dead, I was so taken with her, I'd have done anything she asked.

"You know the rest. I did her bidding for years. I followed her like her trained guard dog. We fought and parted ways for decades at a time, only to pick up where we'd left off. We traveled the world. Witnessed the wonders of technology. Broke up and reunited. Blood and death followed her. I didn't approve of senseless slaughter—no honor in that—but I didn't object. She was my everything, even when there was an ocean between us."

I *did* know this part, from bits and pieces he'd shared about his past the year and a half we'd been together, but I'd never heard this condensed version that showed how important she'd been to him. How deep his feelings for her ran. It wasn't jealousy I felt; in the end, he'd proven he loved me more. Hearing him talk about her with such awe, though, made me hurt for his loss and the hard choice he had to make when he killed her to save me.

"Society changed," Constantine said. "The need to hide our nature became more pronounced, but Ádísa was as reckless as ever. I cleaned her messes because I felt I had to, but as time went by, I became more vocal about questioning her decisions. And then there was Ruby."

My grandma, whom Ádísa left behind for dead and Constantine turned.

"And then there was me," I said.

Constantine's smile was brighter than the sun. "And then there was you." The warmth in his voice tugged at my very core.

I refused to meet his gaze. He's the only vampire I know whose eyes change color to match his emotions, and I didn't trust myself to resist what I'd see there. "Tell me about the scroll." My voice came out gruff and throaty.

He sat back and steepled his fingers on his stomach. "It was torn, but the part I found read, *they can walk under the sun and count finite remaining sunsets once again, requiring breath and sustenance, and growing as nature and God meant Man to.* At the time, I thought it was a blessing. Maybe part of a Christian Orthodox psalm. I knew nothing of their religion.

"I kept my piece in a box, alongside my Viking shield and sword, but never thought to look more into it. When Ruby came to my dream, she told me she'd found a translation of an ancient script in the Romanian mountains. It mentioned a way to revive a specific type of Strigoi, as they call vampires. The latter part of the text matches what I found in Abydos, and it seems it would work on us."

Well, hello, new information. "Us?"

He looked at his fingers. "It speaks about two immortals who've killed the ones who made them, assuming our understanding is correct." His voice was low.

"You're hiding something," I said.

"Not hiding. I'm merely savoring the next part."

I arched an eyebrow. "Spill."

He raised his head to face me. "The ritual involved calls for mutual draining"—mischief danced in his eyes and on his smirk—"during intercourse."

I laughed. The man knew how to relieve tension.

"I'm absolutely serious, I'm afraid," Constantine said. "Though if this is your reaction to the thought of us having sex, I have my work cut out for me."

I was wrong. No tension relieved, and now mental images of Constantine fucking my brains out came to add horniness on top of my stress. "You're serious," I half-said, half-asked.

He gave a slow nod. "It could be worse."

"Yeah. Could involve ritual sacrifice."

"In a way, it does." He frowned. "We're supposed to drink from one another until we both die."

"But then we're reborn."

His shrug was noncommittal. "Have you told your parents you're moving back here?"

"I left a note. I'll fly back tomorrow and get my stuff. Say a proper *goodbye*." Unlike last time, when I had no clue they knew about vampires, and I let them wait for my undead ass for more than six years.

"I'll join you," he said. "But for now, you should get some sleep. We have a long day ahead of us tomorrow. I suppose you'll want to be back in time to see Sheena and the girls off."

Huh? "*Off*, where?"

"They're moving out tomorrow evening. I'm sure we'll be reeled in to help with the last of their stuff."

"They're moving out? You didn't say anything."

"I thought Sheena did. You certainly talked a lot more to her than to me during your absence." *That* didn't sound whiny at all. "They made arrangements while we were in San Louis Obispo. Your chatty friend is returning to her modeling agency and offered to take on the young ladies as clients. Take them in too, I suppose, since she invited them to stay at her place. I didn't think to mention it, because it wasn't about me and it didn't fall into the things-that-affect-you category."

He was right. It didn't affect me. Except for the part where he and I would be left in his sexy mansion with no buffer between us other than an aging human butler. Once the women were gone, Constantine might start running around the mansion without a stitch on. That thought brought back memories of him naked, gleaming in the candlelight as he hovered over me, a wicked smile on his lips, and his blue eyes swirling with violet.

Which made me realize—"You changed the subject."

"I did not." He sounded scandalized, to say the least, so I was pretty certain it was an act.

"You so did. You said we had to drink from each other until we died, and then I said we'd be reborn, and you changed the freaking subject. You promised you wouldn't hide anything else to do with me. *Promised.* Repeatedly." That he'd had reason to do so more than once should've taught me something about his credibility.

Constantine rolled his shoulders and straightened in his seat. When he looked at me, there was no humor in his gaze. "I don't want to tell you."

"Great. Now I *have* to know."

"This is about me. Not you."

I tilted my head to the side and studied his posture. His back was stiff, his shoulders square. His knuckles were even paler than the rest of him. "Is it about the ritual?" I asked.

"Yes."

"Tell me."

"You should decide on your own whether you will return to your human nature or not."

"Tell me," I said again.

He huffed and stood in a fluid motion that had the satin of his pants clinging to him and defining every curve.

"Your ass isn't going to take my mind off this," I told his sculpted back when he turned to look outside.

"This ritual will make us as old as we'd be if we were never turned."

I wasn't sure if he spoke the words or thought them at me, but they chilled me to the core. "That'll make me thirty, but you... You will be—"

"Gone."

I was up and in his face—yes, sandwiched between him and the floor-to-ceiling glass—in no time. "And you didn't think that affects me? Were you not going to tell me at all? I'd wake up human, covered in your fucking dust?" I didn't know what shocked me more—the fact that he'd keep this from me, or the searing agony twisting my gut at the thought of losing him forever. Not too long ago, I'd convinced myself I no longer cared if he lived or died.

"Cherry..."

"No. Fuck you. No." I was crying.

He wrapped his arms around me. "I don't know what I was going to do," he said. "I've been trying to think of a way out, but if there isn't one… You never wanted this life, and I've lived a dozen lifespans. Maybe it's my time."

"No. We're not doing this. You're not dying for me. And you're a bastard for even considering it." I shook off his hold and smacked his chest with my open palm.

He took a step back, and I felt cold. Weird. Vampires don't feel cold, unless we're talking arctic temperatures.

"I thought it was kind of romantic," he said with a shit-eating grin.

I scowled. "Jackass."

"Chivalrous, even."

"Asshole." But a smile tugged at the corners of my lips.

"Yeah, I love you too."

The words were spoken lightly, but they landed like a punch to my stomach. He really did. I believed him before, but now I felt it in my core. And it left me shaken.

"We should get some sleep," I said. I'd adjusted to a human schedule for the past ten days, but being a vampire in L.A. was much easier by night, and I'd apparently remain a bloodsucker after all.

Plus, it was a solid excuse to stop looking into Constantine's soulful eyes.

Chapter Three

It was well after noon, when Constantine and I left for my parents' house. The sun was no longer an issue, but onlookers were, so we couldn't fly there in the middle of the day. Alex had left his car at the mansion, and Constantine suggested we drive.

I shouldn't have agreed.

I hadn't seen Constantine drive since he took me to his place from the Vampire Social Services, early in my unlife. Memories of the debauchery that followed that ride combined with mental images of Alex behind the wheel—or fucking me on the hood, parked outside his mother's house—and amplified the awkward silence between Constantine and me. It was odd, being with him and not talking, but I didn't know what to say.

I leaned against the passenger door, seeking out a semblance of space. It didn't work. I felt Constantine's presence as vividly as if we were pressed together.

Maybe it was the ultra-naughty Constantine-centered dream I had during my beauty sleep. I was able to change it more than once, but my stubborn subconscious fleeted back to him every single time.

Did he insinuate his way into my dreams?

Was he reading my thoughts this very moment?

No. He said he wouldn't, and I'd drive myself crazy if I second-guessed that.

I studied him. He wore jeans and a form fitting T-shirt that had become the norm *after* he and I broke up. While we dated, he was always impeccably dressed and coiffed, but I liked this hair-in-the-wind version more.

His triceps bunched as he shifted gear, and I licked my lips. *Shit.* Better pray for no traffic.

It was a frigging long three-and-a-half hours, and I pretended to sleep through much of it, when I wasn't commenting on the weather.

Mom and Dad were inordinately excited to see Constantine. There was hugging and kissing and pointed looks, rife with innuendo. No pancakes, though.

Once we were done packing and loading the car, Mom ignored my glares and invited us to stay the night.

"It's almost seven, and it *is* a long drive," Constantine said. "It may be a good idea."

It wasn't. Our rooms at the mansion weren't right next to each other. Here, we'd sleep a few feet apart—and Constantine slept in the buff. It was different when I had Alex in bed with me and a threat hung over our heads. Now there would be little to keep my mind occupied.

Luckily, there was a valid reason for us to go back to L.A. tonight. "We can't stay." I tried to sound sorry. "We promised to help the girls with their move."

"Indeed." The look Constantine gave me said he saw right through me. "But there is time for a cup of coffee, and Cherry has some news for you."

Damn it.

I didn't want to get my parents' hopes up, when I saw no way around the pesky issue of needing to sacrifice Constantine to regain my humanity.

"Really?" Mom ushered us to the kitchen and started the coffee maker.

Dad sliced up some cake and joined us at the table. It was all so mundane and normal. I could have that. I slid my gaze to Constantine. *No.* The price was too high.

He smiled. "Go on."

"Constantine may have found a way for me to become human again," I said.

The mug Mom held clanked against the counter. She looked at me, and the hope I meant to avoid shone in her eyes.

It hurt that I had to squash it. "It's not easy, and we don't know if it's even possible."

"It's possible," Constantine said.

Dad reached across the table and covered my hand with his. "Whatever makes you happy makes us happy. We'll love you the same, fangs or no fangs."

I wanted to fly into his arms. Instead, I turned my palm and gave his hand a squeeze. "We'll look into it more. I'll let you know what we find out, but it may not happen."

Constantine shrugged. He took the coffee my mom offered and pulled out a chair for her. "We'll do our best to see it does."

Maybe I didn't mind him dying, after all. I was minutes from staking him where he sat.

A short and awkward conversation later—I mean, what plans *could* I have for the future, Dad?—I was beyond ready to go.

More hugging and kissing and promising to keep in touch, all with a knot in my throat. This *goodbye* wasn't permanent. It didn't have to be a long one either; I could see them every weekend now on. I still wished I could stay with them a while longer. I was supposed to spend a couple months in my childhood home with a little R-n-R, gorging on Mom's food without worrying about calories, and no boy drama. What more could I ask for?

Oh right. To be human again. And I couldn't have that either, without costing Constantine his unlife. *Boo.*

Mom stuffed the trunk of the car with bottles of Ruby's brew. "I've kept some too, just in case," she said.

Constantine gathered her in a hug. "Thank you, Kathleen. If things work out, our little Gertrude won't need it for long," he said.

I didn't know whether to slap him for promising things he couldn't deliver or for using my given name which I'd rather forget.

The moment the car doors were closed and my parents couldn't hear, I plastered a smile on my face and whispered, "Will you stop doing that?"

"What?" Constantine waved at Mom and Dad and peeled off the driveway.

"Making them believe it's possible to have their daughter back."

"You *are* their daughter."

"You know what I'm saying. You let them think I'll be human again."

He shook his head, gaze on the road. "After all this time, you have no faith in my problem-solving abilities."

"I have every faith on your problem-creating abilities, if that helps."

"It doesn't." He sounded sad, which shouldn't bother me but did.

"You said yourself I can only go back if I drain you to dust. That's not an option."

This time, he turned to look at me. "I may have a solution to that."

Now I was the one getting my hopes up. I waited for him to say more. When he didn't, I asked, "Care to elaborate?"

"I've been reading the text in a way that made sense to me, but I was wrong. For both of us to turn human, we must be *consumed*, but not necessarily consume each other. What if I drain you, while you feed from someone else to keep from dusting?"

Someone else who'd be in the room while Constantine and I had sex? "Do you have someone in mind?"

He didn't hesitate. "Alex. He's of your bloodline. It may be an acceptable cheat, and if it doesn't work, there's no real loss."

We'd both still be around. Still vampires.

There was one tiny problem. "How do we pitch that to Alex?"

"Preferably over video chat." Constantine chuckled. "I need to be able to see his face."

Two hours into the drive, I was hungry, and not for blood. I craved something greasy and calorie ridden, to drown out the fantasies wreaking havoc in my head. Constantine gave a moue of distaste when I suggested burgers, but he stopped at a drive-through and let me order.

"Let's pull over somewhere and at least pretend we're having a proper meal," he said when a paper bag full of fatty yumminess was safe on my lap.

I stuffed a handful of fries in my mouth and shrugged.

"You're so sexy like that," he said with a grin.

I tried to blow him a kiss, but the fries wouldn't allow it.

Laughing, he drove to an opening on the road, parked, and got out of the car.

"Where are you going?" I asked.

In lieu of an answer, he pulled a blanket out of the back seat and unfolded it on a grassy spot. He lay on his side and motioned for me to join him. I sat cross legged and placed the food strategically between us. Horizontal Constantine could lead to badness.

The carton-made barrier didn't help. I watched as he wrapped his lips around the fries or bit into a burger like it was the finest delicacy. The man oozed seduction, and my body responded to it. I adjusted my position, to ease the throbbing between my legs. Didn't work. He licked his fingers slowly, and I groaned before I could stop myself.

I blinked, and I was on my back, Constantine covering my body with his.

"Constantine…" My voice was hoarse. Better that it didn't work. I couldn't choose between telling him to stop or to rip off my clothes and fuck me in plain view of anyone who drove by.

"I've been good, Cherry," he whispered in my ear.

My insides clenched at the memory of Alex's weight on top of me, before he tried to kill me. As if he felt it,

Constantine propped himself up on his arms. His eyes were violet but clear. I wasn't afraid of him. Never could be.

He licked his lips. "You've made me *want* to be good, and I plan on keeping it up. I won't pressure you into my bed, and I'll accept your decision if you only come to me for the ritual. But I don't want you to confuse my passiveness for lack of desire."

A tiny shift of my hips, and the proof of his words dug into my thigh. If he kissed me again, I wouldn't stop him.

Spoiler—he didn't.

"I burn for you," he said. "You are the only sunshine I care to touch. Thoughts of you consume my days, and that little sound you just made haunts my dreams. I said I won't be your default choice, and I meant it, but you should know it's sheer torture being this close and not touching you." He raised his hand to my face, let his fingers hover over my cheek for a brief moment, and then formed a fist and punched the ground next to my head.

I was at a loss. My skin hummed in response to his voice, as my brain scrambled to catch up with everything he said.

Constantine rolled off me and sat up. "I don't remember the last time I ate al fresco," he said in a pleasant, conversational tone. His eyes were their usual gorgeous blue again. He'd said his piece and left me in turmoil.

While I'd once blamed sensory memory for my response to his advances, I could no longer deny I wanted him. This was bad. So very bad. It was too soon after Alex to start something new, and the situation would be messy even without Alex in the picture. I couldn't get back together with Constantine, when I was about to give up my immortality.

I dug into my food, avoiding his gaze.

Fuck.

Chapter Four

Female voices reached me as we entered the mansion. The vampettes were used to their new reality—and they didn't have to travel the world for it. I mentally thanked whatever deity sent them to disrupt the tension between Constantine and me.

"I'll take my stuff to my room, and then come help with the move," I said.

Constantine nodded and went straight to the kitchen, while I made my way downstairs. I wasn't over what he'd said. Had he made a bet with himself to drive me nuts, with his *I love you too* and his declarations during our sort-of-a-picnic?

A quick shower washed away road dirt as well as thoughts I shouldn't be entertaining. I'd just put on my underwear and a fresh T-shirt, when Sheena barged in without knocking. My manager-turned-friend-turned-betrayer-turned-friend-again was more hyper than usual, as she hopped on my bed and bounced on her knees.

"Come on, come on, come on," she squealed.

"Someone's excited," I said as grumpily as I could, but I went closer for a hug. In truth, her excitement was refreshing. She'd lived in fear of Willoughby since my turning, and though she never showed weakness, this was the most carefree I'd seen her.

"I sure am," she said. "You're back, and the move is postponed for tomorrow. That means I don't have to carry shit *and* I get to drink."

"Yeah, 'cause you only drink on special days."

"God, I missed you." She laughed and squeezed me before letting go. "Tonight is girls' night in. The vampettes are making drinks, and your presence is mandatory." She hopped to her feet and tossed me my jeans. "Get dressed. The party is their room."

Their room. The one they shared with Constantine. Any lingering heat dissipated.

For a while, I'd done a great job convincing myself there was nothing sexual between my ex and his three protégés—though, let's face it, a man not known for his restraint shared his admittedly humongous bed with three sexy kittens. They sure as hell didn't play Sudoku when the door was closed.

I stretched and pulled my jeans back on. Immortality was supposed to keep me in a good shape, but I felt ancient. Because that was what emotional roller-coasters did to me. What Constantine and his secrets and his stupid confessions of love did to me.

Love. *Pfft.* He meant it, but the word had a different meaning for him. I had to remember it when I considered giving us another chance. When we were together, he'd tried to convince me monogamy wasn't for vampires, and that sex and love were two distinct things. When I'd strongly disagreed, he'd cheated on me with his maker, and when I busted them, he insisted it was okay because he didn't have feelings for her.

Even if I accepted that immortals couldn't do physical fidelity, the lie was unforgivable. It'd be different if I'd agreed to an open relationship. Or a polyamorous one. I could maybe see myself with him and Alex.

I could totally see myself with him and Alex. In this bed. Or on the floor. They'd look so great naked together, Alex's tan contrasted against Constantine's pallor. Could I have them both? At the same time? It would be awkward after, but we could figure things out. And they both loved me. Well, Alex used to. I wasn't sure now.

Wait. Was I consideri—

"Earth to Cherry. Come in, Cherry." Sheena's voice snapped me out of it. She watched me, eyebrows furrowed. "Do I want to know what's in that head of yours?" she asked.

I shook said head.

"That's what I thought. Now button those up and let's go. Momma needs alcohol."

I followed her out of my room. Had I been thinking hard? Did I project my threesome-y thoughts to Constantine?

Speak of the devil... He stood outside his bedroom, tapping something on his phone. There was no sly look of *gotcha* in his eyes when we approached. He barely looked at me, as he said, "Alex called from the airport. He's on his way to London. I texted Ruby, and she and her team will pick him up at Heathrow."

"Did you tell him anything?" About the ritual.

Constantine shook his head. "I thought he should hear it from you."

"He didn't ask for me?" I kept my tone and face impassive, but I must have broadcasted my insecurity. Alex left to find himself. Maybe he also found that he no longer loved me.

And what the hell did I want?

Constantine snorted. "He was about to board. He'll call when he's with Ruby, and you can talk his ear off."

I rolled my eyes and shouldered past him and into the room. "Where's the music?" I asked. "I was promised a party."

"*Hey.*" Sally tackle-hugged me. She wasn't drunk, just naturally perky and friendly. Except for when she thought I meant to stake her. Or last time we spoke, when she was locked inside this room, crying and threatening to starve herself to dust, because she no longer wanted to be a vampire.

Constantine had talked her off the metaphorical ledge, and I'd stopped pretending he wasn't sleeping with her. With all of them. In the bed now covered with giggling girls, platters of snacks, and teetering glasses of margaritas.

I couldn't believe he let them endanger his precious silken sheets.

Sheena nudged me with her hip. "Grab a glass and tell us all about the big fight," she said. "Tall, blond, and dangerous said it's your story to share, and you only gave me the highlights over the phone."

I looked over my shoulder at Constantine, who winked. *"This is girls' night,"* he said inside my head. *"I'll wait it out upstairs, with my best whiskey."*

"Enjoy," I called after him and climbed on the bed. Vampires couldn't drink themselves to oblivion, but I'd give it a solid try.

Liza, unofficial leader of the three fledglings, turned down the music and crawled on the bed to join her two BFFs and Sheena, who sat cross legged in a semi-circle, facing me.

"So?" Sheena said.

"So you know the uber-bitch and her minion were haunting Alex, yes? They lied to him, built on his jealousy, and messed with his mind until he was barely himself." I stuffed a handful of nachos in my mouth and licked some salsa off my lips. "Well, the last night, they convinced him draining me was the only way to keep me from getting back together with Constantine."

"And he believed them?" Sheena asked. "He should have seen how broken you were when you thought he was dead. That boy needs an ass-whopping."

Nods all around.

The next part was hard to remember. Harder to put into words. So I tried to be as detached as possible and present things like an outside observer would. "He dragged me to the forest while I was trapped inside his dream. I woke to his fangs in my neck. My strength had fled and I knew I was almost gone."

Sally gasped. "He did that to you? But he loved you."

"He didn't realize he was killing me. When he did, he stopped. And then Willoughby attacked us." I shook my head, hoping to wipe away the memory of feeling helpless. I wasn't helpless. I won. Willoughby was dead.

"Where was Constantine?" Liza asked.

"Willoughby had staked him to the wall of my parents' basement"—insert collective gasp—"but he freed himself and came to the rescue. He fed me and then helped Alex."

Insert collective swoon. Yeah, yeah. Constantine was awesome.

"There was a fight, and Willoughby staked Alex but missed his heart. Alex pried out the stake and tossed it to me while Willoughby had Constantine pinned on the ground. I still can't believe I hit Willoughby's heart from where I lay half drained." I studied the girls for signs of discomfort. Willoughby had been their maker and was good to them… with the exception of killing them and wanting to turn them into undead assassins.

Carrie sighed. "We felt it when he was gone. We didn't know what we were feeling, but there was a snapping inside. A tearing, and then—"

"Hollowness," I said. I'd felt the same.

"It only lasted for a split second," Liza said. "We knew something big happened, but not what."

"Now you do," I said with a smile that hurt my cheeks. "Sorry I didn't have a more cheerful story for you."

Liza waved off my concern, and Sheena patted my knee. "Alex will be back," she said. "He loves you."

"I know. And he had a good reason for going away." And maybe one day I'd believe that.

"Why did he leave?" the third vampette, Carrie, asked.

Lovely. I had to explain something I barely understood. "He felt bad for attacking me"—for almost perma-killing me— "and he needed some distance to figure out how to fix things. He thought helping out more of the fledglings Willoughby and Ádísa created would be a good step in that direction." Or something.

"So to make up for what he did to you, he left you behind and went to help girls he'd never met?" The scowl was out of place on Sally's lovely face. Especially when she twirled a blond curl around her fingers.

"That makes no sense," Liza added. Her dark eyebrows were pulled together too, shadowing her hazel eyes. "Why not stay and fix things? I appreciate his altruism—got us out of a potentially shitty situation—but it does jack shit for *you*."

"He said he hadn't come to terms with being a vampire. That he wasn't himself since he was turned. He wanted to do good on a larger scale, to feel better, and then come to me in equal terms," I said.

Carrie harrumphed. She was the most level headed of the three, balancing between Liza's quick temper and Sally's naiveté. "What equal terms? He'll still be the jackass who hurt you out of jealousy. He attacked you, Cherry. If you were both humans, he'd be arrested for it."

Or I'd be dead.

"No," I said. Another sip of strawberry-laced tequila might help. "He'll prove to himself he can still be *Alex*, so then he'll know he won't hurt me again." His aggression had horrified me, but I knew it wasn't him. My mind and heart trusted him. In time, my body would learn to do so again too. But he had to be here for that to happen. Instead, he ran away, and I was left defending a decision I didn't agree with.

Liza cupped my shoulder. "But will *you* know?"

Constantine chose that moment to knock on the open door. "You better wrap this up, children. We have a busy day tomorrow."

I was so grateful for the interruption, I didn't care how much he'd heard.

Chapter Five

We moved Sheena and the girls out the next afternoon. It was fun, except for the carrying-stuff-around-while-pretending-to-be-humans thing, and Sheena totally enjoyed ordering us around until the rooms she provided the vampettes were to her liking. We ate and had a drink or two, and then, as much as I delayed the inevitable, Constantine and I had to return to the mansion.

Alone.

My ass buzzed the moment it touched the passenger's seat. I pulled my phone out of my pocket and let out a sigh of relief. Alex. *And* I didn't have to make chitchat with Constantine.

"Hey, you," I said.

Constantine looked at me, and I mouthed *Alex*. He started the car, but we didn't move. So much for this phone call saving us some awkwardness.

"Hey." Alex's voice was warm and sexy as ever. "Wanted to let you know I landed safely."

I glanced at the dashboard clock. "A couple hours ago." Which I hadn't noticed till now. Shame on me.

"I'm sorry. Ruby picked me up at the airport, and we had a bite to eat before driving to the hotel she's staying at. We started talking, and I lost track of time. She's a fascinating lady."

I shouldn't be jealous of my grandma, who really was fascinating. And kickass. And looked like she could be my slightly older sister. And I wouldn't be jealous of her.

"So will you be staying in London," I asked?

"I thought so at first, but Ruby has a plan. We'll be doing recon—fly to a different European city every couple days, verify the location of the fledglings' to be rehabilitated, and make first contact. With Willoughby and Ádísa out of the picture, they may be easier to approach."

"Or they may be panicking."

That was what he wanted to talk about? No *I miss you*?

"That's a possibility too, and we're ready for it. Ruby has made connections with a couple European Masters who'll help us."

It took me a moment to catch up. European vampires have a different social structure. Each area has its own Master, whose word is law for his jurisdiction.

"Please stay safe," I said.

"I will. Honest. I want to get back home in one piece."

He could have said *to you*. He didn't. Should I be reading things into this? "Good. When you have time, there's something else we need to discuss."

"We have a few more seconds. Ruby doesn't want me on this phone longer than that. I'll get a burner phone tomorrow and text you the number."

So very *Cloak and Dagger*. Was there even an enemy they were hiding from, or was this all so our council wouldn't find Ruby? "It's not urgent, and I'd rather do it over video-chat," I told him.

He chuckled. "It may be a while for that. Ruby doesn't trust any online connection but her own, and we won't be in her camp for at least another two weeks."

"I'll wait."

Silence for a second, then— "I'm happy to hear that. I'll call you from the new phone, okay?"

"Okay."

"Love you."

He hadn't said it since he left, and he hung up now before I could say the same. Might be for the best. Even if I had it in me to voice the words, I didn't wanna do so in front of Constantine.

"All good?" Constantine asked.

"Yup. Ruby will drag him all around Europe."

He shook his head. "That woman always has a purpose."

"Yeah." Now what to talk about?

"Wanna go home, get drunk, and fuck like animals?"

I snapped my head toward him and saw his body shake with suppressed laughter. I smacked his leg. "What would you do if I said *yes*?"

Mirth disappearing, he grabbed my wrist and led my hand higher on his thigh. "Say it and see."

Thus began two very torturous weeks.

I don't know if Constantine did it on purpose, but he made it impossible for me to avoid him around the mansion. Every time I left my room, he was there, topless more often than not, and always with that sexy I-know-you-want me smirk.

Despite his obvious availability, our exchanges were polite, bordering on stilted.

Have you fed?

Did you hear from Alex?

Do you need something?

Sheena and the girls are settling in well.

Here are your council bank account details and a credit card.

Let's go over the prophecy again.

The last one never yielded new results. We had to have sex and be sucked near-dry while climaxing. He was convinced forcing Alex's blood through my lips when I was near perma-death would spare Constantine and rehumanize me. And probably Alex too. There was no recorded case of vampires trying this before, but Constantine believed if I turned human again, so would the only vampire I made—Alex. There were no guarantees. At least Constantine wasn't in danger of dusting. Worst case scenario, it didn't work.

Wesley was pulling a vanishing act and only showed his face to bring coffee or reheated blood with Ruby's brew. With the other human and the vampettes out of the mansion, he didn't need to prepare meals for us, and he spent his free time in his rooms or visiting Sheena. He reportedly was teaching her to cook.

To add to the discomfort of my new reality, since Alex's self-actualization journey teamed him up with my grandma, all I heard from him was, *Ruby is so cool* and *Ruby knows what to do* and *You should hear Ruby's rendition of Any-Song-Ever.*

He didn't say those three little words again, but I didn't mind. It made it easier for me to function without constantly wondering about the mess that was our relationship. If there still was such a thing.

The morning before we were supposed to talk on Skype, I couldn't sleep. I tossed and turned, wondering how he'd take the news. Wondering why I cared. *He* left *me*. Now we had a chance for a real life. *I* had a chance for a real life, with or without him. If Alex couldn't push aside his ego and give it a try, Constantine and I would have to find someone else for me to feed on during the ritual.

If I went ahead with the ritual.

I had to put on my big-girl pants and talk to Constantine.

No time like the present.

Fresh out of big-girl pants, I pulled on a pair of sweats and dragged my feet to his door. There'd be time to sort things out after we talked to Alex, but I had to know now—if I became human again, would Constantine have a place in my life? Would he want one?

I tapped my fingertips on his bedroom door. It wasn't two seconds, before his voice in my head said, *"Come in, Cherry."*

I turned the handle and pushed, praying he was dressed or covered, so I could stay focused.

He was propped up in bed, blood-red satin sheets mercifully covering him well above his waist. He was still breathtaking, with his long golden hair draping his muscular shoulders and his angular face cast in the soft glow of candles.

His expression wasn't seductive, though. It was concerned. And I was thankful for it.

"Are you all right?" he said aloud. "Is something the matter?"

"I just want to talk. Is that okay?"

"Of course." He sat up higher, and I was relieved to see the waist of his PJ bottoms peek out from under the sheets. He patted the mattress next to him. How convenient that there was nowhere else to sit in the whole room. He sensed my reluctance, because he said, "No funny business."

I climbed on the humongous bed and sat cross-legged, facing him.

"Is this about Alex?" he asked through our mental link.

"Yes and no." I still felt weird, thinking things at him, so I didn't.

"Tell me," he said with a sigh.

"You really believe the ritual's going to make me human? Alex too?"

A shadow darkened his blue eyes, and he averted his gaze. "I do."

"And it'll keep you safe?"

"It'll keep me from dusting."

Not the same. "But you'll be affected in some way?"

His smile and eyes were brilliant when he looked at me again. "Undoubtedly. The mere thought affects me." He glided his palm down his thigh, and I saw the outline of his erection under the thin fabric of his sheets.

I set my jaw before I did something stupid, like bite my lip and moan. When I regained control of myself, I said, "A *breeze* affects that." We had this exchange before, but it held true. The man was a horndog. "I'm talking about actual physical harm. Will the ritual cause you any?"

"No. I'll remain my devastatingly handsome self long after he's old and senile and can't get it up."

I stared at my hands, folded in my lap. "And if it works, what then?"

"You and Alex get your happily-ever-after, I guess." He sounded like a different man to the one who days ago said he burned for me.

"What will happen to *us*? You and me? Will I still see you?"

He got to his knees and leaned closer. "Why would you want to? You'll get back the life that was stolen from you. You'll build a family with the man you love. Why should I be a part of that?"

I started to say because he was my friend, but it wasn't what he wanted to hear. And it was a lie.

He grabbed my wrists, and I looked up at the storm in his eyes. "If you ask me to be in your life, I will," he whispered, "and it will hurt me with every breath you take. Every time your heart beats, I'll be reminded... Spare me and let me go, Cherry. You've obviously made your decision. Don't make mine for me."

I wanted to scream that this wasn't fair; he'd made decisions for me before. I opened my mouth, but what came out was, "But I love you."

"Then choose me." The hope and yearning in his voice closed like an iron fist around my unbeating heart.

It would mean remaining a vampire. Giving up on normalcy for good. Giving up on Alex.

Did I want Alex back? Shouldn't I have the chance to find out? I knew I loved Constantine the moment I uttered it, but I also loved Alex. Could I be with either of them, after how both relationships ended?

I needed more data, damn it, but one thing was certain.

"I can't," I muttered. I resented my vampire nature for years; I had to give being human again a shot. If I chose Constantine now, I might end up hating him.

He let go, and I felt bereft. "I could erase your memory when you're human," he said. "Make you forget all about us. You might be happier that way."

"No." Out of the question. My past was part of who I was, and nobody tampered with it. Funny how I once thought taking away Alex's memories of me was a good idea.

Constantine nodded. "It might be safer for you to move to Europe, to make sure the council doesn't catch wind of your new situation. Alternatively, you could stage a semi-public staking or walk in the sun and stay here, incognito. Even so, I'd move to a different state. You'll have to find a place. Maybe a job—though I know someone who can funnel money from your council funds into an untraceable account."

My gut twisted at the thought of leaving everything behind. Or maybe it was because of how detached Constantine sounded. As if we'd already said *goodbye*. "I'll stay in L.A.," I said. "I respect that you don't want to see me after, but I'm not starting over again. I'll talk to Sheena. See if I can help her with the agency. I'll find an apartment."

"So your decision is final?"

Was it? Doubt threatened to choke me. "Maybe. No. I'll let you know when it is."

He surprised me by sliding back under the covers and folding one corner back for me. "It's late," he said. "Let's get some sleep."

I slipped in next to him, and he gathered me close, my head on his chest. "I missed this," I murmured, splaying my palm over his bare stomach. I ran my fingertips over the soft down beneath his navel. I was playing with fire, and part of me hoped I'd get burned. That he'd suck me back into the vortex that was loving him, and make me forget my need to see what could be. That he'd fuck me into oblivion and delete all other options from my mind.

He didn't. He tangled his fingers with mine and brought our joined hands to his chest. *"I want nothing more than to bury myself inside you, but I won't be a diversion,"* he said in my head.

Infuriating man.

He held me until I fell asleep, and then he joined me in my dream and lay beside me on the beach till late in the evening.

When we were to talk to Alex.

Chapter Six

"Cherry, can't you see he's lying through his teeth? I can, and I'm in a different continent." Alex shook his head, the motion pixelated by his crappy internet connection. He didn't sound half as upset as he'd have been a month ago. "This is desperate, Cee. What happened to not being the default choice?"

I sighed. "As fucked up as it sounds, I don't think he made up the prophecy. Let him explain."

Constantine sat back in his chair, arms folded over his chest, looking from me to the screen.

"Aren't you gonna say something?" I asked him. Under the harsh artificial lighting, the intimacy we shared earlier was replaced by our usual snarky banter.

"Anything I say at this point will be held against me." A smile curved his full lips. "Besides, this is fun."

"See? He's messing with your head, so you sleep with him."

But I already slept with him, and he made no move to take what was obviously on offer. "There are easier ways to go about that," I said.

"Nice." Alex scowled, but his voice held no anger. It was a refreshing change from the growly, jealous, and ultimately dangerous side of him Ádísa and Willoughby had spent months bringing to the surface. "If vampires could become human again, Ruby would have told me."

Because they were so close. Ugh.

"She told *me*," Constantine said, before I came up with a snarky response. "You've known her for all of a fortnight. I'm her maker. Besides, I happened upon part of the scripture several centuries ago, and Ruby knew that when she discovered the translation." His flared nostrils were the only indication of his annoyance.

What Constantine didn't say was that Ruby didn't want Alex to know. The prophecy was about vampires who'd killed their makers, and Alex's maker was yours truly. If he was determined to become human again, I might be at risk. Constantine convinced her there was no chance Alex would do something like that.

Alex leaned closer to the screen. "How come you're only now mentioning it?" Seeing him in detective mode was familiar. Soothing.

"I didn't know what it meant till Ruby filled in the gaps," Constantine said. "I'm still not entirely certain—"

"I *knew* it. You're working an angle. I can't believe you're using Cherry's grandmother as a cover. She's literally a wall away. I can easily check your story. Good idea, poor execution. You should have gone for something vaguer, man. You're losing your touch."

So my latest ex was giving my previous ex advice on how to… *get in my pants*? "Both of you, shut up," I said, before that thought led me astray. "Constantine, take it from the top. Alex, please don't interrupt this time."

"I'll try." Alex sounded tired.

"Right. As I told Cherry, I was in the Varangian Guard in Byzantium, in the tenth century. Back then, it was called—"

I rolled my eyes. "Without the history lesson this time, please."

Constantine sucked in his cheeks, accentuating his cheekbones. After sleeping in his arms, I found shooing away lustful thoughts about him was harder than ever.

But my lack of a sex life wasn't the focus of this meeting, though it was heavily involved.

"Here is the condensed version, then, for those among us with the attention span of a coleopteron." Constantine smirked. "Our job was to protect the emperor. During the battle of—"

I faked a snore.

"During *a* battle, I was forced to spend the night in a monastery's catacombs. It was completely undignified, having to share a tomb with a freshly interred priest, but in his robes I found a torn parchment."

We'd analyzed the prophecy to death the past couple weeks, but Constantine hadn't mentioned his turning again, so I wasn't surprised he said nothing about it now.

"You searched a dead priest's robes?" Alex asked.

"I was trying to fashion some sort of headrest. I'd elaborate, but Cherry is in a hurry for me to finish the story."

"Yeah, go ahead." I crossed my legs and fiddled with my sneaker's shoelaces.

"Yes, please get to the part that says you and Cherry must have sex, for her to become human again," Alex said.

"I told you that wasn't the right way to preface it," Constantine said to me. "Anyway, at the time it made little sense but provided an opportunity for me to exercise my Greek. Now we have the complete text, the part that applies to us loosely translates to:

If two immortals who have shorn their own roots are consumed to the brink of death while taking each other, they can walk under the sun and count finite remaining sunsets once again, requiring breath and sustenance, and growing as nature and God meant Man to."

"Either the prototype or the translation could be utter bull-crap," Alex said. "Cherry, he may not even speak Greek, for all we know."

"He kind of does," I said. He tried to teach me, years ago, but it didn't take.

"Fluently," Constantine supplied.

"Of course you do," Alex mumbled. "And according to your *fluent* translation, you two are supposed to fuck"—an edge flashed through his voice, before he reined it back in—"while draining each other."

"You can check with Ruby," I said with a sneer.

"We're two vampires who've killed their own makers. Shorn our own roots, in a way," Constantine said. "But there's no mention of draining each other. Only of being drained."

"And then you'll be human again?" Alex asked.

"Cherry will." Constantine shrugged. "I'll be dust. There's a short line about how we'll each revert to what we'd be in human years."

Alex raked the fingers of both hands through his hair. "Cee, if you're lying, you're better at it than I thought. Offering your unlife for a night with Cherry is kind of risky."

His half-assed attempt at a joke didn't make me laugh. "This is serious," I said. "But there may be a way out."

"Of course there is." Alex slapped his thigh. His video shook for a second, before his face came back into focus. "The man is my hero. Now he'll tell us about his brilliant plan that involves the two of you naked and him surviving the prophecy. And when you're still a vampire afterward, you'll have to forgive him, because—hey—he tried."

When Alex and I were together, he'd expressed his distrust of Constantine repeatedly and aggressively. Now he grinned and seemed to admire Constantine for the elaborate scheme he'd supposedly concocted.

Men are weird, but mine are extra wonky.

"Actually, my plan involves all three of us," Constantine said, and I went to my happy place before I could stop myself. "If I take and consume Cherry but she doesn't drain me, she may be the only one turned back."

"Or she dies from exsanguination." Alex's voice dropped to a whisper.

"That's where you come in," Constantine said. "The moment before I drain her completely, you force your blood down her throat."

"So I'll be in the room, while the two of you get it on."

"See the big picture," I said. "Assuming legend and Hollywood"—and Constantine—"have it right, if I turn human, so does my progeny. You get your life back. The council never found out about you, so you don't have to hide."

"You may even pick up a couple of tricks, if you watch closely." Constantine winked at the screen. "Should you feel so inclined, Cherry may finally get the ménage—"

I used my vampire speed to flip down the lid of the laptop. Not the way to end a Skype call, as I always yelled at the TV when actors did it, but it was all I could think of, to keep Alex from hearing the end of that sentence.

"—à trois she and Sheena have been talking about."

I wagged my finger at Constantine. "You weren't supposed to hear that. It was a private conversation."

My phone rang, and I groaned. *Alex.*

"Did he say you want a threesome?" he asked when I picked up.

Could a girl have no secrets?

"He's being a jerk," I said.

"But you believe him?"

"Yes."

"And you want to go through with this?"

I sighed. "I don't know. I want to be human again. I think. It's a big decision."

"There's a flight from Bucharest to L.A. at ten in the morning, local time. If I make it, I'll be there early afternoon. We'll figure it out then."

I was more than a little relieved that Alex didn't press for more information on the threesome thing, but it didn't stop me from glaring at Constantine when I got off the phone.

"What? I was trying to get you your wish." He sounded happy with himself.

"I don't know if I wanna do this. And we were supposed to get Alex to consider it, not scare him away," I said.

"The prospect of sharing you with me may be daunting for your boyfriend, but I doubt he found it scary. He's trying to get back into your good graces. Why would he turn down an opportunity to join us in bed?"

"Because he might want me to himself? Because if he's my boyfriend—like you said—he won't share me, which you seem more than eager to."

"Cherry, I don't want your pussy to myself. I want *you*. I meant what I said about monogamy. After hundreds of years on this world, I don't consider it a prerequisite for a successful relationship."

"Still with that excuse?"

He held up a hand. "Regardless, I should have respected how much it means to you, and I wish I could make that right. But we're no longer together, Alex is a striking man, and the three of us can have an incredible time together before you and he ride off into the sunset."

If he put it this way... I rolled my shoulders and allowed myself two-point-five seconds of daydreaming. It would feel amazing, being pressed between two hard male bodies that defined beauty, but it'd be for a single night. Would having a taste make me crave more?

Constantine stood and stretched, and I was grateful he'd put on a shirt for Alex's sake. I'd seen enough of him the past couple weeks, and I still felt his naked chest against my cheek.

"So you wouldn't mind me sleeping with someone else while we were together?" I asked.

"*Sleeping with*, I'd mind. Fucking, no. I could watch, or you could tell me every sordid detail afterward, while I ravaged you."

Though the idea made me wet, he, Alex, and I had achieved a fragile balance. The ritual could throw a wrench into things. What if having Constantine inside me again made me realize I didn't want to give him up? What if Alex saw the connection I shared with my ex and fled? What if I ended up more confused than I was now *and* with no options?

And Constantine had lost his shirt again.

"Will you stop undressing, while we're talking serious stuff?" I asked. *One. Two. Three. Four...* Had to stop counting abs, but—yup. Six. All there.

He smirked and flexed his pecs. "I thought we were done talking. Alex is flying in tomorrow, and you'll have to make up your mind. Then you and Mr. Marsden can be on your merry way, to have offspring and frolic in the sun, while I return to the debauchery a single male vampire of my stature is supposed to indulge in." Pretentious, run-on sentences were another defense of his, and he used them well, but his tricks didn't work on me.

Until he leaned over me and planted his large palms on the back of my chair. "So unless there's something more you need..."

I was trapped between his arms, having no choice but to look at his chest or straight into his eyes. Violet flecked their usual blue.

Violet meant lust. A hunger I ached to sate but needed to steer clear from.

"Nope. Nothing more for now," I told his chest. Believe it or not, staring at that was the safe choice.

"Good." *Liar.* Regret laced the single word as he straightened and walked toward the stairs leading to the basement.

It would be easy to run after him, tackle him on his bed, and ride him to oblivion, but even if going down that path didn't lead to heartache this time, I had Alex to consider.

My noble Alex, half the world away from L.A. His reactions to our conversation earlier showed he'd done a lot of growing. He was getting used to his new nature, and he had control over his emotions and jealousy.

And Constantine and I were finally at a good place. In retrospect, I was begrudgingly grateful he didn't make a move when I was all over him this morning. We were open about our feelings and enjoying each other's company. Except for the awkward silences and the times I wanted to shred the clothes off him and lick—

What the hell was I doing?

I was faced with the biggest dilemma ever and wasted mental energy on things that didn't matter. I let my feelings for Constantine and my uncertainty about Alex spin me in circles.

I should decide whether or not to go through with the ritual based on the future I wanted, not on which guy I was more into right now.

I ought to do some soul searching of my own. Maybe help other people, like Alex and my grandma did.

After I helped myself to some blood.

I headed downstairs. The mini fridge in the basement was always stocked with blood, and I could call Sheena from my room. She was practical; she'd be a good sounding board.

Chapter Seven

"Do it." Sheena's voice brooked no argument.

"You realize it'll be a new beginning? In all ways?" I didn't consent to my turning, but I hadn't been human in ages. "I can't pick up where I left off. And I'll be thirty, not a frozen-in-time twenty-four."

"Listen, hon. Everything you've told me shows your mind is made up. I know it, you know it, and Tall-Blond-and-Deadly knows it. You told him you can't choose him. We're beating a dead horse."

"You're right, I guess." So was I trying to make sure I made the right choice, or to talk myself out of it?

"Do it," she said again. "If only for the crazy sexytimes. You'll live the fantasy of anyone who's ever laid eyes on those boys. We'll get you a job. And you can stay with me till you find a new place if you don't wanna shack up with Alex. The girls are used to sharing their space, so I've got a spare room."

"But—"

"Stop over thinking it, Cherry. You never wanted to be a vampire. This is your chance. Go for it, and maybe record the ritual, for those less fortunate than you?"

"You're an idiot." But I was chuckling. "And the sex part scares me too. I'm not crazy about the idea of Alex watching me with Constantine."

Sheena harrumphed. "If he's only watching, you're doing it wrong. Give the man a side and let him play."

"A side?"

"Yeah. Does he get in the front or the back? Decide who goes where, and then relax and enjoy it."

"*Sheena.*" I pulled off sounding shocked, while my mind juxtapositioned visuals with different combinations of the three of us. Some didn't have me in the middle.

"Right. I forgot your delicate sensibilities, Ms. I-Wanna-be-a-Porn-Star. This is a one-time thing, correct?"

"Yes." A potentially incredible one-time thing…

"Then why are we having this discussion?"

I didn't know. Not like it was helping me make up my mind. "So you don't think me becoming mortal again is a bad idea?" I asked.

"Hell, no. And if you hate it, you can always go back."

As if.

I spent my vampire years bemoaning the things I'd never do. Now I could do them. I'd stop self-sabotaging and get on with it. Whoever wanted to stick around afterward was more than welcome.

I thanked Sheena for hearing me out and ended the call with a promise to visit as soon as possible. I wanted *everything* to happen as soon as possible. I couldn't take the next step till Alex was here, but I could let Constantine know my decision was final.

"I'll do it," I said, barging into his room.

He wasn't there. Better. He tended to be naked in his room, and I had to stay the course. I flew up the stairs and found him reading the paper in the kitchen, two cups of steaming blood on the table in front of him.

"Sit. Drink," he said.

"I wanna become human again," I blurted and dropped on the chair to his right. "I'm certain."

He rolled the paper and tapped it on the kitchen table, like a makeshift drumstick. "I was hoping you'd change your mind. This world is going to hell. Humans kill each other over imaginary infractions. Politics and religion divide communities and turn the masses into rabid zealots. The people refuse to learn from the past, and humanity is constantly on the brink of several wars. And you want to revert to being one of them."

He let go of the paper and grasped the table with both hands. "You will lose your immortality. Things will be able to hurt you. No superhuman strength. You won't fly or see the colors come to life after sundown. You will no longer have the connection to the world that vampires do. Are you ready for these losses?"

They didn't matter. *He* did, and I was as ready to lose him as I'd ever be—not at all. "But I'll hear my heart beat again, Constantine. I'll be able to have a family. Mortality comes with an expiration date, and that makes life more... *more*."

He clenched his jaw and squeezed his eyes shut. I watched his knuckles whiten with tension. He wasn't getting this.

"When you know you may not be around tomorrow, you seek out experiences. Take risks. Feel things," I said.

Constantine flipped the table straight across the room. It crashed into the fridge, leaving both in shambles. "Vampires fucking *feel* things, Cherry," he roared. When he looked at me, pain swirled in his eyes. "*I* fucking feel things. *You* fucking feel things. You want me as much as I want you. I see it. I feel it in my skin. Your heart doesn't beat, but you love me. This isn't about feeling. This is about doing what you've been taught is right. You don't even want a family, but you'll be a good little girl and force yourself to fit a mold you broke long ago. So I'll fuck the immortality out of you, and then I don't want to see you again."

He stomped out of the kitchen, leaving me plenty of time to stop him. I didn't. Constantine was always composed except for the glimpses of sentiment he allowed me at his most vulnerable or honest moments. His eruption shocked me. And though it didn't scare me—he'd never hurt me—his words landed on me like punches.

I wasn't doing this to fit a mold. I wanted to be human. I'd reclaim all that was stolen from me. I'd be happy. And if Constantine didn't get that, maybe it was best that we never saw each other again afterward.

A huge crack ran along the table's surface, where the impact splintered the wood. The door of the fridge had snapped inward, creating an opening for fruit and blood bags to spill to the floor. The two mugs had shattered against the wall and the floor, their contents making the room look like a crime scene.

Wesley would have someone clean up, and all that was broken would be replaced by morning. But I'd seen the damage, and it would stay with me.

* * * *

Bagged blood wouldn't cut it, after all. I was feeling antsy and didn't want to run into Constantine again. I could go by Sheena's, but I wasn't in the mood for company either. If Alex got on board, this might be my last night as a vampire, and I'd spend it hunting.

The chill in the air was refreshing against my cool skin. I let my eyes adjust and took in the vibrant hues the night brought to life. Constantine was right; I'd miss this. But not enough. I once felt sorry for Alex, because his world was so different to mine. I turned him soon after, to save him from death. Now I could give him his world back and me with it. Vamp-sight was a small price to pay.

I took off for downtown, loving the rush lift-off shot through my veins. I didn't like my donors intoxicated, but a little alcohol in their system gave me a light buzz while I fed, and that was more than welcome tonight.

I got my wish and my fill from a frat boy who was enjoying his friend's drunken misery a little too much. The punk was recording, while the other guy puked his guts out and cried for the boy who broke his heart. I fed on the first one, deleted the video on his phone, and then thralled him to have the world's worst hangover in the morning. Then I turned my vampire gaze to his heartbroken buddy, sobered him up, and sent him to shower. All in a good day's work, huh?

The sun was almost up when I returned to the mansion. I tiptoed inside and was glad to be greeted by darkness and quiet. If Constantine was home, he wasn't on the ground floor.

I didn't see him on the way to my room and heard no sign of him while I got ready for bed. Good. We had more than our share of emotional moments this week.

I was in bed when I heard the front door open and shut again. I kept my eyes closed and listened to Constantine's footsteps cross the living room above me and then descend the stairs to the basement. They stopped outside my door. "Are you awake?"

I wasn't sure if the question was out loud or in my head, but I considered ignoring it either way. *Nah.* "Come in."

He opened the door, and I rolled on my side, to face him. He leaned on the doorframe and folded his arms over his wide chest. "I'm sorry for my outburst earlier."

Outburst was an understatement, but apologizing doesn't come naturally to Constantine, and I appreciated the effort. "It's okay. Your kitchen, your mess."

"That mess is fixed. It's what's between us I hope to mend. I shouldn't have reacted that way. I asked Ruby to let me be the one to tell you about the prophecy because I wanted to make you happy. My actions don't show that. I don't wish to see you when you're human, because I can't watch you die with every day that passes. It's not a punishment for you; it's a way to safeguard me from more sorrow. That said, I'll never turn my back to you. If you need me, I'll be there. I'll cover for you with the council. And I'll love you till the day I dust."

Not a single word could make it past the knot in my throat. I nodded and thought at him, *"Thank you."*

Saying I loved him again would get us nowhere.

Chapter Eight

Constantine offered to pick up Alex at the airport, but Alex said he'd get a cab. Good idea. Safe.

Didn't keep me from pacing the living room from the moment Alex texted he landed in L.A. to when the intercom buzzed for Wesley to let him in the gate.

I threw the front door open, but trepidation trumped excitement when Alex got out of the taxi and ducked back in for his duffel bag. Would reverting to his mortal self write out what he did as a vampire, in my mind or his?

He looked good as ever, his jeans hugging his toned ass and legs, and his polo shirt straining to contain his muscular back and arms. Yummy.

But was I allowed to enjoy the yumminess?

He said he loved me two weeks ago, but not since. He obviously cared, or he wouldn't have hopped on a plane back when I told him about the prophecy. Though maybe he did that because he wanted to become human again.

And how did I feel about the prospect of him touching me? I used to enjoy his touch, but then he'd hurt me. Would my body remember how he made it arch with pleasure, or cling to the terror of his fangs buried in my neck when he almost dusted me?

My smile hurt my face. Did it look fake? Should I hug him? Kiss him?

He saved me from myself by wrapping both arms around me and planting a kiss at the corner of my mouth. "You're a sight for sore eyes."

So he was into me and his proximity didn't make me balk. No panic rushed in. Yay! I held on, enjoying his hard body against mine. "Hey, you. Long time no see," I said.

He let go and offered his hand to Constantine, who came up behind me.

Constantine pulled him in for that half-hug, half-pat-on-the-back thing men do. "Welcome home, Alex."

Home. Not for long. Alex still had his place in the city. I might move in with him.

One step at a time. My new motto.

I tugged him inside the mansion. "Come. Take a nap, and when you wake up, you can tell us everything."

"Want some blood first?" Constantine asked.

"Yeah. I'm starving."

Wesley was already brewing his miracle coffee that could keep vampires awake in mid-day.

"I'll have a cup of that," I said.

"Which I'll pour," Constantine said. He turned to the aging human. "Get some rest, Wesley. We're good here."

"If you say so, sir." Wesley gave a tiny bow and left us.

The three of us.

Alone.

Together.

Did I hammer that point home yet?

No? Let me try again.

I was alone in the kitchen with two men I was incredibly drawn to—whom I loved—and we had to discuss the possibility of me having sex with one while the other watched, so I could cut all ties to the former and maybe spend my human years with the latter.

Just your usual Tuesday.

Alex sank into one of the new kitchen chairs that came with the new kitchen table and looked around. "Did you redecorate?"

I looked at Constantine, who was reheating the blood. He shrugged.

"So how was Europe? How were things with Ruby? Did you locate any of Willoughby's fledglings?" I asked, while

Constantine placed a mug of blood in front of Alex and handed me my coffee.

"Ruby is amazing." Alex beamed. "She's on top of everything. All her leads were good. We found six more women, and Ruby and her team will rehabilitate them. Things are different in Europe. The local Masters were getting restless with new vampires entering their turfs, so they were on Willoughby's trail too. Seems he and Ádísa started over there, to stay under the U.S. council's radar. Their European childer"—that's the plural for *childe*, by the way—"awaited orders for the next step of the plan." To take over the world, using top-model vampire mercenaries. *That* plan. "Most of them weren't happy with the change in regime. Convincing them their makers were the bad guys will take a lot of work, but if anyone can do it—"

It'd be Ruby.

"—it's Ruby."

Cause she was amazing. Ugh.

"Your turn," Alex said to Constantine. "Is the prophecy real?"

Constantine leaned against the counter and crossed his arms. "To the best of my knowledge."

"And if you do the ritual as is, will it kill you?"

"Yes."

Alex blew some air in his mug, then gulped down the contents. "But you'll do it anyway?"

"I don't have a death wish; I'd prefer another vampire to help us. If none will, then yes. I'll do it," Constantine said.

I believed him, and apparently so did Alex, because he said, "I can't let you make all the sacrifices. Doesn't look good for me."

"So you're in?" I asked.

"As long as we're clear on what that entails. Can I wait outside the room till you call me?"

"I'm afraid not," Constantine replied. "Timing is everything, and you'll have to be within reach."

Alex didn't seem pleased, but he said, "Okay. When?"

"When do you want?" I asked.

"The sooner, the better."

"How about midnight tonight?" asked Constantine.

Too soon. I still needed answers. Alex was back, but was he here to stay? And would we get back together? Should we?

One step at a time.

"Midnight it is," I said.

"My room," Constantine said.

Alex nodded and stood. "I'd like a shower and that nap now."

Soon he was in the downstairs bathroom, while I sat on the bed we used to share, listening to the water pelting his skin, while my thoughts wandered. He and I were thrown together by circumstance and bonded by danger. Once we were human again—*if* we were human again—could we have the relationship he wanted? Maybe someday a family?

We had hours till midnight when he emerged from the bathroom. We could fill them with chitchat or talk more about his trip and my forays into the dream-world.

"What happens when we're both human?" I asked instead. "Do we date? Give us a try?"

He studied my face. "Are you open to that? I thought you and Constantine… You smell like him."

Shit. Should have showered. "I slept in his bed, but there's nothing—" *Lie.* There *was* something between Constantine and me. I shook my head. "Nothing happened. I was lonely and confused, and we talked till I fell asleep."

"You still have feelings for him."

After tonight, they wouldn't matter. I could lie now, and Alex would never be the wiser. I didn't. "I always will, like I'll always have feelings for you. But I won't stay with him, and I'm asking if you want us to be something."

I felt like a hypocrite. I wasn't choosing Alex; I was choosing mortality. If the choice were between him and Constantine... No way to know.

"So you forgive me for what I did to you?" he asked.

I did. I had. But could I forget it? Not trusting myself to speak, I nodded.

A timid smile blossomed on his lips. "I want us to be *everything*. I want to have a future with you. To grow old with you."

I couldn't tell if I was elated or suffocated; my head was light, and my feet felt made of lead.

Alex crossed the distance between us and laid a gentle kiss on my lips. "Tomorrow on, when I do this, I'll be able to feel your heartbeat," he said. His palm was on my chest, but there was nothing sexual about the touch.

I let him pull me into his gleeful ramblings. We'd redecorate his apartment. Maybe get a dog. I'd get a job, possibly with Sheena, and he'd see if he could return to the force. We could go somewhere exotic next summer—we earned a sunny vacation, after the crap we dealt with. And his mom would be ecstatic if he told her we were engaged.

What?

"We can pick out a ring together. Anything you want." Alex took my hand and brushed his thumb over my ring finger.

"A ring?" *What what what?*

"I don't mean now. We'll see how things go. But I'll make you happy, Cherry." A shadow crossed his eyes, and he added, "I'll never hurt you again. I swear."

I squeezed his fingers and leaned in closer, my face inches from his. "I know." If we were kissing, we didn't have to talk, and I didn't have to think of how a few weeks of chasing hot women alongside my grandma had freed him from the guilt of almost killing me for good.

Alex crushed his mouth to mine and nibbled on my lower lip before thrusting his tongue between my lips, to find mine. While demanding, his kiss wasn't threatening. I felt bad for allowing memories of a past he couldn't control interfere with this moment. The darkness had washed out of him, and he was my Alex again, now and forever.

Funny how long *forever* sounded when our future was finite.

Chapter Nine

I was surprised when Constantine got the door for us instead of bidding us enter, but then I realized it was to show off how gorgeous he looked in his robe. Sashed around his waist, it accentuated his wide shoulders and narrow waist, and allowed glimpses of his chest. The dark-purple silk made his pallor luminescent.

He was barefoot, and his hair was pulled back in a—

"Is that a man-bun?" I asked.

He flashed a smile. "Carrie showed me an instructional video. The abundance of positive comments convinced me to give it a try."

I wanted to say something snarky, but the updo enhanced his savage beauty. *Shit.* Shouldn't think of him as savagely beautiful.

Alex snorted. "You can pull anything off, huh?"

Constantine stepped aside for us to come in, and I noticed no pants legs were visible beneath his robe, and I knew he always went commando.

I didn't wear panties or a bra for this either, and I was suddenly too aware of my nipples pushing through the cotton of my T-shirt.

Constantine motioned at an armchair and end table at the foot of the bed. They weren't here yesterday. "Thought you'd be more comfortable with some semblance of a distance," he said.

Whether he meant Alex or me, I appreciated his thoughtfulness.

Alex sat, and Constantine produced a bottle of whiskey from his nightstand and filled a glass for him. He cocked an eyebrow at me. *"Liquid courage?"* he asked in my head.

"Yes, please," I replied in the same manner. I downed the drink he poured me and enjoyed the burn, though the buzz from the alcohol fumes would only last a few minutes. Could we make this quick? We had to reach orgasm for the ritual to work, but that didn't take long with Constantine.

Constantine took the empty glass from me, set it aside, and held out his other hand. "Shall we?"

Unsure what else to do, I placed my palm in his.

He twirled me so my back was flush against him, and brought his arms around me, to skate his palms up my thighs. My body's reaction was immediate. I leaned into him, molding to his hard planes. Giving him the lead in our dance.

He rocked his hips, and I let him sway me to his silent rhythm, as he popped the button of my jeans and lowered the zipper. His hard cock dug into the small of my back. I stood on tiptoe, so he'd rub against my ass instead. When he slid his fingers under my T-shirt, I sucked in my stomach, every muscle in my body tense with equal parts anticipation and trepidation. He was the same temperature as me, but his touch set my skin on fire. And Alex could see it.

Constantine chuckled. "Relax."

Right. Alex knew what we were here for.

Constantine nuzzled my cheek and grazed my sides with his fingertips, before closing his large palms over my breasts. His touch was gentle yet confident. He knew my body and remembered what I liked, but he gave me ample opportunity to stop him before he pinched my nipples.

I didn't.

He slipped one hand down my belly and inside the waist of my jeans, to cup my pussy. I pumped my hips forward, willing him lower, but his fingers stilled against my bare flesh.

"This won't be fast," he said, twisting and tugging on one of my nipples until I ached with need. "I have one last time to savor you, and I intend on taking full advantage of it. Unless there are any objections."

I looked at Alex for a reaction; he must have heard Constantine's words.

Alex's expression was unreadable.

Another choice for Cherry to make, then.

I lifted my head and rubbed my cheek against Constantine's. I wanted this as much as he did, and if I was to have something real with Alex, I couldn't hide from him. "No objections"—I was glad I hadn't fed and they couldn't see my embarrassment painted in red all over my face—"but I want you both."

Alex narrowed his eyes and tilted his head. "At the same time?"

"Yes."I didn't expect to have to talk things out.

"Not yet, though." Constantine pushed his hand lower and ran one finger along my slit.

I squeezed my thighs together, trapping him in place until I got a response from Alex.

It took an eternity, but Alex said, "Okay."

Constantine turned me around and tugged off my T-shirt, his fingers lingering on my breasts. I stood before him topless, and he claimed my lips with the same fervor he had on the night he admitted to forging a mental link between us.

And he messed with my head tonight as much as he did then.

If I were to decide now, I'd choose to stay with him. Luckily, my mind was already made up.

He broke the kiss and caught my gaze before helping me lie on the bed. It was custom made so he could fuck standing up—his words—which he demonstrated on several occasions. I had no doubt it was what he had in mind now. I kicked off my flats, closed my eyes, and lifted my hips so he could peel off my jeans. My bravado had been spent on my request and had taken with it all other initiative.

When an eternity passed and Constantine hadn't touched me, I opened my eyes to find him staring down at me. Violet flecks wound around his irises, and his fangs were out.

He was hungry. Starving. For me.

I stopped caring about the ritual, the prophecy, ever becoming human again. My sole purpose was to sate his hunger. I was wet and aching for him. I dipped two fingers between my lower lips and brought them to my mouth, to taste myself.

Constantine growled, and Alex echoed him, as he appeared next to him.

Alex's gaze was dark, but I wasn't afraid. It wasn't jealousy swimming in the depths of his grey eyes, but desire. He pulled his shirt over his head and sent it flying across the room. Hard muscle rippled and flexed, as he undid his jeans and stepped out of them.

I looked at Constantine. "You should be naked too."

He untied the sash and let his robe slide off his shoulders and float to the floor. Next to Alex's tan skin, Constantine looked like he was carved from living marble.

They were night and day and all mine.

Whether Constantine's idea worked as planned or not, this would be the best night of my existence.

Constantine lifted one of my legs and laid an open-mouthed kiss over the ankle. He glided his mouth up my calf and kissed the back of my knee, as he pushed me higher up, so he could climb on the mattress between my legs.

I raised my head, wanting to see him, but Alex hopped on the bed next to me and leaned down for a kiss that left my lips swollen.

Constantine trailed more kisses up my thigh, ignoring my barked orders to go higher still. He took his time nibbling on the tender flesh, and then moved his attentions to my other leg, never touching my aching center.

I reached for his hair, intending to use it as a lever, but Alex grabbed both my wrists and pinned them to the mattress, over my head. His cock nudged my hip, teasing me.

Constantine recaptured my attention by spreading my legs as wide as they'd go and laying a kiss on my pussy.

"Finally," I said.

Constantine shook his head. "Oh, I'm going to make you beg for it."

It didn't take long.

He alternated between flicking my clit with his tongue and sucking on it. He grazed it with his teeth. Pushed his tongue inside me. The sensations drove me to the edge but weren't enough to send me tumbling over it.

Alex kept me in place, his hands on my wrists and a leg pressing down on my knee. I was exposed and needy, and I couldn't get enough of their divine torture.

Which I'd never experience again.

The thought was sobering, but I forgot about it when Constantine worried my clit with his teeth and tapped it with the tip of his tongue.

"Please," I sent through our link. Out loud I added, "More."

Constantine laughed and sat back on his haunches. I thought he wanted me to beg aloud, and I was about to do just that, when he thrust two long, thick fingers in my pussy. I pumped my hips, and he leaned over me to close his lips over my nipple. He hooked his fingers inside me and began slamming his palm against me, so the heel rubbed against my clit.

His fangs descended again, piercing the skin around my nipple, and making me arch into his mouth.

Alex let go of one wrist and pinched my second nipple punishingly. I stretched and grabbed his hard cock. It throbbed in my fist. I couldn't focus on him, though, because my mind—my entire being—was rolled in a ball in my cunt, waiting to erupt through my cells.

I was close. So close.

Constantine fucked me with his hand, rubbing against the bundle of nerves inside while pressing on my sensitive button. I pulsed in time to his thrusts, tasting release but not attaining it.

I let Alex's cock slip out of my grasp. I didn't trust myself not to dig my nails into him. He nuzzled my neck and kneaded my breast, but that wasn't what I yearned for.

In my head, I chanted, *"Please. Please. Please…"*

A million times, I must have said it, before Constantine thought at me, *"Since you ask so nicely…"* He pressed the heel of his hand down on my clit and mentally said, *"This is how I want to remember you. Falling apart with pleasure. For me."*

My body shook with the force of the orgasm that tore through me. I had to clench my jaw, to keep from screaming as white-hot fire radiated from my core to every one of my nerve endings.

I lost control over my senses, and the sounds of the night above reached my ears despite the relative soundproofing of the room. An owl. A passing car. Wesley's heartbeat two floors above us. I was grateful not to catch the scent of the women who lived here till recently. I only smelled Alex and Constantine. Their arousal. Precum dripping from their cocks. My blood.

Constantine slanted his lips over mine, and I tasted myself on his tongue, before melting into his kiss. I dug my hand in his bun and loosened it, letting his golden mane cascade down his shoulders.

"That was amazing," he said out loud.

I didn't answer, too busy regaining my bearings.

And then he flipped me on my stomach.

Stars blinked behind my eyelids when I slid them shut.

Constantine licked down my spine, and his tongue sent tingles along my fingers and toes. His hair tickled my skin. He gave my ass a playful bite, and I shook it with a giggle.

Alex got out of bed and stood in front of me. He fisted his hand in my hair, and tugged me upward. When I propped myself up on my elbows, he found his way into my mouth. This time I paid his cock better attention. I swirled my tongue over the tip, and sucked until my cheeks hollowed. He moaned and pumped his hips against my face, and I touched my teeth to the underside, the way I knew he liked it.

Constantine straddled my legs, and his erection poked at me. Why was he wasting time? Why wasn't he already inside me?

I tried to lift my hips, but he slapped my ass.

Nice.

One slicked finger—saliva?—separated my buttcheeks and pressed against my asshole. I bucked. I'd said I wanted him and Alex at the same time, but I didn't like things going up my ass. Well, except a couple times, when Alex's fingers were more adventurous than usual.

But I couldn't take Constantine's cock.

I mean, have you seen that thing? It was too big for back there, but it perfectly matched my pussy, that craved him desperately.

"You said you wanted both of us," he whispered in my mind. *"I chose first."*

Alex didn't pause his thrusts, and I couldn't speak around the dick in my mouth, so I sent Constantine, *"Don't hurt me."*

"Do you want me to stop?" he sent back.

Maybe? *"Why choose to go there?"* I asked.

"I saw your face contort in bliss for me. I want to hold on to that memory, not watch while life seeps out of you."

Sold. *"Do it."*

He pushed his finger in, past the tight ring of muscle, and I bit my lip. I'd gone this far with Alex and enjoyed it. I forced myself to push back into it until I felt Constantine's knuckles against my pussy. He withdrew slowly, and my flesh gave way more easily when he inched back inside. Soon he was sliding his finger in and out of my ass at the same time Alex fucked my mouth.

Constantine tried to add a second finger, but my body clenched around him. He tilted up my hips and buried himself inside my pussy in one hard thrust. My inner walls fluttered at the intrusion, and he took advantage of my surprise, to drive his second finger in my ass. And it was good. Scratch that—it was great. His cock hit all the right spots, and his fingers in my ass added to the delicious feeling of being filled.

Alex closed his fist over his cock and slipped it out of my mouth. I flattened my upper body to the mattress, watching as he moved his hand lazily along his shaft, like he didn't want to come yet. Of course. He'd soon be inside me too.

Yes.

I met Constantine's thrusts, feeling each down-stroke like a jolt of electricity to my core. I was seconds from coming again.

And then the bastard pulled out.

My mewl of frustration turned into a groan when he positioned the tip of his cock at my asshole. He squeezed the first inch inside, and I wasn't all that thrilled. It burned and stretched me, and I didn't see what people liked about it.

He stilled. "Tell me when you want me to move."

Never?

I nodded and twisted my hands in the sheets. I once wanted to be a porn star, damn it; I could handle anal. And I trusted Constantine to make it good. "I'm okay," I said.

He drove forward slowly, stopping every so often to caress my back or use our link to tell me I'm beautiful and that the memory of this moment would get him hard for years to come. He didn't let his sexy talk get sentimental, but his touch reminded me of how he felt. How he said he'd always feel.

It was too much. *"Can you be quiet?"* I thought at him. *"I'm trying to focus on taking your huge dick in."*

He chuckled and brushed my hair out of the way to kiss the back of my neck, then sent me a mental image of himself buried in my ass. *"Beautiful."*

It kind of was.

He withdrew as slowly as he entered me, until only the tip was inside, and then sheathed himself inside me again, with a little more force. He kept going until the near-unbearable discomfort deepened into a different kind of ache. The burning sweetened into pleasure. The stretching made me feel full and yet want more. *This* was what people loved about it.

A few more lunges, and I was impaling myself on him with abandon. *"So good."* I fed on people and played with their memories, but *this* felt like the naughtiest, dirtiest thing I'd done. And I couldn't get enough. I was a fucking convert.

Constantine laughed and snaked his hand around my hip. I thought he meant to find my clit and send me headfirst into another spiraling release, but he grasped me and used his vampire strength to flip us over.

Ah.

I draped my legs back over Constantine's and arched an eyebrow at Alex.

He didn't need more of an invitation. He crawled between our spread legs and ran his hand up the length of my body. He palmed my breast, and I held his gaze as I closed my fingers around his shaft and guided him inside my pussy. He entered me in one smooth stroke. When I felt his balls slam against Constantine's, I expected one of them to recoil, but neither seemed perturbed or inclined to stop.

My body fought to contain the men stretching and filling me. I thrashed between them, while they found their rhythm, seeking their pleasure in my body. Their cocks rubbed against each other through the thin barrier of my flesh. The sensation hurtled me toward new heights of desire. I wanted them to fuck me raw. To rip me apart and put me back together.

One pushed forward while the other withdrew, never leaving me empty. They moved and positioned me, to better accommodate them. They pinched and caressed every inch of skin they could reach. Fingers dug in my hips. Spread my pussy. Scratched my thighs. Alex lifted my leg, so he could go deeper. Constantine knotted his fist in my hair and pulled to the side, exposing my neck. Mouths closed over my flesh—one nibbling, one piercing. I was a piece of clay, there for them to shape at will. And I loved it.

The stinging in the crook of my neck, where Constantine was feeding on me, pulsed in time to the tugging in my womb. My fangs itched. I locked my gaze with Alex's, and he knew what I wanted.

He leaned down and threw back his head, and I sliced into his shoulder, careful to stay away from major blood vessels. His blood filled my mouth, but I let it dribble down my chin, instead of swallowing. I needed to die on Constantine's lips, shuddering in pleasure around him, before Alex's blood brought me back.

But I wanted to feel this connection to Alex now.

I was seconds from coming again, and could tell neither of the men was far behind. Their thrusts turned shorter. Jerkier. No longer timed to flow together. They pounded me into each other, chasing their completion, and I was in heaven in our jumble of need.

Panic threatened to overtake me when I realized I was no longer moving, just lay there, impaled between the men I loved, as they gave me pleasure and took away my life.

I swallowed down the fear and trusted them to bring me back from this. I wanted to tell Alex it was okay. That we'd make it. My fangs retracted, but my lips were too numb to form words.

Blood loss, pleasure, and Alex's weight on me made my body heavy and my head light. My mind spun, as Constantine—or maybe Alex—found my clit and rubbed.

"I love you," Constantine said in my head. And then, "Now, Alex."

The last things I felt as I shattered in a million pieces were cool cum spilling inside me and a coppery taste on my lips.

Then I fell... fell... fell... into darkness.

Chapter Ten

Who the fuck was hammering?

No. Not hammering.

Blunter. Softer.

A thudding. What was it?

I opened heavy eyelids, to look around. The sound came from close by.

Me.

My heart.

My heart was beating.

I heaved in a breath and felt my lungs expand. I'd forgotten the need to do this. I held my breath for as long as I could, but my lungs constricted, sending the air whooshing out my nose. My *human* lungs. My *human* nose.

I was fucking human again.

And I was back in my jeans and top. My feet were tangled in satin sheets. I was still in Constantine's bed. I stretched, my soles gliding against the smoothness, and bumped my ass against something that yielded. Someone.

"I think she's awake."

I rolled around and saw Alex sitting on the bed next to me, fully dressed. If it weren't for the throbbing in my pussy, I might worry the naughty fun-times he and I shared with Constantine—that Constantine and I shared with Alex—were a dream.

"Hey," I whispered. My throat was raw. I touched my neck gingerly. *Ouch.* There was no stickiness or gaping wounds where Constantine bit me, but the muscle beneath the skin felt battered.

"Hey." Alex smiled and brought my hand to his lips, to lay a gentle kiss on my knuckles. "How are you feeling?"

"Alive." I returned the smile and sat up. Ouch. My ass was sore too. Still, I loved the reminders of last night. Having Alex and Constantine inside me at the same time was incredible.

More—it worked.

And how did I feel about that?

Alex was as excited as a puppy in a ball pit. "We're human again, Cherry. Or do I call you *Gerri* now on? I can get used to *Gertrude*, if I have to, but I prefer Gerri. It's more you." He pulled me in his arms. "We can have a life together. I know we talked about it, but it's really real. I can hear your heart beat. You're *warm*, baby."

"I know." I hugged him more tightly but let my smile slip. My chest felt hollow. Empty. Which was weird, since I felt my heart batting against my ribs.

Constantine sat in the armchair, staring at me as if searching for something. It might be the same thing I was missing.

"Can you still hear me?" I asked in my head.

The void inside widened at his silence.

"Constantine?"

Nothing.

"When do you want to move?" Alex whispered in my ear.

Constantine's eyes burned holes in my soul, the sadness in them near-palpable.

"Today," I whispered back.

Constantine gave a tiny nod, and I returned it. I would respect his wishes.

He stood and mouthed *goodbye*. My stomach churned. I didn't miss this from my human days. I hid my face in Alex's neck and squeezed my eyes shut. My connection to Constantine was severed.

I heard the door of his room open and close. He couldn't hear me, but I sent, *"I'm sorry."*

* * * *

Packing to leave Constantine's mansion was hard. Knowing I could never return had me close to tears the entire time Alex and I folded clothes and shoved them in our bags. Last time I left Constantine, things were different. He'd betrayed me. This was the other way around, and I didn't feel empowered or validated for breaking his heart like he broke mine.

As if the emotional turmoil wasn't enough, I was friggin' tired by the time we were ready to go. My arms ached, and my back was stiff. Perks of being a mortal. I couldn't begrudge Constantine for not offering to help, and I wouldn't ask Wesley to do manual labor, but I wished we had some supernatural assistance. I should have called the vampettes.

I helped Alex shoulder a third duffle bag, and my stomach made a loud gurgling sound. I let out an embarrassed chuckle. "I think I'm hungry."

Alex snorted. "That thing sounds dangerous."

His snort turned into a chortle, and then a full-out belly laugh. The sound was smooth and round and filled the room. I started snickering and couldn't stop. All the pressure and stress and fear and worry bottled up inside found their way out, until tears squeezed out the corners of my eyes and I was short of breath.

"We need to buy food on the way home," Alex said when we composed ourselves again. "Anything left in my fridge is months past its expiration date."

"I vote we throw away the fridge and get a new one." The memory of Constantine flinging the table into his fridge re-soured my mood, but I shook it off. "I can afford it, with my monthly council salary."

Yeah, baby. I was human and rich.

Feeling awesome about it would kick in any minute now.

Alex arched both eyebrows. "You're gonna keep that?"

"Why not? As far as they know, I'm still a member. If I stay away from them, I'm good." I shrugged. Constantine said he'd cover for me, and I trusted him.

"Cool." Alex grinned. "Ready?"

I picked up my suitcase and held out my free hand. He took it with the one not holding a carryon.

We must have looked funny, burdened down by luggage, but we wanted to make as few trips as possible. Or I did. The sooner I was away from here, the sooner I could start getting over my life as a vampire.

"We should say *goodbye*." Alex tilted his head toward the end of the corridor and Constantine's room.

"Should thank him, too." For putting us up. For helping us turn back to human. For giving me a revelation of a sexual experience.

I let go of Alex, so he could knock on Constantine's door. There was no reply. I turned the handle and pushed, and it slid open, to reveal the empty bed. The armchair and table were gone again.

"Maybe he's upstairs." But I didn't believe it. He'd let me go.

Wesley waited for us at the living room, two small envelopes in hand. One had my name scrawled on it, in Constantine's elegant handwriting, the other Alex's.

"Master Constantine asked me to give you these," the human—hey, that could refer to any of us now; I mean Wesley—said as he handed them to us. "He requested that you not share their contents."

Sneaky. I was only back with Alex a few hours, and Constantine was making us keep secrets from each other.

Thinking of him as sneaky made it easier to act disinterested as I flipped open the envelope and pulled out a folded piece of paper.

Forgive me for not being strong enough to walk you out of my eternity. I love you.

~ Constantine

I sniffed, folded the note again, and slid it back in the envelope. As I pushed it in my back pocket, I caught Wesley's gaze. His face was pinched, his eyes red. He was an old man when I met him, but now he seemed ancient. Gaunt. Crumbling.

Without thinking about it, I dropped the suitcase and squeezed him in a tight hug. He felt frail.

After a heartbeat, he squeezed back. "Don't let him convince you he's fine," he whispered in my ear. "He's not. He needs you, and soon he'll need you more."

There was nothing to say to that. I blinked tears away and gave him a peck on the cheek. "I'll miss you."

He trained his gaze to the ground. "I'm sorry to see you go, but I wish you both the best."

We thanked him, and Alex got the door for me. My first step outside was underwhelming. The sun was warm against my skin, but it'd been that way since shortly after I started taking Ruby's potion. The colors hadn't changed either. Good that my first experience with the outside as a human wasn't at night. I'd miss the colors only vampires saw, even if I told Constantine otherwise.

I drew a long breath. Now *this* was different. The air didn't taste of pollution as much. It felt fresh. Rejuvenating. I slipped my hand into Alex's.

He turned a huge grin my way. "Let's get something to eat, and then make plans."

I grinned back. "Sounds good."

We got in his Chrysler and buckled our safety belts. How funny would it be if we managed to become mortal again, only to die in a car crash the same day?

Not funny at all. What's the matter with you?

His note from Constantine peeked out of his shirt pocket.

I pointed at it. "Yours any good?"

Alex slid me a sideways glance.

"Okay. No talking about the notes. Whatever." My stomach made another of those freaky sounds, and my mouth felt full of cotton. "Huh. I'm thirsty too." Human thirst was different to bloodlust. It wasn't all consuming. Just a nagging reminder that I had to have some liquid. I ran the tip of my tongue over my canines. If I were still a vampire, these would be way longer by now—I was hungry, thirsty, and in close proximity to a hot human male.

I wasn't a vampire any more, and I should stop comparing my old reality to this one.

"Burger and a milkshake?" Alex asked as he passed the open gates.

I tried hard not to look behind. "I don't feel like it. How about pizza?" I doubted I'd ever want a burger again. I'd forever associate them with Constantine.

"Sounds good."

And then we'd talk plans. I hoped he wouldn't mention getting engaged again for a very long time. I loved him, but we weren't *there* yet.

I flipped down the sun visor and slid aside the cover of the mirror, to keep myself busy.

And then I shrieked.

Alex hit the brakes. "What? What?"

Honking filled the air, and I said, "Don't stop. It's just—" The woman looking at me from the mirror had thin lines around her eyes and several inches of graying blonde roots. *Which made no sense*, because my hair wasn't any longer than it had been since Willoughby turned me.

And yay to that, by the way. If my hair showed six years' worth of growth, so would my nails, and there'd be a lot of waxing in my immediate future. *Ew*, *ouch*, and *eek* at the same time.

He glanced at me as the car started moving again. "You're beautiful."

"I'm *thirty*."

He laughed. "There's worse. And you're a hot thirty."

I examined my reflection. It wasn't *that* bad; if it happened gradually, I probably wouldn't notice. But it was all at once. Should we skip pizza and go to a beauty salon?

My stomach said *no*.

I expected Alex to stop at a chain pizza place, but he pulled over at the first Italian restaurant we came across.

"Not sure we'll find milkshakes here," I murmured, trying to figure out if my hair looked better in a ponytail. Closer study indicated the color was faded, not grown out. And was it me, or was it no longer perfectly straight?

Alex reached in the map pocket on the driver's side and pulled out a deep blue jockey hat. He held it out to me. "Now can we eat?"

"Yup." I put it on and arranged my bangs under the visor. Not bad, as long as the Italian place wasn't too classy.

My mom told me once that ladies weren't supposed to remove their hats while eating. I'm pretty sure she didn't mean jockeys and was talking about the distant past, but it'd do.

The restaurant was small and cozy, and nobody looked at us twice, even when we ordered two family pizzas. I devoured the first slice before I paid attention to the taste. When I did, I was bummed out. I always loved pepper and added extra to most dishes, but this wasn't a case of the pizza needing a boost of spice. It was loaded with peperoni and sprinkled with jalapenos, and yet it lacked oomph.

"Is something wrong?" Alex asked.

"The flavors are understated. Blunter than I'm used to."

He gobbled down a huge bite. "Tastes fine to me."

Because he'd only been a vampire a short while. Not long enough for his flavor buds to adjust permanently. I could pretend it was my pizza's fault and other things would taste normal, but I knew better.

Still—human, back with a guy I loved, and about to splurge on myself and on renovating his apartment for us. It was all good.

"Let's go shopping," I said, feigning enthusiasm for my food.

"For…?"

"Everything. Clothes, shoes, furniture… But first I have to fix this mess." I indicated my head with a twirl of my finger.

"Your face?"

I glared, before I saw the glint in his eyes. "*My hair*," I said pointedly, but couldn't keep the corners of my lips from tugging up.

Alex reached across the table and took my hand in both of his. "Are you okay with this?"

"With the pizza, or with you implying I need plastic surgery?" By the way, I could finally get some work done. *Hello lipo and new boobs.*

"You know what I mean." When he was in detective mode, there was no changing the subject.

I shrugged and guzzled my soda. "It'll take some getting used to, but I'm more than okay." Except there was a pressure low on my belly I hadn't felt in a while. I jumped up, jostling the table. "Be right back," I said, and ran to the ladies' room.

Running full speed was weird too, like I waded through Jell-O. But the weirdest thing ever was peeing for the first time in half a dozen years. I thought it'd never end. And I'll spare you the horror that's the Ladies' Room Experie—

No, wait. I won't. It's *horrible*. You can't touch anything. Can't sit down. If you're an idiot like me and keep your cell phone in your back pocket, you have to tuck it under your chin and pray it stays put. *While you're hovering over the toilet with your knees half bent.* Killer exercise for the thighs and glutes.

At least the place seemed clean, smelled fresh, and had toilet paper.

I washed my hands and returned to the table.

Alex managed three quarters of a pizza, but I stopped halfway through the third slice.

He sat back and rubbed his stomach. "I'd missed feeling full after a shitload of carbs," he said.

"I know, right?" I popped the button on my jeans. That was something I could do without. I'd have to start watching my diet. My only consolation was that it'd be easier with food tasting like cardboard.

"So what'll you do with your hair?"

Alex's question threw me. "Retouch the red? Maybe grow out the bangs."

"Why don't you go blonde again? It suited you." He'd seen an old picture in my missing person's file shortly after we met.

"It washed me out," I said.

"It'll be different. A fresh start."

A human start. A worrisome thought dawned on me. "Are you trying to erase the woman who... who was in that room, with you and Constantine?"

"No." He answered immediately, but it was the shock in his eyes that convinced me he was being honest. "God, no. If it weren't for *that* woman, I wouldn't have *this* woman with me."

"You know it's the same woman, right? I'm me?"

"I know. And every moment of your life has shaped you. That includes last night, which was mind blowing."

"So it didn't bother you to watch me with Constantine?" I whispered.

He grimaced. "It wasn't my favorite thing ever, but it was necessary."

Time for brutal honesty. "It wasn't necessary for me to be so into it."

He squeezed my leg under the table. "You never denied having feelings for Constantine, and the man makes me bi-curious. Plus, I'd be an ass if I wanted you to have sex you didn't like. What matters is that you're here now. You chose to be with me."

About that... "I decided to go through with the change before you and I said we'd get back together."

"Same result." He leaned closer and brushed his thumb over my cheekbone.

This Alex 2.0 was a curious beast, but I liked how he made me feel about myself and our relationship.

"I'll go blonde," I said.

Chapter Eleven

My stomach churned again, and it had nothing to do with the lustful gazes the colorist doing my high- and low-lights threw Alex.

He looked at odds with the pink hues of the salon's waiting room, but I bet what caught Mircella's gaze wasn't his drab attire, but his gorgeous grey eyes, wide mouth, and sculpted upper body. If he were standing, my bets would be on his ass. Bitable. Seriously.

What would Mircella think, if I told her I spent last night with him and a possibly even hotter male specimen?

No thinking of that. Constantine wanted out of my life; he'd stay out of my head too. Technically, he already was.

I covered my mouth and swallowed a very unladylike burp. Whatever magic kept vampire bodies going after death, conveniently disappeared all sorts of waste in the process. Being a human was messy. My armpits were sweaty—because who would remember to use body spray after not needing it for this long?—and I still tasted the pepperoni. It might be good my taste buds weren't sensitive now, or I wouldn't make through the day without hurling.

Ugh.

I was in serious need of antacids.

Alex caught my gaze in the mirror and smiled.

I returned it. He was so nice to wait for me, instead of spending his time at the electronics' store.

Of course, I waited for him first.

And I shouldn't go there.

A stylist approached us and introduced herself as Gretchen. "Do you have something specific in mind?" she asked.

"I was thinking of growing out my fangs—*bangs*, so maybe layer it a bit? I don't know. Whatever you think will suit me."

Her eyes glazed over with creative mania. "How about an asymmetrical long bob with sidebangs?"

Why not? It was just a hairstyle. Temporary. "Do it."

By the time I was done, I was a new me. Not the girl who left San Luis Obispo to make a career in showbiz, and not the vampire who fucked two men last night.

Loose curls framed my face, one side down to my chin, the other reaching my collarbone. Gretchen did a good job of thinning my bangs and swiping them to the side, so they were half hidden. The overall color was a honey blonde, with pale-beige and light-chestnut streaks. And I loved it.

I thanked the ladies who performed this miracle, paid, and strutted over to Alex.

"Ya like?" I turned this way and that, for him to take in the amazeballs that was my new look.

He stood and pulled me flush against him. "You're gorgeous."

Mircella must have noticed the ass on the man, because she gave me a thumbs-up as I slid my hand in his back pocket.

I felt good, as we strolled out of there. Kind of proud of myself too, for only wondering once what Constantine would think of my makeover. He always liked redheads.

"Next up, nails." If I never painted them red again, it'd be too soon.

Alex shook his head. "I've been around enough estrogen for a day. I'll drive you where you need me to, and then make a couple calls. Maybe swing by my place and empty the fridge. You call me when you're done, and I'll pick you up."

"Okay." A quick search returned the info of three nail salons in the area, and the third one had an opening for an emergency mani-pedi.

Add waxing, and my second first day as a human would be pretty much the same as my first last one.

Lost you, huh?

After my nails, I caught a taxi to the mall. I got *some* groceries, also known as crackers and cheese, and then did some damage with my recently acquired credit card. If the thing had a limit, I didn't find it.

Alex pulled up at the mall's northern entrance, got out, and popped the trunk for me to stash my shopping.

I noticed our luggage wasn't in the back seat. "You unloaded the car?"

"And put everything away. Had enough time to kill." He hummed with pent up energy and seemed more upbeat than when I left him, as he got the passenger door.

"Everything okay?" I asked, as I sank into my seat and carefully laid my brand-sparkling-new Balenciaga bag on my lap—thank you, vampire council.

"More than okay. Perfect. Incredible." He took me in and wolf-whistled. "And I get to take you home."

It was hard to resist his good mood, and I had no reason to try. Things were pretty great. Years ago, I left my home town to make something of myself. Today, I could get started on that, and I didn't have to worry about money. And this hunk of a man was taking me home.

He slammed my door shut and rounded the car to get behind the wheel. I closed my hand over his on the gear stick as he went into first gear. I loved that he drove stick. Gave me an illusion of control over the mechanic beast we rode in. I buckled up again, and we headed for his apartment.

Home.

And I'd never even seen the place.

"So your mysterious calls panned out?" I asked. "Or is this the face of a man with a clean fridge?"

He chuckled. "Both. The fridge wasn't an issue after all."

"And the calls?"

"Don't you want to wait till we're home and can properly celebrate?"

"Tell me. Now. Now now now."

He caressed my little finger with his thumb and shifted to second gear. "I have my job back. Roebuck wants me in, first thing Friday morning."

Day after tomorrow. "He couldn't give us the weekend?" I pouted, but stopped when I remembered I was a thirty-year-old woman now.

Alex let go of the gear shift to give my thigh a gentle squeeze. "He doesn't know this is our first week with a heartbeat. Last we spoke, I demanded he suspend me."

It was Alex's way of keeping his people out of harm's way while he and I looked for Willoughby. After my neighbor Dotty, whom Willoughby kidnaped to shut me up, resurfaced and couldn't give the cops anything about her mystery kidnapper, Alex asked for more time off, to get over his supposed failure.

"He has no hard feelings?" I asked.

Alex gave a small shrug. "He sounded happy to hear from me, and I can usually read him. He said it was about time I pulled my head out of my ass and got with the program."

"Wise man."

Alex snapped his jaws at me, and I laughed. Then something worrisome crossed my mind. "He didn't demote you." Being a detective wasn't safe, but I'd take that over the hazards wearing a uniform entailed.

"Nah. Nothing's changed. It's like the past few months never happened."

But they did.

I tried to keep my mouth shut and failed. "Try not to take any unnecessary risks?"

"You know they're part of the job." We stopped at a traffic light, and he turned to study my face. "Can you handle it?"

I'd known from the beginning that his life was on the line much of the time, but back then he didn't mean this much to me. And then he died.

The air was jammed in my lungs at the memory of watching him bleed to death. The devastation of being unable to save him. The gutting sense of loss, until Constantine brought him back to me...

Alex's death wasn't what I should be thinking of, today of all days. Neither was Constantine. I dug deep for the mood boost that came with the makeover and new clothes—and shoes and cosmetics and a designer bag. "Let's say, if I dump your cute ass, it won't be 'cause of that," I said and immediately regretted it. His ex-fiancée had left him because she couldn't handle his job.

Alex seemed unfazed by my foot-in-mouth moment. Must be getting used to me. "Good to know, but there's not much to worry about. There's a series of muggings gone violent down town he wants me to look into."

That didn't sound too scary.

Alex swerved right, and soon we were leaving traffic behind. Odd. His apartment was in the city, and L.A.'s all about traffic. Odder still, we were heading for the suburbs, down a vaguely familiar road.

When he slowed down, I recognized the street. His mother's house stood near the end of the block. "This is your mom's place," I said.

"Not anymore." He flashed me a grin. "She moved in with Mr. O'Connor while I was in Europe."

"So you get the house?" So many memories in that place. My first night with Alex. Fighting my maker. Falling for Alex.

Losing him.

"*We* get the house. I wanted to surprise you. Is that okay?"

I hadn't lost him. He was right here, beside me.

"*Hell yeah*, that's okay," I said. "There are a couple rooms we haven't fucked in."

Alex left the car with its tail half-hanging out of the driveway, and dragged me to the front door. He fished the key out of his pocket and wedged it in the lock, then shoved the door open until it slammed on the wall behind it.

I let my Balenciaga drop to the floor when he gathered me to him with an arm around my waist. I pulled him down by his lapel, to seal his mouth with mine. While I sucked on his tongue and nibbled on his bottom lip, he undid my jeans and walked me backward to the nearest wall. He inched one hand down the seat of my pants, to cup my ass, and glided the other inside my shirt.

I unbuckled his belt, and was fumbling with his fly when he withdrew both hands with a curse.

"What?" I asked, before noticing the open door. "Oh. Well, close it and get back here."

Alex shook his head while redoing his belt. "Not that. Condoms."

Like a bucket of ice. "Shit. Don't you have any?"

He shook his head again. "I'll be right back."

I kicked the door shut and climbed the stairs to the bathroom. The shower wasn't as quick as I planned. Human-me liked water a lot warmer than vampire-me used to, and I had to keep my hair from getting wet, 'cause it no longer styled itself.

I made it back to the couch and sprawled on it—clean, naked, and grateful for the roll-on deodorant I found in the bathroom cabinet—as Alex reentered the house.

We'd already done it in this room, but oh well.

I motioned him over with my index finger, and he gave me a slow, lazy smile. "I wonder what that means."

I spread my legs. "Come hither."

"Well okay, then." He ripped through the paper bag and box of condoms, and then tore open the condom wrapper with his teeth while he popped his fly one handed. "Let's do this thing."

I laughed. It was good to see him this carefree and silly. And when he pulled his shirt over his head, kicked off his shoes, and dropped his jeans, it was plain good to see him. His midnight-black hair was messy, his grey eyes hooded with desire. His broad shoulders, wide chest, and chiseled abs belonged to a Greek god. I wanted to lose myself in his muscular arms. Feel his wide palms and long fingers map my body. And the rest of him… His legs were long and thick and hard, as was what bobbed between them with every step he took toward me.

He fisted his cock. Two tugs, and he was hard enough to roll the condom down his shaft.

When he knelt with his head between my thighs, I dug my new golden acrylics in his hair and pulled him up my body. "I'm ready for my main course." I needed to connect with him in these new, frail bodies we occupied, as much as I needed to exorcise the ghost hovering at the edge of my consciousness.

Not a ghost. A vampire. Tall and blond and sexy as hell, whose touch lit my body on fire.

I welcomed Alex inside me, pressed my face to his chest and squeezed my eyes against Constantine's memory. Alex slammed his hips against me. I was still tender from last night, and the pain helped anchor me to the now. My new nails dug furrows that wouldn't heal soon in Alex's back. Skipping foreplay might not be the best idea when I lacked vampire healing, but as we rocked together, the ache faded and soon gave its place to pleasure.

Sex with him remained pretty fucking great. It lacked the intimacy of biting, and it was sweaty and sticky, but he had the moves and knew the right places to pinch and rub and stroke, for me to burst like a rocket. The part where my heart tried to leap out of my chest when I came scared the shit out of me, but hyperventilating added to the euphoria of being properly debauched by Alex.

I only fantasized of Constantine being with us for the briefest of moments.

Chapter Twelve

Alex was ecstatic with my new look, and he was pretty vocal about it, which kept my good mood going after clothes were back on and talk shifted from *I love fucking you* to *so what do we do with our future?*

"You're going back to work on Friday. I should find a job too." I played with the thin line of hairs beneath his navel. I lay on the couch, half on top of him, sweat slicking our skin and melding us together.

"I thought you were Ms. Money now. Don't you have a huge allowance for extravagant leather goods?"

I nodded against his chest. "It covers shoes too. But I don't know if anyone keeps track of what comes out of the account. If I use the card for grocery shopping on a regular basis, it may raise flags." Plus, I liked the idea of working again. Weird, I know. Before Constantine dropped the you-can-be-human-again bomb, I didn't mind the rest of my life being a vacation.

"So what will it be?" Alex asked. "Back to modeling?"

"Thought I'd give it a try."

"And the adult movies?"

I sensed the tension beneath his light tone and said, "Nah. I'm over that."

To his credit, he didn't say *good* or anything judgy. "Will you sign with Sheena again?"

I considered it. "She said she'd help me find a job but didn't offer to take me on, and I don't want her to feel like she has to. I'll look for a new agent."

He pulled me closer and kissed the tip of my nose. "Nobody too hot, though." But he was smiling. This wasn't the uncontrollable, irrational jealousy that tore us apart and nearly killed me.

"Define *too hot*." I flicked my tongue over his lower lip. "Someone like you?"

He tangled his fingers in my hair and kissed me hard, but when I closed my fist around his cock, he gently moved my hand away. "Need some time before Round Two."

"Worth the wait." I pressed my lips to his neck, feeling his pulse vibrate beneath the skin.

I don't know which of us drifted off first, but I woke up with a crick in my neck, a stiff lower back, and the pressing need to pee. I climbed over Alex and padded across the carpeted floor and up the stairs to the bathroom. The cold tiles were a shock to my system, but not as bad as the cold water I used, to freshen up once business was done.

"I think there's something wrong with the water heater," I called out on my way downstairs.

"I'll look into it," Alex called back. "Are you dressed?"

I laughed. "Why would I be?"

"Don't worry about me. I've seen it all before," said the woman by the front entrance.

Ruby.

She was dressed in black tights and a long black T-shirt, her auburn hair pulled into a tight low bun. I grew up thinking of her as my awesome aunt, but she was my kickass vampire grandma. And she'd better mean she'd seen *my* all, and not Alex's too.

Alex stood next to her, biting back a smile. He had his jeans on and tossed his T-shirt my way. I snatched it out of the air and pulled it on. Covered to mid-thigh, I hopped the rest of the way down and gave my grandma a hug.

When I pulled away, she was smiling, but tears shone in her dark-brown eyes. "I'm so sorry for everything. I'd have killed Ádísa myself if I knew she'd come after you." Her voice held the faintest hint of an Irish brogue. How did I never notice before? Or was I imagining it now that I knew she was Irish?

"It's okay—umm… What do I call you?"

"I've lost the chance to be your grandma, but you can call me that, if you want. Ruby is fine too."

I studied her. No lines around the eyes. No white hairs. "Ruby for now. It'd be weird calling you Gran, when you look younger than me."

She shook her head. "I watched my husband fade away. I had to uproot my daughter and bring her to a different continent, where she too will grow old and eventually pass on. I'm frozen in time. But you're not. You can be anything you want to be. Have it all." She tilted her head toward Alex and winked at me.

I could also wither and die.

I didn't share the bitter thought.

Alex offered Ruby a drink, which she declined, and we stood there exchanging looks for what seemed like an eternity, before she spoke again.

"Constantine called me. He had me expunge your VSS file." Vampire Social Services—VSS for short—kept records that included details of every registered vampire's turning as well as notes on their whereabouts.

"You can do that?" I asked.

Her grin was smug. "*I* can."

"And nobody will realize?" Alex asked.

"Unless someone requests a hearing, the council holds no meetings in its entirety, for safety reasons," Ruby said. "As long as Gerri avoids seeing them up close, she'll be fine."

Other than getting used to my old name again, it sounded too easy. Not like I'd ever run into any of them by accident. Their hunting grounds were too exclusive for little-old human-me.

"Have you kept your ID?" she asked.

"I have, but can I show it around?"

The smug grin made a reappearance. "You no longer come up as a missing person on electronic records. I didn't manage to follow the paper trail, which means nobody can, and the detective in charge of your case no longer remembers anything about you. So unless you run into a former associate or someone who kept a six-year-old milk carton…"

Alex gathered her in a bear hug before I could. "Thank you. Thank you so much."

I felt like he was trespassing on my sentiment. Stupid, I know, but this was about *me*. I was supposed to be thanking Ruby and squeezing the unlife out of her.

So why were my lips numb when I echoed Alex's gratitude?

Ruby stayed a while longer, to talk with Alex about our future plans and then tell me about places in Europe I absolutely had to visit. Her descriptions of places she traveled to and people she met were so vivid and full of life, I wondered if she realized how much she loved being a vampire.

Her eyes glittered, and her hands drew elegant lines in the air as she spoke of London, Paris, Athens, Rome... "But don't stick solely to big cities. There's a town at the foot of the Carpathians that carries the echoes of German and Hungarian conquerors. The food is divine, and it's got a beautiful little bridge—"

Maybe her previous lamenting of the life she lost was for my benefit. To show me I wasn't missing much by being a mortal.

But I was. Even if I lived to my eighties, which was around the age she'd be if she were human, I'd never lead the life she led till now. I was achy 'cause I slept in an uncomfortable position. I'd never swim naked across the Thames—illegal, by the way—or climb Mount Kilimanjaro.

So what? I had my youth, my health, a man I loved and who loved me, and enough money to do anything I wanted.

Ruby promised to let me break the news to my parents. She said she'd call or write, and then she was off to her hotel or her next adventure. I didn't ask which, and she didn't offer any info.

I felt antsy and exposed. Like my skin was too tight. Too hot. I needed to get dressed. "You said you unpacked?" I asked Alex.

He pointed upstairs. "Master bedroom. Your closet is the one on the right, and I've put lingerie and nightwear in the top two drawers of the dresser."

"Efficient."

"Aim to please."

I blew him a kiss. "You're doing a pretty good job so far."

He gave an exaggerated bow. "So you see exactly how good, I'll even bring in your shopping."

"You're only doing that so I model my new clothes for you."

I was still laughing, when pain sliced my gut and made me double over.

Alex rushed to my side. "Are you okay?" When I didn't answer, he knelt in front of me to meet my gaze.

"Feels like something wrapped its talons in my stomach and pulled," I said through gritted teeth. The description was familiar. *Fuck.* "Can you make a quick supermarket trip?"

He looked at me quizzically.

"I think I'm about to get my period."

* * * *

"Where the fuck are you?" Sheena screeched over the line. "I called the mansion."

"You talked to Constantine?" A dull ache that had nothing to do with period pains settled in my stomach when his name spilled from my lips.

Sheena huffed. "He told me you don't live there anymore. He wouldn't elaborate. Did you have a fight, or…?"

Or. Definitely *or.* He ate me out and fucked me with his fingers and then shoved his magnificent cock up my ass. "Is he okay?" I asked.

"So there *was* fighting?"

"Not the F-ing that transpired, no. But he won't talk to me now, so end result is the same." The ache inside deepened. Widened. Screamed with a need I didn't want to define.

"*You fucked him?*"

I'd like to correct my previous statement; *now* she was screeching.

I filled the yawning void with excuses—it was better not to see Constantine again; he'd only complicate things; Alex and I were building something together; there was no room for third wheels. Besides, Sheena's exuberance was contagious.

I bit my lip and tried to sound nonchalant, when I was dying to share the deets. "Yup," I said. "Totally did."

"And Alex?"

"And Alex."

"No, I mean how did he take it?"

I tugged at a loose curl. "I did all the taking."

"What are yo— Wait. *You fucked Alex and Constantine? At the same time?*"

I laughed. Ibuprofen was a thing of beauty, for subduing the angry T-Rex in my womb. "I did. And you're going supersonic."

She cleared her throat, and when she spoke next, she sounded more normal. "So what now?"

"Oh, I don't know. I sneezed an hour ago, and I swear an ovary fell off."

"What does that have to do with any—" She gasped. "Shit. You sneezed. *You're human again?*"

I put some distance between the phone and my ear, and yelled, "I am. So is Alex. Now can you please tone down the hysterics?"

"*But it's a big thing.*"

"Inside voice. Please."

Sheena snorted. "Not sure you get to be cranky."

"It's been a long day."

"Sure has. What with fucking two gorgeous men at the same time."

"Yeah, well, I'm being punished for that. Got my period." And one of the men was out of my life for good.

"Shit." She laughed. "Welcome back to the world of the living. Mother Nature knows how to throw one hell of a party."

Alex brought me a cup of hot chocolate. I mouthed *thank you,* and he retreated to the kitchen where he'd been since I heavily implied getting me tampons without an applicator indicated he didn't care.

"Not sure I like being the guest of honor," I told Sheena.

"Oh, hush. You're human again. What's a little blood and pain compared to that?"

I blew on my chocolate and touched my lips to the cup. Too hot to drink, and no marshmallows. Didn't I deserve a good, yummy, *marshmallowy* hot chocolate I could drink?

"There's the bitching too," I said. "Alex isn't happy with me being an emotional mess."

"That's a Cherry thing, not a human thing."

"Fuck you." But I was grinning.

"Well, since you're making the rounds…"

I barked out a surprised laugh. "For shame, woman."

"Yeah, yeah. I'm blushing. But before I forget—now that the visual is fresh in your memory, who's got a bigger cock?"

Her question evoked images of Constantine and Alex naked. Constantine was longer, but Alex was thicker. And I took them inside at the same time. Stretched to accommodate them. Let them fuck me to oblivion.

"Not answering that," I said.

Sheena made a sound of disappointment. "Can I at least know if it was good?"

I peeked toward the kitchen, made sure Alex wasn't in sight, and then whispered, "It was fucking amazing. I'll walk bowlegged for days, but it was incredible, Sheena." And I wished I could do it again.

"Was there… double penetration? Did you give one of those boys your tight little apple? I mean your ass."

"I know what you mean, and *ew* to that description. Seriously."

"Yeah, you did." She chuckled.

"Yeah, I did."

We acted like horny teens exchanging sex stories for a little longer—well, I did most of the talking, while she gasped, giggled, and made snide remarks.

"And how are you feeling about all of this?" She sounded far more serious than a second ago. I thought she was talking about being human, but she went on. "Back in a relationship with Alex after... I mean it's soon. Moving in together already, cutting all ties to Constantine..."

"That last part wasn't my choice," I said.

"But you're okay with it?"

"Not like I can change things." I hated the waver in my voice. "He's right, if you think about it. I'll eventually see things his way."

"Are you over him?"

The question landed like a slap on my face. The painkillers were wearing off, my lower abdomen hurt, and my gut churned. I should take something for this. "I thought I was."

"And now?"

Now I had to be.

Alex came in, to ask if I needed anything else. I shook my head and smiled at him, and he laid a kiss on my forehead before getting his car keys. "I'll get some food," he whispered.

I shoved Constantine's memory aside, squeezed it into a tiny little box and buried it where it wouldn't mess with me. "I love Alex," I told Sheena when Alex was out the door. "I'll make it work."

She must have caught on to my need to change the subject, because she said, "Any plans for tomorrow? Wanna get lunch?"

"How about Friday? I want to cook for Alex tomorrow, to make up for all the nagging." And for missing Constantine.

I could practically hear Sheena roll her eyes, as she said, "May the Lord have mercy on that boy."

Chapter Thirteen

I'd woken up next to Alex several times before, but this was entirely new, and not because of the foul taste in my mouth.

Alex was spread out across the bed as usual, one leg across mine, and an arm on my stomach. It was annoying when I was a vampire, but sweltering hot when we were both above room temperature and under the sheets.

I slid out of bed and hurried to the bathroom, to brush my teeth and relieve the pressure in my bladder. I hated the human morning routine. As a vampire, all I did most mornings was sleep through them.

All freshened up, I slipped back into bed. Alex had rolled away. I ran my hand down the length of his body, but he lay still. I listened for his heart beat, panicked, and then remembered I couldn't hear heartbeats anymore.

I pressed closer until his heart thudded against my chest. Or maybe it was the other way around. I wedged my arm underneath his and wrapped it around his waist.

"Are we being naughty or cuddly?" he asked.

"Cuddly." I rubbed my nose between his shoulder blades. It was too hot under the covers. I flicked them up and folded a leg over them. Better. Now I could stay like this for a couple minutes.

"I love waking up with you again," he said.

I nodded against his skin. A trickle of sweat tickled the small of my back. Couple of minutes had to be up. "I need coffee." I laid a kiss on his shoulder and got out of bed.

"Me too. And something to eat."

"Grilled cheese okay? Lunch will be something more elaborate. Honest."

He laughed and kicked the sheets away. I stole a glimpse of his naked body as he strolled to the bathroom. His morning arousal was unaffected by his breathing status.

I went down the stairs with a smile on my face that wilted when I saw the dirty dishes in the sink. They were a couple of plates and three glasses, but the last few months with Wesley around and a cleaning service on call had spoiled me.

I turned on the coffee maker and got to washing up. I was living here rent free; I could at least help with the chores, though I planned on covering my share of utilities and expenses too. Alex and I had to have a talk.

"Will you take out the trash?" I asked when he came down in a pair of boxer shorts. He smelled amazing, and if it weren't for the current no-entry policy in my lady parts, I'd be all over him.

"Can it wait for after breakfast?"

"Sure." I covered four slices of bread with grated cheddar and put them in the oven, then turned on the grill.

Alex poured us two cups of coffee, added a heap of sugar to mine, and brought our mugs and a carton of milk to the table. I towel dried the dishes while waiting for the cheese to melt.

"I was thinking I should chip in. I mean, if I'm going to live here, I need to pay my way. Cover half of the utilities. Maybe a little extra, since I'm not paying rent?"

Alex looked at me like I'd grown a second head. "You're not paying rent *because you're my girlfriend*. I'm not going to take money from you for staying here. We can share the bills, yeah, but no more than that."

"Okay. Cool. Yeah." It still felt weird. I had no problem not paying for anything while we stayed at the mansion, but Constantine didn't need the money. "And I'll pay for half of the new furniture we get."

"Like half a sofa, half a table, and so on?"

I smacked the back of his head with the dishtowel, then used it to take our breakfast out of the oven.

"This isn't a sandwich," Alex said when I placed his plate in front of him.

"It's an open-faced sandwich."

"So a slice of bread."

"Two slices."

He waggled his eyebrows. "Still not a sandwich."

I grabbed one slice and flipped it over the other. "There. Now it is."

Alex laughed, and I joined him. This was nice. Relaxed. Fun. Couple-y. I'd stick to it, and soon my blood-drinking days would be behind me, and I'd stop comparing *now* to *then*.

We spent the rest of the day watching TV shows—I may have developed an unhealthy attraction to a fictional demon hunter—and talking about mundane things like leasing out his apartment and transferring the house's utilities to his name.

My belly hurt, but the pain was dulled. The same should eventually happen to the sense of loss that came with scratching out the last few years of my existence.

Lunch was late and consisted of a pretty *not* bad Salisbury steak and mashed potatoes that came out of a box. I was proud of myself for producing a dish that was neither undercooked nor burned, even if it tasted like boiled chicken to me.

Alex was pleasantly surprised, which would be insulting if I hadn't warned him that we might have to order in.

The small talk flowed between us while we ate, and then I picked up the table, while he went to get chocolate soufflé.

My heart broke a little with the first spoon full, but I finished my portion and thanked him for getting it. And I felt super-petty for thinking he should have known better than to rub my face into my inability to enjoy my once-favorite dessert.

Alex went to the living room, while I stashed the empty patisserie box in the trash. "You didn't take out the garbage," I called out. Yesterday's leftovers were getting rank in the summer heat.

"I will. Come sit with me. You'll miss me tomorrow, when I'm at work."

"Oh, I don't know… I may go furniture shopping." I joined him on the couch, and he made room for me to stretch out beside him. Hot again. I was getting a ceiling fan for each room.

We put on a movie. Took a nap. Ate more. I felt like a lazy bum with an expanding waist line, but Alex and I deserved some peace and quiet.

"Did you call any agencies?" he asked during the first action sequence.

I paused the movie. "When? We've been together all day. Did you see me calling?"

"You're right. Sorry."

"It's okay." I pressed *Play* again

Alex said, "My laptop is upstairs, if you want to look online for modeling agencies."

"Thanks. I will. When the movie is over." I kept my finger over the *Play/Pause* button, waiting to see if he was done.

He wasn't. "I thought you might want to call while it's early in the day. Looks more professional."

Long story short, we didn't see the movie, and I called four agents, the last of which not only picked up her own phone, but also agreed to meet me tomorrow morning.

"I don't feel like a thriller." Alex scrunched his face when I said maybe now we could see the rest. "Wanna try something else?"

I hate, hate, *hate* not watching something to the end, but this was *our* day, and I'd compromise. "Like what?"

"Cooking show?"

I rubbed my full stomach. "No, thank you. I should be cutting down on food, if I ever want to work again."

He placed his hand over mine. "You could join the gym."

Burn.

I diverted my insecurities from his suggestion, and asked, "Comedy?"

"Can't think of any I want to see. You?"

I shook my head.

We watched a basketball game.

Actually, *he* watched it, while I moved my contacts to the new smartphone I bought during yesterday's shopping spree.

I didn't mind the me-time.

I minded that the trash was still in the kitchen.

Human. In love. Good prospects.

Couldn't have everything, but I had a lot.

I took the garbage bag out myself.

It was late, and the first sprinkle of stars lit up the night sky. I sat on the front porch and looked up at them. The darkness felt unfamiliar. The shadows held no shapes I could decipher. No colors blazed through the black.

I knew I'd miss my night vision, but I didn't believe it'd sting so much.

I lay back and folded my hands on my stomach, seeking out the sounds of the night. An owl made its presence known, somewhere nearby. A neighbor's cat meowed. A car engine roared. It all sounded so very far away. So disassociated from me. As an anomaly of nature, I'd felt more a part of it than I did now that warm blood flowed in my veins.

It'd pass.

I'd adapt. Humans always do; they can't afford not to, with time wearing them down.

The door opened behind me, and seconds later, Alex lay down next to me. "Looking for shooting stars?" he asked.

"Reminiscing," I said.

"Missing the mansion?" Tension lined his voice.

I shrugged and turned to look at him. "If you saw a shooting star now, what would you wish for?"

He propped himself up on his elbow and leaned in, to slant his mouth over mine. "All my wishes have come true," he whispered against my lips.

I kissed him again before he could ask me the same question, because I had no answer for either of us. I loved him, and I loved having a real chance to be with him, but I didn't feel complete, and although I missed Constantine, he wasn't the reason.

I'd made my peace with what Alex had done when he was being used against me, and I felt safe with him again, but the bubble we'd built around us to keep the world out felt restrictive. He was so clear about what he wanted, so determined to move forward, and I still couldn't adjust the shower temperature.

Was something wrong with me? Did my time as a vampire jade me? Was I damaged?

Chapter Fourteen

I was still bloated in the morning. I couldn't zip up my jeans without sucking in my stomach and lying on the bed. It did wonders for my self-esteem, when I was about to visit agencies and ask for work.

An agency. So far, Anastasia Looks was the only one to offer me an appointment. I never heard of them before, but they'd be good for practice. My people skills were rusty from disuse, and I was bloated and pissy. I was cool with starting from the bottom up.

I wore a fitted white T-shirt and checked my hair for the millionth time. Despite my best efforts, my curls came nowhere near what I left the hair salon with, but a few hairpins did wonders for that messy-bun look.

Blazer and pumps on, and I looked good. Polished. Professional.

I was glad Alex left early for work. He didn't need to see more of my insecurities. I texted him, *I'm off.*

My phone chimed a second later. *Good luck. Love you.*

Good thing he did, because Anastasia clearly didn't.

She looked at me over her turtle-shell glasses and tapped a finger on my portfolio, which she hadn't bothered to flip through. "Will your daughter be joining us?"

Huh? "My daughter?"

"Yes. How old is she?"

"I don't have a daughter."

The widening of her eyes was so exaggerated, her surprise was obviously fake. "You mean *you* want to work with us?"

My vampire gaze would come in handy at this point, but I no longer had it, and snark might backfire. I toned down my glare. "I was thinking maybe catalog work. I know runway and editorials have different standards."

"Listen, Ms. Mosby." She said my last name with such disdain, I regretted not using my stage name. "You're what? Thirty-two? Thirty-four?"

"Thirty," I said through gritted teeth.

"Thirty is too old for our industry. Twenty-five is too old. You can't show up now and expect to become a model."

"I've worked as a model before."

"So you say." Her voice dripped disbelief.

I sat straighter. "I have. I did."

She huffed and looked at her smartphone. "Yet you have nothing to show for it. In any case, you're well outside our age bracket."

I pointed at my portfolio. "If you just—"

"Have a nice day." She didn't raise her gaze from her phone.

I was dismissed. Worse, I was humiliated. I snatched my folder and strolled out of there with my head held high, and my stomach sinking lower with each step.

What was a girl to do, to lift her spirits?

Something I wanted for a while.

I scrolled down my contacts list till I reached *P*.

Plastic Surgeon – Dr. King

His receptionist informed me the doctor had no opening for a consultation for another month, but she promised to let me know if there was a cancellation. If she didn't call before Tuesday, I'd drop by and throw cash at her till she fit me in his schedule. Who needed class when I could buy boobs?

The thought of finally getting the upgrades I wanted since I was to star in *Knotting Cherry Stem* made me feel better, but only marginally.

I had the uncontrollable urge to call Constantine and let him know how weird it was to be human after this long. Tell him about the need to pee, and sneezing when there was dust in the room, and fucking menstrual cycles. He might get a kick out of the latter; he was still a bloodsucker.

For four whole years after we broke up, he called me on a daily basis, and for some unexplainable reason I always picked up, if only to tell him to leave me alone. His excuse for ignoring my need for distance was that talking on the phone was different than meeting up close. I could use the same loophole.

I held my thumb over his cell phone number for a second, before I called the mansion instead. The replica of an old rotary phone in the living room had no caller-ID feature. Maybe I'd get lucky and Constantine would pick up.

He didn't. "Good morning. How may I help you?" Wesley's familiar voice sounded tired.

"Hey. It's Cherry. Miss me yet?"

"Of course. The mansion is too quiet without you," he deadpanned.

I laughed. "Does Constantine maybe feel the same way?"

He was silent for a heartbeat or two, and then said, "Master Constantine inquires whether this is an urgent matter."

I could lie and say it was, but it was no use. I kept my voice chipper. "Nah. I wanted to say *hi*. See how he's doing. Maybe tell him about my day."

"I'm afraid he believes keeping in touch is a bad idea. He wishes you the best and asks that you only contact him again in case of emergency."

I swallowed hard and blinked back unbidden tears. "Yeah. I get it."

A door closed somewhere in the background. I was about to say *goodbye*, when Wesley whispered, "Don't give up on him. Please."

I had no warning before a sob burbled up my throat and I could no longer breathe through the snot in my nose. "I got to go," I said.

Wesley wished me a good day and the line went dead.

Constantine was right, I told myself again. I wasn't convinced, but I'd repeat it till I hammered in the need to keep my human life separate from his immortal one. My chest constricted. It felt like my heart stopped beating again. My throat went tight. I gasped for air and leaned against a wall for support until I managed a proper breath.

It would pass. It would all pass, and I'd survive. With Alex by my side. I had him and Sheena, and maybe the vampettes in my corner. And my parents…

I didn't tell my parents I was alive.

I should call now. Or get Alex to drive me over there tomorrow. Or maybe wait until I got the hang of things.

Yeah. No reason to call them yet.

I was staring at my cell phone, when the screen came to life. Sheena. I took the call before the ringtone kicked in. "Hey."

"How did it go?" she asked.

How did she know I called Constantine? *Oh.* She meant the interview that wasn't. I mentioned it in passing last night, when she called to see if Alex survived my cooking. "It didn't go. I'm too old for this shit," I said now.

"I could have told you that."

I frowned. "Great. Kick me when I'm down, why don't you?"

"Cherry, baby, I mean that with love. For all intents and purposes, you're a newcomer to an industry that doesn't take newcomers past their teenage years. You didn't have a strong enough career to call this a comeback, and maybe it's for the best, or people from your past might be suing for breach of contract. Modeling isn't all you can do, though."

I shrugged, though she couldn't see me. I wasn't up for a pep-talk. "Whatever. Are we on for lunch?"

"Sure thing. Meet you there in half an hour."

By *there*, she meant the Italian place Alex and I had our first all-mortal meal at. I'd mentioned it to Sheena, and she wanted to try the pizza. I hoped she'd enjoy it more than I did.

I took a taxi there, got seated, and had a couple glasses of white wine while waiting for her. Not the best idea on an empty stomach, but I didn't mind how it dulled the edges of my thoughts.

Sheena planted a kiss on my cheek and dropped into the chair across from me. I was used to seeing her in bright colors, and this lilac pantsuit seemed too pale against her mocha-color skin. Her black hair was pulled up in a neat bun, with enough product to smooth the kink, and she had on barely-there makeup.

"What's with the transformation?" I asked.

"Trying on a new style. You like?" Before I could answer, she waved the waiter over and pointed at my glass. "We'll have this in bottle form, as well as a large pepperoni pizza."

The man disappeared between tables, while Sheena scrutinized me, her dark eyes narrowed. "What's wrong?"

"Nothing. The job. I didn't like how Anastasia turned me down."

Sheena harrumphed. "You're not seriously letting her get to you."

"It's not just that. It's… I don't know. Everything is so. Fucking. Slow. I can't fly up the stairs, chase someone down, or even get to the kitchen, sneak a snack, and return before Alex knows I'm gone."

Her expression was flat. "I can see how being unable to sneak food past Lover Boy may be upsetting."

"And the shower water's all wrong, no matter how many times I adjust the temperature."

"It would make anyone cranky."

I took a sip of my wine. "You're making fun of me."

"Only 'cause you're being a whiny little shit. You're living my reality. Everyone's reality. It just takes time for it to sink in."

"I guess I'm still getting used to things." I twirled the stem of my glass between thumb and forefinger. The glass teetered, and I flattened my other hand over it, to keep it from toppling over. "I hate the lack of coordination."

"That might be the wine," she said.

It wasn't. I never tripped while I was a member of the undead society. *Almost* never. Okay, all the time, but I recovered pretty damn well. I gave her a half-shrug.

"How's Alex?" she asked.

The waiter approached with a bottle in hand, so I downed the rest of my wine and held my glass out for a refill. He poured another glass for Sheena and left us the bottle, saying the pizza would be right out.

"Alex is *fine*. He's ecstatic. And he's at work now, because *he* could get his job back," I said.

"*He* was only gone a few months. You were off the grid for years. And you can have another job."

She wasn't being very understanding or supportive. So much for having her in my corner. I sulked. "Like what?"

"Like becoming a partner in Sheena's Models. Silent partner. And you'd have to help with day-to-day operations, interviews, bookings—the whole shebang."

"Seriously?" My head was light, and she looked a little blurry. I squinted, to bring her to focus.

She guzzled her wine and added more. "Seriously. The vampettes scared Barbie away. You'll be doing me a favor."

Barbie was her latest assistant. I didn't like her much, but she loved her job and was good at it. The vampettes must have done something horrible, to make her quit.

"Okay. Yeah. When do I start?" *Hold on.* "No illegal, under-the-table crap this time, yes?"

In the past, Sheena maintained a second business in her ex-husband's name. What she did was organize the shooting of adult films starring her models, without her name showing, and without paying taxes for her cut. She'd booked me a couple projects, and ultimately *Knotting Cherry Stem*, for which I changed my name.

She shook her head like the thought never crossed her mind. "None of that. No shady stuff, and it'll all be down on paper. We'll draw a contract that says you're buying fifty percent of my company. Humans need paper trails. You'll need something to show the IRS."

How did other council members explain their never-depleting bank accounts? Where did council money come from? And were these questions a good enough reason for Constantine to take my call?

"We need to settle on a price," I said. "And a salary."

"We'll figure it all out. But first"—she tilted her head toward the waiter, who arrived with a huge pizza and hastily made room for it in the center of our table.

"Enjoy," he said.

Sheena cut a slice and brought it to her plate. I looked at the golden crust and the melted mozzarella rushing to fill in the gap left behind. The smell of pepperoni made my stomach rumble.

I took a slice too, hoping against hope that the taste would match the heavenly scents wafting from it.

It didn't.

Focus on the positive.

Human life. Incredible boyfriend. Now a job.

Would I trade any of it for tasty pizza?

Possibly. But only because I was hormonal.

Sheena insisted on buying, and I let her. The wine made me mellow and sleepy, and all I wanted was to go home, lose the tight jeans and high heels, and take a nap.

"I think you need to walk off the alcohol," Sheena said.

Bad Sheena, harshing my buzz. "Can't we call an Uber? The shoes are killing me."

"I'm parked three blocks from here. I'll drive you home. Wouldn't want Lover Boy to come after me for letting a stranger drive you home drunk."

Why would he care? "He doesn't care. He won't take my calls. And Wesley says not to give up, but I have to. Can't pine over him."

She frowned. "Over Al—? Oh. You mean Constantine."

"Don't say his name. He's out of my life." I covered both ears with my palms as we rounded the corner into an alley.

We were twenty feet from the main road, but it felt like a different city. No business people milling about. The cars looked older, the buildings more worn down.

I was too warm. I took off my blazer. I'd get a funny tan with the short sleeves, because now I could tan. I could do all sorts of things.

I didn't see where the man came from. I was tucking my blazer neatly around the handles of my Balenciaga, when he wrapped one arm around Sheena's waist and held his other fist out to me.

Something glinted in the early afternoon sun.

A blade. Too short to do much damage.

"Gimme the bag," the man told me.

I clutched it to my chest. Did the stupid human think he could come between me and my designer bag?

"Now, bitch." He looked over his shoulder. He seemed antsy.

Instead of offering a way out, my mind decided to absorb every little detail about our mugger. His beady eyes were red and puffy. He was missing his right upper lateral incisor. His shirt was filthy and strewn with burn holes, his arms full of tattoos, and he smelled rank. He shifted his weight from one foot to the other and sniffed. I looked into his eyes again. Feverish. In a moment of surprising clarity, I understood he was sick or high. I wouldn't feed on him if you paid me.

While Constantine and I were together, we spent an hour every evening sparring. He showed me mostly defensive moves, but also how to attack and feed from a human without causing lasting damage. It'd been a while since I last practiced, but I remembered most of it.

I went for the knife, feeling too slow. No. I didn't *feel* slow; I *was* slow. Human-slow. No longer supernatural. Stupid fuzzy brain.

The blade was sharp. It sliced through my forearm like a hot knife through butter. Blood pooled along the cut and then dripped on the fine leather.

I screamed.

The man grabbed Sheena's clutch, and then hugged her tight, before dropping her and running away.

"That was close," I whispered. My throat was tight again. So was my chest. The pizza and wine threatened to make a reappearance. "Let's go to your car. I'll call Alex, to meet us there."

Sheena didn't speak. She didn't move, either. She lay curled op on her side, where she fell.

Why did he hug her?

The blade.

Not a hug. A stab.

a series of muggings gone violent down town

Alex's case.

My knees buckled, and I welcomed the pain when they hit the sidewalk. I rolled Sheena on her back and saw a splotch of red spreading across her lilac jacket. Acid burned my throat, and a sour taste hit the roof of my mouth. I barely had time to turn away before emptying the contents of my stomach.

I wiped my mouth with the back of my hand, my head marginally clearer. Her chest rose and fell. Her skin had paled to a grayish hue, and her eyes were shut, but she moved her lips.

I pressed one palm on the side of her stomach, over the wound. Her blood seeping between my fingers reminded me of when Alex lay dying in his childhood bed, ripped bloody by Willoughby.

I'd saved Alex by sealing his wounds with my saliva and feeding him my blood.

I wasn't a vampire any longer. I couldn't heal Sheena with my blood or saliva. Couldn't fly her to the hospital.

I could only make a call and pray.

Chapter Fifteen

My fingers were slippery and sticky, and it took forever to find my phone and call up Constantine's cell on the touch screen.

I brought the phone to my ear. The ringing was interrupted by the *beep* that signified the battery was dying.

Fuck.

Pick up, pick up, pick up, I chanted in my head.

Sheena was still breathing. There was no blood coming out of her mouth. It was a good thing. Had to be. We'd save her. Constantine would save her.

"I'm sorry," I whispered, on the fourth ring. "I should have given him the stupid bag." Fresh tears ran down my cheeks.

"Not your fault, idiot." Her voice was barely audible and her eyes closed, but she was joking. We'd make it.

"Cherry, your persistence is doing neither of us any good." Constantine sounded sad more than annoyed.

"This is an emergency," I said. "Sheena was stabbed. I need you."

"Where are you?"

Beep. Battery.

I hurried to give him the street name and basic directions, and he said, "Don't move her. I'll be right there."

I tossed the phone in my purse and waited, watching Sheena's breathing.

It felt like an eternity before he flew in like a rocket and landed inches from Sheena and me. Without a glance my way, he knelt by her other side and lifted her shirt. A new bout of nausea made me avert my gaze. I couldn't watch him lick the wound closed.

Instead I went over the attack. God, I was stupid. I should have handed the mugger my bag. I could afford to replace it; I couldn't afford to lose Sheena. He could have killed us both. If I were a vampire, this wouldn't have happened. She wouldn't be in danger when she was with me. I'd be the predator, not the prey.

"The wound is deep," Constantine said. "If I close it on the outside, it may fester. I'll give her blood, to help her heal from the inside." He wouldn't meet my gaze, which gave me time to study him. Though the physical appearance of a vampire never changed, he looked haggard. His eyes seemed sunken, his cheeks hollow.

"What happened?" he asked.

"It was one man. He tried to get my bag. I thought I could disarm him," I mumbled.

"You obviously couldn't." He rolled up his sleeve, bit into his arm, and dripped blood into Sheena's mouth. She made a moue of distaste, but I saw her throat working a couple times. It should be enough.

"You're wounded too. I can smell it," Constantine said.

"It's nothing. Just a scrape." I held up my arm. Blood oozed to the surface but no longer dripped.

He flared his nostrils. "Smells different." He reached for my wrist and licked it clean. I felt the edges of the cut strain and the flesh bind together again. The sensation of his tongue on my skin sent a thrill down my spine and moisture pooling between my legs.

Not the right time. *So* not the right time.

"Constantine…" What could I say to make it all better between us?

He stood. "I've called for an ambulance. They should be here shortly. Sheena will be stable by then."

"Thank you," I said, as he turned away.

"I liked the red hair more," he said without looking back. When he reached the corner, he took off.

The ambulance showed up minutes later. Sheena had stopped bleeding. The EMTs cleaned and bandaged her cut, which was now only a flesh wound, and let me ride in the back with her.

Sheena seemed alert, but the painkillers she was administered en route apparently killed her brain-to-mouth filter, because she told the handsome Latino paramedic by her side that he had an amazing ass and could make hard cash as a stripper.

The paramedic laughed. "It's my second job, chica."

"*Sheena.*" I scowled at her, but all I felt was relief. She'd be okay. Thanks to Constantine.

As if she picked his name from my thoughts, she said, "Your ex is too hot for words. Bet I could make him famous, if he didn't have that immortality problem."

"She's a little loopy," I told the paramedic.

"It's the drugs. Don't worry about it."

Sheena snorted. "If I wasn't bleeding like a stuck pig when he raised my shirt, I'd show him a trick or two."

The man glanced at her stomach.

I beamed a smile at him. "Must be awesome drugs, huh?"

He gave a slow nod. "Better than I thought." A heartbeat later, he asked, "Where is the guy who called in the incident?"

"He came, he fed, he left her pining," Sheena muttered. Then she giggled. It was odd seeing her like this.

"He was a bystander. I think he chased our attacker," I said.

We didn't talk much till we reached the hospital. I expected the police to be waiting there for us to report the mugging, but the ambulance doors opened to reveal Liza's familiar face.

"Sheena said you're human now. Bummer," she told me with a wink, and then told our paramedic and the EMT driving that the women they'd picked up had nothing more serious than a case of food poisoning.

She also intervened when the hospital staff wouldn't let me know how Sheena was doing, and then thralled them to remember treating her for dehydration, not blood loss.

Sheena got a suite with round-the-clock care. Liza arranged everything, while I watched from the sidelines.

I cleaned up as well as I could and sat by Sheena's bed to hold her hand, while she drifted off for the tenth time after more lewd remarks about Constantine and his tongue.

Liza came to the room and pulled up a chair next to mine. "All done. No record of the attack. Constantine asked me and the girls to find the guy for him, but I said I'd ask what you want to do."

"I think it's Alex's case. He'll want to be involved."

She nodded. "Is he at the scene now?"

Shit-crap-fuck. "I haven't called him yet." Because I forgot all about him.

Though really, my best friend lay bleeding on the street. A vampire had a better chance of helping than a cop did. I was right to call Constantine first.

But I didn't call Alex second. Or at all.

I fished for my phone in my bag. The screen was still smudged. I used a wipe with disinfectant to clean it, but I couldn't call him. The phone was out of juice. It was as good an excuse as any to put off a discussion I didn't want to have.

A male nurse came in to shoo me off near sundown. Visiting hours were over.

I looked at Liza, expecting her to work her vampire mojo, but she shook her head. "I'll stay the night. You need to go home. Get some rest. Come back in the morning."

"Yeah, you look like shit," Sheena croaked.

I flipped her the bird, but it was with love. She and Liza were right. I needed rest and a hot shower. And to stop thinking of how Constantine rushed to Sheena's rescue but didn't spare me a glance. And of how his dismissal cut deeper than our mugger's blade.

Why couldn't I forget about Constantine? He was my past, and a rocky one at that.

Alex was my future.

And he was naked when he opened the door and pulled me inside the house. Our house. "Ta *dah*," he said with flourish. Then he got a better look at me. "What the fuck? What happened? Are you okay?"

"Yes. I'm fine." I motioned at the blood soaking my T-shirt. "Not mine. Sheena and I went for lunch. As we were leaving, a guy went for my purse. I tried to stop him, and he stabbed her." My voice broke. "It was all my fault."

More tears? I should be dehydrated by now.

Alex gathered me in his arms and kissed the top of my head. "Shhh, baby. It's all right. You're okay. Is Sheena...?"

I may have wiped snot on his bare chest. Disgusting, I know, but it's the human condition. Suck it up. "She's in the hospital. Constantine managed to save her life, but she needed stitches and they're keeping her for a couple days, to monitor her."

"Constantine was there? I thought he didn't want to see you again." He didn't sound upset, but he had mad interrogating skills and a crazy-good poker face.

I didn't try to hide the truth. "She was losing too much blood to make it to the hospital. I called him because he could make that stop." I looked into Alex's eyes, so he'd read the truth in mine. I didn't choose Constantine over him; I simply thought of Constantine first because he was the best man for the specific job.

"Did you call the police?" Alex asked.

"No. We didn't know how to explain that Sheena was already healing. I think the guy who did it might be the one you're looking for. He had nothing to gain by stabbing her, but he did anyway. It made no sense, Alex. Does human life matter so little?"

He hesitated, then said, "You drank human blood till a couple days ago."

"But I didn't kill them. I don't get how someone would do this for a few bucks."

He pulled me close again and tucked my head under his chin. His hard body supported and anchored me. "It's one of the things I love about you. Despite your choices, despite the porn, despite everything, you're a good, decent person inside."

His words were meant as praise, but they were a misogynist load of crap. I was too tired to point out that there was no *despite* here. My choices made me.

Alex was a good man. He didn't realize he insulted me. I'd talk to him about it in the morning.

"Go wash off the grime," he said. "I've made pasta. We'll eat, and you'll tell me about your attacker."

"Okay."

His priorities were right. This was what he needed to know. But when I plugged my phone to the charger and saw no missed calls from him, it pissed me off that he hadn't cared to ask about my job interview.

I was being irrational. Irritable. But last time I brushed off my worries and made excuses for him, he went psycho on me.

As the too-hot—no, too-cold… wait, too hot again—water soaked my head and ran down my body to form pale red rivulets beneath my feet, I went over Alex's behavior the past couple days. No red flags. No irrational jealousy. No outbursts. Maybe he saw certain things a different way than I did. That was to be expected. With time, our ragged edges would grind against one another and smoothen out until we fit together comfortably.

'Cause that was what solid human relationships became, once bodies aged and passion faded. Comfortable.

Thirty was too young for me to be thinking like this. I was okay. Sheena was okay. I had a job. I had Alex.

Mentally repeating the reminder as a mantra was soothing.

The void inside mocked me. I had to woman up and face it, instead of sidestepping along its ledge.

I missed Constantine. I hadn't been ready to lose him. Having him inside me again after all this time had brought to the surface feelings I'd done a great job of ignoring for a long while. I knew I loved him when I agreed to give him up, but I didn't expect it to hurt this much, like part of me was stolen. Like a weight pressed on my heart with every breath.

It didn't change the facts. I was human, and I was with Alex. Constantine wanted nothing to do with me. Besides, even if I hadn't chosen humanity, there was no happily-ever-after that involved all three of us.

The pasta was creamy and cheesy and filling, but it didn't help me feel better. My sense of taste remained suppressed, and hearing Alex's delighted moan at the first bite of bacon, chicken, and parm linguini only made me gloomier.

I described our attacker, surprised at the effort it took to recall details I knew I'd noticed.

Alex asked questions from time to time. He told me how brave I was for fighting back. That I thought clearly under pressure and my actions saved my friend's life. That he loved me.

He cupped my cheek, and I leaned into his touch. "I love you too," I said. It would have to be enough.

Chapter Sixteen

I was back by Sheena's bedside bright and early the next morning. Liza spent the night here, as she promised. I secretly envied the spryness in her step when she stood to greet me. If I spent last night in a chair, I'd need a spa day to loosen my muscles this morning.

"She's still asleep," Liza said. "I think it's more her lifestyle catching up to her than the knife wound. She hasn't been sleeping much these days, with… work." Before I could ask what it was about work that kept Sheena up at night, Liza added, "I fed her more blood, and she's mostly healed. She should be able to go home when she wakes up."

I hugged her and held on despite her stiff posture. "Thank you. I don't know what we'd do if it weren't for Constantine and you."

"No problem. Constantine found her purse nearby. Seemed like only cash and credit cards were missing."

I opened my mouth to speak, but Liza said, "He already arranged for her cards to be cancelled. Sally will get Sheena's car and come by in a few hours. She'll help you check Sheena out without questions."

God, I was a horrible friend. I didn't think of any of the practical stuff. I thanked her again, took her place in the uncomfortable chair, and waited.

Sheena's eyes moved under her closed lids. Her chest rose and fell with unhindered, long breaths. Nurses checked her pulse and temperature, then mmmed approvingly. She was okay, no thanks to me.

It was around noon, and I was dozing off, when Sheena whispered, "Hope you brought me a donut." She had one eye open.

I laughed and squeezed her hand. "I'll buy you a dozen when we're out of here."

She opened her second eye, sat up, and patted her hair, which was a fluffy dark cloud around her head. "Who messed with the hair?"

"They checked you for a concussion last night. The bun got in the way. You're lucky Liza didn't let them shave you."

She grumbled. I handed her a hairband and watched her tame her frizzy mane into submission.

"When can we leave?" she asked.

"As soon as Sally gets here."

As if I conjured her, Sally stepped in the room. With her hair pulled back in a ponytail, she looked like a teenager.

"Were you waiting outside till someone called your name?" Sheena sounded cheerful. As if she hadn't had a near-death experience. Maybe Liza helped with that.

"Huh?" Sally said.

I had the feeling it didn't take much to confuse her, but she was a sweetheart. "Will you get a doctor to sign off on Sheena's release?" I asked.

"I did you one better." Sally bounced on her toes, a grin threatening to slice her face in half. "No staff members remember you being here. Let's go." For someone who weeks ago would rather kill herself than remain a vampire, she certainly enjoyed her mind-control abilities.

We helped Sheena get dressed in a clean change of clothes Sally brought—why didn't I think of that?—and the three of us exited the hospital with no trouble whatsoever.

"I parked over there." Sally pointed to Sheena's car right outside the sliding doors. "And don't yell, but I cancelled your appointments for Monday and Tuesday. You need to take it easy. You could have died."

Sheena gave her a death glare, but all she said was, "I'm fine."

"Are you sure?" I asked. "You didn't even threaten to mop the floor with her ass."

"I'm too hungry to be throwing around threats, but I'm pain free and well rested. I don't think I've slept this well in ages."

Lucky her.

Sally drove, despite Sheena's protests. We got donuts on the way, and I called Alex and let him know Sally and I would be taking Sheena home and spending the day with her.

At Sheena's, I made us a salad, which we proceeded to ignore in favor of the donuts.

Sally offered to do our nails "—since I can't do my own." She looked so crestfallen as she looked at her perma-nude fingernails, I let her do mine, though I paid for a manicure three days ago.

"You know, Cherry will be working with me now on," Sheena said, washing down her bite with a glass of Chianti.

I glared. "Should you be drinking that?"

"Liza said my liver's as good a new. I have to break it in."

Sally giggled, then sobered up. "So Barbie isn't coming back?"

Sheena looked at the glass she held, then the rest of the donut in her other hand. Then she dunked the donut in the wine and bit into it. "Doubtful." To me, she said, "All three of them vamped out when she accidentally stapled her finger. You should've seen them. They were offering first aid, fangs out. Barbie flew out the door and emailed me her resignation the same evening. Poor thing."

"Poor thing," Sally echoed, but she was giggling again.

I loved the time with the two of them, and things only got better when Liza and Carrie came home with tacos. I was shocked when the first bite tasted like heaven, and wolfed down three of them before pacing myself with the fourth. It seemed my sense of taste was returning. Good day, all around.

The girls and I were discussing work—jobs the vampettes wanted to book, new clients Sheena hoped to woo, time schedules and days off for me—when Alex called. He wanted to drop by and see the girls, since he hadn't spoken to them in a while. I saw the young vampires exchange uncertain looks, so I told him Sheena was tired and I was about to go home anyway.

"What was that about?" I asked when I hung up.

"What?" Carrie slathered sour cream on her taco, looking all too innocent.

"The looks. Do you have a problem with Alex?"

Liza shook her head. "No. No problem."

"Good, because he died saving your undead asses."

Sally turned her gaze to the floor. "Alex is great, but we don't like what he did to you."

"And we're worried he might do it again," Liza added.

"And Const—" Whatever Sally was about to say was hushed by the three others.

"What about him?" My voice sounded louder than I was going for.

"Nothing," Sheena said. "He's fine. We're all fine. You and Alex should drop by for dinner sometime this week."

I narrowed my eyes. "What aren't you telling me?"

"Nothing."

I looked at the vampires. "Nothing?"

They shook their heads. Sally avoided my gaze. I'd get to the bottom of this, but not now.

"I should be going," I said.

Sheena offered to give me a ride to work on Monday. Carrie said she'd drop by. See how things were. She and Sheena exchanged another of those weird looks. Hmm…

I called a cab. I should buy a car. Or maybe Alex could drive me to work every morning. Nah. I'd get a car. Maybe a driver too.

The evening got chilly while I waited outside. I regretted not taking a jacket with this morning—not that I planned to be out all day. I hugged myself. Days ago, this would be the perfect temperature.

Days ago, everything was different.

Tonight, Alex was waiting for me at home.

The cab driver wasn't chatty, which left me alone with my thoughts. I had way too much time to myself lately. Work would fix that. Work and focusing on Alex. On being his girlfriend. His return to his human life was seamless. If I took my cues from him and tried to be normal, maybe it'd come back to me, like my taste did.

The door was unlocked, so I let myself in. Alex was cooking. He had on his mother's apron, and I smiled at the memory of the first time I saw him wear it. He'd been naked underneath. Now he wore his jeans and a T-shirt that hugged his broad shoulders as he chopped lettuce.

"Hey you," he said, without raising his gaze. "Hungry? I was going for a Caesar's, but there's no bacon."

I leaned my hip on the table behind him. "I've eaten, and it's always a *no* to no bacon."

He washed his hands, patted them dry on a dishtowel hanging from the glass cupboard, and gave me a light kiss on the corner of my lips. "How's Sheena?"

"She ate her weight in donuts and didn't keel over, so I guess she's fine." I laughed, but I felt so very tired, all of a sudden.

He got a roasted chicken fillet from the fridge and began slicing it. "We have a suspect for the muggings. We put out an APB, but nothing yet. Roebuck wouldn't let me sign out his file, but if you drop by the precinct tomorrow or Monday, you can go over some mug shots."

"Monday, I guess. Maybe after work."

He abandoned the chicken and faced me again. "Work? The meeting yesterday went well? I meant to ask, but with everything that happened…"

He didn't know anything happened till I got home last night. He could have asked. And I was being selfish. Yesterday was his first day back to work. I didn't ask how that went, either.

"The meeting was horrible, but Sheena offered me half of her agency. We'll be partners." I grinned, and so did he. This was normal.

"That's awesome. We should celebrate. Screw the salad—we're going out." He pulled me toward the door, but I planted my feet on the ground.

"I'm tired. Maybe tomorrow? Or your next day off?"

He brought my hand to his lips and kissed my knuckles. The gesture reminded me of Constantine.

I pulled away as soon as I could without making it seem like I hated his touch. "Any news on Ruby? I didn't ask her when she's leaving again."

Alex returned to preparing his dinner. "She called this morning. She's back in Romania."

"That was fast. Thought she'd want to stay a little longer." Maybe visit her old friend Constantine.

"We came back on Tuesday so"—he counted days on his fingers—"that's four days. Huh. I thought it was longer. Anyway, she was in a hurry to return to Europe."

But I was stuck on the first part of his answer. "You flew in together? How come she didn't come to the mansion with you?"

Alex shook his head. "Ruby doesn't do commercial flights. She used Constantine's jet and landed here a few hours later. It needed to refuel and go through security checks, and I couldn't wait that long."

Aw, he'd been in a hurry to come home to me.

"Ruby dropped by your parents'. They didn't mention anything about your… reversal, so she didn't say anything, but she said you should call them."

"I wanted to tell them up close. Maybe next weekend."

"Gerri"—there was my real name again, not the one he met me under, because I was no longer that person to him—"you're human. Don't you think they'd like to know as soon as possible? I mean, they can be grandparents now."

I was lightheaded. It felt a lot like blood loss. Had to be my period. "I'll call them. Tomorrow."

Salad ready, he asked once more if I wanted some, and when I said no, sat at the table while I pulled out a chair across from him.

I should change out of the clothes I wore all day. I felt heat more intensely when I was undead, but I didn't sweat back then. I kicked off my ballet pumps and wiggled my toes. Freedom. I sat there, listening to Alex go on about his day and work and how happy the guys at the precinct were to see him, while I itched to get out of my clothes and have a shower. If flavors were returning to what they used to be, I might finally get used to the water jet.

I escaped upstairs as soon as Alex put the last bit of lettuce in his mouth, and only went back down once I was squeaky clean and in shorts and a tank top. I drifted off on the couch and woke up in bed the next morning, in the same clothes.

I didn't change out of them on Sunday, most of which Alex and I spent online shopping. After hours in front of his laptop, we bought a state-of-the-art widescreen TV, a new double bed with a memory foam mattress, and finally—to Alex's utter horror and despite his numerable protests—a car for me.

While I didn't mind splurging on other things, in this case, I went with a used Toyota Prius. My driving skills were rusty, and I didn't trust myself with anything bigger, faster, or more expensive. I did pay a little extra, to have it delivered to our doorstep Monday afternoon.

Chapter Seventeen

Sheena drove me to the station before work, to unofficially identify the guy who stabbed her. She waited in the car; she hadn't seen enough of him to recognize his picture. Alex was swamped, so we didn't talk much. I basically pointed to the right pic, said I'd be home for dinner, and blew him a kiss.

Sheena stopped for smoothies on the way to the office. I watched her for signs of discomfort as she exited and reentered the car, and I was happy to see no stiffness in her movements. She really was fine—physically, at least.

"They give potential clients a good example," she said, as she handed me a kale-something mixture. She placed hers in the driver's side cup holder.

I took a sip and wished my sense of taste was still numb. "Yuck."

"I didn't say you should drink it. Carry it around. Maybe swirl the straw while you interview someone." She wasn't all the way back to her usual color combinations, but the fuchsia button-down shirt she wore with her black slacks was a step in that direction.

"I'm gonna need coffee," I said.

"Just keep it in your drawer. We're supposed to be all about healthy living."

As we pulled into traffic again, I flashed back to the chocolate-glazed fried bites of sin we indulged in on Saturday. "Since when?"

"Since Sally suggested that as our new pitch. Everyone has thin models, but with the rise of the clean-living movement, we can provide companies with people who take care of themselves.”

“People? We’re taking on men now too?”

“We’re more inclusive, in general.”

“Is that also Sally’s idea?”

Sheena nodded. “The girl is a marketing genius.”

“Or she hopes to meet hot guys,” I said with a smirk.

Sheena laughed. “Then she’s an evil genius.”

We parked in an above-ground parking garage and walked a couple of blocks. The building entrance was open. I went in first, and called the elevator.

“Not that way.” Sheena grabbed my elbow, almost making me spill my kale-flavored vileness—and wouldn’t that be a crying shame?—and led me toward the stairs. “It’s only three flights.”

Come. Fucking. On.

By the third floor landing, my thighs burned with exertion. I needed to work out more. Or at all.

Sheena moved to unlock the door, while I studied the Sheena’s Models sign.

“Will my name go up there too?” I asked.

“Sure. Who doesn’t want to be signed up by Gertrude Mosby? No, you won’t go up there, doofus.” She flicked my ear and led the way in. “This is your desk.”

“I know my way around. Thanks.” It used to be Barbie’s desk. “And I know what’s in here.” I opened the top drawer, expecting to see the huge-ass folder Barbie kept client info in, but nada.

Sheena crossed her arms over her chest and gave me her best you-don’t-know-shit look. “We’ve gone fully electronic. It’s planet-friendly. You’ll be lucky to find a pack of Post-It notes in the entire office.”

O... kay. “Sally’s idea?”

“Nope. Carrie digitalized everything. I’ll ask her to show you when she gets here, because I don’t know my way around her system yet.”

Sheena disappeared into the small kitchenette. When she returned, she jingled two keys in her hand. “For you. Main entrance and front door." She tossed them at me, and I reached for them, but I missed and they hit my smoothie, which sloshed all over my desk.

"You did that on purpose." Sheena arched an eyebrow.

I shook my head. "But I'm not gonna mourn its loss."

I cleaned the green goop from my desk and the floor, and by the time I was properly caffeinated, Carrie showed up.

"Everything okay?" Sheena asked her, as she let her in.

Carrie gave a quick shake of the head I supposed I wasn't meant to see, and then said, "Why wouldn't it be?"

"No reason. Never mind me. Been on edge since the mugging."

No, she wasn't. With the exception of her outfits, she seemed like her usual self.

I planted my fists on my hips. "Oh, come on. Tell me what's wrong."

They looked at each other, then back at me. "Constantine doesn't want you involved," Carrie said.

My very being protested that sentence. I shouldn't be involved, but Sheena was?

Then again, Sheena hadn't hurt him...

"Okay. But if he's in any danger, you let me know," I said to Carrie.

"I will."

I studied her. I was used to seeing her around the house and had stopped being amazed at how beautiful she was. In her ripped jeans, tight tank top, and ballet flats, with her long brown hair falling down her shoulders and her makeup expertly applied, she looked a hundred percent the swimsuit model she was—the woman Willoughby killed and recruited to his and Ádísa's army of gorgeous undead killers.

And she was apparently a computer whiz.

She spent a couple hours showing me her filing system and the online backup she kept, on *the cloud*, and I pretended to understand everything.

When she asked, "Got it?" I nodded.

"I'll call you if I have any questions." I'd better add her number to speed-dial.

The doorbell rang, and Carrie pulled up the schedule on the list. "I think it's your first walk-in."

Sheena rushed to her glass-walled office and closed the door behind her. I buzzed in the newcomer and steepled my fingers, trying to look like I knew what I was doing. Inside, I berated myself for feeling jittery. But think about it—I hadn't had a job in half a dozen years. Never had a *desk* job before that.

A tall, ethereal blonde stepped inside. She marched to my desk on impossibly long legs, hugging a folder to her chest. "Good morning. I'm Cecilia Torrent, and I want to become a model." Her smile was dazzling.

I kept my expression professional. "Do you have an appointment?"

The corners of her lips wobbled, before her expression turned upbeat again. "I do not. I was hoping Ms. Herring would see me today. I'm only in town for a few hours."

And she hadn't thought to call ahead. I knew the system. Act like the agent is intruding on your time.

I liked Cecilia Torrent's attitude.

"I'll see if she'll fit you in." I let myself in Sheena's office and whispered, "She's gorgeous. Has the right style. Nothing overdone. She's like a sexy blonde gazelle."

Sheena replied in the same tone, "Have her wait. Maybe next time she'll make an appointment."

I returned to my desk, sat, and looked up at her. "Please take a seat." I motioned to the waiting area.

"Thank you so much." Her smile grew wider, and I couldn't keep from returning it this time.

"You didn't get her info," Carrie whispered from behind me.

Shit. "I'll do it when she's on the way out."

"You're supposed to log all meetings."

"I will. After she leaves." I bit out the words.

"Okay. Maybe offer her something to drink?"

"Maybe stop backseat driving?"

Carrie relented, and I opened a new file for Cecilia, with just her name for now.

I rocked the shit out of Candy Crush Soda on my phone, until Sheena told me to send Cecilia in.

Fifteen, then twenty minutes ticked by, and she wasn't coming back out. Good for her. Sheena weighed people at a glance, and for her to still be talking to Cecilia, it was good news.

The skip in Cecilia's step when she returned to my desk confirmed it. She started to speak, when the phone rang. I held up a finger for her to wait.

"Make an appointment for her with Jade this afternoon," Sheena said over the line. New hairdo, and with Sheena's own stylist. "Then call Trent. I need new portfolio pics tomorrow. If he's a diva about it, remind him he owes me."

This Trent guy was her new photographer, then. Carrie called up *Associates* on the screen and scrolled down to his number. This electronic filing was cool.

"Yes, Ms. Herring." I hung up and turned to Cecilia. "I thought you were only in town for a few hours."

She blushed and lowered her head. "I'm sorry. I really wanted to see Ms. Herring, and when I called on Friday I was told I'd have to wait a month for an appointment."

She must have talked to Sally.

I asked for her info, and she was more than forthcoming with the details. She was born and raised in L.A. Always wanted to be a model, but her parents wouldn't let her until she graduated high school. She just moved in with her boyfriend, and she was eighteen. Twelve years younger than me.

I felt old.

I booked Cecilia an appointment, convinced Trent—who sounded friendly once I mentioned Sheena—to meet her at his studio at seven in the morning, and sent her on her merry way.

Then I called Dr. King again. And was told there were still no openings.

Carrie checked her phone and grimaced. "It's almost two."

"If you need to go, go. I'm good for now. I'll call you if I need help." *If.* Ha.

"I'll wait for Sally to get here first."

Huh. "Have you left Sheena's side since Friday?" I asked.

"I wasn't with her on Friday," she said.

"But Liza was. And then Sally on Saturday. Is there a reason you're guarding her round the clock?"

Carrie huffed. "You weren't supposed to know, but we worry about you."

Not Sheena? "Me? Why?"

"Because all this is new, and you may need time to process, and something may happen while you're processing."

"Like what?"

"Like get mugged again. I don't know. We worry. You, Sheena, and Wesley are our human family now—Alex too, but more like a distant cousin—and we wanna keep you around."

This gorgeous vampire would *not* make me cry.

I hugged her. "I'm okay."

"Well, good," she said stiffly, "but we'll still check from time to time."

Sally let herself in, chirping about a guy who flirted with her on the way here. "He was *so* hot. Like *oh my God* hot."

Emotional moment diffused.

Carrie left, and Sally and I ordered something to eat. It was a salad, but I felt every single flavor. *Win.* Sheena joined us, and then said we could call it a day.

"Can we make a detour on the way home?" I asked her.

"Sure. What for?"

"Upgrades." To Sally I said, "I need your help with something."

She widened her eyes. "What is it? It won't get me in trouble with Constantine, will it?"

Hearing his name was no easier than uttering it. It twisted my insides. I needed a distraction. Needed to do something for me. And Sally could… facilitate that.

"I need you to get me a doctor's appointment ASAP," I said.

"Oh no. Are you sick? Please say you're not dying." Tears welled in her eyes.

This goes to show everyone that vampires aren't monsters, by the way.

I hurried to reassure her. "I'm fine. It's a plastic surgeon. Being a human takes a toll on the body, and I want to firm some things up. Maybe enlarge others?"

"Oh." She looked me over and nodded, like she recognized the problem areas. "I can do that. We'll have you looking thirty again in no time."

Grumble grumble.

We locked up, and I found Dr. King's address while we got the car. Maybe I'd ask for a facelift too.

* * * *

I was relieved when Dr. King didn't remember me. Of course he saw thousands of patients every year, but I took the lack of recognition in his gaze as extra confirmation that my makeover worked.

Sheena waited in the car, while Sally used her vampire gaze to book me a breast augmentation—despite my efforts, the doctor wouldn't call it a boob job—and liposuction for Monday after next. Sally promised to assist with the healing, bless her. In two weeks, I'd have the body I always wanted. Though Dr. King mentioned collagen depletion and crow's feet more than once, I wouldn't have him work on my face. I'd invest in a good day cream instead. Okay, and possibly get fillers around the eyes.

Chapter Eighteen

As Sheena swerved into our street, I saw a sight that made me squeal. A silver Prius sat in our driveway.

Sheena pulled up behind it, and I flew—well, not really, because I couldn't do that now—out of the back seat.

"Do you like my new ride?" I hovered my palm over the roof, and felt the heat of the day reflected back at me.

Sally cheered from the passenger seat, while Sheena gave me a thumbs-up. "Goes with our new brand too."

I laughed. "That's a happy coincidence. But it's here early."

A sound came from behind, and I turned startled toward the house, to see Alex walking out the door. "They needed someone to sign for the delivery, and called me. You must have given them the wrong number."

"Sorry I made you leave work."

"It's okay. Had to pick up something else too. These are the temporary plates. Guy said you need to go sort out the paperwork and get the final ones in a week." He came down the porch stairs to give me a kiss, and then continued toward the girls.

I felt a tightening in my chest that loosened when they both got out of the car and gave him hugs and pecks on the cheek.

"Are you coming inside? I can make coffee. I have an hour before I go back in," Alex said.

Sheena and Sally thanked him for the offer but declined.

"Where are the keys? I'm taking you out for coffee," I said once they were gone. "I'll drop you off at work after."

He fished a key fob out of his pocket and dangled it in the air as he approached me. I snatched it and unlocked the car, but Alex stopped me before I reached for the door handle.

"I have something for you too." He produced a small velvet box from his other pocket.

And I froze.

I don't mean I couldn't move; an icy hand ran down my spine, and the numbness spread to my limbs. I tried to smile. My chest felt tight, my heart slammed against my ribs, and my stupid lungs refused to let air in.

Was he going to propose?

I zeroed in on his hand raising the lid of the box, and the image slowed. Flickered. Broke. Like I was watching an old film reel.

What would I say if he did? He'd mentioned getting engaged, but this was too soon. Way too soon. He sometimes left dirty dishes in the sink and forgot to take out the trash and talked during movies and—

Was I hyperventilating?

I was hyperventilating.

I had to stop him from opening the box, but no words came out of my mouth and I couldn't raise my hand to place it over his. Was this what a heart attack felt like? Nah. It was just cold feet. Right?

I couldn't say *yes*. Would *no* mean we were breaking up? Should I accept and then stall?

No. No no no no no.

We were back together less than a week. Too soon. We didn't know if we were compatible. We'd been together longer as vampires, but the circumstances were different.

He opened the box. The box was open.

Oh thank fuck.

There was something shiny in it, but it wasn't a ring. I gulped in air and willed my heartrate to return to normal. "A key?" I smiled with relief. "It's a key for the house."

"It was about time you had your own." Alex held it out to me. The keyring was a bejeweled *G*. For *Gerri*.

I took it with shaking hands and burrowed in Alex's arms. "Thank you." The pressure in my chest was lighter but still there.

He kissed the crown of my head. "You're very welcome, but this is your place too."

I pulled him down for a deep kiss that soothed my nerves more. "It's Key-Day for Cherry," I said when we broke apart. "Got a set for the agency too."

"Sounds like a day for celebration." He winked.

"French press and handmade crostini will have to do for now, but I'll get a bottle of wine for tonight, and maybe we can…" I waggled my eyebrows.

He glanced beneath my waist. "So we're—"

"Cleared for landing."

"Wanna skip coffee?"

"Tempting, but I want to take this baby for a ride." I tilted my head toward the car.

He gave an exaggerated roll of the eyes. "If you haffta."

I slid in behind the wheel and adjusted the seat and the mirrors while Alex got in next to me.

Now, I'm the first to admit I reversed a little faster than I should have, but there was no reason for him to yell. I didn't hit anything, and the rest of the drive was smooth. Parking took a couple more tries than I'd like, but it was all coming back to me fast, which did wonders for my mood.

Until we were seated at the brasserie, and Alex asked, "Why did you freak out earlier?"

"Earlier?" I hid behind my menu.

"When you thought there was a ring in that box." Alex took the plasticized card from me. "I'm a cop; I'm good at reading body language. Though I didn't need my training in this case. You were like a deer caught in the headlights."

"I was surprised."

The waiter came for our order, and Alex asked for more time, before returning to me. "You were terrified."

I gulped. "It's too soon, Alex." Possibly for everything.

He nodded. "Which is why I wasn't proposing. But you're open to the idea in the future." He said it as a statement, but it was a question.

Saying I was would be the end of it, and we could enjoy our afternoon till he had to return to work, but I didn't want to lie. "Maybe?"

"Are you asking *me*?"

"I don't know, Alex. I love you. I'm sure about that. But I don't see me getting married or having kids anytime soon. My priorities are different right now." My phone rang, and I pulled it out to see Dr. King's number flashing on the screen. "Sorry. I have to get this," I said.

It was the doctor's assistant, to confirm the date for the procedure and give me instructions not to eat or drink for hours beforehand.

I asked Alex for his pen and a page of the little notebook he always carried about, and jotted everything down.

When I ended the call, he was looking at me, brow furrowed.

Shit. I should have told him. "I'm getting cosmetic surgery in two weeks. I only booked it today. Literally just before I got home. Sally *convinced* the guy to see me when his assistant was out, so she called for the details."

"I didn't know you were considering it."

"Sure you did." I tried to sound playful, hoping to diffuse the situation. "I told you in the car, when I saw myself in the mirror."

"I thought you were joking." He clenched his jaw. So much for diffusing the situation. "I was kidding about the wrinkles. You know that."

I waved him off. "Not touching the face, but I've always wanted a slimmer waist and maybe something more on the cleavage area."

He pointed a finger at me. "You're beautiful the way you are, Gerri. Belly and all. You have nothing to prove."

I loved the part about being beautiful. The assumption that I'd alter my body to *prove* something, not so much. "I'm doing this for me," I said slowly. "It's my body."

"I know it is, but you want to change it because you think it'll make you more attractive. Do you realize you won't be able to get pregnant for the next three or four years? What'll you tell your parents and my mom when they ask why we're waiting?"

Lipo isn't a tummy tuck. They don't tighten your muscles, and you don't have to wait years to get pregnant, but that wasn't the point. "I wasn't planning on getting knocked up anytime soon, and I don't generally base my decisions on how I'll explain them to others." My eyes burned. I wanted to be a vampire for ten seconds, so I could thrall this discussion to an end.

He glared. "You obviously don't care what *others* have to say, but it's not all about you anymore. You can't do anything you please and damn the consequences. And when will you want to have kids? Neither of us is getting any younger."

You know how sometimes you can't tell the moment a relationship died? Well, that was when I realized ours had run its course, and it wasn't 'cause of his jibe about my age.

What I felt when I saw him with the box wasn't cold feet. It was a fucking full-on panic attack, and I felt it resurging inside, clouding my reason. My first instinct was to pick a fight—tell Alex I didn't care about his opinion and he wouldn't see the new boobs anyway, because we were over. But I wasn't pissed off; I was sad. And Alex was the one who taught me not to translate all my feelings into anger just because it was easier to handle.

I threw the approaching waiter a death-glare that kept him at bay. "Alex, this isn't working. *We* are not working." The words burned my lips, but I didn't want to take them back. Whether things between us were more broken than I thought when we got back together, or we simply weren't at the same place, this wasn't working.

"Because we're disagreeing on liposuction?"

"It's not this disagreement." Hell, when I thought about it, I didn't want the lipo anymore. I was no longer the girl who considered her value to be reversely proportional to the circumference of her waist. Becoming human again had confused me for a while, but I saw clearly now. The boobs I very much wanted, though. For me. Not to be more attractive.

I made a fist, digging my nails in my palm to keep from screaming. "When we met, I thought we couldn't have a future because I was a vampire. Then you got turned, and the problem was that you weren't used to your new reality. I believed with both of us human, we'd be good, but I was wrong. You want a serious girlfriend, someone you can marry, and I'm not that girl."

He cupped my fist with both hands. "But you can be. If you're set on doing this, let's talk about it."

I squeezed more tightly. There was nothing to talk about. "You're not listening. I'm saying I don't want to be the perfect woman you have in your head. I'm not ready for all this relationship entails, and I don't know if I'll ever—"

Alex glanced at the ceiling. When he zeroed in on me again, his expression was flat. "This is about Constantine, isn't it?"

I withdrew from his grip so fast, I hit my hand on the wall. It hurt. "This is about you and me," I whispered, frustration and pain choking me. Anything else, we could overcome, but we weren't compatible in our core. "We're not meant to be, Alex. I don't want the picket fence and the family you always dreamed of." Realization dawned, and I added, "Not now, not ever."

"Gerri, I love you. We can work this out." He didn't say he didn't care about anything but me.

"I love you too, but we'll never see eye to eye, and this isn't fixable." I stood.

Alex got up to block my way. He reached for me but didn't touch me. "Come home with me. Stay the night." His steel-grey eyes were mesmerizing, and I wanted to say *yes*.

It was tempting. I really did love him, and I'd never *not* be attracted to him, but another night together would only prolong our misery.

I leaned into him and pressed my lips to his. He tasted salty with the tears that ran down my cheeks. I handed him the key fob. "I'll call Sheena to pick me up. Take my car to work. I'll come pick it up and get my stuff tomorrow morning, and I'll leave the house key."

Leaving him behind looking like a lost pup hurt like hell, but I also felt liberated. No Constantine. No Alex. Just me, and time to figure out who I was and what I wanted.

I called Sheena and got a vampire lift to her place.

I can't see myself as a wife and mom. I don't want it. And if I don't want it now that it's a fucking miracle, I never will."

"Woman, your timing sucks," Sheena said. "Couldn't you have thought of all that before becoming human again? But then you'd have missed out on that threesome, so…"

So the subject was changed to something marginally less uncomfortable, as questions and comments were thrown my way. I answered a few, dodged many others, and soon I was half-drunk and giggling and thanking the powers that be for having girlfriends.

Me and the vampettes, *girlfriends*. Sheena, who handed us all to Willoughby, my best friend. Things changed from one day to the next. Hell, within a week, I'd gone from sleeping with both the men I loved to talking to neither of them. I'd gone from vampire to human. Maybe I'd been too hasty to leave Alex. I might change my mind.

No. Breaking up with Alex was a good choice, and I shouldn't let insecurities change my mind. Even now, I missed talking to Constantine—in my dreams, in my head, and in reality.

Going to work did me good. It took my mind off things. Sally had to fly me in to Cecilia's photo shoot at the butt crack of dawn, because Sheena wouldn't hear of waking up that early. Cecilia was a darling. She was cooperative and took direction like a pro.

"Thank you so much." She wrapped me in a tight hug when the headshots were done.

Her hair was still long, but Sheena's stylist had given it volume, and it flowed and swung with grace every time she bounced on the balls of her feet. Which was a lot.

As she tucked it behind her ear, I saw a faint bruise on the side of her neck.

She saw me looking and covered it with her hand. "My boyfriend got a little overzealous. I tried to cover it with makeup, but…" She grimaced.

We could edit it out if it showed on her pictures, but I advised her to avoid this much passion in the future.

Trent called for her to change into a bikini for her body shots, and I spent the better part of the next two hours telling myself I looked great for my age.

I arranged for Trent to send the photos to Sheena, hugged Cecilia goodbye, and Sally and I took a cab to the agency. It was too late in the morning for us to fly. Sheena drove in, and Carrie brought my car. She and Sheena picked it up together with my stuff.

Alex was home when they showed up, and he was surprised not to see me. He asked them to tell me to call if I needed anything. It was nice of him. Alex was always nice, and I was a bitch for stealing the last few months from him.

No.

We'd been in the relationship together, both made mistakes, and now we went on our separate ways. Like mature adults.

God. I hated these mood swings.

The vampettes stayed with Sheena and me throughout another short workday, and then joined us for lunch and shoe shopping. It felt very *Sex and the City*, but in L.A. and with several of the ladies preferring a high-hemoglobin lunch. I loved my time with them and their efforts to keep me from thinking too hard about my life.

Work picked up from Wednesday on, with more appointments to juggle and companies to contact for Sheena. I got the hang of the computerized system, but Carrie dropped by once a day anyway. As did Sally. Liza had a catwalk in New York, so we didn't see much of her.

I stayed at Sheena's a few nights, enjoying the camaraderie and coddling of the other women, but being around them twenty-four-seven made me crave some space.

Finding an apartment on South Park was shockingly easy when I said the words *money is not an issue*, and the realtor Sheena hired for me had me moved into my own place before the end of the week.

By the way, I loved not having a budget, but I was also aware of the unfairness—the council had unlimited funds, but new vamps got a tiny nest egg. I should talk to Constantine about that.

Or not.

Alex and I exchanged a few texts. He was tired but good. He hadn't been sleeping well. We missed each other, but I said this was for the best, and he agreed. He reminded me I should get my final license plates, and I said I was on it. He said *good*. He insisted I should have the new stuff we bought for his place. Instead, I convinced him to buy off my share, and I spent the weekend shopping for my new sixth-floor apartment.

I had two large bedrooms, a kitchen, and a living room to furnish and decorate. And I had a *nook*—a bay window with a bench seat in my living room. I smothered it in pillows and lined the walls on either side with black-and-white photos of places I wanted to visit. I knew better than to think real plants would survive in my care, so I went with fake ones instead— all the beauty and none of the fuss. I wasn't up for a deeper commitment.

By Sunday evening, I was mostly unpacked and settled in, but fully exhausted and happy. Truly happy, in my open spaces and surrounded by bright colors.

I opened the last suitcase Sheena got from Alex's. Towels and sheets. No hurry to put those away; I'd bought new ones. I stuffed the suitcase in the back of my closet, to be dealt with another day.

I should have the girls over for drinks, to thank them properly for all their help, but not tonight. Tonight I'd enjoy my peace and quiet.

I poured myself a glass of white wine, put on some music, and picked up a book. An actual book. Romance, if you wanna know. The ceiling fan kept the room cool, but I opened the window and looked down at the lit street. I thought I saw movement to my right, and I swiveled my head, but there was nothing there.

If I'd never been a vampire, I'd say I imagined it, but my racing pulse hinted otherwise. I leaned out further, before I remembered I was no longer gravity resistant and would make a decent splatter if I lost my balance. I jumped back inside and closed the window, to be safe. If there was a vampire nearby, it'd be one of the vampettes, checking in on me. I should probably invite her in, but as I said—peace and quiet time.

* * * *

I started my week being all responsible and going by the auto dealership for my final license plates and the transfer of ownership. I think the salesman flirted with me, but I was in a hurry to get to work and really not interested.

Talent, old and new, paraded by the agency on a daily basis. My job was to log everything in, keep notes, and track their schedules. I also took it upon myself to take the arrogant, entitled ones down a peg or two. Most of them weren't a horror to work with, but Cecilia was the only one to bring us cookies—organic, low carb, and gluten free—and stole a couple minutes to ask about my day. No surprise that she was my favorite.

She visited a lot this week, to arrange for seminars, talk schedules with Sheena, or talk with her about a meeting, and she was always bright eyed and bushy tailed.

Which was why we were all worried to see her sad and exhausted when she came in on Thursday.

"You okay, hon?" Once Sheena decided you were one of hers, she was protective of you for life.

"Yeah. Sure." Cecilia sounded distracted.

"Is something wrong? You can tell us," I said.

Cecilia rubbed her eyes. "Had a long night. Nothing to worry about."

Sheena tapped her phone repeatedly. "You went out? I didn't have anything on your schedule for last night."

"No, no. I was home. Just stayed up late." She avoided our gazes.

My phone chimed with a text from Sally, who was across the room. I glanced at her, a *what the fuck?* in my gaze. When I read the text, I understood.

Should I mojo her for answers?

I shook my head. It was one thing to thrall our way into an early appointment, and another to use vampire powers to extract answers from someone against their will, on what was obviously a personal matter.

Cecilia looked no better the next day, and I happened to notice another bruise on the other side of her neck.

Okay, so I looked for it, but the point is that it was there, and I was no longer sure it was a hickey. I shared my finding with Sheena and Carrie, who was our designated undead babysitter du jour.

"So she's into kink." Sheena shrugged. "It's always the quiet, vanilla-looking ones."

But that's not where my mind went. "I don't think that's it. I mean, think about it. She's tired, moody—"

"She could be on her period," Carrie said.

"And the bruises? Nah uh. I think she has a vampire problem." Bet I impressed them with my mad deductive skills.

Sheena grabbed her tote and motioned for Carrie and me to get out so she could lock. "Because of two hickeys? You should be a mystery writer."

Carrie snorted. "Anything to take her away from the agency, huh?"

Sheena glared and took off down the stairs. Carrie hovered next to her, and I chased after them. "What was that about?"

"Nothing," Sheena said over her shoulder.

If I heard that again, I'd flip out. "Say *nothing* one more time, and I'm throttling you."

She kept going, while I hobbled on my heels three or four steps behind. "You can't say this is your dream job," she said.

"No, but—"

"I mean, you keep rolling your eyes at people."

"So do you," I said with more force than I meant to.

"I'm the *boss*, and you roll your eyes at me too, which is fine at home, but not at work."

I made it down to the ground floor with no shortness of breath and no ache in my knees. *Go me.* "You're right," I said. *Not* panting.

"And you're snappy. Bordering on rude, more often than not," Carrie supplied with a grin.

"Okay, okay. I get it. I'll be better next week."

Sheena rolled her eyes. See? "You won't be here next week. Surgery, remember?"

Right. I'd go up a cup size or two. Though I wasn't going with the double-Ds that would benefit my old career.

"I won't need the whole week; Sally said she'd help me recuperate."

Carrie scrunched her nose. "I'm not sure that'll be good. Implants are foreign objects. Vampire blood may make your body reject them."

Why didn't I think of that? "So I'll be out of commission for a few days."

Carrie cupped her breasts. "More like a few weeks, unless things changed since I got these babies."

I didn't know those were fake. "Weeks?" I caught myself stealing glances at her cleavage and raised my gaze to her face. "I don't want to be down for weeks. And if Sally doesn't heal the incision points, there'll be scarring."

"Then don't get the boob job," Sheena said.

Fuck. "I'll think about it. This being-human thing is losing its glamour day by day, though."

We stopped at the crossing, and I noticed a car at the street light. What looked like a very upset Cecilia was in the passenger seat, shaking her head and moving her hands animatedly. I couldn't make out the driver. "Hey, is that Cecilia?" I pointed at the car.

"Might be. She lives nearby." Carrie turned to look, but the light changed, and the car sped off.

"I think we should check in on her tonight," I said, breast augmentation taking a back seat in my thoughts. "Whatever is bugging her may be paranormal."

"Or she's having a difficult week with her boyfriend," Sheena said, leading the way toward the parking garage.

"And I guess by *we should check in on her*, you mean me?" Carrie harrumphed. She took out her phone and searched for something I couldn't see.

"I'll tell the girls you'll be late," Sheena said.

"Got Cecilia's address. I'll walk there. It's too early for me to fly after them." Carrie turned to me. "If it's nothing, you owe me big time."

"Totally." But I was thinking about my upcoming procedure again. Should I go through with it? Larger breast had been a dream of mine since I was out of puberty with my current set. Trying to make it in the adult-movie industry was a good excuse to bite the bullet and buy myself a pair, but my life had changed since. I had changed. And with how my back complained if I stood for too long, I doubted it'd thank me for the extra weight.

Or I was a wimp and didn't care for the painful recovery. Younger me was braver, stupider, or had a greater tolerance for pain.

I could live with that. And without implants.

Damn. Was this what maturity felt like?

Should I also try accountability on for size? "Hold on, Carrie. I'll come with," I said.

Chapter Twenty

Cecilia didn't have a vampire problem. She had an asshole-boyfriend problem.

Carrie rounded the building and flew to the first floor windows, where she thralled a tenant to buzz me in. I waited for her, and we went up floor by floor, looking for Cecilia's apartment. Full disclosure—without Sheena around, I used the lift.

We heard yelling coming from a fourth-floor apartment, and I recognized Cecilia's voice. I was about to point out the door to Carrie, when she started banging on it. Made sense she'd hear Cecilia before I could. She was a vampire.

A guy yelled, "Go away," from the other side of the door.

Carrie mouthed *human*. When I whispered, "You sure?" she nodded and pointed to her ear and then the left side of her chest. She'd heard his heart.

I was searching for something to say that would convince him to let us in, when Carrie kicked in the door.

A shirtless human man in his early twenties was flung backward, yelling, "What the fuck?"

I followed Carrie in the apartment and saw Cecilia cowering at the corner of the living room. There was blood at the corner of her lip.

"You hit her." I wished I could rip him limb from limb.

"I'm going to kill you, bitches. You can't break into my—"

He didn't get to finish his sentence, because Carrie had him by the throat. She raised her arm, and his feet stopped touching the ground.

I rushed to Cecilia, and she averted her face.

"We're here to help," I said. "Has he hurt you anywhere else?"

She shook her head. "Not today. But you have to go. He has a gun."

I looked at the man, who kicked and thrashed. "Don't worry about him," I told Cecilia.

"Bitch. Let me down. What the fuck are you?" he yelled.

Carrie shook him and looked at me. "I need a catchy phrase, for when assholes ask that. How about, *your worst nightmare?*"

"Eh. Maybe, *someone who'll kick your ass?*" I asked.

Carrie grimaced. "I don't hate it, but... Oh, I know. We're the monsters under the bed."

This cracked me up, and I felt horrible, because Cecilia was trembling next to me. I gathered her in my arms and whispered, "I swear to God you'll never have to worry about him again. Believe me." I wished I had my vampire mojo and could thrall away her fear.

The man kept cursing and threatening us. He kicked Carrie in the face, and I winced. Now he was done for.

Carrie wiped her mouth with the back of her free hand. "You like hitting girls, huh? Helps you feel like a man? Does it make up for your tiny dick?"

He was weirdly quiet. I looked at his face, which was turning blue. She was crushing his windpipe and hadn't popped a fang. I was proud.

"Please," he squeaked and raked his fingers at her hand around his neck. "Please."

She punched him in the balls, and while he was crying with pain, lowered him so she could look him in the eye. "The moment I let you go, you're going to pack your stuff, take your car, and move to a different state. You will never contact

Cecilia again. And every time you *think* of hurting another woman, you'll hurt yourself instead."

He nodded. He was cupping his balls but his face was slack, his gaze locked on hers.

"Go. Before I change my mind and end you right now." She dropped him, and he punched himself in the nose. Horrified shock etched on his features, he hobbled to the other room. When he reappeared, he was carrying a tattered suitcase. He didn't glance our way.

Carrie waited until he was out the door for good, and then she approached Cecilia and me slowly, like she didn't want to scare the cowering girl more. "Do I need to heal her?" she asked me.

I saw no wounds, and Cecilia's lip was no longer bleeding, but there could be internal damage. "Honey, are you sure he didn't hit you anywhere else?"

"No. Just a slap. I fell on the couch, and he pushed up my skirt, and then you knocked." She spoke dispassionately, like she was talking about someone else.

I remembered the feeling. "Cecilia, if you want, Carrie can make you forget all that happened," I said. "You can forget he ever existed."

Cecilia pressed the heels of her palms against her eyes. "I wish I could."

"You can." Carrie knelt in front of her.

When Cecilia lowered her hands, she no longer looked afraid, but determined. "I should remember. I should know there is such ugliness out there. And you… I don't know what you are, but thank you. You saved me today. And you saved the next girl too." She took Carrie's hand and squeezed. "Thank you."

Carrie grinned. "My pleasure. Totally. Just… if possible—"

"I'm not telling anyone," Cecilia said. "What would I say? That you're Superwoman?"

I offered to take Cecilia in for the night, but she said even with a busted door she felt safe at home now. Carrie made a call—she said it was to Sheena, but I had my doubts—and promised someone would be over to fix that door in an hour.

By the time I was tucked under my Egyptian cotton sheets in my heavenly double bed, in my super-amazing apartment, I knew what I wanted to do with my life.

I bet Sheena would be relieved when I told her.

I was too antsy to stay in bed after sunup. I got up and Googled what it took to become a licensed private investigator in California. Hmmm… lots of qualifications I didn't have. I knew who could help me acquire documentation, though. I waited until I wasn't risking Sheena's wrath, and made a breakfast run to the nearest bakery.

I called Sheena as I was pulling onto her street. "Hey. Can I come over? I'll bring coffee and pastries."

"Sure." She sounded groggy. "What time is it?"

I ignored her question. "I'll be at the door in five."

Sally got the door, and she and Sheena seemed not to mind the early visit. Carrie was asleep, and Liza was busy. Outside. On a Saturday morning. I suspected none of the girls had much of a life outside Sheena and the agency, and that was another reason they were always around. I wondered what Liza might be doing. Maybe she was visiting Constantine? Now that no women lived with him, she could make a move more easily.

Sheena bit into a Nutella-filled croissant and moaned. "After a week of healthy crap, this and a cup of java are a godsend."

"You're welcome," I said.

She arched a perfectly shaped eyebrow. "So you got your ass out of bed at this ungodly hour to bring us breakfast?"

I sipped my coffee and tried to look innocent. "Carrie told you about last night?"

"She did. Good catch. She said the guy was dangerous."

No mention of having Cecilia's door replaced. So Carrie hadn't called her. My PI-brain was on already. *Yes.*

"I think maybe this is something worth pursuing," I said.

Sally was playing with her phone. "Dangerous guys?" she asked without looking up from her screen.

"That too. Sheena, I'm sorry, but I have to quit. I'll still buy half of the agency, if you—"

"Praise the Lord." She laughed. "I adore you, you're my best friend, and I loved spending time with you, but you're a horrible assistant. Carrie had to go over all your entries remotely and fix your mistakes every night."

"She did? Why didn't you tell me?" I was too relieved, to sound indignant.

"You had enough on your plate. But what will you do for work? Or will you become a socialite instead?"

I closed my eyes, composed myself, and then opened them again and smiled. "I want to be a private investigator."

Sheena choked on her coffee and spat her mouthful back into her cup. "You wanna be what?"

"I wanna take weird cases that other PIs wouldn't touch with a ten-foot pole. I know the paranormal exists, so I'll have more options. And I'll need your realtor friend again. I wanna start looking for a place first thing Monday morning."

For the first time, Sally looked away from her phone. "Don't you have an appointment with Dr. K. Monday?"

"About that…" I chewed on my lower lip. "Not doing it."

"No lipo and no boobs?" Sally sounded shocked.

"No. I'll join a gym. Maybe."

"But you broke up with Alex *because* you wanted to have work done?"

"I broke up with him because I wanted the option. I wanted to be able to do anything I want."

She'd lost interest. She was typing things on her phone again.

"Thing is I need six thousand hours of paid investigative work the past three years, and I don't have them," I said.

"We can thrall someone for you," was her distracted reply. "Sorry, I need to put this post on my blog, and then I'll help you."

I gawked. "You have a blog?"

"Lifestyle," Sheena said. "She's promoting the agency through it."

"There. Done." Sally put the phone aside and smiled at me. "Who do we go see?"

"Alex or Constantine." I scrunched my nose. "I stupidly didn't get Ruby's number when she was here, and my mom has no way of contacting her, because Ruby doesn't want to leave a trail. But she's the only hacker I know."

"Tell me exactly what you need, and I'll get Constantine to ask her," Sally said.

And with that out of the way, I was out of excuses not to tell my parents of my current situation.

No, that didn't come out right.

It wasn't that I didn't want them to know I was human; I was afraid I wouldn't share their excitement at my news, when all I had to show was two lost lovers and a job that didn't fulfill me. Now I knew what I wanted to do with my life, it was easier to sound upbeat.

I still didn't do it face to face, though. After all, I was busy. There were classes to take and licenses to apply for and spaces to rent—and I wasn't sure I could look them in the eye when they asked how I was turned back.

I called that afternoon, and Mom answered. We exchanged the usual pleasantries, said we missed each other and I should visit soon, and then she asked, "How is Constantine?"

Umm...

Mom's radar was always on point. "Cherry, hon, is everything okay?"

I loved that she called me that. "Everything is fine. Mostly. Mom, I'm human again."

"Oh my God. *That's amazing.*" She yelled, "*Greg,* she's human again," then in a quieter voice said, "How? And are you... Is everything as it was? Organically? Hell, I mean, there are no lingering issues from being undead?" She barely caught her breath between questions.

I smiled, though she couldn't see me. "Everything seems to be in working order."

"But how did it—?"

"Constantine found a ritual." No more details.

She laughed. "That man is our official benefactor—turning Ruby so she wouldn't die, helping you out with that man, and now turning you back and letting you stay with him…"

"I moved out. He won't talk to me, Mom. He said he doesn't want to watch me grow old and die. And Alex and I… We said we'd try to work things out, but we weren't compatible." I felt like crying. Apologizing for not wanting to give her grandkids. But this wasn't about her or anyone other than me. "He sees a big family in his future, and I don't."

The pause that followed raised my hackles, but when she spoke again, she didn't try to change my mind. "So where are you staying now? Do you want to come home?"

Her words warmed me up inside. "I'm renting an amazing apartment. You and Dad should come over. You can stay the weekend." I told her all about my color scheme and my view and my new career.

"Please be careful," she said. "There are all sorts of dangers out there."

It hadn't occurred to me that when I was a vampire they at least didn't need to worry when I went out alone at night. "I'll be careful. I promise."

We said our goodbyes, and I was about to end the call, when she asked, "Are you happy, baby?"

I gave it some thought. I was lonely, but I wasn't settling, and I was pursuing something I liked. "Most of the time."

Chapter Twenty-one

The vampires in my life came through for me again, and by Tuesday I had more than enough registered hours of investigative work.

Carrie accompanied me to get fingerprinted, sit for an exam, and submit my application packet. She used her gaze enough to make sure I wouldn't have to wait more than a week for my license, but she wouldn't help me get a firearms permit without completing the training course for real.

It took a month and a little help from my friends, but I had my office set up on the first floor of my building. It had a leather couch in the waiting room, and a huge mahogany desk with a winged desk chair in my inner sanctum. And a full bar, because PIs always served their clients alcohol in old movies.

The girls had insisted I needed a door like the ones in those movies, with a glass upper part and my name printed on it. I told them to go ahead and order one.

I saw the result at the unveiling ceremony, also known as *the first day we drank at my office.*

It read:

CHERRY STEM
Paranormal Private Investigator

The *Paranormal* part lead to a yelling match, with me saying nobody would take me seriously, and Sally insisting L.A. was all about the paranormal these days.

If it didn't get us clients, she said, she'd pay to have it taken out of the sign. And to print me new cards. Because I apparently had ten thousand of them as *Cherry Stem – PPI*.

Notice the *us* before? *If it didn't get* us *clients?*

I didn't give the word much thought at the time, but when I stumbled down the stairs the next morning, Sally stood outside my office door, dressed in all black and wearing sensible shoes, which up to that moment I doubted she owned.

And she had a tall latte in each hand.

She grinned and held out one of them. "Ready for our first day, boss?"

Come again?

I raised both hands, to show her I has holding a coffee mug and a set of keys and couldn't accept her offering. "*Our* first day?" I asked as I unlocked the door and walked in.

"Yup. I'm going to help you with this thing."

Saying I didn't need help would be lying, and I didn't want to hurt her feelings, but I wanted this to be my thing. Though it wasn't a horrible idea to have a vampire tagging along when I needed things done. "I didn't realize you wanted to be an investigator too," I said.

"Eh, modeling is cool, but it's not a long-term career. People will notice my appearance doesn't change. And I love to blog, but there's only so much experience I can gather by hanging with Sheena and the girls all the time. You, on the other hand, seem to know where to find trouble. You keep things interesting. And I'm sup—I like hanging out with you. So am I hired? You'll only have to cover meals and expenses." She waggled her eyebrows, and I wished for a scarf to cover my neck. Did she want to feed from me?

"Define *meals*," I said.

"Pizza? Chinese? Anything I feel like for lunch, whether we're at the office or working a case." Human food doesn't sustain vampires, but it tastes great, and for someone who'd been counting calories most of her life that was an amazing perk to going undead.

"You've got yourself a deal," I said.

"*Awesome.*" She wrapped her arms around me in an awkward hug, as she balanced the coffees. "I'm going to need a desk and a chair. And supplies. Do I use a company credit card, or—"

"*Sally.*" I glared.

"Never mind. I'll spend wisely, and you can pay me back when I return." Her glee was near-palpable, as she all but flew out the door, taking both coffees with her.

I should make her switch to decaf.

* * * *

"Any calls?" I cradled the received between my shoulder and ear and clicked on a pair of boots. They were stylish but seemed sturdy. Added to my shopping bag.

"Nothing since you last checked." Sally's reply carried down the line and from the other side of the door separating my office from the waiting area. "Wanna get something to eat?"

"No. I want a client." This was our daily routine for a fortnight now. We'd wait at our desks, play online games or shop, have lunch, wait longer, then go home.

I was bored.

I wanted to work.

To do *something.*

"Should we be like ambulance chasers?" Sally asked.

"Go to situations where people are guaranteed to have spouses cheat on them or business partners steal from them?" I infused my question with a healthy dosage of sarcasm.

"I was thinking more like go to haunted houses or look into unsolved mysteries." She tossed my sarcasm back to me.

I'd spent time with Sally when we both lived with Constantine, but not one on one. The more I got to know her now, the more I realized the airhead spiel was just that. An act.

Still… "We're not ghost busters. We're private investigators."

"*Paranormal* ones." She hung up, and moments later let herself into my office. "We need to play up the paranormal angle. People here love it. They believe in mediums and fortune tellers, and we're the real deal, Cherry."

I'd never seen a ghost, and as a human, odds were I never would. "*You're* the real deal; I'm in the know."

"More than anyone else has going for them. Let's get ourselves out there. I should write about this place on my blog. Get word out."

We already had that conversation and agreed it was better that her followers not know where she worked. Besides, investigative work had nothing to do with outfit-of-the-day posts.

"You don't need to worry about promo; I'm in charge of the administrative stuff," I said. Because I had to do something. This was supposed to be my newly found calling, but she had more ideas than I did.

"Well, administrate. Or let me? I'm so freaking good at PR, you can't even imagine. I'll have clients swarming in. Honest." Sally perched her cute butt on my shiny new desk. "Let me put an ad in the paper? It'll be awesome, you'll see."

"Okay, but I'm still the brains of the operation. You're the brawn."

"She said okay," Sally yelled.

Carrie showed up behind her.

I smiled, confused. "Hey. I didn't know you were co—"

"Told ya," Carrie said to Sally. She tossed a folded newspaper on my desk. "The ad ran today, in print and online. Now we sit back and wait."

We.

"Did I hire you too?" I flipped through the paper, and sure enough, there was a half-page ad with my name in block capitals. Beneath it read:

Is a ghost haunting your house?
Do you suspect your boyfriend is a vampire?
Could your neighbor be a pet-eating shifter?
Whatever your supernatural problem, we'll kick its butt back to the hell that spawned it.

A nervous giggle bubbled up my chest and spilled from my lips. "Who thought of this?"

"I did." Sally arched an eyebrow. "And it's on my blog and Instagram too."

I tried to stop laughing, but I couldn't. Until I remembered the vampire council, and the laugh got lodged in my throat. "We need to take it down now. It has to disappear. If the council catches wind of this…"

"Oh, I'm sure Constantine will take care of it." Sally waved off my concern.

"But you don't know it. You haven't cleared it with him." Panic sent bile churning up my throat. "The council will have us all killed if they decide this might expose us. Expose you, I mean."

Carrie planted her hands on her hips. "Don't be a drama queen. It's no worse than any vampire movie. Those who already believe in us will see it as confirmation we exist. The rest will see it as a gimmick to bring in the gullible. And we don't say *we're* vampires. We say we know how to deal with them."

I forced my thoughts away from the gruesome scenarios running in my head. "Okay. We don't take it down. But you don't run it again either. Whatever happens happens."

"But Cherry—" Sally was probably about to protest my decision, but we'd never know, because the unimaginable happened.

My desk phone rang.

I looked from her to the phone and back again. If she was here, she wasn't calling me. Was it a potential client?

"Hel—Cherry Stem, Private Investigator." I didn't trust myself to say the *paranormal* part without laughing.

"I heard you take on cases others have no interest in." The male voice on the other end of the line was deep and smooth and reminded me of dark chocolate. And of Constantine. I hadn't thought of him much while I kept myself busy preparing my business, but his memory never stopped calling to an ache deep inside.

"What is this about?" I asked with as much authority as I could muster.

"It's a sensitive matter. I'd rather discuss it in person."

I wanted to tell him to please drop by *now now now*, and save us from the boredom of the past way-too-many days, but I pulled the threads of my professionalism together. "I'll connect you to my assistant, and you can arrange an appointment." I waved frantically at Sally, who flew to her desk, and then I realized I didn't know how to forward the call.

Carrie shook her head, her expression a mixture of exasperation and amusement. She came closer, grabbed the receiver, and said, "This is Ms. Stem's assistant. How may I help you?"

I listened to her tell the man we were very busy this morning but had an opening in the afternoon.

"Ms. Stem will see you at nine, Mr...." Pause. "Mr. Hunt. Thank you. Have a nice day."

"Nine in the evening?" I asked when she hung up.

She shrugged. "He said he has to work late but needs to see you today."

Chapter Twenty-two

Sally was gone when Mr. Hunt showed up, so I answered the door, and *damn*, he looked as delicious as he sounded. He was tall—though not as tall as Alex and Constantine—with dark skin and eyes a brown so light, they looked almost amber. His wide shoulders, narrow waist, and long legs were well defined by a designer suit, and I could see my reflection on his patent shoes as I introduced myself and invited him in.

The man was poise personified, with his elegant moves and perfect manners, but there was a sense of repressed energy coming from him. Like he hid a volcano beneath the sleek exterior. It made me think of Constantine again, and not because I missed him. Mr. Hunt hummed with power that didn't come with his lawyer career.

He followed me to my office and took a seat across the desk from me. I offered him a drink from my well-stocked bar, but he turned it down. His lips curved at the corners in a permanent hint of a smile, even while he described how his house was broken into and a precious stone stolen from him.

"Can you describe the gem?" I asked. "Any specific characteristics?"

He let out a chuckle that belonged in the Top Ten list of Sexiest Sounds Ever. "You'll know it when you see it. It's a sapphire, cornflower blue and two inches in diameter."

An alarm went off in my head. I doubted there were several stones that fit the bill, and last I'd seen one of them was in a dream, a couple months ago—a vivid, lifelike dream that almost cost me my unlife. And the queen bitch wore it around her neck.

If he was talking about that sapphire, odds were he either knew vampires were real or he was a jewelry thief. Either way, he wasn't *just* the big-shot lawyer he presented himself as. "Mr. Hunt—"

"It's just *Hunt*."

His last-name-for-first-name thing added to my suspicions. "Hunt, then. When you called, you asked if we take cases others turn down. It seems to me like the police would be able to help you with this. It's a straightforward burglary, and I'm sure your insurance will cover the gem."

"I didn't report the incident to the police."

"And why is that, if you're the legal owner?"

"Because there is no record of purchase for this sapphire, and whoever stole it wasn't interested in its monetary value, or they would have also taken the diamond bracelet that was stored in the same safe." He sounded calm and very much in control, despite basically saying he'd stolen the thing first.

"Do you have any idea who would steal it?"

"I suspect my wife's family. The stone belonged to her, and after Katje was gone"—his tone wavered for the first time—"they demanded I return it to them."

I wanted to comfort him, but the power he emanated filled the room, suffocating me. Was he a vampire? Was he thralling me right now? "I'm sorry for your loss," I managed.

He shook his head. "It was a very long time ago. But I need your help. You have to find the sapphire as soon as possible."

"I'll do my best. Can you tell me your wife's full name and any next of kin that live in the wider Los Angeles area?"

"Her name was Catharina Kappel. Her brother Filippus lives in L.A." He gave me the name and address, and I jotted it down, though the first place I meant to look at was Ádísa's old place. By vampire law, it had passed to her oldest childe, Constantine, and if I played my cards right, I might get to see him again.

"I'm prepared to pay anything to get the stone back," Hunt stood and produced a plump envelope from his jacket's inner pocket. "I trust this will cover the retainer and expenses for a few days."

He left the envelope on my desk, and I itched to tear it open and count the cash, to see how much this case meant to him. Instead I stood too. "Thank you, Mr. Hunt. I'll be in touch."

As I walked him to the waiting area, he said, "Would you have dinner with me this Friday?"

The cogs in my brain halted. If he was a vampire, he was dangerous. For all I knew, he was another of Ádísa's childer, out for blood. But then why wasn't he pouncing? He had to realize I was human now. He'd hear my heartbeat. His invitation had to be a trap, but if I turned him down, it might take forever to find out what he was up to.

Sally chose the worst day to leave early, damn it.

An idea slapped me full force, and I beamed a smile at him. "I'm busy Friday evening, but how about lunch, Saturday?"

As far as I knew, only Ruby's nearest and dearest vamps could move around during the day. If Hunt accepted the invitation and showed up, he wasn't one of the evil undead.

"I'm afraid I'll be out of town this weekend."

Of course. "Another time, then."

As I closed the door behind him, it occurred to me we never shook hands.

It was late, but I wasn't sleepy. Instead of going home, I locked up and went to my desk. I should call Constantine and ask for access to Ádísa's manor, but I needed to steel myself first for his negative reaction to hearing my voice. Maybe tomorrow... First, I was curious about the history of the gem. More so about how Catharina Kappel died.

An extensive search in public records came up with no results on her life or death. I tried *Catharina Hunt* too, and again got zilch, but if Hunt was a vampire, his wife might have been one too. Or she was never in the States, and he moved here after she passed. I looked for *Hunt* in California and decided not to bother wading through the pages of results. It'd help if I had a second name for him.

I could lift his fingerprints off the envelope and have someone run them through the system. Where *someone* equaled *Alex*. No. Bad idea.

Next time I saw Hunt, I'd shake his hand. See if he was warmer than room temperature. If he wasn't, I'd ask Constantine or Ruby to check the U.S. vampire census for me.

My eyes felt gritty. I rubbed them with the heels of my hands and checked my phone for the time. After three, and I had to be in at eight. The five floors to my bedroom seemed impossibly far. I made myself comfortable on the sofa in the waiting room and was out like a light before I thought to set an alarm clock.

I was startled awake by knocking. "Did you forget your keys?" I yelled, thinking it was Sally.

"I'm pretty sure you didn't give me any." That voice didn't belong to Sally or any other woman I knew.

"Hunt?" I glanced at the window and the sun sneaking in through the shutters. Daytime. Not a vampire.

I ran my fingers through my hair—never a good idea when your hair isn't straight, which I kept forgetting mine no longer was—and let him in.

He was dressed in tight jeans and a black T-shirt that defined every single muscle on his torso. He held up a carton with two coffee cups, and a paper bag from a bagel place I knew and loved. "Since you can't do dinner and I can't do lunch, I thought we'd settle for breakfast," he said.

I opened my mouth to respond but didn't know whether to thank him or say I was busy. I stepped back and waved for him to come in.

"Sorry, sorry. I have a good reason for being late. Honest." Sally squeezed in between us, rummaging through her bag. "I swear I tossed the keys in here this morn—" She froze, flared her nostrils, and turned to face Hunt.

"It's okay," I said. "Hunt, this is Sally. She's my receptionist-slash-assistant."

I expected him to offer his hand, but instead he returned Sally's expression, tilting his head to the side. The power I felt from him yesterday surged all around me, and I took a step back. Sally gave a light shake of her head and relaxed her shoulders. "Good to meet you, Mr. Hunt. I assume you're our new client."

I was glad she didn't say *first* client.

"Nice to meet you too." He gave a small bow. "I've only brought two coffees, but you can have mine, and there are enough bagels for all of us."

I thought of offering to go make a coffee at my place, but I didn't want him to know where I lived. I wasn't sure I appreciated his gesture. It was undeniably a little creepy.

Sally turned down his coffee, but she was more than happy to partake of the bagels, and was soon moaning over a corn-beef-and-mustard one with extra onion, while texting.

Hunt handed me my coffee, and I touched his fingers on purpose. He felt feverish. I withdrew more quickly than I meant to, and he smiled. "Everything okay?"

"Yeah. Let's eat here, and then I have a few more questions for you." I felt bolder with Sally around. My phone chimed. A text from Sally. This time I knew better than to look at her. I made sure Hunt couldn't see the screen, and I read her message. *He doesn't smell human. He has a heartbeat, but his scent is all wrong. Nothing I've smelled before.*

He definitely wasn't a ghost. A shifter? I thought they were near-extinct. I swiped back a quick, *Stick around.* I planned on getting to the bottom of this, and I needed some muscle, in case Hunt wasn't as friendly as he acted. My coffee was sweet and strong. "This is perfect," I told Hunt, as I stuffed half a bagel with cream cheese, lox, and capers in my mouth. "I forgot to eat last night."

He chuckled. "I like a woman with a healthy appetite." He was flirting with me, but I didn't feel any erotic interest from him. It was like he was going through the motions. Or he pretended to be attracted to me, to keep an eye on me, *because he wasn't human.*

We devoured breakfast, and then retreated to my office, where my desk acted as a buffer and a barrier between us.

I pulled in front of me the printouts of gems that matched his description, and flicked through them, to gain time as I gathered my thoughts. "*Ow.*" Paper cuts freakin' hurt. I brought my index finger to my mouth and licked the cut. Though my sense of taste had returned, blood tasted wrong. I splayed my hand and looked at the tiny beads forming a red line across the pad of my finger.

Hunt frowned, and I watched him watch my blood pool along the cut. "How much of a *paranormal* investigator are you?" he asked.

I frowned and licked my finger again. There wasn't enough blood to get Sally running in here, but better safe than sorry. "Not sure I know what you mean."

He stood and closed the door, and I opened my first drawer, ready to go for my gun. He rounded the desk, and I tensed, though his posture wasn't threatening. He leaned so close I could feel his breath, and whispered, "Do you know your receptionist is a vampire?"

My first reaction was to laugh, but I schooled my face into an impassive mask. "I know. I don't know what you are."

He sat down again, no longer bothering to keep his voice low. "She'll probably tell you, but I'm a shifter. Panther."

Of course. I should have known by the sleek muscles and feline grace. "I've never met a shifter before. Should I be afraid?"

"Not of me. Others may take offense in the company you keep."

"Others? I thought you were all… gone."

He gave me a half-nod, half-shake of the head that meant nothing.

When I was with the VSS, Constantine told me shifters and vampire were non-mixy, but since there were a handful of shifters left in the world, I didn't expect it to be an issue. "And what do you want from me? For real, this time."

He sat back and crossed his arms. "I really want you to find that stone for me."

"What about the rest of your story? Did you even have a wife? I found no record of her in the States."

Sadness darkened his eyes. "She existed. Part of her still does, which is why I need the sapphire. Katje and I met at a different time, when magic… Never mind. Vampires and shifters were enemies, and though I had no ties to sever, her maker and his other childer opposed our mating. For centuries"—so shifters were immortal too?—"we ran and hid from them, as well as from bigots who hated our other differences, but fifty years ago her maker found us. He trapped the part of her soul that loved me, along with all her memories of me, in one of four soul sapphires."

Four. And one of them had been around Ádísa's neck in Alex's dream.

"Am I boring you?" Hunt asked with the same smile that wouldn't leave his lips yesterday.

"I'm sorry. It's a lot to absorb."

"And there is more. Last year, I tracked down her brother in L.A. and stole the stone, but I couldn't use it until I found where they kept Katje. I stuck around, in case he had her with him, but I've never seen her enter or exit his house. A few days ago, someone started following me. I don't see them, but every now and then I feel a presence nearby. Then, day before yesterday, the sapphire disappeared. I need to find it and find my mate. I need to make her whole again." His voice broke.

"I'll help you," I said. "We'll find them both." Someone around here deserved a happily-ever-after, damn it.

Chapter Twenty-three

Sally came in without knocking. "I couldn't help but overhear..."

I arched an eyebrow.

"Okay, so I listened in. I want to help, and I'm sure the girls will be on board. They need the distraction. Constantine too. The more the merrier, right?"

"You're a vampire," Hunt said. "Why help?"

Sally batted her eyelashes. "I'm a sucker for a good love story. Do we know how many vampires will be at the brother's house?"

Hope softened the hard angles of his face. "Two that live with him. A couple others that come and go." He frowned. "I just realized you're out in the daylight."

She opened her mouth to answer, but I cut in. "You have your secrets, we have ours."

Shit. I shouldn't have said *we*. I felt his scrutiny like a physical weight. To divert him, I asked, "Why were you flirting with me, if you're so set on finding your wife? Why the dinner invitation and the breakfast?"

"I had to know whether you were a hack or the real thing, so I meant to stay close."

As I imagined.

Sally asked Liza and Carrie over. While we waited for them, I left her and Hunt talking about the layout of Filippus Kappel's estate and went to her desk, to call Constantine. Sally could have done it, but I wanted to hear his voice. I missed him, okay?

"Cherry." His greeting lacked emotion.

"Hi." Now I had him on the line, I didn't know what to say.

"Is this an emergency?"

"It may be council business."

"I'm listening."

"I have a were-panther in my office." Which might make more sense if Constantine knew what I did with my life. "I'm a private investigat—"

"I know. But a were-panther? I was led to believe—"

"Yeah, me too." If he could interrupt, so would I. "I didn't ask him to shift or anything, but he says that's what he is, and I believe him. The thing is he's mated to a vampire, and her... *kiss* I think it's called? Anyway, they locked away the part of her that loves him in a sapphire like the one Ádísa had in Alex's dreams. A soul sapphire?"

Constantine cursed, and hearing him lose his cool was soothing. The cold version of him broke my heart.

Like I broke his.

"You've heard of soul sapphires?" I asked.

"I have, and I feel like an imbecile for not recognizing it when I saw it. I believed she haunted Alex's dreams because of who she was before she became a vampire. I didn't think..."

"This isn't about her. She's gone, and we need to help Hunt and Katje."

"Your new shifter friend and his mate? What can the council do for them? Are they registered in the U.S.? We have no authority over European vampires."

"I don't know. Can't you check the census? Please?" After Ádísa and Johnny-boy's deaths in our hands, the council decreed a census, to record all vampires in the United States. Even if the Kappels weren't registered as natives, we might find useful information about them. Like whether Catharina was in the country.

He let out a tortured sigh. "You realize you're still a council member. You could do the research yourself."

"I'm trying to stay under the radar. If one of the others decides to drop by and ask why I'm looking into things, they'll know I'm human."

"I hate when you're right, but I'll look into it. Have your Mr. Hunt call me tonight. If the council can't help him, I will."

"What about me?"

"You will not get involved." His tone brooked no argument. "I will not have you risk your precious humanity." He spat out the last word like it had a foul taste.

"This is my case. You can't tell me what to do."

"I know. But if you want my help, we do it my way." He hung up, and I felt empty.

Hearing his voice for a couple minutes wasn't enough. I needed to see him—touch him. I couldn't. I went to the small WC and splashed water on my face, then studied my reflection. I'd changed my hair back to red this month. It felt more *me*. There were black circles under my eyes, but I looked good. Self-assured. Like I knew what I was doing.

Ha.

I went back to my office and found Sally and Hunt laughing.

"Your assistant-slash-receptionist is a delight," Hunt said. "She has given me hope I can be with my Katje once again."

I told him about my call to Constantine.

"Another vampire willing to assist?" Hunt's expression was a mix of incredulity and suspicion.

"If the Kappels aren't registered with the vampire council, this is vampire business," I said.

"Is Katje in danger, if she's found in the country unregistered?" he asked.

I hoped not. "Constantine will be in charge of the case, and he'll make sure she's safe. I trust him with my life."

"Plus he's a big softy deep down," Sally said. If Constantine ever heard that, there might be an evisceration in her near future.

Hunt stood and all but crushed me in a giant hug. "I will owe you forever," he said.

I wouldn't be around that long.

Carrie and Liza joined us, and I stayed and tossed ideas for a Plan B with them. If the council couldn't intervene, they'd have to storm Kappel's place. Deep down, I hoped Constantine would drop by and help with the planning. He didn't.

By 1 p.m. my lids were drooping and my temples throbbed with the beginnings of a headache. Another thing to add to the *con* list for being human.

"I need a shower, a nap, and some downtime. Call me if you need me, otherwise forward calls to my cell and lock when you're done," I told Sally.

"Sure thing, boss." She didn't glance my way, too engrossed in her discussion with Hunt and the girls. She was so excited, I smiled despite myself.

I had my usual fight with the water temperature, but managed a semi-decent shower and was under the covers in no time. My new sheets were crisp and cool and inviting, but sleep wouldn't come until I took some ibuprofen for the pain.

Even then, Hunt's story, my relationship with Alex, and my brief talk with Constantine rattled in my head. Hunt and Katje made it work despite ignorant racists and lethal supernaturals, and I couldn't commit to a wonderful man who wanted a future with me. I was honest when I told Alex I didn't want the same things out of life that he did, but I finally admitted to myself he was right too. It was also about Constantine.

I was supposed to get over him, but I thought of him whenever I had a moment to myself. Like now, when I should be sleeping.

I squeezed my eyes shut and willed away the thoughts. It must have worked, because the next thing I knew was an incoming text waking me up.

Unsurprisingly, it was from Sally. *Forwarded incoming calls to my cell, so you'd rest. Hunt called. He dropped his wallet at the office. He can be there in an hour, and I'm busy. Will you get it for him?*

I looked at the time. 8:15. I'd slept the afternoon away. I couldn't bother typing, so I pressed *Call*, but she declined my call and sent, *Can't talk. Hunt will fill you in.*

I got dressed and went downstairs to wait for him and see if I could find anything online about soul sapphires.

Hunt was on time, and I let him in and handed him his wallet. "Sally said you'd fill me in," I said. "Do you have a plan?"

He nodded. "I spoke with Constantine. He didn't find Katje's family in your council's records, but his search unfortunately raised a red flag. Enforcers went to Filippus' estate at sundown. He has forty-eight hours to leave the States peacefully. They found two more vampires with him, but no sign of Katje. Constantine and Liza will break into his place tomorrow during the day, to look for the stone. Carrie and Sally will help me lure whoever's shadowing me, and use them to get to Katje. I'm not losing her again."

His determination again brought to mind Constantine—not that he was ever far from my thoughts these days. "How did you make it work for centuries?" I asked.

He smiled. "We built a relationship that suited us both, and we never let external factors get between us. If we needed space or a diversion, we took it, but we talked about everything. And had regular, passionate intimate moments."

I only half-smiled, because my next question weighed on my chest. "After all these years, are you sure she's alive?"

"We're mated, Cherry. When she dies, so do I."

I was trying to wrap my mind around the love and certainty it took to tie your lifespan to someone else's, when I heard glass breaking in the inner room. I rushed to see what happened, but the moment I opened the door to my private office, someone rushed me.

My attacker was too fast for me to see a face, but it was a woman, judging by the shrieking and the breasts pressing against mine, as she body-slammed me to the floor. She yanked my hair aside painfully, baring my neck.

I looked up in horror, as fangs descended toward me. In that moment, I forgot my training. I forgot how to move. I forgot how to speak. I lay there and waited for the furious blonde to rip into my throat.

As if the night wasn't surreal enough, a low growl came from my left. The vampire on top of me froze, and I followed her gaze to a huge beast prowling toward us. It was a panther, almost twice my length and black as midnight, its coat sleek and its yellow eyes shining under the overhead light. The clothes Hunt wore were strewn in tatters behind him.

I hated being the only human in the room. Also, could shifters tell friend from foe when in animal form?

The vampire, who I strongly suspected was Katje, narrowed her eyes at Hunt and hissed. She sat back, and as the panther leapt for her, I kicked her off and rolled on my stomach, to crawl away as fast as my trembling limbs allowed.

"Get off me, mutt," Katje screeched. Hunt had her cornered, and she flailed and scratched him. Why didn't she toss him across the room? Huge or not, he couldn't weigh more than a car, and vamps can lift cars.

I found my phone, miraculously unscathed despite my landing on my ass, and called Sally.

Can't talk, she texted again, after cancelling my call.

Vampire attack at the office, I wrote back. I should get out of there, but I watched in sick fascination as the animal lowered its jaws toward the woman he loved. I squeezed my eyes shut, not wanting to see him kill her, but when she shrieked again, it wasn't in horror but fury.

Hunt said, "You smell different."

I opened my eyes and saw him pressed against her in all his naked man-shaped glory. He sniffed her. "Look at me, Katje. Remember me. I'd never hurt you."

She screamed for him to leave her alone and raised welts on his back with her fingernails, but he wrapped his arms around her and held on.

"Don't touch me." Her screams had faded to pleading. "I don't want you near me. You mean nothing to me."

"Then why did you follow me here? Why attack this woman?"

"*I don't know.*" The yell broke into a sob. "I can't get you out of my mind since I saw you at my brother's house. You sneaked in and stole my sapphire, and I need it back."

"Were you the one following me?"

"I wanted to kill you"—she was crying in earnest now—"but I couldn't bring myself to pull the trigger. Why can't I kill you and get you out of my system?"

"Because you love me."

These crazy kids would have their happy ending after all, and I was intruding. I convinced my legs it was time to stand, and was reaching for the handle when I heard Sally say, "Wait. I have a key."

Constantine broke down the door. He rushed the huddled couple, and I yelled for him to wait, but Carrie and Sally managed to hold him back. He fought to get free, but Liza grabbed his face, and they span him to look at me.

"She's here. She's fine," Liza said.

Constantine had a wild look in his eyes, that tonight were the dark blue of stormy sea. Was all this pain and worry for me?

"Constantine…" I took a step toward him, and the vampettes let go, but he slid his impassive mask over his features.

"You're all right. Good," he said. "Now if you'll excuse me, I'll have to retrieve the sapphire tonight, if we're to save this woman's sanity. Liza, join me?"

I reached for his hand as he passed by me. I expected him to avoid my touch, but he gave my fingers a tiny squeeze before walking out the ruined door.

Katje was thrashing under Hunt, trying to throw him off, denying the truth of his words.

"Will she be safe if we get you both to your place?" Carrie asked Hunt.

"I have built a room that will detain her until she can be restored," he said.

"Good. Sally, help me?"

The two vampettes held Katje still until Hunt got on his feet. He was very naked, and his clothes were unwearable.

"I'll see if I have something you can wear," I said. Five minutes later I was back with a tracksuit that was too tight and short for him but wouldn't get him arrested for indecent exposure.

Katje oscillated between threats and pleas, but the three of them managed to get her outside.

"Do you want my car?" I asked.

"Better to fly them," Sally said. "Something tells me she'll be a horrible passenger."

"Call me when it's all over?" I kept away from the unstable vampire snapping her jaws at me.

"I will," Sally said.

"Let Sheena know where we are," Carrie told me. To Sally she said, "Ready?" and all four of them took off toward the night sky.

Chapter Twenty-four

I bypassed the mess that was my office and went straight home, to call Sheena. "Drinks while our vampires save the day?"

"Cherry. Hey. Everyone okay? Sally said you were attacked." She sounded like she was crying. Was she afraid something happened to me?

"We're all fine," I said.

"Good. I was worried." But she didn't sound relieved; she sounded like shit. "Did it have to do with your case?"

"Yeah. How much has Sally told you about it?"

"I know a gorgeous were-panther is looking for his bespelled vampire bride and a sapphire that holds her soul or something." Her tired voice belied her humorous words.

"Well, the vampire bride came after me, and the shifter grabbed her," I said. "The gang is going to get the jewel tonight, so you and I can have a slumber party while we wait for news."

"Nah. I'm tired, and you could use some rest."

I wouldn't take *no* for an answer. She needed the company, and so did I, if I were to stop thinking of how Constantine ran to my rescue and then took off instead of talking to me. Constantine never fled from anything. "If you don't come over, I'll come to you, and then you'll have four of us all up in your space tonight," I told Sheena. "Come *on*. We'll order in, and veg out in front of the TV. I'll even let you sleep in tomorrow."

"I don't know..."

"*Please?*"

"Okay. But no chic flicks."

I ordered a couple of huge, greasy, calorie- and fat-ridden hot dogs with bacon, mustard, and extra relish, and fries. Praise the Powers that Be for all the stair climbing, or I soon wouldn't fit in my jeans. I added a salad, to assuage the guilt. There was beer and white wine in the fridge, and I found *Fast & Furious 6* on Netflix.

Sheena looked exhausted when I let her in. Her eyes were bloodshot and sunken.

"What happened?" I asked as she threw her arms around me.

"Me? You were the one attacked."

"My door and window got the brunt of it." I studied her face. "What's the matter, hon?"

"Nothing. I'm tired. There's never any quiet around the house."

"Now tell me the truth."

"I am." She looked away.

"Are you sick? Is your wound acting up?"

She shook her head and met my gaze. "I'm fine. A friend passed away earlier today. I knew it was coming, but I miss him already."

My pulse thudded in my ears. Sheena didn't have many friends. "I'm sorry for your loss." I hugged her, and a niggling fear tied my stomach into a knot. "Was it someone I knew?"

"Have you talked to Constantine recently?" Why did she change the subject?

"I saw him today. He broke down my door, saw I was okay, and left. Didn't even look at me. But he knew I'm a PI, when I called to ask about this case. Guess the girls told him."

"Guess so. Did he seem well?"

She was leading to something my brain refused to puzzle out. "Yeah, except for the wanting-nothing-to-do-with-me part." My heart was racing, but she'd tell me if there was something wrong with him.

Sheena rolled her eyes. "He loves you. You chose not to be with him; he gets to choose not to be your friend."

The intercom buzzed, and I jumped before I remembered the hot dogs.

I got the door and returned with an armful of drool-worthy artery cloggers. We got some food into our systems, and then drowned our sorrows while watching sexy people wreak havoc.

Sheena yawned, and I paused the film to go make the guest bed for her. The king-size sheets I bought when I moved in were too big for the queen bed in the spare room. I was resigned to tucking in a lot of fabric, when I remembered I had the right size covers in the suitcase stashed in my bedroom closet. As I tried to pull out a set without laying the suitcase flat and opening it all the way, a folded piece of paper slipped out and floated to the hardwood floor. *Alex* was scribbled on it, in Constantine's handwriting.

It was Constantine's note to Alex, and Alex wanted me to have it.

It took me three tries to pick it up; my hands shook.

"Need any help?" called Sheena from the living room.

"I'm good," I called back and opened the note.

Alex,

I never expected to consider you a friend, but I do, so I mean it when I wish you and Cherry a long, happy life together.

This woman is my world, however, and should you ever hurt her, I will become your worst nightmare. Letting go of her is only possible because I know she'll be happy with you. If she's not, let her free. Cherry isn't meant to fit in the norms you were brought up to embrace. If she chooses to do so, make it worth her while.

Be good, my friend. Be healthy. Be happy.

> *Sincerely,*
> *Constantine*

Tears fell from my eyes and soaked the paper in my hands. I felt lightheaded and sat on the bed, rereading the note.

"Is this from him?" Sheena asked from the doorway. "Did he tell you about Wesley?"

I snapped my gaze to her. "Wesley?"

"Shit. Constantine made me promise not to tell you."

"What happened?" That came out shrill.

"The last of Wesley's great grandkids passed months ago, and Wesley decided he didn't want to live any longer. He passed away tonight."

"Oh God. Poor Wesley." The tears came harder.

"He asked us not to cry for him." But tears beaded her eyelids. She blinked them back. "He had a full life, and it was his choice. He stopped taking Constantine's blood about when you came back from your parents."

I wiped my face. "Constantine's blood?"

"That's what kept Wesley going. How else do you think he got to live almost a hundred and eighty years, and still be spry?"

I sniffled. "I didn't know. I thought he was old, not *old* old." Because I never cared to ask. Because I was too absorbed with my drama to get to know the gentle old man who took care of everyone. "I didn't even know that was possible." *Someone* could have told me when I was a vampire dating a human.

I'd miss Wesley. He was ancient—literally, apparently—but I never thought of him dying. He was a constant in my life and in Constantine's. "Constantine…"

"It destroyed him. Between losing you and waiting for his closest friend to pass, he became a hermit. When we went to visit Wesley, Constantine made himself scarce. This case is the first the girls saw him in weeks."

"Why didn't any of you tell me? I wanted to say *goodbye*."

"Wesley said you did, and Constantine didn't want you to return to him out of pity. He wanted your new life to be filled with happiness."

I remembered Sally telling me I should go to him. That we were both alone. "Doesn't he know Alex and I broke up?"

"Carrie called him when we found out—sorry, but we're his friends too—and when she mentioned you, he stopped her and said he only wants to know if you're in trouble or need help."

Stupid, stubborn man. "But he knew I was a PI."

"Which none of us told him."

I shook my head. "I'm sorry. A good man is dead, and I'm making it all about my nonexistent love life."

"Wesley would be happy if you and Constantine made things work," she said with a sad smile.

"Too bad that's not gonna happen, huh?"

She came to sit next to me. "Hon, you know your situation isn't irreversible, yes?"

"He said he doesn't want to—"

"No, woman. I mean you don't have to stay human if you don't want to."

Be a vampire again? Did I want to? Would Constantine turn me if I asked?

But did I want to?

"Do you love him?" Sheena asked.

"Yes, but I loved Alex too, and—"

She didn't let me finish. "Do you love being human?"

"I don't hate it. It's cool, I guess, now I can tell flavors apart."

She gave me a light smack upside the head. "Focus. Do you love being a human?"

I thought about it. Being human was about growing, experiencing all stages of life, and not outliving everyone you forged a connection to. With the exception of Sheena and my parents, my nearest and dearest were all undead. Humans could walk in the sun, but with Ruby's brew, so could vampires, and they didn't get period pains or migraines or hunger pangs.

"What if one day I decide I want children?" I asked.

"You adopt. Or you take the girls in. Or get a dog."

I thought of the night I shared with Alex and Constantine. The choice I made that night wasn't between the two of them; it was about the life I craved. I loved Alex—I really did—but I didn't choose *him*. He was the added bonus.

Would I do it all again? Yes, because I needed to see what I'd missed out on.

Would I make the same choice today?

I planted a kiss on Sheena's cheek. "Thank you."

"I won't wait up," she said, kicking her shoes and making herself comfortable on my bed.

Chapter Twenty-five

The Uber dropped me off at the mansion's gate.

I considered pressing the intercom button, but my inebriated brain insisted it was better to climb the wrought iron fence.

Using the gate for support and the strength-boost alcohol afforded me, I lifted my weight up the end post. My jeans didn't offer enough friction, and my hands hurt. It took several tries, and I berated me my stupidity the whole time it took to reach the top. My relief when I swung my right leg over the top rail was squelched when one of my belt loops got snagged on the spike behind me and I couldn't move either way.

Screw it. I'd call Constantine, and if he left me hanging—literally—I'd threaten to call 911.

I pulled out my phone, but my fingers were clumsy and sweaty with the effort it took to get up here. The phone slipped through them. I watched horrified as it landed on a rock and the back jumped off, spilling out the battery and sim card.

Awesome.

"*Constantine,*" I yelled. "Hey! Help me down. Your stupid fence has taken me hostage." He was a vampire. He should be able to hear me.

Sometime later, I realized he couldn't. As far as I knew, he was still out, looking for the soul sapphire. Fuck.

I don't know how I managed to fall asleep in the most uncomfortable position imaginable, or how the jeans held my weight and saved me from plummeting to the ground when I half-slid off the iron rail I straddled, but Constantine's face was inches from mine when he said, "What the fuck are you doing,

Cherry?" His expression wavered between amused and angry. And maybe concerned?

"Waiting for you?" My eyes burned again. I was supposed to throw myself in his arms and profess my love. Instead, I was dangling upside down like meat at the butcher's, and I couldn't figure out where to start. I looked around. I was on the inner side of the fence. I'd count that as a win.

He helped me down and handed me the remains of my phone. "What do you want?" he asked, holding the gate open for me to exit.

I leaned my weight against it, but his grip kept it from closing. "I need to talk to you," I said.

"Is it another case? The girls can help you. My part in this one is done. Kappel's place was empty when we went in for the sapphire. Since he didn't follow protocol, he's a fugitive in the U.S., so I expect he left the country. Hunt will apply for Katje to stay legally. He'll call you."

"Thank you, but that's not why I came."

"Why *did* you? I've repeatedly asked you to keep your distance." He glowered, violet and grey swirling in his eyes and confusing me.

"I'm sorry. About Wesley, not for being here. Sheena saw me crying, and she thought I knew. He was a good, decent man, and I'm so sorry he's gone." I cupped Constantine's face, but he shied away from my touch.

"I'm tired, Cherry," he croaked. "Tonight I lost the best friend I've had in centuries, and I ran to do your bidding before his body was cold."

"I didn't know—"

"I'm tired of hurting." He trapped me between his body and the gate. "I'm tired of missing you and being lonely, and I'm tired of you not getting that seeing you and not having you is torture."

"But—"

"I don't want to hear how you miss me too and want us to be friends. I don't want to be your friend. I want you to leave me alone."

"Constantine, I love you."

He huffed. "But not enough. Why do you torment me? Are you enjo—"

"Oh, will you shut the fuck up?" That shocked him into silence long enough for me to add, "I'm not here to torture you. I love you enough. I want to be with you."

He widened his eyes and took a step back. "Best case scenario, I can delay your aging, but I can't watch you wither away like Wesley. I won't do that."

Was he always this dense?

"No, you insufferable man. I want to be a vampire again, and I want you to be my maker."

He leaned in close, and I closed my eyes, thinking he'd kiss me. Instead, I heard him sniff. "You've been drinking," he said. "You don't know what you're saying."

I glared. My thoughts had never been clearer. "I'm not drunk. I want this as much as you do. Unless you're not that into me when I'm actually available."

"And what does Alex think about this?" Constantine asked, his voice dripping honey all of a sudden.

"Alex and I are done."

"That's why you came back. We're interchangeable for you. It didn't work out with one, so you'll scurry to the other. I told you before—I won't be the consolation prize."

How could he love me and be such an ass about it? I poked him in the chest hard enough to hurt my finger, though it had no effect on him. "I broke up with Alex weeks ago, because I don't want a family. I tried to be human, but I didn't like it. I tried to live without you, but you're the only thing on my fucking mind. Now, will you get over yourself and kiss me already?"

I didn't expect it to work without further groveling, but he snatched my finger and pulled me into him. An electric current ran through me when our lips met. How did I ever survive without him?

He deepened the kiss, and I felt lightheaded. My feet no longer touched the ground. Constantine flew us across his gardens, kicked down his own front door, and took me to his bed.

He wasn't gentle with my clothes, ripping my jeans in two and tearing my T-shirt off me. "Forgive me, but I've waited too long. Too long."

"Don't worry. I have other clothes," I said, fighting to pull his shirt over his head.

He snapped the elastic in my thong and pulled down his jeans without unbuttoning them. "Foreplay next time. You have my word." He pulled me to the edge of the mattress by the ankles, lifted my legs in the air, and slid inside me in one long thrust.

This. This was what I needed. Not a hard cock, but the connection with Constantine. Feeling him inside me. Spreading me. He draped his body over mine, folding me in half. My legs dangled over his arms as rammed into me time and again.

I arched up to find his lips and breathed into his mouth. I didn't know if my human body could withstand the way he contorted me, but I didn't care.

He folded one of my legs around his hips and splayed his hand over my chest. "Are you sure you no longer want this?"

It took a second to realize he meant my heartbeat. "I'm sure." I bucked against him, urging him deeper. Faster. I wanted him to take me to my limit. To throw me over the edge. To end me and breathe new life into me.

His skin was cold against mine, but he scorched me when he palmed my breasts and squeezed, using them to drive his thrusts. He hurt me in the most delicious ways, and I couldn't wait till I was a vampire and could take more of it. More of him.

"It doesn't have to be now." He punctuated each word with a thrust. "We can have a romantic evening. Candlelight. Strawberries. Chocolate. I want to make it special for you this time."

"You're all I need," I whispered. "Don't ever stop fucking me."

"Not planning on it anytime soon." He kissed me again, plunging his tongue into my mouth as he pumped his cock inside me, hard and demanding.

I bit his lip with enough force to draw blood. It drove him wild. His rhythm became punishing, and I thought I'd faint with pleasure.

My body tightened around him, and I felt the ball of fire in my belly prepare to erupt. I tossed my head to the side and swept my hair out of the way. "Now. Please."

Constantine kissed along my jaw line and down my neck, while he inched his hand toward my cunt. He pierced the flesh with his fangs at the same time he pressed his thumb on my clit and twisted.

I came apart. My legs thrashed of their own accord, as my heart pounded in my chest. I dug my nails in his shoulders, and felt the skin give way, but I didn't care. I latched on to him and rode out my orgasm, as I felt my life's blood fill his mouth and trickle to pool on the sheets under my head.

Constantine wedged an arm under my shoulders to hold me close. He kept fucking me and drinking me down, prolonging my release while he drove me to yet another death.

I slid into darkness like more than once before, but this time I didn't panic. I was where I belonged.

"I love you."

Epilogue

I opened my eyes, and smiled when I saw Constantine's beautiful face. He lay on his side next to me, one leg between mine. The darkness did nothing to hide him from me, but brought out his beauty in stark relief. I took in his sparkling eyes. His generous lips. His perfect teeth. The angle of his prominent cheekbones. With his halo of golden hair, he could be a wicked angel.

"Good morning," he said. His eyes were their normal light blue and no longer looked haunted.

"Mmm…" I stretched and brought my fingers to my neck, where he bit me—was it this morning? "What day is it?"

"You were only out a few hours." He ran his fingers through my hair. "I love this color on you, but you were just as fetching when you went blonde. I was being a jerk when I said otherwise."

"Thanks." If I were human, I'd blush. I wasn't, so I blew him a kiss. How did I ever stay away?

"You came back to me." For an older-than-dirt vampire, he had the boyish grin down pat.

"And you were a bastard about it." I teased the light sprinkling of hair below his navel, and his cock bumped against my hip.

"I didn't expect you to change your mind, especially after you got your own place and made the effort to register as an investigator."

I sat up and looked down at him. "Sheena said you wouldn't let anyone talk about me. How did you know?"

He squeezed his eyes shut. "I may have checked in on you once or twice."

That was rich. "You checked in on me, when I wasn't allowed to call you? You're horrible." I batted his shoulder, but I was grinning. If he hadn't insisted on keeping his distance, I might settle for having him around, and we'd remain in limbo.

He clasped my hand and placed it on his chest. "Maybe once a week, tops. I had to know you were okay."

"So you knew Alex and I broke up?" I asked.

He turned his gaze to my bare breasts. "I did. I didn't know why, though."

"And this morning you threw him into the conversation because…"

He raked his fingers through his hair and sighed. "I had to know if you were choosing me, or if I was all you had left."

He knew me better than that. I should be upset, but it was comfy here, and I didn't need to pee, and I could eat anything I felt like and never take the stairs anywhere again, and we were both naked, and I was happy.

Truly very happy.

"Round two?" Constantine asked, as I said, "I'm keeping my apartment and my job."

"Sure," I replied, as he said, "Whatever makes you happy."

He made me happy. And he made me happier by kissing and licking his way down my body, teasing, pinching, and nibbling until I begged him to eat me out.

Which he did. With gusto. Then he bit my inner thigh and drunk from me again.

Later, I'll ride him to oblivion and feed from his neck while he whispers my name like a prayer.

At some point I need to get out of bed and check my phone. It rang a couple times during the day. Might be Hunt. Sheena knows I won't be back for a few days. She'll tell Sally, but I have to call Mom and Dad and update them on my situation.

I should talk with Constantine too. If this is going to work, we must do it right this time. I'm keeping my place, though I don't mind spending every night with him. And he can help me with my PI-ing. If we change our working hours and vet clients properly, we may even get council sanctioning.

At some point, I should tell Alex I'm a vampire again. We're not together, and I owe him no explanation, but I want him to know he did nothing wrong. I just wasn't cut out for mortality.

Constantine stirs beside me. The man is insatiable, and I match his appetite. I straddle him and rub my wet slit along his shaft.

Without opening his eyes, he says, "You'll be the end of me."

No, wait. He didn't move his lips.

Euphoria spills through my veins, making my nerve endings tingle, and he's not even touching me. *"Can you hear me?"* I ask in my head.

He looks at me, startled. "Shouldn't I?"

I send, *"I didn't speak."*

I feel my joy fill his chest. I feel my weight on top of him. I feel my slickness against him. He bucks his hips and enters me, and I'm both of us at once.

"I love you." The thought is in my head, but I don't know if it's mine or his.

I'm happy. I'm whole.

I'm home.

The End

(but you should keep reading)

<h1 style="text-align:center;font-style:italic;">Later that night</h1>

"I knew you'd find your way back to him."

I snapped my head toward the foot of the bed and saw Wesley's simmering form smiling at us.

I squealed and pulled the sheets over my naked body. Constantine jumped up and looked around in alarm, but his gaze glided over the specter now hovering next to me.

"He can't see me." A hint of sadness tinged Wesley's voice. "You've died more times. You're closer to us."

"To… ghosts?" I blinked, and he turned brighter, making the rest of the room fade behind him.

"Cherry? Who are you talking to?" Constantine grabbed my arm and shook me. In my head, I heard, *"If someone's haunting your dreams—"*

"It's okay." I met his gaze long enough for him to see I was awake and aware of my surroundings. "It's Wesley."

Constantine started to ask more, but I shushed him and used our mental link to project to him what I saw. "How are you here?" I asked Wesley.

"My unfinished business was to see Master Constantine happy. Now I can rest. Thank you. Take care of him for me." He cupped my cheek, and I felt his touch, but when he tried to straighten the candle on the nightstand, his fingers passed through it.

"I will," I said. "Thank you for everything."

"Goodbye, my friend." Constantine sounded as choked up as I felt.

Wesley brightened into a ball of pure white light, and then dissolved into a million sparkles that disappeared before they hit the floor.

"So now I see ghosts, apparently," I said.

He sat back wide eyed and gathered me to him. "Apparently."

If only that was the last of the surprises coming our way.

We got a whole week to ourselves, before Alex called the mansion. It wasn't about me.

Constantine had asked Ruby to look into soul sapphires, and she enlisted Alex's help. Don't ask me why.

According to her, there aren't four soul gems, but ten, and they're not all sapphires. Their original name was Petradia tis Anamonis, which translates to *stones of waiting*, and they put things or people into stasis.

I think they're no more real than the Excalibur, but Constantine believes there's more to them. He's afraid Ádísa's essence is still trapped in one of them, and we're not done with her yet. We'll go check her place tomorrow, and then look into Willoughby's last known residence, but I don't expect to find something.

Upside to this phone call was that Alex seemed fine with me and Constantine being together. We said we'll all have drinks together.

There we go again, with the freaky civility.

I should write a book about these guys.

Keep up to date with all the latest news and information
from Sotia Lazu at http://SotiaLazu.com

Acknowledgments

Thank you, Marilyn and Lorraine, for working with me for months to shape up Cherry Stem this story and for keeping my morale high when I was about to give up.

Thank you, Melina, for getting me a laptop when mine gave up on me. I wouldn't have written Cherry Blossom without you. Thank you, January M. for being the best content editor ever, and for always making time for me and my stories. Thank you, Diane Saxon, for making Cherry Blossom a much smoother read.

Thank you, Allyson Lindt and Sofia Grey, for sticking with me throughout Cherry's journey, beta reading, cheerleading, and virtually kicking my ass when needed. I couldn't have finished the series without you. Thank you, Milana and Camilla, for loving Cherry and her boys and asking for more when I felt too overwhelmed to write.

Thank you, Andrei, for reading it over and over when I was sure I'd messed up, and for all your solid advice. And for putting up with me during my writing sprees. I love you.

Last but not least, a great big thank you to everyone who's followed this series to the end. I hope you give my other books a chance, and that when I'm ready to return to Cherry's world, you'll make the leap with me.

Sotia loves romances with a twist and urban fantasy novels, always with vivid erotic elements. Her favorite characters to write are not conventional hero-material at first glance, and she enjoys making them fight for their happiness.

She shares her life and living quarters with her husband, their son, and two rescue dogs, one of which may be part-pony. Sappy movies make her bawl like a baby, and she wishes she could take in all the stray dogs in the world.

Also, she hates mornings.

www.ingramcontent.com/pod-product-compliance
Lightning Source LLC
Chambersburg PA
CBHW070729120726
47910CB00001B/26